MILES ERRANT

MILES ERRANT

LOIS McMASTER BUJOLD

BAEN

MILES ERRANT

A Baen Books Original Omnibus

Baen Publishing Enterprises
P.O. Box 1403
Riverdale, NY 10471
www.baen.com

ISBN: 0-7434-3558-3

Cover art by Steven Hickman

First printing, September 2002

Library of Congress Cataloging-in-Publication Data

Bujold, Lois McMaster.
    Miles errant / by Lois McMaster Bujold.
      p. cm.
    "A Baen Books original omnibus"—T.p. verso.
    Contents: Borders of infinity—Brothers in arms—Mirror Dance.
    ISBN 0-7434-3558-3 (pbk.)
    1. Vorkosigan, Miles (Ficticious character)—Fiction. 2. Science fiction, American.
I. Title.

PS3552.U39 A6 2002
813'.54—dc21   2002071158

Distributed by Simon & Schuster
1230 Avenue of the Americas
New York, NY 10020

Production by Windhaven Press, Auburn, NH
Printed in the United States of America

10   9   8   7   6   5   4   3   2   1

CONTENTS

"THE BORDERS OF INFINITY"

How could I have died and gone to hell without noticing the transition?

The opalescent force dome capped a surreal and alien landscape, frozen for a moment by Miles's disorientation and dismay. The dome defined a perfect circle, half a kilometer in diameter. Miles stood just inside its edge, where the glowing concave surface dove into the hard-packed dirt and disappeared. His imagination followed the arc buried beneath his feet to the far side, where it erupted again to complete the sphere. It was like being trapped inside an eggshell. An unbreakable eggshell.

Within was a scene from an ancient limbo. Dispirited men and women sat, or stood, or mostly lay down, singly or in scattered irregular groups, across the breadth of the arena. Miles's eye searched anxiously for some remnant of order or military grouping, but the inhabitants seemed splashed randomly as a liquid across the ground.

Perhaps he had been killed just now, just entering this prison camp. Perhaps his captors had betrayed him to his death, like those ancient Earth soldiers who had lured their victims sheeplike into poisoned showers, diverting and soothing their suspicions with stone soap, until their final enlightenment burst upon them in a choking cloud. Perhaps the annihilation of his body had been so swift, his neurons had not had time to carry the information to his brain. Why else did so many antique myths agree that hell was a circular place?

1

Dagoola IV Top Security Prison Camp #3. This was it? This naked . . . dinner plate? Miles had vaguely visioned barracks, marching guards, daily head counts, secret tunnels, escape committees.

It was the dome that made it all so simple, Miles realized. What need for barracks to shelter prisoners from the elements? The dome did it. What need for guards? The dome was generated from without. Nothing inside could breach it. No need for guards, or head counts. Tunnels were a futility, escape committees an absurdity. The dome did it all.

The only structures were what appeared to be big gray plastic mushrooms evenly placed about every hundred meters around the perimeter of the dome. What little activity there was seemed clustered around them. Latrines, Miles recognized.

Miles and his three fellow prisoners had entered through a temporary portal, which had closed behind them before the brief bulge of force dome containing their entry vanished in front of them. The nearest inhabitant of the dome, a man, lay a few meters away upon a sleeping mat identical to the one Miles now clutched. He turned his head slightly to stare at the little party of newcomers, smiled sourly, and rolled over on his side with his back to them. Nobody else nearby even bothered to look up.

"Holy shit," muttered one of Miles's companions.

He and his two buddies drew together unconsciously. The three had been from the same unit once, they'd said. Miles had met them bare minutes ago, in their final stages of processing, where they had all been issued their total supply of worldly goods for life in Dagoola #3.

A single pair of loose gray trousers. A matching short-sleeved gray tunic. A rectangular sleeping mat, rolled up. A plastic cup. That was all. That, and the new numbers encoded upon their skins. It bothered Miles intensely that their captors had chosen to locate the numbers in the middle of their backs, where they couldn't see them. He resisted a futile urge to twist and crane his neck anyway, though his hand snaked up under his shirt to scratch a purely psychosomatic itch. You couldn't feel the encode either.

Some motion appeared in the tableau. A group of four or five men approaching. The welcoming committee at last? Miles was desperate for information. Where among all these countless gray men and women—no, not countless, Miles told himself firmly. They were all accounted for here.

The battered remnants of the 3rd and 4th Armored All-Terrain Rangers. The ingenious and tenacious civilian defenders of Garson

Transfer Station. Winoweh's 2nd Battalion had been captured almost intact. And the 14th Commandos, survivors of the high-tech fortress at Fallow Core. Particularly the survivors of Fallow Core. Ten thousand, two hundred fourteen exactly. The planet Marilac's finest. Ten thousand, two hundred fifteen, counting himself. Ought he to count himself?

The welcoming committee drew up in a ragged bunch a few meters away. They looked tough and tall and muscular and not noticeably friendly. Dull, sullen eyes, full of a deadly boredom that even their present calculation did not lighten.

The two groups, the five and the three, sized each other up. The three turned, and started walking stiffly and prudently away. Miles realized belatedly that he, not a part of either group, was thus left alone.

Alone and immensely conspicuous. Self-consciousness, body-consciousness, normally held at bay by the simple fact that he didn't have time to waste on it, returned to him with a rush. Too short, too odd-looking—his legs were even in length now, after the last operation, but surely not long enough to outrun these five. And where did one run to, in this place? He crossed off flight as an option.

Fight? Get serious.

This isn't going to work, he realized sadly, even as he started walking toward them. But it was more dignified than being chased down with the same result.

He tried to make his smile austere rather than foolish. No telling whether he succeeded. "Hi, there. Can you tell me where to find Colonel Guy Tremont's 14th Commando Division?"

One of the five snorted sardonically. Two moved behind Miles.

Well, a snort was almost speech. Expression, anyway. A start, a toehold. Miles focused on that one. "What's your name and rank and company, soldier?"

"No ranks in here, mutant. No companies. No soldiers. No nothing."

Miles glanced around. Surrounded, of course. Naturally. "You got some friends, anyway."

The talker almost smiled. "You don't."

Miles wondered if perhaps he had been premature in crossing off flight as an option. "I wouldn't count on that if I were—*unh!*" The kick to his kidneys, from behind, cut him off—he damn near bit his tongue—he fell, dropping bedroll and cup and landing in a tangle. A barefoot kick, no combat boots this time, thank God—

by the rules of Newtonian physics, his attacker's foot ought to hurt just as much as his back. Fine. Jolly. Maybe they'd bruise their knuckles, punching him out. . . .

One of the gang gathered up Miles's late wealth, cup and bed-roll. "Want his clothes? They're too little for me."

"Naw."

"Yeah," said the talker. "Take 'em anyway. Maybe bribe one of the women."

The tunic was jerked off over Miles's head, the pants over his feet. Miles was too busy protecting his head from random kicks to fight much for his clothes, trying obliquely to take as many hits as possible on his belly or ribcage, not arms or legs or jaw. A cracked rib was surely the most injury he could afford right now, here, at the beginning. A broken jaw would be the worst.

His assailants desisted only a little before they discovered by experimentation the secret weakness of his bones.

"*That's* how it is in here, mutant," said the talker, slightly winded.

"I was born naked," Miles panted from the dirt. "Didn't stop me."

"Cocky little shit," said the talker.

"Slow learner," remarked another.

The second beating was worse than the first. Two cracked ribs at least—his jaw barely escaped being smashed, at the cost of something painfully wrong in his left wrist, flung up as a shield. This time Miles resisted the impulse to offer any verbal parting shots.

He lay in the dirt and wished he could pass out.

He lay a long time, cradled in pain. He was not sure how long. The illumination from the force dome was even and shadowless, unchanging. Timeless, like eternity. Hell was eternal, was it not? This place had too damn many congruencies with hell, that was certain.

And here came another demon. . . . Miles blinked the approaching figure into focus. A man, as bruised and naked as Miles himself, gaunt-ribbed, starveling, knelt in the dirt a few meters away. His face was bony, aged by stress—he might have been forty, or fifty—or twenty-five.

His eyes were unnaturally prominent, due to the shrinking of his flesh. Their whites seemed to gleam feverishly against the dirt darkening his skin. Dirt, not beard stubble—every prisoner in here, male and female, had their hair cut short and the hair follicles stunned to prevent re-growth. Perpetually clean-shaved and crew-cut. Miles had undergone the same process bare hours ago. But whoever had processed this fellow must have been in a hurry. The hair stunner had missed a line on his cheek and a few dozen hairs grew there like a stripe on a badly-mown lawn. Even curled as they were, Miles could see they were several centimeters long, draggling down past the man's jaw. If only he knew how fast hair grew, he could calculate how long this fellow had been here. *Too long, whatever the numbers,* Miles thought with an inward sigh.

The man had the broken-off bottom half of a plastic cup, which he pushed cautiously toward Miles. His breath whistled raggedly past his yellowish teeth, from exertion or excitement or disease—probably not disease, they were all well immunized here. Escape, even through death, was not that easy. Miles rolled over and propped himself stiffly on his elbow, regarding his visitor through the thinning haze of his aches and pains.

The man scrabbled back slightly, smiled nervously. He nodded toward the cup. "Water. Better drink. The cup's cracked, and it all leaks out if you wait too long."

"Thanks," croaked Miles. A week ago, or in a previous lifetime, depending on how you counted time, Miles had dawdled over a selection of wines, dissatisfied with this or that nuance of flavor. His lips cracked as he grinned in memory. He drank. It was perfectly ordinary water, lukewarm, faintly redolent of chlorine and sulfur. *A refined body, but the bouquet is a bit presumptuous. . . .*

The man squatted in studied politeness until Miles finished drinking, then leaned forward on his knuckles in restrained urgency. "Are you the One?"

Miles blinked. "Am I the what?"

"The One. The *other* one, I should say. The scripture says there has to be two."

"Uh," Miles hesitated cautiously, "what exactly does the scripture say?"

The man's right hand wrapped over his knobby left wrist, around which was tied a rag screwed into a sort of rope. He closed his eyes; his lips moved a moment, and then he recited aloud, " . . . but the pilgrims went up that hill with ease, because they had these two men to lead them by the arms; also they had left their garments behind them, for though they went in with them, they came out without them." His eyes popped back open to stare hopefully at Miles.

So, now we begin to see why this guy seems to be all by

himself. . . . "Are you, perchance, the other One?" Miles shot at a venture.

The man nodded shyly.

"I see. Um . . ." How was it that he always attracted the nut cases? He licked the last drops of water from his lips. The fellow might have some screws loose, but he was certainly an improvement over the last lot, always presuming he didn't have another personality or two of the homicidal loonie variety tucked away in his head. No, in that case he'd be introducing himself as the Chosen Two, and not be looking for outside assistance. "Um . . . what's your name?"

"Suegar."

"Suegar. Right, all right. My name is Miles, by the way."

"Huh." Suegar grimaced in a sort of pleased irony. "Your name means 'soldier,' did you know?"

"Uh, yeah, so I've been told."

"But you're not a soldier . . . ?"

No subtle expensive trick of clothing line or uniform style here to hide from himself, if no one else, the peculiarities of his body. Miles flushed. "They were taking anything, toward the end. They made me a recruiting clerk. I never did get to fire my gun. Listen, Suegar—how did you come to know you were the One, or at any rate one of the Ones? Is it something you've always known?"

"It came on me gradually," confessed Suegar, shifting to sit cross-legged. "I'm the only one in here with the words, y'see." He caressed his rag rope again. "I've hunted all up and down the camp, but they only mock me. It was a kind of process of elimination, y'see, when they all gave up but me."

"Ah." Miles too sat up, only gasping a little in pain. Those ribs were going to be murder for the next few days. He nodded toward the rope bracelet. "Is that where you keep your scripture? Can I see it?" And how the hell had Suegar ever gotten a plastic flimsy, or loose piece of paper or whatever, in here?

Suegar clutched his arms protectively to his chest and shook his head. "They've been trying to take them from me for months, y'see. I can't be too careful. Until you prove you're the One. The devil can quote scripture, y'know."

Yes, that was rather what I had in mind. . . . Who knew what opportunities Suegar's "scripture" might contain? Well, maybe later. For now, keep dancing. "Are there any other signs?" asked Miles. "You see, I don't know that I'm your One, but on the other hand I don't know I'm not, either. I just got here, after all."

Suegar shook his head again. "It's only five or six sentences, y'see. You have to interpolate a lot."

I'll bet. Miles did not voice the comment aloud. "However did you come by it? Or get it in here?"

"It was at Port Lisma, y'see, just before we were captured," said Suegar. "House-to-house fighting. One of my boot heels had come a bit loose, and it clicked when I walked. Funny, with all that barrage coming down around our ears, how a little thing like that can get under your skin. There was this bookcase with a glass front, real antique books made of paper—I smashed it open with my gun butt and tore out part of a page from one, and folded it up to stick in my boot heel, to make a sort of shim, y'see, and stop the clicking. Didn't look at the book. Didn't even know it was scripture till later. At least, I think it's scripture. It sounds like scripture, anyway. It must be scripture."

Suegar twisted his beard hairs nervously around his finger. "When we were waiting to be processed, I'd pulled it out of my boot, just idle-like, y'know. I had it in my hand—the processing guard saw it, but he just didn't take it away from me. Probably thought it was just a harmless piece of paper. Didn't know it was scripture. I still had it in my hand when we were dumped in here. D'you know, it's the only piece of writing in this whole camp?" he added rather proudly. "It must be scripture."

"Well . . . you take good care of it, then," advised Miles kindly. "If you've preserved it this long, it was obviously meant to be your job."

"Yeah . . ." Suegar blinked. Tears? "I'm the only one in here with a job, aren't I? So I must be one of the Ones."

"Sounds good to me," said Miles agreeably. "Say, ah," he glanced around the vast featureless dome, "how do you find your way around in here, anyway?" The place was decidedly undersupplied with landmarks. It reminded Miles of nothing so much as a penguin rookery. Yet penguins seemed able to find their rocky nests. He was going to have to start thinking like a penguin—or get a penguin to direct him. He studied his guide bird, who had gone absent and was doodling in the dirt. Circles, naturally.

"Where's the mess hall?" Miles asked more loudly. "Where did you get that water?"

"Water taps are on the outside of the latrines," said Suegar, "but they only work part of the time. No mess hall. We just get rat bars. Sometimes."

"Sometimes?" said Miles angrily. He could count Suegar's ribs.

"Dammit, the Cetagandans are claiming loudly to be treating their POW's by Interstellar Judiciary Commission rules. So many square meters of space per person, 3,000 calories a day, at least fifty grams of protein, two liters of drinking water—you should be getting at least two IJC standard ration bars a day. Are they starving you?"

"After a while," Suegar sighed, "you don't really care if you get yours or not." The animation that his interest in Miles as a new and hopeful object in his world had lent Suegar seemed to be falling away. His breathing had slowed, his posture slumped. He seemed about to lie down in the dirt. Miles wondered if Suegar's sleeping mat had suffered the same fate as his own. Quite some time ago, probably.

"Look, Suegar—I think I may have a relative in this camp somewhere. A cousin of my mother's. D'you think you could help me find him?"

"It might be good for you, to have a relative," Suegar agreed. "It's not good to be by yourself, here."

"Yeah, I found that out. But how can you find anyone? It doesn't look too organized."

"Oh, there's—there's groups and groups. Everyone pretty much stays in the same place after a while."

"He was in the Fourteenth Commandos. Where are they?"

"None of the *old* groups are left, much."

"He was Colonel Tremont. Colonel Guy Tremont."

"Oh, an officer." Suegar's forehead wrinkled in worry. "That makes it harder. You weren't an officer, were you? Better not let on, if you were—"

"I was a clerk," repeated Miles.

"—because there's groups here who don't like officers. A clerk. You're probably OK, then."

"Were you an officer, Suegar?" asked Miles curiously.

Suegar frowned at him, twisted his beard hairs. "Marilac Army's gone. If there's no army, it can't have officers, can it?"

Miles wondered briefly if he might get farther faster by just walking away from Suegar and trying to strike up a conversation with the next random prisoner he came across. Groups and groups. And, presumably, groups, like the five burly surly brothers. He decided to stick with Suegar for a while longer. For one thing, he wouldn't feel quite so naked if he wasn't naked by himself.

"Can you take me to anybody who used to be in the 14th?" Miles urged Suegar anew. "Anybody, who might know Tremont by sight."

"You don't know him?"

"We'd never met in person. I've seen vids of him. But I'm afraid his appearance may be . . . changed, by now."

Suegar touched his own face pensively. "Yeah, probably."

Miles clambered painfully to his feet. The temperature in the dome was just a little cool, without clothes. A voiceless draft raised the hairs on his arms. If he could just get one garment back, would he prefer his pants, to cover his genitals, or his shirt, to disguise his crooked back? Screw it. No time. He held out a hand to help Suegar up. "Come on."

Suegar glanced up at him. "You can always tell a newcomer. You're still in a hurry. In here, you slow down. Your brain slows down. . . ."

"Your scripture got anything to say on that?" inquired Miles impatiently.

" ' . . . they therefore went up here with much agility and speed, through the foundation of the city . . .' " Twin verticals appeared between Suegar's eyebrows, as he frowned speculatively at Miles.

Thank you, thought Miles. *I'll take it.* He pulled Suegar up. "Come on, then."

Neither agility nor speed, but at least progress. Suegar led him on a shambling walk across a quarter of the camp, through some groups, in wide arcs around others. Miles saw the surly brothers again at a distance, sitting on their collection of mats. Miles upped his estimation of the size of the tribe from five to about fifteen. Some men sat in twos or threes or sixes, a few sat alone, as far as possible from any others, which still wasn't very far.

The largest group by far consisted entirely of women. Miles studied them with electric interest as soon as his eye picked up the size of their unmarked boundary. There were several hundred of them at least. None were matless, although some shared. Their perimeter was actually patrolled, by groups of half a dozen or so strolling slowly about. They apparently defended two latrines for their exclusive use.

"Tell me about the girls, Suegar," Miles urged his companion, with a nod toward their group.

"Forget the girls." Suegar's grin actually had a sardonic edge. "They do not put out."

"What, not at all? None of them? I mean, here we all are, with nothing to do but entertain each other. I'd think at least some of them would be interested." Miles's reason raced ahead of Suegar's answer, mired in unpleasantness. How unpleasant did it get in here?

For answer, Suegar pointed upward to the dome. "You know

we're all monitored in here. They can see everything, pick up every word if they want. That is, if there's still anybody out there. They may have all gone away, and just forgotten to turn the dome off. I have dreams about that, sometimes. I dream that I'm here, in this dome, forever. Then I wake up, and I'm here, in this dome. . . . Sometimes I'm not sure if I'm awake or asleep. Except that the food is still coming, and once in while—not so often, anymore— somebody new, like you. The food could be automated, though, I suppose. You could be a dream. . . ."

"They're still out there," said Miles grimly.

Suegar sighed. "You know, in a way, I'm almost glad."

Monitored, yes. Miles knew all about the monitoring. He put down an urge to wave and call *Hi, Mom!* Monitoring must be a stultifying job for the goons out there. He wished they might be bored to death. "But what's that got to do with the girls, Suegar?"

"Well, at first everybody was pretty inhibited by that—" He pointed skywards again. "Then after a while we discovered that they didn't interfere with anything we did. At all. There were some rapes. . . . Since then things have been—deteriorating."

"Hm. Then I suppose the idea of starting a riot, and breaching the dome when they bring troops inside to restore order, is a no-go?"

"That was tried once, a long time ago. Don't know how long." Suegar twisted his hairs. "They don't have to come inside to stop a riot. They can reduce the dome's diameter—they reduced it to about a hundred meters, that time. Nothing to stop them reducing it down to one meter, with all of us still inside, if they choose. It stopped the riot, anyway. Or they can reduce the gas permeability of the dome to zilch and just let us breathe ourselves into a coma. That's happened twice."

"I see," said Miles. It made his neck crawl.

A bare hundred or so meters away, the side of the dome began to bulge inward like an aneurysm. Miles touched Suegar's arm. "What's happening there? More new prisoners being delivered?"

Suegar glanced around. "Uh oh. We're not in a real good position, here." He hovered a moment, as if uncertain whether to go forward or back.

A wave of movement rippled through the camp from the bulge outward, of people getting to their feet. Faces turned magnetically toward the side of the dome. Little knots of men came together; a few sprinters began running. Some people didn't get up at all.

Miles glanced back towards the women's group. About half of them were forming rapidly into a sort of phalanx.

"We're so close—what the hell, maybe we've got a chance," said Suegar. "Come on!" He started toward the bulge at his most rapid pace, a jog. Miles perforce jogged too, trying to jar his ribs as little as possible. But he was quickly winded, and his rapid breathing added an excruciating torque to his torso.

"What are we doing?" Miles started to pant to Suegar, before the dome's extruding bulge dissolved with a fading twinkle, and he saw what they were doing, saw it all.

Before the force dome's shimmering barrier now sat a dark brown pile, roughly a meter high, two meters deep, three meters wide. IJC standard ration bars, Miles recognized. Rat bars, apocryphally named after their supposed principal ingredient. Fifteen hundred calories each. Twenty-five grams of protein, fifty percent of the human MDR for vitamins A, B, C, and the rest of the alphabet—tasted like a shingle sprinkled with sugar and would sustain life and health forever or for as long as you could stand to keep eating them.

Shall we have a contest, children, to guess how many rat bars are in that pile? Miles thought. *No contest. I don't even have to measure the height and divide by three centimeters. It has to be 10,215 exactly. How ingenious.*

The Cetagandan Psy Ops corps must contain some remarkable minds. If they ever fell into his hands, Miles wondered, should he recruit them—or exterminate them? This brief fantasy was overwhelmed by the need to keep to his feet in the present reality, as 10,000 or so people, minus the wholly despairing and those too weak to move, all tried to descend on the same six square meters of the camp at once.

The first sprinters reached the pile, grabbed up armloads of rat bars, and started to sprint off. Some made it to the protection of friends, divided their spoils, and started to move away from the center of the growing human maelstrom. Others failed to dodge clots of operators like the burly surly brothers, and were violently relieved of their prizes. The second wave of sprinters, who didn't get away in time, were pinned up against the side of the dome by the incoming bodies.

Miles and Suegar, unfortunately, were in this second category. Miles's view was reduced to a sweating, heaving, stinking, swearing mass of elbows and chests and backs.

"Eat, eat!" Suegar urged around stuffed cheeks as he and Miles were separated by the pack. But the bar Miles had grabbed was twisted out of his hands before he had gathered his wits enough to follow Suegar's advice. Anyway, his hunger was nothing to his terror of being crushed, or worse, falling underfoot. His own feet pummeled over something soft, but he was unable to push back with enough strength to give the person—man, woman, who knew?—a chance to get up again.

In time the press lessened, and Miles found the edge of the crowd and broke free again. He staggered a little way off and fell to the dirt to sit, shaken and shaking, pale and cold. His breath rasped unevenly in his throat. It took him a long time to get hold of himself again.

Sheer chance, that this had hit his rawest nerve, his darkest fears, threatened his most dangerous weakness. *I could die here,* he realized, *without ever seeing the enemy's face.* But there seemed to be no new bones broken, except possibly in his left foot. He was not too sure about his left foot. The elephant who had trod on it was surely getting more than his fair share of rat bars.

All right, Miles thought at last. *That's enough time spent on R&R. On your feet, soldier.* It was time to go find Colonel Tremont.

Guy Tremont. The real hero of the siege of Fallow Core. The defiant one, the one who'd held, and held, and held, after General Xian fled, after Baneri was killed.

Xian had sworn to return, but then Xian had run into that meat grinder at Vassily Station. HQ had promised re-supply, but then HQ and its vital shuttleport had been taken by the Cetagandans.

But by this time Tremont and his troops had lost communication. So they held, waiting, and hoping. Eventually resources were reduced to hope and rocks. Rocks were versatile; they could either be boiled for soup or thrown at the enemy. At last Fallow Core was taken. Not surrendered. Taken.

Guy Tremont. Miles wanted very much to meet Guy Tremont.

On his feet and looking around, Miles spotted a distant shambling scarecrow being pelted off from a group with clods of dirt. Suegar paused out of range of their missiles, still pointing to the rag on his wrist and talking. The three or four men he was haranguing turned their backs to him by way of a broad hint.

Miles sighed and started trudging toward him. "Hey, Suegar!" he called and waved when he got closer.

"Oh, there you are." Suegar turned and brightened, and joined him. "I lost you." Suegar rubbed dirt out of his eyebrows. "Nobody wants to listen, y'know?"

"Yeah, well, most of them have heard you at least once by now, right?"

"Pro'bly twenty times. I keep thinking I might have missed one, y'see. Maybe the very One, the other One."

"Well, I'd be glad to listen to you, but I've really got to find Colonel Tremont first. You said you knew somebody . . . ?"

"Oh, right. This way." Suegar led off again.

"Thanks. Say, is every chow call like that last one?"

"Pretty much."

"What's to keep some—group—from just taking over that arc of the dome?"

"It's never issued at the same place twice. They move it all around the perimeter. There was a lot of strategy debated at one time, as to whether it was better to be at the center, so's you're never more than half a diameter away, or near the edge, so's to be up front at least part of the time. Some guys had even worked out the mathematics of it, probabilities and all that."

"Which do you favor?"

"Oh, I don't have a spot, I move around and take my chances." His right hand touched his rag. "It's not the most important thing, anyway. Still, it was good to eat—today. Whatever day this is."

"Today is November 2, '97, Earth Common Era."

"Oh? Is that all?" Suegar pulled his beard strands out straight and rolled his eyes, attempting to look across his face at them. "Thought I'd been here longer than that. Why, it hasn't even been three years. Huh." He added apologetically, "In here it's always today."

"Mm," said Miles. "So the rat bars are always delivered in a pile like that, eh?"

"Yeah."

"Damned ingenious."

"Yeah," Suegar sighed. Rage, barely breathed, was camouflaged in that sigh, in the twitch of Suegar's hands. *So, my madman is not so simple. . . .*

"Here we are," Suegar added. They paused before a group defined by half a dozen sleeping mats in a rough circle. One man looked up and glowered.

"Go away, Suegar. I ain't in the mood for a sermon."

"That the colonel?" whispered Miles.

"Naw, his name's Oliver. I knew him—a long time ago. He was

at Fallow Core, though," Suegar whispered back. "He can take you to him."

Suegar bundled Miles forward. "This is Miles. He's new. Wants to talk to you." Suegar himself backed away. Helpfully, Miles realized. Suegar was aware of his unpopularity, it seemed.

Miles studied the next link in his chain. Oliver had managed to retain his gray pajamas, sleeping mat, and cup intact, which reminded Miles again of his own nakedness. On the other hand, Oliver did not seem to be in possession of any ill-gotten duplicates. Oliver might be as burly as the surly brothers, but was not otherwise related. That was good. Not that Miles in his present state need have any more worries about thievery.

Oliver stared at Miles without favor, then seemed to relent. "What d'you want?" he growled.

Miles opened his hands. "I'm looking for Colonel Guy Tremont."

"Ain't no colonels in here, boy."

"He was a cousin of my mother's. Nobody in the family—nobody in the outside world—has heard anything from or about him since Fallow Core fell. I—I'm not from any of the other units or pieces of units that are in here. Colonel Tremont is the only person I know anything about at all." Miles clasped his hands together and tried to look waif-like. Real doubt shook him, drew down his brows. "Is he still alive, even?"

Oliver frowned. "Relative, eh?" He scratched the side of his nose with a thick finger. "I suppose you got a right. But it won't do you any good, boy, if that's what you're thinking."

"I . . ." Miles shook his head. "At this point, I just want to *know.*"

"Come on, then." Oliver levered himself to his feet with a grunt and lumbered off without looking over his shoulder.

Miles limped in his wake. "Are you taking me to him?"

Oliver made no answer until they'd finished their journey, only a few dozen meters, among and between sleeping mats. One man swore, one spat; most ignored them.

One mat lay at the edge of a group, almost far enough away to look alone. A figure lay curled up on his side with his back to them. Oliver stood silent, big fists on hips, and regarded it.

"Is that the colonel?" Miles whispered urgently.

"No, boy." Oliver sucked on his lower lip. "Only his remains."

Miles, alarmed, knelt down. Oliver was speaking poetically, Miles realized with relief. The man breathed. "Colonel Tremont? Sir?"

Miles's heart sank again, as he saw that breathing was about all that Tremont did. He lay inert, his eyes open but fixed on nothing.

They did not even flick toward Miles and dismiss him with contempt. He was thin, thinner than Suegar even. Miles traced the angle of his jaw, the shape of his ear, from the holovids he'd studied. The remains of a face, like the ruined fortress of Fallow Core. It took nearly an archeologist's insight to recognize the connections between past and present.

He was dressed, his cup sat upright by his head, but the dirt around his mat was churned to acrid, stinking mud. From urine, Miles realized. Tremont's elbows were marked with lesions, the beginning of decubiti, bedsores. A damp patch on the gray fabric of his trousers over his bony hips hinted at more advanced and horrible sores beneath.

Yet somebody must be tending him, Miles thought, *or he wouldn't be looking even this good.*

Oliver knelt beside Miles, bare toes squishing in the mud, and pulled a hunk of rat bar from beneath the elastic waistband of his trousers. He crumbled a bit between his thick fingers and pushed it between Tremont's lips. "Eat," he whispered. The lips almost moved; the crumbs dribbled to the mat. Oliver tried again, seemed to become conscious of Miles's eyes upon him, and stuffed the rest of the rat bar back into his pants with an unintelligible grumble.

"Was—was he injured when Fallow Core was overrun?" asked Miles. "Head injury?"

Oliver shook his head. "Fallow Core wasn't stormed, boy."

"But it fell on October 6th, it was reported, and—"

"It fell on October 5th. Fallow Core was betrayed." Oliver turned and walked away before his stiffened face could betray any emotion.

Miles knelt in the mud and let his breath trickle out slowly.

So. And so.

Was this the end of his quest, then?

He wanted to pace and think, but walking still hurt too much. He hobbled a little way off, trying not to accidentally infringe upon the territory of any sizeable group, and sat, then lay in the dirt with his hands behind his head, staring up at the pearly glow of the dome sealed like a lid over them all.

He considered his options, one, two, three. He considered them carefully. It didn't take long.

I thought you didn't believe in good guys and bad guys? He had cauterized his emotions, he'd thought, coming in here, for his own protection, but he could feel his carefully cultivated impartiality slipping. He was beginning to hate that dome in a really intimate, personal way. Aesthetically elegant, form united with function as perfectly as an eggshell, a marvel of physics—perverted into an instrument of torture.

Subtle torture . . . Miles reviewed the Interstellar Judiciary Commission's rules for the treatment of POW's, to which Cetaganda was a signatory. So many square meters of space per person, yes, they were certainly supplied with that. No prisoner to be solitarily confined for a period exceeding twenty-four hours— right, no solitude in here except by withdrawal into madness. No dark periods longer than twelve hours, that was easy, no dark periods at all, the perpetual glare of noon instead. No beatings— indeed, the guards could say with truth that they never laid a hand on their prisoners. They just watched, while the prisoners beat each other up instead. Rapes, even more strictly forbidden, doubtless handled the same way.

Miles had seen what they could do with their issue of two IJC standard ration bars per person per day. The rat bar riot was a particularly neat touch, he thought. No one could fail to participate (he rubbed his growling stomach). The enemy might have seeded the initial breakdown by sending in a short pile. But maybe not—the first person who snatched two instead of one left another foodless. Maybe next time that one took three, to make up for it, and so it quickly snowballed. Breaking down any hope of order, pitting group against group, person against person in a scrambling dogfight, a twice-a-day reminder of their powerlessness and degradation. None could afford for long to hold themselves aloof unless they wished to embrace slow starvation.

No forced labor—hah, check. That would require the imposition of order. Access to medical personnel—right, the various units' own medics must be mixed in out there somewhere. He re-ran the wording of that paragraph through his memory again—by God, it *did* say "personnel," didn't it? No medicine, just medical personnel. Empty-handed, naked doctors and medtechs. His lips drew back in a mirthless grin. Accurate lists of prisoners taken had been duly dispatched, as required. But no other communication . . .

Communication. This lack of word from the outside world might drive even him crazy shortly. It was as bad as prayer, talking to a God who never talked back. No wonder they all seemed touched with a sort of solipsistic schizophrenia here. Their doubts infected him. *Was* anybody still out there? Could his voice be heard and understood?

Ah, blind faith. The leap of faith. His right hand clenched, as if crushing an eggshell. "This," he enunciated clearly, "calls for a major change of plans."

He drove himself to his feet to go find Suegar again.

Miles found him not far off, hunkered in the dirt doodling. Suegar looked up with a brief smile. "Did Oliver take you to—to your cousin?"

"Yes, but I came too late. He's dying."

"Yeah . . . I was afraid that might be the case. Sorry."

"Me too." Miles was momentarily distracted from his purpose by a practical curiosity. "Suegar, what do they do with dead bodies here?"

"There's a rubbish pile of sorts, over against one side of the dome. The dome sort of extrudes and laps it up every once in a while, same way as food and new prisoners are introduced. Usually by the time a body swells and starts to stink, somebody'll drag it over there. I take 'em sometimes."

"No chance of anybody sneaking out in the rubbish pile, I suppose?"

"They microwave-incinerate it all before the portal's opened."

"Ah." Miles took a deep breath, and launched himself. "Suegar, it's come to me. I *am* the other One."

Suegar nodded serenely, unsurprised. "I'd had it figured."

Miles paused, nonplused. Was that all the response . . . ? He had expected something more energetic, either pro or con. "It came to me in a vision," he declared dramatically, following his script anyway.

"Oh, yeah?" Suegar's attention sharpened gratifyingly. "I've never gotten a vision," he added with envy. "Had to figure it all out, y'know, from context. What's it like? A trance?"

Shit, and here I thought this guy talked with elves and angels. . . . Miles backed down slightly. "No, it's like a thought, only more compelling. It storms your will—burns like lust, only not so easy to satisfy. Not like a trance, because it drives you outward, not inward." He hesitated, unsettled, having spoken more truth than he'd intended.

Suegar looked vastly encouraged. "Oh, good. I was afraid for a second you might be one of those guys who start talking to people nobody else can see."

Miles glanced upward involuntarily, returned his gaze straightly to Suegar.

"—so that's a vision. Why, I've felt like that." His eyes seemed to focus and intensify.

"Didn't you recognize it in yourself?" asked Miles blandly.

"Not by name . . . it's not a comfortable thing, to be chosen so. I tried to evade it for a long time, but God finds ways of dealing with draft dodgers."

"You're too modest, Suegar. You've believed in your scripture, but not in yourself. Don't you know that when you're given a task, you're given the power to accomplish it as well?"

Suegar sighed in joyous satisfaction. "I knew it was a job for two. It's just like the scripture said."

"Uh, right. So now we are two. But we must be more. I guess we'd better start with your friends."

"That won't take much time," said Suegar wryly. "You got a step two in mind, I hope?"

"Then we'll start with your enemies. Or your nodding acquaintances. We'll start with the first bleeding body that crosses our path. It doesn't matter where we start, because I mean to have them all, in the end. All, to the last and least." A particularly apt quote shot across his memory, and he declaimed vigorously, " 'Those who have ears, let them hear.' All." Miles sent a real prayer up from his heart with that one.

"All right," Miles pulled Suegar to his feet, "let's go preach to the unconverted."

Suegar laughed suddenly. "I had a top kick once who used to say, 'Let's go kick some ass,' in just that tone of voice."

"That, too." Miles grimaced. "You understand, universal membership in this congregation won't come all voluntary. But you leave the recruiting to me, hear?"

Suegar stroked his beard hairs, regarded Miles from beneath raised brows. "A clerk, eh?"

"Right."

"Yes, sir."

They started with Oliver.

Miles gestured. "May we step into your office?"

Oliver rubbed his nose with the back of his hand and sniffed. "Let me give you a piece of advice, boy. You ain't gonna make it in here as a stand-up comic. Every joke that can possibly be made has been run into the ground. Even the sick ones."

"Very well." Miles sat cross-legged, near Oliver's mat but not too near. Suegar hunkered down behind Miles's shoulder, not so welded to the ground, as if ready to skip backwards if necessary. "I'll lay it out straight, then. I don't like the way things are run around here."

Oliver's mouth twisted sardonically; he did not comment aloud. He didn't need to.

"I'm going to change them," Miles added.

"Shit," said Oliver, and rolled back over.

"Starting here and now."

After a moment's silence Oliver added, "Go away or I'll pound you."

Suegar started to get up; Miles irritably motioned him back down.

"He was a commando," Suegar whispered worriedly. "He can break you in half."

"Nine-tenths of the people in this camp can break me in half, including the girls," Miles whispered back. "It's not a significant consideration."

Miles leaned forward, grasped Oliver's chin, and twisted his face back toward him. Suegar sucked his breath through his teeth with a whistle at this dangerous tactic.

"Now, there's this about cynicism, Sergeant. It's the universe's most supine moral position. Real comfortable. If nothing can be done, then you're not some kind of shit for not doing it, and you can lie there and stink to yourself in perfect peace."

Oliver batted Miles's hand down, but did not turn away again. Rage flared in his eyes. "Suegar tell you I was a sergeant?" he hissed.

"No, it's written on your forehead in letters of fire. Listen up, Oliver—"

Oliver rolled over and up as far as supporting his upper body with his knuckles on his sleeping mat. Suegar flinched, but did not flee.

"You listen up, mutant," Oliver snarled. "We've done it all already. We've done drill, and games, and clean living, exercise, and cold showers, except there ain't no cold showers. We've done group sings and floor shows. We've done it by the numbers, by the book, by candlelight. We've done it by force, and made real war on each other. After that we did sin and sex and sadism till we were ready to puke. We've done it all at least ten times. You think you're the first reformer to come through here?"

"No, Oliver." Miles leaned into his face, his eyes boring into Oliver's burning eyes unscorched. His voice fell to a whisper. "I think I'm the last."

Oliver was silent a moment, then barked a laugh. "By God,

Suegar has found his soul-mate at last. Two loonies together, just like his scripture says."

Miles paused thoughtfully, sat up as straight as his spine would allow. "Read me your scripture again, Suegar. The full text." He closed his eyes for total concentration, also to discourage interruptions from Oliver.

Suegar rustled around and cleared his throat nervously. "'For those that shall be the heirs of salvation,'" he began. "'Thus they went along toward the gate. Now you must note that the city stood upon a mighty hill, but the pilgrims went up that hill with ease, because they had these two men to lead them by the arms; also they had left their mortal garments behind them in the river, for though they went in with them, they came out without them. They therefore went up here with much agility and speed, through the foundation upon which the city was framed higher than the clouds. They therefore went up through the regions of the air . . .'" He added apologetically, "It breaks off there. That's where I tore the page. Not sure what that signifies."

"Probably means that after that you're supposed to improvise for yourself," Miles suggested, opening his eyes again. So, that was the raw material he was building on. He had to admit the last line in particular gave him a turn, a chill like a belly full of cold worms. So be it. Forward.

"There you are, Oliver. That's what I'm offering. The only hope worth breathing for. Salvation itself."

"Very uplifting," sneered Oliver.

"'Uplifted' is just what I intend you all to be. You've got to understand, Oliver, I'm a fundamentalist. I take my scriptures *very* literally."

Oliver opened his mouth, then closed it with a snap. Miles had his utter attention.

Communication at last, Miles breathed inwardly. *We have connected.*

"It would take a miracle," said Oliver at last, "to uplift this whole place."

"Mine is not a theology of the elect. I intend to preach to the masses. Even," he was definitely getting into the swing of this, "the sinners. Heaven is for everyone.

"But miracles, by their very nature, must break in from outside. We don't carry them in our pockets—"

"You don't, that's for sure," muttered Oliver with a glance at Miles's undress.

"—we can only pray, and prepare ourselves for a better world. But miracles come only to the prepared. Are you prepared, Oliver?" Miles leaned forward, his voice vibrating with energy.

"Sh . . ." Oliver's voice trailed off. He glanced for confirmation, oddly enough, at Suegar. "Is this guy for real?"

"He thinks he's faking it," said Suegar blandly, "but he's not. He's the One, all right and tight."

The cold worms writhed again. Dealing with Suegar, Miles decided, was like fencing in a hall of mirrors. Your target, though real, was never quite where it looked as if it should be.

Oliver inhaled. Hope and fear, belief and doubt, intermingled in his face. "How shall we be saved, Rev'rend?"

"Ah—call me Brother Miles, I think. Yes. Tell me—how many converts can you deliver on your own naked, unsupported authority?"

Oliver looked extremely thoughtful. "Just let them see *that* light, and they'll follow it anywhere."

"Well . . . well . . . salvation is for all, to be sure, but there may be certain temporary practical advantages to maintaining a priesthood. I mean, blessed also are they who do not see, and yet believe."

"It's true," agreed Oliver, "that if your religion failed to deliver a miracle, that a human sacrifice would certainly follow."

"Ah . . . quite," Miles gulped. "You are a man of acute insight."

"That's not an insight," said Oliver. "That's a personal guarantee."

"Yes, well . . . to return to my question. How many followers can you raise? I'm talking bodies here, not souls."

Oliver frowned, cautious still. "Maybe twenty."

"Can any of them bring in others? Branch out, hook in more?"

"Maybe."

"Make them your corporals, then. I think we had better disregard any previous ranks here. Call it, ah, the Army of the Reborn. No. The Reformation Army. That scans better. We shall be re-formed. The body has disintegrated like the caterpillar in its chrysalis, into nasty green gook, but we shall re-form into the butterfly and fly away."

Oliver sniffed again. "Just what reforms you planning?"

"Just one, I think. The food."

Oliver gave him a disbelieving stare. "You sure this isn't just a scam to get yourself a free meal?"

"True, I *am* getting hungry . . ." Miles backed off from the joke as Oliver remained icily unimpressed. "But so are a lot of other people. By tomorrow, we can have them all eating out of our hands."

"When would you want these twenty guys?"

"By the next chow call." Good, he'd startled the man.

"That soon?"

"You understand, Oliver, the belief that you have all the time in the world is an illusion this place fosters on purpose. Resist it."

"You're sure in a hurry."

"So, you got a dental appointment? I think not. Besides, I'm only half your mass. I gotta move twice as fast just to keep up the momentum. Twenty, plus. By next chow call."

"What the hell do you think you're gonna be able to do with twenty guys?"

"We're going to take the food pile."

Oliver's lips tightened in disgust. "Not with twenty guys, you're not. No go. Besides, it's been done. I told you we'd made real war in here. It'd be a quick massacre."

"—and then, after we've taken it—we re-distribute it. Fair and square, one rat bar per customer, all controlled and quartermasterly. To sinners and all. By the next chow call everybody who's ever been shorted will be coming over to us. And then we'll be in a position to deal with the hard cases."

"You're nuts. You can't do it. Not with twenty guys."

"Did I say we were only going to have twenty guys? Suegar, did I say that?"

Suegar, listening in rapt fascination, shook his head.

"Well, I ain't sticking my neck out to get pounded unless you can produce some visible means of support," said Oliver. "This could get us killed."

"Can do," Miles promised recklessly. One had to start lifting somewhere; his imaginary bootstraps would do well enough. "I will deliver 500 troops to the sacred cause by chow call."

"You do that, and I'll walk the perimeter of this camp naked on my hands," retorted Oliver.

Miles grinned. "I may hold you to that, Sergeant. Twenty plus. By chow call." Miles stood. "Come on, Suegar."

Oliver waved them off irritably. They retreated in good order. When Miles looked back over his shoulder, Oliver had arisen, and was walking toward a group of occupied mats tangential to his own, waving down an apparent acquaintance.

✧   ✧   ✧

"So where do we get 500 troops before next chow call?" Suegar asked. "I better warn you, Oliver was the best thing I had. The next is bound to be tougher."

"What," said Miles, "is your faith wavering so soon?"

"I believe," said Suegar, "I just don't see. Maybe that makes me blessed, I dunno."

"I'm surprised. I thought it was pretty obvious. There." Miles pointed across the camp toward the unmarked border of the women's group.

"Oh." Suegar stopped short. "Oh, oh. I don't think so, Miles."

"Yes. Let's go."

"You won't get in there without a change-of-sex operation."

"What, as God-driven as you are, haven't you tried to preach your scripture to them?"

"I tried. Got pounded. Tried elsewhere after that."

Miles paused, and pursed his lips, studying Suegar. "It wasn't defeat, or you wouldn't have hung on long enough to meet me. Was it—ah, shame, that drained your usual resolve? You got something to work off in that quarter?"

Suegar shook his head. "Not personally. Except maybe, sins of omission. I just didn't have the heart to harass 'em any more."

"This whole place is suffering from sins of omission." A relief, that Suegar wasn't some sort of self-confessed rapist. Miles's eyes swept the scene, teasing out the pattern from the limited cues of position, grouping, activity. "Yes . . . predator pressure produces herd behavior. Social—fragmentation here being what it is, the pressure must be pretty high, to hold a group of that size together. But I hadn't noticed any incidents since I got here. . . ."

"It comes and goes," said Suegar. "Phases of the moon or something."

Phases of the moon, right. Miles sent up a prayer of thanks in his heart to whatever gods might be—to Whom it may concern—that the Cetagandans appeared to have implanted some standard time-release anti-ovulant in all their female prisoners, along with their other immunizations. Bless the forgotten individual who'd put *that* clause in the IJC rules, forcing the Cetagandans into more subtle forms of legal torture. And yet, would the presence of pregnancies, infants, and children among the prisoners have been another destabilizing stress—or a stabilizing force deeper and stronger than all the previous loyalties the Cetagandans seemed to have so successfully broken down? From a purely logistical viewpoint, Miles was elated that the question was theoretical.

"Well . . ." Miles took a deep breath, and pulled an imaginary hat down over his eyes at an aggressive angle. "I'm new here, and so temporarily unembarrassed. Let he who is without sin cast the first lure. Besides, I have an advantage for this sort of negotiation. I'm clearly not a threat." He marched forward.

"I'll wait for you here," called Suegar helpfully, and hunkered down where he was.

Miles timed his forward march to intersect a patrol of six women strolling down their perimeter. He arranged himself in front of them and swept off his imaginary hat to hold strategically over his crotch. "Good afternoon, ladies. Allow me to apologize for m'beh—"

His opening line was interrupted by a mouthful of dirt abruptly acquired as his legs were swept backward and his shoulders forward by the four women who had parted around him, dumping him neatly on his face. He had not even managed to spit it out when he found himself plucked up and whirled dizzily through the air, still face-down, by hands grasping his arms and legs. A muttered count of three, and he was soaring in a short forlorn arc, to land in a heap not far from Suegar. The patrollers walked on without another word.

"See what I mean?" said Suegar.

Miles turned his head to look at him. "You had that trajectory calculated to the centimeter, didn't you?" he said smearily.

"Just about," agreed Suegar. "I figured they could heave you quite a bit farther than usual, on account of your size."

Miles scrambled back up to a sitting position, still trying to get his wind. Damn the ribs, which had grown almost bearable, but which now wrung his chest with electric agony at every breath. In a few minutes he got up and brushed himself off. As an afterthought, he picked up his invisible hat, too. Dizzied, he had to brace his hands on his knees a moment.

"All right," he muttered, "back we go."

"Miles—"

"It's gotta be done, Suegar. No other choice. Anyway, I can't quit, once I've started. I've been told I'm pathologically persistent. I *can't* quit."

Suegar opened his mouth to object, then swallowed his protest. "Right," he said. He settled down cross-legged, his right hand unconsciously caressing his rag rope library. "I'll wait till you call me in." He seemed to fall into a reverie, or meditation—or maybe a doze.

Miles's second foray ended precisely like the first, except that his trajectory was perhaps a little wider and a little higher. The third attempt went the same way, but his flight was much shorter.

"Good," he muttered to himself. "Must be tiring 'em out."

This time he skipped in parallel to the patrol, out of reach but well within hearing. "Look," he panted, "you don't have to do this piecemeal. Let me make it easy for you. I have this teratogenic bone disorder—I'm not a mutant, you understand, my genes are normal, it's just their expression got distorted, from my mother being exposed to a certain poison while she was pregnant—it was a one-shot thing, won't affect any children *I* might have—I always felt it was easier to get dates when that was clearly understood, *not* a mutant—anyway, my bones are brittle, in fact any one of you could probably break every one in my body. You may wonder why I'm telling you all this—in fact, I usually prefer not to advertise it—you have to stop and listen to me. I'm not a threat—do I look like a threat?—a challenge, maybe, not a threat—are you going to make me run all around this camp after you? Slow down, for God's sake—" He would be out of wind, and therefore verbal ammunition, very shortly at this rate. He hopped around in front of them and planted himself, arms outstretched.

"—so if you *are* planning to break every bone in my body, please do it now and get it over with, because I'm going to keep coming back here until you do."

At a brief hand signal from their leader the patrol stopped, facing him.

"Take him at his word," suggested a tall redhead. Her short brush of electric copper hair fascinated Miles to distraction; he pictured missing masses of it having fallen to the floor at the clippers of the ruthless Cetagandan prison processors. "I'll break the left arm if you'll break the right, Conr," she continued.

"If that's what it takes to get you to stop and listen to me for five minutes, so be it," Miles responded, not retreating. The redhead stepped forward and braced herself, locking his left elbow in an arm bar, putting on the pressure.

"Five minutes, right?" Miles added desperately as the pressure mounted. Her stare scorched his profile. He licked his lips, closed his eyes, held his breath, and waited. The pressure reached critical—he rose on his toes . . .

She released him abruptly, so that he staggered. "Men," she commented disgustedly. "Always gotta make everything a peeing contest."

"Biology is Destiny," gasped Miles, popping his eyes back open.

"—or are you some kind of pervert—do you get off on being beaten up by women?"

God, I hope not. He remained unbetrayed by unauthorized salutes from his nether parts, just barely. If he was going to be around that redhead much he was definitely going to have to get his pants back somehow. "If I said yes, would you refrain, just to punish me?" he offered.

"Shit, no."

"It was just a thought—"

"Cut the crap, Beatrice," said the patrol leader. At a jerk of her head the redhead stepped back into formation. "All right, runt, you've got your five minutes. Maybe."

"Thank you, ma'am." Miles took a breath, and reordered himself as best he could with no uniform to adjust. "First, let me apologize for intruding upon your privacy in this undress. Practically the first persons I met upon entering this camp were a self-help group— they helped themselves to my clothes, among other things—"

"I saw that," confirmed Beatrice-the-redhead unexpectedly. "Pitt's bunch."

Miles pulled off his hat and swept her a bow with it. "Yes, thank you."

"You moon people behind you when you do that," she commented dispassionately.

"That's their look-out," responded Miles. "For myself, I want to talk to your leader, or leaders. I have a serious plan for improving the tone of this place with which I wish to invite your group to collaborate. Bluntly, you are the largest remaining pocket of civilization, not to mention military order, in here. I'd like to see you expand your borders."

"It takes everything we've got to keep our borders from being overrun, son," replied the leader. "No can do. So take yourself off."

"Jack yourself off, too," suggested Beatrice. "You ain't gettin' any in here."

Miles sighed, and turned his hat around in his hands by its wide brim. He spun it for a moment on one finger, and locked eyes with the redhead. "Note my hat. It was the one garment I managed to keep from the ravages of the burly surly brothers—Pitt's bunch, you say."

She snorted at the turn of phrase. "Those jerks . . . why just a hat? Why not pants? Why not a full-dress uniform while you're at it?" she added sarcastically.

"A hat is a more useful object for communicating. You can make broad gestures," he did so, "denote sincerity," he held it over his heart, "or indicate embarrassment," over his genitals, with a hang-dog crouch, "or rage—" he flung it to earth as if he might drive it into the ground, then picked it up and brushed it off carefully, "or determination—" he jammed it on his head and yanked the brim down over his eyes, "or make courtesies." He swept it off again in salute to her. "Do you see the hat?"

She was beginning to be amused. "Yes . . ."

"Do you see the feathers on the hat?"

"Yes . . ."

"Describe them."

"Oh—plumey things."

"How many?"

"Two. Bunched together."

"Do you see the color of the feathers?"

She drew back, suddenly self-conscious again, with a sidewise glance at her companions. "No."

"When you can see the color of the feathers," said Miles softly, "you'll also understand how you can expand your borders to infinity."

She was silent, her face closed and locked. But the patrol leader muttered, "Maybe this little runt better talk to Tris. Just this once."

The woman in charge had clearly been a front line trooper once, not a tech like the majority of the females. She had certainly not acquired the muscles that flowed like braided leather cords beneath her skin from crouching by the hour in front of a holovid display in some rear-echelon underground post. She had toted the real weapons that spat real death, and sometimes broke down; had rammed against the limits of what could really be done by flesh and bone and metal, and been marked by that deforming press. Illusion had been burned out of her like an infection, leaving a cauterized scar. Rage burned permanently in her eyes like a fire in a coal seam, underground and unquenchable. She might be thirty-five, or forty.

God, I'm in love, thought Miles. *Brother Miles wants YOU for the Reformation Army . . .* then got hold of his thoughts. Here, now, was the make-or-break point for his scheme, and all the persiflage, verbal misdirection, charm, chutzpah, and bullshit he could muster weren't going to be enough, not even tied up with a big blue bow.

The wounded want power, nothing else; they think it will keep them from being hurt again. This one will not be interested in Suegar's strange message—at least, not yet. . . . Miles took a deep breath.

"Ma'am, I'm here to offer you command of this camp."

She stared at him as if he were something she'd found growing on the walls in a dark corner of the latrine. Her eyes raked over his nudity; Miles could feel the claw marks glowing from his chin to his toes.

"Which you store in your duffel bag, no doubt," she growled. "Command of this camp doesn't exist, mutant. So it's not yours to give. Deliver him to our perimeter in pieces, Beatrice."

He ducked the redhead. He would pursue correction of the mutant business later. "Command of this camp is mine to *create*," he asserted. "Note, please, that what I offer is power, not revenge. Revenge is too expensive a luxury. Commanders can't afford it."

Tris uncoiled from her sleeping mat to her full height, then had to bend her knees to bring her face level to his, hissing, "Too bad, little turd. You almost interest me. Because I *want* revenge. On every man in this camp."

"Then the Cetagandans have succeeded; you've forgotten who your real enemy is."

"Say, rather, that I've discovered who my real enemy is. Do you want to know the things they've done to us—our own guys—"

"The Cetagandans want you to believe this," a wave of his hand embraced the camp, "is something you're doing to each other. So fighting each other, you become their puppets. They watch you all the time, you know, voyeurs of your humiliation."

Her glance flicked upward, infinitesimally; good. It was almost a disease among these people, that they would look in any direction at all in preference to up at the dome.

"Power is better than revenge," suggested Miles, not flinching before her snake-cold, set face, her hot coal eyes. "Power is a live thing, by which you reach out to grasp the future. Revenge is a dead thing, reaching out from the past to grasp you."

"—and you're a bullshit artist," she interrupted, "reaching out to grasp whatever's going down. I've got you pegged now. *This* is power." She flexed her arm under his nose, muscles coiling and loosing. "This is the only power that exists in here. You haven't got it, and you're looking for some to cover your ass. But you've come to the wrong store."

"No," Miles denied, and tapped his forehead. "*This* is power. And I own the store. This controls that," he slapped his bunched fist.

"Men may move mountains, but ideas move men. Minds can be reached through bodies—what else is the point of all this," he waved at the camp, "but to reach your minds through your bodies. But that power flows both ways, and the outflow is the stronger tide.

"When you have allowed the Cetagandans to reduce your power to *that* alone," he squeezed her bicep for emphasis—it was like squeezing a rock covered in velvet, and she tensed, enraged at the liberty, "then you have allowed them to reduce you to your weakest part. And they win."

"They win anyway," she snapped, shrugging him off. He breathed relief that she hadn't chosen to break his arm. "Nothing that we do within this circle will result in any net change. We're still prisoners, whatever we do. They can cut off the food, or the damned air, or squeeze us to mush. And time's on their side. If we spill our guts restoring order—if that's what you're trying to work up to—all they have to do is wait for it to break down again. We're *beaten*. We're *taken*. There's nobody left *out there*. We're here forever. And you'd better start getting used to the idea."

"I've heard that song before," said Miles. "Use your head. If they meant to keep you forever, they could have incinerated you at the start, and saved the considerable expense of operating this camp. No. It's your minds they want. You are all here because you were Marilac's best and brightest, the hardest fighters, the strongest, baddest, most dangerous. The ones any potential resisters to the occupation would look to for leadership. It's the Cetagandans' plan to break you, and then return you to your world like little innoculated infections, counseling surrender to your people.

"When this is killed," he touched her forehead, oh so lightly, "then the Cetagandans have nothing more to fear from this," one finger on her bicep, "and you will all go free. To a world whose horizon will encircle you just like this dome, and just as inescapably. The war's not over. You are *here* because the Cetagandans are still waiting for the surrender of Fallow Core."

He thought for a moment she might murder him, strangle him on the spot. She must certainly prefer ripping him apart to letting him see her weep.

She regained her protective bitter tension with a toss of her head, a gulp of air. "If that's true, then following you puts us farther from freedom, not closer."

Damn, a logician to boot. She didn't have to pound him, she could parse him to death if he didn't scramble. He scrambled.

"There is a subtle difference between being a prisoner and being a slave. I don't mistake either for being free. Neither do you."

She fell silent, staring at him through slitted eyes, pulling unconsciously on her lower lip. "You're an odd one," she said at last. "Why do you say 'you' and not 'we'?"

Miles shrugged casually. Blast—he rapidly reviewed his pitch—she was right, he had. A little too close to the edge, there. He might yet make an opportunity of the mistake, though. "Do I look like the flower of Marilac's military might? I'm an outsider, trapped in a world I never made. A traveler—a pilgrim—just passing through. Ask Suegar."

She snorted. "That loonie."

She'd missed the catch. Rats, as Elli would say. He missed Elli. Try again later. "Don't discount Suegar. He has a message for you. I found it fascinating."

"I've heard it. I find it irritating. . . . So, what do you want out of this? And don't tell me 'nothing,' 'cause I won't believe you. Frankly, I think you're after command of the camp yourself, and I'm not volunteering to be your stepping stone in some empire-building scheme."

She was thinking at speed now, and constructively, actually following out trains of thought besides that of having him removed to her border in bits. He was getting warmer. . . .

"I only wish to be your spiritual advisor. I do not want—indeed, can't use—command. Just an advisor."

It must have been something about the term "advisor" that clicked, some old association of hers. Her eyes flicked fully open suddenly. He was close enough to see her pupils dilate. She leaned forward, and her index finger traced the faint indentations on his face beside his nose caused by certain control leads in a space armor helmet. She straightened again, and her first two fingers in a V caressed the deeper marks permanently flanking her own nose. "What did you say you were, before?"

"A clerk. Recruiting office," Miles replied sturdily.

"I . . . see."

And if what she saw was the absurdity of someone claiming to be a rear-echelon clerk having worn combat armor often and long enough to have picked up its stigmata, he was in. Maybe.

She coiled herself back up on her sleeping mat, and gestured toward its other end. "Sit down, chaplain. And keep talking."

✧　　✧　　✧

Suegar was genuinely asleep when Miles found him again, sitting up cross-legged and snoring. Miles tapped him on the shoulder.

"Wake up, Suegar, we're home."

He snorted to consciousness. "God, I miss coffee. Huh?" He blinked at Miles. "You're still in one piece?"

"It was a near thing. Look, this garments-in-the-river bit—now that we've found each other, do we have to go *on* being naked? Or is the prophecy sufficiently fulfilled?"

"Huh?"

"Can we get dressed now?" Miles repeated patiently.

"Why—I don't know. I suppose, if we were meant to have clothes, they'd be given to us—"

Miles prodded and pointed. "There. They're given to us."

Beatrice stood a few meters away in a hip-shot pose of bored exasperation, a bundle of gray cloth under her arm. "You two loonies want this stuff or not? I'm going back."

"You got them to give you clothes?" Suegar whispered in amazement.

"Us, Suegar, us." Miles motioned to Beatrice. "I think it's all right."

She fired the bundle at him, sniffed, and stalked away.

"Thanks," Miles called. He shook out the fabric. Two sets of gray pajamas, one small, one large. Miles had only to turn up the bottoms of the pants legs one fold to keep them from catching under his heels. They were stained and stiff with old sweat and dirt, and had probably been peeled off a corpse, Miles reflected. Suegar crawled into his and stood fingering the gray fabric in wonder.

"They gave us clothes. *Gave* us," he muttered. "How'd you do that?"

"They gave us everything, Suegar. Come on, I've got to talk to Oliver again." Miles dragged Suegar off determinedly. "I wonder how much time we've actually got before the next chow call? Two in each twenty-four-hour cycle, to be sure, but I wouldn't be surprised if it's irregular, to increase your temporal disorientation— after all, it's the only clock in here . . ."

Movement caught Miles's eye, a man running. It wasn't the occasional flurry of someone outrunning a hostile group; this one just ran, head down, flat out, bare feet thumping the dirt in frantic rhythm. He followed the perimeter generally, except for a detour around the border of the women's group. As he ran, he wept.

"What's this?" Miles asked Suegar, with a nod at the approaching figure.

Suegar shrugged. "It takes you like that sometimes. When you can't stand sitting in here any more. I saw a guy run till he died, once. Around and around and around . . ."

"Well," Miles decided, "this one's running to us."

"He's gonna be running away from us in a second."

"Then help me catch him."

Miles hit him low and Suegar high. Suegar sat on his chest. Miles sat on his right arm, halving his effective resistance. He must have been a very young soldier when he was captured—maybe he had lied about his age at induction—for even now he had a boy's face, ravaged by tears and his personal eternity inside this hollow pearl. He inhaled in sobbing gasps and exhaled in garbled obscenities. After a time he quieted.

Miles leaned into his face and grinned wolfishly. "You a party animal, boy?"

"Yeah . . ." His white-rimmed eyes rolled, right and left, but no rescue approached.

"How 'bout your friends? They party animals too?"

"The best," the boy asserted, perhaps secretly shaken by the suspicion that he'd fallen into the hands of someone even crazier than himself. "You better clear off me, mutant, or they'll take you apart."

"I want to invite you and your friends to a *major* party," Miles chanted. "We gonna have a party tonight that's an his-tor-i-cal event. You know where to find Sergeant Oliver, late of the 14th Commandos?"

"Yeah . . ." the boy admitted cautiously.

"Well, you go get your friends and report to him. You better reserve your seat aboard his ve-hic-le now, 'cause if you're not on it, you gonna be *under* it. The Reformation Army is moving out. You copy?"

"Copy," he gasped, as Suegar pressed his fist into the boy's solar plexus for emphasis.

"Tell him Brother Miles sent you," Miles called as the boy staggered off, glancing nervously over his shoulder. "You can't hide in here. If you don't show, I'll send the Cosmic Commandos to find you."

Suegar shook out his cramped limbs, his new used clothes. "Think he'll come?"

Miles grinned. "Fight or flight. That one'll be all right." He stretched himself, recaptured his original orientation. "Oliver."

✧   ✧   ✧

In the end they had not twenty, but 200. Oliver had picked up forty-six. The running boy brought in eighteen. The signs of order and activity in the area brought in the curious—a drifter at the edge of the group had only to ask, "What's going on?" to be inducted and promoted to corporal on the spot. Interest among the spectators was aroused to a fever when Oliver's troops marched up to the women's border—and were admitted within. They picked up another seventy-five volunteers instantly.

"Do you know what's going on?" Miles asked one such, as he fed them through a short gauntlet of inspection and sent them off to one of the fourteen command groups he had devised.

"No," the man admitted. He waved an arm eagerly toward the center of the women's group. "But I wanta go where *they're* going . . ."

Miles cut the admissions off at 200 total in deference to Tris's growing nervousness at this infiltration of her borders, and promptly turned the courtesy into a card in his own hand in their still-continuing strategy debate. Tris wanted to divide her group in the usual way, half for the attack, half to maintain home base and keep the borders from collapsing. Miles was insisting on an all-out effort.

"If we win, you won't need guards anymore."

"What if we lose?"

Miles lowered his voice. "We don't dare lose. This is the only time we'll have surprise on our side. Yes, we can fall back—re-group—try again—I for one am prepared—no, compelled—to keep trying till it kills me. But after this, what we're trying to do will be fully apparent to any counter-group, and they'll have time to plan counter-strategies of their own. I have a particular aversion to stale-mates. I prefer winning wars to prolonging them."

She sighed, momentarily drained, tired, old. "I've been at war a long time, y'know? After a while even losing a war can start to look preferable to prolonging it."

He could feel his own resolve slip, sucked into the vortex of that same black doubt. He pointed upwards, dropping his voice to a rasping whisper. "But not, surely, to *those* bastards."

She glanced upwards. Her shoulders straightened. "No. Not to those . . ." She took a deep breath. "All right, chaplain. You'll get your all-out effort. Just once . . ."

Oliver returned from a circuit of the command groups and squatted beside them. "They've got their orders. How many's Tris contributing to each group?"

"Commandant Tris," Miles quickly corrected for her as her brows beetled. "It's gonna be an all-out shot. You'll get every walking body in here."

Oliver made a quick calculation in the dirt with his finger for a stylus. "That'll put about fifty in each group—ought to be enough . . . matter of fact, what say we set up twenty groups? It'll speed distribution when we get the lines set up. Could make the difference between bringing this off, and not."

"No," Miles cut in quickly as Tris began to nod agreement. "It has to be fourteen. Fourteen battle groups make fourteen lines for fourteen piles. Fourteen is—is a theologically significant number," he added as they stared doubtfully at him.

"Why?" asked Tris.

"For the fourteen apostles," Miles intoned, tenting his hands piously.

Tris shrugged. Suegar scratched his head, started to speak—Miles speared him with a baleful glance, and he stilled.

Oliver eyed him narrowly. "Huh." But he did not argue further.

Then came the waiting. Miles stopped worrying about his uppermost fear—that their captors would introduce the next food pile early, before his plans were in place—and started worrying about his second greatest fear, that the food pile would come so late he'd lose control of his troops and they would start to wander off, bored and discouraged. Getting them all assembled had made Miles feel like a man pulling on a goat with a rope made of water. Never had the insubstantial nature of the Idea seemed more self-apparent.

Oliver tapped him on the shoulder and pointed. "Here we go . . ."

A side of the dome about a third of the way around the edge from them began to bulge inward.

The timing was perfect. His troops were at the peak of readiness. Too perfect . . . the Centagandans had been watching all this, surely they wouldn't miss an opportunity to make life more difficult for their prisoners. If the food pile wasn't early, it had to be late. Or . . .

Miles bounded to his feet, screaming, "Wait! Wait! Wait for my order!"

His sprint groups wavered, drawn toward the anticipated goal. But Oliver had chosen his group commanders well—they held, and held their groups, and looked to Oliver. They *had* been soldiers once. Oliver looked to Tris, flanked by her lieutenant Beatrice, and Tris looked to Miles, angrily.

"What is it now? We're gonna lose our advantage . . ." she began, as the general stampede throughout the camp started toward the bulge.

"If I'm wrong," Miles moaned, "I'm going to kill myself— wait, dammit! On my order. I can't see— Suegar, give me a boost—" He clambered up on the thin man's shoulders and stared toward the bulge. The force wall had only half twinkled out when the first distant cries of disappointment met his straining ears. Miles's head swiveled frantically. How many wheels within wheels—if the Cetagandans knew, and he knew they knew, and they knew he knew they knew, and . . . He cut off his internal gibber as a second bulge began, on the opposite side of the camp from the first.

Miles's arm flung out, pointing toward it like a man rolling dice. "There! There! Go, go, go!"

Tris caught on then, whistling and shooting him a look of startled respect, before whirling and dashing off to double-time the main body of their troops after the sprint groups. Miles slithered off Suegar and started limping after.

He glanced back over his shoulder, as the rolling gray mass of humanity crashed up against the opposite side of the dome and reversed itself. He felt suddenly like a man trying to outrun a tidal wave. He indulged himself with one brief anticipatory whimper, and limped faster.

One more chance to be mortally wrong—no. His sprint groups had reached the pile, and the pile was really there. Already they were starting to break it down. The support troops surrounded them with a wall of bodies as they began to spread out along the perimeter of the dome. The Cetagandans had outfoxed themselves. This time.

Miles was reduced from the commander's eagle overview to the grunt's worm's-eye as the tidal wave overtook him. Someone shoved him from behind, and his face hit the dirt. He thought he recognized the back of the surly Pitt, vaulting over him, but he wasn't certain—surely Pitt would have stepped on, not over him. Suegar yanked him up by the left arm, and Miles bit back a scream of pain. There was enough howling already.

Miles recognized the running boy, squaring off with another tough. Miles shoved past him with a shouted reminder—"You're supposed to be yelling *Get in line!*, NOT *Get fucked!* . . . The signal always gets degraded in combat," he muttered to himself. "Always . . ."

Beatrice materialized beside him. Miles clung to her instantly. Beatrice had personal space, her own private perimeter, maintained even as Miles watched by a casual elbow to somebody's jaw with a quite sickening crack. It he tried that, Miles reflected enviously, not only would he smash his own elbow, but his opponent's nipple would probably be quite undamaged. Speaking of nipples, he found himself face to—well, not face—confronting the redhead. He resisted the urge to cuddle into the soft gray fabric covering home base with a contented sigh on the grounds that it would certainly get both his arms broken. He uncrossed his eyes and looked up into her face.

"C'mon," she said, and dragged him off through the mob. Was the noise level dropping? The human wall of his own troops parted just enough to let them squeeze through.

They were near the exit point of the chow line. It was working, by God it was working. The fourteen command groups, still bunched rather too closely along the dome wall—but that could be improved next run—were admitting the hungry supplicants one at a time. The expediters kept the lines moving at top speed, and channeled the already-supplied along the perimeter behind the human shield wall in a steady stream, to flow back out into the larger camp at the edge of the mob. Oliver had put his toughest-looking bravos to work in pairs, patrolling the outflow and making sure no one's rat bar was taken by force.

It was a long time since anyone here had had a chance to be a hero. Not a few of the newly-appointed policemen were approaching their work with great enthusiasm—maybe some personal grudges being worked off there—Miles recognized one of the burly surlys prone beneath a pair of patrollers, apparently getting his face beaten in. Miles, remembering what he was about, tried not to find music in the meaty thunks of fist on flesh.

Miles and Beatrice and Suegar bucked the stream of rat bar-clutching prisoners back toward the distribution piles. With a slightly regretful sigh, Miles sought out Oliver and dispatched him to the exit to restore order among his order-keepers.

Tris had the distribution piles and their immediate lines under tight control. Miles congratulated himself on having the women hand out the food. He had definitely tuned into a deep emotional resonance there. Not a few of the prisoners even muttered a sheepish "thank you" as their rat bars were shoved into their hands, and so did the ones in line behind them, when their turns came.

Nyah! Miles thought upward to the bland and silent dome. *You don't have the monopoly on psychological warfare any more, you bastards. We're gonna reverse your peristalsis, and I hope you barf your bowels out—*

An altercation at one of the food piles interrupted his meditations. Miles's lip curled with annoyance as he saw Pitt in the middle of it. He limped hastily toward it.

Pitt, it appeared, had repaid his rat bar not with a "thank you" but with a leer, a jeer, and a filthy remark. At least three of the women within hearing were trying to rip him apart, without success; he was big and beefy and had no inhibitions about fighting back. One of the females, not much taller than Miles himself, was knocked back in a heap and didn't get up again. In the meantime, the line was jammed, and the smooth civilized flow of would-be diners totally disrupted. Miles cursed under his breath.

"You, you, you, and—you," Miles tapped shoulders, "grab that guy. Get him out of here—back to the dome wall—"

Miles's draftees were not terribly pleased with their assignment, but by this time Tris and Beatrice had run up and led the attack with rather more science. Pitt was seized and pulled away, behind the lines. Miles made sure the rat bar distribution pile was running again before turning his attention to the savage, foul-mouthed Pitt. Oliver and Suegar had joined him by this time.

"I'm gonna rip the bastard's balls off," Tris was saying. "I command—"

"A military command," Miles interrupted. "If this one is accused of disorderly conduct, you should court martial him."

"He is a rapist and a murderer," she replied icily. "Execution's too good for him. He's got to die *slowly.*"

Miles pulled Suegar aside. "It's tempting, but I feel real uneasy about handing him over to her just now. And yet . . . real uneasy. Why is that?"

Suegar eyed him respectfully. "I think you're right. You see, there's—there's too many guilty."

Pitt, now in a foaming fury, spotted Miles. "You! You little cunt-licking wimp—you think *they* can protect you?" He jerked his head toward Tris and Beatrice. "They ain't got the muscle. We've run 'em over before and we'll run 'em over again. We wouldn'ta lost the damn war if we'd had real soldiers—like the Barrayarans. They didn't fill their army with cunts and cunt-lickers. And they ran the Cetagandans right off their planet—"

"Somehow," Miles growled, drawn in, "I doubt you're an expert in the Barrayarans' defense of their homeworld in the First Cetagandan War. Or you might have learned something—"

"Did Tris make you an honorary girl, mutant?" jeered Pitt in return. "It wouldn't take much—"

Why am I standing here bandying words with this low-life crazy? Miles asked himself as Pitt raved on. *No time. Let's finish it.*

Miles stepped back and folded his arms. "Has it occurred to any of you yet that this man is clearly a Cetagandan agent?"

Even Pitt was shocked to silence.

"The evidence is plain," Miles went on forcefully, raising his voice so all bystanders could hear. "He is a ringleader in your disruption. By example and guile he has corrupted the honest soldiers around him, set them one against another. You were Marilac's best. The Cetagandans could not count on your fall. So they planted a seed of evil among you. Just to make sure. And it worked—wonderfully well. You never suspected—"

Oliver grabbed Miles's ear and muttered, "Brother Miles—I know this guy. He's no Cetagandan agent. He's just one of a whole lot of—"

"Oliver," Miles hissed back through clenched teeth, *"shut up."* And continued in his clearest parade-ground bellow, "Of course he's a Cetagandan spy. A mole. And all this time you thought this was something you were doing to *yourselves.*"

And where the devil does not exist, Miles thought to himself, *it may become expedient to invent him.* His stomach churned, but he kept his face set in righteous rage. He glanced at the faces around him. Not a few were as white as his must be, though for a different reason. A low mutter rose among them, partly bewildered, partly ominous.

"Pull off his shirt," Miles ordered, "and lay him down on his face. Suegar, give me your cup."

Suegar's plastic cup had a jagged point along its broken edge. Miles sat on Pitt's buttocks, and using the point as a stylus scratched the words

CETA

SPY

across Pitt's back in large print. He dug deep and ruthlessly, and the blood welled. Pitt screamed and swore and bucked.

Miles scrambled to his feet, shaking and breathless from more than just the physical exertion.

"Now," he ordered, "give him his rat bar and escort him to the exit."

Tris's teeth opened in objection, clicked back down. Her eyes burned into Pitt's back as he was hustled off. Her gaze turned rather more doubtfully to Miles, as she stood on one side of him and Oliver on the other.

"Do you really think he was a Cetagandan?" she asked Miles lowly.

"No way," scoffed Oliver. "What the hell's the charade all about, Brother Miles?"

"I don't doubt Tris's accusation of his other crimes," said Miles tightly. "You must know. But he couldn't be punished for them without dividing the camp, and so undermining Tris's authority. This way, Tris and the women have their revenge without half the men being set against them. The commandant's hands are clean, yet justice is done on a criminal, and a hard case who would doubtless be stockade bait outside is removed from under our feet. Furthermore, any like-minded souls are handed a warning they can't ignore. It works on every level."

Oliver's face had grown expressionless. After a silent moment he remarked, "You fight dirty, Brother Miles."

"I can't afford to lose." Miles shot him a black look from beneath his own lowered brows. "Can you?"

Oliver's lips tightened. "No."

Tris made no comment at all.

Miles personally oversaw the delivery of rat bars to all those prisoners too sick or weak or beaten to have attempted the chow line.

Colonel Tremont lay too still upon his mat, curled up, staring blankly. Oliver knelt and closed the drying, fixed eyes. The colonel might have died any time in the last few hours.

"I'm sorry," said Miles sincerely. "Sorry I came so late."

"Well . . ." said Oliver, "well . . ." He stood, chewing on his lip, shook his head, and said no more. Miles and Suegar, Tris and Beatrice, helped Oliver carry the body, mat, clothes, cup and all, to the rubbish pile. Oliver shoved the rat bar he had reserved under the dead man's arm. No one attempted to strip the corpse after they had turned away, although another one stiffening there had already been so robbed, lying naked and tumbled.

They stumbled across Pitt's body shortly thereafter. The cause of death was most probably strangulation, but the face was so battered that its empurpling was not a certain clue.

Tris, squatting beside it, looked up at Miles in slow re-estimation. "I think you may be right about power after all, little man."

"And revenge?"

"I thought I could never get my fill of it," she sighed, contemplating the thing beside her. "Yeah . . . that too."

"Thank you." Miles prodded the body with his toe. "Make no mistake, *that* is a loss for our side."

Miles made Suegar let somebody else drag it to the rubbish pile.

Miles held a council of war immediately after chow call. Tremont's pallbearers, whom Miles had begun to think of as his general staff, and the fourteen group leaders gathered around him at a spot near the borders of the women's group. Miles paced back and forth before them, gesturing energetically.

"I commend the group leaders for an excellent job, and Sergeant Oliver for choosing them. By bringing this off, we have bought not only the allegiance of the greater part of the camp, but time as well. Each chow call after this should run a little easier, a little smoother, each become a real-life practice drill for the next.

"And make no mistake, this is a military exercise. We're at war again. We've already suckered the Cetagandans into breaking their carefully calculated routine and making a counter-move. We acted. They reacted. Strange as it may all seem to you, *we* had the offensive advantage.

"Now we start planning our next strategies. I want your thinking on what the next Cetagandan challenge will be." *Actually, I want you thinking, period.* "So much for the sermon—Commandant Tris, take over." Miles forced himself to sit down cross-legged, yielding the floor to his chosen one whether she wanted it or not. He reminded himself that Tris had been a field officer, not a staff officer; she needed the practice more than he did.

"Of course, they can send in short piles again, like they did before," she began after clearing her throat. "It's been suggested that's how this mess got started in the first place." Her glance crossed Miles's, who nodded encouragingly. "This means we're going to have to start keeping head counts, and work out a strict rotation schedule in advance of people to divide their rations with the short-changed. Each group leader must choose a quartermaster and a couple of accountants to double-check his count."

"An equally disruptive move the Cetagandans may try," Miles couldn't help putting in, "is to send in an overstock, giving us the interesting problem of how to equitably divide the extras. I'd provide for that, too, if I were you." He smiled blandly up at Tris.

She raised an eyebrow at him, and continued. "They may also try dividing the chow pile, complicating our problem of capturing it so as to strictly control its re-distribution. Are there any other really dirty tricks any of you can anticipate?" She couldn't help glancing at Miles.

One of the group leaders raised his hand hesitantly. "Ma'am—they're listening to all this. Aren't we doing their thinking for them?"

Miles rose to answer that one, loud and clear. "Of course they're listening. We've doubtless got their quivering attention." He made a rude gesture domewards. "Let them. Every move they make is a message from outside, a shadow marking their shape, information about them. We'll take it."

"Suppose," said another group leader even more hesitantly, "they cut off our air again? Permanently?"

"Then," said Miles smoothly, "they lose their hard-won position one-up on the IJC, which they've gone to enormous trouble to gain. It's a propaganda coup they've been making much of lately, particularly since our side, in the stress of the way things are going back home, hasn't been able to maintain its own troops in style, let alone any captured Cetagandans. The Cetagandans, whose published view is that they're sharing their Imperial government with us out of cultural generosity, are claiming this as a demonstration of their superior civilization and good manners—"

Some jeers and catcalls marked the prisoners' view of this assertion, and Miles smiled and went on. "The death rate reported for this camp is so extraordinary, it's caught the IJC's attention. The Cetagandans have managed to account for it so far, through three separate IJC inspections, but 100% would be a bit extreme even for them to justify." A shiver of agreement, compressed rage, ran through his rapt listeners.

Miles sat again. Oliver leaned over to him to whisper, "How the hell did you come by all that information?"

Miles smirked. "Did it sound convincing? Good."

Oliver sat back, looking unnerved. "You don't have any inhibitions at all, do you?"

"Not in combat."

Tris and her group leaders spent the next two hours laying out chow call scenario flow charts, and their tactical responses at each branching. They broke up to let the group leaders pass it on to their chosen subordinates, and Oliver to his crew of supplementary Enforcers.

Tris paused before Miles, who had succumbed to gravity sometime during the second hour and now lay in the dirt staring somewhat blankly at the dome, blinking in an effort to keep his blurring eyes open. He had not slept in the day and a half before entering this place. He was not sure how much time had passed since then.

"I thought of one more scenario," Tris remarked. "What do we do if they do nothing at all? Do nothing, change nothing."

Miles smiled sleepily. "It seems most probable. That attempted double-cross on the last chow call was a slip on their part, I think."

"But in the absence of an enemy, how long can we go on pretending we're an army?" she persisted. "You scraped us up off the bottom for this. When it runs down at last, what then?"

Miles curled up on his side, drowning in weird and shapeless thoughts, and enticed by the hint of an erotic dream about a tall aggressive redhead. His yawn cracked his face. "Then we pray for a miracle. Remind me to discuss miracles with you . . . later. . . ."

He half-woke once when somebody shoved a sleeping mat under him. He gave Beatrice a sleepy bedroom smile.

"Crazy mutant," she snarled at him, and rolled him roughly onto the pad. "Don't you go thinking this was my idea."

"Why Suegar," Miles muttered, "I think she *likes* me." He cuddled back into the entwining limbs of the dream-Beatrice in fleeting peace.

To Miles's secret dismay, his analysis proved right. The Cetagandans returned to their original rat bar routine, unresponsive again to their prisoners' internal permutations. Miles was not sure he liked that. True, it gave him ample opportunity to fine-tune his distribution scheme. But some harassment from the dome would have directed the prisoners' attention outward, given them a foe again, above all broken the paralyzing boredom of their lives. In the long run, Tris must prove right.

"I hate an enemy who doesn't make mistakes," Miles muttered irritably, and flung his efforts into events he could control.

He found a phlegmatic prisoner with a steady heartbeat to lie in the dirt and count his own pulse, and began timing distribution, and then working on reducing timing.

"It's a spiritual exercise," he announced when he had his fourteen quartermasters start issuing the rat bars 200 at a time, with thirty-minute breaks between groups.

"It's a change of pace," he explained in an aside to Tris. "If we can't induce the Cetagandans to provide some variety, we'll just have to do it ourselves." He also finally got an accurate head count of the surviving prisoners. Miles was everywhere, exhorting, prodding, pushing, restraining.

"If you really want it to go faster, make more bleeding piles," Oliver protested.

"Don't blaspheme," said Miles, and went to work inducing his groups to cart their rat bars away to distribution piles spaced evenly around the perimeter.

At the end of the nineteenth chow call since he had entered the camp, Miles judged his distribution system complete and theologically correct. Calling every two chow calls a "day," he had been there nine days.

"I'm all done," he realized with a groan, "and it's *too early*."

"Weeping because you have no more worlds to conquer?" inquired Tris with a sarcastic grin.

By the thirty-second chow call, the system was still running smoothly, but Miles was getting frayed.

"Welcome to the long haul," said Beatrice dryly. "You better start pacing yourself, Brother Miles. If what Tris says is true, we're going to be in here even longer because of you. I must remember to thank you for that properly sometime." She treated him to a threatening smirk, and Miles prudently remembered an errand on the opposite side of the camp.

She was right, Miles thought, depressed. Most prisoners here counted their captivity not in days and weeks, but months and years. He himself was likely to be gibbering nuts in a space of time that most of them would regard as a mere breath. He wondered glumly what form his madness would take, Manic, inspired by the glittering delusion that he was—say—the Conquerer of Komarr? Or depressive, like Tremont, curling up in himself until he was no one at all, a sort of human black hole?

Miracles. There had been leaders throughout history who had been wrong in their timing for armageddon, leading their shorn flocks up the mountain to await an apotheosis that never came. Their later lives were usually marked by obscurity and drinking problems. Nothing to drink in here. Miles wanted about six doubles, right now.

Now. Now. Now.

✧　　✧　　✧

Miles took to walking the dome perimeter after each chow call, partly to make or at least pretend to inspection, partly to burn off a little of his uncomfortably accumulating nervous energy. It was getting harder and harder to sleep. There had been a period of quiet in the camp after the chow calls were successfully regulated, as if their ordering had been a crystal dropped in a supersaturated solution. But in the last few days the number of fistfights broken up by the Enforcers had risen. The Enforcers themselves were getting quicker to violence, acquiring a potentially unsavory swagger. Phases of the moon. Who could outrace the moon?

"Slow down, Miles," complained Suegar, ambling along beside him.

"Sorry." Miles restrained his stride and broke his self-absorption to look around. The glowing dome rose on his left hand, seeming to pulse to an unsettling hum just out of the range of his hearing. Quiet spread out on his right, groups of people mostly sitting. Not that much visible change since his first day in here. Maybe a little less tension, maybe a little more concerted care being taken of the injured or ill. Phases of the moon. He shook off his unease and smiled cheerfully at Suegar.

"You getting any more positive responses to your sermons these days?" Miles asked.

"Well—nobody tries to beat me up anymore," said Suegar. "But then, I haven't been preaching so often, being busy with the chow calls and all. And then, there are the Enforcers now. It's hard to say.

"You going to keep trying?"

"Oh, yes." Suegar paused. "I've seen worse places than this, y'know. I was at a mining camp once, when I was scarcely more than a kid. A fire gem strike. For a change, instead of one big company or the government muscling in, it had gotten divided up into hundreds and hundreds of little claims, usually about two meters square. Guys dug out there by hand, with trowels and whisk brooms—big fire gems are delicate, y'know, they'll shatter at a careless blow—they dug under the broiling sun, day after day. A lot of these guys had less clothes than us now. A lot of 'em didn't eat as good, or as regular. Working their butts off. More accidents, more disease than here. There were fights, too, in plenty.

"But they lived for the future. Performed the most incredible feats of physical endurance for hope, all voluntary. They were obsessed. They were—well, you remind me a lot of them. They wouldn't quit for *nothing*. They turned a mountain into a chasm in a year, with hand trowels. It was nuts. I loved it.

"This place," Suegar glanced around, "just makes me scared shitless." His right hand touched his rag rope bracelet. "It'll suck up your future, swallow you down—it's like death is just a formality, after that. Zombie town, suicide city. The day I stop trying, this place'll eat me."

"Mm," agreed Miles. They were nearing what Miles thought of as the farthest point of their circuit, across the camp from the women's group at whose now-permeable borders Miles and Suegar kept their sleeping mats.

A couple of men walking the perimeter from the opposite direction coalesced with another gray-pajama'd pair. As if casually and spontaneously, three more arose from their mats on Miles's right. He could not be sure without turning his head, but Miles thought he caught more peripheral motion closing in behind him.

The approaching four stopped a few meters in front of them. Miles and Suegar hesitated. Gray-clad men, all variously larger than Miles—who wasn't?—frowning, full of a fierce tension that arced to Miles and scree'd down his nerves. Miles recognized only one of them, an ex-surly brother he'd seen in Pitt's company. Miles didn't bother taking his eyes off Pitt's lieutenant to look around for Enforcers. For one thing, he was pretty sure one of the men in the company facing them *was* an Enforcer.

And the worst of it was, getting cornered—if you could call it that in here—was his own fault, for letting his movements fall into a predictable daily routine. A stupid, basic, beginner's mistake, that; inexcusable.

Pitt's lieutenant stepped forward, chewing on his lip, staring at Miles with hollowed eyes. *He's psyching himself up*, Miles realized. *If all he wanted was to beat me to a pulp, he could do it in his sleep.* The man slid a carefully-braided rag rope through his fingers. A strangling cord . . . no, it wasn't going to be another beating. This time, it was going to be premeditated murder.

"You," said Pitt's lieutenant hoarsely. "I couldn't figure you out at first. You're not one of us. You could never have been one of us. Mutant . . . You gave me the clue yourself. Pitt wasn't a Cetagandan spy. *You* are!" And lunged forward.

Miles dodged, overwhelmed by onslaught and insight. Damn, he'd known there must be a good reason scragging Pitt that way had felt so much like a mistake despite its efficiency. The false accusation was two-edged, as dangerous to its wielder as its

victim—Pitt's lieutenant might even believe *his* accusation true—
Miles had started a witch-hunt. Poetic justice, that he be its first
victim, but where would it end? No wonder their captors hadn't
interfered lately. Their silent Cetagandan watchers must be falling off their station chairs laughing right now—mistake piled on
mistake, culminating here by dying stupidly like vermin at the
hands of vermin in this verminous hole. . . .

Hands grabbed him; he contorted spasmodically, kicking out,
but only half-broke their hold. Beside him Suegar whirled, kicked,
struck, shouted with demonic energy. He had reach, but lacked
mass. Miles lacked both reach and mass. Still Suegar managed to
break an assailant's hold on Miles for a moment.

Suegar's left arm, lashing out for a backhand blow, was caught
and locked. Miles winced in sympathetic anticipation of the familiar
muffled crack of breaking bones, but instead the man stripped off
the rag rope bracelet from Suegar's wrist.

"Hey, Suegar!" the man taunted, dancing backward. "Look what
I got!"

Suegar's head swiveled, his attention wrenched from his determined defense of Miles. The man peeled the wrinkled, tattered piece
of paper from its cloth covering and waved it in the air. Suegar
cried out in dismay and started to plunge toward him, but found
himself blocked by two other bodies. The man tore the paper in
half twice, then paused, as if momentarily puzzled how to dispose
of it—then, with a sudden grin, stuffed the pieces in his mouth
and started chewing. Suegar screamed.

"Dammit," cried Miles furiously, "it was me you wanted! You
didn't have to do that—" He jammed his fist with all his strength
into the smirking face of the nearest attacker, whose attention had
been temporarily distracted by Suegar's show.

He could feel his bones shatter all the way back through his
wrist. He was so damned *tired* of the bones, tired of being hurt
again and again. . . .

Suegar was screaming and sobbing and trying to gain on the
paper chewer, who stood and chewed on through his grin. Suegar
had lost all science in his attack, flailing like a windmill. Miles saw
him go down, then had no attention left for anything but the
anaconda coil of the strangling cord, settling over his own neck.
He managed to get one hand between the cord and his throat, but
it was the broken one. Cables of pain shuddered up his arm, seeming to burrow under his skin all the way to his shoulder. The
pressure in his head mounted to bursting, closing down his

vision. Dark purple and yellow moiré-patterned clouds boiled up in his eyes like thunder heads. A flashing brush of red hair sizzled past his tunneling vision. . . .

He was on the ground then, with blood, wonderful blood, thudding back into his oxygen-starved brain. It hurt good, hot and pulsing. He lay for a moment not caring about anything else. It would be so good not to have to get up again. . . .

The damned dome, cold and white and featureless, mocked his returning vision. Miles jerked onto his knees, staring around wildly. Beatrice, some Enforcers, and some of Oliver's commando buddies were chasing Miles's would-be assassins across the camp. Miles had probably only passed out for a few seconds. Suegar lay on the ground a couple of meters off.

Miles crawled over to Suegar. The thin man lay curled up around his stomach, his face pale green and clammy, involuntary shivers coursing through his body. Not good. Shocky. Keep patient warm and administer synergine. No synergine. Miles peeled clumsily out of his tunic and laid it over Suegar. "Suegar? You all right? Beatrice chased the barbarians off . . ."

Suegar looked up and smiled briefly, but the smile was reabsorbed almost immediately by distancing pain.

Beatrice came back eventually, mussed and breathing heavily. "You loonies," she greeted them dispassionately. "You don't need a bodyguard, you need a bloody keeper." She flopped onto her knees beside Miles to stare at Suegar. Her lips thinned to a white slit. She glanced at Miles, her eyes darkening, the creases between her brows deepening.

I've changed my mind, Miles thought. *Don't start caring for me, Beatrice, don't start caring for anybody. You'll only get hurt. Over and over and over . . .*

"You better come back to my group," said Beatrice.

"I don't think Suegar can walk."

Beatrice rounded up some muscle, and the thin man was rolled onto a sleeping mat and carried, too much like Colonel Tremont's corpse for Miles's taste, back to their now-usual sleeping place.

"Find a doctor for him," Miles demanded.

Beatrice came back, strong-arming an angry, older woman.

"He's probably got a busted belly," snarled the doctor. "If I had a diagnostic viewer, I could tell you just what was busted. You got a diagnostic viewer? He needs synergine and plasma. You got any? I could cut him, and glue him back together, and speed his healing with electra-stim, if I had an operating theatre. Put him back on his feet in three days, no sweat. You got an operating theatre? I thought not.

"Stop looking at me like that. I used to think I was a healer. It took this place to teach me I was nothing but an interface between the technology and the patient. Now the technology is gone, and I'm just nothing."

"But what can we do?" asked Miles.

"Cover him up. In a few days he'll either get better or die, depending on what got busted. That's all." She paused, standing with folded arms and regarding Suegar with rancor, as if his injury was a personal affront. And so it was, for her: another load of grief and failure, grinding her hard-won healer's pride into the dirt. "I think he's going to die," she added.

"I think so too," said Miles.

"Then what did you want me for?" She stomped off.

Later she came back with a sleeping mat and a couple of extra rags, and helped put them around and over Suegar for added insulation, then stomped off again.

Tris reported to Miles. "We got those guys who tried to kill you rounded up. What do you want done with 'em?"

"Let them go," said Miles wearily. "They're not the enemy."

"The hell they're not!"

"They're not my enemies, anyway. It was just a case of mistaken identity. I'm just a hapless traveler, passing through."

"Wake up, little man. I don't happen to share Oliver's belief in your 'miracle.' You're not passing through here. This is the last stop."

Miles sighed. "I'm beginning to think you're right." He glanced at Suegar, breathing shallowly and too fast, beside whom he crouched in watch. "You're almost certainly right, by this time. Nevertheless—let them go."

"Why?" she wailed, outraged.

"Because I said to. Because I asked you to. Would you have me beg for them?"

"Aargh! No. All right!" She wheeled away, running her hands through her clipped hair and muttering under her breath.

A timeless time passed. Suegar lay on his side not speaking, though his eyes flicked open now and then to stare unseeing. Miles moistened his lips with water periodically. A chow call came and went without incident or Miles's participation; Beatrice passed by and dropped two rat bars beside them, stared at them with a carefully-hardened gaze of general disapproval, and stalked off.

Miles cradled his injured hand and sat cross-legged, mentally reviewing the catalogue of errors that had brought him to this pass. He contemplated his seeming genius for getting his friends killed. He had a sick premonition that Suegar's death was going to be almost as bad as Sergeant Bothari's, six years ago, and he had known Suegar only weeks, not years. Repeated pain, as he had reason to know, made one more afraid of injury, not less, a growing, gut-wrenching dread. Not again, never again . . .

He lay back and stared at the dome, the white, unblinking eye of a dead god. And had more friends than he knew already been killed by this megalomanic escapade? It would be just like the Cetagandans, to leave him in here all unknowing, and let the growing doubt and fear gradually drive him crazy.

Swiftly drive him crazy—the god's eye blinked.

Miles blinked in sympathetic nervous recoil, opened his eyes wide, stared at the dome as if his eyes could bore right through it. Had it blinked? Had the flicker been hallucinatory? Was he losing it?

It flickered again. Miles shot to his feet, inhaling, inhaling, inhaling.

The dome blinked out. For a brief instant, planetary night swept in, fog and drizzle and the kiss of a cold wet wind. This planet's unfiltered air smelled like rotten eggs. The unaccustomed dark was blinding.

"CHOW CALL!" Miles screamed at the top of his lungs.

Then limbo transmuted to chaos in the brilliant flash of a smart bomb going off beyond a cluster of buildings. Red light glared off the underside of an enormous billowing cloud of debris, blasting upward.

A racketing string of similar hits encircled the camp, peeled back the night, deafened the unprotected. Miles, still screaming, could not hear his own voice. A returning fire from the ground clawed the clouds with lines of colored light.

Tris, her eyes stunned, rocketed past him. Miles grabbed her by the arm with his good hand and dug in his heels to brake her, yanking her down so he could scream in her ear.

"This is it! Get the fourteen group leaders organized, make 'em get their first blocks of 200 lined up and waiting all around the perimeter. Find Oliver, we've *got* to get the Enforcers moving to get the rest waiting their turn under control. If this goes exactly as we drilled it, we'll all get off." *I hope.* "But if they mob the shuttles like they used to mob the rat bar pile, none of us will. You copy?"

"I never believed—I didn't think—*shuttles?*"

"You don't have to think. We've drilled this fifty times. Just follow the chow drill. The *drill!*"

"You *sneaky* little sonofabitch!" The acknowledging wave of her arm, as she dashed off, was very like a salute.

A string of flares erupted in the sky above the camp, as if a white strobe of lightning went on and on, casting a ghastly illumination on the scene below. The camp seethed like a termite mound kicked over. Men and women were running every which way in shouting confusion. Not exactly the orderly vision Miles had had in mind—why, for example, had his people chosen a night drop and not a daytime one?—he would grill his staff later on that point, after he got done kissing their feet—

"Beatrice!" Miles waved her down. "Start passing the word! We're doing the chow call drill. But instead of a rat bar, each person gets a shuttle seat. Make 'em understand that—don't let anybody go haring off into the night or they'll miss their flight. Then come back here and stay by Suegar. I don't want him getting lost or trampled on. *Guard,* you copy?"

"I'm not a damn dog. What shuttles?"

The sound Miles's ears had been straining for penetrated the din at last, a high-pitched, multi-faceted whine that grew louder and louder. They loomed down out of the boiling scarlet-tinged clouds like monstrous beetles, carapaced and winged, feet extending even as they watched. Fully armored combat-drop shuttles, two, three, six . . . seven, eight . . . Miles's lips moved as he counted. Thirteen, fourteen, by God. They *had* managed to get #B-7 out of the shop in time.

Miles pointed. *"My shuttles."*

Beatrice stood with her mouth open, staring upward. "My God. They're beautiful." He could almost see her mind start to ratchet forward. "But they're not *ours.* Not Cetagandan either. Who the hell . . . ?"

Miles bowed. "This is a paid political rescue."

"Mercenaries?"

"We're not something wriggling with too many legs that you found in your sleeping bag. The proper tone of voice is *Mercenaries!*—with a glad cry."

"But—but—but—"

"Go, dammit. Argue *later."*

She flung up her hands and ran.

Miles himself started tackling every person within reach, passing on the order of the day. He captured one of Oliver's tall commando buddies and demanded a boost on his shoulders. A quick look around showed fourteen coagulating knots of people in the mob scattered around the perimeter in nearly the right positions. The shuttles hovered, engines howling, then thumped to the ground one by one all around the camp.

"It'll have to do," Miles muttered to himself. He slapped the commando's shoulder. "Down."

He forced himself to walk to the nearest shuttle, a run on the shuttles being just the scenario he had poured out blood and bone and pride these last—three, four?—weeks to avoid.

A quartet of fully-armed and half-armored troops were the first down the shuttle ramp, taking up guard positions. Good. They even had their weapons pointed in the right direction, toward the prisoners they were here to rescue. A larger patrol, fully armored, followed to gallop off double time, leapfrogging their own covering-fire range into the dark toward the Cetagandan installations surrounding the dome circle. Hard to judge which direction held the most danger—from the continuing fireworks, his fighter shuttles were providing plenty of external distraction for the Cetagandans.

At last came the man Miles most wanted to see, the shuttle's comm officer.

"Lieutenant, uh," he connected face and name, "Murka! Over here!"

Murka spotted him. He fumbled excitedly with his equipment and called into his audio pick-up, "Commodore Tung! He's *here,* I *got* him!"

Miles peeled the comm set ruthlessly from the lieutenant's head, who obligingly ducked down to permit the theft, and jammed it on his own head left-handed in time to hear Tung's voice reply tinnily, "Well, for God's sake don't lose him again, Murka. Sit on him if you have to."

"I want my staff," called Miles into the pick-up. "Have you retrieved Elli and Elena yet? How much time have we got for this?"

"Yes, sir, no, and about two hours—if we're lucky," Tung's voice snapped back. "Good to have you back aboard, Admiral Naismith."

"You're telling me . . . Get Elena and Elli. Priority One."

"Working. Tung out."

Miles turned to find that the rat bar group leader in this section had actually succeeded in marshaling his first group of 200, and was engaged in making the second 200 sit back down in a block to wait their turns. Excellent. The prisoners were being channeled up the ramp one at a time through a strange gauntlet. A mercenary slit the back of each gray tunic with a swift slice from a vibra-knife. A second mercenary slapped each prisoner across the back with a medical stunner. A third made a pass with a surgical hand-tractor, roughly ripping out the Cetagandan serial numbers encoded beneath the skin. He didn't bother to waste time on bandaging after. "Go to the front and sit five across, go to the front and sit five across, go to the front . . ." he chanted, droning in time to his hypnotically moving device.

Miles's sometime-adjutant Captain Thorne appeared, hurrying out of the glare and black shadows, flanked by one of the fleet's ship's surgeons and—praise be—a soldier carrying some of Miles's clothes, and boots. Miles dove for the boots, but was captured instead by the surgeon.

She ran a med stunner between his bare uneven shoulderblades, and zipped a hand-tractor across in its path.

"Ow!" Miles yelped. "Couldn't you wait one bleeding second for the stun to cut in?" The pain faded rapidly to numbness as Miles's left hand patted for the damage. "What's this all about?"

"Sorry, sir," said the surgeon insincerely. "Stop that, your fingers are dirty." She applied a plastic bandage. Rank hath its privileges. "Captain Bothari-Jesek and Commander Quinn learned something from their fellow Cetagandan prison monitors that we hadn't known before you went in. These encodes are permeated with drug beads, whose lipid membranes are kept aligned by a low-power magnetic field the Cetagandans were generating in the dome. An hour out of the dome, and the membranes start to break down, releasing a poison. About four hours later the subject dies—very unpleasantly. A little insurance against escapes, I guess."

Miles shuddered, and said faintly, "I see." He cleared his throat, and added more loudly, "Captain Thorne, mark a commendation— with *highest* honors—to Commander Elli Quinn and Captain Elena Bothari-Jesek. The, ah, our employer's intelligence service didn't even have that one. In fact, our employer's intelligence data lacked on a truly vast number of points. I shall have to speak to them— sharply—when I present the bill for this expanded operation. Before you put that away, doctor, numb my hand, please." Miles stuck out his right hand for the surgeon's inspection.

"Did it again, did you?" muttered the surgeon. "I'd think you'd learn . . ." A pass with the medical stunner, and Miles's swollen hand disappeared from his senses entirely, nothing left from the wrist down. Only his eyes assured him it was still attached to his arm.

"Yes, but will they pay for the expanded operation?" asked Captain Thorne anxiously. "This started out as a one-shot lightning strike to hook out one guy, just the sort of thing little outfits like us specialize in—now it's straining the whole Dendarii fleet. These damned prisoners outnumber *us* two to one. This wasn't in the original contract. What if our perennial mystery employer decides to stiff us?"

"They won't," said Miles. "My word. But—there's no doubt I'll have to deliver the bill in person."

"God help them, then," muttered the surgeon, and took herself off to continue pulling encodes from the waiting prisoners.

Commodore Ky Tung, a squat, middle-aged Eurasian in half-armor and a command channel headset, turned up at Miles's elbow as the first shuttles loaded with prisoners clapped their locks shut and screamed up into the black fog. They took off in first-come first-served positions, no waiting. Knowing Tung's passion for tight formations, Miles judged time must be their most dangerous limiting factor.

"What are we loading these guys onto, upstairs?" Miles asked Tung.

"We gutted a couple of used freighters. We can cram about 5,000 in the holds of each. The ride out is going to be fast and nasty. They'll all have to lie down and breathe as little as possible."

"What are the Cetagandans scrambling to catch us?"

"Right now, barely more than some police shuttles. Most of their local space military contingent just happens to be on the other side of their sun just now, which is why we just happened to pick this moment to drop by . . . we had to wait for their practice maneuvers again, in case you were starting to wonder what was keeping us. In other words, the same scenario as our original plan to pull Colonel Tremont."

"Except expanded by a factor of 10,000. And we've got to get in—what, four lifts? instead of one," said Miles.

"Yeah, but get this," grinned Tung. "They sited these prison camps on this miserable outpost planet so's they wouldn't have to expend troops and equipment guarding them—counted on distance from Marilac, and the downgearing of the war there, to discourage rescue attempts. But in the period since you went in, half of their original guard complement has been pulled to other hot spots. Half!"

"They were relying on the dome." Miles eyed him. "And for the bad news?" he murmured.

Tung's smile soured. "This round, our total time window is only two hours."

"Ouch. Half their local space fleet is still too many. And they'll be back in two hours?"

"One hour, forty minutes, now." A sidewise flick of Tung's eyes betrayed the location of his ops clock, holovid-projected by his command headset into the air at a corner of his vision.

Miles did a calculation in his head, and lowered his voice. "Are we going to be able to lift the last load?"

"Depends on how fast we can lift the first three," said Tung. His ordinarily stoic face was more unreadable than ever, betraying neither hope nor fear.

Which depends in turn on how effectively I managed to drill them all . . . What was done was done; what was coming was not yet. Miles wrenched his attention to the immediate now.

"Have you found Elli and Elena yet?"

"I have three patrols out searching."

He hadn't found them yet. Miles's guts tightened. "I wouldn't have even attempted to expand this operation in midstream if I hadn't known they were monitoring me, and could translate all those oblique hints back into orders."

"Did they get 'em all right?" asked Tung. "We argued over some of their interpretations of your double-talk on the vids."

Miles glanced around. 'They got 'em right . . . you got vids of all this?" A startled wave of Miles's hand took in the circle of the camp.

"Of you, anyway. Right off the Cetagandan monitors. They burst-transmitted them all daily. Very—er—entertaining, sir," Tung added blandly.

Some people would find entertainment in watching someone swallow slugs, Miles reflected. "Very dangerous . . . when was your last communication with them?"

"Yesterday." Tung's hand clamped on Miles's arm, restraining an involuntary leap. "You can't do better than my three patrols, sir, and I haven't any to spare to go looking for *you*."

"Yah, yah." Miles slapped his right fist into his left palm in frustration before remembering that was a bad idea. His two co-agents, his vital link between the dome and the Dendarii, missing. The

Cetagandans shot spies with depressing consistency. After, usually, a series of interrogations that rendered death a welcome
release. . . . He tried to reassure himself with logic. If they'd blown
their covers as Cetagandan monitor techs, and been interrogated,
Tung would have run into a meat grinder here. He hadn't, ergo, they
hadn't. Of course, they might have been killed by friendly fire, just
now. . . . Friends. He had too many friends to stay sane in this crazy
business.

"You," Miles retrieved his clothes from the still-waiting soldier,
"go over there," he pointed, "and find a redhaired lady named
Beatrice and an injured man named Suegar. Bring them to me.
Carry him carefully, he has internal injuries."

The soldier saluted and marched off. Ah, the pleasure again of
being able to give a command without having to follow it up with
a supporting theological argument. Miles sighed. Exhaustion waited
to swallow him, lurking at the edge of his adrenaline-spurred
bubble of hyperconsciousness. All the factors—shuttles, timing,
the approaching enemy, distance to the getaway jump point, formed
and reformed in all their possible permutations in his mind. Small
variations in timing in particular multiplied into major troubles.
But he'd known it would be like this back when he'd started. A
miracle they'd got this far. No—he glanced at Tung, at Thorne—
not a miracle, but the extraordinary initiative and devotion of his
people. *Well done, oh, well done. . . .*

Thorne helped him as he fumbled to dress himself one-handed.
"Where the hell is my command headset?" Miles asked.

"We were told you were injured, sir, and in a state of exhaustion. You were scheduled for immediate evacuation."

"Damn presumptuous of somebody . . ." Miles bit back ire. No
place in this schedule for running errands topside. Besides, if he
had his headset, he'd be tempted to start giving orders, and he
wasn't yet sufficiently briefed on the internal complexities of the
operation from the Dendarii fleet's point of view. Miles swallowed
his observer status without further comment. It did free him for
rear guard.

Miles's batman reappeared, with Beatrice and four drafted
prisoners, carrying Suegar on his mat to lay at Miles's feet.

"Get my surgeon," Miles said. His soldier obediently trotted off
and found her. She knelt beside the semi-conscious Suegar and
pulled the encode from his back. A knot of tension unwound in
Miles's neck at the reassuring hiss of a hypospray of synergine.

"How bad?" Miles demanded.

"Not good," the surgeon admitted, checking her diagnostic viewer. "Burst spleen, oozing hemorrhage in the stomach—this one had better go direct to surgery on the command ship. Medtech—" she motioned to a Dendarii waiting with the guards for the return of the shuttle, and gave triage instructions. The medtech swathed Suegar in a thin foil heat wrap.

"I'll make sure he gets there," promised Miles. He shivered, envying the heat wrap a little as the drizzly acid fog beaded in his hair and coiled into his bones.

Tung's expression and attention were abruptly absorbed by a message from his comm set. Miles, who had yielded Lieutenant Murka's headset back to him so that he might continue his duties, shifted from foot to foot in agony for news. *Elena, Elli, if I've killed you . . .*

Tung spoke into his pick-up. "Good. Well done. Report to the A7 drop site." A jerk of his chin switched channels. "Sim, Nout, fall back with your patrols to your shuttle drop site perimeters. They've been found."

Miles found himself bent over with his hand supported on gelid knees, waiting for his head to clear, his heart lurching in huge slow gulps. "Elli and Elena? Are they all right?"

"They didn't call for a medtech . . . you sure you don't need one yourself? You're green."

"I'm all right." Miles's heart steadied, and he straightened up, to meet Beatrice's questing eyes. "Beatrice, would you please go get Tris and Oliver for me? I need to talk to them before the next shuttle relay goes up."

She shook her head helplessly and wheeled away. She did not salute. On the other hand, she didn't argue, either. Miles was insensibly cheered.

The booming racket around the dome circle had died down to the occasional whine of small-arms fire, human cry, or blurred amplified voice. Fires burned in the distance, red-orange glows in the muffling fog. Not a surgically clean operation . . . the Cetagandans were going to be extremely pissed when they'd counted their casualties, Miles judged. Time to be gone, and long gone. He tried to keep the poisoned encodes in mind, as anodyne to the vision of Cetagandan clerks and techs crushed in the rubble of their burning buildings, but the two nightmares seemed to amplify instead of cancelling each other out.

Here came Tris and Oliver, both looking a little wild-eyed. Beatrice took up station at Tris's right shoulder.

"Congratulations," Miles began, before they could speak. He had a lot of ground to cover and not much time left. "You have achieved an army." A wave of his arm swept the orderly array of prisoners—ex-prisoners—spread across the camp in their shuttle groups. They waited quietly, most seated on the ground. Or was it the Cetagandans who had ingrained such patience in them? Whatever.

"Temporarily," said Tris. "This is the lull, I believe. If things hot up, if you lose one or more shuttles, if somebody panics and it spreads—"

"You can tell anybody who's inclined to panic they can ride up with me if it'll make them feel better. Ah—better also mention that I'm going up in the *last* load," said Miles.

Tung, dividing his attention between this confab and his headset, grimaced in exasperation at this news.

"That'll settle 'em." Oliver grinned.

"Give them something to think about, anyway," conceded Tris.

"Now I'm going to give you something to think about. The new Marilac resistance. You're it," said Miles. "My employer originally engaged me to rescue Colonel Tremont, that he might raise a new army and carry on the fight. When I found him . . . as he was, dying, I had to decide whether to follow the letter of my contract, and deliver a catatonic or a corpse, or the spirit—and deliver an army. I chose this, and I chose you two. *You* must carry on Colonel Tremont's work."

"I was only a field lieutenant," began Tris in horror, in chorus with Oliver's, "I'm a grunt, not a staff officer. Colonel Tremont was a genius—"

"You are his heirs now. *I* say so. Look around you. Do I make mistakes in choosing my subordinates?"

After a moment's silence Tris muttered, "Apparently not."

"Build yourselves a staff. Find your tactics geniuses, your technical wizards, and put 'em to work for you. But the drive, and the decisions, and the direction, must be yours, forged in this pit. It is you two who will remember this place, and so remember what it is you are doing, and why, always."

Oliver spoke quietly. "And when do we muster out of this army, Brother Miles? My time was up during the siege of Fallow Core. If I'd been anywhere else, I could have gone home."

"Until the Cetagandan army of occupation rolled down your street."

"Even then. The odds aren't good."

"The odds were worse for Barrayar, in its day, and they ran the Cetagandans right off. It took twenty years, and more blood than either of you have seen in your lives combined, but they did it," asserted Miles.

Oliver seemed more struck by this historical precedent than Tris, who said skeptically, "Barrayar had those crazy Vor warriors. Nuts who rushed into battle, who *liked* to die. Marilac just doesn't have that sort of cultural tradition. We're civilized—or we were, once. . . ."

"Let me tell you about the Barrayaran Vor," cut in Miles. "The loonies who sought a glorious death in battle found it very early on. This rapidly cleared the chain of command of the accumulated fools. The survivors were those who learned to fight dirty, and live, and fight another day, and win, and win, and win, and for whom nothing, not comfort, or security, not family or friends or their immortal souls, was more important than winning. Dead men are losers by definition. Survival and victory. They weren't supermen, or immune to pain. They sweated in confusion and darkness. And with not one-half the physical resources Marilac possesses even now, they won. When you're Vor," Miles ran down a little, "there is no mustering out."

After a silence Tris said, "Even a volunteer patriotic army must eat. And we won't beat the Cetagandans by firing spitballs at them."

"There will be financial and military aid forthcoming through a covert channel other than myself. If there is a Resistance command to deliver it to."

Tris measured Oliver by eye. The fire in her burned closer to the surface than Miles had ever seen it, coursing down those corded muscles. The whine of the first returning shuttles pierced the fog. She spoke quite softly. "And here I thought I was the atheist, Sergeant, and you were the believer. Are you coming with me— or mustering out?"

Oliver's shoulders bowed. With the weight of history, Miles realized, not defeat, for the heat in his eyes matched Tris's. "Coming," he grunted.

Miles caught Tung's eyes. "How we doing?"

Tung shook his head, held up fingers. "About six minutes slow, unloading upstairs."

"Right." Miles turned back to Tris and Oliver. "I want you both to go up on this wave, in separate shuttles, one to each troopship. When you get there, start expediting the off-loading of your people.

Lieutenant Murka will give you your shuttle assignment—" He motioned Murka over and packed them off.

Beatrice lingered. "I'm inclined to panic," she informed Miles in a distant tone. Her bare toe smudged whorls in the dampening dirt.

"I don't need a bodyguard anymore," Miles said. He grinned. "A keeper, maybe . . ."

A smile lighted her eyes that did not yet reach her mouth. Later, Miles promised himself. Later, he would make that mouth laugh.

The second wave of shuttles began to lift, even as the remnants of the returning first wave were still landing. Miles prayed everyone's sensors were operating properly, passing each other in this fog. Their timing could only get more ragged from now on. The fog itself was coagulating into a cold rain, silver needles pelting down.

The focus of the operation was narrowing rapidly now, more of machines and numbers and timing, less of loyalties and souls and fearsome obligations. An emotionally pathological mind, devoid of love and fear, might even call it fun, Miles thought. He began jotting scores left-handed in the dirt, numbers up, down, in transit, remaining, but the dirt was turning to gluey black mud and did not retain the impressions.

"Shit," Tung hissed suddenly through clenched teeth. The air before his face blurred in a flurry of vid-projected incoming information, his eyes flicking through it with practiced rapidity. His right hand bunched and twitched, as if tempted to wrench off his headset and stamp it into the mud in frustration and disgust. "That tears it. We just lost two shuttles out of the second wave."

Which two? Miles's mind screamed. *Oliver, Tris . . .* He forced his first question to be, "How?" *I swear, if they crashed into each other, I'm going to go find a wall and beat my head on it till I go numb. . . .*

"Cetagandan fighter broke through our cordon. He was going for the troop freighters, but we nailed him in time. Almost in time."

"You got identifications on which two shuttles? And were they loaded or returning?"

Tung's lips moved in subvocalization. "A-4, fully loaded. B-7, returning empty. Loss total, no survivors. Fighter shuttle 5 from the *Triumph* is disabled by enemy fire; pilot recovery now in progress."

He hadn't lost his commanders. His hand-picked and carefully nurtured successors to Colonel Tremont were safe. He opened his eyes, squeezed shut in pain, to find Beatrice, to whom the shuttle IDs meant nothing, waiting anxiously for interpretation.

"Two hundred dead?" she whispered.

"Two hundred six," Miles corrected. The faces, names, voices of the six familiar Dendarii fluttered through his memory. The 200 ciphers must have had faces too. He blocked them out, as too crushing an overload.

"These things happen," Beatrice muttered numbly.

"You all right?"

"Of course I'm all right. These things happen. Inevitable. I am not a weepy wimp who folds under fire." She blinked rapidly, lifting her chin. "Give me . . . something to do. Anything."

Quickly, Miles added for her. *Right.* He pointed across the camp. "Go to Pel and Liant. Divide their remaining shuttle groups into blocks of thirty-three, and add them to each of the remaining third-wave shuttle groups. We'll have to send the third wave up over-loaded. Then report back to me. Go quick, the rest will be back in minutes."

"Yessir," she saluted. For her sake, not his; for order, structure, rationality, a lifeline. He returned the salute gravely.

"They were already overloaded," objected Tung as soon as she was out of earshot. "They're going to fly like bricks with 233 squeezed on board. And they'll take longer to load on here and unload topside."

"Yes. God." Miles gave up scratching figures in the useless mud. "Run the numbers through the computer for me, Ky. I don't trust myself to add two and two just now. How far behind will we be by the time the main body of the Cetagandans comes in range? Come close as you can, no fudge factors, please."

Tung mumbled into his headset, reeled off numbers, margins, timing. Miles tracked every detail with predatory intensity. Tung concluded bluntly. "At the end of the last wave, five shuttles are still going to be waiting to unload when the Cetagandan fire fries us."

A thousand men and women.

"May I respectfully suggest, sir, that the time has come to start cutting our losses?" added Tung.

"You may, Commodore."

"Option One, maximally efficient; only drop seven shuttles in the last wave. Leave the last five shuttle loads of prisoners on the ground. They'll be re-taken, but at least they'll be alive." Tung's voice grew persuasive on this last line.

"Only one problem, Ky. *I* don't want to stay here."

"You can still be on the last shuttle up, just like you said. By the way, sir, have I expressed myself yet, sir, on what a genuinely dumbshit piece of grandstanding that is?"

"Eloquently, with your eyebrows, a while ago. And while I'm inclined to agree with you, have you noticed yet how closely the remaining prisoners keep watching me? Have you ever watched a cat sneaking up on a horned hopper?"

Tung stirred uneasily, eyes taking in the phenomenon Miles described.

"I don't fancy gunning down the last thousand in order to get my shuttle into the air."

"Skewed as we are, they might not realize there were no more shuttles coming till after you were in the air."

"So we just leave them standing there, waiting for us?" *The sheep look up, but are not fed . . .*

"Right."

"You like that option, Ky?"

"Makes me want to puke, but—consider the 9,000 others. And the Dendarii fleet. The idea of dropping them all down the rat hole in a pre-doomed effort to pack up all these—miserable sinners of yours, makes me want to puke a lot more. Nine-tenths of a loaf is *much* better than none."

"Point taken. Let us go on to option two, please. The flight out of orbit is calculated on the speed of the slowest ship, which is . . . ?"

"The freighters."

"And the *Triumph* remains the swiftest?"

"Betcher ass." Tung had captained the *Triumph* once.

"And the best armored."

"Yo. So?" Tung saw perfectly well where he was being driven. His obtuseness was but a form of oblique balking.

"So. The first seven shuttles up on the last wave lock onto the troop freighters and boost on schedule. We call back five of the *Triumph's* fighter pilots and dump and destroy their craft. One's damaged already, right? The last five of these drop shuttles clamp to the *Triumph* in their place, protected from the now-arriving fire of the Cetagandan ships by the *Triumph's* full shielding. Pack the prisoners into the *Triumph's* corridors, lock shuttle hatches, boost like hell."

"The added mass of a thousand people—"

"Would be less than that of a couple of the drop shuttles. Dump and blow them too, if you have to, to fit the mass/acceleration window."

"—would overload life support—"

"The emergency oxygen will take us to the worm-hole jump point. After jump the prisoners can be distributed among the other ships at our leisure."

Tung's voice grew anguished. "Those combat-drop shuttles are *brand new*. And my fighters—*five* of them—do you realize how hard it will be to recoup the funds to replace 'em? It comes to—"

"I asked you to calculate the time, Ky, not the price tag," said Miles through his teeth. He added more quietly, "I'll tack them on to our bill for services rendered."

"You ever hear the term *cost overrun*, boy? You will. . . ." Tung switched his attention back to his headset, itself but an extension of the tactics room aboard the *Triumph*. Calculations were made, new orders entered and executed.

"It flies," sighed Tung. "Buys a damned expensive fifteen minutes. If nothing else goes wrong . . ." he trailed off in a frustrated mumble, as impatient as Miles himself with his inability to be three places at once.

"There comes my shuttle back," Tung noted aloud. He glanced at Miles, plainly unwilling to leave his admiral to his own devices, as plainly itching to be out of the acid rain and dark and mud and closer to the nerve center of operations.

"Get gone," said Miles. "You can't ride up with me anyway, it's against procedure."

"Procedure, hah," said Tung blackly.

With the lift-off of the third wave, there were barely 2,000 prisoners left on the ground. Things were thinning out, winding down; the armored combat patrols were falling back now from their penetration of the surrounding Cetagandan installations, back toward their assigned shuttle landing sites. A dangerous turning of the tide, should some surviving Cetagandan officer recover enough organization to harry their retreat.

"See you aboard the *Triumph*," Tung emphasized. He paused to brace Lieutenant Murka, out of Miles's earshot. Miles grinned in sympathy for the overworked lieutenant, in no doubt about the orders Tung was now laying on him. If Murka didn't come back with Miles in tow, he'd probably be wisest not to come back at all.

Nothing left now but a little last waiting. Hurry up and wait. Waiting, Miles realized, was very bad for him. It allowed his self-generated adrenaline to wear off, allowed him to feel how tired and hurt he really was. The illuminating flares were dying to a red glow.

There was really very little time between the fading of the labored thunder of the last third wave shuttle to depart, and the screaming whine of the first fourth wave shuttle plunging back. Alas that this had more to do with being skewed than being swift. The Marilacans still waited in their rat bar blocks, discipline still holding. Of course, nobody'd told them about the little problem in timing they faced. But the nervous Dendarii patrols, chivvying them up the ramps, kept things moving at a pace to Miles's taste. Rear guard was never a popular position to draw, even among the lunatic fringe who defaced their weapons with notches and giggled among themselves while speculating upon newer and more grotesque methods of blowing away their enemies.

Miles saw the semi-conscious Suegar carried up the ramp first. Suegar would actually reach the *Triumph's* sickbay faster in his company, Miles calculated, on this direct flight, than had he been sent on an earlier shuttle to one of the troop freighters and had to await a safe moment to transfer.

The arena they were leaving had grown silent and dark, sodden and sad, ghostly. *I will break the doors of hell, and bring up the dead* . . . there was something not quite right about the half-remembered quote. No matter.

This shuttle's armored patrol, the last, drew back out of the fog and darkness, electronically whistled in like a pack of sheepdogs by their master Murka, who stood at the foot of the ramp as liaison between the ground patrol and the shuttle pilot, who was expressing her anxiety to be gone with little whining revs on the engines.

Then from the darkness—plasma fire, sizzling through the rain-sodden, saturated air. Some Cetagandan hero—officer, troop, tech, who knew?—had crawled up out of the rubble and found a weapon—and an enemy to fire it at. Splintered afterimages, red and green, danced in Miles's eyes. A Dendarii patroller rolled out of the dark, a glowing line across the back of his armor smoking and sparking until quenched in the black mud. His armor legs seized up, and he lay wriggling like a frantic fish in an effort to peel out of it. A second plasma burst, ill-aimed, spent itself turning a few kilometers of fog and rain to superheated steam on a straight line to some unknown infinity.

Just what they needed, to be pinned down by sniper fire *now*. . . . A pair of Dendarii rear guards started back into the fog. An excited prisoner—ye gods, it was Pitt's lieutenant again—grabbed up the armor-paralyzed soldier's weapon and made to join them.

"No! Come back later and fight on your own time, you jerk!" Miles sloshed toward Murka. "Fall back, load up, get in the air! Don't stop to fight! No time!"

Some of the last of the prisoners had fallen flat to the ground, burrowing like mudpuppies, a sound sensible reflex in any other context. Miles dashed among them, slapping rumps. "Get *aboard,* up the *ramp,* go, go, go!" Beatrice popped up out of the mud and mimicked him, shakily driving her fellows before her.

Miles skidded to a stop beside his fallen Dendarii and snapped the armor clamps open left-handed. The soldier kicked off his fatal carapace, rolled to his feet, and limped for the safety of the shuttle. Miles ran close behind him.

Murka and one patrolman waited at the foot of the ramp.

"Get ready to pull in the ramp and lift on my mark," Murka began to the shuttle pilot. "R—" His words were lost in an explosive pop as the plasma beam sliced across his neck. Miles could feel the searing heat from it pass centimeters above his head as he stood next to his lieutenant. Murka's body crumpled.

Miles dodged, paused to yank off Murka's comm headset. The head came too. Miles had to brace it with his numb hand to pull the headset free. The weight of the head, its density and roundness, hammered into his senses. The precise memory of it would surely be with him until his dying day. He let it fall by Murka's body.

He staggered up the ramp, a last armored Dendarii pulling on his arm. He could feel the ramp sag peculiarly under their feet, glanced down to see a half-melted seam across it where the plasma arc that had killed Murka had passed on.

He fell through the hatchway, clutching the headset and yelling into it, "Lift, lift! Mark, now! Go!"

"Who is this?" came the shuttle pilot's voice back.

"Naismith."

"Yes, *sir.*"

The shuttle heaved off the ground, engines roaring, even before the ramp had withdrawn. The ramp mechanism labored, metal and plastic complaining—then jammed on the twisted distortion of the melt.

"Get that hatch sealed back there!" the shuttle pilot's voice yowled over the headset.

"Ramp's jammed," Miles yowled back. "Jettison it!"

The ramp mechanism skreeled and shrieked, reversing itself. The ramp shuddered, jammed again. Hands reached out to thump on it urgently. "You'll never get it that way!" Beatrice, across the hatch from Miles, yelled fiercely, and twisted around to kick at it with her bare feet. The wind of their flight screamed over the open hatchway, buffeting and vibrating the shuttle like a giant blowing across the top of a bottle.

To a chorus of shouting, thumping, and swearing, the shuttle lurched abruptly onto its side. Men, women, and loose equipment tangled across the tilting deck. Beatrice kicked bloodily at a final buggered bolt. The ramp tore loose at last. Beatrice, sliding, fell with it.

Miles dove at her, lunging across the hatchway. If he connected, he never knew, for his right hand was a senseless blob. He saw her face only as a white blur as she whipped away into the blackness.

It was like a silence, a great silence, in his head. Although the roar of wind and engines, screaming and swearing and yelling, went on as before, it was lost somewhere between his ears and his brain, and went unregistered. He saw only a white blur, smearing into the darkness, repeated again and again, replaying like a looping vid.

He found himself crouched on his hands and knees, the shuttle's acceleration sucking him to the deck. They'd gotten the hatch closed. The merely human babble within seemed muffled and thin, now that the roaring voices of the gods were silenced. He looked up into the pale face of Pitt's lieutenant, crouched beside him still clutching the unfired Dendarii weapon he'd grabbed up in that other lifetime.

"You'd better kill a whole lot of Cetagandans for Marilac, boy," Miles rasped to him at last. "You better be worth something to *somebody*, 'cause I've sure paid too much for you."

The Marilacan's face twitched uncertainly, too cowed even to try to look apologetic. Miles wondered what his own face must look like. From the reflection in that mirror, strange, very strange.

Miles began to crawl forward, looking for something, some-body. . . . Formless flashes made yellow streaks in the corners of his vision. An armored Dendarii, her helmet off, pulled him to his feet.

"Sir? Hadn't you better come forward to the pilot's compartment, sir?"

"Yes, all right . . ."

She got an arm around him, under his arm, so he didn't fall

down again. They picked their way forward in the crowded shuttle, through Marilacans and Dendarii mixed. Faces were drawn to him, marked him fearfully, but none dared an expression of any kind. Miles's eye was caught by a silver cocoon, as they neared the forward end.

"Wait . . ."

He fell to his knees beside Suegar. A hit of hope . . . "Suegar. Hey, Suegar!"

Suegar opened his eyes to slits. No telling how much of this he was taking in, through the pain and the shock and the drugs.

"You're on your way now. We made it, made the timing. With all ease. With agility and speed. Up through the regions of the air, higher than the clouds. You had the scripture right, you did."

Suegar's lips moved. Miles bent his head closer.

" . . . wasn't really a scripture," Suegar whispered. "I knew it . . . you knew it . . . don't shit me . . ."

Miles paused, cold-stoned. Then he leaned forward again. "No, brother," he whispered. "For though we went in clothed, we have surely come out naked."

Suegar's lips puffed on a dry laugh.

Miles didn't weep until after they'd made the wormhole jump.

Brothers in Arms

For Martha and Andy

CHAPTER ONE

His combat-drop shuttle crouched still and silent in the repairs docking bay—malevolent, to Miles's jaundiced eye. Its metal and fibreplas surface was scarred, pitted and burned. It had seemed such a proud, gleaming, efficient vessel when it was new. Perhaps it had undergone psychotic personality change from its traumas. It had been new such a short few months ago. . . .

Miles rubbed his face wearily, and blew out his breath. If there was any incipient psychosis floating around here, it wasn't contained in the machinery. In the eye of the beholder indeed. He took his booted foot off the bench he'd been draped over and straightened up, at least to the degree his crooked spine permitted. Commander Quinn, alert to his every move, fell in behind him.

"There," Miles limped down the length of the fuselage and pointed to the shuttle's portside lock, "is the design defect I'm chiefly concerned about."

He motioned the sales engineer from Kaymer Orbital Shipyards closer. "The ramp from this lock extends and retracts automatically, with a manual override—fine so far. But its recessed slot is inside the hatch, which means that if for any reason the ramp gets hung up, the door can't be sealed. The consequences of which I trust you can imagine." Miles didn't have to imagine them; they had burned in his memory for the last three months. Instant replay without an off switch.

"Did you find this out the hard way at Dagoola IV, Admiral Naismith?" the engineer inquired in a tone of genuine interest.

"Yeah. We lost . . . personnel. I was damned near one of them."

"I see," said the engineer respectfully. But his brows quirked.

How dare you be amused. . . . Fortunately for his health, the engineer did not smile. A thin man of slightly above average height, he reached up the side of the shuttle to run his hands along the slot in question, pull himself up chin-up fashion, peer about and mutter notes into his recorder. Miles resisted an urge to jump up and down like a frog to try to see what he was looking at. Undignified. With his own eye-level even with the engineer's chest, Miles would need about a one-meter stepladder even to reach the ramp slot on tiptoe. And he was too damned tired for calisthenics just now, nor was he about to ask Elli Quinn to give him a boost. He jerked his chin up in the old involuntary nervous tic, and waited in a posture of parade rest appropriate to his uniform, his hands clasped behind his back.

The engineer dropped back to the docking bay deck with a thump. "Yes, Admiral, I think Kaymer can take care of this for you all right. How many of these drop shuttles did you say you had?"

"Twelve." Fourteen minus two equalled twelve. Except in Dendarii Free Mercenary Fleet mathematics, where fourteen minus two shuttles equalled two hundred and seven dead. *Stop that,* Miles told the calculating jeerer in the back of his head firmly. *It does no one any good now.*

"Twelve." The engineer made a note. "What else?" He eyed the battered shuttle.

"My own engineering department will be handling the minor repairs, now that it looks as if we'll actually be holding still in one place for a while. I wanted to see to this ramp problem personally, but my second in command, Commodore Jesek, is chief engineer for my fleet, and he wants to talk to your jump tech people about re-calibrating some of our Necklin rods. I have a jump pilot with a head wound, but jumpset implant micro-neurosurgery is not one of Kaymer's specialties, I understand. Nor weapons systems?"

"No, indeed," the engineer agreed hastily. He touched a burn on the shuttle's scarred surface, perhaps fascinated by the violence it silently witnessed, for he added, "Kaymer Orbital mainly services merchant vessels. A mercenary fleet is something a bit unusual in this part of the wormhole nexus. Why did you come to us?"

"You were the lowest bidder."

"Oh—not Kaymer Corporation. Earth. I was wondering why you came to Earth? We're rather off the main trade routes, except for the tourists and historians. Er . . . peaceful."

He wonders if we have a contract here, Miles realized. Here, on a planet of nine billion souls, whose combined military forces would make pocket change of the Dendarii's five thousand—right. *He thinks I'm out to make trouble on old mother Earth? Or that I'd break security and tell him even if I was. . . .* "Peaceful, precisely," Miles said smoothly. "The Dendarii are in need of rest and refitting. A peaceful planet off the main nexus channels is just what the doctor ordered." He cringed inwardly, thinking of the doctor bill pending.

It hadn't been Dagoola. The rescue operation had been a tactical triumph, a military miracle almost. His own staff had assured him of this over and over, so perhaps he could begin to believe it true.

The break-out on Dagoola IV had been the third largest prisoner-of-war escape in history, Commodore Tung said. Military history being Tung's obsessive hobby, he ought to know. The Dendarii had snatched over ten thousand captured soldiers, an entire POW camp, from under the nose of the Cetagandan Empire, and made them into the nucleus of a new guerrilla army on a planet the Cetagandans had formerly counted on as an easy conquest. The costs had been so small, compared to the spectacular results—except for the individuals who'd paid for the triumph with their lives, for whom the price was something infinite, divided by zero.

It had been Dagoola's aftermath that had cost the Dendarii too much, the infuriated Cetagandans' vengeful pursuit. They had followed with ships till the Dendarii had slipped through political jurisdictions that Cetagandan military vessels could not traverse; hunted on with secret assassination and sabotage teams thereafter. Miles trusted they had outrun the assassination teams at last.

"Did you take all this fire at Dagoola IV?" the engineer went on, still intrigued by the shuttle.

"Dagoola was a covert operation," Miles said stiffly. "We don't discuss it."

"It made a big splash in the news a few months back," the Earthman assured him.

My head hurts. . . . Miles pressed his palm to his forehead, crossed his arms, and rested his chin in his hand, twitching a smile at the engineer. "Wonderful," he muttered. Commander Quinn winced.

"Is it true the Cetagandans have put a price on your life?" the engineer asked cheerfully.

Miles sighed. "Yes."

"Oh," said the engineer. "Ah. I'd thought that was just a story."

He moved away just slightly, as if embarrassed, or as if the air of morbid violence clinging to the mercenary were a contagion that could somehow rub off on him, if he got too close. He just might be right. He cleared his throat. "Now, about the payment schedule for the design modifications—what had you in mind?"

"Cash on delivery," said Miles promptly, "acceptance to follow my engineering staff's inspection and approval of the completed work. Those were the terms of your bid, I believe."

"Ah—yes. Hm." The Earthman tore his attention away from the machinery itself; Miles felt he could see him switching from technical to business mode. "Those are the terms we normally offer our established corporate customers."

"The Dendarii Free Mercenary Fleet is an established corporation. Registered out of Jackson's Whole."

"Mm, yes, but—how shall I put this—the most exotic risk our normal customers usually run is bankruptcy, for which we have assorted legal protections. Your mercenary fleet is, um . . ."

He's wondering how to collect payment from a corpse, Miles thought.

"—a lot riskier," the engineer finished candidly. He shrugged an apology.

An honest man, at least.

"We shall not raise our recorded bid. But I'm afraid we're going to have to ask for payment up front."

As long as we're down to trading insults . . . "But that gives us no protection against shoddy workmanship," said Miles.

"You can sue," remarked the engineer, "just like anybody else."

"I can blow your—" Miles's fingers drummed against his trouser seam where no holster was tied. Earth, old Earth, old civilized Earth. Commander Quinn, at his shoulder, touched his elbow in a fleeting gesture of restraint. He shot her a brief reassuring smile— no, he was not about to let himself get carried away by the— exotic—possibilities of Admiral Miles Naismith, Commanding, Dendarii Free Mercenary Fleet. He was merely tired, his smile said. A slight widening of her brilliant brown eyes replied, *Bullshit, sir.* But that was another argument, which they would not continue here, out loud, in public.

"You can look," said the engineer neutrally, "for a better offer if you wish."

"We have looked," said Miles shortly. *As you well know.* "Right. Um . . . what about . . . half up front and half on delivery?"

The Earthman frowned, shook his head. "Kaymer does not pad

its estimates, Admiral Naismith. And our cost overruns are among the lowest in the business. That's a point of pride."

The term *cost overrun* made Miles's teeth hurt, in light of Dagoola. How much did these people really know about Dagoola, anyway?

"If you're truly worried about our workmanship, the monies could be placed in an escrow account in the control of a neutral third party, such as a bank, until you accept delivery. Not a very satisfactory compromise from Kaymer's point of view, but—that's as far as I can go."

A neutral third *Earther* party, thought Miles. If he hadn't checked up on Kaymer's workmanship, he wouldn't be here. It was his own cash flow Miles was thinking about. Which was definitely not Kaymer's business.

"You having cash flow problems, Admiral?" inquired the Earther with interest. Miles fancied he could see the price rising in his eyes.

"Not at all," Miles lied blandly. Rumors afloat about the Dendarii's liquidity difficulties could sabotage a lot more than just this repair deal. "Very well. Cash up front to be held in escrow." If he wasn't to have the use of his funds, neither should Kaymer. Beside him, Elli Quinn drew air in through her teeth. The Earther engineer and the mercenary leader shook hands solemnly.

Following the sales engineer back toward his own office, Miles paused a moment by a viewport that framed a fine view of Earth from orbit. The engineer smiled and waited politely, even proudly, watching his gaze.

Earth. Old, romantic, historic Earth, the big blue marble itself. Miles had always expected to travel here someday, although not, surely, under these conditions.

Earth was still the largest, richest, most varied and populous planet in scattered humanity's entire worm-hole nexus of explored space. Its dearth of good exit points in solar local space and governmental disunity left it militarily and strategically minor from the greater galactic point of view. But Earth still reigned, if it did not rule, culturally supreme. More war-scarred than Barrayar, as technically advanced as Beta Colony, the end-point of all pilgrimages both religious and secular—in light of which, major embassies from every world that could afford one were collected here. Including, Miles reflected, nibbling gently on the side of his index finger, the Cetagandan. Admiral Naismith must use all means to avoid them.

"Sir?" Elli Quinn interrupted his meditations. He smiled briefly up at her sculptured face, the most beautiful his money had been able to buy after the plasma burn and yet, thanks to the genius of the surgeons, still unmistakably Elli. Would that every combat casualty taken in his service could be so redeemed. "Commodore Tung is on the comconsole for you," she went on.

His smile sagged. What now? He abandoned the view and marched off after her to take over the sales engineer's office with a polite, relentless, "Will you excuse us, please?"

His Eurasian third officer's bland, broad face formed above the vid plate.

"Yes, Ky?"

Ky Tung, already out of uniform and into civilian gear, gave him a brief nod in lieu of a salute. "I've just finished making arrangements at the rehab center for our nine severely-wounded. Prognoses are good, for the most part. And they think they will be able to retrieve four of the eight frozen dead, maybe five if they're lucky. The surgeons here even think they'll be able to repair Demmi's jumpset, once the neural tissue itself has healed. For a price, of course . . ." Tung named the price in GSA Federal credits; Miles mentally converted it to Barrayaran Imperial marks, and made a small squeaking noise.

Tung grinned dry appreciation. "Yeah. Unless you want to give up on that repair. It's equal to all the rest put together."

Miles shook his head, grimacing. "There are a number of people in the universe I'd be willing to double-cross, but my own wounded aren't among 'em."

"Thank you," said Tung, "I agree. Now, I'm just about ready to leave this place. Last thing I have to do is sign a chit taking personal responsibility for the bill. Are you quite sure you're going to be able to collect the pay owed us for the Dagoola operation here?"

"I'm on my way to do that next," Miles promised. "Go ahead and sign, I'll make it right."

"Very good, sir," said Tung. "Am I released for my home leave after that?"

Tung the Earth man, the only Earther Miles had ever met— which probably accounted for the unconscious favorable feelings he had about this place, Miles reflected. "How much time off do we owe you by now, Ky, about a year and a half?" *With pay, alas,* a small voice added in his mind, and was suppressed as unworthy. "You can take all you want."

"Thank you." Tung's face softened. "I just talked to my daughter. I have a brand-new grandson!"

"Congratulations," said Miles. "Your first?"

"Yes."

"Go on, then. If anything comes up, we'll take care of it. You're only indispensable in combat, eh? Uh . . . where will you be?"

"My sister's home. Brazil. I have about four hundred cousins there."

"Brazil, right. All right." Where the devil was Brazil? "Have a good time."

"I shall." Tung's departing semi-salute was distinctly breezy. His face faded from the vid.

"Damn," Miles sighed, "I'm sorry to lose him even to a leave. Well, he deserves it."

Elli leaned over the back of his comconsole chair. Her breath barely stirred his dark hair, his dark thoughts. "May I suggest, Miles, that he's not the only senior officer who could use some time off? Even you need to dump stress sometimes. And you were wounded too."

"Wounded?" Tension clamped Miles's jaw. "Oh, the bones. Broken bones don't count. I've had the damned brittle bones all my life. I just have to learn to resist the temptation to play field officer. The place for my ass is in a nice padded tactics-room chair, not on the line. If I'd known in advance that Dagoola was going to get so—physical, I'd have sent somebody else in as the fake POW. Anyway, there you are. I had my leave in sickbay."

"And then spent a month wandering around like a cryo-corpse who'd been warmed up in the microwave. When you walked into a room it was like a visit from the Undead."

"I ran the Dagoola rig on pure hysteria. You can't be up that long and not pay for it after with a little down. At least, I can't."

"My impression was there was more to it than that."

He whirled the chair around to face her with a snarl. "Will you back off! Yes, we lost some good people. I don't like losing good people. I cry real tears—in private, if you don't mind!"

She recoiled, her face falling. He softened his voice, deeply ashamed of his outburst. "Sorry, Elli. I know I've been edgy. The death of that poor POW who fell from the shuttle shook me more than . . . more than I should have let it. I can't seem to . . ."

"I was out of line, sir."

The "sir" was like a needle through some voodoo doll she held of him. Miles winced. "Not at all."

Why, why, why, of all the idiotic things he'd done as Admiral Naismith, had he ever established as explicit policy not to seek physical intimacy with anyone in his own organization? It had seemed like a good idea at the time. Tung had approved. Tung was a grandfather, for God's sake; his gonads had probably withered years ago. Miles remembered how he had deflected the first pass Elli had ever made at him. "A good officer doesn't go shopping in the company store," he'd explained gently. Why hadn't she belted him in the jaw for that fatuousness? She had absorbed the unintended insult without comment, and never tried again. Had she ever realized he'd meant that to apply to himself, not her?

When he was with the fleet for extended periods, he usually tried to send her on detached duties, from which she invariably returned with superb results. She had headed the advance team to Earth, and had Kaymer and most of their other suppliers all lined up by the time the Dendarii fleet made orbit. A good officer; after Tung, probably his best. What would he not give to dive into that lithe body and lose himself now? Too late. He'd lost his option.

Her velvet mouth crimped quizzically. She gave him a—sisterly, perhaps—shrug. "I won't hassle you about it any more. But at least think about it. I don't think I've ever seen a human being who needed to get laid worse than you do now."

Oh, God, what a straight line—what did those words really mean? His chest tightened. Comradely comment, or invitation? If mere comment, and he mistook it for invitation, would she think he was leaning on her for sexual favors? If the reverse, would she be insulted again and not breathe on him for years to come? He grinned in panic. "Paid," he blurted. "What I need right now is paid, not laid. After that—after that, um . . . maybe we could go see some of the sights. It seems practically criminal to come all this way and not see any of Old Earth, even if it was by accident. I'm supposed to have a bodyguard at all times downside anyway; we could double up."

She was sighing, straightening up. "Yes, duty first, of course."

Yes, duty first. And his next duty was to report in to Admiral Naismith's employers. After that, all his troubles would be vastly simplified.

Miles wished he could have changed to civilian clothes before embarking on this expedition. His crisp gray-and-white Dendarii admiral's uniform was as conspicuous as hell in this shopping arcade. Or at least made Elli change—they could have pretended to be a soldier on leave and his girlfriend. But his civilian gear had been stashed in a crate several planets back—would he ever retrieve it? The clothes had been tailor-made and expensive, not so much as a mark of status as pure necessity.

Usually he could forget the peculiarities of his body—oversized head exaggerated by a short neck set on a twisted spine, all squashed down to a height of four-foot-nine, the legacy of a congenital accident—but nothing highlighted his defects in his own mind more sharply than trying to borrow clothes from someone of normal size and shape. *You sure it's the uniform that feels conspicuous, boy?* he thought to himself. *Or are you playing foolie-foolie games with your head again? Stop it.*

He returned his attention to his surroundings. The spaceport city of London, a jigsaw of nearly two millennia of clashing architectural styles, was a fascination. The sunlight falling through the arcade's patterned glass arch was an astonishing rich color, breathtaking. It alone might have led him to guess his eye had been returned to its ancestral planet. Perhaps later he'd have a chance to visit more historical sites, such as a submarine tour of Lake Los Angeles, or New York behind the great dikes

Elli made another nervous circuit of the bench beneath the light-clock, scanning the crowd. This seemed a most unlikely spot for Cetagandan hit squads to pop up, but still he was glad of her alertness, that allowed him to be tired. *You can come look for assassins under my bed anytime, love. . . .*

"In a way, I'm glad we ended up here," he remarked to her. "This might prove an excellent opportunity for Admiral Naismith to disappear up his own existence for a while. Take the heat off the Dendarii. The Cetagandans are a lot like the Barrayarans, really; they take a very personal view of command."

"You're pretty damned casual about it."

"Early conditioning. Total strangers trying to kill me make me feel right at home." A thought struck him with a certain macabre cheer. "You know, this is the first time anybody has tried to kill me for myself, and not because of who I'm related to? Have I ever told you about what my grandfather really did when I was . . ."

She cut off his babble with a lift of her chin. "I think this is it."

He followed her gaze. He *was* tired; she'd spotted their contact before he had. The man coming toward them with the inquiring look on his face wore stylish Earther clothes, but his hair was clipped in a Barrayaran military burr. A non-com, perhaps. Officers favored a slightly less severe Roman patrician style. *I need a haircut,* thought Miles, his collar suddenly ticklish.

"My lord?" said the man.

"Sergeant Barth?" said Miles.

The man nodded, glanced at Elli. "Who is this?"

"My bodyguard."

"Ah."

So slight a compression of the lips and widening of the eyes, to convey so much amusement and contempt. Miles could feel the muscles coil in his neck. "She is outstanding at her job."

"I'm sure, sir. Come this way, please." He turned and led off.

The bland face was laughing at him, he could feel it, tell by looking at the back of the head. Elli, aware only of the sudden increase of tension in the air, gave him a look of dismay. *It's all right,* he thought at her, tucking her hand in his arm.

They strolled after their guide, through a shop, down a lift tube and then some stairs, then picked up the pace. The underground utility level was a maze of tunnels, conduits, and power optics. They traversed, Miles guessed, a couple of blocks. Their guide opened a door with a palm-lock. Another short tunnel led to another door. This one had a live human guard by it, extremely neat in Barrayaran Imperial dress greens, who scrambled up from his comconsole seat where he monitored scanners to barely resist saluting their civilian-clothed guide.

"We dump our weapons here," Miles told Elli. "All of them. I mean really all."

Elli raised her brows at the sudden shift of Miles's accent, from the flat Betan twang of Admiral Naismith to the warm gutturals of his native Barrayar. She seldom heard his Barrayaran voice, at that—which one would seem put-on to her? There was no doubt which one would seem a put-on to the embassy personnel, though, and Miles cleared his throat, to be sure of fully disciplining his voice to the new order.

Miles's contributions to the pile on the guard's console were a pocket stunner and a long steel knife in a lizard-skin sheath. The guard scanned the knife, popped the silver cap off the end of its jewelled hilt to reveal a patterned seal, and handed it back carefully to Miles. Their guide raised his brows at the miniaturized technical arsenal Elli unloaded. *So there,* Miles thought to him. *Stuff that up your regulation nose.* He followed on feeling rather more serene.

Up a lift tube, and suddenly the ambience changed to a hushed, plush, understated dignity. "The Barrayaran Imperial Embassy," Miles whispered to Elli.

The ambassador's wife must have taste, Miles thought. But the building had a strange hermetically-sealed flavor to it, redolent to Miles's experienced nose as paranoid security in action. *Ah, yes, a planet's embassy is that planet's soil. Feels just like home.*

Their guide led them down another lift tube into what was clearly an office corridor—Miles spotted the sensor scanners in a carved arch as they passed—then through two sets of automatic doors into a small, quiet office.

"Lieutenant Lord Miles Vorkosigan, sir," their guide announced, standing at attention. "And—bodyguard."

Miles's hands twitched. Only a Barrayaran could convey such a delicate shade of insult in a half-second pause between two words. Home again.

"Thank you, Sergeant, dismissed," said the captain behind the comconsole desk. Imperial dress greens again—the embassy must maintain a formal tone.

Miles gazed curiously at the man who was to be, will or nill, his new commanding officer. The captain gazed back with equal intensity.

An arresting-looking man, though far from pretty. Dark hair. Hooded, nutmeg-brown eyes. A hard, guarded mouth, fleshy blade of a nose sweeping down a Roman profile that matched his officer's haircut. His hands were blunt and clean, steepled now together in a still tension. In his early thirties, Miles guessed.

But why is this guy looking at me like I'm a puppy that just piddled on his carpet? Miles wondered. *I just got here. I haven't had time to offend him yet. Oh, God, I hope he's not one of those rural Barrayaran hicks who see me as a mutant, a refugee from a botched abortion.* . . .

"So," said the captain, leaning back in his chair with a sigh, "you're the Great Man's son, eh?"

Miles's smile became absolutely fixed. A red haze clouded his vision. He could hear his blood beating in his ears like a death march. Elli, watching him, stood quite still, barely breathing. Miles's lips moved; he swallowed. He tried again. "Yes, sir," he heard himself saying, as from a great distance. "And who are you?"

He managed, just barely, not to let it come out as *And whose son are you?* The fury bunching his stomach must not be allowed to show; he was going to have to work with this man. It might not even have been an intentional insult. Couldn't have been— how could this stranger know how much blood Miles had sweated fighting off charges of privilege, slurs on his competence? *The mutant's only here because his father got him in.* . . . He could hear his father's voice, countering, *For God's sake get your head out of your ass, boy!* He let the rage stream out on a long, calming breath, and cocked his head brightly.

"Oh," said the captain, "yes, you only talked to my aide, didn't you. I'm Captain Duv Galeni. Senior military attaché for the embassy, and by default chief of Imperial Security, as well as Service Security, here. And, I confess, rather startled to have you appear in my chain of command. It is not entirely clear to me what I'm supposed to do with you."

Not a rural accent; the captain's voice was cool, educated, blandly urban. Miles could not place it in Barrayaran geography. "I'm not surprised, sir," said Miles. "I did not myself expect to be reporting in at Earth, nor so late. I was originally supposed to report back to Imperial Security Command at Sector Two HQ on Tau Ceti, over a month ago. But the Dendarii Free Mercenary Fleet was driven out of Mahata Solaris local space by a surprise Cetagandan attack. Since we were not being paid to make war directly on the Cetagandans, we ran, and ended up unable to get back by any shorter route. This is literally my first opportunity to report in anywhere since we delivered the refugees to their new base."

"I was not—" the captain paused, his mouth twitching, and began again, "I had not been aware that the extraordinary escape at Dagoola was a covert operation of Barrayaran Intelligence. Wasn't it perilously close to being an act of outright war on the Cetagandan Empire?"

"Precisely why the Dendarii mercenaries were used for it, sir. It was actually supposed to be a somewhat smaller operation, but things got a little out of hand. In the field, as it were." Beside him, Elli kept her eyes straight ahead, and didn't even choke. "I, uh . . . have a complete report."

The captain appeared to be having an internal struggle. "Just what is the relationship between the Dendarii Free Mercenary Fleet and Imperial Security, Lieutenant?" he finally said. There was something almost plaintive in his tone.

"Er . . . what do you know already, sir?"

Captain Galeni turned his hands palm-up. "I hadn't even heard of them, except peripherally, until you made contact by vid yesterday. My files—my Security files!—say exactly three things about the organization. They are not to be attacked, any requests for emergency assistance should be met with all due speed, and for further information I must apply to Sector Two Security Head-quarters."

"Oh, yeah," said Miles, "that's right. This is only a Class III embassy, isn't it. Um, well, the relationship is fairly simple. The Dendarii are kept on retainer for highly covert operations which are either out of Imperial Security's range, or for which any direct, traceable connection with Barrayar would be politically embarrassing. Dagoola was both. Orders are passed from the General Staff, with the advice and consent of the Emperor, through Chief of Imperial Security Illyan to me. It's a very short chain of command. I'm the go-between, supposedly the sole connection. I leave Imperial HQ as Lieutenant Vorkosigan, and pop up—wherever—as Admiral Naismith, waving a new contract. We go do whatever we've been assigned to do, and then, from the Dendarii point of view, I vanish as mysteriously as I came. God knows what they think I do in my spare time."

"Do you really want to know?" Elli asked, her eyes alight.

"Later," he muttered out of the corner of his mouth.

The captain drummed his fingers on his desk console and glanced down at a display. "None of this is in your official dossier. Twenty-four years old—aren't you a little young for your rank, ah—Admiral?" His tone was dry; his eyes passed mockingly over the Dendarii uniform.

Miles tried to ignore the tone. "It's a long story. Commodore Tung, a very senior Dendarii officer, is the real brains of the outfit. I just play the part."

Elli's eyes widened in outrage; a severe glance from Miles tried to compel her to silence. "You do a lot more than that," she objected.

"If you're the sole connection," frowned Galeni, "who the devil is this woman?" His wording rendered her, if not a non-person, certainly a non-soldier.

"Yes, sir. Well, in case of emergencies, there are three Dendarii who know my real identity. Commander Quinn, who was in on the beginning of the whole scam, is one of them. I'm under orders from Illyan to maintain a bodyguard at all times, so Commander Quinn fills in whenever I have to change identities. I trust her implicitly." *You will respect my people, damn your mocking eyes, whatever you think of me. . . .*

"How long has this been going on, Lieutenant?"

"Ah," Miles glanced at Elli, "seven years, isn't it?"

Elli's bright eyes glinted. "It seems like only yesterday," she cooed blandly. It seemed she was finding it hard to ignore the tone too; Miles trusted she would keep her edged sense of humor under control.

The captain regarded his fingernails, then sharply stared at Miles. "Well, I'm going to apply to Sector Two Security, Lieutenant. And if I find out that this is another Vor lordling's idea of a practical joke, I shall do my level best to see that you are brought up on charges for it. No matter who your father is."

"It's all true, sir. My word as Vorkosigan."

"Just so," said Captain Galeni through his teeth.

Miles, infuriated, drew breath—then placed Galeni's regional accent at last. He jerked up his chin. "Are you—Komarran, sir?"

Galeni gave him a wary nod. Miles returned it gravely, rather frozen. Elli nudged him, whispering, "What the hell—?"

"Later," Miles muttered back. "Barrayaran internal politics."

"Will I need to take notes?"

"Probably." He raised his voice. "I must get in touch with my actual superiors, Captain Galeni. I have no idea what my next orders even are."

Galeni pursed his lips, and remarked mildly, "I am actually a superior of yours, Lieutenant Vorkosigan."

And chapped as hell, Miles judged, to be cut out of his own command chain—and who could blame him? Softly, now . . . "Of course, sir. What are my orders?"

Galeni's hands clenched briefly in frustration, his mouth set in irony. "I will have to add you to my staff, I suppose, while we all await clarification. Third assistant military attaché."

"Ideal, sir, thank you," said Miles. "Admiral Naismith needs very much to vanish just now. The Cetagandans put a price on his— my—head after Dagoola. I've been lucky twice."

It was Galeni's turn to freeze. "Are you joking?"

"I had four dead and sixteen wounded Dendarii because of it," said Miles stiffly. "I don't find it amusing at all."

"In that case," said Galeni grimly, "you may consider yourself confined to the Embassy compound."

And miss Earth? Miles sighed reluctance. "Yes, sir," he agreed in a dull tone. "As long as Commander Quinn here can be my go-between to the Dendarii."

"Why do you need further contact with the Dendarii?"

"They're my people, sir."

"I thought you said this Commodore Tung ran the show."

"He's on home leave right now. But all I really need before

Admiral Naismith departs into the woodwork is to pay some bills. If you could advance me their immediate expenses, I could wrap up this mission."

Galeni sighed; his fingers danced over his comconsole and paused. "Assistance with all due speed. Right. Just how much do they require?"

"Roughly eighteen million marks, sir."

Galeni's fingers hung paralyzed. "Lieutenant," he said carefully, "that is more than ten times the budget for this entire embassy for a year. Several tens of times the budget for this department!"

Miles spread his hands. "Operating expenses for five thousand troops and techs and eleven ships for over six months, plus equipment losses—we lost a hell of a lot of gear at Dagoola—payroll, food, clothing, fuel, medical expenses, ammunition, repairs—I can show you the spreadsheets, sir."

Galeni sat back. "No doubt. But Sector Security Headquarters is going to have to handle this one. Funds in that amount don't even exist here."

Miles chewed on the side of his index finger. "Oh." Oh, indeed. He would not panic. . . . "In that case, sir, may I request you send to Sector HQ as soon as possible?"

"Believe me, Lieutenant, I consider getting you transferred to someone else's command an object of the highest priority." He rose. "Excuse me. Wait here." He exited the office shaking his head.

"What the hell?" prodded Elli. "I thought you were about to try and dismantle the guy, captain or no captain—and then you just stopped. What's so magic about being Komarran, and where can I get some?"

"Not magic," said Miles. "Definitely not magic. But very important."

"More important than being a Vor lord?"

"In a weird way, yes, right now. Look, you know the planet Komarr was Barrayar's first interstellar Imperial conquest, right?"

"I thought you called it an annexation."

"A rose by any other name. We took it for its wormholes, because it sat across our only nexus connection, because it was strangling our trade, and most of all because it accepted a bribe to let the Cetagandan fleet pass through it when Cetaganda first tried to annex *us*. You may also recall who was the chief conquistador."

"Your dad. Back when he was only Admiral Lord Vorkosigan, before he became regent. It made his reputation."

"Yeah, well, it made more than one reputation for him. You ever want to see smoke come out of his ears, whisper, 'the Butcher of Komarr' in his hearing. They actually called him that."

"Thirty years ago, Miles." She paused. "Was there any truth to it?"

Miles sighed. "There was something. I've never been able to get the whole story out of him, but I'm damn sure what's in the history books isn't it. Anyway, the conquest of Komarr got messy. As a result, in the fourth year he was Imperial Regent came the Komarr Revolt, and that got really messy. Komarran terrorists have been a security nightmare for the Imperium ever since. It was pretty repressive there, I guess.

"Anyway, so time's gone on, things have calmed down a bit, anyone from either planet with energy to spare is off settling newly-opened Sergyar. There's been a movement among the Progressives—spearheaded by my father—to fully integrate Komarr into the Empire. It's not a real popular idea with the Barrayaran right. It's a bit of an obsession with the old man—'Between justice and geno-cide there is, in the long run, no middle ground,'" Miles intoned. "He gets real eloquent about it. So, all right, the route to the top on dear old caste-conscious, army-mad Barrayar was and always has been through the Imperial Military Service. It was opened to Komarrans for the first time just eight years ago.

"That means any Komarran in the service now is on the spot. They have to prove their loyalty the way I have to prove my—" he faltered, "prove myself. It also follows that if I'm working with or under any Komarran, and I turn up unusually dead one day, that Komarran is dog meat. Because my father was the Butcher, and no one will believe it wasn't some sort of revenge.

"And not just that Komarran. Every other Komarran in the Imperial Service would be shadowed by the same cloud. It'd put things back years in Barrayaran politics. If I got assassinated now," he shrugged helplessly, "my father would kill me."

"I trust you weren't planning on it," she choked.

"So now we come to Galeni," Miles went on hastily. "He's in the Service—an officer—has a post in Security itself. Must have worked his tail off to get here. Highly trusted—for a Komarran. But not at a major or strategic post; certain critical kinds of security infor-mation are deliberately withheld from him; and here I come along and rub his nose in it. And if he did have any relatives in the Komarr Revolt—well . . . here I am again. I doubt if he loves me, but he's going to have to guard me like the apple of his eye. And I, God help me, am going to have to let him. It's a real tricky situation."

She patted him on the arm. "You can handle it."

"Hm," he grunted glumly. "Oh, God, Elli," he wailed suddenly, letting his forehead fall against her shoulder, "and I didn't get the money for the Dendarii—can't, till God knows when—what will I tell Ky? I gave him my word . . . !"

She patted him on the head, this time. But she didn't say anything.

CHAPTER TWO

He let his head rest against the crisp cloth of her uniform jacket a moment longer. She shifted, her arms reaching toward him. Was she about to hug him? If she did, Miles decided, he was going to grab her and kiss her right there. And then see what happened—

Behind him, Galeni's office doors swished open. Elli and he both flinched away from each other, Elli coming to parade rest with a toss of her short dark curls, Miles just standing and cursing inwardly at the interruption.

He heard and knew the familiar, drawling voice before he turned.

"—brilliant, sure, but hyper as hell. You think he's going to slip his flywheel any second. Watch out when he starts talking too fast. Oh, yeah, that's him all right."

"Ivan," Miles breathed, closing his eyes. "How, God, have I sinned against You, that You have given me Ivan—*here.* . . ."

God not deigning to answer, Miles smiled crookedly and turned. Elli had her head tilted, frowning, listening in sudden concentration.

Galeni had returned with a tall young lieutenant in tow. Indolent as he was, Ivan Vorpatril had obviously been keeping in shape, for his athletic physique set off his dress greens to perfection. His affable, open face was even-featured, framed by wavy dark hair in a neat patrician clip. Miles could not help glancing at Elli, covertly alert for her reaction. With her face and figure Elli tended to make anyone standing next to her look grubby, but Ivan might actually play the stem to her rose and not be overshadowed.

86

"Hi, Miles," said Ivan. "What are you doing here?"

"I might ask you the same thing," said Miles.

"I'm second assistant military attaché. They assigned me here to get cultured, I guess. Earth, y'know."

"Oh," said Galeni, one corner of his mouth twitching upward, "is that what you're here for. I'd wondered."

Ivan grinned sheepishly. "How's life with the irregulars these days?" he asked Miles. "You still getting away with your Admiral Naismith scam?"

"Just barely," said Miles. "The Dendarii are with me now. They're in orbit," he jabbed his finger skyward, "eating their heads off even as we speak."

Galeni looked as if he'd bitten into something sour. "Does everybody know about this covert operation but me? You, Vorpatril—I know your security clearance is no higher than my own!"

Ivan shrugged. "A previous encounter. It was in the family."

"Damned Vor power network," muttered Galeni.

"Oh," said Elli Quinn in a tone of sudden enlightenment, "this is your *cousin* Ivan! I'd always wondered what he looked like."

Ivan, who had been sneaking little peeks at her ever since he'd entered the room, came to attention with all the quivering alertness of a bird dog pointing. He smiled blindingly and bowed over Elli's hand. "Delighted to meet you, m'lady. The Dendarii must be improving, if you are a fair sample. The fairest, surely."

Elli repossessed her hand. "We've met."

"Surely not. I couldn't forget that face."

"I didn't have this face. 'A head just like an onion' was the way you phrased it, as I recall." Her eyes glittered. "Since I was blinded at the time, I had no idea how bad the plastiskin prosthesis really looked. Until you told me. Miles never mentioned it."

Ivan's smile had gone limp. "Ah. The plasma-burn lady."

Miles smirked and edged closer to Elli, who put her hand possessively through the crook of his elbow and favored Ivan with a cold samurai smile. Ivan, trying to bleed with dignity, looked to Captain Galeni.

"Since you know each other, Lieutenant Vorkosigan, I've assigned Lieutenant Vorpatril here to take you in tow and orient you to the Embassy, and to your duties here," said Galeni. "Vor or no Vor, as long as you're on the Emperor's payroll, the Emperor might as well get some use of you. I trust some clarification of your status will arrive promptly."

"I trust the Dendarii payroll will arrive as promptly," said Miles.

"Your mercenary—bodyguard—can return to her outfit. If for any reason you need to leave the Embassy compound, I'll assign you one of my men."

"Yes, sir," sighed Miles. "But I still have to be able to get in touch with the Dendarii, in case of emergencies."

"I'll see that Commander Quinn gets a secured comm link before she leaves. As a matter of fact," he touched his comconsole, "Sergeant Barth?" he spoke into it.

"Yes, sir?" a voice replied.

"Do you have that comm link ready yet?"

"Just finished encoding it, sir."

"Good, bring it to my office."

Barth, still in his civvies, appeared within moments. Galeni shepherded Elli out. "Sergeant Barth will escort you out of the embassy compound, Commander Quinn." She glanced back over her shoulder at Miles, who sketched her a reassuring salute.

"What will I tell the Dendarii?" she asked.

"Tell them—tell them their funds are in transit," Miles called. The doors hissed shut, eclipsing her.

Galeni returned to his comconsole, which was blinking for his attention. "Vorpatril, please make getting your cousin out of that . . . costume, and into a correct uniform your 'first priority."

Does Admiral Naismith spook you—just a little . . . sir? Miles wondered irritably. "The Dendarii uniform is as real as your own, sir."

Galeni glowered at him, across his flickering desk. "I wouldn't know, Lieutenant. My father could only afford toy soldiers for me when I was a boy. You two are dismissed."

Miles, fuming, waited until the doors had closed behind them before tearing off his gray-and-white jacket and throwing it to the corridor floor. "Costume! Toy soldiers! I think I'm gonna kill that Komarran son-of-a-bitch!"

"Oooh," said Ivan. "Aren't we touchy today."

"You heard what he said!"

"Yeah, so . . . Galeni's all right. A bit regulation, maybe. There's a dozen little tin-pot mercenary outfits running around in oddball corners of the worm-hole nexus. Some of them tread a real fine line between legal and illegal. How's he supposed to know your Dendarii aren't next door to being hijackers?"

Miles picked up his uniform jacket, shook it out, and folded it carefully over his arm. "Huh."

"Come on," said Ivan. "I'll take you down to Stores and get you a kit in a color more to his taste."

"They got anything in my size?"

"They make a laser-map of your body and produce the stuff one-off, computer controlled, just like that overpriced sartorial pirate you take yourself to in Vorbarr Sultana. This is Earth, son."

"My man on Barrayar's been doing my clothes for ten years. He has some tricks that aren't in the computer. . . . Well, I guess I can live with it. Can the embassy computer do civilian clothes?"

Ivan grimaced. "If your tastes are conservative. If you want something in style to wow the local girls, you have to go farther afield."

"With Galeni for a duenna, I have a feeling I'm not going to get a chance to go very far afield," Miles sighed. "It'll have to do."

Miles sighted down the forest-green sleeve of his Barrayaran dress uniform, adjusted the cuff, and jerked his chin up, the better to settle his head on the high collar. He'd half-forgotten just how uncomfortable that damned collar was, with his short neck. In front the red rectangles of his lieutenant's rank seemed to poke into his jaw; in back it pinched his still-uncut hair. And the boots were hot. The bone he'd broken in his left foot at Dagoola still twinged, even now after being re-broken, set straight, and treated with electra-stim.

Still, the green uniform was home. His true self. Maybe it was time for a vacation from Admiral Naismith and his intractable responsibilities, time to remember the more reasonable problems of Lieutenant Vorkosigan, whose sole task now was to learn the procedures of one small office and put up with Ivan Vorpatril. The Dendarii didn't need him to hold their hand for routine rest and refit, nor could he have arranged any more safe and thorough a disappearance for Admiral Naismith.

Ivan's particular charge was this tiny windowless room deep in the bowels of the embassy compound; his job, to feed hundreds of data disks to a secured computer that concentrated them into a weekly report on the status of Earth, to be sent back to Security Chief Illyan and the general staff on Barrayar. Where, Miles supposed, it was computer-collated with hundreds of other such reports to create Barrayar's vision of the universe. Miles hoped devoutly that Ivan wasn't adding kilowatts and megawatts in the same column.

"By far the bulk of this stuff is public statistics," Ivan was explaining, seated before his console and actually looking at ease in his dress greens. "Population shifts, agricultural and manufacturing production figures, the various political divisions' published military budgets. The computer adds 'em up sixteen different ways, and blinks for attention when things don't match. Since all the originators have computers too, this doesn't happen too often— all the lies are embedded before it ever gets to us, Galeni says. More important to Barrayar are records of ship movements in and out of Earth local space.

"Then we get to the more interesting stuff, real spy work. There're several hundred people on Earth this embassy tries to keep track of, for one security reason or another. One of the biggest groups is the Komarran rebel expatriates." A wave of Ivan's hand, and dozens of faces flickered one after another above the vid plate.

"Oh, yeah?" said Miles, interested in spite of himself. "Does Galeni have secret contacts and so on with them? Is that why he's assigned here? Double agent—triple agent . . ."

"I bet Illyan wishes," said Ivan. "As far as I know, they regard Galeni as a leper. Evil collaborator with the imperialist oppressors and all that."

"Surely they're no great threat to Barrayar at this late date and distance. Refugees . . ."

"Some of these were the smart refugees, though, the ones who got their money out before the boom dropped. Some were involved in financing the Komarr Revolt during the Regency—they're mostly a lot poorer now. They're aging, though. Another half generation, if your father's integration policies succeed, and they'll have totally lost momentum, Captain Galeni says."

Ivan picked up another data disk. "And then we come to the real hot stuff, which is keeping track of what the other embassies are doing. Such as the Cetagandan."

"I hope they're on the other side of the planet," said Miles sincerely.

"No, most of the galactic embassies and consuls are concentrated right here in London. Makes watching each other ever so much more convenient."

"Ye gods," moaned Miles, "don't tell me they're across the street or some damned thing."

Ivan grinned. "Almost. They're about two kilometers away. We go to each other's parties a lot, to practice being snide, and play I-know-you-know-I-know games."

Miles sat, hyperventilating slightly. "Oh, shit."

"What's up you, coz?"

"Those people are trying to kill me."

"No they're not. It'd start a war. We're at peace right now, sort of, remember?"

"Well, they're trying to kill Admiral Naismith, anyway."

"Who vanished yesterday."

"Yeah, but—one of the reasons this whole Dendarii scam has held up for so long is distance. Admiral Naismith and Lieutenant Vorkosigan never show up within hundreds of light years of each other. We've never been trapped on the same planet together, let alone the same city."

"As long as you leave your Dendarii uniform in my closet, what's to connect?"

"Ivan, how many four-foot-nine-inch black-haired gray-eyed hunchbacks can there be on this damned planet? D'you think you trip over twitchy dwarfs on every street corner?"

"On a planet of nine billion," said Ivan, "there's got to be at least six of everything. Calm down!" He paused. "Y'know, that's the first time I've ever heard you use that word."

"What word?"

"Hunchback. You're not really, you know." Ivan eyed him with friendly worry.

Miles's fist closed, opened in a sharp throw-away gesture. "Anyway, Cetagandans. If they have a counterpart doing what you're doing—"

Ivan nodded. "I've met him. His name's ghem-lieutenant Tabor."

"Then they know the Dendarii are here, and know Admiral Naismith's been seen. They probably have a list of every purchase order we've put through the comm net, or will soon enough, when they turn their attention to it. They're tracking."

"They may be tracking, but they can't get orders from higher up any faster than we can," said Ivan reasonably. "And in any case they've got a manpower shortage. Our security staff is four times the size of theirs, on account of the Komarrans. I mean, this may be Earth, but it's still a minor embassy, even more so for them than us. Never fear," he struck a pose in his station chair, hand across his chest, "Cousin Ivan will protect you."

"That's so reassuring," Miles muttered.

Ivan grinned at the sarcasm and turned back to his work.

The day wore on interminably in the quiet, changeless room. His claustrophobia, Miles discovered, was developed to a much higher pitch than it used to be. He absorbed lessons from Ivan, and paced from wall to wall between times.

"You could do that about twice as fast, you know," Miles observed to Ivan, plugging away at his data analysis.

"But then I'd be done right after lunch," said Ivan, "and then I wouldn't have anything to do at all."

"Surely Galeni could find something."

"That's what I'm afraid of," said Ivan. "Quitting time rolls around soon enough. Then we go party."

"No, then you go party. I go to my room, as ordered. Maybe I'll catch up on my sleep, finally."

"That's it, think positive," said Ivan. "I'll work out with you in the embassy gym, if you want. You don't look so good, you know. Pale and, um . . . pale."

Old, thought Miles, *is the word you just edited.* He glanced at the distorted reflection of his face in a bit of chrome plating on the console. *That bad, eh?*

"Exercise," Ivan thumped his chest, "will be good for you."

"No doubt," muttered Miles.

The days fell quickly into a set pattern. Miles was awakened by Ivan in the room they shared, did a stint in the gym, showered, breakfasted, and went to work in the data room. He began to wonder if he would ever be permitted to see Earth's beautiful sunlight again. After three days Miles took the computer-stuffing job away from Ivan and started finishing it by noon, so that he might at least have the later hours for reading and study. He devoured embassy and security procedures, Earth history, galactic news. In the later afternoon they knocked off for another grueling workout in the gym. On the nights Ivan stayed in, Miles watched vid dramas with him; on the nights he went out, travelogues of all the sites of interest he wasn't allowed to go visit.

Elli reported in daily on the secured comm link on the status of the Dendarii fleet, still holding in orbit. Miles, closeting himself with the comm link, found himself increasingly hungry for that outside voice. Her reports were succinct. But afterwards they drifted off into inconsequential small talk, as Miles found it harder and harder to cut her off, and she never hung up on him. Miles fantasized about courting her in his own persona—would a commander accept a date from a mere lieutenant? Would she even like Lord Vorkosigan? Would Galeni ever let him leave the embassy to find out?

✧   ✧   ✧

Ten days of clean living, exercise, and regular hours had been bad for him, Miles decided. His energy level was up. Up, and bottled in the immobilized persona of Lord Vorkosigan, while the list of chores facing Admiral Naismith piled up and up and up. . . .

"Will you stop fidgeting, Miles?" Ivan complained. "Sit down. Take a deep breath. Hold still for five minutes. You can do it if you try."

Miles made one more circuit of the computer room, then flung himself into a chair. "Why hasn't Galeni called me yet? The courier from Sector HQ got in an hour ago!"

"So, give the man time to go to the bathroom and get a cup of coffee. Give Galeni time to read his reports. This is peacetime, everybody's got lots of leisure to sit around writing reports. They'd be hurt if nobody read 'em."

"That's the trouble with your government-supported troops," said Miles. "You're spoiled. You get paid not to make war."

"Wasn't there a mercenary fleet that did that once? They'd show up in orbit somewhere, and get paid—to *not* make war. Worked, didn't it? You're just not a creative enough mercenary commander, Miles."

"Yeah, LaVarr's fleet. It worked real good till the Tau Cetan Navy caught up with 'em, and then LaVarr was sent to the disintegration chamber."

"No sense of humor, the Tau Cetans."

"None," Miles agreed. "Neither has my father."

"Too true. Well—"

The comconsole blinked. Ivan had to duck out of the way as Miles pounced on it. "Yes sir?" said Miles breathlessly.

"Come to my office, Lieutenant Vorkosigan," said Galeni. His face was as saturnine as ever, no cues there.

"Yes, sir, thank you sir." Miles cut the com and plunged for the door. "My eighteen million marks, at last!"

"Either that," said Ivan genially, "or he's found a job for you in inventory. Maybe you're going to get to count all the goldfish in the fountain in the main reception court."

"Sure, Ivan."

"Hey, it's a real challenge! They keep moving around, you know."

"How do you know?" Miles paused, his eyes lighting. "Ivan, did he actually make you do that?"

"It had to do with a suspected security breach," said Ivan. "It's a long story."

"I'll bet." Miles beat a brief tattoo on the desk and vaulted around its corner. "Later. I'm gone."

Miles found Captain Galeni sitting staring dubiously at the display on his comconsole, as if it was still in code.

"Sir?"

"Hm." Galeni leaned back in his chair. "Well, your orders have arrived from Sector HQ, Lieutenant Vorkosigan."

"And?"

Galeni's mouth tightened. "And they confirm your temporary assignment to my staff. Officially and publicly. You may now draw your lieutenant's pay from my department as of ten days ago. As for the rest of your orders, they read the same as Vorpatril's—in fact, they could be templated from Vorpatril's orders with the name changed. You are to assist me as required, hold yourself at the disposal of the ambassador and his lady for escort duties, and as time permits take advantage of educational opportunities unique to Earth and appropriate to your status as an Imperial officer and lord of the Vor."

"What? This can't be right! What the devil are escort duties?" *Sounds like a call-girl.*

A slight smile turned one corner of Galeni's mouth. "Mostly, standing around in parade dress at official embassy social functions and being Vor for the natives. There are a surprising number of people who find aristocrats—even off-planet aristocrats—peculiarly fascinating." Galeni's tone made it clear that he found this fascination peculiar indeed. "You will eat, drink, dance perhaps . . ." his tone grew doubtful for a second, "and generally be exquisitely polite to anyone the ambassador wants to, ah, impress. Sometimes, you will be asked to remember and report conversations. Vorpatril does it all very well, rather to my surprise. He can fill in the details for you."

I don't need to take social notes from Ivan, Miles thought. *And the Vor are a military caste, not an aristocracy.* What the hell was HQ thinking of? It seemed extraordinarily obtuse even for them.

Yet if they had no new project on line for the Dendarii, why not use the opportunity for Count Vorkosigan's son to acquire a little more diplomatic polish? No one doubted that he was destined for the most rarified levels of the service—he would hardly be exposed to less varied experience than Ivan. It wasn't the content of the orders, it was only the lack of separation from his other persona that was so . . . unexpected.

Still . . . *report conversations.* Could this be the start of some special spy work? Perhaps further, clarifying details were en route.

He didn't even want to think about the possibility that HQ had decided it was finally time to shut down Dendarii covert ops altogether.

"Well," said Miles grudgingly, "all right."

"So glad," murmured Galeni, "you find your orders to your taste, Lieutenant."

Miles flushed, closing his mouth tightly. But if only he could get his Dendarii taken care of, the rest didn't matter. "And my eighteen million marks, sir?" he asked, taking care to keep his tone humble this time.

Galeni drummed his fingers on his desk. "No such credit order arrived with this courier, Lieutenant. Nor any mention of one."

"What!" shrieked Miles. "There's got to be!" He almost lunged across Galeni's desk to examine the vid himself, caught himself up just in time. "I calculated ten days for all the . . ." His brain dumped unwanted data, streaming past his consciousness—fuel, orbital docking fees, re-supply, medical-dental-surgical, the depleted ordnance inventory, payroll, roll-over, liquidity, margin. . . . "Dammit, we bled for Barrayar! They can't—there must be some mistake!"

Galeni spread his hands helplessly. "No doubt. But not one in my power to repair."

"Send again—sir!"

"Oh, I shall."

"Better yet—let me go as courier. If I talked to HQ in person—"

"Hm." Galeni rubbed his lips. "A tempting idea . . . no, better not. Your orders, at least, were clear. Your Dendarii will simply have to wait for the next courier. If all is as you *say,*" his emphasis was not lost on Miles, "I'm sure it will all be straightened out."

Miles waited an endless moment, but Galeni offered nothing more. "Yes, sir." He saluted and faced about. Ten days . . . ten more days . . . ten more days at least. They could wait out ten more days. But he hoped HQ would get the oxygen back to its collective brain by then.

The highest-ranking female guest at the afternoon reception was the ambassador from Tau Ceti. She was a slender woman of indeterminate age, fascinating facial bone structure, and penetrating eyes. Miles suspected her conversation would be an education in itself, political, subtle, and scintillating. Alas, as the Barrayaran ambassador had monopolized her, Miles doubted he was going to get a chance to find out.

The dowager Miles had been assigned to squire about held her rank by virtue of her husband, who was the Lord Mayor of London and now being entertained by the ambassador's wife. The mayor's lady seemed able to chatter on interminably, mainly about the clothing worn by the other guests. A passing servant of rather military bearing (all the human servants in the embassy were members of Galeni's department) offered Miles a wine glass full of straw-pale liquid from a gold tray, which Miles accepted with alacrity. Yes, two or three of those, with his low tolerance for alcohol, and he would be numb enough to endure even this. Was this not exactly the constrained social scene he had sweated his way, despite his physical handicaps, into the Imperial Service to escape? Of course, more than three glasses, and he would be stretched out asleep on the inlaid floor with a silly smile on his face, and deep in trouble when he woke up.

Miles took a large sip, and almost choked. *Apple juice.* . . . Damn Galeni, he was thorough. A quick glance around confirmed that this was not the same beverage being served to the guests. Miles ran his thumb around the high collar of his uniform jacket and smiled tightly.

"Something wrong with your wine, Lord Vorkosigan?" the dowager inquired with concern.

"The vintage is a trifle, ah . . . young," Miles murmured. "I may suggest to the ambassador that he keep this one in his cellars a little longer." *Like till I get off this planet.*

The main reception court was a high-arched, skylighted, elegantly appointed chamber that looked as if it should echo cavernously, but was strangely hushed for the large crowd its levels and niches could enclose. Sound absorbers concealed somewhere, Miles thought—and, he bet, if you knew just where to stand, secure cones to baffle eavesdroppers both human and electronic. He noted where the Barrayaran and Tau Cetan ambassadors were standing, for future reference; yes, even their lip movements seemed shadowed and blurred somehow. Certain right-of-passage treaties through Tau Cetan local space were coming up for renegotiation soon.

Miles and his charge drifted toward the architectural center of the room, the fountain and its pool. It was a cool, trickling sort of sculptured thing, with color-coordinated ferns and mosses. Red-gold shapes moved mysteriously in the shadowed waters.

Miles stiffened, then forced his spine to relax. A young man in black Cetagandan dress uniform with the yellow and black face-paint markings of a ghem-lieutenant approached, smiling and watchful. They exchanged wary nods.

"Welcome to Earth, Lord Vorkosigan," murmured the Cetagandan. "Is this an official visit, or are you on a grand tour?"

"A little of both." Miles shrugged. "I've been assigned to the embassy for my, ah, education. But I believe you have the advantage of me, sir." He didn't, of course; both the two Cetagandans who were in uniform and the two who were not, plus three individuals suspected of being their covert jackals, had been pointed out to Miles first thing.

"Ghem-lieutenant Tabor, military attaché, Cetagandan Embassy," Tabor recited politely. They exchanged nods again. "Will you be here long, my lord?"

"I don't expect so. And yourself?"

"I have taken up the art of bonsai for a hobby. The ancient Japanese are said to have worked on a single tree for as long as a hundred years. Or perhaps it only seemed like it."

Miles suspected Tabor of humor, but the lieutenant kept his face so straight it was hard to tell. Perhaps he feared cracking his paint job.

A trill of laughter, mellow like bells, drew their attention toward the far end of the fountain. Ivan Vorpatril was leaning against the chrome railing down there, dark head bent close to a blonde confection. She wore something in salmon pink and silver that seemed to waft even when she was standing still, as now. Artfully artless golden hair cascaded across one white shoulder. Her fingernails flashed silver-pink as she gestured animatedly.

Tabor hissed slightly, bowed exquisitely over the dowager's hand, and passed on. Miles next saw him on the other side of the fountain jockeying for position near Ivan—but somehow Miles felt it was not military secrets Tabor was prowling for. No wonder he'd seemed only marginally interested in Miles. But Tabor's stalk on the blonde was interrupted by a signal from his ambassador, and he perforce followed the dignitaries out.

"Such a nice young man, Lord Vorpatril," Miles's dowager cooed. "We like him very much here. The ambassador's lady tells me you two are related?" She cocked her head at him, brightly expectant.

"Cousins, of a sort," Miles explained. "Ah—who is the young lady with him?"

The dowager smiled proudly. "That's my daughter, Sylveth."

Daughter, of course. The ambassador and his lady had a keen
Barrayaran appreciation of the nuances of social rank. Miles, being
of the senior family line, not to mention the son of Prime Minister Count Vorkosigan, outranked Ivan socially if not militarily.
Which meant, oh God, he was doomed. He'd be stuck with
the VIP dowagers forever while Ivan—Ivan carried off *all* the
daughters. . . .

"A lovely couple," said Miles thickly.

"Aren't they? Just what sort of cousins, Lord Vorkosigan?"

"Uh? Oh, Ivan and me, yes. Our grandmothers were sisters. My
grandmother was Prince Xav Vorbarra's eldest child, Ivan's was his
youngest."

"Princesses? How romantic."

Miles considered describing in detail how his grandmother, her
brother, and most of their children had been blown into hamburger
during Mad Emperor Yuri's reign of terror. No, the mayor's lady
might find it merely a shivery and outré tale, or even worse,
romantic. He doubted she'd grasp the true violent stupidity of
Yuri's affairs, with their consequences escaping in all directions to
warp Barrayaran history to this day.

"Does Lord Vorpatril own a castle?" she inquired archly.

"Ah, no. His mother, my Aunt Vorpatril," *who is a social barra-
cuda who would eat you alive,* "has a very nice flat in the capital
city of Vorbarr Sultana." Miles paused. "We used to have a castle.
But it was burned down at the end of the Time of Isolation."

"A ruined castle. That's almost as good."

"Picturesque as hell," Miles assured her.

Someone had left a small plate with the remains of their hors
d'oeuvres sitting on the railing by the fountain. Miles took the
roll and started breaking off bits for the goldfish. They glided up
to snap at the crumbs with a brief gurgle.

One refused to rise to the bait, lurking in the depths. How interesting, a goldfish that did not eat—now, there was a solution to
Ivan's fish-inventory problem. Perhaps the stubborn one was a
fiendish Cetagandan construct, whose cold scales glittered like gold
because they were.

He might pluck it out with a feline pounce, stamping it underfoot with a mechanical crunch and electric sizzle, then hold it up
with a triumphal cry—"Ah! Through my quick wits and reflexes,
I have discovered the spy among you!"

But if his guess were wrong, ah. The *squish!* under his boot, the
dowager's recoil, and the Barrayaran prime minister's son would

have acquired an instant reputation as a young man with *serious emotional difficulties*. . . . "Ah ha!" he pictured himself cackling to the horrified woman as the fish guts slithered underfoot, "you should see what I do to kittens!"

The big goldfish rose lazily at last, and took a crumb with a splash that marred Miles's polished boots. *Thank you, fish,* Miles thought to it. *You have just saved me from considerable social embarrassment.* Of course, if the Cetagandan artificers were really clever, they might have designed a mechanical fish that really ate, and excreted little . . .

The mayor's lady had just asked another leading question about Ivan, which Miles in his absorption failed to completely catch. "Yes, most unfortunate about his disease," Miles purred, and prepared to launch a monologue maligning Ivan's genes involving inbred aristocracies, radiation areas left from the First Cetagandan War, and Mad Emperor Yuri, when the secured comm link in his pocket beeped.

"Excuse me, ma'am. I'm being paged." *Bless you, Elli,* he thought as he fled the dowager to find a quiet corner to answer it. No Cetagandans in sight. He found an unoccupied niche on the second level made private by green plants, and opened the channel.

"Yes, Commander Quinn?"

"Miles, thank God." Her voice was hurried. "We seem to have us a Situation down there, and you're the closest Dendarii officer."

"What sort of situation?" He didn't care for situations that came capitalized. Elli was not normally inclined to panicky exaggerations. His stomach tightened nervously.

"I haven't been able to get details I can trust, but it appears that four or five of our soldiers on downside leave in London have barricaded themselves in some sort of shop with a hostage, holding off the police. They're armed."

"Our guys, or the police?"

"Both, unfortunately. The police commander I talked to sounded like he was prepared for blood on the walls. Very soon."

"Worse and worse. What the hell do they think they're doing?"

"Damned if I know. I'm in orbit right now, preparing to leave, but it'll be forty-five minutes to an hour before I can get down there. Tung's in worse position, it'd be a two-hour suborbital flight from Brazil. But I think you could be there in about ten minutes. Here, I'll key the address into your comm link."

"How were our guys permitted to take Dendarii weaponry off-ship?"

"A good question, but I'm afraid we'll have to save it for the post-mortem. So to speak," she said grimly. "Can you find the place?"

Miles glanced at the address on his readout. "I think so. I'll meet you there." Somehow . . .

"Right. Quinn out." The channel snapped closed.

CHAPTER THREE

Miles pocketed the comm link and gazed around the main reception court. The reception had peaked. There were perhaps a hundred people present, in a blinding variety of Earth and galactic fashions, and a fair sprinkling of uniforms besides Barrayaran. A few of the earlier arrivals were cutting out already, ushered past security by their Barrayaran escorts. The Cetagandans appeared to be truly gone, along with their friends. His escape must be opportune rather than clever, it appeared.

Ivan was still chatting with his beautiful charge down at the end of the fountain. Miles bore down upon him ruthlessly.

"Ivan. Meet me by the main doors in five minutes."

"What?"

"It's an emergency. I'll explain later."

"What sort of—?" Ivan began, but Miles was already slipping out of the room and making his way toward the back lift tubes. He had to force himself not to run.

When the door to his and Ivan's room slid shut behind him he tore off his boots, peeled out of the dress greens, and catapulted for the closet. He yanked on the black tee-shirt and gray trousers of his Dendarii uniform. Barrayaran boots were descended from a cavalry tradition; Dendarii had evolved from foot-soldiers' gear. In the presence of a horse the Barrayaran were the more practical, although Miles had never been able to explain that to Elli. It would take two hours or so in the saddle on heavy cross-country terrain, and her calves rubbed to bleeding blisters,

101

to convince her that the design had a purpose besides looks. No horses here.

He sealed the Dendarii combat boots and adjusted the gray-and-white jacket in midair, tumbling back down the lift tube at max drop. He paused at the bottom to pull down his jacket, jerk up his chin, and take a deep breath. One could not saunter inconspicuously while gasping. He took an alternate corridor, around the main court to the front entrance. Still no Cetagandans, thank God.

Ivan's eyes widened as he saw Miles approach. He flashed a smile at the blonde, excusing himself, and backed Miles against a potted plant as if to hide him from view. "What the hell—?" he hissed.

"You've got to walk me out of here. Past the guards."

"Oh, no I don't! Galeni will have your hide for a doormat if he sees you in that get-up."

"Ivan, I don't have time to argue and I don't have time to explain, which is precisely why I'm sidestepping Galeni. Quinn wouldn't have called me if she didn't need me. I've got to go *now*."

"You'll be AWOL!"

"Not if I'm not missed. Tell them—tell them I retired to our room due to excruciating pain in my bones."

"Is that osteo-joint thing of yours acting up again? I bet the embassy physician could get that anti-inflammatory med for you—"

"No, no—no more than usual, anyway—but at least it's something real. There's a chance they'll believe it. Come on. Bring her." Miles gestured with his chin toward Sylveth, waiting out of earshot for Ivan with an inquiring look on her flower-petal face.

"What for?"

"Camouflage." Smiling through his teeth, Miles propelled Ivan by his elbow toward the main doors.

"How do you do?" Miles nattered to Sylveth, capturing her hand and tucking it through his arm. "So nice to meet you. Are you enjoying the party? Wonderful town, London. . . ."

He and Sylveth made a lovely couple too, Miles decided. He glanced at the guards from the corner of his eye as they passed. They noticed her. With any luck, he would be a short gray blur in their memories.

Sylveth glanced in bewilderment at Ivan, but by this time they had stepped into the sunlight.

"You don't have a bodyguard," Ivan objected.

"I'll be meeting Quinn in a short time."

"How are you going to get back in the embassy?"

Miles paused. "You'll have until I get back to figure that out."

"Ngh! When's that?"

"I don't know."

The outside guards' attention was drawn to a groundcar hissing up to the embassy entrance. Abandoning Ivan, Miles darted across the street and dove into the entrance to the tubeway system.

Ten minutes and two connections later, he emerged to find himself in a very much older section of town, restored 22nd-century architecture. He didn't have to check for street numbers to spot his destination. The crowd, the barricades, the flashing lights, the police hovercars, fire equipment, ambulance . . . "Damnation," Miles muttered, and started down that side street. He rolled the words back through his mouth, switching gears to Admiral Naismith's flat Betan accent, "Aw, *shit* . . ."

Miles guessed the policeman in charge was the one with the amplifier comm, and not one of the half-dozen in body armor toting plasma rifles. He pushed his way through the crowd and hopped over the barricade. "Are you the officer in charge?"

The constable's head snapped around in bewilderment, then he looked down. At first purely startled, he frowned as he took in Miles's uniform. "Are you one of those psychopaths?" he demanded.

Miles rocked back on his heels, wondering how to answer that one. He suppressed all three of the initial retorts that came to his mind, and chose instead, "I'm Admiral Miles Naismith, commanding, Dendarii Free Mercenary Fleet. What's happened here?" He interrupted himself to slowly and delicately extend one index finger and push skyward the muzzle of a plasma rifle being held on him by an armored woman. "Please, dear, I'm on your side, really." Her eyes flashed mistrustfully at him through her faceplate, but the police commander jerked his head, and she faded back a few paces.

"Attempted robbery," said the constable. "When the clerk tried to foil it, they attacked her."

"Robbery?" said Miles. "Excuse me, but that makes no sense. I thought all transactions were by computer credit transfer here. There's no cash to rob. There must be some misunderstanding."

"Not cash," said the constable. "Stock."

The store, Miles noticed out of the corner of his eye, was a wineshop. A display window was cracked and starred. He suppressed a queasy feeling of unease, and plunged on, keeping his voice light. "In any case, I fail to understand this stand-off with deadly weapons over a case of shoplifting. Aren't you overreacting a trifle? Where are your stunners?"

"They hold the woman hostage," said the constable grimly.

"So? Stun them all, God will recognize his own."

The constable gave Miles a peculiar look. He didn't read his own history, Miles guessed—the source of that quote was just across the water from here, for pity's sake.

"They claim to have arranged some sort of dead-man switch. They claim this whole block will go up in flames." The constable paused. "Is this possible?"

Miles paused too. "Have you got ID's on any of these guys yet?"

"No."

"How are you communicating with them?"

"Through the comconsole. At least, we were—they appear to have destroyed it a few minutes ago."

"We will, of course, pay damages," Miles choked.

"That's not all you'll pay," growled the constable.

"Well . . ." Out of the corner of his eye Miles saw a hovercar labeled EURONEWS NETWORK dropping down to the street. "I think it's time to break this up."

He started toward the wineshop.

"What are you going to do?" asked the constable.

"Arrest them. They face Dendarii charges for taking ordnance off-ship."

"All by yourself? They'll shoot you. They're crazy-drunk."

"I don't think so. If I were going to be shot by my own troops, they've had much better opportunities than this."

The constable frowned, but did not stop him.

The autodoors were not working. Miles stood baffled before the glass a moment, then pounded on it. There was shadowy movement behind the iridescent shimmer. A very long pause, and the doors slid open about a third of a meter; Miles turned sideways and slipped through. A man inside shoved them shut again by hand and jammed a metal brace in their slot.

The interior of the wineshop was a shambles. Miles gasped at the fumes in the air, aromatic vapors from shattered bottles. *You could get plastered just from breathing. . . .* The carpeting squished underfoot.

Miles glanced around, to determine who he wanted to murder first. The one who'd unblocked the door stood out, as he was wearing only underwear.

"'S Admiral Naismith," the doorman hissed. He came to a tilted attention, and saluted.

"Whose army are you in, soldier?" Miles growled at him. The

man's hands made little waving motions, as if to offer explanations by mime. Miles couldn't dredge up his name.

Another Dendarii, in uniform this time, was sitting on the floor with his back to a pillar. Miles squatted down, considering hauling him to his feet, or at least his knees, by his jacket and bracing him. Miles stared into his face. Little red eyes like coals in the caverns of his eye-sockets stared back without recognition. "Eugh," muttered Miles, and rose without further attempt to communicate. That one's consciousness was somewhere in wormhole space.

"Who cares?" came a hoarse voice from the floor behind a display rack, one of the few that hadn't been violently upended. "Who t'hell cares?"

Oh, we've got the best and brightest here today, don't we? Miles thought sourly. An upright person emerged around the end of the display rack, saying, "Can't be, he's disappeared again . . ."

At last, someone Miles knew by name. All too well. Further explanation for the scene was almost redundant. "Ah, Private Danio. Fancy meeting you here."

Danio shambled to a species of attention, towering over Miles. An antique pistol, its grip defaced with notches, dangled menacingly from his ham hand. Miles nodded toward it. "Is that the deadly weapon I was called away from my affairs to come collect? They talked as though you had half our bleeding arsenal down here."

"No, sir!" said Danio. "That would be against regs." He patted the gun fondly. "Jus' my personal property. Because you never know. The crazies are everywhere."

"Are you carrying any other weapons among you?"

"Yalen has his bowie knife."

Miles controlled a twinge of relief as premature. Still, if these morons were on their own, the Dendarii fleet might not have to get officially sucked into their morass after all. "Did you know that carrying any weapon is a criminal offense in this jurisdiction?"

Danio thought this over. "Wimps," he said at last.

"Nevertheless," said Miles firmly, "I'm going to have to collect them and take them back to the flagship." Miles peered around the display rack. The one on the floor—Yalen, presumably—lay clutching an unsheathed hunk of steel suitable for butchering an entire steer, should he encounter one mooing down the metalled streets and skyways of London. Miles thought it through, and pointed. "Bring me that knife, Private Danio."

Danio pried the weapon from his comrade's grip. "Nooo . . ." said the horizontal one.

Miles breathed easier when he had both weapons in his poss-ession. "Now, Danio—quickly, because they're getting nervous out there—exactly what happened here?"

"Well, sir, we were having a party. We'd rented a room." He jerked his head toward the demi-naked doorman who hovered listening. "We ran out of supplies, and came here to buy more, 'cause it was close by. Got everything all picked out and piled up, and then the bitch wouldn't take our credit! Good Dendarii credit!"

"The bitch . . . ?" Miles looked around, stepping over the disarmed Yalen. *Oh, ye gods. . . .* The store clerk, a plump, middle-aged woman, lay on her side on the floor at the other end of the display rack, gagged, trussed up in the naked soldier's twisted jacket and pants by way of makeshift restraints.

Miles pulled the bowie knife out of his belt and headed for her. She made hysterical gurgling noises down in her throat.

"I wouldn't let her loose if I were you," warned the naked soldier. "She makes a lot of noise."

Miles paused and studied the woman. Her graying hair stuck out wildly, except where it was plastered to her forehead and neck by sweat. Her terrorized eyes rolled whitely; she bucked against her bonds.

"Mm." Miles thrust the knife back in his belt temporarily. He caught the naked soldier's name off his uniform at last, and made an unwelcome mental connection. "Xaveria. Yes, I remember you now. You did well at Dagoola." Xaveria stood straighter.

Damn. So much for his nascent plan of throwing the entire lot to the local authorities and praying they were all still incarcerated when the fleet broke orbit. Could Xaveria be detached from his worthless comrades somehow? Alas, it looked as if they were all in this together.

"So she wouldn't take your credit cards. You, Xaveria—what happened next?"

"Er—insults were exchanged, sir."

"And?"

"And tempers kind of got out of hand. Bottles were thrown, and thrown on the floor. The police were called. She was punched out." Xaveria eyed Danio warily.

Miles contemplated the sudden absence of actors from all this action, in Xaveria's syntax. "And?"

"And the police got here. And we told them we'd blow the place up if they tried to come in."

"And do you actually have the means to carry out that threat, Private Xaveria?"

"No, sir. It was pure bluff. I was trying to think—well—what you would do in the situation, sir."

This one is too damned observant. Even when he's potted, Miles thought dryly. He sighed and ran his hands through his hair. "Why wouldn't she take your credit cards? Aren't they the Earth Universals you were issued at the shuttleport? You weren't trying to use the ones left over from Mahata Solaris, were you?"

"No, sir," said Xaveria. He produced his card by way of evidence. It looked all right. Miles turned, to test it in the comconsole at the checkout, only to discover that the comconsole had been shot. The final bullet hole in the holovid plate was precisely centered; it must have been intended as the coup de grace, although the console still emitted little wheezing popping noises now and then. He added the price of it to the running tally in his head and winced.

"Actually," Xaveria cleared his throat, "it was the machine that spat it up, sir."

"It shouldn't have done that," Miles began, "unless—" *Unless there's something wrong with the central account,* his thought finished. The pit of his stomach felt suddenly very cold. "I'll check it out," he promised. "Meanwhile we have to wrap this up and get you out of here without your being fried by the local constables."

Danio nodded excitedly toward the pistol in Miles's hand. "We could blast our way out the back. Make a run for the nearest tubeway."

Miles, momentarily bereft of speech, envisioned plugging Danio with his own pistol. Danio was saved only by Miles's reflection that the recoil might break his arm. He'd smashed his right hand at Dagoola, and the memory of the pain was still fresh.

"No, Danio," Miles said when he could command his voice. "We are going to walk quietly—very quietly—out the front door and surrender."

"But the Dendarii never surrender," said Xaveria.

"This is not a firebase," said Miles patiently. "It is a wineshop. Or at any rate, it was. Furthermore, it is not even our wineshop." *Though I shall no doubt be compelled to buy it.* "Think of the London police not as your enemies, but as your dearest friends. They are, you know. Because," he fixed Xaveria with a cold eye, "until they get done with you, I can't start."

"Ah," said Xaveria, quelled at last. He touched Danio on the arm. "Yeah. Maybe—maybe we better let the Admiral take us home, eh, Danio?"

Xaveria hauled the ex-bowie knife owner to his feet. After a moment's thought, Miles walked quietly behind red-eye, pulled out his pocket stunner, and placed a light blast to the base of his skull. Red-eye toppled sideways. Miles sent up a short prayer that this final stimulus wouldn't send him into trauma-shock. God alone knew what chemical cocktail it chased, except that it clearly wasn't alcohol alone.

"You take his head," Miles directed Danio, "and you, Yalen, take his feet." There, that effectively immobilized all three of them. "Xaveria, open the door, place your hands on top of your head, and walk, do not run, to where you will submit quietly to arrest. Danio, you follow. That's an order."

"Wish we had the rest of the troops," muttered Danio.

"The only troop you need is a troop of legal experts," said Miles. He eyed Xaveria, and sighed. "I'll send you one."

"Thank you, sir," said Xaveria, and lurched gravely forward. Miles brought up the rear, gritting his teeth.

Miles blinked in the sunlight of the street. His little patrol fell into the arms of the waiting police. Danio did not fight when they started to frisk him, though Miles only relaxed when he saw the tangle-field finally turned on. The constable commander approached, inhaling for speech.

A soft *foomp!* broke from the door of the wine-shop. Blue flames licked out over the slidewalk.

Miles cried out, wheeled, and sprinted explosively from his standing start, gulping a huge breath and holding it. He hurtled through the wineshop doors, into darkness shot through with twisting heat, around the display case. The alcohol-soaked carpeting was growing flames, like stands of golden wheat running in a crazy pattern following concentrations of fumes. Fire was advancing on the bound woman on the floor; in a moment, her hair would be a terrible halo. . . .

Miles dove for her, wriggled his shoulder under her, grunted to his feet. He swore he could feel his bones bend. She kicked unhelpfully. Miles staggered for the door, bright like the mouth of a tunnel, like the gate of life. His lungs pulsed, straining for oxygen against his tightly-closed lips. Total elapsed time, eleven seconds.

In the twelfth second, the room behind them brightened, roaring.

Miles and his burden fell to the slidewalk, rolling—he rolled her over and over—flames were lapping over their clothing. People were screaming and yelling at an unintelligible distance. His Dendarii uniform cloth, combat-rated, would neither melt nor burn, but still made a dandy wick for the volatile liquids splashed on it. The effect was bloody spectacular. But the poor clerk's clothing offered no such protection—

He choked on a faceful of foam, sprayed on them by the fireman who had rushed forward. He must have been standing at the ready all this time. The frightened-looking policewoman hovered anxiously clutching her thoroughly redundant plasma-rifle. The fire extinguisher foam was like being rolled in beer suds, only not so tasty—Miles spat vile chemicals and lay a moment gasping. God, air was good. Nobody praised air enough.

"A bomb!" cried the constable commander.

Miles wriggled onto his back, appreciating the blue slice of sky seen through eyes miraculously unglazed, unburst, unslagged. "No," he panted sadly, "brandy. Lots and lots of very expensive brandy. And cheap grain alcohol. Prob'ly set off by a short circuit in the comconsole."

He rolled out of the way as firemen in white protective garments bearing the tools of their trade stampeded forward. A fireman pulled him to his feet, farther away from the now-blazing building. He came up staring at a person pointing a piece of equipment at him resembling, for a disoriented moment, a microwave cannon. The adrenaline rush washed over him without effect; there was no response left in him. The person was babbling at him. Miles blinked dizzily, and the microwave cannon fell into more sensible focus as a holovid camera.

He wished it had been a microwave cannon. . . .

The clerk, released at last, was pointing at him and crying and screaming. For someone he'd just saved from a horrible death, she didn't sound very grateful. The holovid swung her way for a moment, until she was led away by the ambulance personnel. He hoped they'd supply her with a sedative. He pictured her arriving home that night, to husband and children— "And how was the shop today, dear . . . ?" He wondered if she'd accept hush-money, and if so, how much it would be.

Money, oh God . . .

"Miles!" Elli Quinn's voice over his shoulder made him jump. "Do you have everything under control?"

✧   ✧   ✧

They collected stares, on the tubeway ride to the London shuttleport. Miles, catching a glimpse of himself in a mirrored wall while Elli credited their tokens, was not surprised. The sleek, polished Lord Vorkosigan he'd last seen looking back at him before the embassy reception has been transmuted, werewolf-like, into a most degraded little monster. His scorched, damp, bedraggled uniform was flecked with little fluffy bits of drying foam. The white placket down the jacket front was filthy. His face was smudged, his voice a croak, his eyes red and feral from smoke irritation. He reeked of smoke and sweat and drink, especially drink. He'd been rolling in it, after all. People near them in line caught one whiff and started edging away. The constables, thank God, had relieved him of knife and pistol, impounded as evidence. Still he and Elli had their end of the bubble-car all to themselves.

Miles sank into his seat with a groan. "Some bodyguard you are," he said to Elli. "Why didn't you protect me from that interviewer?"

"She wasn't trying to shoot you. Besides, I'd just got there. I couldn't tell her what had been going on."

"But you're far more photogenic. It would have improved the image of the Dendarii Fleet."

"Holovids make me tongue-tied. But you sounded calm enough."

"I was trying to downplay it all. 'Boys will be boys' chuckles Admiral Naismith, while in the background his troops burn down London. . . .'"

Elli grinned. "'Sides, they weren't interested in me. I wasn't the hero who'd dashed into a burning building—by the gods, when you came rolling out all on fire—"

"You saw that?" Miles was vaguely cheered. "Did it look good in the long shots? Maybe it'll make up for Danio and his jolly crew, in the minds of our host city."

"It looked properly terrifying." She shuddered appreciation. "I'm surprised you're not more badly burned."

Miles twitched singed eyebrows, and tucked his blistered left hand unobtrusively under his right arm. "It was nothing. Protective clothing. I'm glad not all our equipment design is faulty."

"I don't know. To tell the truth, I've been shy of fire ever since . . ." Her hand touched her face.

"As well you should be. The whole thing was carried out by my spinal reflexes. When my brain finally caught up with my body, it was all over, and then I had the shakes. I've seen a few fires, in combat. The only thing I could think of was speed, because when fires hit that certain point, they expand *fast*."

Miles bit back confiding his further worries about the security aspects of that damned interview. It was too late now, though his imagination played with the idea of a secret Dendarii raid on Euronews Network to destroy the vid disk. Maybe war would break out, or a shuttle would crash, or the government would fall in a major sex scandal, and the whole wineshop incident would be shelved in the rush of other news events. Besides, the Cetagandans surely already knew Admiral Naismith had been seen on Earth. He would disappear back into Lord Vorkosigan soon enough, perhaps permanently this time.

Miles staggered off the tubeway clutching his back.

"Bones?" said Elli worriedly. "Did you do something to your spine?"

"I'm not sure." He stomped along beside her, rather bent. "Muscle spasms—that poor woman must have been fatter than I thought. Adrenaline'll fool you. . . ."

It was no better by the time their little personnel shuttle docked at the *Triumph*, the Dendarii flagship in orbit. Elli insisted on a detour to sickbay.

"Pulled muscles," said his fleet surgeon unsympathetically after scanning him. "Go lie down for a week."

Miles made false promises and exited clutching a packet of pills in his bandaged hand. He was pretty sure the surgeon's diagnosis was correct, for the pain was easing, now that he was aboard his own flagship. He could feel the tension uncoiling in his neck at least, and hoped it would continue all the way down. He was coming down off his adrenaline-induced high, too—better finish his business here while he could still walk and talk at the same time.

He straightened his jacket, brushing rather futilely at the white flecks, and jerked up his chin, before marching into his fleet finance officer's inner sanctum.

It was evening, ship-time, only an hour skewed from London downside time, but the mercenary accountant was still at her post. Vicky Bone was a precise, middle-aged woman, heavy-set, definitely a tech not a troop, whose normal tone of voice was a calming drawl. Now she spun in her station chair and squealed at him, "Oh, sir! Do you have the credit transfer . . . ?" She took in his appearance and her voice dropped to a more usual timbre. "Good God, what happened to you?" As an afterthought, she saluted.

"That's what I'm here to find out, Lieutenant Bone." He hooked a second seat into its floor brackets and swung it around to sit backwards, his arms draped over its back. As an afterthought, he returned her salute. "I thought you reported yesterday that all our resupply orders not essential for orbital life-support were on hold, and that our Earthside credit was under control."

"Temporarily under control," she replied. "Fourteen days ago you told me we'd have a credit transfer in ten days. I tried to time as many expenses as possible to come in after that. Four days ago you told me it would be another ten days—"

"At least," Miles confirmed glumly.

"I've put off as much stuff as I can again, but some of it had to be paid off, in order to get credit extended another week. We've dipped dangerously far into reserve funds since Mahata Solaris."

Miles rubbed a finger tiredly over the seat back. "Yeah, maybe we should have pushed on straight to Tau Ceti." Too late now. If only he were dealing with Sector II Security Headquarters directly. . .

"We would have had to drop three-fourths of the fleet at Earth anyway, sir."

"And I didn't want to break up the set, I know. We stay here much longer, and none of us will be able to leave—a financial black hole. . . . Look, tap your programs and tell me what happened to the downside personnel credit account about 1600 London time tonight."

"Hm?" Her fingers conjured up arcane and colorful data displays from her holovid console. "Oh, dear. It shouldn't have done that. Now where did the money go . . . ? Ah, direct override. That explains it."

"Explain it to me," Miles prodded.

"Well," she turned to him, "of course when the fleet is on station for long at any place with any kind of financial net at all, we don't just leave our liquid assets sitting around."

"We don't?"

"No, no. Anything that isn't actually outgoing is held for as long as possible in some sort of short-term, interest-generating investment. So all our credit accounts are set to ride along at the legal minimum; when a bill comes due, I cycle it through the computer and shoot just enough to cover it from the invest-ment account into the credit account."

"Is this, er, worth the risk?"

"Risk? It's basic good practice! We made over four thousand GSA federal credits on interest and dividends last week, until we fell out of the minimum amount bracket."

"Oh," said Miles. He had a momentary flash about giving up war and playing the stock market instead. The Dendarii Free Mercenary Holding Company? Alas, the Emperor might have a word or two to say about that.

"But these morons," Lieutenant Bone gestured at the schematic representing her version of Danio's adventures that afternoon, "attempted to tap the account directly through its number, instead of through Fleet Central Accounting as everyone has been told and told to do. And because we're riding so low at the moment, it bounced. Sometimes I think I'm talking to the deaf." More lurid bar graphs fountained up at her fingertips. "But I can only run it round and round for so long, sir! The investment account is now empty, so of course it's generating no extra money. I'm not sure we can even make it six more days. And if the credit transfer doesn't arrive then . . ." she flung up her hands, "the whole Dendarii fleet could start to slide, piecemeal, into receivership!"

"Oh." Miles rubbed his neck. He'd been mistaken; his headache wasn't waning. "Isn't there some way you can shift the stuff around from account to account to create, er . . . virtual money? Temporarily?"

"Virtual money?" Her lips curled in loathing.

"To save the fleet. Just like in combat. Mercenary accounting." He clasped his hands together, between his knees, and smiled up at her hopefully. "Of course, if it's beyond your abilities . . ."

Her nostrils flared. "Of course it's not. But the kind of thing you're talking about relies mostly on time lags. Earth's financial network is totally integrated; there are no time lags unless you want to start working it interstellar. I'll tell you what would work, though . . ." Her voice trailed off. "Well, maybe not."

"What?"

"Go to a major bank and get a short-term loan against, say, some major capital equipment." Her eyes, glancing around by implication through the walls to the *Triumph*, revealed what order of capital equipment she had in mind. "We might have to conceal certain other outstanding liens from them, and the extent of depreciation, not to mention certain ambiguities about what is and is not owned by the Fleet corporation versus the Captain-owners—but at least it would be real money."

And what would Commodore Tung say when he found out that Miles had mortgaged his command ship? But Tung wasn't here. Tung was on leave. It could be all over by the time Tung got back.

"We'd have to ask for two or three times the amount we really needed, to be sure of getting enough," Lieutenant Bone went on. "You would have to sign for it, as senior corporation officer."

Admiral Naismith would have to sign for it, Miles reflected. A man whose legal existence was strictly—virtual, not that an Earth bank could be expected to find that out. The Dendarii fleet propped his identity most convincingly. This could be almost the safest thing he'd ever done. "Go ahead and set it up, Lieutenant Bone. Um . . . use the *Triumph*, it's the biggest thing we've got."

She nodded, her shoulders straightening as she regained some of her accustomed serenity. "Yes, sir. Thank you, sir."

Miles sighed and shoved to his feet. Sitting down had been a mistake; his tired muscles were seizing up. Her nostrils wrinkled as he passed upwind of her. Perhaps he'd better take a few minutes to clean up. It would be hard enough to explain his disappearance, when he returned to the embassy, without explaining his remarkable appearance as well.

"Virtual money," he heard Lieutenant Bone mutter disapprovingly to her comconsole as he exited. "Good God."

CHAPTER FOUR

By the time Miles had showered, groomed, and donned a fresh uniform and glossy spare boots, his pills had cut in and he was feeling no pain at all. When he caught himself whistling as he splashed on after-shave and adjusted a rather flashy and only demi-regulation black silk scarf around his neck, tucked into his gray-and-white jacket, he decided he'd better cut the dosage in half next round. He was feeling much too good.

Too bad the Dendarii uniform did not include a beret one could tilt at a suitably rakish angle, though. He might order one added. Tung would probably approve; Tung had theories about how spiffy uniforms helped recruiting and morale. Miles was not entirely sure this wouldn't just result in acquiring a lot of recruits who wanted to play dress-up. Private Danio might like a beret . . . Miles abandoned the notion.

Elli Quinn was waiting patiently for him in the *Triumph's* number six shuttle hatch corridor. She swung gracefully to her feet and ahead of him into their shuttle, remarking, "We'd better hustle. How long do you think your cousin can cover for you at the embassy?"

"I suspect it's already a lost cause," Miles said, strapping himself in beside her. In light of the warnings on the pain pill packet about operating equipment, he let her take the pilot's seat again. The little shuttle broke smoothly away from the side of the flag-ship and began to drop through its orbital clearance pattern.

Miles meditated morosely on his probable reception when he

showed up back at the embassy. Confined-to-quarters was the least he might expect, though he plead mitigating circumstances for all he was worth. He did not feel at all like hustling back to that doom. Here he was on Earth on a warm summer night, with a glamorous, brilliant woman friend. It was only—he glanced at his chronometer—2300. Night life should just be getting rolling. London, with its huge population, was an around-the-clock town. His heart rose inexplicably.

Yet what might they do? Drinking was out; God knew what would happen if he dropped alcohol on top of his current pharmaceutical load, with his peculiar physiology, except that it could be guaranteed not to improve his coordination. A show? It would immobilize them for a rather long time in one spot, security-wise. Better to do something that kept them moving.

To hell with the Cetagandans. He was damned if he would become hostage to the mere fear of them. Let Admiral Naismith have one last fling, before being hung back in the closet. The lights of the shuttleport flashed beneath them, reached up to pull them in. As they rolled into their rented hardstand (140 GSA federals per diem) with its waiting Dendarii guard, Miles blurted, "Hey, Elli. Let's go—let's go window shopping."

And so it was they found themselves strolling in a fashionable arcade at midnight. Not just Earth's but the galaxy's wares were spread out for the visitor with funds. The passers-by were a parade worth watching in their own right, for the student of fad and fashion. Feathers were in this year, and synthetic silk, leather, and fur, in revival of primitive natural fabrics from the past. And Earth had such a lot of past to revive. The young lady in the—the Aztec-Viking outfit, Miles guessed—leaning on the arm of the young man in faintly 24th-century boots and plumes particularly caught his eye. Perhaps a Dendarii beret wouldn't be too unprofessionally archaic after all.

Elli, Miles observed sadly, was not relaxing and enjoying this. Her attention on the passers-by was more in the nature of a hunt for concealed weapons and sudden movements. But she paused at last in real intrigue before a shop discreetly labeled, CULTURED FURS: A DIVISION OF GALACTECH BIOENGINEERING. Miles eased her inside.

The display area was spacious, a sure tip-off to the price range they were operating in. Red fox coats, white tiger carpets, extinct leopard jackets, gaudy Tau Cetan beaded lizard bags and boots and belts, black and white macaque monkey vests—a holovid display ran a continuous program explaining the stock's origins not in the slaughter of live animals, but in the test tubes and vats of GalacTech's R&D division. Nineteen extinct species were offered in natural colors. Coming up for the fall line, the vid assured them, were rainbow rhino leather and triple-length white fox in designer pastels. Elli buried her hands to the wrists in something that looked like an explosion of apricot Persian cat.

"Does it shed?" Miles inquired bemusedly.

"Not at all," the salesman assured them. "GalacTech cultured furs are guaranteed not to shed, fade, or discolor. They are also soil-resistant."

An enormous width of silky black fur poured through Elli's arms. "What is this? Not a coat."

"Ah, that's a very popular new item," said the salesman. "The very latest in biomechanical feedback systems. Most of the fur items you see here are ordinary tanned leathers—but this is a live fur. This model is suitable for a blanket, spread, or throw rug. Various sorts of outerwear are upcoming from R&D next year."

"A live fur?" Her eyebrows rose enchantingly. The salesman rose on his toes in unconscious echo—Elli's face was having its usual effect on the uninitiated.

"A live fur," the salesman nodded, "but with none of the defects of a live animal. It neither sheds nor eats nor," he coughed discreetly, "requires a litter box."

"Hold on," said Miles. "How can you advertise it as living, then? Where's it getting its energy from, if not the chemical breakdown of food?"

"An electromagnetic net in the cellular level passively gathers energy from the environment. Holovid carrier waves and the like. And every month or so, if it seems to be running down, you can give it a boost by placing it in your microwave for a few minutes on the lowest setting. Cultured Furs cannot be responsible, however, for the results if the owner accidently sets it on high."

"That still doesn't make it alive," Miles objected.

"I assure you," said the salesman, "this blanket was blended from the very finest assortment of *felis domesticus* genes. We also have the white Persian and the chocolate-point Siamese stripe in stock, in the natural colors, and I have samples of decorator colors that can be ordered in any size."

"They did *that* to a cat?" Miles choked as Elli gathered up the whole huge boneless double-armful.

"Pet it," the salesman instructed Elli eagerly.

She did so, and laughed. "It purrs!"

"Yes. It also has programmable thermotaxic orientation—in other words, it snuggles up."

Elli wrapped it around herself completely, black fur cascading over her feet like the train of a queen's robe, and rubbed her cheek into the silky shimmer. "What won't they think of next? Oh, my. You want to rub it all over your skin."

"You do?" muttered Miles dubiously. Then his eyes widened as he pictured Elli, in all her lovely skin, lolling on the hairy thing. "You do?" he said in an entirely changed tone. His lips peeled back in a hungry grin. He turned to the salesman. "We'll take it."

The embarrassment came when he pulled out his credit card, stared at it, and realized he couldn't use it. It was Lieutenant Vorkosigan's, chock full of his embassy pay and utterly compromising to his present cover. Quinn, beside him, glanced over his shoulder at his hesitation. He tilted the card toward her to see, shielded in his palm, and their eyes met.

"Ah . . . no," she agreed. "No, no." She reached for her wallet.

I should have asked the price first, Miles thought to himself as they exited the shop carting the unwieldy bundle in its elegant silver plastic wrappings. The package, the salesman had finally convinced them, did not require air-holes. Well, the fur had delighted Elli, and a chance to delight Elli was not to be lost for mere imprudence— or pride—on his part. He wanted to delight her. He would pay her back later.

But now, where could they go to try it out? He tried to think, as they exited the arcade and made their way to the nearest tubeway access port. He didn't want the night to end. He didn't know what he did want. No, he knew perfectly well what he wanted, he just didn't know if he could have it.

Elli, he suspected, didn't know how far his thought had taken him either. A little romance on the side was one thing; the change of career he was thinking of proposing to her—nice turn of phrase, that—would overturn her existence. Elli the space-born, who called all downsiders dirtsuckers in careless moments, Elli with a career agenda of her own. Elli who walked on land with all the dubious distaste of a mermaid out of water. Elli was an independent country. Elli was an island. And he was an idiot and this couldn't go on unresolved much longer or he would burst.

A view of Earth's famous moon, Miles figured, was what they needed, preferably shining on water. The town's old river, unfortunately, went underground in this sector, absorbed into arterial pipes below the 23rd-century building boom that had domed the half of the landscape not occupied by dizzily soaring spires and preserved historic architecture. Quietude, some fine and private place, was not easy to come by in a city of roiling millions.

The grave's a fine and private place, but none, I think, do there embrace. . . . The deathly flashbacks to Dagoola had faded of late weeks, but this one took him unawares in an ordinary public lift tube descending to the bubble-car system. Elli was falling, torn out of his numb grip by a vicious vortex—design defect in the anti-grav system—swallowed by darkness—

"Miles, ow!" Elli objected. "Let go of my arm! What's the matter?"

"Falling," Miles gasped.

"Of course we're falling, this is the down-tube. Are you all right? Let me see the pupils of your eyes." She grabbed a handgrip and pulled them to the side of the tube, out of the central fast traffic zone. Midnight Londoners continued to flow past them. Hell had been modernized, Miles decided wildly, and this was a river of lost souls gurgling down some cosmic drain, faster and faster.

The pupils of *her* eyes were large and dark. . . .

"Do your eyes get dilated or constricted when you get one of your weird drug reactions?" she demanded in worry, her face centimeters from his.

"What are they doing now?"

"Pulsing."

"I'm all right." Miles swallowed. "The surgeon double-checks anything she puts me on, now. It may make me a little dizzy, she told me that." He had not loosed his grip.

In the lift tube, Miles realized suddenly, their height difference was voided. They hung face to face, his boots dangling above her ankles—he didn't even need to hunt up a box to stand on, nor risk a twist in his neck—impulsively, his lips dove onto hers. There was a split-second wail of terror in his mind, like the moment after he'd plunged from the rocks into thirty meters of clear green water that he knew was icy cold, after he'd surrendered all choice to gravity but before the consequences engulfed him.

The water was warm, warm. . . . Her eyes widened in surprise. He hesitated, losing his precious forward momentum, and began to withdraw. Her lips parted for him, and her arm clamped around the back of his neck. She was an athletic woman; the grip was a non-regulation but effective immobilization. Surely the first time his being pinned to the mat had meant *he'd* won. He devoured her lips ravenously, kissed her cheeks, eyelids, brow, nose, chin—where was the sweet well of her mouth? there, yes. . . .

The bulky package containing the live fur began to drift, bumping down the lift tube. They were jostled by a descending woman who frowned at them, a teenage boy shooting down the center of the tube hooted and made rude, explicit gestures, and the beeper in Elli's pocket went off.

Awkwardly, they recaptured the fur and scrambled off the first exit they came to, fleeing the tube's field through an archway onto a bubble-car platform. They staggered into the open and stared at each other, shaken. In one lunatic moment, Miles realized, he'd upended their carefully-balanced working relationship, and what were they now? Officer and subordinate? Man and woman? Friend and friend, lover and lover? It could be a fatal error.

It could also be fatal without the error; Dagoola had thrust that lesson home. The person inside the uniform was larger than the soldier, the man more complex than his role. Death could take not just him but her tomorrow, and a universe of possibilities, not just a military officer, would be extinguished. He would kiss her again—damn, he could only reach her ivory throat now—

The ivory throat emitted a dismayed growl, and she keyed open the channel on the secure comm link, saying, "What the hell . . . ? It can't be you, you're here. Quinn here!"

"Commander Quinn?" Ivan Vorpatril's voice came small but clear. "Is Miles with you?"

Miles's lips rippled in a snarl of frustration. Ivan's timing was supernatural, as ever.

"Yes, why?" said Quinn to the comm link.

"Well, tell him to get his ass back here. I'm holding a hole in the security net for him, but I can't hold it much longer. Hell, I can't stay awake much longer." A long gasp that Miles interpreted as a yawn wheezed from the comm link.

"My God, I didn't think he could really do it," Miles muttered. He grabbed the comm link. "Ivan? Can you really get me back in without being seen?"

"For about fifteen more minutes. And I had to bend regs all to hell and gone to do it, too. I'm holding down the guard post on the third sub-level, where the municipal power and sewer connections come through. I can loop the vid record and cut out the shot of your entry, but only if you get back here before Corporal Veli does. I don't mind putting my tail on the line for you, but I object to putting my tail on the line for nothing, you copy?"

Elli was studying the colorful holovid display mapping the tubeway system. "You can just make it, I think."

"It won't do any good—"

She grabbed his elbow and marched him toward the bubble cars, the firm gleam of duty crowding out the softer light in her eyes. "We'll have ten more minutes together on the way."

Miles massaged his face, as she went to credit their tokens, trying to rub his escaping rationality back through his skin by force. He looked up to see his own dim reflection staring back at him from the mirrored wall, shadowed by a pillar, face suffused with frustration and terror. He squeezed his eyes shut and looked again, moving in front of the pillar and staring. Most unpleasant—for a second, he had seen himself wearing his green Barrayaran uniform. Damn the pain pills. Was his subconscious trying to tell him something? Well, he didn't suppose he was in real trouble until a brain scan taken of him in his two different uniforms produced two different patterns.

Upon reflection, the idea was suddenly not funny.

He embraced Quinn upon her return with more complicated feelings than sexual desire alone. They stole kisses in the bubble car—more pain than pleasure; by the time they reached their destination Miles was in the most physically uncomfortable state of arousal he could ever recall. Surely all his blood had departed his brains to engorge his loins, rendering him moronic by hypoxia and lust.

She left him on the platform in the embassy district with an anguished whisper of "Later . . . !" It was only after the tubeway had swallowed her that Miles realized she'd left him holding the bag, which was vibrating with a rhythmic purr.

"Nice kitty." Miles hoisted it with a sigh, and began walking—hobbling—home.

He awoke blearily the next morning engulfed in rumbling black fur.

"Friendly thing, isn't it?" remarked Ivan.

Miles fought his way clear, spitting fuzz. The salesman had lied: clearly the near-beast ate people, not radiation. It enveloped them secretly in the night and ingested them like an amoeba—he'd left it on the foot of his bed, dammit. Thousands of little kids, sliding under their blankets to protect them from the monsters in their closets, were in for a shocking surprise. The cultured fur salesman was clearly a Cetagandan agent-provocateur assassin. . . .

Ivan, wearing his underwear and with his toothbrush sticking jauntily out between gleaming incisors, paused to run his hands through the black silk. It rippled, as if trying to arch into the strokes. "'At's amazing," Ivan's unshaven jaw worked, shifting the toothbrush around. "You want to rub it all over your skin."

Miles pictured Ivan, lolling. . . . "Yech." He shuddered. "God. Where'sa coffee?"

"Downstairs. After you're dressed all nice and regulation. Try to at least look as if you'd been in bed since yesterday afternoon."

Miles smelled trouble instantly when Galeni called him, alone, into his office a half hour after their work-shift started.

"Good morning, Lieutenant Vorkosigan." Galeni smiled, falsely affable. Galeni's false smile was as horrendous as his rare real one was charming.

"Morning, sir." Miles nodded warily.

"All over your acute osteo-inflammatory attack, I see."

"Yes, sir."

"Do sit down."

"Thank you, sir." Miles sat, gingerly—no pain pills this morning. After last night's adventure, topped by that unsettling hallucination in the tubeway, Miles had flushed them, and made a mental note to tell his fleet surgeon that there was yet another med she could cross off his list. Galeni's eyebrows drew down in a flash of doubt. Then his eye fell on Miles's bandaged right hand. Miles shifted in his seat, and tried to be casual about tucking it behind the small of his back. Galeni grimaced sourly and keyed up his holovid display.

"I picked up a fascinating item on the local news this morning," said Galeni. "I thought you'd like to see it too."

I think I'd rather drop dead on your carpet, sir. Miles had no doubt about what was coming. Damn, and he'd only worried about the Cetagandan embassy picking it up.

The journalist from Euronews Network began her introduction—clearly, this part had been made a little later, for the wineshop fire was dying down in the background. When the cut with Admiral Naismith's smudged, strained face came on, it was still burning merrily. ". . . unfortunate misunderstanding," Miles heard his own Betan voice coughing. "—I promise a full investigation . . ." The long shot of himself and the unhappy clerk rolling out the front door on fire was only moderately spectacular. Too bad it couldn't have been nighttime, to bring out the full splendor of the pyrotechnics. The frightened fury in the holovid Naismith's face was faintly echoed in Galeni's. Miles felt a certain sympathy. It was no pleasure commanding subordinates who failed to follow orders and sprang dangerous idiocies on you. Galeni was not going to be happy about this.

The news clip ended at last, and Galeni flipped the off-switch. He leaned back in his chair and regarded Miles steadily. "Well?"

This was not, Miles's instincts warned him, the time to get cute. "Sir, Commander Quinn called me away from the embassy yesterday afternoon to handle this situation because I was the closest ranking Dendarii officer. In the event, her fears proved fully justified. My prompt intervention did prevent unnecessary injuries, perhaps deaths. I must apologize for absenting myself without leave. I cannot regret it, however."

"Apologize?" purred Galeni, suppressing fury. "You were out, AWOL, unguarded in direct defiance of standing orders. I missed the pleasure, evidently by seconds, of making my next report to Security HQ a query of where to ship your broiled body. Most interesting of all you managed to, apparently, teleport in and out of the embassy without leaving a ripple in my security records. And you plan to wave it all off with an apology? I think not, Lieutenant."

Miles stood the only ground he had. "I was not without a bodyguard, sir. Commander Quinn was present. I wave off nothing."

"Then you can begin by explaining precisely how you passed out, and back in, through my security net without anyone noticing you." Galeni leaned back in his chair with his arms folded, frowning fiercely.

"I . . ." Here was the fork of the thing. Confession might be good for his soul, but should he rat on Ivan? "I left in a group of guests departing the reception through the main public entrance. Since I was wearing my Dendarii uniform, the guards assumed I was one of them."

"And your return?"

Miles fell silent. Galeni ought to be put in full possession of the facts, in order to repair his net, but among other things Miles didn't know himself exactly how Ivan had diddled the vid scanners, not to mention the guard corporal. He'd fallen into bed without asking the details.

"You cannot protect Vorpatril, Lieutenant," remarked Galeni. "He's my meat next after you."

"What makes you think Ivan was involved?" Miles's mouth went on, buying time to think. No, he should have thought first.

Galeni looked disgusted. "Get serious, Vorkosigan."

Miles took a breath. "Everything Ivan did, he did at my command. The responsibility is entirely mine. If you'll agree that no charges will fall upon him, I'll ask him to give you a complete report on how he created the temporary hole in the net."

"You will, eh?" Galeni's lips twisted. "Has it occurred to you yet that Lieutenant Vorpatril is *above* you in this chain of command?"

"No, sir," gulped Miles. "It, er . . . slipped my mind."

"His too, it appears."

"Sir. I had originally planned to be gone only a short time, and arranging my return was the least of my worries. As the situation extended itself, it was apparent to me that I should return openly, but when I did get back it was two in the morning and he'd gone to a great deal of trouble—it seemed ungrateful—"

"And besides," Galeni interpolated *sotto voce*, "it looked like it might work. . . ."

Miles suppressed an involuntary grin. "Ivan is an innocent party. Charge me as you wish, sir."

"Thank you, Lieutenant, for your kind permission."

Goaded, Miles snapped, "Dammit, sir, what would you have of me? The Dendarii are as much Barrayaran troops as any who wear the Emperor's uniform, even if they don't know it. They are my assigned charge. I cannot neglect their urgent needs even to play the part of Lieutenant Vorkosigan."

Galeni rocked back in his chair, his eyebrows shooting up. "*Play the part* of Lieutenant Vorkosigan? Who do you think you *are*?"

"I'm . . ." Miles fell silent, seized by a sudden vertigo, like falling down a defective lift tube. For a dizzy moment, he could not even make sense of the question. The silence lengthened.

Galeni folded his hands on his desk with an unsettled frown. His voice went mild. "Lose track, did you?"

"I'm . . ." Miles's hands opened helplessly. "It's my duty, when I'm Admiral Naismith, to be Admiral Naismith as hard as I can. I don't usually have to switch back and forth like this."

Galeni cocked his head. "But Naismith isn't real. You said so yourself."

"Uh . . . right, sir. Naismith isn't real." Miles inhaled. "But his duties are. We must set up some more rational arrangement for me to be able to carry them out."

Galeni did not seem to realize that when Miles had, however inadvertantly, entered his chain of command, it had expanded not by one but by five thousand. Yet if he did awake to the fact, might he start messing with the Dendarii? Miles's teeth closed on the impulse to point out this possibility in any way. A hot flash of—jealousy?—shot through him. Let Galeni continue, please God, to think of the Dendarii as Miles's personal affair.

"Hm." Galeni rubbed his forehead. "Yes, well—in the meantime, when Admiral Naismith's duties call, you come to me first, Lieutenant Vorkosigan." He sighed. "Consider yourself on probation. I would order you confined to quarters, but the ambassador has specifically requested your presence for escort duties this afternoon. But be aware that I could have made serious charges. Disobeying a direct order, for instance."

"I'm . . . keenly aware of that, sir. Uh . . . and Ivan?"

"We'll see about Ivan." Galeni shook his head, apparently contemplating Ivan. Miles couldn't blame him.

"Yes, sir," said Miles, deciding he'd pushed as hard as he dared, for now.

"Dismissed."

Great, thought Miles sardonically, exiting Galeni's office. *First he thought I was insubordinate. Now he just thinks I'm crazy.*

Whoever I am.

The afternoon's political-social event was a reception and dinner in honor of a visit to Earth of the Baba of Lairouba. The Baba, hereditary head-of-state of his planet, was combining political and religious duties. After completing his pilgrimage to Mecca he had come to London for participation in the right-of-passage talks for the Western Orion Arm group of planets. Tau Ceti was the hub of this nexus, and Komarr connected to it through two routes, hence Barrayar's interest.

Miles's duties were the usual. In this case he found himself partnering one of the Baba's four wives. He wasn't sure whether to classify her as a dread dowager or not—her bright brown eyes and smooth chocolate hands were pretty enough, but the rest of her was swathed in yards of creamy silk edged with gold embroidery that suggested a zaftig pulchritude, like a very enticing mattress.

Her wit he could not gauge, as she spoke neither English, French, Russian nor Greek in their Barrayaran dialects or any other, and he spoke neither Lairouban nor Arabic. The box of keyed translator earbugs had unfortunately been mis-delivered to an unknown address on the other side of London, leaving half the diplomats present able only to stare at their counterparts and smile. Miles

and the lady communicated basic needs by mime—salt, ma'am?—
with good will through dinner, and he made her laugh twice. He
wished he knew why.

Even more unfortunately, before the after-dinner speeches could
be cancelled a box of replacement ear-bugs was delivered by a panting caterer's assistant. There followed several speeches in a variety
of tongues for the benefit of the press corps. Things broke up, the
zaftig lady was swept off Miles's hands by two of her co-wives, and
he began to make his way across the room back to the Barrayaran
ambassador's party. Rounding a soaring alabaster pillar holding up
the arched ceiling, he came face to face with the lady journalist from
Euronews Network.

"*Mon Dieu*, it's the little admiral," she said cheerfully. "What are
you doing here?"

Ignoring the anguished scream inside his skull, Miles schooled
his features to an—exquisitely—polite blankness. "I beg your
pardon, ma'am?"

"Admiral Naismith. Or . . ." She took in his uniform, her eyes
lighting with interest. "Is this some mercenary covert operation,
Admiral?"

A beat passed. Miles allowed his eyes to widen, his hand to stray
to his weaponless trouser seam and twitch there. "My God," he
choked in a voice of horror—not hard, that—"Do you mean to
tell me Admiral Naismith has been seen on Earth?"

Her chin lifted, and her lips parted in a little half-smile of
disbelief. "In your mirror, surely."

Were his eyebrows visibly singed? His right hand was still bandaged. *Not a burn, ma'am*, Miles thought wildly. *I cut it shaving. . . .*

Miles came to full attention, snapping his polished boot heels
together, and favored her with a small, formal bow. In a proud,
hard, and thickly Barrayaran-accented voice, he said, "You are
mistaken, ma'am. I am Lord Miles Vorkosigan of Barrayar. Lieutenant in the Imperial Service. Not that I don't aspire to the rank
you name, but it's a trifle premature."

She smiled sweetly. "Are you entirely recovered from your burns,
sir?"

Miles's eyebrows rose—no, he shouldn't have drawn attention to
them—"Naismith's been burned? You have seen him? When? Can
we speak of this? The man you name is of the greatest interest to
Barrayaran Imperial Security."

She looked him up and down. "So I would imagine, since you
are one and the same."

"Come, come over here." And how was he going to get out of this one? He took her by the elbow and steered her toward a private corner. "Of course we are the same. Admiral Naismith of the Dendarii Mercenaries is my—" Illegitimate twin brother? No, that didn't scan. Light didn't just dawn, it came like a nuclear flash at ground zero. "—clone," Miles finished smoothly.

"What?" Her certainty cracked; her attention riveted upon him.

"My clone," Miles repeated in a firmer voice. "He's an extraordinary creation. We think, though we've never been able to confirm it, that he was the result of an intended Cetagandan covert operation that went greatly awry. The Cetagandans are certainly capable of the medical end of it, anyway. The real facts of their military genetic experiments would horrify you." Miles paused. That last was true enough. "Who are you, by the way?"

"Lise Vallerie." She flashed her press cube at him, "Euronews Network."

The very fact she was willing to reintroduce herself confirmed he'd chosen the right tack. "Ah." He drew back from her slightly. "The news services. I didn't realize. Excuse me, ma'am. I should not be talking to you without permission from my superiors." He made to turn away.

"No, wait—ah—-Lord Vorkosigan. Oh—you're not related to *that* Vorkosigan, are you?"

He jerked up his chin and tried to look stern. "My father."

"Oh," she breathed in a tone of enlightenment, "that explains it."

Thought it might, Miles thought smugly. He made a few more little escaping motions. She clamped to him like a limpet. "No, please . . . if you don't tell me, I shall surely investigate it on my own."

"Well . . ." Miles paused. "It's all rather old data, from our point of view. I can tell you a few things, I suppose, since it impinges upon me so personally. But it is not for public dissemination. You must give me your word of that, first."

"A Barrayaran Vor lord's word is his bond, is it not?" she said. "I never reveal my sources."

"Very well." Miles nodded, pretending he was under the impression she'd promised, though her words in fact had said nothing of the sort. He nabbed a pair of chairs, and they settled themselves out of the way of the roboservers clearing the banquet debris. Miles cleared his throat and launched himself.

"The biological construct who calls himself Admiral Naismith is . . . perhaps the most dangerous man in the galaxy. Cunning—resolute—both Cetagandan and Barrayaran Security have attempted, in the past, to assassinate him, without success. He's started to build himself a power-base, with his Dendarii Mercenaries. We still don't know what his long-range plans for this private army are, except that he must have some."

Vallerie's finger went to her lips doubtfully. "He seemed—pleasant enough, when I spoke with him. Allowing for the circumstance. A brave man, certainly."

"Aye, there's the genius and the wonder of the man," cried Miles, then decided he'd better tone it down a bit. "Charisma. Surely the Cetagandans, if it was the Cetagandans, must have intended something extraordinary for him. He's a military genius, you know."

"Wait a moment," she said. "He is a true clone, you say—not just an exterior copy? Then he must be even younger than yourself."

"Yes. His growth, his education, were artificially accelerated, apparently to the limits of the process. But where have you seen him?"

"Here in London," she answered, started to say more, and then stopped. "But you say Barrayar is trying to kill him?" She drew away from him slightly. "I think perhaps I'd better let you trace him yourselves."

"Oh, not anymore." Miles laughed shortly. "Now we just keep track of him. He'd dropped out of sight recently, you see, which makes my own security extremely nervous. Clearly, he must have been originally created for some sort of substitution plot aimed ultimately against my father. But seven years ago he went renegade, broke away from his captors-creators, and started working for himself. We—Barrayar—know too much about him now, and he and I have diverged too much, for him to attempt to replace me at this late date."

She eyed him. "He could. He really could."

"Almost." Miles smiled grimly. "But if you could ever get us in the same room, you'd see I was almost two centimeters taller than he is. Late growth, on my part. Hormone treatments . . ." His invention must give out soon—he babbled on. . . .

"The Cetagandans, however, are still trying to kill him. So far, that's the best proof we have that he's actually their creation. Clearly, he must know too much about something. We'd dearly love to know what." He favored her with an inviting canine smile, horribly false. She drew back slightly more.

Miles let his fists close angrily. "The most offensive thing about the man is his nerve. He might at least have picked another name for himself, but he flaunts mine. Perhaps he became used to it when he was training to be me, as he must have done once. He speaks with a Betan accent, and takes my mother's Betan maiden name for his surname, Betan-style, and do you know why?"

Yeah, why, why . . . ?

She shook her head mutely, staring at him in repelled fascination.

"Because by Betan law regarding clones, he would actually be my legal brother, that's why! He attempts to gain a false legitimacy for himself. I'm not sure why. It may be a key to his weakness. He must have a weakness, somewhere, some chink in his armor—" Besides hereditary insanity, of course— He broke off, panting slightly. Let her think it was from suppressed rage, and not suppressed terror.

The ambassador, thank God, was motioning at him from across the room, his party assembling to depart. "Pardon me, ma'am." Miles rose. "I must leave you. But, ah . . . if you encounter the false Naismith again, I should consider it a great service if you would get in touch with me at the Barrayaran embassy."

Pour quoi? her lips moved slightly. Rather warily, she rose too. Miles bowed over her hand, executed a neat about-face, and fled.

He had to restrain himself from skipping down the steps to the Palais de London in the ambassador's wake. Genius. He was a frigging genius. Why hadn't he thought of this cover story years ago? Imperial Security Chief Illyan was going to love it. Even Galeni might be slightly cheered.

CHAPTER FIVE

Miles camped in the corridor outside Captain Galeni's office the day the courier returned for the second time from Sector HQ. Exercising great restraint, Miles did not trample the man in the doorway as he exited, but he let him clear the frame before plunging within.

Miles came to parade rest before Galeni's desk. "Sir?"

"Yes, yes, Lieutenant, I know," said Galeni irritably, waving him to wait. Silence fell while screen after screen of data scrolled above Galeni's vid plate. At the end Galeni sat back, creases deepening between his eyes.

"Sir?" Miles reiterated urgently.

Galeni, still frowning, rose and motioned Miles to his station. "See for yourself."

Miles ran it through twice. "Sir—there's nothing *here*."

"So I noticed."

Miles spun to face him. "No credit chit—no orders—no explanation—no nothing. No reference to my affairs at all. We've waited here twenty bleeding days for nothing. We could have walked to Tau Ceti and back in that time. This is insane. This is *impossible*."

Galeni leaned thoughtfully on his desk on one splayed hand, staring at the silent vid plate. "Impossible? No. I've seen orders lost before. Bureaucratic screw-ups. Important data misaddressed. Urgent requests filed away while waiting for someone to return from leave. That sort of thing happens."

"It doesn't happen to me," hissed Miles through his teeth.

One of Galeni's eyebrows rose. "You are an arrogant little vorling." He straightened. "But I suspect you speak the truth. That sort of thing wouldn't happen to you. Anybody else, yes. Not you. Of course," he almost smiled, "there's a first time for everything."

"This is the second time," Miles pointed out. He glowered suspiciously at Galeni, wild accusations boiling behind his lips. Was this some bourgeois Komarran's idea of a practical joke? If the orders and credit chit weren't there, they had to have been intercepted. Unless the queries hadn't been sent at all. He had only Galeni's word that they had. But it was inconceivable that Galeni would risk his career merely to inconvenience an irritating subordinate. Not that a Barrayaran captain's pay was much loss, as Miles well knew.

Not like eighteen million marks.

Miles's eyes widened, and his teeth closed behind set lips. A poor man, a man whose family had lost all its great wealth in, say, the Conquest of Komarr, could conceivably find eighteen million marks tempting indeed. Worth risking—much for. It wasn't the way he would have read Galeni, but what, after all, did Miles really know about the man? Galeni hadn't spoken one word about his personal history in twenty days' acquaintance.

"What are you going to do now, sir?" Miles jerked out stiffly.

Galeni spread his hands. "Send again."

"Send again. That's all?"

"I can't pull your eighteen million marks out of my pocket, Lieutenant."

Oh, no? We'll just see about that. . . . He had to get out of here, out of the embassy and back to the Dendarii. The Dendarii, where he had left his own fully professional information-gathering experts gathering dust, while he'd wasted twenty days in immobilized paralysis. . . . If Galeni had indeed diddled him to that extent, Miles swore silently, there wasn't going to be a hole deep enough for him to hide in with his eighteen million stolen marks.

Galeni straightened and cocked his head, eyes narrowed and absent. "It's a mystery to me." He added lowly, almost to himself, " . . . and I don't like mysteries."

Nervy . . . cool . . . Miles was struck with admiration for an acting ability almost equal to his own. Yet if Galeni had embezzled his money, why was he not long gone? What was he waiting around for? Some signal Miles didn't know about? But he would find out, oh, yes he would. "Ten more days," said Miles. "Again."

"Sorry, Lieutenant," said Galeni, still abstracted.

You will be. . . . "Sir, I must have a day with the Dendarii. Admiral Naismith's duties are piling up. For one thing, thanks to this delay we're now absolutely forced to raise a temporary loan from commercial sources to stay current with our expenses. I have to arrange it."

"I regard your personal security with the Dendarii as totally insufficient, Vorkosigan."

"So add some from the embassy if you feel you have to. The clone story surely took some of the pressure off."

"The clone story was idiotic," snapped Galeni, coming out of himself.

"It was brilliant," said Miles, offended at this criticism of his creation. "It completely compartmentalizes Naismith and Vorkosigan at last. It disposes of the most dangerous ongoing weakness of the whole scam, my . . . unique and memorable appearance. Undercover operatives shouldn't be memorable."

"What makes you think that vid reporter will ever share her discoveries with the Cetagandans anyway?"

"We were seen together. By millions on the holovid, for God's sake. Oh, they'll be around to ask her questions, all right, one way or another." A slight twinge of fear—but surely the Cetagandans would send somebody to pump the woman subtly. Not just snatch, drain, and dispose of her, not a publicly prominent Earth citizen right here on Earth.

"In that case, why the hell did you pick the Cetagandans as Admiral Naismith's putative creators? The one thing they'll know for sure is that they didn't do it."

"Verisimilitude," explained Miles. "If even *we* don't know where the clone really came from, they might not be so surprised that they hadn't heard of him till now either."

"Your logic has a few glaring weaknesses," sneered Galeni. "It may help your long-term scam, possibly. But it doesn't help me. Having Admiral Naismith's corpse on my hands would be just as embarrassing as having Lord Vorkosigan's. Schizoid or no, not even you can compartmentalize yourself to that extent."

"I am not schizoid," Miles bit off. "A little manic-depressive, maybe," he admitted in afterthought.

Galeni's lips twitched. "Know thyself."

"We try, sir."

Galeni paused, then chose perhaps wisely to ignore that one. He snorted and went on. "Very well, Lieutenant Vorkosigan. I'll assign Sergeant Barth to supply you with a security perimeter. But I want you to report in no less than every eight hours by secured comm link. You may have twenty-four hours' leave."

Miles, drawing breath to marshall his next argument, was bereft of speech. "Oh," he managed. "Thank you, sir." And why the hell did Galeni just flip-flop like that? Miles would give blood and bone to know what was going on behind that deadpan Roman profile right now.

Miles withdrew in good order before Galeni could change his mind again.

The Dendarii had chosen the most distant hardstand of those available for rent at the London shuttleport for security, not economy. The fact that the distance also made it the cheapest was merely an added and delightful bonus. The hardstand was actually in the open, at the far end of the field, surrounded by lots of empty, naked tarmac. Nothing could sneak up on it without being seen. And if any—untoward activity—did happen to take place around it, Miles reflected, it was therefore less likely to fatally involve innocent civilian bystanders. The choice had been a logical one.

It was also a damned long walk. Miles tried to step out briskly, and not scurry like a spider across a kitchen floor. Was he getting a trifle paranoid, as well as schizoid and manic-depressive? Sergeant Barth, marching along beside him uncomfortably in civvies, had wanted to deliver him to the shuttle's hatch in the embassy's armored groundcar. With difficulty Miles had persuaded him that seven years of painfully careful subterfuge would go up in smoke if Admiral Naismith was ever seen getting out of a Barrayaran official vehicle. The good view from the shuttle hardstand was something that cut two ways, alas. Still, nothing could sneak up on them.

Unless it was psychologically disguised, of course. Take that big shuttleport maintenance float truck over there, for instance, speeding along busily, hugging the ground. They were all over the place; the eye quickly became used to their irregular passing. If he were going to launch an attack, Miles decided, one of those would definitely be the vehicle of choice. It was wonderfully doubtful. Until it fired first, no defending Dendarii could be sure he or she wasn't about to randomly murder some hapless stray shuttleport employee. Criminally embarrassing, that, the sort of mistake that wrecked careers.

The float truck shifted its route. Barth twitched and Miles

stiffened. It looked awfully like an interception course. But dammit, no windows or doors were opening, no armed men were leaning out to take aim with so much as a slingshot. Miles and Barth both drew their legal stunners anyway. Miles tried to separate himself from Barth as Barth tried to step in front of him, another precious moment's confusion.

And then the now-hurtling float truck was upon them, rising into the air, blotting out the bright morning sky. Its smooth sealed surface offered no target a stunner would matter to. The method of his assassination was at last clear to Miles. It was to be death by squashing.

Miles squeaked and spun and scrambled, trying to get up a sprint. The float truck fell like a monstrous brick as its anti-grav was abruptly switched off. It seemed like overkill, somehow; didn't they know *his* bones could be shattered by an overloaded grocery pallet? There'd be nothing left of him but a revolting wet smear on the tarmac.

He dove, rolled—only the blast of displaced air as the truck boomed to the pavement saved him. He opened his eyes to find the skirt of the truck centimeters in front of his nose, and recoiled onto his feet as the maintenance vehicle rose again. Where was Barth? The useless stunner was still clutched convulsively in Miles's right hand, his knuckles scraped and bleeding.

Ladder handholds were recessed into a channel on the truck's gleaming side. If he were *on* it he couldn't be *under* it— Miles shook the stunner from his grip and sprang, almost too late, to cling to the hand-holds. The truck lurched sideways and flopped again, obliterating the spot where he'd just been lying. It rose and fell again with an angry crash. Like an hysterical giant trying to smash a spider with a slipper. The impact knocked Miles from his precarious perch, and he hit the pavement rolling, trying to save his bones. There was no crack in the floor here to scuttle into and hide.

A line of light widened under the truck as it rose again. Miles looked for a reddened lump on the tarmac, saw none. Barth? No, over there, crouched at a distance screaming into his wrist comm. Miles shot to his feet, zigged, zagged. His heart was pounding so hard it seemed his blood was about to burst from his ears on adrenaline overload, his breathing half-stopped despite his straining lungs. Sky and tarmac spun around him, he'd lost the shuttle— no, there—he started to sprint toward it. Running had never been his best sport. They'd been right, the people who'd wanted to disbar him from officer's training on the basis of his physicals. With a deep vile whine the maintenance truck clawed its way into the air behind him.

The violent white blast blew him forward onto his face, skidding over the tarmac. Shards of metal, glass, and boiling plastic spewed across him. Something glanced numbingly across the back of his skull. He clapped his arms over his head and tried to melt a hole down into the pavement by heat of fear alone. His ears hammered but he could only hear a kind of roaring white noise.

A millisecond more, and he realized he was a stopped target. He jerked onto his side, glaring up and around for the falling truck. There was no more falling truck.

A shiny black aircar, however, was dropping swiftly and illegally through shuttleport traffic control space, no doubt lighting up boards and setting off alarms on the Londoners' control computers. Well, it was a lost cause now to try to be inconspicuous. Miles had it pegged as Barrayaran outer-perimeter backup even before he glimpsed the green uniforms within, by virtue of the fact that Barth was running toward it eagerly. No guarantee that the three Dendarii sprinting toward them from his personnel shuffle had drawn the same conclusions, though. Miles sprang to his—hands and knees. The abrupt if aborted movement rendered him dizzy and sick. On the second attempt he made it to his feet.

Barth was trying to drag him by the elbow toward the settling aircar. "Back to the embassy, sir!" he urged.

A cursing gray-uniformed Dendarii skidded to a halt a few meters away and aimed his plasma arc at Barth. "Back off, you!" the Dendarii snarled.

Miles stepped hastily between the two as Barth's hand went to his jacket. "Friends, friends!" he cried, flipping his hands palm-out toward both combatants. The Dendarii paused, doubtful and suspicious, and Barth clenched his fists at his sides with an effort.

Elli Quinn cantered up, swinging a rocket-launcher one-handed, its stock nestled in her armpit, smoke still trickling from its five-centimeters-wide muzzle. She must have fired from the hip. Her face was flushed and terrorized.

Sergeant Barth eyed the rocket-launcher with suppressed fury. "That was a little close, don't you think?" he snapped at Elli. "You damn near blew him up with your target." Jealous, Miles realized, because *he* hadn't had a rocket launcher.

Elli's eyes widened in outrage. "It was better than nothing. Which was what you came equipped with, apparently!"

Miles raised his right hand—his left shoulder spasmed when he tried to raise the other arm—and dabbed gingerly at the back of his head. His hand came away red and wet. Scalp wound, bleeding like a stuck pig but not dangerous. Another clean uniform shot.

"It's awkward to carry major ordnance on the tubeway, Elli," Miles intervened mildly, "nor could we have gotten it through shuttleport security." He paused and eyed the smoking remnant of the float truck. "Even they couldn't get weapons through shuttleport security, it seems. Whoever they were." He nodded significantly toward the second Dendarii who, taking the hint, went off to investigate.

"Come away, sir!" Barth urged anew. "You're injured. The police will be here. You shouldn't be mixed up in this."

Lieutenant Lord Vorkosigan shouldn't be mixed up in this, he meant, and he was absolutely right. "God, yes, Sergeant. Go. Take a circuitous route back to the embassy. Don't let anyone trace you."

"But sir—"

"My own security—which has just demonstrated its effectiveness, I think—will take over now. Go."

"Captain Galeni will have my head on a platter if—"

"Sergeant, Simon Illyan himself will have my head on a platter if my cover is blown. That's an order. Go!"

The dreaded Chief of Imperial Security was a name to conjure with. Torn and distressed, Barth allowed Miles to chivvy him toward the aircar. Miles breathed a sigh of relief as it streaked away. Galeni really would lock him in the basement forever if he went back now.

The Dendarii guard was returning, grim and a little green, from the scattered remains of the float truck. "Two men, sir," he reported. "At least, I think they were male, and there were at least two, judging from the number of, um, parts remaining."

Miles looked at Elli and sighed. "Nothing left to question, eh?"

She shrugged an insincere apology. "Oh—you're bleeding . . ." She closed on him fussily.

Damn. If there had been something left to question, Miles would have been in favor of shoveling it onto the shuttle and taking off, clearance or no clearance, to continue his investigation in the *Triumph's* sickbay unimpeded by the legal constraints that would doubtless delay the local authorities. The London constables could scarcely be more unhappy with him anyway. From the looks of things he'd be dealing with them again shortly. Fire equipment and shuttleport vehicles were converging on them even now.

Still, the London police employed some 60,000 individuals, an army much larger, if less heavily equipped, than his own. Maybe he could sic them on the Cetagandans, or whoever was behind this.

"Who were those guys?" asked the Dendarii guard, glancing in the direction the black aircar had gone.

"Never mind," said Miles. "They weren't here, you never saw 'em."

"Yes, sir."

He loved the Dendarii. They didn't *argue* with him. He submitted to Elli's first aid, and began mentally marshaling his story for the police. The police and he were doubtless going to be quite tired of each other before his visit to Earth was over.

Before the forensic lab team had even arrived on the tarmac, Miles turned to find Lise Vallerie at his elbow. He should have expected her. Since Lord Vorkosigan had exerted himself to repel her, Admiral Naismith now marshaled his charm, struggling to remember just which of his personas had told her what.

"Admiral Naismith. Trouble certainly seems to follow you!" she began.

"This did," he said affably, smiling up at her with what fragmented calm he could muster under the circumstances. The holovid man was off recording elsewhere on-site—she must be trying to set up something more than an off-the-cuff spot interview.

"Who were those men?"

"A very good question, now in the lap of the London police. My personal theory is that they were Cetagandan, seeking revenge for certain Dendarii operations, ah, not against them, but in support of one of their victims. But you had better not quote that. No proof. You could be sued for defamation or something."

"Not if it's a quote. You don't think they were Barrayarans?"

"Barrayarans! What do you know of Barrayar?" He let startlement segue into bemusement.

"I've been looking into your past." She smiled.

"By asking the Barrayarans? I trust you don't believe everything they say of me."

"I didn't. *They* think you were created by the Cetagandans. I've been looking for independent corroboration, from my own private sources. I found an immigrant who used to work in a cloning laboratory. His memory was somewhat lacking in detail, unfortunately. He had been forcibly debriefed at the time he was fired. What he could remember was appalling. The Dendarii Free Mercenary Fleet is officially registered out of Jackson's Whole, is it not?"

"A legal convenience only. We're not connected in any other way, if that's what you're asking. You've been doing some homework, eh?" Miles craned his neck. Over by a police groundcar, Elli Quinn was gesticulating vividly to an earnest constable captain.

"Of course," said Vallerie. "I'd like, with your cooperation, to do an in-depth feature on you. I think it would be extremely interesting to our viewers."

"Ah . . . The Dendarii do not seek publicity. Quite the reverse. It could endanger our operations and operatives."

"You personally, then. Nothing current. How you came to this. Who had you cloned, and why—I already know from whom. Your early memories. I understand you underwent accelerated growth and hypnotic training. What was it like? And so on."

"It was unpleasant," he said shortly. Her offered feature was a tempting notion indeed, apart from the fact that after Galeni had him skinned, Illyan would have him stuffed and mounted. And he rather liked Vallerie. It was all very well to float a few useful fictions into the air through her, but too close an association with him just now—he glanced across the tarmac at the police lab team now arrived and poking about the remains of the float truck—could be bad for her health. "I have a better idea. Why don't you do an expose on the civilian illegal cloning business?"

"It's been done."

"Yet the practices still go on. Apparently not enough has been done."

She looked less than thrilled. "If you would work closely with me, Admiral Naismith, you would have some input into the feature. If you don't—well, you are news. Fair game."

He shook his head reluctantly. "Sorry. You're on your own." The scene by the police groundcar compelled his attention. "Excuse me," he said distractedly. She shrugged and went to catch up with her vid-man as Miles jogged off.

They were taking Elli away.

"Don't worry, Miles, I've been arrested before," she tried to reassure him. "It's no big deal."

"Commander Quinn is my personal bodyguard," Miles protested to the police captain, "and she was on duty. Manifestly. She still is. I need her!"

"Sh, Miles, calm down," Elli whispered to him, "or they could end up taking you too."

"Me! I'm the bloody victim! It's those two goons who tried to flatten me who should be under arrest."

"Well, they're taking them away too, as soon as the forensics guys get the bags filled. You can't expect the authorities to just take our word for it all. They'll check out the facts, they'll corroborate our story, then they'll release me." She twinkled a smile at the captain, who melted visibly. "Policemen are human too."

"Didn't your mother ever tell you never to get in a car with strangers?" Miles muttered. But she was right. If he kicked up much more fuss it might occur to the constables to order his shuttle grounded, or worse. He wondered if the Dendarii would ever get back the rocket-launcher, now impounded as the murder weapon. He wondered if getting his key bodyguard arrested was step one of a deep-laid plot against him. He wondered if his fleet surgeon had any psychoactive drugs to treat galloping paranoia. If she did, he'd probably be allergic to them. He ground his teeth and took a deep, calming breath.

A two-man Dendarii mini-shuttle was rolling up to the hardstand. What was this, now? Miles glanced at his wrist chrono and realized he'd lost almost five hours out of his precious twenty-four fooling around here at the shuttleport. Knowing what time it was, he knew who had arrived, and swore in frustration under his breath. Elli used the new distraction to prod the police captain into motion, sketching Miles a breezy, reassuring salute by way of farewell. The reporter, thank God, had gone off to interview the shuttleport authorities.

Lieutenant Bone, squeaky-clean, polished, and striking in her best velvet dress grays, exited her shuttle and approached the remnant of men left at the foot of the larger shuttle's ramp. "Admiral Naismith, sir? Are you ready for our appointment . . . Oh, *dear.*"

He flashed her a toothy grin from his bruised and dirt-smudged face, conscious of his hair, matted and sticky with drying blood, his blood-soaked collar and spattered jacket and ripped trouser knees. "Would you buy a used pocket dreadnought from this man?" he chirped at her.

"It won't do," she sighed. "The bank we're dealing with is *very* conservative."

"No sense of humor?"

"Not where their money is concerned."

"Right." He bit short further quips; they were too close to nervous-involuntary. He made to run his hands through his hair, winced, and changed the gesture to a gentle probing touch around the temporary plas dressing. "And all my spare uniforms are in orbit—and I'm not anxious to go carting around London without Quinn at my back. Not now, anyway. And I need to see the surgeon about this shoulder, there's something still not right—" throbbing agony, if you wanted to get technical about it—"and there are some new and serious doubts about just where our outstanding credit transfer went."

"Oh?" she said, alert to the essential point.

"Nasty doubts, which I need to check out. All right," he sighed, yielding to the inevitable, "cancel our appointment at the bank for today. Set up another one for tomorrow if you can."

"Yes, sir." She saluted and moved off.

"Ah," he called after her, "you needn't mention why I was unavoidably detained, eh?"

One corner of her mouth tugged upward. "I wouldn't dream of it," she assured him fervently.

Back in close Earth orbit aboard the *Triumph*, a visit to his fleet surgeon revealed a hairline crack in Miles's left scapula, a diagnosis which surprised him not at all. The surgeon treated it with electra-stim and put his left arm in an excessively annoying plastic immobilizer. Miles bitched until the surgeon threatened to put his entire body in a plastic immobilizer. He slunk out of sickbay as soon as she was done treating the gouge on the back of his head, before she got carried away with the obvious medical merit of the idea.

After getting cleaned up, Miles tracked down Captain Elena Bothari-Jesek, one of the triumvirate of Dendarii who knew his real identity, the other being her husband and Miles's fleet engineer, Commodore Baz Jesek. Elena in fact probably knew as much about Miles as he did himself. She was the daughter of his late bodyguard, and they had grown up together. She had become an officer of the Dendarii by Miles's fiat back when he'd created them, or found them lying around, or however one wanted to describe the chaotic beginnings of this whole hideously overextended covert op. Been named an officer, rather; she had become one since then by sweat and guts and fierce study. Her concentration was intense and her fidelity was absolute, and Miles was as proud of her as if he'd invented her himself. His other feelings about her were no one's business.

As he entered the wardroom, Elena sketched him a greeting that was halfway between a wave and a salute, and smiled her somber smile. Miles returned her a nod and slid into a seat at her table. "Hello, Elena. I've got a security mission for you."

Her long, lithe body was folded into her chair, her dark eyes luminous with curiosity. Her short black hair was a smooth cap framing her face: pale skin, features not beautiful yet elegant, sculptured like a hunting wolfhound. Miles regarded his own short square hands, folded on the table, lest he lose his eye in the subtle planes of that face. Still. Always.

"Ah . . ." Miles glanced around the room and caught the eye of a couple of interested techs at a nearby table. "Sorry, fellows, not for you." He jerked his thumb, and they grinned and took the hint and their coffee and clattered out.

"What sort of security mission?" she said, biting into her sandwich.

"This one is to be sealed on both ends, from both the Dendarii point of view and that of the Barrayaran embassy here on Earth. Especially from the embassy. A courier job. I want you to get a ticket on the fastest available commercial transport to Tau Ceti, and take a message from Lieutenant Vorkosigan to the Imperial Security Sector Headquarters at the embassy there. My Barrayaran commanding officer here on Earth doesn't know I'm sending you, and I'd like to keep it that way."

"I'm . . . not anxious to deal with the Barrayaran command structure," she said mildly after a moment. Watching her own hands, she was.

"I know. But since this involves both my identities, it has to be either you, Baz, or Elli Quinn. The London police have Elli under arrest, and I can't very well send your husband; some confused underling on Tau Ceti might try to arrest him."

Elena glanced up from her hands at that. "Why were the desertion charges against Baz never dropped by Barrayar?"

"I tried. I thought I almost had them persuaded. But then Simon Illyan had a spasm of twitchiness and decided leaving the arrest warrant outstanding, if not actually pursued, gave him an extra handle on Baz in case of, er, emergencies. It also gives a little artistic depth to the Dendarii's cover as a truly independent outfit. I thought Illyan was wrong—in fact, I told him so, till he finally ordered me to shut up on the subject. Someday, when I'm giving the orders, I'll see that's changed."

Her eyebrow quirked. "It could be a long wait, at your present rate of promotion—Lieutenant."

"My Dad's sensitive to charges of nepotism. Captain." He picked up the sealed data disk he'd been pushing about one-handed on the table top. "I want you to give this into the hand of the senior military attaché on Tau Ceti, Commodore Destang. Don't send it in via anyone else, because among my other suspicions is the nasty one that there may be a leak in the Barrayaran courier channel between here and there. I think the problem's on this end, but if I'm wrong . . . God, I hope it isn't Destang himself."

"Paranoid?" she inquired solicitously.

"Getting more so by the minute. Having Mad Emperor Yuri in my family tree doesn't help a bit. I'm always wondering if I'm starting to come down with his disease. Can you be paranoid about being paranoid?"

She smiled sweetly. "If anyone can, it's you."

"Hm. Well, this particular paranoia is a classic. I softened the language in the message to Destang—you better read it before you embark. After all, what would you think of a young officer who was convinced his superiors were out to get him?"

She tilted her head, winged eyebrows climbing.

"Quite." Miles nodded. He tapped the disk with one forefinger. "The purpose of your trip is to test a hypothesis—only a hypothesis, mind you—that the reason our eighteen million marks aren't here is that they disappeared en route. Just possibly into dear Captain Galeni's pockets. No corroborative evidence yet, such as Galeni's sudden and permanent disappearance, and it's not the sort of charge a young and ambitious officer had better make by mistake. I've embedded it in four other theories, in the report, but that's the one I'm hot about. You must find out if HQ ever dispatched our money."

"You don't sound hot. You sound unhappy."

"Yes, well, it's certainly the messiest possibility. It has a deal of forceful logic behind it."

"So what's the hook?"

"Galeni's a Komarran."

"Who cares? So much the more likely that you're right, then."

I care. Miles shook his head. What, after all, were Barrayaran internal politics to Elena, who had sworn passionately never to set foot on her hated home world again?

She shrugged and uncoiled to her feet, pocketing the disk.

He did not attempt to capture her hands. He did not make a single move that might embarrass them both. Old friends were harder to come by than new lovers.

Oh, my oldest friend.

Still. Always.

CHAPTER SIX

He ate a sandwich and slurped coffee for dinner in his cabin while he perused Dendarii fleet status reports. Repairs had been completed and approved on the *Triumph's* surviving combat-drop shuttles. And paid for, alas, the money now passed beyond recall. Refit chores were all caught up throughout the fleet, downside leaves used up, spit spat and polish polished off. Boredom was setting in. Boredom and bankruptcy.

The Cetagandans had it all wrong, Miles decided bitterly. It wasn't war that would destroy the Dendarii, it was peace. If their enemies would just stay their hands and wait patiently, the Dendarii, his creation, would collapse all on its own without any outside assistance.

His cabin buzzer blatted, a welcome interruption to the dark and winding chain of his thoughts. He keyed the comm on his desk. "Yes?"

"It's Elli."

His hand leapt eagerly to tap the lock control. "Enter! You're back before I'd expected. I was afraid you'd be stuck down there like Danio. Or worse, with Danio."

He wheeled his chair around, the room seeming suddenly brighter as the door hissed open, though a lumen-meter might not have registered it. Elli waved him a salute and hitched a hip over the edge of his desk. She smiled, but her eyes looked tired.

"Told you," she said. "In fact there was some talk of making me a permanent guest. I was sweet, I was cooperative, I was nearly

143

prim, trying to convince them I wasn't a homicidal menace to society and they really could let me back out on the streets, but I was making no headway till their computers suddenly hit the jackpot. The lab came back with ID's on those two men I . . . killed, at the shuttleport."

Miles understood the little hesitation before her choice of terms. Someone else might have picked a breezier euphemism—*blew away,* or *offed*—distancing himself from the consequences of his action. Not Quinn.

"Interesting, I take it," he said encouragingly. He made his voice calm, drained of any hint of judgment. *Would that the ghosts of your enemies only escorted you to hell. But no, they had to hang about your shoulder interminably, waiting until that service was called for. Maybe the notches Danio gouged in the hilts of his weapons weren't such a tasteless idea after all. Surely it was a greater sin to forget a single dead man in your tally.* "Tell me about them."

"They turned out to be both known to and desired by the Eurolaw Net. They were—how shall I put this—soldiers of the sub-economy. Professional hit men. Locals."

Miles winced. "Good God, what have I ever done to them?"

"I doubt they were after you of their own accord. They were almost certainly hirelings, contracted by a third party or parties unknown, though I imagine we could both give it a good guess."

"Oh, no. The Cetagandan Embassy is sub-contracting my assassination now? I suppose it makes sense. Galeni said they were understaffed. But do you realize—" he rose and began to pace in his agitation, "this means I could be attacked again from any quarter. Anywhere, any time. By totally un-personally-motivated strangers."

"A security nightmare," she agreed.

"I don't suppose the police were able to trace their employer?"

"No such luck. Not yet, anyway. I did direct their attention to the Cetagandans, as candidates for the motive leg of any method-motive-opportunity triangle they may try to put together."

"Good. Can we make anything of the method and opportunity parts ourselves?" Miles wondered aloud. "The end results of their attempt would seem to indicate they were a trifle underprepared for their task."

"From my point of view their method looked like it came awfully damn close to working," she remarked. "It suggests, though, that opportunity might have been their limiting factor. I mean, Admiral Naismith doesn't just go into hiding when you go

downside, tricky as it would be to find one man among nine billion. He literally ceases to exist anywhere, zip! There was evidence
these guys had been hanging around the shuttleport for some days
waiting for you."

"Ugh." His visit to Earth was quite spoiled. Admiral Naismith
was, it appeared, a danger to himself and others. Earth was too
congested. What if his assailants next tried to blow up a whole
tubeway car or restaurant to reach their target? An escort to hell
by the souls of his enemies was one thing, but what if he were
standing beside a class of primary-school children next round?

"Oh, by the way, I did see Private Danio when I was downside,"
Elli added, examining a chipped fingernail. "His case is coming
up for judicial review in a couple of days, and he asked me to
ask you to come."

Miles snarled under his breath. "Oh, sure. A potentially unlimited
number of total strangers are trying to off me, and he wants me
to schedule a public appearance. For target practice, no doubt."

Elli grinned and nibbled her fingernail off evenly. "He wants a
character witness by someone who knows him."

"Character witness! I wish I knew where he hid his scalp collection; I'd bring it just to show the judge. Sociopath therapy was
invented for people like him. No, no. The last person he wants for
a character witness is someone who knows him." Miles sighed,
subsiding. "Send Captain Thorne. Betan, got a lot of cosmopoli-
tan *savoir faire*, should be able to lie well on the witness stand."

"Good choice," Elli applauded. "It's about time you started
delegating some of your work load."

"I delegate all the time," he objected. "I am extremely glad, for
instance, that I delegated my personal security to you."

She flipped up a hand, grimacing, as if to bat away the implied
compliment before it could land. Did his words bite? "I was slow."

"You were fast enough." Miles wheeled and came to face her,
or at any rate her throat. She had folded back her jacket for
comfort, and the arc of her black tee-shirt intersected her collarbone in a kind of abstract, aesthetic sculpture. The scent of her—
no perfume, just woman—rose warm from her skin.

"I think you were right," she said. "Officers shouldn't go shopping
in the company store—"

Dammit, thought Miles, *I only said that back then because I was
in love with Baz Jesek's wife and didn't want to say so—better to
never say so—*

"—it really does distract from duty. I watched you, walking

toward us across the shuttleport, and for a couple of minutes, critical minutes, security was the last thing on my mind."

"What was the first thing on your mind?" Miles asked hopefully, before his better sense could stop him. *Wake up man; you could fumble your whole future in the next thirty seconds.*

Her smile was rather pained. "I was wondering what you'd done with that stupid cat blanket, actually," she said lightly.

"I left it at the embassy. I was going to bring it," and what wouldn't he give to whip it out now, and invite her to sit with him on the edge of his bed? "but I had some other things on my mind. I haven't told you yet about the latest wrinkle in our tangled finances. I suspect—" dammit, business again, intruding into this personal moment, this would-be personal moment. "I'll tell you about that later. Right now I want to talk about us. I have to talk about us."

She moved back from him slightly; Miles amended his words hastily, "and about duty." She stopped retreating. His right hand touched her uniform collar, turned it over, slid over the smooth cool surface of her rank insignia. Nervous as lint-picking. He drew his hand back, clenched it over his breast to control it.

"I . . . have a lot of duties, you see. Sort of a double dose. There's Admiral Naismith's duties, and there's Lieutenant Vorkosigan's duties. And then there's Lord Vorkosigan's duties. A triple dose."

Her eyebrows were arched, her lips pursed, her eyes blandly inquiring; supernal patience, yes, she'd wait for him to make an ass of himself at his own pace. His pace was becoming headlong.

"You're familiar with Admiral Naismith's duties. But they're the least of my troubles, really. Admiral Naismith is subordinate to Lieutenant Vorkosigan, who exists only to serve Barrayaran Imperial Security, to which he has been posted by the wisdom and mercy of his Emperor. Well, his Emperor's advisors, anyway. In short, Dad. You know that story."

She nodded.

"That business about not getting personally involved with anyone on his staff may be true enough for Admiral Naismith . . ."

"I'd wondered, later, whether that . . . incident in the lift tube might have been some kind of test," she said reflectively.

This took a moment to sink in. "Eugh! No!" Miles yelped. "What a repulsively lowdown, mean and scurvy trick that would have been—no. No test. Quite real."

"Ah," she said, but failed to reassure him of her conviction with, say, a heartfelt hug. A heartfelt hug would be very reassuring just now. But she just stood there, regarding him, in a stance uncomfortably like parade rest.

"But you have to remember, Admiral Naismith isn't a real man. He's a construct. I invented him. With some important parts missing, in retrospect."

"Oh, rubbish, Miles." She touched his cheek lightly. "What is this, ectoplasm?"

"Let's get back, all the way back, to Lord Vorkosigan," Miles forged on desperately. He cleared his throat and with an effort dropped his voice back into his Barrayaran accent. "You've barely met Lord Vorkosigan."

She grinned at his change of voice. "I've heard you do his accent. It's charming if, um, rather incongruous."

"I don't do his accent, he does mine. That is—I think—" He stopped, tangled. "Barrayar is bred in my bones."

Her eyebrows lifted, their ironic tilt blunted by her clear good will. "Literally, as I understand it. I shouldn't think you'd thank them, for poisoning you before you'd even managed to get born."

"They weren't after me, they were after my father. My mother—" Considering just where he was attempting to steer this conversation, it might be better to avoid expanding upon the misfired assassination attempts of the last twenty-five years. "Anyway, that kind of thing hardly ever happens any more."

"What was that out there on the shuttleport today, street ballet?"

"It wasn't a Barrayaran assassination."

"You don't know that," she remarked cheerfully.

Miles opened his mouth and hung, stunned by a new and even more horrible paranoia. Captain Galeni was a subtle man, if Miles had read him aright. Captain Galeni could be far ahead down any linked chain of logic of interest to him. Suppose he was indeed guilty of embezzlement. And suppose he had anticipated Miles's suspicions. And suppose he'd spotted a way to keep money and career both, by eliminating his accuser. Galeni, after all, had known just when Miles was to be at the shuttleport. Any local dealer in death that the Cetagandan embassy could hire, the Barrayaran embassy could hire just as readily, just as covertly. "We'll talk about that—later— too," he choked.

"Why not now?"

"BECAUSE I'M—" he stopped, took a deep breath, "trying to say something else," he continued in a small, tightly contained voice.

There was a pause. "Say on," Elli encouraged.

"Um, duties. Well, just as Lieutenant Vorkosigan contains all of

Admiral Naismith's duties, plus others of his own, so Lord Vorkosigan contains all of Lieutenant Vorkosigan, plus duties of his own. Political duties separate from and overarching a lieutenant's military duties. And, um . . . family duties." His palm was damp; he rubbed it unobtrusively on the seam of his trousers. This was even harder than he'd thought it would be. But no harder, surely, than someone who'd had her face blown away once having to face plasma fire again.

"You make yourself sound like a Venn diagram. 'The set of all sets which are members of themselves' or something."

"I feel like it," he admitted. "But I've got to keep track somehow."

"What contains Lord Vorkosigan?" she asked curiously. "When you look in the mirror when you step out of the shower, what looks back? Do you say to yourself, Hi, Lord Vorkosigan?"

I avoid looking in mirrors. . . . "Miles, I guess. Just Miles."

"And what contains Miles?"

His right index finger traced over the back of his immobilized left hand. "This skin."

"And that's the last, outer perimeter?"

"I guess."

"Gods," she muttered. "I've fallen in love with a man who thinks he's an onion."

Miles snickered; he couldn't help it. But—*fallen in love?* His heart lifted in vast encouragement.

"Better than my ancestress who was supposed to have thought herself—" No, better not bring that one up either.

But Elli's curiosity was insatiable; it was why he'd first assigned her to Dendarii Intelligence, after all, where she'd been so spectacularly successful. "What?"

Miles cleared his throat. "The fifth Countess Vorkosigan was said to suffer from the periodic delusion that she was made of glass."

"What finally happened to her?" asked Elli in a tone of fascination.

"One of her irritated relations eventually dropped and broke her."

"The delusion was that intense?"

"It was off a twenty-meter-tall turret. I don't know," he said impatiently. "I'm not responsible for my weird ancestors. Quite the reverse. Exactly the inverse." He swallowed. "You see, one of Lord Vorkosigan's non-military duties is to eventually, sometime, somewhere, come up with a Lady Vorkosigan. The eleventh Countess-Vorkosigan-to-be. It's rather expected from a man from a strictly patrilinear culture, y'see. You do know," his throat seemed to be stuffed with cotton, his accent wavered back and forth, "that these, uh, physical problems of mine," his hand swept vaguely down the length, or lack of it, of his body, "were teratogenic. Not genetic. My children should be normal. A fact which may have saved my life, in view of Barrayar's traditional ruthless attitude toward mutations. I don't think my grandfather was ever totally convinced of it. I've always wished he could have lived to see my children, just to prove it. . . ."

"Miles," Elli interrupted him gently.

"Yes?" he said breathlessly.

"You're babbling. Why are you babbling? I could listen by the hour, but it's worrisome when you get stuck on fast-forward."

"I'm nervous," he confessed. He smiled blindingly at her.

"Delayed reaction, from this afternoon?" She slipped closer to him, comfortingly. "I can understand that."

He eased his right arm around her waist. "No. Yes, well, maybe a little. Would you like to be Countess Vorkosigan?"

She grinned. "Made of glass? Not my style, thanks. Really, though, the title sounds more like something that would go with black leather and chromium studs."

The mental image of Elli so attired was so arresting, it took him a full half minute of silence to trace back to the wrong turn. "Let me rephrase that," he said at last. "Will you marry me?"

The silence this time was much longer.

"I thought you were working up to asking me to go to bed with you," she said finally, "and I was laughing. At your nerves." She wasn't laughing now.

"No," said Miles. "That would have been easy."

"You don't want much, do you? Just to completely rearrange the rest of my life."

"It's good that you understand that part. It's not just a marriage. There's a whole job description that goes with it."

"On Barrayar. Downside."

"Yes. Well, there might be some travel."

She was quiet for too long, then said, "I was born in space. Grew up on a deep-space transfer station. Worked most of my adult life aboard ships. The time I've spent with my feet on real dirt can be measured in months."

"It would be a change," Miles admitted uneasily.

"And what would happen to the future Admiral Quinn, free mercenary?"

"Presumably—hopefully—she would find the work of Lady Vorkosigan equally interesting."

"Let me guess. The work of Lady Vorkosigan would not include ship command."

"The security risks of allowing such a career would appall even me. My mother gave up a ship command—Betan Astronomical Survey—to go to Barrayar."

"Are you telling me you're looking for a girl just like Mom?"

"She has to be smart—she has to be fast—she has to be a determined survivor," Miles explained unhappily. "Anything less would be a slaughter of the innocent. Maybe for her, maybe for our children with her. Bodyguards, as you know, can only do so much."

Her breath blew out in a long, silent whistle, watching him watching her. The slippage between the distress in her eyes and the smile on her lips tore at him. *Didn't want to hurt you— the best I can offer shouldn't be pain to you—is it too much, too little . . . too awful?*

"Oh, love," she breathed sadly, "you aren't thinking."

"I think the world of you."

"And so you want to maroon me for the rest of my life on a, sorry, backwater dirtball that's just barely climbed out of feudalism, that treats women like chattel—or cattle—that would deny me the use of every military skill I've learned in the past twelve years from shuttle docking to interrogation chemistry . . . I'm sorry. I'm not an anthropologist, I'm not a saint, and I'm not crazy."

"You don't have to say no right away," said Miles in a small voice.

"Oh, yes I do," she said. "Before looking at you makes me any weaker in the knees. Or in the head."

And what am I to say to that? If you really loved me, you'd be delighted to immolate your entire personal history on my behalf? Oh, sure. She's not into immolation. This makes her strong, her strength makes me want her, and so we come full circle. "It's Barrayar that's the problem, then."

"Of course. What female human in her right mind would voluntarily move to that planet? With the exception of your mother, apparently."

"She is exceptional. But . . . when she and Barrayar collide, it's Barrayar that changes. I've seen it. You could be a force of change like that."

Elli was shaking her head. "I know my limits."

"No one knows their limits till they've gone beyond them."

She eyed him. "*You* would naturally think so. What's with you and Barrayar, anyway? You let them push you around like . . . I've never understood why you've never just grabbed the Dendarii and taken off. You could make it go, better than Admiral Oser ever did, better than Tung even. You could end up emperor of your own rock by the time you were done."

"With you at my side?" He grinned strangely. "Are you seriously suggesting I embark on a plan of galactic conquest with five thousand guys?"

She chuckled. "At least I wouldn't have to give up fleet command. No, really seriously. If you're so obsessed with being a professional soldier, what do you need Barrayar for? A mercenary fleet sees ten times the action of a planetary one. A dirtball may see war once a generation, if it's lucky—"

"Or unlucky," Miles interpolated.

"A mercenary fleet follows it around."

"That statistical fact has been noted in the Barrayaran high command. It's one of the chief reasons I'm here. I've had more actual combat experience, albeit on a small scale, in the past four years than most other Imperial officers have seen in the last fourteen. Nepotism works in strange ways." He ran a finger along the clean line of her jaw. "I see it now. You are in love with Admiral Naismith."

"Of course."

"Not Lord Vorkosigan."

"I am *annoyed* with Lord Vorkosigan. He sells you short, love."

He let the double entendre pass. So, the gulf that yawned between them was deeper than he'd truly realized. To her, it was Lord Vorkosigan who wasn't real. His fingers entwined around the back of her neck, and he breathed her breath as she asked, "Why do you let Barrayar screw you over?"

"It's the hand I was dealt."

"By whom? I don't get it."

"It's all right. It just happens to be very important to me to win with the hand I was dealt. So be it."

"Your funeral." Her lips were muffled on his mouth.

"Mmm."

She drew back a moment. "Can I still jump your bones? Carefully, of course. You'll not go away mad, for turning you down? Turning Barrayar down, that is. Not you, never you . . ."

I'm getting used to it. Almost numb. "Am I to sulk?" he inquired lightly. "Because I can't have it all, take none, and go off in a huff? I'd hope you'd bounce me down the corridor on my pointed head if I were so dense."

She laughed. It was all right, if he could still make her laugh. If Naismith was all she wanted, she could surely have him. Half a loaf for half a man. They tilted bedward, hungry-mouthed. It was easy, with Quinn; she made it so.

Pillow talk with Quinn turned out to be shop talk. Miles was unsurprised. Along with a sleepy body-rub that turned him to liquid in danger of pouring over the edge of the bed into a puddle on the deck, he absorbed the rest of her complete report on the activities and discoveries of the London police. He in turn brought her up to date on the events of the embassy, and the mission on which he'd dispatched Elena Bothari-Jesek. And all these years he'd thought he needed a conference room for debriefing. Clearly, he'd stumbled into an unsuspected universe of alternative command style. Sybaritic had it all over cybernetic.

"Ten more days," Miles complained smearily into his mattress, "until Elena can possibly return from Tau Ceti. And there's no guarantee she can bring the missing money with her even then. Particularly if it's already been sent once. While the Dendarii fleet hangs idly in orbit. You know what we need?"

"A contract."

"Damn straight. We've taken interim contracts before, in spite of Barrayaran Imperial Security having us on permanent retainer. They even like it; it gives their budget a break. After all, the less taxes they have to squeeze out of the peasantry, the easier security gets on the domestic side. It's a wonder they've never tried to make the Dendarii Mercenaries a revenue-generating project. I'd have sent our contract people out hunting weeks ago if we weren't stuck in Earth orbit till this mess at the embassy gets straightened out."

"Too bad we can't put the fleet to work right here on Earth," said Elli. "Peace seems to have broken out all over the planet, unfortunately." Her hands unknotted the muscles in his calves, fiber by fiber. He wondered if he could persuade her to work on his feet next. He'd done hers a while ago, after all, albeit with higher goals in view. Oh, joy, he wasn't even going to have to persuade her . . . he wriggled his toes in delight. He'd never suspected that his toes were sexy until Elli'd pointed it out. In fact, his satisfaction with his entire pleasure-drenched body was at an all-time high.

"There's a blockage in my thinking," he decided. "I'm looking wrong at something. Let's see. The Dendarii fleet isn't tied to the embassy, though I am. I could send you all off . . ."

Elli whimpered. It was such an unlikely noise, coming from her, that he risked muscle spasm to twist his neck and look over his shoulder at her. "Brainstorming," he apologized.

"Well, don't stop with *that* one."

"And anyway, because of the mess at the embassy, I'm not anxious to strip myself of my private backup. It's—there's something very wrong going on there. Which means that any more sitting around waiting for the embassy to come through is dumber than rocks. Well. One problem at a time. The Dendarii. Money. Odd jobs . . . hey!"

"Hey?"

"What says I've got to contract out the entire fleet at a time? Work. Odd jobs. Interim cash flow. Divide and conquer! Security guards, computer techs, anything and everything anyone can come up with that will generate a little cash income—"

"Bank robberies?" said Elli in a tone of rising interest.

"And you say the police let you out? Don't get carried away. But I'm sitting on a labor pool of five thousand variously and highly trained people. Surely that's a resource of even greater value than the *Triumph*. Delegate! Let *them* spread out and go scare up some bloody cash!"

Elli, sitting cross-legged on the foot of his bed, remarked in aggravation, "I worked for an hour to get you relaxed, and now look! What are you, memory-plastic? Your whole body is coiling back up right before my eyes . . . Where are you going?"

"To put the idea into action, what else?"

"*Most* people go to *sleep* at this point. . . ." Yawning, she helped him sort through the pile of uniform bits on the floor nearby. The black tee-shirts proved nearly interchangable. Elli's was distinguishable by the faint scent of her body lingering in it—Miles almost didn't want to give it back, but reflected that keeping his girlfriend's underwear to sniff probably wouldn't score him points in the savoir-faire department. The agreement was unspoken but plain: this phase of their relationship must stop discreetly at the bedroom door, if they were to disprove Admiral Naismith's fatuous dictum.

The initial Dendarii staff conference, at the start of a mission when Miles arrived on fleet station with a new contract in hand, always gave him the sense of seeing double. He was an interface, conscious of both halves, trying to be a one-way mirror between the Dendarii and their true employer the Emperor. This unpleasant sensation usually faded rapidly, as he concentrated his faculties around the mission in question, re-centering his personality; Admiral Naismith came very near to occupying his whole skin then. "Relaxing" wasn't quite the right term for this alpha-state, given Naismith's driving personality; "unconstrained" came closer.

He had been with the Dendarii an unprecedented five months straight, and the sudden re-intrusion of Lieutenant Vorkosigan into his life had been unusually disruptive this time. Of course, it wasn't normally the *Barrayaran* side of things that was screwed up. He'd always counted on that command structure to be solid, the axiom from which all action flowed, the standard by which subsequent success or failure was measured. Not this time.

This night he stood in the *Triumph's* briefing room before his hastily called department heads and ship captains, and was seized by a sudden, schizoid paralysis: what was he to say to them? *You're on your own, suckers. . . .*

"We're on our own for a while," Admiral Naismith began, emerging from whatever cave in Miles's brain he dwelt in, and he was off and running. The news, made public at last, that there was a glitch in their contract payment inspired the expected dismay; more baffling was their apparently serene reassurance when he told them, his voice heavy with menacing emphasis, that he was personally investigating it. Well, at least it accounted from the Dendarii point of view for all the time he'd spent stuffing the computers in the bowels of the Barrayaran embassy. *God, I swear I could sell them all radioactive farmland.*

But when challenged they unleashed an impressive flurry of ideas for short-term cash creation. Miles was intensely relieved, and left them to it. After all, nobody arrived on the Dendarii general staff by being dense. His own brain seemed drained. He hoped it was because its circuits were subconsciously working on the Barrayaran half of the problem, and not a symptom of premature senile decay.

He slept alone and badly, and woke tired and sore. He attended to some routine internal matters, and approved the seven least harebrained schemes for cash creation evolved by his people during the night. One officer had actually come up with a security guard contract for a squad of twenty, never mind that it was for the grand opening of a shopping mall in—where the hell was Xian?

He arrayed himself carefully in his best—gray velvet dress tunic with the silver buttons on the shoulders, trousers with the blinding white side trim, his shiniest boots—and accompanied Lieutenant Bone downside to the London bank. Elli Quinn backed him with two of his largest uniformed Dendarii and an unseen perimeter, before and behind, of civilian-dressed guards with scanners.

At the bank Admiral Naismith, quite polished and urbane for a man who didn't exist, signed away questionable rights to a warship he did not own to a financial organization who did not need or want it. As Lieutenant Bone pointed out, at least the money was real. Instead of a piecemeal collapse beginning that afternoon—the hour when Lieutenant Bone had calculated the first Dendarii payroll chits would start bouncing—it would be just one great crash at an undefined future date. Hooray.

He peeled off guards, as he approached the Barrayaran Embassy, until only Elli remained. They paused before a door in the underground utility tunnels marked DANGER: TOXIC: AUTHORIZED PERSONNEL ONLY.

"We're under the scanners now," Miles remarked in warning.

Elli touched her finger to her lips, considering. "On the other hand, you may go in there to find orders have arrived to spirit you off to Barrayar, and I won't see you for another year. Or ever."

"I would resist that—" he began, but she touched the finger to his lips now, bottling whatever stupidity he'd been about to utter, transferring the kiss. "Right." He smiled slightly. "I'll be in touch, Commander Quinn."

A straightening of her spine, a small ironic nod, an impressionistic version of a salute, and she was gone. He sighed and palmed open the intimidating door's lock.

On the other side of the second door, past the uniformed guard at the scanner console, Ivan Vorpatril was waiting for him. Shifting from foot to foot with a strained smile. Oh, God, now what? It was doubtless too much to hope that the man merely had to take a leak.

"Glad you're back, Miles," Ivan said. "Right on time."

"I didn't want to abuse the privilege. I might want it again. Not that I'm likely to get it—I was surprised that Galeni didn't just yank me back to the embassy permanently after that little episode at the shuttleport yesterday."

"Yes, well, there's a reason for that," said Ivan.

"Oh?" said Miles, in a voice drained to neutrality.

"Captain Galeni left the embassy about half an hour after you did yesterday. He hasn't been seen since."

CHAPTER SEVEN

The ambassador let them into Galeni's locked office. He concealed his nerves rather better than Ivan, merely remarking quietly, "Let me know what you find, Lieutenant Vorpatril. Some certain indication as to whether or not it's time to notify the local authorities would be particularly desirable." So, the ambassador, who had known Duv Galeni some two years, thought in terms of multiple possibilities too. A complex man, their missing captain.

Ivan sat at the desk console and ran through the routine files, searching for recent memos, while Miles wandered the perimeter of the room looking for—what? A message scrawled in blood on the wall at the level of his kneecap? Alien vegetable fiber on the carpet? A note of assignation on heavily perfumed paper? Any or all would have been preferable to the bland blankness he found.

Ivan threw up his hands. "Nothing here but the usual."

"Move over." Miles wriggled the back of Galeni's swivel chair to evict his big cousin and slid into his place. "I have a burning curiosity as to Captain Galeni's personal finances. This is a golden opportunity to check them out."

"Miles," said Ivan with trepidation, "isn't that a little, um, invasive?"

"You have the instincts of a gentleman, Ivan," said Miles, absorbed in breaking into the coded files. "How did you ever get into Security?"

"I don't know," said Ivan. "I wanted ship duty."

"Don't we all? Ah," said Miles as the holoscreen began to disgorge data. "I love these Earth Universal Credit Cards. So revealing."

"What do you expect to find in Galeni's charge account, for God's sake?"

"Well, first of all," Miles muttered, tapping keys, "let's check the totals for the last few months and find out if his outgo exceeds his income."

It was the work of a moment to answer that one. Miles frowned slight disappointment. The two were in balance; there was even a small end-of-month surplus, readily traceable to a modest personal savings fund. It proved nothing one way or another, alas. If Galeni were in some kind of serious money trouble he had both the wit and the know-how not to leave evidence against himself. Miles began going down the itemized list of purchases.

Ivan shifted impatiently. "Now what are you looking for?"

"Secret vices."

"How?"

"Easy. Or it would be, if . . . compare, for example, the records of Galeni's accounts with yours for the same three-month period." Miles split the screen and called up his cousin's data.

"Why not compare it with yours?" said Ivan, miffed.

Miles smiled in scientific virtue. "I haven't been here long enough for a comparable baseline. You make a much better control. For example—well, well. Look at this. A lace nightgown, Ivan? What a confection. It's totally non-regulation, y'know."

"That's none of your business," said Ivan grumpily.

"Just so. And you don't have a sister, and it's not your mother's style. Inherent in this purchase is either a girl in your life or transvestism."

"You will note it's not my size," said Ivan with dignity.

"Yes, it would look rather abbreviated on you. A sylph-like girl, then. Whom you know well enough to buy intimate presents. See how much I know about you already, from just that one purchase. Was it Sylveth, by chance?"

"It's Galeni you're supposed to be checking," Ivan reminded him.

"Yes. So what kind of presents does Galeni buy?" He scrolled on. It didn't take long; there wasn't that much.

"Wine," Ivan pointed out. "Beer."

Miles ran a cross check. "About one-third the amount you drank in the same period. But he buys book-discs in a ratio of thirty-five to—just two, Ivan?"

Ivan cleared his throat uncomfortably.

Miles sighed. "No girls here. No boys either, I don't think . . . eh? You've been working with him for a year."

"Mm," said Ivan. "I've run across one or two of that sort in the Service, but . . . they have ways of letting you know. Not Galeni, I don't think either."

Miles glanced up at his cousin's even profile. Yes, Ivan probably had collected passes from both sexes, by this time. Scratch off yet another lead. "Is the man a monk?" Miles muttered. "Not an android, judging from the music, books, and beer, but . . . terribly elusive."

He killed the file with an irritated tap on the controls. After a moment of thought he called up Galeni's Service records instead. "Huh. Now that's unusual. Did you know Captain Galeni had a doctorate in history before he ever joined the Imperial Service?"

"What? No, he never mentioned that. . . ." Ivan leaned over Miles's shoulder, gentlemanly instincts overcome by curiosity at last.

"A Ph.D. with honors in Modern History and Political Science from the Imperial University at Vorbarr Sultana. My God, look at the dates. At the age of twenty-six Dr. Duv Galeni gave up a brand-new faculty position at the College of Belgravia on Barrayar, to go back to the Imperial Service Academy with a bunch of eighteen-year-olds. On a cadet's pittance." *Not* the behavior of a man to whom money was an all-consuming object.

"Huh," said Ivan. "He must have been an upperclassman when we entered. He got out just two years ahead of us. And he's a captain already!"

"He must have been one of the first Komarrans permitted to enter the military. Within weeks of the ruling. And he's been on the fast track ever since. Extra training—languages, information analysis, a posting at the Imperial HQ—and then this plum of a post on Earth. Duvie is our darling, clearly." Miles could see why. A brilliant, educated, liberal officer—Galeni was a walking advertisement for the success of the New Order. An Example. Miles knew all about being an Example. He drew in his breath, a long, thoughtful inhalation hissing cold through his front teeth.

"What?" prodded Ivan.

"I'm beginning to get scared."

"Why?"

"Because this whole thing is acquiring a subtle political odor. And anyone who isn't alarmed when things Barrayaran start smelling political hasn't studied . . . history." He uttered the last word with a subsiding, ironic sibilant, hunching in the chair. After a moment he hit the file again, searching on.

"Jack. Pot."

"Eh?"

Miles pointed. "Sealed file. Nobody under the rank of an Imperial Staff officer can access this part."

"That lets us out."

"Not necessarily."

"Miles . . ." Ivan moaned.

"I'm not contemplating anything illegal," Miles reassured him. "Yet. Go get the ambassador."

The ambassador, upon arrival, pulled up a chair next to Miles. "Yes, I do have an emergency access code that will override that one," he admitted when Miles pressed him. "The emergency in mind was something on the order of war breaking out, however."

Miles nibbled the side of his index finger. "Captain Galeni's been with you two years now. What's your impression of him?"

"As an officer, or as a man?"

"Both, sir."

"Very conscientious in his duties. His unusual educational background—"

"Oh, you knew of it?"

"Of course. But it makes him an extraordinarily good pick for Earth. He's very good, very at ease on the social side, a brilliant conversationalist. The officer who preceded him in the post was a Security man of the old school. Competent, but dull. Almost . . . ahem! . . . boorish. Galeni accomplishes the same duties, but more smoothly. Smooth security is invisible security, invisible security does not disturb my diplomatic guests, and so my job becomes that much easier. That goes double for the, er, information-gathering activities. As an officer I'm extremely pleased with him."

"What's his fault as a man?"

" 'Fault' is perhaps too strong a term, Lieutenant Vorkosigan. He's rather . . . cool. In general I find this restful. I do notice that in any given conversation he will come away knowing a great deal more about you than you of him."

"Ha." What a very diplomatic way of putting it. And, Miles reflected, thinking back over his own brushes with the missing officer, dead-on.

The ambassador frowned. "Do you think some clue to his disappearance may be in that file, Lieutenant Vorkosigan?"

Miles shrugged unhappily. "It isn't anywhere else."

"I am reluctant . . ." The ambassador trailed off, eyeing the strongly worded access restrictions on the vid.

"We could wait a little longer," said Ivan. "Suppose he's just found a girlfriend. If you were so worried about that as to make that other suggestion, Miles, you ought to be glad for the man. He isn't going to be too happy, coming back from his first night out in years, to find we've turned his files inside out."

Miles recognized the singsong tone of Ivan playing dumb, playing devil's advocate, the ploy of a sharp but lazy intellect to get others to do its work. *Right, Ivan.*

"When you spend nights out, don't you leave notice where you'll be and when you'll return?" asked Miles.

"Well, yes."

"And don't you return on time?"

"I've been known to oversleep a time or two," Ivan admitted.

"What happens then?"

"They track me down. 'Good morning, Lieutenant Vorpatril, this is your wake-up call.'" Galeni's precise, sardonic accent came through clearly in Ivan's parody. It had to be a direct quote.

"D'you think Galeni's the sort to make one rule for subordinates and another for himself, then?"

"No," said Ivan and the ambassador in unison, and glanced sideways at each other.

Miles took a deep breath, jerked up his chin, and pointed at the holovid. "Open it."

The ambassador pursed his lips and did so.

"I'll be damned," whispered Ivan after a few minutes of scrolling. Miles elbowed into the center place and began speed-reading in earnest. The file was enormous: Galeni's missing family history at last.

David Galen had been the name to which he was born. *Those* Galens, owners of the Galen Orbital Transshipping Warehouse Cartel, strong among the oligarchy of powerful families who had run Komarr, straddling its important wormhole connections like ancient Rhine River robber barons. Its wormholes had made Komarr rich; it was from the power and wealth pouring through them that its jewel-like domed cities sprang, not grubbed up from the planet's dire, barren soil by sweaty labor.

Miles could hear his father's voice, ticking off the points that had made the conquest of Komarr Admiral Vorkosigan's textbook war. *A small population concentrated in climate-controlled cities; no place for guerillas to fall back and regroup. No allies; we had only to let it be known that we were dropping their twenty-five-percent cut of everything that passed through their wormhole nexus to fifteen percent and the neighbors that should have supported them fell into our pockets. They didn't even want to do their own fighting, till the mercenaries they'd hired saw what they were up against and turned tail. . . .*

Of course, the unspoken heart of the matter was the sins of the Komarran fathers a generation earlier, who had accepted the bribe to let the Cetagandan invasion fleet pass through for the quick and easy conquest of poor, newly rediscovered, semi-feudal Barrayar. Which had proved neither quick, nor easy, nor a conquest; twenty years and a river of blood later the last of the Cetagandan warships withdrew back the way they had come, through "neutral" Komarr.

Barrayarans might have been backward, but no one could accuse them of being slow learners. Among Miles's grandfather's generation, who came to power in the harsh school of the Cetagandan occupation, there grew an obsessed determination that such an invasion must never be permitted to happen again. It had fallen on Miles's father's generation to turn the obsession into fact, by taking absolute and final control of Barrayar's Komarran gateway.

The avowed aim of the Barrayaran invasion fleet, its lightning speed and painstaking strategic subtleties, was to take Komarr's wealth-generating economy intact, with minimal damage. Conquest, not revenge, was to be the Emperor's glory. Imperial Fleet Commander Admiral Lord Aral Vorkosigan had made that abundantly and explicitly clear, he'd thought.

The Komarran oligarchy, supple middlemen that they were, were brought into alignment with that aim, their surrender eased in every possible way. Promises were made, guarantees given; subordinate life and reduced property were life and property still, calculatedly leavened with hope for future recovery. Living well was to be the best revenge all round.

Then came the Solstice Massacre.

An overeager subordinate, growled Admiral Lord Vorkosigan. Secret orders, cried the surviving families of the two hundred Komarran Counsellors gunned down in a gymnasium by Barrayaran Security forces. Truth, or at any rate certainty, lay among the victims. Miles himself was not sure any historian could resurrect it. Only Admiral Vorkosigan and the security commander knew for sure, and it was Admiral Vorkosigan's word that was on trial. The security commander lay dead without trial at the admiral's own furious hands. Justly executed, or killed to keep from talking, take your pick according to your prejudices.

In absolute terms Miles was disinclined to get excited about the Solstice Massacre. After all, Cetagandan atomics had taken out the entire city of Vorkosigan Vashnoi, killing not hundreds but thousands, and nobody rioted in the streets about *that.* Yet it was the Solstice Massacre that got the attention, captured an eager public imagination; it was the name of Vorkosigan that acquired the sobriquet "Butcher" with a capital letter, and the word of a Vorkosigan that was besmirched. And that made it all a very personal bit of ancient history indeed.

Thirty years ago. Miles hadn't even been born. David Galen had been four years old on the very day his aunt, Komarran Counsellor Rebecca Galen, had died in the gym at the domed city of Solstice.

The Barrayaran High Command had argued the matter of twenty-six-year-old Duv Galeni's admittance to the Imperial Service back and forth in the frankest personal terms.

" . . . I can't recommend the choice," Imperial Security Chief Illyan wrote in a private memo to Prime Minister Count Aral Vorkosigan. "I suspect you're being quixotic about this one out of guilt. And guilt is a luxury you cannot afford. If you're acquiring a secret desire to be shot in the back, please let me know at least twenty-four hours in advance, so I can activate my retirement. —Simon."

The return memo was handwritten in the crabbed scrawl of a thick-fingered man for whom all pens were too tiny, a handwriting achingly familiar to Miles. " . . . guilt? Perhaps. I had a little tour of that damned gym, soon after, before the thickest blood had quite dried. Pudding-like. Some details burn themselves permanently in the memory. But I happen to remember Rebecca Galen particularly because of the way she'd been shot. She was one of the few who died facing her murderers. I doubt very much if it will ever be my back that's in danger from 'Duv Galeni.'

"The involvement of his father in the later Resistance worries me rather less. It wasn't just for us that the boy altered his name to the Barrayaran form.

"But if we can capture this one's true allegiance, it will be something like what I'd had in mind for Komarr in the first place. A generation late, true, and after a long and bloody detour, but— since you bring up these theological terms—a sort of redemption. Of course he has political ambitions, but I beg to suggest they are both more complex and more constructive than mere assassination.

"Put him back on the list, Simon, and leave him there this time. This issue tires me, and I don't want to be dragged over it again. Let him run, and prove himself—if he can."

The closing signature was the usual hasty scribble.

After that, Cadet Galeni became the concern of officers much lower in the Imperial hierarchy, his record the public and accessible one Miles had viewed earlier.

"The trouble with all this," Miles spoke aloud into the thick, ticking silence that had enveloped the room for the last thirty minutes, "fascinating as it all is, is that it doesn't narrow the possibilities. It multiplies them. Dammit."

Including, Miles reflected, his own pet theory of embezzlement and desertion. There was nothing here that actually disproved it, just rendered it more painful if true. And the shuttleport assassination idea took on new and sinister overtones.

"He might also," Ivan Vorpatril put in, "just be the victim of some perfectly ordinary accident."

The ambassador grunted, and pushed to his feet, shaking his head. "Most ambiguous. They were right to seal it. It could be very prejudicial to the man's career. I think, Lieutenant Vorpatril, I will have you go ahead and file a missing person report now with the local authorities. Seal that back up, Vorkosigan." Ivan followed the ambassador out.

Before he closed the console, Miles traced through the documents pertinent to the tantalizing reference to Galeni's father. After his sister was killed in the Solstice Massacre, the senior Galen had apparently become an active leader in the Komarran underground. What wealth the Barrayaran conquest had left to the once-proud family evaporated entirely at the time of the violent Revolt six years later. Old Barrayaran Security records explicitly traced some of it, transformed into smuggled weapons, payroll, and expenses of the terrorist army; later, bribes for exit visas and transport off-planet for the survivors. No transport off Komarr for Galeni's father, though; he'd been blown up with one of his own bombs during the last, futile, exhausted attack on a Barrayaran Security HQ. Along with Galeni's older brother, incidentally.

Thoughtfully, Miles ran a cross-check. Rather to his relief there were no more stray Galen relations among the Earthbound refugees listed in the embassy's Security files.

Of course, Galeni had had plenty of opportunity to edit those files, in the last two years.

Miles rubbed his aching head. Galeni had been fifteen when the last spasm of the Revolt had petered out. Was stamped out. Too young, Miles hoped, to have been actively involved. And whatever his involvement, Simon Illyan had apparently known of it and been willing to let it pass into history. A closed book. Miles resealed the file.

Miles permitted Ivan to do all the dealing with the local police. True, with the clone story now afloat he was in part protected from the chance of meeting the same people in both his personas, but there was no point in pushing it. The police could be expected to be more alert and suspicious than most others, and he hadn't counted on being a two-headed crime wave.

At least the police seemed to take the military attaché's disappearance with proper seriousness, promising cooperation even to the extent of honoring the ambassador's request that the matter not be given to the news media. The police, manned and equipped for such things, could take over the routine legwork such as checking the identities of any unexplained human body parts found in trash receptacles, etc. Miles appointed himself official detective for all matters inside the embassy walls. Ivan, as senior man now, suddenly found all of Galeni's normal routine dumped in his lap; Miles heartlessly left it there.

Twenty-four hours passed, for Miles mostly in a console station chair cross-checking embassy records on Komarran refugees. Unfortunately, the embassy had amassed huge quantities of such information. If there was something significant, it was well camouflaged in the tons of irrelevencies. It simply wasn't a one-man job.

At two in the morning, cross-eyed, Miles gave it up, called Elli Quinn, and dumped the whole problem on the Dendarii Mercenaries' Intelligence Department.

Dumped was the word for it: mass data transfer via comm link from the embassy's secured computers to the *Triumph* in orbit. Galeni would have had convulsions; screw Galeni, it was all his fault for disappearing in the first place. Miles thoughtfully didn't ask Ivan, either. Miles's legal position, if it came to that, was that the Dendarii were de facto Barrayaran troops and the data transfer therefore internal to the Imperial military. Technically. Miles included all of Galeni's personnel files too, in fully accessed form. Miles's legal position there was that the seal was only to protect Galeni from the prejudice of Barrayaran patriots, which the Dendarii clearly were not. One argument or the other had to work.

"Tell the spooks that finding Galeni is a contract," Miles told Elli, "part of the fleet-wide fund-raising drive. We only get paid for producing the man. That could actually be true, come to think of it."

He fell into bed hoping his subconscious would work it out during what was left of the night, but woke blank and bleary as before. He set Barth and a couple of the other non-coms to rechecking the movements of the courier officer, the other possible weak link in the chain. He sat tight, waiting for the police to call, his imagination weaving daisy chains of ever more gaudy and bizarre explanatory scenarios. Sat still as stone in a darkened room, one foot tapping uncontrollably, feeling as if the top of his head was about to blow off.

On the third day Elli Quinn called in.

He snapped the comm link into place in the holovid, hungry for the pleasure of seeing her face. It bore a most peculiar smirk.

"I thought this might interest you," she purred. "Captain Thorne was just contacted with a *fascinating* contract offer for the Dendarii."

"Does it have a fascinating price?" Miles inquired. The gears in his head seemed to grind as he tried to switch back to Admiral Naismith's problems, which had been overwhelmed and forgotten in the past two days' uncertain tensions.

"A hundred thousand Betan dollars. In untraceable cash."

"Ah . . ." That came to close to half a million Imperial marks. "I thought I'd made it clear we weren't going to touch anything illegal this time. We're in enough trouble as it is."

"How does a kidnapping grab you?" She giggled inexplicably.

"Absolutely not!"

"Oh, you're going to make an exception in this case," she predicted with confidence, even verve.

"Elli . . ." he growled in warning.

She controlled her humor with a deep breath, though her eyes remained alight. "But Miles—our mysterious and wealthy strangers want to hire Admiral Naismith to kidnap Lord Miles Vorkosigan from the Barrayaran embassy."

"It's got to be a trap," Ivan jittered nervously, guiding the groundcar Elli had rented through the levels of the city. Midnight was scarcely less well lit than daytime, though the shadows of their faces shifted as the sources of illumination flitted by outside the bubble canopy.

The gray Dendarii sergeant's uniform Ivan wore flattered him no less than his Barrayaran dress greens, Miles noted glumly. The man just looked good in uniform, any uniform. Elli, sitting on Miles's other side, seemed Ivan's female twin. She simulated ease, lithe body stretched out, one arm flung carelessly and protectively across the back of the seat above Miles's head. But she had taken to biting her nails again, Miles noted. Miles sat between them in Lord Vorkosigan's Barrayaran dress greens, feeling like a piece of wilted watercress between two slices of moldy bread. Too damned tired for these late-night parties.

"Of course it's a trap," said Miles. "Who set it and why, is what we want to find out. And how much they know. Have they set this up because they believe Admiral Naismith and Lord Vorkosigan to be two separate people—or because they don't? If the latter, will it compromise Barrayar's covert connection with the Dendarii Mercenaries in future operations?"

Elli's sideways glance met Miles's. Indeed. And if the Naismith game were over, what future had they?

"Or maybe," said Ivan helpfully, "it's something totally unrelated, like local criminals looking for a spot of ransom. Or something really tortuous, like the Cetagandans trying to get Admiral Naismith in deep trouble with Barrayar, in hopes that we'd have better luck killing the little spook than they have. Or maybe—"

"Maybe you're the evil genius behind it all, Ivan," Miles suggested affably, "clearing the chain of command of competition so you can have the embassy all to yourself."

Elli glanced at him sharply, to be sure he was joking. Ivan just grinned. "Ooh, I like that one."

"The only thing we can be sure of is that it's not a Cetagandan assassination attempt." Miles sighed.

"I wish I was as sure as you seem to be," muttered Elli. It was late evening of the fourth day since Galeni's disappearance. The thirty-six hours since the Dendarii had been offered their peculiar contract had given Elli time for reflection; the initial charm had worn off for her even as Miles had become increasingly drawn in by the possibilities.

"Look at the logic of it," argued Miles. "The Cetagandans either still think I'm two separate people, or they don't. It's Admiral Naismith they want to kill, not the Barrayaran prime minister's son. Killing Lord Vorkosigan could restart a bloody war. In fact, we'll know my cover's been blown the day they stop trying to assassinate Naismith—and start making a great and embarrassing public flap about Dendarii operations against them instead. They wouldn't miss that diplomatic opportunity for anything. Particularly now, with the right-of-passage treaty through Tau Ceti up in the air. They could cripple our galactic trade in one move."

"They could be trying to prove your connection, as step one of just that plan," said Ivan, looking thoughtful.

"I didn't say it wasn't the Cetagandans," said Miles mildly. "I just said that if it was, this isn't an assassination."

Elli groaned.

Miles looked at his chrono. "Time for the last check."

Elli activated her wrist comm. "Are you still up there, Bel?"

Captain Thorne's alto voice lilted back, signalling from the aircar that followed with its troop of Dendarii soldiers. "I have you in my sights."

"All right, keep us that way. You watch the back from above, we'll watch the front. This will be the last voice contact till we invite you to drop in."

"We'll be waiting. Bel out."

Miles rubbed the back of his neck nervously. Quinn, watching the gesture, remarked, "I'm really not crazy about springing the trap by letting them take you."

"I have no intention of letting them take me. The moment they show their hand, Bel drops in and we take them instead. But if it doesn't look like they want to kill me outright, we could learn a lot by letting their operation run on a few steps further. In view of the, ah, Situation at the embassy, it could be worth a little risk."

She shook her head in mute disapproval.

The next few minutes passed in silence. Miles was about half-way through a mental review of all the branching possibilities they had hammered out for this evening's action when they pulled up in front of a row of ancient, three-story houses crammed together along a crescent street. They seemed very dark and quiet, unoccupied, apparently in process of condemnation or renovation.

Elli glanced at the numbers on the doors and swung up the bubble canopy. Miles slid out to stand beside her. From the groundcar, Ivan ran the scanners. "There's nobody home," he reported, squinting at his readouts.

"What? Not possible," said Elli.

"We could be early."

"Rats," said Elli. "As Miles is so fond of saying, look at the logic. The people who want to buy Lord Vorkosigan didn't give us this rendezvous till the last second. Why? So we couldn't get here first and check it out. They have to be set up and waiting." She leaned back into the car's cockpit, reaching over Ivan's shoulder. He turned his hands palm-out in acquiescence as she ran the scan again. "You're right," she admitted, "but it still feels wrong."

Was it chance vandalism that a couple of streetlights were broken out, just here? Miles peered into the night. "Don't like it," Elli murmured. "Let's not tie your hands."

"Can you handle me, all by yourself?"

"You're drugged to the eyeballs."

Miles shrugged, and let his jaw hang slack and his eyes track randomly and not quite in unison. He shambled beside her as her hand pinched his upper arm, guiding him up the steps. She tried the door, an old-fashioned one hung on hinges. "It's open." It swung wide squeaking, revealing blackness.

Elli reluctantly reholstered her stunner and unhooked a handlight from her belt, flashing it into the darkness. An entry hall; rickety-looking stairs ascended to the left. Twin archways on either side led into empty, dirty front rooms. She sighed and stepped cautiously across the threshold. "Anybody here?" she called softly. Silence. They entered the left-hand room, the beam of the handlight darting from corner to corner.

"We're not early," she muttered, "not late, the address is right . . . where are they?"

He could not very well answer and stay in character. Elli released him, switched the light to her left hand, and re-drew her stunner. "You're too tanked to wander far," she decided, as if talking to herself. "I'm going to take a look around."

One of Miles's eyelids shivered in acknowledgement. Until she finished checking for remote bugs and scanner beams, he had better keep playing Lord Vorkosigan in a convincingly kidnapped state. After a moment's hesitation, she took to the stairs. Taking the light with her, dammit.

He was still listening to the swift, faint creak of her footsteps overhead when the hand closed over his mouth and the back of his neck was kissed by a stunner on very light power, zero range.

He convulsed, kicking, trying to shout, trying to bite. His assailant hissed in pain and clutched harder. There were two—his hands were yanked up behind his back, a gag stuffed into his mouth before his teeth could snap closed on the hand that fed him. The gag was permeated with some sweet, penetrating drug; his nostrils flared wildly, but his vocal cords went involuntarily slack. He seemed out of touch with his body, as if it had moved leaving no forwarding address. Then a pale light came up.

Two large men, one younger, one older, dressed in Earther clothing, shifted in the shadows, faintly blurred. Scanner shields, dammit! And very, very good ones, to beat the Dendarii equipment. Miles spotted the boxes belted to their waists—a tenth the size of the latest thing his people had. Such tiny power packs—they looked new. The Barrayaran embassy was going to have to update its secured areas ... He went cross-eyed, for a mad moment, trying to read the maker's mark on them, until he saw the third man.

Oh, the third. *I've lost it,* Miles's panicked thought gyrated. *Gone right over the edge.* The third man was himself.

The alter-Miles, neatly turned out in Barrayaran dress greens, stepped forward to stare long and strangely, hungrily, into his face as he was held up by the two younger men. He began emptying the contents of Miles's pockets into his own. Stunner ... IDs ... half a pack of clove breath mints ... He frowned at the breath mints as if momentarily puzzled, then pocketed them with a shrug. He pointed to Miles's waist.

Miles's grandfather's dagger had been willed explicitly to him. The 300-year-old blade was still flexible as rubber, sharp as glass. Its jewelled hilt concealed the Vorkosigan seal. They took it from beneath his jacket. The alter-Miles shrugged the sheath-strap over his shoulder and refastened his tunic. Finally, he unhooked the scanner-shield belt from his own waist and slipped it swiftly around Miles.

The alter-Miles's eyes were hot with an exhilarated terror, as he paused to sweep one last glance over Miles. Miles had seen the look once before, in his own face in the mirrored wall of a tube station.

No.

He'd seen it on *this one's* face in the mirrored wall of a tube station.

He must have been standing feet away that night, behind Miles at an angle. In the wrong uniform. The green one, at a moment Miles was wearing his Dendarii grays.

Looks like they managed to get it right this time, though. . . .

"Perfect," growled the alter-Miles, freed of the scanner-shield's sonic muffling. "We didn't even have to stun the woman. She'll suspect nothing. Told you this would work." He inhaled, jerked up his chin, and smiled sardonically at Miles.

Posturing little martinet, Miles thought poisonously. *I'll get you for that.*

Well, I always was my own worst enemy.

The switch had taken only seconds. They carried Miles through the doorway at the back of the room. With a heroic twitch, he managed to bump his head on the frame, going through.

"What was that?" Elli's voice called instantly from upstairs.

"Me," the alter-Miles called back promptly. "I just checked around. There's nobody down here either. This is a wash-out."

"You think?" Miles heard her cantering down the stairs. "We could wait a while."

Elli's wristcom chimed. "Elli?" came Ivan's voice thinly. "I just got a funny blip in the scanners a minute ago."

Miles's heart lurched in hope.

"Check again." The alter-Miles's voice was cool.

"Nothing, now."

"Nothing here either. I'm afraid something's panicked them, and they've aborted. Pull in the perimeter and take me back to the embassy, Commander Quinn."

"So soon? You sure?"

"Now, yes. That's an order."

"You're the boss. Damn," said Elli regretfully, "I had my heart set on that hundred thousand Betan dollars."

Their syncopated footsteps echoed out the hallway and were muted by the closing door. The purr of a groundcar faded in the distance. Darkness, silence scored by breathing.

They dragged Miles along again, out a back door, through a narrow mews and into the back seat of a groundcar parked in the alley. They sat him up like a mannequin between them, while a third kidnapper drove. Miles's thoughts spun dizzily along the edge of consciousness. Goddamn scanners . . . five-year-old technology from the rim zone, which put it maybe ten years behind Earth's—they'd have to bite the budget bullet and scrap the Dendarii scanner system fleet-wide, now—if he lived to order it. . . . Scanners, hell. The fault didn't lie in the scanners. Wasn't the formerly-mythical unicorn hunted with mirrors, to fascinate the vainglorious beast while its killers circled for the strike? Must be a virgin around here somewhere. . . .

This was an ancient district. The tortuous route the groundcar was taking could be either to confuse him or merely the best shortcut local knowledge could supply. After about a quarter hour they dove into an underground parking garage and hissed to a halt. The garage was small, clearly private, with room for only a few vehicles.

They hauled him to a lift tube and ascended one level to a short hallway. One of the goons pulled off Miles's boots and scanner-shield belt. The stun was starting to wear off. His legs were rubbery, shot with pins and needles, but at least they propped him up. They released his wrists; clumsily, he tried to rub his aching arms. They popped the gag from his mouth. He emitted a wordless croak.

They unlocked a door in front of him and bundled him into a windowless room. The door closed behind with a click like trap jaws snapping. He staggered and stood, feet spread a little, panting.

A sealed light fixture in the ceiling illuminated a narrow room furnished only with two hard benches along the walls. To the left a doorframe with the door removed led to a tiny, windowless washroom.

A man, wearing only green trousers, cream shirt, and socks, lay curled on one of the benches, facing the wall. Stiffly, gingerly, he rolled over and sat up. One hand flung up automatically, as if to shield his reddened eyes from some too-bright light; the other pressed the bench to keep him from toppling. Dark hair mussed, a four-day beard stubble. His shirt collar hung open in a V, revealing a throat strangely vulnerable, in contrast to the usual turtle-armored effect of the high, closed Barrayaran tunic collar. His face was furrowed.

The impeccable Captain Galeni. Rather the worse for wear.

CHAPTER EIGHT

Galeni squinted at Miles. "Bloody hell," he said in a flattened voice.

"Same to you," Miles rasped back.

Galeni sat up straighter, bleary eyes narrowing with suspicion. "Or—is it you?"

"I don't know." Miles considered this. "Which me were you expecting?" He staggered over to the bench opposite before his knees gave way and sat, his back against the wall, feet not quite reaching the floor. They were both silent for a few minutes, taking in the details of the other.

"It would be pointless to throw us together in the same room unless it was monitored," said Miles at last.

For answer Galeni flipped an index finger up toward the light fixture.

"Ah. Visual too?"

"Yes."

Miles bared his teeth and smiled upward.

Galeni was still regarding him with wary, almost painful uncertainty.

Miles cleared his throat. There was a bitter tang lingering in his mouth. "I take it you've met my alter-ego?"

"Yesterday. I think it was yesterday." Galeni glanced at the light.

His kidnappers had relieved Miles of his own chrono, too. "It's now about one in the morning, of the start of the fifth day since you disappeared from the embassy," Miles supplied, answering

172

Galeni's unspoken question. "Do they leave that light on all the time?"

"Yes."

"Ah." Miles fought down a queasy twinge of associative memory. Continuous illumination was a Cetagandan prison technique for inducing temporal disorientation. Admiral Naismith was intimately familiar with it.

"I saw him for just a few seconds," Miles went on, "when they made the switch." His hand touched the absence of a dagger, massaged the back of his neck. "Do I—really look like that?"

"I thought it was you. Till the end. He told me he was practicing. Testing."

"Did he pass?"

"He was in here for four or five hours."

Miles winced. "That's bad. That's very bad."

"I thought so."

"I see." A sticky silence filled the room. "Well, historian. And how do you tell a forgery from the real thing?"

Galeni shook his head, then touched his hand to his temple as though he wished he hadn't; blinding headache, apparently. Miles had one too. "I don't believe I know anymore." Galeni added reflectively, "He saluted."

A dry grin cracked one corner of Miles's mouth. "Of course, there could be just one of me, and all this a ploy to drive you crazy. . . ."

"Stop that!" Galeni almost shouted. A ghastly answering smile lit his face for a moment nonetheless.

Miles glanced up at the light. "Well, whoever I am, you should still be able to tell me who they are. Ah—I hope it's not the Cetagandans? I would find that just a little too weird for comfort, in light of my . . . duplicate. He's a surgical construct, I trust." *Not a clone—please, don't let him be my clone. . . .*

"He said he was a clone," said Galeni. "Of course, at least half of what he said was lies, whoever he was."

"Oh." Stronger exclamations seemed wholly inadequate.

"Yes. It made me rather wonder about you. The original you, that is."

"Ah . . . hem! Yes. I think I know now why I popped out with that . . . that story when the reporter cornered me. I'd seen him once before. In the tubeway, when I was out with Commander Quinn. Eight, ten days ago now. They must have been maneuvering in to make the switch. I thought I was seeing myself in the mirror. But he was wearing the wrong uniform, and they must have aborted."

Galeni glanced down at his own sleeve. "Didn't you notice?"

"I had a lot on my mind."

"You never reported this!"

"I was on some pain meds. I thought it might be a little hallucination. I was a bit stressed out. By the time I'd got back to the embassy I'd forgotten about it. And besides," he smirked weakly, "I didn't think our working relationship would benefit from planting serious doubts about my sanity."

Galeni's lips compressed with exasperation, then softened with something like despair. "Perhaps not."

It alarmed Miles, to see despair in Galeni's face. He babbled on, "Anyway, I was relieved to realize I hadn't suddenly become clairvoyant. I'm afraid my subconscious must be brighter than the rest of my brain. I just didn't get its message." He pointed upward again. "Not Cetagandans?"

"No." Galeni leaned back against the far wall, stone-faced. "Komarrans."

"Ah," Miles choked. "A Komarran plot. How . . . fraught."

Galeni's mouth twisted. "Quite."

"Well," said Miles thinly, "they haven't killed us yet. There must be some reason to keep us alive."

Galeni's lips drew back on a deathly grin, his eyes crinkling. "None whatsoever." The words came out in a *whee*ing chuckle, abruptly cut off. A private joke between Galeni and the light fixture, apparently. "He imagines he has reason," Galeni explained, "but he's very mistaken." The bitter thrust of those words was also directed upward.

"Well, don't tell *them*," said Miles through his teeth. He took a deep breath. "Come on, Galeni, spill it. What happened the morning you disappeared from the embassy?"

Galeni sighed, and seemed to compose himself. "I got a call that morning. From an old . . . Komarran acquaintance. Asking me to meet him."

"There was no log of a call. Ivan checked your comconsole."

"I erased it. That was a mistake, though I didn't realize it at the time. But something he'd said led me to think this might be a lead into the mystery of your peculiar orders."

"So I did convince you my orders had to have been screwed up."

"Oh, yes. But it was clear that if that were so, my embassy

Security had been penetrated, compromised from the inside. It was probably through the courier. But I dared not lay such a charge without adducing objective evidence."

"The courier, yes," said Miles. "That was my second choice."

Galeni's brows lifted. "What was your first choice?"

"You, I'm afraid."

Galeni's sour smile said it all.

Miles shrugged in embarrassment. "I figured you'd made off with my eighteen million marks. Except if you had, why hadn't you absconded? And then you absconded."

"Oh," said Galeni in turn.

"All the facts fit, then," Miles explained. "I had you pegged as an embezzler, deserter, thief, and all-around Komarran son of a bitch."

"So what kept you from laying charges to that effect?"

"Nothing, unfortunately." Miles cleared his throat. "Sorry."

Galeni's face went faintly green, too dismayed even to get up a convincing glare, though he tried.

"Too right," said Miles. "If we don't get out of here, your name is going to be mud."

"All for nothing . . ." Galeni braced his back to the wall, his head tilting back against it for support, eyes closing as if in pain.

Miles contemplated the probable political consequences, should he and Galeni disappear now without further trace. Investigators must find his embezzlement theory even more exciting than he had, compounded now by kidnapping, murder, elopement, God knew what. The scandal could be guaranteed to rock the Komarran integration effort to its foundations, perhaps destroy it altogether. Miles glanced across the room at the man his father had chosen to take a chance on. *A kind of redemption . . .*

That alone could be enough reason for the Komarran underground to murder them both. But the existence of the—oh God, not a clone!—alter-Miles suggested that this slander upon Galeni's character, courtesy of Miles, was merely a happy bonus from the Komarran viewpoint. He wondered if they'd be properly grateful.

"So you went to meet this man," Miles prodded. "Without taking a beeper or a backup."

"Yes."

"And promptly got yourself kidnapped. And you criticize my security techniques!"

"Yes." Galeni's eyes opened. "Well, no. We had lunch first."

"You sat down to lunch with this guy? Or—was she pretty?"

Miles awoke to Galeni's choice of pronoun, back when he'd been addressing edged remarks to the light fixture. No, not a pretty.

"Hardly. But he did attempt to suborn me."

"Did he succeed?"

At Galeni's withering glare, Miles explained, "Making this entire conversation a play for my benefit, y'see."

Galeni grimaced, half irritation, half wry agreement. Forgeries and originals, truth and lies, how were they to be tested here?

"I told him to get stuffed." Galeni said this loudly enough that the light fixture couldn't possibly miss it. "I should have realized, in the course of our argument, that he had told me entirely too much about what was really going on to dare let me go. But we exchanged guarantees, I turned my back on him . . . let sentiment cloud my judgment. He did not. And so I ended up here." Galeni glanced around their narrow cell, "For a little time yet. Until he gets over his surge of sentiment. As he will, eventually." Defiance, glared at the light fixture.

Miles drew breath cold, cold through his teeth. "Must have been a pretty compelling old acquaintance."

"Oh yes." Galeni closed his eyes again, as if he contemplated escaping Miles, and this whole tangle, by retreating into sleep.

Galeni's stiff, halting movements hinted of torture. . . . "They been urging you to change your mind? Or interrogating you the old hard way?"

Galeni's eyes slitted open; he touched the purple splotch under the left one. "No, they have fast-penta for interrogation. No need to get physical. I've been round on it, three, four times. There's not much they don't know about embassy security by now."

"Why the contusions, then?"

"I made a break for it . . . yesterday, I guess. The three fellows who tackled me look worse, I assure you. They must still be hoping I'll change my mind."

"Couldn't you have pretended to cooperate at least long enough to get away?" said Miles in exasperation.

Galeni's eyes snapped in truculence. "Never," he hissed. The spasm of rage evaporated with a weary sigh. "I suppose I should have. Too late now."

Had they scrambled the captain's brains with their drugs? If old cold Galeni had let emotion ambush his reason to that extent, well—it must be a bloody strong emotion. The down-deep deadlies that IQ could do nothing about.

"I don't suppose they'd buy an offer to cooperate from me," Miles said glumly.

Galeni's voice returned to its original drawl. "Hardly."

"Right."

A few minutes later Miles remarked, "It can't be a clone, y'know."

"Why not?" said Galeni.

"Any clone of mine, grown from my body cells, ought to look—well, rather like Ivan. Six feet tall or so and not . . . distorted in his face and spine. With good bones, not these chalk-sticks. Unless," horrid thought, "the medics have been lying to me all my life about my genes."

"He must have been distorted to match," Galeni offered thoughtfully. "Chemically or surgically or both. No harder to do that to your clone than to any other surgical construct. Maybe easier."

"But what happened to me was so random an accident—even the repairs were experimental—my own doctors didn't know what they'd have till it was over."

"Getting the duplicate right must have been tricky. But obviously not impossible. Perhaps the . . . individual we saw represents the last in a series of trials."

"In that case, what have they done with the discards?" Miles asked wildly. A parade of clones passed through his imagination like a chart of evolution run in reverse, upright Ivanish Cro-Magnon devolving through missing links into chimpanzee-Miles.

"I imagine they were disposed of." Galeni's voice was high and mild, not so much denying as defying horror.

Miles's belly shivered. "Ruthless."

"Oh, yes," Galeni agreed in that same soft tone.

Miles groped for logic. "In that case, he—the clone—" *my twin brother,* there, he had thought the thought flat out, "must be significantly younger than myself."

"Several years," agreed Galeni. "At a guess, six."

"Why six?"

"Arithmetic. You were about six when the Komarran revolt ended. That would have been the time this group would have been forced to turn its attention toward some other, less direct plan of attack on Barrayar. The idea would not have interested them earlier. Much later, and the clone would still be too young to replace you even with accelerated growth. Too young to carry off the act. It appears he must act as well as look like you, for a time."

"But why a clone at all? Why a clone of me?"

"I believe he's intended for some sabotage timed with an uprising on Komarr."

"Barrayar will never let Komarr go. Never. You're our front gate."

"I know," said Galeni tiredly. "But some people would rather drown our domes in blood than learn from history. Or learn anything at all." He glanced involuntarily at the light.

Miles swallowed, rallied his will, spoke into the silence. "How long have you known your father hadn't been blown up with that bomb?"

Galeni's eyes flashed back to him; his body froze, then relaxed, if so grating a motion could be called relaxation. But he said merely, "Five days." After a time he added, "How did you know?"

"We cracked open your personnel files. He was your only close relative with no morgue record."

"We believed he was dead." Galeni's voice was distant, level. "My brother certainly was. Barrayaran Security came and got my mother and me, to identify what was left. There wasn't much left. It was no effort to believe there was literally nothing left of my father, who'd been reported much closer to the center of the explosion."

The man was in knots, fraying before Miles's eyes. Miles found he did not relish the idea of watching Galeni come apart. Very wasteful of an officer, from the Imperium's viewpoint. Like an assassination. Or an abortion.

"My father spoke constantly of Komarr's freedom," Galeni went on softly. To Miles, to the light fixture, to himself? "Of the sacrifices we must all make for the freedom of Komarr. He was very big on sacrifices. Human or otherwise. But he never seemed to care much about the freedom of anyone *on* Komarr. It wasn't until the day the revolt died that I became a free man. The day he died. Free to look with my own eyes, make my own judgments, choose my own life. Or so I thought. Life," the lilt of Galeni's voice was infinitely sarcastic, "is full of surprises." He favored the light fixture with a vulpine smile.

Miles squeezed his eyes shut, trying to think straight. Not easy, with Galeni sitting two meters away emanating murderous tension on red-line overload. Miles had the unpleasant feeling that his nominal superior had lost sight of the larger strategic picture just now, locked in some private struggle with old ghosts. Or old non-ghosts. It was up to Miles.

Up to Miles to do—what? He rose and prowled the room on shaky legs. Galeni watched him through slitted eyes without comment. No exit but the one. He scratched at the walls with his fingernails. They were impervious. The seams at floor and ceiling—he hopped up on the bench and reached dizzily—yielded not at all. He passed into the half-bath, relieved himself, washed his hands and face and sour mouth at the sink—cold water only— drank from his cupped hands. No glass, not even a plastic cup. The water sloshed nauseatingly in his stomach; his hands twitched from the aftereffects of the stun. He wondered what the result might be of stuffing the drain with his shirt and running the water. That seemed to be the maximum possible vandalism. He returned to his bench, wiping his hands on his trousers, and sat down before he fell down.

"Do they feed you?" he asked.

"Two or three times a day," said Galeni. "Some of whatever they're cooking upstairs. Several people seem to be living in this house."

"That would seem to be the one time you could make a break, then."

"It was," agreed Galeni.

Was, right. Their captors' guard would be redoubled now, after Galeni's attempt. Not an attempt that Miles dared duplicate; a beating like the one Galeni had taken would incapacitate him completely.

Galeni contemplated the locked door. "It does provide a certain amount of entertainment. You never know, when the door opens, if it's going to be dinner or death."

Miles got the impression Galeni was rather hoping for death. *Bloody kamikaze.* Miles knew the fey mood inside out. You could fall in love with that grave-narrow option—it was the enemy of creative strategic thought. It was the enemy, period.

But his resolve failed to find a practical form, though he spun it round and round inside his head. Surely Ivan must recognize the imposter immediately. Or would he just put down any mistakes the clone made to Miles having an off day? There was certainly precedent for that. And if the Komarrans had spent four days pumping Galeni dry on embassy procedures, it was quite possible the clone would be able to carry out Miles's routine duties error-free. After all, if the creature were truly a clone, he should be just as smart as Miles.

Or just as stupid . . . Miles hung on to that comforting thought. If Miles made mistakes, in his desperate dance through life, the clone could make just as many. Trouble was, would anyone be able to tell their mistakes apart?

But what about the Dendarii? His Dendarii, fallen into the hands of a—a what? What were the Komarrans' plans? How much did they know about the Dendarii? And how the hell could the clone duplicate both Lord Vorkosigan and Admiral Naismith, when Miles himself had to make them up as he went along?

And Elli—if Elli hadn't been able to tell the difference in the abandoned house, could she tell the difference in bed? Would that filthy little imposter dare swive Quinn? But what human being of any of the three sexes could possibly resist an invitation to cavort between the sheets with the brilliant and beautiful. . . ? Miles's imagination curdled with detailed pictures of the clone, out there, Doing Things to his Quinn, most of which Miles hadn't even had time to try yet himself. He found his hands writhing in a white-knuckled grip on the edge of the bench, in danger of snapping his finger-bones.

He let up. Surely the clone must try to avoid intimate situations with people who knew Miles well, where he would be in most danger of getting tripped up. Unless he was a cocky little shit with a compulsive experimental bent, like the one Miles shaved daily in his mirror. Miles and Elli had just begun to get intimate—would she, wouldn't she know the difference? If she—Miles swallowed, and tried to bring his mind back to the larger political scenario.

The clone hadn't been created just to drive him crazy; that was merely a fringe benefit. The clone had been forged as a weapon, directed against Barrayar. Through Prime Minister Count Aral Vorkosigan against Barrayar, as if the two were one. Miles had no illusions; it wasn't for his own self's sake that this plot had been gotten up. He could think of a dozen ways a false Miles might be used against his father, ranging from relatively benign to horrifically cruel. He glanced across the cell at Galeni, sprawled coolly, waiting for his own father to kill him. Or using that very coolness to force his father to kill him, proving . . . what? Miles quietly dropped the benign scenarios off his list of possibilities.

In the end exhaustion overtook him, and he slept on the hard bench.

He slept badly, swimming up repeatedly out of some unpleasant dream only to re-encounter the even more unpleasant reality—cold bench, cramped muscles, Galeni flung across the bench opposite twisting in equal discomfort, his eyes gleaming through the fringe of his lashes not revealing whether he woke or dozed—then wavering back down to dreamland in self-defense. Miles's sense of the passage of time became totally distorted, though when he finally sat up his creaking muscles and the water-clock of his bladder suggested he'd slept long. By the time he made a trip to the washroom, splashed cold water on his now-stubbled face, and drank, his mind was churning back into high gear, rendering farther sleep impossible. He wished he had his cat-blanket.

The door clicked. Galeni snapped from his apparent doze into a sitting position, feet under his center of gravity, face utterly closed. But this time it was dinner. Or breakfast, judging from the ingredients: lukewarm scrambled eggs, sweet raisin bread, blessed coffee in a flimsy cup, one spoon each. It was delivered by one of the poker-faced young men Miles had seen the night before. Another hovered in the doorway, stunner at ready. Eyeing Galeni, the man set the food down on the end of one bench and backed quickly out.

Miles regarded the food warily. But Galeni collected his and ate without hesitation. Did he know it wasn't drugged or poisoned, or did he just not give a damn anymore? Miles shrugged and ate too.

Miles swallowed his last precious drops of coffee and asked, "Have you picked up any hint of what the purpose of this whole masquerade is? They must have gone to incredible lengths to produce this ... duplicate me. It can't be a minor plot."

Galeni, looking a bit less pale by virtue of the decent food, rolled his cup carefully between his hands. "I know what they've told me. I don't know if what they've told me is the truth."

"Right, go on."

"You've got to understand, my father's group is a radical splinter of the main Komarran underground. The groups haven't spoken to each other in years, which is one of the reasons we—Barrayaran Security," a faint ironic smile played around his lips, "—missed them. The main body has been losing momentum over the last decade. The expatriates' children, with no memory of Komarr, have been growing up as citizens of other planets. And the older ones have been—well, growing old. Dying off. And with things becoming not so bad at home, they're not making new converts. It's a shrinking power base, critically shrinking."

"I can see that would make the radicals itchy to make some move. While they still had a chance," Miles remarked.

"Yes. They're in a squeeze." Galeni crushed his cup slowly in his fist. "Reduced to wild gambles."

"This one seems pretty damned exotic, to bet—sixteen, eighteen years on? How the devil did they assemble the medical resources? Was your father a doctor?"

Galeni snorted. "Hardly. The medical half was the easy part, apparently, once they'd got hold of the stolen tissue sample from Barrayar. Though how they did that—"

"I spent the first six years of my life getting prodded, probed, biopsied, scanned, sampled, sliced and diced by doctors. There must have been kilograms of me floating around in various medical labs to choose from, a regular tissue smorgasbord. That was the easy part. But the actual cloning—"

"Was hired out. To some shady medical laboratory on the planet of Jackson's Whole, as I understand it, that would do anything for a price."

Miles's mouth, opening, gaped for a moment. "Oh. Them."

"Do you know about Jackson's Whole?"

"I've—encountered their work in another context. Damned if I can't name the lab most likely to have done it, too. They're experts at cloning. Among other things, they do the illegal brain-transfer operations—illegal anywhere but Jackson's Whole, that is—where the young clone is grown in a vat, and the old brain is transferred into it—the old rich brain, needless to say—and, um, they've done some bioengineering work that I can't talk about, and . . . yes. And all this time they had a copy of me in the back room—those sons of bitches, they're going to find out they're not as bloody untouchable as they think they are this time . . . !" Miles controlled incipient hyperventilation. Personal revenge upon Jackson's Whole must wait for some more propitious time. "So. The Komarran underground invested nothing except money in the project for the first ten or fifteen years. No wonder it was never traced."

"Yes," said Galeni. "So a few years ago, the decision was made to pull this card out of their sleeve. They picked up the completed clone, now a young teenager, from Jackson's Whole and began training him to be you."

"Why?"

"They're apparently going for the Imperium."

"What?!" Miles cried. "No! Not with *me*—!"

"That . . . individual . . . stood right there," Galeni pointed to a spot near the door, "two days ago and told me I was looking at the next Emperor of Barrayar."

"They would have to kill both Emperor Gregor and my father to mount anything of a sort—" Miles began frantically.

"I would imagine," said Galeni dryly, "they're looking forward to just that." He lay back on his bench, eyes glinting, hands locked behind his neck for a pillow, and purred, "Over my dead body, of course."

"Over both our dead bodies. They don't dare let us live. . . ."

"I believe I mentioned that yesterday."

"Still, if anything goes wrong," Miles's gaze flickered toward the light fixture, "it might be handy for them to have hostages." He enunciated this idea clearly, emphasizing the plural. Though he feared that from the Barrayaran point of view, only one of them had value as a hostage. Galeni was no fool; he knew who the goat was too.

Damn, damn, damn. Miles had walked into this trap, knowing it was a trap, in hopes of gaining just the sort of information he now possessed. But he hadn't meant to stay trapped. He rubbed the back of his neck in utter frustration—what joy it would have been to call down a Dendarii strike force on this—this nest of rebels—right now—

The door clicked. It was too early for lunch. Miles whipped around, hoping for a wild instant to find Commander Quinn leading a patrol to his rescue—no. It was just the two goons again, and a third in the doorway with a stunner.

One gestured at Miles. "You. Come along."

"Where to?" Miles asked suspiciously. Could this be the end already—to be taken back down to the garage sub-level and shot or have his neck broken? He felt disinclined to walk voluntarily to his own execution.

Something like that must have been passing through Galeni's mind too, for as the pair grabbed Miles unceremoniously by the arms, Galeni lunged for them. The one with the stunner dropped him before he was halfway across the floor. Galeni convulsed, teeth bared, in desperate resistance, then lay still.

Numbly, Miles allowed himself to be bundled out the door. If his death were coming, he wanted to at least stay conscious, to spit in its eye one last time as it closed on him.

CHAPTER NINE

To Miles's temporary relief, they took him up, not down the lift tube. Not that they couldn't perfectly well kill him someplace other than the garage sublevel. Galeni, now, they might murder in the garage to avoid having to lug the body, but Miles's own dead weight, so to speak, would not present nearly the logistic load.

The room into which the two men now shoved him was some sort of study or private office, bright despite the polarized window. Library data files filled a transparent shelf on the wall; an ordinary comconsole desk occupied one corner. The comconsole vid was presently displaying a fish-eye view of Miles's cell. Galeni still lay stunned on the floor.

The older man who had seemed in charge of Miles's kidnapping the night before sat on a beige-padded chrome bench before the darkened window, examining a hypospray just taken from its case, which lay open beside him. So. Interrogation, not execution, was the plan. Or at any rate, interrogation before execution. Unless they simply contemplated poisoning him.

Miles tore his gaze from the glittering hypo as the man shifted, his head tilting to study Miles through narrowed blue eyes. A flick of his gaze checked the comconsole. It was a momentary accident of posture, a handgripping the edge of the bench, that snapped Miles's realization into place, for the man did not greatly resemble Captain Galeni except perhaps in the paleness of his skin. He appeared to be about sixty. Clipped graying hair, lined face, body thickening with age, clearly not that of an outdoorsman or athlete. He wore conservative Earther clothes a generation removed from the historical fashions of the parading teenagers that Miles had enjoyed in the shopping arcade. He might have been a businessman or a teacher, anything but a hairy terrorist.

Except for the murderous tension. In that, in the coil of the hands, flare of the nostril, iron of the mouth, stiffness of the neck, Ser Galen and Duv Galeni were as one.

Galen rose and stalked slowly around Miles with the air of a man studying a sculpture by an inferior artist. Miles stood very still, feeling smaller than usual in his sock feet, stubbled and grubby. He had come to the center at last, the secret source from which all his coiling troubles had been emanating these past weeks. And the center was this man, who orbited him staring back with hungry hate. Or perhaps he and Galen were both centers, like the twin foci of an ellipse, brought together and superimposed at last to create some diabolical perfect circle.

Miles felt very small and very brittle. Galen could very well begin by breaking Miles's arms with the same absent, nervous air that Elli Quinn bit her nails, just to release tension. *Does he see me at all? Or am I an object, a symbol representing the enemy—will he murder me for the sake of sheer allegory?*

"So," Ser Galen spoke. "This is the real thing at last. Not very impressive, to have seduced my son's loyalty. What can he see in you? Still, you represent Barrayar very well. The monster son of a monster father, Aral Vorkosigan's secret moral genotype made flesh for all to see. Perhaps there is some justice in the universe after all."

"Very poetic," choked Miles, "but biologically inaccurate, as you must know, having cloned me."

Galen smiled sourly. "I won't insist on it." He completed his circuit and faced Miles. "I suppose you couldn't help being born. But why have you never revolted from the monster? He made you what you are—" an expansive gesture of Galen's open hand summed up Miles's stunted and twisted frame. "What dictator's charisma does the man possess, that he's able to hypnotize not only his own son but everyone else's too?" The prone figure in the vid console seemed to pluck at Galen's eye. "Why do you follow him? Why does David? What corrupt kick can my son get out of crawling into a Barrayaran goon-uniform and marching behind *Vorkosigan?*" Galen's voice feigned light banter very badly; the undertones twisted with anguish.

Miles, glowering, clipped out, "For one thing, my father has never abandoned me in the presence of an enemy."

Galen's head jerked back, all pretense of banter extinguished. He turned abruptly away and went to take up the hypospray from the bench.

Miles silently cursed his own tongue. But for that stupid impulse to grab the last word, to return the cut, he might have kept the man talking, and learned something. Now the talking, and the learning, would all be going the other way.

The two guards took him by the elbows. The one on the left pushed up his shirt sleeve. Here it came. Galen pressed the hypospray against the vein on the inside of Miles's elbow, a hiss, a prickling bite. "What is it?" Miles had just time to ask. His voice sounded unfortunately weak and nervous in his own ears.

"Fast-penta, of course," replied Galen easily.

Miles was not surprised, though he cringed inwardly, knowing what was to come. He had studied fast-penta's pharmacology, effects, and proper use in the Security course at the Barrayaran Imperial Academy. It was the drug of choice for interrogation, not only for the Imperial Service but galaxy-wide. The near-perfect truth serum, irresistible, harmless to the subject even with repeated doses. Irresistible and harmless, that is, except to the unfortunate few who had either a natural or artificially-induced allergic reaction to it. Miles had never even been considered as a candidate for this last conditioning, his person being judged more valuable than any secret information he might contain. Other espionage agents were less lucky. Anaphylactic shock was an even less heroic death than the disintegration chamber usually reserved for convicted spies.

Despairing, Miles waited to go ga-ga. Admiral Naismith had sat in on more than one real fast-penta interrogation. The drug washed all reason out to sea on a flood of benign good feeling and charitable cheer. Like a cat on catnip, it was highly amusing to watch— in somebody else. In moments he would be mellow to the point of drooling idiocy.

Ugly, to think of the resolute Captain Galeni having been so shamefully reduced. Four times running, he'd said. No wonder he was twitchy.

Miles could feel his heart racing, as though he'd overdosed on caffeine. His vision seemed to sharpen to an almost painful focus. The edge lines of every object in the room glowed, the masses they enclosed palpable to his exacerbated senses. Galen, standing back by the pulsing window, was a live wiring diagram, electric and dangerous, loaded with deadly voltage awaiting some triggering discharge.

Mellow, this wasn't.

He had to be slipping into natural shock. Miles took his last breath. Would his interrogator ever be surprised. . . .

Rather to Miles's own surprise, he kept on panting. Not anaphylactic shock, then. Just another damned idiosyncratic drug reaction. He hoped the stuff wouldn't bring on those ghastly hallucinations like that bloody sedative he'd been given once by an unsuspecting surgeon. He wanted to scream. His eyes flashed white-edged to follow Galen's least motion.

One of the guards shoved a chair up behind him and sat him down. Miles fell into it gratefully, shivering uncontrollably. His thoughts seemed to explode in fragments and reform, like fireworks being run forward and then in reverse through a vid. Galen frowned down at him.

"Describe the security procedures for entry and exit from the Barrayaran embassy."

Surely they must have squeezed this basic information out of Captain Galeni already—it must merely be a question to check the effect of the fast-penta, " . . . of the fast-penta," Miles heard his own voice echoing his thoughts. Oh, hell. He'd hoped his odd reaction to the drug might have included the ability to resist spilling his mind out his mouth. "—what a repulsive image . . ." Head swaying, he stared down at the floor in front of his feet as if he might see a pile of bloody brains vomited there.

Ser Galen strode forward and yanked his head up by the hair, and repeated through his teeth, "Describe the security procedures for entry and exit from the Barrayaran embassy!"

"Sergeant Barth's in charge," Miles began impulsively. "Obnoxious bigot. No savoir faire at all, and a jock to boot—" Unable to stop himself Miles poured out not only codes, passwords, scanner perimeters, but also personnel schedules, his private opinions of each and every individual, and a scathing critique of the Security net's defects. One thought triggered another and then the next in an explosive chain like a string of firecrackers. He couldn't stop; he babbled.

Not only could he not stop himself, Galen couldn't stop him either. Prisoners on fast-penta tended to wander by free association from the topic unless kept on track by frequent cues from their interrogators. Miles found himself doing the same on fast-forward.

Normal victims could be brought up short by a word, but only when Galen struck him hard and repeatedly across the face, shouting him down, did Miles halt, and sit panting.

Torture was not a part of fast-penta interrogation because the happily drugged subjects were impervious to it. For Miles the pain pulsed in and out, at one moment detached and distant, the next flooding his body and whiting out his mind like a burst of static. To his own horror, he began to cry. Then stopped with a sudden hiccup.

Galen stood staring at him in repelled fascination.

"It's not right," muttered one of the guards. "He shouldn't be like that. Is he beating the fast-penta, some kind of new conditioning?"

"He's not beating it, though," Galen pointed out. He glanced at his wrist chrono. "He's not withholding information. He's giving more. Too much more."

The comconsole began chiming insistently.

"I'll get it," volunteered Miles. "It's probably for me." He surged up out of his seat, his knees gave way, and he fell flat on his face on the carpet. It prickled against his bruised cheek. The two guards dragged him off the floor and propped him back up in the chair. The room jerked in a slow circle around him. Galen answered the comconsole.

"Reporting in." Miles's own crisp voice in its Barrayaran-accented incarnation rang from the vid.

The clone's face seemed not quite as familiar as the one Miles shaved daily in his mirror. "His hair's parted on the wrong side if he wants to be me," Miles observed to no one in particular. "No, it's not . . ." No one was listening, anyway. Miles considered angles of incidence and angles of reflection, his thoughts bouncing at the speed of light back and forth between the mirrored walls of his empty skull.

"How's it going?" Galen leaned anxiously across the comconsole.

"I nearly lost it all in the first five minutes last night. That big Dendarii sergeant-driver turned out to be the damned cousin." The clone's voice was low and tense. "Blind luck, I was able to carry off my first mistake as a joke. But they've got me rooming with the bastard. And he snores."

"Too true," Miles remarked, unasked. "For real entertainment, wait'll he starts making love in his sleep. Damn, I wish I had dreams like Ivan's. All I get are anxiety nightmares—playing polo naked against a lot of dead Cetagandans with Lieutenant Murka's

severed head for the ball. It screamed every time I hit it toward
the goal. Falling off and getting trampled . . ." Miles's mutter trailed
off as they continued to ignore him.

"You're going to have to deal with all kinds of people who
knew him, before this is done," said Galen roughly to the vid.
"But if you can fool Vorpatril, you'll be able to carry it off
anywhere—"

"You can fool all of the people some of the time," chirped Miles,
"and some of the people all of the time, but you can fool Ivan
anytime. He doesn't pay attention."

Galen glanced over at him in irritation. "The embassy is a perfect
isolated test-microcosm," he went on to the vid, "before you go
on to the larger arena of Barrayar itself. Vorpatril's presence makes
it an ideal practice opportunity. If he tumbles to you, we can find
some way to eliminate him."

"Mm." The clone seemed scarcely reassured. "Before we started,
I thought you'd managed to stuff my head with everything it was
possible to know about Miles Vorkosigan. Then at the last minute
you find out he's been leading a double life all this time—what
else have you missed?"

"Miles, we've been over that—"

Miles realized with a start that Galen was addressing the clone
with his name. Had he been so thoroughly conditioned to his role
that he had no name of his own? Strange . . .

"We knew there'd be gaps over which you'd have to improvise.
But we'll never have a better opportunity than this chance visit
of his to Earth has given us. Better than waiting another six months
and trying to maneuver in on Barrayar. No. It's now or never."
Galen took a calming breath. "So. You got through the night all
right."

The clone snorted. "Yeah, if you don't count waking up being
strangled by a damned animated fur coat."

"What? Oh, the live fur. Didn't he give it to his woman?"

"Evidently not. I nearly peed myself before I realized what it
was. Woke up the cousin."

"Did he suspect anything?" Galen asked urgently.

"I passed it off as a nightmare. It seems Vorkosigan has them
fairly often."

Miles nodded sagely. "That's what I told you. Severed heads . . .
broken bones . . . mutilated relatives . . . unusual alterations to
important parts of my body . . ." The drug seemed to be
imparting some odd memory effects, part of what made fast-penta

so effective for interrogation, no doubt. His recent dreams were coming back to him far more clearly than he'd ever consciously remembered them. All in all, he was glad he usually tended to forget them.

"Did Vorpatril say anything about it in the morning?" asked Galen.

"No. I'm not talking much."

"That's out of character," Miles observed helpfully.

"I'm pretending to have a mild episode of one of those depressions in his psych report—who is that, anyway?" The clone craned his neck.

"Vorkosigan himself. We've got him on fast-penta."

"Ah, good. I've been getting calls all morning over a secured comm link from his mercenaries, asking for orders."

"We agreed you'd avoid the mercenaries."

"Fine, tell them."

"How soon can you get orders cut getting you out of the embassy and back to Barrayar?"

"Not soon enough to avoid the Dendarii completely. I broached it to the ambassador, but it appears Vorkosigan's in charge of the search for Captain Galeni. He seemed surprised I'd want to leave, so I backed off for now. Has the captain changed his mind about cooperating yet? If not, you'll have to generate my return-home orders from out there and slip them in with the courier or something."

Galen hesitated visibly. "I'll see what I can do. In the meantime, keep trying."

Doesn't Galen know we know the courier's compromised? Miles thought in a flash of near-normal clarity. He managed to keep the vocalization to a low mumble.

"Right. Well, you promised me you'd keep him alive for questions until I left, so here's one. Who is Lieutenant Bone, and what is she supposed to do about the surplusage from the *Triumph*? She didn't say what it was a surplus of."

One of the guards prodded Miles. "Answer the question."

Miles struggled for clarity of thought and expression. "She's my fleet accountant. I suppose she should dump it into her investment account and play with it as usual. It's a surplus of money," he felt compelled to explain, then cackled bitterly. "Temporary, I'm sure."

"Will that do?" asked Galen.

"I think so. I told her she was an experienced officer and to use her discretion, and she seemed to go off satisfied, but I sure wondered what I'd just ordered her to do. All right, next. Who is Rosalie Crew, and why is she suing Admiral Naismith for half a million GSA federal credits?"

"Who?" gaped Miles in genuine astonishment as the guard prodded him again. "What?" Miles was confusedly unable to convert half a million GSA credits to Barrayaran Imperial marks in his drug-scrambled head with any precision beyond "lots and lots and lots"; for a moment the association of the name remained blocked, then clicked in. "Ye gods, it's that poor clerk from the wine shop. I saved her from burning up. Why sue me? Why not sue Danio, he burned down her store—of course, he's broke . . ."

"But what do I do about it?" asked the clone.

"You wanted to be me," said Miles in a surly voice, "you figure it out." His mental processes clicked on anyway. "Slap her with a countersuit for medical damages. I think I threw my back out, lifting her. It still hurts."

Galen overrode this. "Ignore it," he instructed. "You'll be out of there before anything can come of it."

"All right," said the Miles-clone doubtfully.

"And leave the Dendarii holding the bag?" said Miles angrily. He squeezed his eyes shut, trying desperately to think in the wavering room. "But of course, you don't care anything about the Dendarii, do you? You must care! They put their lives on the line for you—me—it's wrong—you'll betray them, casually, without even thinking about it, you scarcely know what they are—"

"Quite," sighed the clone, "and speaking of what they are, just what is his relationship with this Commander Quinn, anyway? Did you finally decide he was screwing her, or not?"

"We're just good friends," caroled Miles, and laughed hysterically. He lunged for the comconsole—the guards grabbed for him and missed—and climbing across the desk snarled into the vid, "Stay away from her, you little shit! She's mine, you hear, mine, mine, all mine—Quinn, Quinn, beautiful Quinn, Quinn of the evening, beautiful Quinn," he sang off-key as the guards dragged him back. Blows ran him down into silence.

"I thought you had him on fast-penta," said the clone to Galen.
"We do."

"It doesn't sound like fast-penta!"

"Yes. There's something wrong. Yet he's not supposed to have been conditioned. . . . I'm beginning to seriously doubt the utility of keeping him alive any longer as a data bank if we can't trust his answers."

"That's just great." The clone scowled. He glanced over his shoulder. "I've got to go. I'll report again tonight. If I'm still alive by then." He vanished with an irritated bleep.

Galen turned back to Miles with a list of questions, about Barrayaran Imperial Headquarters, about Emperor Gregor, about Miles's usual activities when quartered in Barrayar's capital city of Vorbarr Sultana, and question after question about the Dendarii Mercenaries. Miles, writhing, answered and answered and answered, unable to stop his own rapid gabble. But partway through he hit on a line of poetry, and ended by reciting the whole sonnet. Galen's slaps could not derail him; the strings of association were too strong to break into. After that he managed to jump off the interrogation repeatedly. Works with strong meter and rhyme worked best, bad narrative verse, obscene Dendarii drinking songs, anything a chance word or phrase from his interrogators could trigger. His memory seemed phenomenal. Galen's face was darkening with frustration.

"At this rate we'll be here till next winter," said one of the guards in disgust.

Miles's bleeding lips peeled back in a maniacal grin. " 'Now is the winter of our discontent,' " he cried, " 'made glorious summer by this sun of York—' "

It had been years since he'd memorized the ancient play, but the vivid iambic pentameter carried him along relentlessly. Short of beating him into unconsciousness, there seemed nothing Galen could do to turn him off. Miles was not even to the end of Act I when the two guards dragged him back down the lift tube and threw him roughly back into his prison room.

Once there, his rapid-firing neurons drove him from wall to wall, pacing and reciting, jumping up and down off the bench at appropriate moments, doing all the women's parts in a high falsetto. He got all the way through to the last Amen! before he collapsed on the floor and lay gasping.

Captain Galeni, who had been scrunched into the corner on his bench with his arms wrapped protectively around his ears for the last hour, lifted his head cautiously from their circle. "Are you quite finished?" he said mildly.

Miles rolled over on his back and stared blankly up at the light. "Three cheers for literacy . . . I feel sick."

"I'm not surprised." Galeni looked pale and ill himself, still shaky from the aftereffects of the stun. "What was that?"

"The play, or the drug?"

"I recognized the play, thank you. What drug?"

"Fast-penta."

"You're joking."

"Not joking. I have several weird drug reactions. There's a whole chemical class of sedatives I can't touch. Apparently this is related."

"What a piece of good fortune!"

I seriously doubt the utility of keeping him alive.... "I don't think so," Miles said distantly. He lurched to his feet, ricocheted into the bathroom, threw up, and passed out.

He awoke with the unblinking glare of the overhead light needling his eyes, and flung an arm over his face to shut it out. Someone—Galeni?—had put him back on his bench. Galeni was asleep now across the room, breathing heavily. A meal, cold and congealed, sat on a plate at the end of Miles's bench. It must be deep night. Miles contemplated the food queasily, then put it down out of sight under his bench. Time stretched inexorably as he tossed, turned, sat up, lay down, aching and nauseated, escape even into sleep receding out of reach.

The next morning after breakfast they came and took not Miles but Galeni. The captain left with a look of grim distaste in his eyes. Sounds of a violent altercation came from the hallway, Galeni trying to get himself stunned, a draconian but surely effective way of avoiding interrogation. He did not succeed. Their captors returned him, giggling vacuously, after a marathon number of hours.

He lay limply on his bench giving vent to an occasional snicker for what might have been another hour before slipping into torpid sleep. Miles gallantly resisted taking advantage of the residual effects of the drug to get in a few questions of his own. Alas, fast-penta subjects remembered their experiences. Miles was fairly certain by now that one of Galeni's personal triggers was in the key word *betrayal.*

Galeni returned to a thick but cold consciousness at last, looking ill. Fast-penta hangover was a remarkably unpleasant experience; in that, Miles's response to the drug had not been at all idiosyncratic.

Miles winced in sympathy as Galeni made his own trip to the washroom.

Galeni returned to sit heavily on his bench. His eye fell on his cold dinner plate; he prodded it dubiously with an experimental forefinger. "You want this?" he asked Miles.

"No, thanks."

"Mm." Galeni shoved the plate out of sight under his bench and sat back rather nervelessly.

"What were they after," Miles jerked his head doorward, "in your interrogation?"

"Personal history, mostly, this time." Galeni contemplated his socks, which were getting stiff with grime; but Miles was not sure Galeni was seeing what he was looking at. "He seems to have this strange difficulty grasping that I actually mean what I say. He had apparently genuinely convinced himself that he had only to reveal himself, to whistle, to bring me to his heel as I had run when I was fourteen. As if the weight of my entire adult life counted for nothing. As if I'd put on this uniform for a joke, or out of despair or confusion—anything but a reasoned and principled decision."

No need to ask who "he" was. Miles grinned sourly. "What, it wasn't for the spiffy boots?"

"I'm just dazzled by the glittering tinsel of neo-fascism," Galeni informed him blandly.

"Is that how he phrased it? Anyway, it's feudalism, not fascism, apart maybe from some of the late Emperor Ezar Vorbarra's experiments in centralization. The glittering tinsel of neo-feudalism I will grant you."

"I am thoroughly familiar with the principles of Barrayaran government, thank you," remarked Dr. Galeni.

"Such as they are," muttered Miles. "It was all arrived at by improvisation, y'know."

"Yes, I do. Glad to know you aren't as historically illiterate as the average young officer coming up these days."

"So . . ." Miles said, "if it wasn't for the gold braid and the shiny boots, why *are* you with us?"

"Oh, of *course*," Galeni rolled his eyes toward the light fixture, "I get a sadistic psychosexual kick out of being a bully, goon, and thug. It's a power trip."

"Hi," Miles waved from across the room, "talk to me, not him, huh? He had his turn."

"Mm." Galeni crossed his arms glumly. "In a sense, it's true, I suppose. I am on a power trip. Or I was."

"For what it's worth, that's not a secret to the Barrayaran high command."

"Nor to any Barrayaran, though people from outside your society seem to miss it regularly. How do they imagine such an apparently caste-rigid society has survived the incredible stresses of the century since the end of the Time of Isolation without exploding? In a way, the Imperial Service has performed something of the same social function as the medieval church once did here on Earth, as a safety valve. Through it, anyone of talent can launder his caste origins. Twenty years of Imperial service, and they step out for all practical purposes an honorary Vor. The names may not have changed since Dorca Vorbarra's day, when the Vor were a closed caste of self-serving horse goons—"

Miles grinned at this description of his great-grandfather's generation.

"—but the substance has altered out of all recognition. And yet through it all the Vor have managed, however desperately, to hang on to certain vital principles of service and sacrifice. To the knowledge that it is possible for a man who would not stop and stoop to take, to yet run down the street for a chance to give. . . ." He stopped short and cleared his throat, flushing. "My Ph.D. thesis, y'know. 'The Barrayaran Imperial Service, A Century of Change.'"

"I see."

"I wanted to serve Komarr—"

"As your father before you," Miles finished. Galeni glanced up sharply, suspecting sarcasm, but found, Miles trusted, only sympathetic irony in his eyes.

Galeni's hand opened in a brief gesture of agreement and understanding. "Yes. And no. None of the cadets who entered the service when I did have yet seen a shooting war. I saw one from street level—"

"I had suspected you were more intimately acquainted with the Komarr Revolt than the Security reports seemed to believe," remarked Miles.

"As a drafted apprentice to my father," Galeni confirmed. "Some night forays, other missions of sabotage—I was small for my age. There are places a child, idly playing, can pass where an adult would be stopped. Before my fourteenth birthday I had helped kill men. . . . I have no illusions about the glorious Imperial troops during the Komarr Revolt. I saw men wearing this uniform," he waved a hand down the piped length of his green trousers, "do shameful things. In anger or fear, in frustration or desperation, sometimes just in idle viciousness. But I could not see that it made any practical difference to the corpses, ordinary people caught in the cross fire, whether they were burned down by evil invader plasma fire, or blown to bits by good patriotic gravitic implosions. Freedom? We can scarcely pretend that Komarr was a democracy even before the Barrayarans came. My father cried that Barrayar had destroyed Komarr, but when I looked around, Komarr was still there."

"You can't tax a wasteland," Miles murmured.

"I saw a little girl once—" He stopped, bit his lip, plunged on. "What makes a practical difference is that there not be war. I mean—I meant—to make that practical difference. A Service career, an honorable retirement, leverage to a ministerial appointment— then up through the ranks on the civil side, then . . ."

"The viceroyalty of Komarr?" suggested Miles.

"That hope would be slightly megalomanic," said Galeni. "An appointment on his staff, though, certainly." His vision faded, palpably, as he glanced around their cell-room, and his lips puffed on a silent, self-derisive laugh. "My father, on the other hand, wants revenge. Foreign domination of Komarr being not merely prone to abuse, but intrinsically evil by first principle. Trying to make it un-foreign by integration is not compromise, it's collaboration, capitulation. Komarran revolutionaries died for my sins. And so on. And on."

"He's still attempting to persuade you to come over to his side, then."

"Oh, yes. I believe he will keep talking till he pulls the trigger."

"Not that I'm asking you to, um, compromise your principles or anything, but I really don't see that it would be any extra skin off my nose if you were to, say, plead for your own life," Miles mentioned diffidently. " 'He who fights and runs away lives to fight another day,' and all that."

Galeni shook his head. "For precisely that logic, I cannot surrender. Not will not—*can* not. He can't trust me. If I reversed, he would too, and be compelled to argue himself into killing me as hard as he now feigns to be arguing himself out. He's already sacrificed my brother. In a sense, my mother's death came ultimately from that loss, and others he inflicted on her in the name of the cause." He added in a flash of self-consciousness, "I suppose that makes this all seem very oedipal. But—the anguish of making the hard choices has always appealed to the romance in his soul."

Miles shook his head. "I'll allow you know the man better than I do. And yet . . . well, people do get hypnotized by the hard choices.

And stop looking for alternatives. The will to be stupid is a very powerful force—"

This surprised a brief laugh from Galeni, and a thoughtful look.

"—but there are always alternatives. Surely it's more important to be loyal to a person than a principle."

Galeni raised his eyebrows. "I suppose that shouldn't surprise me, coming from a Barrayaran. From a society that traditionally organizes itself by internal oaths of fealty instead of an external framework of abstract law—is that your father's politics showing?"

Miles cleared his throat. "My mother's theology, actually. From two completely different starting points they arrive at this odd intersection in their views. Her theory is that principles come and go, but that human souls are immortal, and you should therefore throw in your lot with the greater part. My mother tends to be extremely logical. Betan, y'know."

Galeni sat forward in interest, his hands loosely clasped between his knees. "It surprises me more that your mother had anything to do with your upbringing at all. Barrayaran society tends to be so, er, aggressively patriarchal. And Countess Vorkosigan has the reputation of being the most invisible of political wives."

"Yeah, invisible," Miles agreed cheerfully, "like air. If it disappeared you'd hardly miss it. Till the next time you came to inhale." He suppressed a twinge of homesickness, and a fiercer fear—*if I don't make it back this time. . . .*

Galeni smiled polite disbelief. "It's hard to imagine that Great Admiral yielding to, ah, uxorial blandishments."

Miles shrugged. "He yields to logic. My mother is one of the few people I know who has almost completely conquered the will to be stupid." Miles frowned introspectively. "Your father's a fairly bright man, is he not? I mean, given his premises. He's eluded Security, he's been able to put together at least temporarily effective courses of action, he's got follow-through, he's certainly persistent. . . ."

"Yes, I suppose so," said Galeni.

"Hm."

"What?"

"Well . . . there's something about this whole plot that bothers me."

"I should think there's a great deal!"

"Not personally. Logically. In the abstract. As a plot, *qua* plot, there's something that doesn't quite add up even from his point of view. Of course it's a scramble—chances must be taken, it's always like that when you try to convert any plan into action—but over and above the practical problems. Something intrinsically screwy."

"It's daring. But if he succeeds, he'll have it all. If your clone takes the Imperium, he'll stand in the center of Barrayar's power structure. He'll control it all. Absolute power."

"Bullshit," said Miles.

Galeni's brows rose.

"Just because Barrayar's system of checks and balances is unwritten doesn't mean it's not there. You must know the Emperor's power consists of no more than the cooperation he is able to extract, from the military, from the counts, from the ministries, from the people generally. Terrible things happen to emperors who fail to perform their function to the satisfaction of all these groups. The Dismemberment of Mad Emperor Yuri wasn't so very long ago. My father was actually present for that remarkably gory execution, as a boy. And yet people still wonder why he's never tried to take the Imperium for himself!

"So here we have a picture of this imitation me, grabbing for the throne in a bloody coup, followed by a rapid transfer of power and privilege to Komarr, say even granting its independence. Results?"

"Go on," said Galeni, fascinated.

"The military will be offended, because I'm throwing away their hard-won victories. The counts will be offended, because I'll have promoted myself above them. The ministries will be offended, because the loss of Komarr as a tax farm and trade nexus will reduce their power. The people will be offended for all these reasons plus the fact that I am in their eyes a mutant, physically unclean in Barrayaran tradition. Infanticide for obvious birth defects is still going on secretly in the back country, do you know, despite its being outlawed for four decades? If you can think of any fate nastier than being dismembered alive, well, that poor clone is headed straight for it. I'm not sure even I could ride the Imperium and survive, even without the Komarran complications. And that kid's only—what—-seventeen, eighteen years old?" Miles subsided. "It's a stupid plot. Or . . ."

"Or?"

"Or it's some other plot."

"Hm."

"Besides," said Miles more slowly, "why should Ser Galen, who if I'm reading him right hates my father more than he loves—anybody, be going to all this trouble to put Vorkosigan blood on the Barrayaran Imperial throne? It's a most obscure revenge. And how, if by some miracle he succeeds in getting the boy Imperial power, does he then propose to control him?"

"Conditioning?" suggested Galeni. "Threats to expose him?"

"Mm, maybe." At this impasse, Miles fell silent. After long moments he spoke again.

"I think the real plot is much simpler and smarter. He means to drop the clone into the middle of a power struggle just to create chaos on Barrayar. The results of that struggle are irrelevant. The clone is merely a pawn. A revolt on Komarr is timed to rise during the point of maximum uproar, the bloodier the better, back on Barrayar. He must have an ally in the woodwork prepared to step in with enough military force to block Barrayar's wormhole exit. God, I hope he hasn't made a devil's deal with the Cetagandans for that."

"Trading a Barrayaran occupation for a Cetagandan one strikes me as a zero-sum move in the extreme—surely he's not that mad. But what happens to your rather expensive clone?" said Galeni, puzzling out the threads.

Miles smiled crookedly. "Ser Galen doesn't care. He's just a means to an end." His mouth opened, closed, opened again. "Except that—I keep hearing my mother's voice, in my head. That's where I picked up that perfect Betan accent, y'know, that I use for Admiral Naismith. I can hear her now."

"And what does she say?" Galeni's brows twitched in amusement.

"Miles—she says—*what have you done with your baby brother?!"*

"Your clone is hardly that!" choked Galeni.

"On the contrary, by Betan law my clone is *exactly* that."

"Madness." Galeni paused. "Your mother could not possibly expect you to look out for this creature."

"Oh, yes she could." Miles sighed glumly. A knot of unspoken panic made a lump in his chest. Complex, too complex . . .

"And this is the woman that—you claim—is behind the man who's behind the Barrayaran Imperium? I don't see it. Count Vorkosigan is the most pragmatic of politicians. Look at the entire Komarr integration scheme."

"Yes," said Miles cordially. "Look at it."

Galeni shot him a suspicious glance. "Persons before principles, eh?" he said slowly at last.

"Yep."

Galeni subsided wearily on his bench. After a time one corner of his mouth twitched up. "My father," he murmured, "was always a man of great—principles."

CHAPTER TEN

With every passing minute, the chances of rescue seemed bleaker. In time another breakfast-type meal was delivered, making this, if such a clock was to be relied upon, the third day of Miles's incarceration. The clone, it appeared, had not made any immediate and obvious mistake to reveal his true nature to Ivan or Elli. And if he could pass Ivan and Elli, he could pass anywhere. Miles shivered.

He inhaled deeply, swung from his bench, and put himself through a series of calisthenics, trying to clear the residual mush of drug from his body and brain. Galeni, sunk this morning in an unpleasant mixture of drug hangover, depression, and helpless rage, sprawled on his bench and watched without comment.

Wheezing, sweating, and dizzy, Miles paced the cell to cool down. The place was beginning to stink, and this wasn't helping. Not too hopefully, he went to the washroom and tried the sock-down-the-drain trick. As he had suspected, the same sensor system that turned on the water with a pass of his hand turned it off prior to overflow. The toilet worked fail-safe the same way. And even if by some miracle he managed to get their captors to open the door, Galeni had demonstrated how poor the chance was of fighting their way out against stunners.

No. His sole point of contact with the enemy lay in the flow of information they hoped to squeeze from him. It was after all the only reason he was still alive. As levers went it was potentially very powerful. Informational sabotage. If the clone wasn't going to make mistakes on his own, perhaps he needed a little push. But how could Miles work it, tanked on fast-penta? He could stand in the center of the cell and make spurious confidences to the light fixture, à la Captain Galeni, but could hardly expect to be taken seriously.

He was sitting on his bench frowning at his cold toes—the clammy wet socks were laid out to dry—when the door clicked open. Two guards with stunners. One covered Galeni, who sneered back without moving. The guard's finger twitched tensely on the trigger; no hesitation there. They did not need Galeni conscious today. The other one gestured Miles out. If Captain Galeni was to be stunned instantly, there was not a great deal of point in Miles tackling the guards unilaterally; he sighed and obeyed, stepping into the corridor.

Miles exhaled in startlement. The clone stood waiting, staring at him with devouring eyes.

The alter-Miles was dressed in his Dendarii admiral's uniform. It fit perfectly, right down to the combat boots.

Rather breathlessly, the clone directed the guards to escort Miles to the study. This time he was tied firmly to a chair in the middle of the room. Interestingly, Galen was not there.

"Wait outside the door," the clone told the guards. They looked at each other, shrugged, and obeyed, hauling a couple of padded chairs with them for comfort.

The silence when the door closed was profound. His duplicate walked slowly around Miles at the safe distance of a meter, as though Miles were a snake that might suddenly strike. He fetched up to face him a good meter and a half away, leaning hip-slung against the comconsole desk, one booted foot swinging. Miles recognized the posture as his own. He would never be able to use it again without being painfully self-aware—a little piece of himself the clone had stolen from him. One of many little pieces. He felt suddenly perforated, frayed, tattered. And afraid.

"How, ah," Miles began, and had to pause and clear his thick, dry throat, "however did you manage to escape the embassy?"

"I've just spent the morning attending to Admiral Naismith's duties," the clone told him. Smugly, Miles fancied. "Your body-guard thought she was handing me back to Barrayaran embassy security. The Barrayarans will think my Komarran guard is a Dendarii. And I win myself a little slice of unaccounted time. Neat, no?"

"Risky," remarked Miles. "What do you hope to gain that's worth it? Fast-penta doesn't exactly work on me, y'know." In fact, Miles noticed, the hypospray was nowhere in sight. Missing, like Ser Galen. Curious.

"It doesn't matter." The clone made a sharp throwaway gesture, another piece torn from Miles, *twang.* "I don't care if you talk truth or lies. I just want to hear you talk. To see you, just once. You, you, you—" the clone's voice dropped to a whisper, *twang,* "how I've come to hate you."

Miles cleared his throat again. "I might point out that, in point of fact, we met for the very first time three nights ago. Whatever was done to you was not done by me."

"You," said the clone, "screwed me over just by existing. It hurts me that you breathe." He spread a hand across his chest. "However, that will be cured very shortly. But Galen promised me an interview first." He wheeled off the desk and began to pace; Miles's feet twitched. "He promised me."

"And where is Ser Galen this morning, by the way?" Miles inquired mildly.

"Out." The clone favored him with a sour grin. "For a little slice of time."

Miles's brows rose. "This conversation is unauthorized?"

"He promised me. But then he reneged. Wouldn't say why."

"Ah—hm. Since yesterday?"

"Yes." The clone paused in his pacing to regard Miles through narrowed eyes. "Why?"

"I think it may have been something I said. Thinking out loud," Miles said. "I'm afraid I figured out one too many things about his plot. Something even you weren't supposed to know. He was afraid I'd spill it under fast-penta. That suited me. The less you were able to pump from me, the more likely you'd be to make a mistake." Miles waited, barely breathing, to see which way this bait would be taken. A whiff of the exhilarated hyperconsciousness of combat thrilled along his nerves.

"I'll bite," said the clone agreeably. His eyes gleamed, sardonic. "Spill it, then."

When he was seventeen, this clone's age, he'd been—inventing the Dendarii Mercenaries, Miles recalled. Perhaps it would be better not to underestimate him. What would it be like to be a clone? How far under the skin did their similarity end? "You're a sacrifice," Miles stated bluntly. "He does not intend for you to make it alive to the Barrayaran Imperium."

"Do you think I haven't figured that out?" the clone scoffed.

"I know he doesn't think I can make it. Nobody thinks I can make it—"

Miles's breath caught as from a blow. This *twang* bit bone-deep.

"But I'll show them. Ser Galen," the clone's eyes glittered, "is going to be very surprised at what happens when I come to power."

"So will you," Miles predicted morosely.

"D'you think I'm stupid?" the clone demanded.

Miles shook his head. "I know *exactly* how stupid you are, I'm afraid."

The clone smiled tightly. "Galen and his friends spent a month farting around London, chasing you, just trying to set up for the switch. It was I who told them to have you kidnap yourself. I've studied you longer than any of them, harder than all of them. I knew you couldn't resist. I can outthink you."

Demonstrably true, alas, at least in this instance. Miles fought off a wave of despair. The kid was good, too good—he had it all, right down to the screaming tension radiating from every muscle in his body. *Twang.* Or was that home-grown? Could different pressures produce the same warps? What would it be like, behind those eyes . . . ?

Miles's eye fell on the Dendarii uniform. His own insignia winked back at him malevolently as the clone paced. "But you can outthink Admiral Naismith?"

The clone smiled proudly. "I got your soldiers released from jail this morning. Something you hadn't been able to do, evidently."

"Danio?" Miles croaked, fascinated. *No, no, say it isn't so. . . .*

"He's back on duty." The clone nodded incisively.

Miles suppressed a small moan.

The clone paused, glanced at Miles intently, some of his decisiveness falling away. "Speaking of Admiral Naismith—are you sleeping with that woman?"

What kind of life had this kid led? Miles wondered anew. Secret—always watched, constantly force-tutored, allowed contact with only a few selected persons—almost cloistered. Had the Komarrans thought to include *that* in his training, or was he a seventeen-year-old virgin? In which case he must be obsessed with sex . . . "Quinn," said Miles, "is six years older than *me*. Extremely experienced. And demanding. Accustomed to a high degree of finesse in her chosen partner. Are you an initiate in the variant practices of the Deeva Tau love cults as practiced on Kline Station?" A safe challenge, Miles judged, as he'd just this minute invented them. "Are you familiar with the Seven Secret Roads of

Female Pleasure? After she's climaxed four or five times, though, she'll usually let you up—"

The clone circled him, looking distinctly unsettled. "You're lying. I think."

"Maybe." Miles smiled toothily, only wishing the improvised fantasy were true. "Consider what you'd risk, finding out."

The clone glowered at him. He glowered back.

"Do your bones break like mine?" Miles asked suddenly. Horrible thought. Suppose, for every blow Miles had suffered, they had broken this one's bones to match. Suppose for every miscalculated foolish risk of Miles's, the clone had paid full measure—reason indeed to hate.

"No."

Miles breathed concealed relief. So, their med-sensor readings wouldn't exactly match. "It must be a short-term plot, eh?"

"I mean to be on top in six months."

"So I'd understood. And whose space fleet will bottle all the chaos on Barrayar, behind its wormhole exit, while Komarr rises again?" Miles made his voice light, trying to appear only casually interested in this vital bit of intelligence.

"We were going to call in the Cetagandans. That's been broken off."

His worst fears . . . "Broken off? I'm delighted, but why, in an escapade singularly lacking in sanity, should you have come to your senses on that one?"

"We found something better, ready to hand." The clone smirked strangely. "An independent military force, highly experienced in space blockade duties, with no unfortunate ties to other planetary neighbors who might be tempted to muscle in on the action. And personally and fiercely loyal, it appears, to my slightest whim. The Dendarii Mercenaries."

Miles tried to lunge for the clone's throat. The clone recoiled. Being still firmly tied to the chair, Miles and it toppled forward, mashing his face painfully into the carpet. "No, no, no!" he gibbered, bucking, trying to kick loose. "You moron! It'd be a slaughter—!"

The two Komarran guards tumbled through the door. "What, what happened?"

"Nothing." The clone, pale, ventured out from behind the comconsole desk where he'd retreated. "He fell over. Straighten him back, will you?"

"Fell or was pushed," muttered one of the Komarrans as the pair of them yanked the chair back upright. Miles perforce came with it. The guard stared with interest at his face. A warm wetness, rapidly cooling, trickled itchily down Miles's upper lip and three-day moustache stubble. Bloody nose? He glanced down cross-eyed, and licked at it. Calm. Calm. The clone could never get that far with the Dendarii. His future failure would be little consolation to a dead Miles, though.

"Do you, ah, need some help for this part?" the older of the two Komarrans asked the clone. "There is a kind of science in torture, you know. To get the maximum pain for the minimum damage. I had an uncle who told me what the Barrayaran Security goons used to do. . . . Given that the fast-penta is useless."

"He doesn't need help," snapped Miles, at the same moment that the clone began, "I don't want help—" then both paused to stare at each other, Miles self-possessed again, regaining his wind, the clone taken slightly aback.

But for the outward and visible marker of the damned beard, now would be the perfect time to begin screaming that Vorkosigan had overpowered and changed clothes with him, he was the clone, couldn't they tell the difference and untie me you cretins! A non-opportunity, alas.

The clone straightened, trying to regain some dignity. "Leave us, please. When I want you, I'll call you."

"Or maybe I will," remarked Miles sunnily. The clone glared. The two Komarrans exited with doubtful backward glances.

"It's a stupid idea," Miles began immediately they were alone. "You've got to grasp, the Dendarii are an elite bunch—largely—but by planetary standards they are a small force. *Small,* you understand *small?* Small is for covert operations, hit and run, intelligence gathering. Not all-out slogging matches for a fixed spatial field with a whole developed planet's resources and will backing the enemy. You've got no sense of the economics of war! I swear to God, you're not thinking past that first six months. Not that you need to—you'll be dead before the end of the year, I expect."

The clone's smile was razor-thin. "The Dendarii, like myself, are intended as a sacrifice. Dead mercenaries, after all, don't need to be paid." He paused and looked at Miles curiously. "How far ahead do you think?"

"These days, about twenty years," Miles admitted glumly. And a fat lot of good it did him. Consider Captain Galeni. In his mind Miles already saw him as the best viceroy Komarr was ever likely to get—his death, not the loss of a minor Imperial officer of dubious origins, but of the first link in a chain of thousands of lives striving for a less tormented future. A future when Lieutenant Miles Vorkosigan would surely be subsumed by Count Miles Vorkosigan, and need sane friends in high places. If he could bring Galeni through this mess alive, and sane . . . "I admit," Miles added, "when I was your age I got through about one quarter hour at a time."

The clone snorted. "A century ago, was it?"

"Seems like it. I've always had the sense that I'd better live fast, if I'm to fit it all in."

"Prescient of you. See how much you can fit into the next twenty-four hours. That's when I have my orders to ship out. At which point you will become—redundant."

So soon. . . . No time left for experiments. No time left for anything but to be right, once.

Miles swallowed. "The prime minister's death must be planned, or the destabilization of the Barrayaran government will not occur, even if Emperor Gregor is assassinated. So tell me," he said carefully, "what fate do you and Galen have planned for our father?"

The clone's head jerked back. "Oh, no you don't. You are not my brother, and the Butcher of Komarr was never a father to me."

"How about your mother?"

"I have none. I came out of a replicator."

"So did I," Miles remarked, "before the medics were done. It never made any difference to her that I could see. Being Betan, she's quite free of anti-birth-technology prejudices. It doesn't matter to her how you got here, but only what you do after you arrive. I'm afraid having a mother is a fate you can't avoid, from the moment she discovers your existence."

The clone waved the phantom Countess Vorkosigan away. "A null factor. She is nothing in Barrayaran politics."

"Is that so?" Miles muttered, then controlled his tongue. No time. "And yet you'd continue, knowing Ser Galen means to betray you to your death?"

"When I am Emperor of Barrayar—then we shall see about Ser Galen."

"If you mean to betray him anyway, why wait?"

The clone cocked his head, eyes narrowing. "Ha?"

"There's another alternative for you." Miles made his voice calm, persuasive. "Let me go now. And come with me. Back to Barrayar. You are my brother—like it or not; it's a biological fact, and it won't ever go away. Nobody gets to choose their relatives anyway, clone or no. I mean, given a choice, would you pick Ivan Vorpatril for your cousin?"

The clone choked slightly, but did not interrupt. He was beginning to look faintly fascinated.

"But there he is. And he's exactly as much your cousin as mine. Did you realize you have a name?" Miles demanded suddenly. "That's another thing you don't get to choose on Barrayar. Second son—that's you, my twin-six-years-delayed—gets the second names of his maternal and paternal grandfathers, just as the first son gets stuck with their first names. That makes you Mark Pierre. Sorry about the Pierre. Grandfather always hated it. You are Lord Mark Pierre Vorkosigan, in your own right, on Barrayar." He spoke faster and faster, inspired by the clone's arrested eyes.

"What have you ever dreamed of being? Any education you want, Mother will see that you get. Betans are very big on education. Have you dreamed of escape—how about Licensed Star Pilot Mark Vorkosigan? Commerce? Farming? We have a family wine business, from grape vines to export crates—does science interest you? You could go live with your Grandmother Naismith on Beta Colony, study at the best research academies. You have an aunt and uncle there too, do you realize? Two cousins and a second cousin. If backward benighted Barrayar doesn't appeal to you, there's a whole 'nother life waiting on Beta Colony, to which Barrayar and all its troubles is scarcely a wrinkle on the event horizon. Your cloned origin wouldn't be novel enough to be worth mentioning, there. Any life you want. The galaxy at your fingertips. Choice—freedom—ask, and it's yours." He had to stop for breath.

The clone's face was white. "You lie," he hissed. "Barrayaran Security would never let me live."

Not, alas, a fear without force. "But imagine for one minute it is, it could be real. It could be yours. My word as Vorkosigan. My protection as Lord Vorkosigan, against all comers up to and including Imperial Security." Miles gulped a little as he made this promise. "Galen offers you death on a silver platter. I can get you life. I can get it for you wholesale, for God's sake."

Was this informational sabotage? He'd meant to set the clone up for a fall, if he could . . . *what have you done with your baby brother?*

The clone threw back his head and laughed, a sharp hysterical bark. "My God, look at yourself! A prisoner, tied to a chair, hours from death—" He swept Miles a huge, ironic bow. "Oh noble lord, I am overwhelmed by your generosity. But somehow, I don't think your protection is worth spit, just now." He strode up to Miles, the closest he had yet ventured. "Flaming megalomaniac. You can't even protect yourself—" impulsively, he slapped Miles across the face, across yesterday's bruises, *"can* you?" He stepped back, startled by the force of his own experiment, and unconsciously held his stinging hand to his mouth a moment. Miles's bleeding lips peeled back in a grin, and the clone dropped his hand hastily.

So. This one has never struck a man for real before. Nor killed either, I wager. Oh, little virgin, are you ever in for a bloody deflowering.

"Can you?" the clone finished.

Gah! He takes my truth for lies, when I meant to have him take my lies for truth—some saboteur I am. Why am I compelled to speak the truth to him?

Because he is my brother, and we have failed him. Failed to discover him earlier—failed to mount a rescue— "Did you ever dream of rescue?" Miles asked suddenly. "After you knew who you were— or even before? What kind of childhood did you have, anyway? Orphans are supposed to dream of golden parents, riding to their rescue—for you, it could have been true."

The clone snorted bitter contempt. "Hardly. I always knew the score. I knew what I was from the beginning. The clones of Jackson's Whole are farmed out, y'see, to paid foster parents, to raise them to maturity. Vat-raised clones tend to have unpleasant health problems—susceptibility to infection, bad cardio-vascular conditioning—the people who are paying to have their brains transplanted expect to wake up in a healthy body.

"I had a kind of foster-brother once—a little older than me—" the clone paused, took a deep breath, "raised with me. But not educated with me. I taught him to read, a little. . . . Shortly before the Komarrans came and got me, the laboratory people took him away. It was sheer chance that I saw him again afterwards. I'd been sent on an errand to pick up a package at the shuttleport, though I wasn't supposed to go into town. I saw him across the concourse, entering the first-class passenger lounge. Ran up to him. Only it wasn't him any more. There was some horrible rich old man, sitting in his head. His bodyguard shoved me back. . . ."

The clone wheeled, and snarled at Miles. "Oh, I knew the score. But once, once, just this once, a Jackson's Whole clone is turning it around. Instead of you cannibalizing my life, I shall have yours."

"Then where will your life be?" asked Miles desperately. "Buried in an imitation of Miles, where will Mark be then? Are you sure it will be only me, lying in my grave?"

The clone flinched. "When I am emperor of Barrayar," he said through his teeth, "no one will be able to get at me. Power is safety."

"Let me give you a hint," said Miles. "There is no safety. Only varying states of risk. And failure." And was he letting his old only-child loneliness betray him, at this late date? Was there anybody home, behind those too-familiar gray eyes staring back at him so fiercely? What snare would hook him? Beginnings, the clone clearly understood beginnings; it was endings he lacked experience of. . . .

"I always knew," said Miles softly—the clone leaned closer—"why my parents never had another child. Besides the tissue damage from the soltoxin gas. But they could have had another child, with the technologies then available on Beta Colony. My father always pretended it was because he didn't dare leave Barrayar, but my mother could have taken his genetic sample and gone alone.

"The reason was me. These deformities. If a whole son had existed, there would have been horrendous social pressure put on them to disinherit me and put him in my place as heir. You think I'm exaggerating, the horror Barrayar has of mutation? My own grandfather tried to force the issue by smothering me in my cradle, when I was an infant, after he lost the abortion argument. Sergeant Bothari—I had a bodyguard from birth—who stood about two meters tall, didn't dare draw a weapon on the Great General. So the sergeant just picked him up, and held him over his head, quite apologetically—on a third-story balcony— until General Piotr asked, equally politely, to be let down. After that, they had an understanding. I had this story from my grandfather, much later; the sergeant didn't talk much.

"Later, my grandfather taught me to ride. And gave me that dagger you have stuck in your shirt. And willed me half his lands, most of which still glow in the dark from Cetagandan nuclears. And stood behind me in a hundred excruciating, peculiarly Barrayaran social situations, and wouldn't let me run away, till I was forced to learn to handle them or die. I did consider death.

"My parents, on the other hand, were so *kind*, and *careful*—their absolute lack of suggestion spoke louder than shouting. Overprotected me even as they let me risk my bones in every sport, in the military career—because they let me stifle my siblings before they could even be born. Lest I think, for one moment, that I wasn't good enough to please them. . . ." Miles ran down abruptly, then added, "Perhaps you're lucky not to have a family. They only drive you crazy after all."

And how am I to rescue this brother I never knew I had? Not to mention survive, escape, foil the Komarran plot, rescue Captain Galeni from his father, save the emperor and my father from assassination, and prevent the Dendarii Mercenaries from being put through a meat grinder?

No. If only I can save my brother, all the rest must follow. I'm right. Here, now, is the place to push, to fight, before the first weapon is ever drawn. Snap the first link, and the whole chain comes loose.

"I know exactly what I am," said the clone. "You won't make a dead fool of me."

"You are what you do. Choose again, and change."

The clone hesitated, meeting Miles's eyes directly for almost the first time. "What guarantee could you possibly give me, that I could trust?"

"My word as Vorkosigan?"

"Bah!"

Miles considered this problem seriously, from the clone's— Mark's—point of view. "Your entire life to date has been centered on betrayal, on one level or another. Since you've had zero experience with unbroken trust, naturally you cannot judge with confidence. Suppose you tell *me* what guarantee you would believe?"

The clone opened his mouth, closed it, and stood silent, reddening slightly.

Miles almost smiled. "You see the little fork, eh?" he said softly. "The logical flaw? The man who assumes everything is a lie is at least as mistaken as the one who assumes everything is true. If no guarantee can suit you, perhaps the flaw is not in the guarantee, but in you. And you're the only one who can do anything about that."

"What can I do?" muttered the clone. For a moment, anguished doubt flickered in his eyes.

"Test it," breathed Miles.

The clone stood locked. Miles's nostrils flared. He was so close— so close—he almost had him—

The door burst open. Galen, dusky with fury, stormed in, flanked by the startled Komarran guards.

"Damn, the time . . . !" the clone hissed. He straightened guiltily, his chin jerking up.

Damn the timing! Miles screamed silently in his head. If he had had just a few more minutes—

"What the hell do you think you're doing?" demanded Galen. His voice blurred with rage, like a sled over gravel.

"Improving my chances of survival past the first five minutes I set foot on Barrayar, I trust," said the clone coolly. "You do need me to survive a little while, even to serve your purposes, no?"

"I told you, it was too damn dangerous!" Galen was almost, but not quite, shouting. "I've had a lifetime of experience fighting the Vorkosigans. They are the most insidious propagandists ever to cloak self-serving greed with pseudo-patriotism. And this one is stamped from the same mold. His lies will trip you, trap you— he's a subtle little bastard, and he never takes his eye off the main chance."

"But his choice of lies was very interesting." The clone moved about like a nervous horse, kicking at the carpet, half-defiant, half-placating. "You've had me study how he moves, talks, writes. But I've never been really clear on how he thinks."

"And now?" purred Galen dangerously.

The clone shrugged. "He's loony. I think he really believes his own propaganda."

"The question is, do you?"

Do you, do you? thought Miles frantically.

"Of course not." The clone sniffed, jerked up his chin, *twang.*

Galen jerked his head toward Miles, gathering in the guards by eye. "Take him back and lock him up."

He followed on untrustingly as Miles was untied and dragged out. Miles saw his clone, beyond Galen's shoulder, staring at the floor, still scuffing one booted foot across the carpet.

"Your name is Mark!" Miles shouted back to him as the door shut. "Mark!"

Galen gritted his teeth and swung on Miles, a sincere, unscientific, roundhouse blow. Miles, held by the guards, could not dodge, but did flinch far enough that Galen's fist landed glancingly and did not shatter his jaw. Fortunately, Galen shook out his fist and did not strike again, regaining a thin crust of control.

"Was that for me, or him?" Miles inquired sweetly through an expanding bubble of pain.

"Lock him up," growled Galen to the guards, "and don't let him out again until I, personally, tell you to." He pivoted and swung away up the hall, back to the study.

Two on two, thought Miles sharply as the guards prodded him down the lift tube to the next level. *Or at any rate, two on one and a half. The odds will never be better, and the time margin can only get worse.*

As the door to his cell-room swung open, Miles saw Galeni—asleep on his bench, the sodden, sullen, despairing ploy of a man shutting out inescapable pain in the only way left to him. He'd spent most of last night pacing the cell silently, restless to the point of being frantic—the sleep that had eluded him then was now captured. Wonderful. *Now,* just when Miles needed him on his feet and primed like an overtightened spring.

Try anyway. "Galeni!" Miles yelled. "Now, Galeni! Come on!"

Simultaneously, he plunged backward into the nearest guard, going for a nerve-pinching grip on the hand that held the stunner. A joint snapped in one of Miles's fingers, but he shook the stunner loose and kicked it across the floor toward Galeni, who was lumbering bewilderedly up off his bench like a wart-hog out of the mud. Despite his half-conscious state, he reacted fast and accurately, lunging for the stunner, scooping it up, and rolling across the floor out of the line of fire from the door.

Miles's guard wrapped an arm around Miles's neck and lifted him off his feet, lurching around to face the second guard. The little gray rectangle of the business end of the second guard's weapon was so close Miles almost had to cross his eyes to bring it into focus. As the Komarran's finger tightened on the trigger the stunner's buzz fragmented, and Miles's head seemed to explode in a burst of pain and colored lights.

CHAPTER ELEVEN

He woke in a hospital bed, an unwelcome but familiar environment. In the distance, out his window, the towers of the skyline of Vorbarr Sultana, capital city of Barrayar, glowed strangely green in the darkness. Imp Mil, then, the Imperial Military Hospital. This room was undecorated in the same severe style he had known as a child, when he'd been in and out of its clinical laboratories and surgeries for painful therapies so often Imp Mil had seemed his home away from home.

A doctor entered. He appeared to be about sixty: clipped graying hair, pale lined face, body thickening with age. DR. GALEN, his name badge read. Hyposprays clanked together in his pockets. Copulating and breeding more, perhaps. Miles had always wondered where hyposprays came from.

"Ah, you're awake," said the doctor gladly. "You're not going to go away on us again this time, now, are you?"

"Go away?" He was tied down with tubes and sensor wires, drips and control leads. It hardly seemed he was going anywhere.

"Catatonia. Cloud-cuckoo-land. Ga-ga. In short, insane. In short is the only way you can go, I suppose, eh? It runs in the family. Blood will tell."

Miles could hear the susurration of his red blood cells in his ears, whispering thousands of military secrets to each other, cavorting drunkenly in a country dance with molecules of fast-penta which were flipping their hydroxyl groups at him like petticoats. He blinked away the image.

Galen's hand rummaged in his pocket; then his face changed. "Ow!" He yanked his hand out, shook off a hypospray, and sucked at his bleeding thumb. "The little bugger *bit* me." He glanced down, where the young hypospray skittered about uncertainly on its spindly metal legs, and crunched it underfoot. It died with a tiny squeak.

"This sort of mental slippage is not at all unusual in a revived cryo-corpse, of course. You'll get over it," Dr. Galen reassured him.

"Was I dead?"

"Killed outright, on Earth. You spent a year in cryogenic suspension."

Oddly enough, Miles could remember that part. Lying in a glass coffin like a fairy-tale princess under a cruel spell, while figures flitted silent and ghostlike beyond the frosted panels.

"And you revived me?"

"Oh, no. You spoiled. Worst case of freezer-burn you ever saw."

"Oh," Miles paused, nonplused, and added in a small voice, "Am I still dead, then? Can I have horses at my funeral, like Grandfather?"

"No, no, no, of course not." Dr. Galen clucked like a mother hen. "You aren't allowed to die, your parents would never permit it. We transplanted your brain into a replacement body. Fortunately, there was one ready to hand. Pre-owned, but hardly used. Congratulations, you're a virgin again. Was it not clever of me, to get your clone all ready for you?"

"My cl— my brother? Mark?" Miles sat bolt upright, tubes falling away from him. Shivering, he pulled out his tray table and stared into the mirror of its polished metal surface. A dotted line of big black stitches ran across his forehead. He stared at his hands, turning them over in horror. "My God. I'm wearing a *corpse.*"

He looked up at Galen. "If I'm in here, what have you done with Mark? Where did you put the brain that used to be in this head?"

Galen pointed.

On the table at Miles's bedside squatted a large glass jar. In it a whole brain, like a mushroom on a stem, floated rubbery, dead, and malevolent. The pickling liquid was thick and greenish.

"No, no, no!" cried Miles. "No, no, no!" He struggled out of bed and clutched up the jar. The liquid sloshed cold down over his hands. He ran out into the hall, barefoot, his patient gown flapping open behind him. There had to be spare bodies around here; this was Imp Mil. Suddenly, he remembered where he'd left one.

He burst through another door and found himself in the combat-drop shuttle over Dagoola IV. The shuttle hatch was jammed open; black clouds shot with yellow dendrites of lightning boiled beyond. The shuttle lurched, and muddy, wounded men and women in scorched Dendarii combat gear slid and screamed and swore. Miles skidded to the open hatch, still clutching the jar, and stepped out.

Part of the time he floated, part of the time he fell. A crying woman plummeted past him, arms reaching for help, but he couldn't let go of the jar. Her body burst on impact with the ground.

Miles landed feet first on rubbery legs and almost dropped the jar. The mud was thick and black and sucked at his knees.

Lieutenant Murka's body, and Lieutenant Murka's head, lay just where he'd left them on the battleground. His hands cold and shaking, Miles pulled the brain from the jar and tried to shove the brainstem down the plasma-bolt-cauterized neck. It stubbornly refused to hook in.

"He doesn't have a face anyway," criticized Lieutenant Murka's head from where it lay a few meters off. "He's going to look ugly as sin, walking around on my body with that thing sticking up."

"Shut up, you don't get a vote, you're dead," snarled Miles. The slippery brain slithered through his fingers into the mud. He picked it back out and tried clumsily to rub the black goop off on the sleeve of his Dendarii Admiral's uniform, but the harsh cloth scrubbed up the convoluted surface of Mark's brain, damaging it. Miles patted the tissue surreptitiously back into place, hoping no one would notice, and kept trying to shove the brain stem back in the neck.

Miles's eyes flipped open and stared wide. His breath caught. He was shaking and damp with sweat. The light fixture burned steadily in the unwavering ceiling of the cell; the bench was hard and cold on his back. "God. Thank God," he breathed.

Galeni loomed over him in worry, one arm supporting himself against the wall. "You all right?"

Miles swallowed, breathed deeply. "You know it's a bad dream when waking up *here* is an improvement."

One of his hands caressed the cool, reassuring solidity of the bench. The other found no stitches across his forehead, though his head did feel as if somebody had been doing amateur surgery on it. He blinked, squeezed his eyes shut, opened them again, and with an effort made it up on his right elbow. His left hand was swollen and throbbing. "What happened?"

"It was a draw. One of the guards and I stunned each other. Unfortunately, that left one guard still on his feet. I woke up maybe an hour ago. It was max stun. I don't know how much time we've lost."

"Too much. It was a good try, though. *Dammit.*" He stopped just short of pounding his bad hand on the bench in frustration. "I was so close. I almost had him."

"The guard? It looked like he had you."

"No, my clone. My brother. Whatever he is." Flashes of his dream came back to him, and he shuddered. "Skittish fellow. I think he's afraid he's going to end up in a jar."

"Eh?"

"Eugh." Miles attempted to sit up. The stun had left him feeling nauseated. Muscles spasmed jerkily in his arms and legs. Galeni, clearly in no better shape, tottered back to his own bench and sat.

Some time later the door opened. *Dinner,* thought Miles.

The guard jerked his stunner at them. "Both of you. Out." The second guard backed him up from behind, several meters beyond hope of reach, with another stunner. Miles did not like the looks on their faces, one solemn and pale, the other smiling nervously.

"Captain Galeni," Miles suggested in a voice rather higher in pitch than he'd meant it to come out as they exited, "I think it might be a good time for you to talk to your father, now."

A variety of expressions chased across Galeni's face: anger, mulish stubbornness, thoughtful appraisal, doubt.

"That way." The guard gestured them toward the lift tube. They dropped down, toward the garage level.

"You can do this, I can't," Miles coaxed Galeni in a *sotto voce* singsong out of the corner of his mouth.

Galeni hissed through his teeth: frustration, acquiescence, resolve. As they entered the garage, he turned abruptly to the closer guard and jerked out unwillingly, "I wish to speak to my father."

"You can't."

"I think you had better let me." Galeni's voice was dangerous, edged, at last, with fear.

"It's not up to me. He gave us our orders and left. He's not here."

"Call him."

"He didn't tell me where he would be." The guard's voice was tight and irritated. "And if he had, I wouldn't anyway. Stand over there by that lightflyer."

"How are you going to do it?" asked Miles suddenly. "I really am curious to know. Think of it as my last request." He sidled over toward the lightflyer, his eyes shifting in search of cover, any cover. If he could vault over or dodge around the vehicle before they fired . . .

"Stun you, fly you out over the south coast, drop you in the water," the guard recited. "If the weights work loose and you wash ashore, the autopsy would show only that you'd drowned."

"Not exactly a hands-on murder," Miles observed. "Easier for you that way, I expect." These men were not professional killers, if Miles read them right. Still, there was a first time for everything. That pillar over there was not wide enough to stop a stun bolt. The array of tools on the far wall presented possibilities . . . his legs were cramping furiously. . . .

"And so the Butcher of Komarr gets his at last," the solemn guard observed in a detached voice. "Indirectly." He raised his stunner.

"Wait!" squeaked Miles.

"What for?"

Miles was still groping for a reply when the garage doors slid open.

"Me!" yelled Elli Quinn. "Freeze!"

A Dendarii patrol streamed past her. In the instant it took the Komarran guard to shift his aim, a Dendarii marksman dropped him. The second guard panicked and bolted for the lift tube. A sprinting Dendarii tackled him from behind, and had him laid out face down on the floor with his hands locked behind him within seconds.

Elli strolled up to Miles and Galeni, pulling a sonic eavesdropper-sensor from her ear. "Gods, Miles, I couldn't believe it was your voice. How did you *do* that?" As she took in his appearance, an expression of extreme disquiet stole over her face.

Miles captured her hands and kissed them. A salute might have been more proper, but his adrenaline was still pumping and this was more heartfelt. Besides, he wasn't in uniform. "Elli, you genius! I should have known the clone couldn't fool you!"

She stared at him, almost recoiling, her voice circling upward in pitch. "What clone?"

"What do you mean, what clone? That's why you're here, isn't it? He blew it—and you came to rescue me—didn't you?"

"Rescue you from what? Miles, you ordered me a week ago to find Captain Galeni, remember?"

"Oh," said Miles. "Yes. So I did."

"So we did. We've been sitting outside this block of housing units all night, waiting to pick up a positive voiceprint analysis on him, so we could notify the local authorities. They don't appreciate false alarms. But what finally came over the sensors suggested we'd better not wait for the local authorities, so we took a chance—visions of us being arrested en masse for breaking and entering dancing in my head—"

A Dendarii sergeant drifted up and saluted. "Damn, sir, how'd you do that?" He trotted on waving a scanner without waiting for reply.

"Only to find you'd beaten us to it."

"Well, in a sense, yes . . ." Miles massaged his throbbing forehead. Galeni stood scratching his beard and taking it all in without comment. Galeni could say nothing at noticeable volume.

"Remember, three or four nights ago when you took me to be kidnapped so's I could penetrate the opposition and find out who they were and what they wanted?"

"Yeah . . ."

"Well," Miles took a deep breath, "it worked. Congratulations. You have just converted an absolute disaster into a major intelligence coup. Thank you, Commander Quinn. By the way, the guy you walked out of that empty house with—wasn't me."

Elli's eyes widened; her hand went to her mouth. Then the dark glints narrowed in furious thought. "Sonofabitch," she breathed. "But Miles—I thought the clone story was something you'd made up!"

"So did I. It's thrown everyone off, I expect."

"Then he was—he is—a real clone?"

"So he claims. Fingerprints—retina—voiceprint—all the same. There is, thank God, one objective difference. You radiograph my bones, you'll find a crazy-quilt pattern of old breaks, except for the synthetics in my legs. His bones have none. Or so he says." Miles cradled his throbbing left hand. "I think I'll leave the beard on for the moment, just in case."

Miles turned to Captain Galeni. "How shall we—Imperial Security—handle this, sir?" he said deferentially. "Do we really want to call in the local authorities?"

"Oh, so I'm 'sir' again, am I?" muttered Galeni. "Of course we want the police. We can't extradite these people. But now that they're guilty of a crime right here on Earth, the Eurolaw authorities will hold them for us. It'll break up this whole radical splinter group."

Miles tamped down his personal urgency, trying to make his voice cool and logical. "But a public trial would bring out the whole clone story. In all its details. It would attract a lot of undesirable attention to me, from a security viewpoint. Including, you may be sure, Cetagandan attention."

"It's too late to put a lid on this."

"I'm not so sure. Yes, rumors will float, but a few sufficiently confused rumors might actually be useful. Those two," Miles gestured to the captured guards, "are small fry. My clone knows more than they do, and he's already back at the embassy. Which is, legally, Barrayaran soil. What do we need them for? Now that we have you back, and have the clone, the plot is void. Put this group under surveillance like the rest of the Komarran expatriates here on Earth, and they're no further danger to us."

Galeni met his eyes, then looked away, pale profile tense with the unspoken corollary: *and your career will be uncompromised by a splashy public scandal. And you won't have to confront your father.* "I . . . don't know."

"I do," said Miles confidently. He gestured a waiting Dendarii over. "Sergeant. Take a couple of techs upstairs and suck out these people's comconsole files. Take a fast scan around for secret files. And while you're about it, search the house for a couple of anti-personnel-scan devices on belts, should be stored somewhere. Take them to Commodore Jesek and tell him I want him to find the manufacturer. As soon as you call the all-clear, we decamp."

"Now, that *is* illegal," Elli remarked.

"What are they going to do, go to the police and complain? I think not. Ah—you want to leave any messages on the comconsole, Captain?"

"No," said Galeni softly after a moment. "No messages."

"Right."

A Dendarii rendered first aid to Miles's broken finger and numbed his hand. The sergeant was back down in less than half an hour, anti-scan belts hung over his shoulder, and flipped a data disc at Miles. "You got it, sir."

"Thank you."

Galen had not yet returned. All things considered, Miles counted that as a plus.

Miles knelt by the still-conscious Komarran and held a stunner to his temple.

"What are you going to do?" croaked the man.

Miles's lips peeled back in a grin, cracking to bleed. "Why— stun you, of course, fly you out over the south coast, and drop you in. What else? Nighty-night." The stunner buzzed, and the struggling Komarran jerked and slumped. The Dendarii soldier retrieved his restraints, and Miles left the two Komarrans lying side by side on the garage floor. They let themselves out and keyed the garage doors closed carefully.

"Back to the embassy, then, and nail the little bastard," said Elli Quinn grimly, calling up the route to their destination from her rented car's console. The rest of the patrol withdrew to covert observation positions.

Miles and Galeni settled back. Galeni looked as exhausted as Miles felt.

"Bastard?" sighed Miles. "No. That's the one thing he is not, I'm afraid."

"Nail him first," Galeni murmured. "Define him later."

"Agreed," said Miles.

"How shall we go in?" asked Galeni as they approached the embassy in the late-morning light.

"Only one way," said Miles. "Through the front door. Marching. Pull up at the front, Elli."

Miles and Galeni looked at each other and snickered. Miles's beard was well behind Galeni's in development—Galeni's after all had a four-day head start—but his split lips, bruises, and the dried blood on his shirt made up for it, Miles figured, in augmenting his general air of seedy degradation. Besides, Galeni had found his boots and uniform jacket back at the Komarrans' house, and Miles had not. Carried off by the clone, perhaps. Miles was not sure which of them smelled worse—Galeni had been incarcerated longer, but Miles fancied he'd sweated harder—and he wasn't going to ask Elli Quinn to sniff and rate them. From Galeni's twitching lips and crinkling eyes Miles thought he might be undergoing the same delayed reaction of lunatic relief that was presently bubbling up through his own chest. They were alive, and it was a miracle and a wonderment.

They matched steps, going up the ramp. Elli sauntered behind, watching the performance with interest.

The guard at the entrance saluted by reflex even as astonishment spread over his face. "Captain Galeni! You're back! And, er. . ." he glanced at Miles, opened and closed his mouth, "you. Sir."

Galeni returned the salute blandly. "Call Lieutenant Vorpatril up here for me, will you? Vorpatril only."

"Yes, sir." The embassy guard spoke into his wrist comm, not taking his eyes off them; he kept looking sideways at Miles with a very puzzled expression. "Er—glad to have you back, Captain."

"Glad to be back, Corporal."

In a moment, Ivan popped out of a lift tube and came running across the marble-paved foyer.

"My God, sir, where have you been?" he cried, grabbing Galeni by the shoulders. He remembered himself belatedly, and saluted.

"My absence wasn't voluntary, I assure you." Galeni tugged on one earlobe, blinking, and ran the hand through his beard stubble, clearly a little touched by Ivan's enthusiasm. "As I shall explain in detail, later. Right now—Lieutenant Vorkosigan? It is perhaps time to surprise your, er, other relative."

Ivan glanced at Miles. "They let you out, then?" He looked more closely, then stared. "Miles . . ."

Miles bared his teeth and moved them out of earshot of the mesmerized corporal. "All shall be revealed when we arrest the other me. Where am I, by the way?"

Ivan's lips wrinkled in dawning dismay. "Miles . . . are you trying to diddle my head? It's not very funny. . . ."

"No diddle. And not funny. The individual you've been rooming with for the last four days—wasn't me. I've been rooming with Captain Galeni, here. A Komarran revolutionary group tried to plant a ringer on you, Ivan. The sucker is my clone, for real. Don't tell me you never noticed anything!"

"Well . . ." said Ivan. Belief, and growing embarrassment, began to suffuse his features. "You did seem sort of, um, off your feed, the last couple of days."

Elli nodded thoughtfully, highly sympathetic to Ivan's embarrassment.

"In what way?" asked Miles.

"Well . . . I've seen you manic. And I've seen you depressive. But I've never seen you—well—*neutral.*"

"I had to ask. And yet you never suspected anything? He was that good?"

"Oh, I wondered about it the very first night!"

"And what?" yelped Miles. He felt like tearing his hair.

"And I decided it couldn't be. After all, you'd made that clone story up yourself a few days ago."

"I shall now demonstrate my amazing prescience. Where is he?"

"Well, that's why I was so surprised to see you, see."

Galeni was now standing with his arms crossed and his hand to his forehead, supportingly; Miles could not read his lips, though they were moving slightly—counting to ten, perhaps. "Why, Ivan?" said Galeni, and waited.

"My God, he hasn't left for Barrayar already, has he?" said Miles urgently. "We've got to stop him—"

"No, no," said Ivan. "It was the locals. That's why we're all in such a flap, here."

"*Where is he?*" snarled Miles, going for a grip on Ivan's green uniform jacket with his good hand.

"Calm down, that's what I'm trying to tell you!" Ivan glanced down at Miles's white-knuckled fist. "Yeah, it's you all right, isn't it? The local police came through here a couple of hours ago and arrested you—him—whatever. Well, not arrested, exactly, but they had a detention order, forbidding you to leave this legal jurisdiction. You—he—was frantic 'cause it meant you'd miss your ship. You were shipping out tonight. They subpoenaed you for questioning, before the municipal bench's investigator, to ascertain if there was enough evidence to file formal charges."

"Charges for *what,* what are you babbling about, *Ivan!*"

"Well, that's it, why it's such a mess. Somewhere, they got this short circuit in their brains about embassies—they came and arrested you, Lieutenant Vorkosigan, for suspicion of conspiracy to commit murder. To wit, you are suspected of hiring those two goons who tried to assassinate Admiral Naismith at the shuttleport last week."

Miles stamped in a circle. "Ah. Ah. Agh!"

"The ambassador is filing protests all over the place. Naturally, we couldn't tell them why we thought they were mistaken."

Miles clutched Quinn's elbow. "Don't panic."

"I'm not panicking," Quinn observed, "I'm watching you panic. It's more entertaining."

Miles pressed his forehead. "Right. Right. Let us begin by assuming all is not lost. Let us assume the kid hasn't panicked—hasn't broken. Yet. Suppose he has climbed up on an aristocratic high horse and is sneering a lot of no-comments at them. He'd do that well, it's how he thinks Vor are supposed to act. Little schmuck. Assume he's holding out."

"Assume away," remarked Ivan. "So what?"

"If we hurry, we can save—"

"Your reputation?" said Ivan.

"Your . . . brother?" ventured Galeni.

"Our asses?" said Elli.

"Admiral Naismith," Miles finished. "He's the one at risk, now." Miles's gaze crossed Elli's; her eyebrows arched in dawning worry. "The key word is *cover,* as in *blown*—or, just possibly, permanently assured.

"You and I," he nodded to Galeni, "have to get cleaned up. Meet me back here in fifteen minutes. Ivan, bring a sandwich. Two sandwiches. We'll take you along for muscle." Ivan was well endowed in that resource. "Elli, you drive."

"Drive where?" asked Quinn.

"The Assizes. We go to the rescue of poor, misunderstood Lieutenant Vorkosigan. Who will return with us gratefully, whether he wants to or not. Ivan, better bring a hypospray with two cc's of tholizone, in addition to those sandwiches."

"Hold it, Miles," said Ivan. "If the ambassador couldn't get him sprung, how do you expect us to?"

Miles grinned. "Not us. Admiral Naismith."

The London Municipal Assizes was a big black crystal of a building some two centuries old. A slash of similar architecture erupted unevenly through a district of even older styles, representing the bombings and fires of the Fifth Civil Disturbance. Urban renewal here seemed to wait on disaster. London was so filled up, a cramped jigsaw of juxtaposed eras, with Londoners stubbornly hanging on to bits of their past; there was even a committee to save the singularly ugly disintegrating remnants of the late twentieth century. Miles wondered if Vorbarr Sultana, presently expanding madly, would look like this in a thousand years, or whether it would obliterate its history in the rush to modernize.

Miles paused in the Assizes's soaring foyer to adjust his Dendarii admiral's uniform. "Do I look respectable?" he asked Quinn.

"The beard makes you look, um . . ."

Miles had hastily trimmed the edges. "Distinguished? Older?"

"Hung over."

"Ha."

The four of them took the lift tube to the ninety-seventh level.

"Chamber W," the reception panel directed them after accessing its files. "Cubicle 19."

Cubicle 19 proved to contain a secured Euronet JusticeComp terminal and a live human being, a serious young man.

"Ah, Investigator Reed." Elli smiled winningly at him as they entered. "We meet again."

The briefest glance showed Investigator Reed to be alone. Miles cleared a twinge of panic from his throat.

"Investigator Reed is in charge of looking into that unpleasant incident at the shuttleport, sir," Elli explained, mistaking his choke for a request for an introduction and slipping back into professional mode. "Investigator Reed, Admiral Naismith. We had a long talk on my last trip here."

"I see," said Miles. He kept his face blandly polite.

Reed was frankly staring at him. "Uncanny. So you really are Vorkosigan's clone!"

"I prefer to think of him as my twin brother," Miles flung off, "once removed. We generally prefer to stay as far removed from each other as possible. So you've spoken to him."

"At some length. I did not find him very cooperative." Reed glanced back and forth uncertainly from Miles and Elli to the two uniformed Barrayarans. "Obstructive. Indeed, rather unpleasant."

"So I would imagine. You were treading on his toes. He's quite sensitive about me. Prefers not to be reminded of my embarrassing existence."

"Ah? Why?"

"Sibling rivalry," Miles extemporized. "I've gotten farther in my military career than he has in his. He takes it as a reproach, a slur on his own perfectly reasonable achievements." *God, somebody, give me another straight line*—Reed's stare was becoming piercing.

"To the point, please, Admiral Naismith," Captain Galeni rumbled.

Thank you. "Quite. Investigator Reed—I do not pretend that Vorkosigan and I are friends, but how did you come by this curious misapprehension that he tried to arrange my rather messy death?"

"Your case has not been easy. The two would-be killers," Reed glanced at Elli, "were a dead end. So we went to other leads."

"Not Lise Vallerie, was it? I'm afraid I've been guilty of leading her slightly astray. An untimely sense of humor, I fear. It's an affliction . . ."

" . . . we all must bear," murmured Elli.

"I found Vallerie's suggestions interesting, not conclusive," said Reed. "In the past I've found her to be a careful investigator in her own right, unimpeded by certain rules of order that hamper, say, me. And most helpful in passing on items of interest."

"What's she investigating these days?" inquired Miles.

Reed gave him a bland look. "Illegal cloning. Perhaps you might give her some tips."

"Ah—I fear my experiences are some two decades out of date for your purposes."

"Well, that's neither here nor there. In this case the lead was quite objective. An aircar was seen leaving the shuttleport at the time of the attack, passing illegally through a traffic control space. We traced it to the Barrayaran embassy."

Sergeant Barth. Galeni looked as if he wanted to spit; Ivan was acquiring that pleasant, slightly moronic expression he'd found so useful in the past for evading any accusation of responsibility.

"Oh, that," said Miles airily. "That was merely Barrayar's usual tedious surveillance of me. Frankly, the embassy I would suspect of having a hand in this is the Cetagandan. Recent Dendarii operations in their area of influence—far outside your jurisdiction—displeased them exceedingly. But it was not a charge in my power to prove, which was why I was content to leave it to your people."

"Ah, the remarkable rescue at Dagoola. I'd heard of it. A compelling motive."

"More compelling, I would suggest, than the ancient history I confided to Lise Vallerie. Does that straighten out the contratemps?"

"And are you getting something in return for this charitable service to the Barrayaran embassy, Admiral?"

"My good deed for the day? No, you're right, I warned you about my sense of humor. Let's just say, my reward is sufficient."

"Nothing that could be construed as an obstruction of justice, I trust?" Reed's eyebrows rose dryly.

"I'm the *victim,* remember?" Miles bit his tongue. "My reward has nothing to do with London's criminal code, I assure you. In the meantime, can I ask you to return poor Lieutenant Vorkosigan to the custody, say, of his commanding officer, Captain Galeni, here?"

Reed's face was a study in suspicion, his alertness multiplied. *What's wrong, dammit?* wondered Miles. *This is supposed to be lulling him. . . .*

Reed steepled his hands, leaned back, and cocked his head. "Lieutenant Vorkosigan left with a man who introduced himself as Captain Galeni an hour ago."

"Aaah . . ." said Miles. "An older man in civilian dress? Graying hair, heavyset?"

"Yes . . ."

Miles inhaled, smiling fixedly. "Thank you, Investigator Reed. We won't take any more of your valuable time."

Back in the foyer Ivan said, "Now what?"

"I think," said Captain Galeni, "it is time to return to the embassy. And send a full report to HQ."

The urge to confess, eh? "No, no, never send interim reports," said Miles. "Only final ones. Interim reports tend to elicit orders. Which you must then either obey, or spend valuable time and energy evading, which you could be using to solve the problem."

"An interesting command philosophy; I must keep it in mind. Do you share it, Commander Quinn?"

"Oh, yes."

"The Dendarii Mercenaries must be a *fascinating* outfit to work for."

Quinn smirked. "I find it so."

CHAPTER TWELVE

They returned to the embassy nonetheless, Galeni to galvanize his staff into an all-out investigation of the now highly-suspect courier officer, Miles to change back into his Barrayaran dress greens and visit the embassy physician to have his hand properly set. If there was a lull in his life after this mess was cleared up, Miles reflected, perhaps he'd better take the time to go get the bones and joints in his arms and hands, not just the long bones of his legs, replaced with synthetics. Getting the legs done had been painful and tedious, but putting off the arms wasn't going to make it any better. And he certainly couldn't pretend he was going to do any more growing.

Somewhat morose with these thoughts, he left the embassy clinic and wandered down to Security's office sub-level. He found Galeni sitting alone at his comconsole desk, having generated a flurry of orders that dispatched subordinates in all directions. The lights in the office were dimmed. Galeni was leaning back with his feet on the desk, crossed at the ankles, and Miles had the impression that he would have preferred a bottle of something potently alcoholic in his hand to the light pen he now turned over and over.

Galeni smiled bleakly, sat up, and took to tapping the pen on the desk as Miles entered. "I've been thinking it over, Vorkosigan. I'm afraid we may not be able to avoid calling in the local authorities in this."

"I wish you wouldn't do that, sir." Miles pulled up a chair and sat astride it, arms athwart its back. "Involve them, and the consequences pass beyond our control."

"It will take a small army to find those two on Earth now."

"I have a small army," Miles reminded him, "which had just demonstrated its effectiveness for this sort of thing, I think."

"Ha. True."

"Let the embassy hire the Dendarii Mercenaries to find our . . . missing persons."

"Hire? I thought Barrayar was already paying for them!"

Miles blinked innocently. "But sir, it's part of their covert status that that relationship is unknown even to the Dendarii themselves. If the embassy hires them in a formal contract for this job, it—covers the cover, so to speak."

Galeni raised his brows sardonically. "I see. And how do you propose to explain your clone to them?"

"If necessary, as a clone—of Admiral Naismith."

"Three of you, now?" said Galeni dubiously.

"Just set them to find your—find Ser Galen. Where he is, the clone will be too. It worked once."

"Hm," said Galeni.

"There's just one thing," Miles added. He ran one finger thoughtfully along the top of the chair back. "If we do succeed in catching them—just what is it that we plan to do with 'em?"

The light pen tapped. "There are," said Galeni, "only two or three possibilities. One, they can be arrested, tried, and incarcerated for the crimes committed here on Earth."

"During the course of which," Miles observed seriously, "Admiral Naismith's cover as a supposedly independent operator will almost certainly be compromised, his true identity publicly revealed. I can't pretend the Barrayaran Empire will stand or fall on the Dendarii Mercenaries, but Security has found us useful in the past. Command may—I hope may—regard this as a poor trade. Besides, has my clone in fact committed any crimes he can be held for? I think he may even be a minor, by Eurolaw rules."

"Second alternative," Galeni recited. "Kidnap them and returned them secretly to Barrayar for trial, evading Earth's non-extradition status. If we had an order from on high, my guess is this would be it, the minimum proper paranoid Security response."

"For trial," said Miles, "or to be held indefinitely in some oubliette . . . For my—brother, that might not turn out as bad as he'd at first think. He has a friend in a very high place. If he can escape being secretly murdered by some—overexcited underling first, en route." Galeni and Miles exchanged glances. "But nobody's going to intercede for your father. Barrayar has always taken the killings in the Komarr Revolt to be civil crimes, not acts of war, and he never submitted to the loyalty oath and amnesty. He'll be up on capital charges. His execution will inevitably follow."

"Inevitably." Galeni pursed his lips, staring down at the toes of his boots. "The third possibility being—as you said—an order coming down for their secret assassination."

"Criminal orders can be successfully resisted," Miles observed, "if you have a strong enough stomach for it. High command isn't as free with that sort of thing as they were back in Emperor Ezar's day, fortunately. I submit a fourth possibility. It might be better not to catch these—awkward relatives—in the first place."

"Bluntly, Miles, if I fail to produce Ser Galen, my career will be smoke. I must already be suspect, for having failed to turn him up any time these last two years. Your suggestion skirts—not insubordination, that seems to be your normal mode of operation—but something worse."

"What about your predecessor here, who failed to discover him in five years? And if you do produce him now, will your career be any better off? You'll be suspect anyway, in the minds of those who are determined to be suspicious."

"I wish," Galeni's face had an inward look, deathly calm, his voice a reflective murmur, "I wish he had stayed dead in the first place. His first death was a much better one, glorious in the heat of battle. He had his place in history, and I was alone, past pain, without mother or father to torment me. How fortunate that science hasn't cracked human immortality. It's a great blessing that we can outlive old wars. And old warriors."

Miles mulled over the dilemma. In jail on Earth, Galen destroyed both Galeni's career and Admiral Naismith's, but lived. Shipped to Barrayar, he died; Galeni's career would be a little better off, but Galeni himself—would not be quite sane, Miles rather thought. The patricide would not have the rooted serenity to serve Komarr's complex future needs, certainly. *But Naismith would live,* his thought whispered temptingly. Left loose, the persistent Galen and Mark remained a threat of unknown, and so intolerable, proportion; if Miles and Galeni did nothing, high command would most certainly take the choice from them, issuing who-knew-what orders sealing the fate of their perceived enemies.

Miles loathed the thought of sacrificing Galeni's promising career to this crabbed old revolutionary who refused to give up. Yet Galen's destruction would also damage Galeni, just as certainly. Dammit, why couldn't the old man have pensioned himself off to some tropical paradise, instead of hanging around making trouble for the younger generation on the grounds, no doubt, that it was good for 'em? Mandatory retirement for revolutionaries, that's what they needed now.

What do you choose when all choices are bad?

"This choice is mine," said Galeni. "We have to go after them."

They stared at each other, both very tired.

"Compromise," suggested Miles. "Send the Dendarii Mercenaries out to locate, track, and monitor them. Don't attempt to pick them up yet. This will permit you to put all the embassy's resources to work on the problem of the courier, a purely Barrayaran-internal matter on any scale."

There was a silence. "Agreed," Galeni said at last. "But whatever finally happens—I want to get it over with quickly."

"Agreed," said Miles.

Miles found Elli sitting alone in the embassy cafeteria, leaning tired and a little blank over the remains of her dinner, ignoring the covert stares and hesitant smiles of various embassy personnel. He grabbed a snack and tea and slid into the seat across from her. Their hands gripped briefly across the table, then she rested her chin on her cupped palms again, elbows propped.

"So, what's next?" she asked.

"What's the traditional reward for a job well done in this man's army?"

Her dark eyes crinkled. "Another job."

"You got it. I've persuaded Captain Galeni to let the Dendarii Mercenaries find Galen, just as you found us. How did you find us, by the way?"

"Lotta damn work, that's how. We started by crunching through that awful pile of data you beamed up from the embassy files about Komarrans. We eliminated the well-documented ones, the young children, and so on. Then we put the Intelligence computer team downside to break into the economic net and pull out credit files, and into the Eurolaw net—*that* was tricky—and pull out criminal files, and started looking for anomalies. That's where we found the break. About a year ago, the Earth-born son of a Komarran expatriate was picked up by the Eurolaw cops on some minor misdemeanor and found to have an unregistered stunner in his possession. Not being a deadly weapon, it merely cost him a fine, and as far as Eurolaw was concerned, that was that. But the stunner wasn't of Earth manufacture. It was old Barrayaran military issue.

"We began following him, both physically and through the computer net, finding out who his friends were, people who weren't in the embassy's computer. We were following up several other leads at the same time that failed to pan out. But this is where I got a compelling hunch. One of this kid's frequent contacts, a man named Van der Poole, was registered as an immigrant to Earth from the planet Frost IV. Now, during that investigation I did a couple of years back involving the stolen genes, I passed through Jackson's Whole—"

Miles nodded in memory.

"So I knew you could buy documented pasts there—one of the little high-profit-margin services certain laboratories sell to go along with the new faces and voices and finger- and retina-prints they offer. One of the planets they frequently use for this is Frost IV, on account of the tectonic disaster having wrecked their computer net—not to mention the rest of the place—twenty-eight years ago. A lot of perfectly legitimate people who left Frost IV then have uncheckable documentation. If you're over twenty-eight years old, Jackson's Whole can fit you right in. So whenever I see somebody above a certain age who claims to be from Frost IV, I'm automatically suspicious. Van der Poole was Galen, of course."

"Of course. My clone was another fine product of Jackson's Whole, by the way."

"Ah. It all fits, how nice."

"My congratulations to you and the whole Intelligence department. Remind me to make that an official commendation, when I next make it back to the *Triumph.*"

"Which is when?" She crunched a piece of ice from the bottom of her glass and swirled the remainder around, trying to look only professionally interested.

Her mouth would taste cool, and tangy. . . . Miles blinked back into professional mode himself, conscious of the curious eyes of embassy personnel upon them. "Dunno. We're sure not done here yet. We should certainly transfer all the new data the Dendarii collected back to embassy files. Ivan's working now on what we pulled from Galen's comconsole. It's going to be harder this time. Galen—Van der Poole—will be hiding. And he's had a lot of experience at serious disappearing. But if and when you do turn him up—ah—report directly to me. I'll report to the embassy."

"Report what to the embassy?" Elli inquired, alert to his undertones.

Miles shook his head. "I'm not sure yet. I may be too tired to think straight. I'll see if it seems to make any more sense in the morning."

Elli nodded and rose.

"Where are you going?" asked Miles in alarm.

"Back to the *Triumph*, to put the mass in motion, of course."

"But you can tight-beam— Who's on duty up there right now?"

"Bel Thorne."

"Right, all right. Let's go find Ivan, we can tight-beam the data swap right from here, and the orders as well." He studied the dark circles under her luminous eyes. "And how long have you been on your feet, anyway?"

"Oh, about the last, um," she glanced at her chrono, "thirty hours."

"Who has trouble delegating work, Commander Quinn? Send the orders, not yourself. And take a sleep shift before you start making mistakes too. I'll find you a place to bunk here at the embassy—" she met his eyes, suddenly grinning, "if you like," Miles added hastily.

"Will you, now?" she said softly. "I'd like that fine."

They paid a visit to Ivan, harried at his comconsole, and made the secured data link to the *Triumph*. Ivan, Miles noted happily, had lots and lots of work left to do. He escorted Elli up the lift tubes to his quarters.

Elli dove for the bathroom by right of first dibs. While hanging up his uniform Miles found his cat blanket bunged lumpily into a dark corner of his closet, doubtless where his terrified clone had thrown it his first night. The black fur broke into ecstatic rumbling when he picked it up. He spread it out carefully on his bed, patting it into place. "There."

Elli emerged from the shower in remarkably few minutes, fluffing her short wet curls out with her fingers, a towel slung attractively around her hips. She spotted the cat blanket, smiled, and hopped up and wriggled her bare toes in it. It shivered and purred louder.

"Ah," sighed Miles, contemplating them both in perfect contentment. Then doubt snaked through his garden of delight. Elli was looking around his room with interest. He swallowed. "Is this, ah, the first time you've been up here?" he asked in what he hoped was a casual tone.

"Uh-huh. I don't know why I was expecting something medieval.

Looks more like an ordinary hotel room than what I would have expected of Barrayar."

"This is Earth," Miles pointed out, "and the Time of Isolation has been over for a hundred years. You have some odd ideas about Barrayar. But I just wondered, if my clone had, uh . . . are you sure you never sensed any difference at *all* during the four days? He was that good?" He smiled wretchedly, hanging on her answer. What if she'd noticed nothing? Was he really so transparent and simple that anyone could play him? Worse, what if she had noticed a difference—and liked the clone better?

Elli looked embarrassed. "Noticed, yes. But to jump from sensing there was something wrong with you, to realizing it *wasn't* you . . . maybe if we'd had more time together. We only talked by comm link, except for one two-hour trip downtown to spring Danio and his merry men from the locals, during which I thought you'd lost your mind. Then I decided you must have something up your sleeve, and just weren't telling me 'cause I'd . . ." her voice went suddenly smaller, "fallen out of favor, somehow."

Miles calculated, and breathed relief. So the clone hadn't had time to . . . ahem. He smiled wryly up at her.

"You see, when you look at me," she went on to explain, "it makes me feel—well—good. Not in the warm and fuzzy sense, though there's that too—"

"Warm and fuzzy," sighed Miles happily, leaning on her.

"Stop it, you goof, I'm serious." But she slipped her arms around him. Firmly, as if prepared to do immediate battle with any wight who might attempt to snatch him away again. "Good, like—I can do. Competent. You make me un-afraid. Unafraid to try, unafraid of what others might think. Your—clone, good gods what a relief to know that—made me start wondering what was wrong with me. Though when I think how easily they took you, that night in the empty house, I could—"

"Sh, sh," Miles stopped her lips with one finger. "There is nothing wrong with you, Elli," he said, pleasantly muffled. "You are most perfectly Quinn." *His* Quinn . . .

"See what I mean? I suppose it saved your life. I'd been meaning to keep you—him—up to date on the hunt for Galeni, even it if was just an interim no-progress report. Which would have been *his* first tip-off that there was a hunt going on."

"Which he would have ordered stopped."

"Precisely. But then, when the break in the case came, I—thought I'd better be sure. Save it up, surprise you with the final result all wrapped up in a big bow—win back your regard, to be frank. In a way, he kept me from reporting to him."

"If it's any consolation, it wasn't dislike. You terrified him. Your face—not to mention the rest of you—has that effect on some men."

"Yes, the face . . ." Her hand touched one cheek, half-consciously, then fell more tenderly to ruffle his hair. "I think you've put your finger on it, what felt so wrong. You knew me when I had my old face, and *no* face, and the new face, and for you alone, it was all the same face."

His unbandaged hand traced over the arch of her brows, perfect nose, paused at her lips to collect a kiss, then down the ideal angle of her chin and velvet skin of her throat. "Yes, the face . . . I was young and dumb then. It seemed like a good idea at the time. It was only later that I realized it could be a handicap for you."

"Me, too," sighed Elli. "For the first six months, I was delighted. But the second time a soldier made a pass at me instead of following an order, I knew I definitely had a problem. I had to discover and teach myself all kinds of tricks to get people to respond to the inside of me, and not the outside."

"I understand," said Miles.

"By the gods, you would." She looked at him for a moment as if seeing him for the very first time, then dropped a kiss on his forehead. "I just now realized how many of those tricks I learned from you. How I love you!"

When they came up for air from the kiss that followed, Elli offered, "Rub you?"

"You're a drunkard's dream, Quinn." Miles flopped down with his face in the fur and let her have her way with him. Five minutes at her strong hands parted him from all ambitions but two. Those satisfied, they both slept like stones, untroubled by any vile dream that Miles could later remember.

Miles woke muzzily to the sound of knocking at the door.

"Go 'way, Ivan," Miles moaned into the flesh and fur he clutched. "Go sleep on a bench somewhere, hunh . . . ?"

The flesh shook him loose decisively. Elli hit the light, swung out of bed, slipping into her black tee-shirt and gray uniform trousers, and padded to the door, ignoring Miles's mumbled "No, no, doan' let 'im in . . ." The knocking grew louder and more insistent.

"Miles!" Ivan fell through the door. "Oh, hi, Elli. Miles!" Ivan shook him by the shoulder.

Miles tried to burrow underneath his fur. "All right, y'can have your bed," he muttered. "Y'don't need me to tuck you in . . ."

"Get *up*, Miles!"

Miles stuck his head out, eyes scrunched against the light. "Why? What time is it?"

"About midnight."

"Ergh." He went back under. Three hours of sleep hardly counted, after what he'd been through the last four days. Displaying a cruel and ruthless streak Miles would never have suspected, Ivan pulled the live fur from his twitching hands and tossed it aside.

"You have to get up," Ivan insisted. "Dressed. Peel off the face fungus. I hope you've got a clean uniform in here somewhere—" Ivan was rooting through his closet. "Here!"

Miles clutched numbly at the green cloth Ivan flung at him. "Embassy on fire?" he inquired.

"Damn near. Elena Bothari-Jesek just blew in from Tau Ceti. I didn't even know you'd sent her!"

"Oh!" Miles came awake. Quinn was by now fully dressed, including boots, and checking her stunner in its holster. "Yes. Gotta get dressed, sure. She won't mind the beard, though."

"Not being subject to beard burn," Elli muttered under her breath, scratching a thigh absently. Miles suppressed a grin; one of her eyelids shivered at him.

"Maybe not," said Ivan grimly, "but I don't think Commodore Destang will be too thrilled by it."

"Destang's *here?*" Miles came fully awake. He still had a little adrenaline left, apparently. "Why?" Then he thought back over some of the suspicions he'd included in his report sent with Elena, and realized why the Sector Two Security chief might have been inspired to investigate in person. "Oh, God . . . gotta get him straightened out before he shoots poor Galeni on sight—"

He ran the shower on cold, needle-spray; Elli shoved a cup of coffee into his working hand as he exited, and inspected the effect when he was dressed.

"Everything's fine but the face," she informed him, "and you can't do anything about that."

He ran a hand over his now-naked chin. "Did I miss a patch with the depilator?"

"No, I was admiring the bruises. And the eyes. I've seen brighter eyes on a strung-out juba freak three days after the supplies ran out."

"Thanks."

"You asked."

Miles considered what he knew of Destang, as they descended the lift tubes. His previous contacts with the commodore had been brief, official, and as far as Miles knew, satisfactory to both sides. The Sector Two Security commander was an experienced officer, accustomed to carrying out his varied duties—coordinating intelligence-gathering, overseeing the security of Barrayaran embassies, consulates, and visiting VIP's, rescuing the occasional Barrayaran subject in trouble—with little direct supervision from distant Barrayar. During the two or three operations the Dendarii had conducted in Sector Two areas, orders and money had flowed down, and Miles's final reports back up, through his command without impediment.

Commodore Destang was seated centrally in Galeni's office chair at Galeni's lit-up comconsole as Miles, Ivan, and Elli entered. Captain Galeni was standing, though extra chairs were available by the wall; his stiff posture worn like armor, his eyes hooded and face blank as a visor. Elena Bothari-Jesek hovered uncertainly in the background, with the worried look of one witnessing a chain of events they had started but no longer controlled. Her eyes lit with relief as she saw Miles, and she saluted—improperly, as he was not in Dendarii uniform; it was more an unstated transfer of responsibility, like someone ridding herself of a bag of live snakes, *Here, this one's all yours. . . .* He returned her a nod, *All right.*

"Sir." Miles saluted.

Destang returned the salute and glowered at him, reminding Miles in a faint twinge of nostalgia of the early Galeni. Another harried commander. Destang was a man of about sixty, lean, with gray hair, shorter than what was middle height for a Barrayaran. Doubtless born just after the end of the Cetagandan occupation, when widespread malnutrition had robbed many of their full growth potential. He would have been a young officer at the time of the Conquest of Komarr, of middle rank during its later Revolt; combat-experienced, like all who had lived through that war-torn past.

"Has anyone brought you up to date yet, sir?" Miles began anxiously. "My original memo is extremely obsolete."

"I've just read Captain Galeni's version." Destang nodded at the comconsole.

Galeni *would* insist on writing reports. Miles sighed inwardly. It was an old academic reflex, no doubt. He restrained himself from craning his neck to try to see.

"You don't seem to have made one yet," Destang noted.

Miles waved his bandaged left hand vaguely. "I've been in the infirmary, sir. But have you realized yet the Komarrans must have had control of the embassy's courier officer?"

"We arrested the courier six days ago on Tau Ceti," Destang said.

Miles exhaled in relief. "And was he—?"

"It was the usual sordid story." Destang frowned. "He committed a little sin; it gave them leverage to extract larger and larger ones, until there was no going back."

A curious mental judo, that sort of blackmail, reflected Miles. In the final analysis, it was fear of his own side, not fear of the Komarrans, that had delivered the courier into the enemy's hands. So a system meant to enforce loyalty ended by destroying it—some flaw, there . . .

"He's been owned by them for at least three years," continued Destang. "Anything that's gone in or out of the embassy since then may have passed before their eyes."

"Ouch." Miles suppressed a grin, substituting, he hoped, an expression of proper horror. So the subversion of the courier clearly predated the arrival of Galeni on Earth. Good.

"Yeah," said Ivan, "I just found copies of some of our stuff a little while ago in that mass data dump you pulled from Ser Galen's comconsole, Miles. It was quite a shock."

"I thought it might be there," said Miles. "There weren't too many other possibilities, once I realized we were being diddled. I trust the interrogation of the courier has cleared Captain Galeni of all suspicion?"

"If he was involved with the Komarran expatriates on Earth," said Destang neutrally, "the courier didn't know of it."

Not exactly an affirmation of heartfelt trust, that. "It was quite clear," Miles said, "that the captain was a card Ser Galen thought he was holding in reserve. But the card refused to play. At the risk of his life. It was chance, after all, that assigned Captain Galeni to Earth—" Galeni was shaking his head, lips compressed, "wasn't it?"

"No," said Galeni, still at parade rest. "I requested Earth."

"Oh. Well, it was certainly chance that brought me here," Miles scrambled over the gap, "chance and my wounded and cryo-corpses who needed the attention of a major medical center as soon as possible. Speaking of the Dendarii Mercenaries, Commodore, did the courier divert the eighteen million marks Barrayar owes them?"

"It was never sent," said Destang. "Until Captain Bothari-Jesek here arrived at my office, our last contact with your mercenaries was the report you sent from Mahata Solaris wrapping up the Dagoola affair. Then you vanished. From the viewpoint of Sector Two Headquarters, you've been missing for over two months. To our consternation. Particularly when the weekly requests for updates on your status from Imperial Security Chief Illyan turned into daily ones."

"I—see, sir. Then you never received our urgent requests for funds? Then I was never actually assigned to the embassy!"

A very small noise, as of deep and muffled pain, escaped the otherwise deadpan Galeni.

Destang said, "Only by the Komarrans. Apparently it was a ploy to keep you immobilized until they could make their attempted switch."

"I'd guessed as much. Ah—you wouldn't by chance happen to have brought my eighteen million marks with you now, have you? That part hasn't changed. I did mention it in my memo."

"Several times," said Destang dryly. "Yes, Lieutenant, we will fund your irregulars. As usual."

"Ah." Miles melted within, and smiled blindingly. "Thank you, sir. That is a very great relief."

Destang cocked his head curiously. "What have they been living on, the past month?"

"It's—been a bit complicated, sir."

Destang opened his mouth as if to ask more, then apparently thought better of it. "I see. Well, Lieutenant, you may return to your outfit. Your part here is done. You should never have appeared on Earth as Lord Vorkosigan in the first place."

"To which outfit—to the Dendarii Mercenaries, you mean, sir?"

"I doubt Simon Illyan was sending out urgent inquiries for them because he was lonely. It's a safe assumption that new orders will be following on as soon as your location is known to HQ. You should be ready to move out."

Elli and Elena, who had been conferring in very low tones in the corner during all this, looked up brightly at this news; Ivan looked more stricken.

"Yes, sir," said Miles. "What's going to happen here?"

"Since you have not, thank God, involved the Earth authorities, we're free to clear up this aborted bit of treason ourselves. I brought a team from Tau Ceti—"

The team was a cleanup crew, Miles guessed, Intelligence commandos ready, at Destang's order, to restore order to a treason-riddled embassy with whatever force or guile might be required.

"Ser Galen would have been on our most-wanted list long before this if we hadn't believed him already dead. Galen!" Destang shook his head as though he still couldn't believe it himself. "Here on Earth, all this time. You know, I served during the Komarr Revolt—it's where I got my start in Security. I was on the team that dug through the rubble of the Halomar Barracks, after the bastards blew it up in the middle of the night—looking for survivors and evidence, finding bodies and damned few clues... There were a lot of new openings for posts in Security that morning. Damn. How it all comes back. If we can find Galen again, after you let him slip through your hands," Destang's eyes fell without favor on Galeni, "accidentally or otherwise, we'll take him back to Barrayar to answer for that bloody morning if nothing else. I wish he could be made to answer for it all, but there's not enough of him to go around. Rather like Mad Emperor Yuri."

"A laudable plan, sir," said Miles carefully. Galeni had his jaw clamped shut, no help there. "But there are a dozen Komarran ex-rebels on Earth with pasts just as bloody as Ser Galen's. Now that he's been exposed, he's no more threat to us than they are."

"They've been inactive for years," said Destang. "Galen, clearly, has been quite the reverse."

"But if you're contemplating an illegal kidnapping, it could damage our diplomatic relations with Earth. Is it worth it?"

"Permanent justice is well worth a temporary offended protest, I can assure you, Lieutenant."

Galen was dead meat to Destang. Well, and so. "On what grounds would you kidnap my—clone, then, sir? He's never committed a crime on Barrayar. He's never even been to Barrayar."

Shut up, Miles! Ivan, with a look of increasing alarm on his face, mouthed silently from behind Destang. *You don't argue with a commodore!* Miles ignored him.

"The fate of my clone concerns me closely, sir,"

"I can imagine. I hope we can eliminate the danger of further confusion between you soon."

Miles hoped that didn't mean what he thought it did. If he had to derail Destang... "There's no danger of confusion, sir. A simple medical scan can tell the difference between us. His bones are normal, mine are not. By what charge or claim do we have any further interest in him?"

"Treason, of course. Conspiracy against the Imperium."

The second part being demonstrably true, Miles concentrated on the first part. "Treason? He was born on Jackson's Whole. He's not an Imperial subject by conquest or place of birth. To charge him with treason," Miles took a breath, "you must allow him to be an Imperial subject by blood. And if he's that, he's that all the way, a lord of the Vor with all the rights of his rank including trial by his peers—the Council of Counts in full session."

Destang's brows rose. "Would he think to attempt such an outré defense?"

If he didn't, I'd point it out to him. "Why not?"

"Thank you, Lieutenant. That's a complication I had not considered." Destang looked thoughtful indeed, and increasingly steely.

Miles's plan to convince Destang that letting the clone go was his own idea seemed to be slipping dangerously retrograde. He had to know— "Do you see assassination as an option, sir?"

"A compelling one." Destang's spine straightened decisively.

"There could be a legal problem, here, sir. Either he's not an Imperial subject, and we have no claim on him in the first place, or he is, and the full protection of Imperial law should apply to him. In either case, his murder would—" Miles moistened his lips; Galeni, who alone knew where he was heading, shut his eyes like a man watching an accident about to happen, "be a criminal order. Sir."

Destang looked rather impatient. "I had not planned to give *you* the order, Lieutenant."

He thinks I want to keep my hands clean. . . . If Miles pushed the confrontation with Destang to its logical conclusion, with two Imperial officers witnessing, there was a chance the commodore would back down; there was at least an equal chance Miles would find himself in very deep—deepness. If the confrontation went all the way to a messy court-martial, neither of them would emerge undamaged. Even if Miles won, Barrayar would not be well served, and Destang's forty years of Imperial service did not deserve such an ignoble end. And if he got himself confined to quarters now, all alternate courses of action (and what was he contemplating, for God's sake?) would be closed to him. He did not want to be locked up in another room. Meanwhile, Destang's team would carry out any order he gave them without hesitation. . . .

He bared his teeth in a smile, of sorts, and said only, "Thank you, sir." Ivan looked relieved.

Destang paused. "Legality is an unusual concern for a covert operations specialist, at this late date, isn't it?"

"We all have our illogical moments."

Quinn's attention was now riveted upon him; a slight twitch of her eyebrow asked, *What the hell . . . ?*

"Try not to have too many of them, Lieutenant Vorkosigan," said Destang dryly. "My aide has the nontraceable credit chit for your eighteen million marks. See him on your way out. Take all these women with you." He waved at the two uniformed Dendarii.

Ivan, reminded, smiled at them. *They're my officers, dammit, not my harem,* Miles's thought snarled silently. But no Barrayaran officer of Destang's age would see it that way. Some attitudes couldn't be changed; they just had to be outlived.

Destang's words were a clear dismissal. Miles ignored them at his peril. Yet Destang had not mentioned—

"Yes, Lieutenant, run along." Captain Galeni's voice was utmost-bland. "I never finished writing my report. I'll give you one Mark, against the commodore's eighteen million, if you take the Dendarii off with you now."

Miles's eyes widened just slightly, hearing the capital M. *Galeni hasn't told Destang yet that the Dendarii are on the case. Therefore, he can't order them off, can he?* A head start—if he could find Galen and Mark before Destang's team did— "That's a bargain, Captain," Miles heard his own voice saying. "It's amazing, how much one Mark can weigh."

Galeni nodded once and turned back to Destang.

Miles fled.

CHAPTER THIRTEEN

Ivan trailed along as Miles returned to their quarters to change clothes for the last time back into the Dendarii admiral's uniform in which he'd arrived, a lifetime and a half ago.

"I don't think I really want to watch, downstairs," Ivan explained. "Destang's well launched into a bloody reaming. Bet he'll keep Galeni on his feet all night, trying to break him if he can."

"Damn it!" Miles bundled his green Barrayaran jacket into a wad and flung it against the far wall, but it didn't carry enough momentum to begin to vent his frustration. He flopped down on a bed, pulled off a boot, hefted it, then shook his head and dropped it in disgust. "It burns me. Galeni deserves a medal, not a load of grief. Well—if Ser Galen couldn't break him, I don't suppose Destang will either. But it's not right, not right . . ." He brooded. "And I helped set him up for it, too. Damn, damn, damn . . ."

Elli handed him his gray uniform without comment. Ivan was not so wise.

"Yeah, nice going, Miles. I'll think of you, safely up in orbit, while Destang's headquarters crew are cleaning house down here. Suspicious as hell—they wouldn't trust their own grandmothers. We're all in for it. Scrubbed, rinsed, and hung out to dry in the cold, cold wind." He wandered over to his own bed and regarded it with longing. "No use turning in; they'll be after me before morning for something." He sat down on it glumly.

Miles looked up at Ivan in sudden speculation. "Huh. Yeah, you are going to be rather in the middle of things for the next few days, aren't you?"

Ivan, alert to the change in his tone, eyed him suspiciously. "Too right. So what?"

Miles shook out his trousers. His half of the secured comm link fell onto the bed. He pulled on his Dendarii grays. "Suppose I remember to turn in my comm link before I leave. And suppose Elli forgets to turn in hers." Miles held up a restraining finger, and Elli stopped fishing in her jacket. "And suppose you stick it in your pocket, meaning to turn it back in to Sergeant Barth as soon as you get the other half." He tossed the comm link to Ivan, who caught it automatically, but then held it away from himself between thumb and forefingers as if it were something he'd found writhing under a rock.

"And suppose I remember what happened to me the last time I helped you sub-rosa?" said Ivan truculently. "That little sleight of hand I pulled to get you back in the embassy the night you tried to burn down London is on my record, now. Destang's bird-dogs will have spasms as soon as they turn that up, in light of the present circumstances. Suppose I stick it up your—" his eyes fell on Elli, "ear, instead?"

Miles thrust his head and arms up through his black tee-shirt and pulled it down, grinning slightly. He began stuffing his feet into his Dendarii-issue combat boots. "It's only a precaution. May never use it. Just in case I need a private line into the embassy in an emergency."

"I cannot imagine," said Ivan primly, "any emergency that a loyal junior officer can't confide to his very own sector security com-mander." His voice grew stern. "Neither would Destang. Just what are you hatching in the back of your twisty little mind, Coz?"

Miles sealed his boots and paused in seriousness. "I'm not sure. But I may yet see a chance to save . . . something, from this mess."

Elli, listening intently, remarked, "I thought we had saved some-thing. We uncovered a traitor, plugged a security leak, foiled a kidnapping, and broke up a major plot against the Barrayaran Imperium. And we got paid. What more do you want for one week?"

"Well, it would have been nice if any of that had been on purpose, instead of by accident," Miles mused.

Ivan and Elli looked at each other across the top of Miles's head, their faces beginning to mirror a similar unease. "What more do you want to save, Miles?" Ivan echoed.

Miles's frown, directed to his boots, deepened. "Something. A future. A second chance. A . . . possibility."

"It's the clone, isn't it?" said Ivan, his mouth hardening. "You've gone and let yourself get obsessed with that goddamn clone."

"Flesh of my flesh, Ivan." Miles turned his hands over, staring at them. "On some planets, he would be called my brother. On others he might even be called my son, depending on the laws regarding cloning."

"One cell! On Barrayar," said Ivan, "they call it your enemy when it's shooting at you. You having a little short-term memory trouble? Those people just tried to kill you! This—yesterday morning!"

Miles smiled briefly up at Ivan without replying.

"You know," Elli said cautiously, "if you decided you really wanted a clone, you could have one made. Without the, ah, problems of the present one. You have trillions of cells . . ."

"I don't want a clone," said Miles. *I want a brother.* "But I seem to have been . . . issued this one."

"I thought Ser Galen bought and paid for him," complained Elli. "The only thing that Komarran meant to issue you was death. By Jackson's Whole law, the planet of his origin, the clone clearly belongs to Galen."

Jockey of Norfolk, be not bold, the old quote whispered through Miles's memory, *for Dickon thy master is bought and sold. . . .* "Even on Barrayar," he said mildly, "no human being can own another. Galen descended far, in pursuit of his . . . principle of liberty."

"In any case," said Ivan, "you're out of the picture now. High command has taken over. I heard your marching orders."

"Did you also hear Destang say he meant to kill my—the clone, if he can?"

"Yeah, so?" Ivan was looking mulish indeed, an almost panicked stubbornness. "I didn't like him anyway. Surly little sneak."

"Destang has mastered the art of the final report too," said Miles. "Even if I went AWOL right now, it would be physically impossible for me to get back to Barrayar, beg the clone's life from my father, have him lean on Simon Illyan for a countermand, and get the order back here to Earth before the deed was done."

Ivan looked shocked. "Miles—I always figured to be embarrassed to ask Uncle Aral for a career favor, but I thought you'd let yourself be peeled and boiled before you'd cry to your Dad for anything! And you want to start by hopscotching a commodore? No C.O. in the service would want you after that!"

"I would rather die," agreed Miles tonelessly, "but I can't ask another to die for me. But it's irrelevant. It couldn't succeed."

"Thank God." Ivan stared at him, thoroughly unsettled.

If I cannot convince two of my best friends I'm right, thought Miles, *maybe I'm wrong.*

Or maybe I have to do this one alone.

"I just want to keep a line open, Ivan," he said. "I'm not asking you to do anything—"

"Yet," came Ivan's glum interpolation.

"I'd give the comm link to Captain Galeni, but he will certainly be closely watched. They'd just take it away from him, and it would look . . . ambiguous."

"So on me it looks good?" asked Ivan plaintively.

"Do it." Miles finished fastening his jacket, stood, and held out his hand to Ivan for the return of the comm link. "Or don't."

"Argh." Ivan broke off his gaze, and shoved the comm link disconsolately into his trouser pocket. "I'll think about it."

Miles tilted his head in thanks.

They caught a Dendarii shuttle just about to lift from the London shuttleport, returning personnel from leave. Actually, Elli called ahead and had it held for them; Miles rather relished the sensation of not having to rush for it, and might have outright sauntered if the pressures of Admiral Naismith's duties, now boiling up in his head, hadn't automatically quickened his steps.

Their delay was another's gain. A last duffel-swinging Dendarii sprinted across the tarmac as the engines revved and just made it up the retracting ramp. The alert guard at the door put up his weapon as he recognized the sprinter, and gave him a hand in as the shuttle began to roll.

Miles, Elli Quinn, and Elena Bothari-Jesek held seats in the rear. The running soldier, pausing to catch his breath, spotted Miles, grinned, and saluted.

Miles returned both. "Ah, Sergeant Siembieda." Ryann Siembieda was a conscientious tech sergeant from Engineering, in charge of maintenance and repair of battle armor and other light equipment. "You're thawed out."

"Yes, sir."

"They told me your prognosis was good."

"They threw me out of the hospital two weeks ago. I've been on leave. You too, sir?" Siembieda nodded toward the silver shopping bag at Miles's feet containing the live fur.

Miles shoved it unobtrusively under his seat with his boot heel. "Yes and no. Actually, while you were playing, I was working. As a result, we will all be working again soon. It's good you got your leave while you could."

"Earth was great," sighed Siembieda. "It was quite a surprise to wake up here. Did you see the Unicorn Park? It's right here on this island. I was there yesterday."

"I didn't see much, I'm afraid," said Miles in regret.

Siembieda dug a holocube out of his pocket and handed it over.

The Unicorn and Wild Animal Park (a division of GalacTech Bioengineering) occupied the grounds of the great and historical estate of Wooton, Surrey, the guide cube informed him. In the vid display, a shining white beast that looked like a cross between a horse and a deer, and probably was, bounded across the greensward into the topiary.

"They let you feed the tame lions," Siembieda informed him.

Miles blinked at an unbidden mental image of Ivan in a toga being tossed out the back of a float truck to a herd of hungry, tawny cats galloping excitedly along behind. He'd been reading too much Earth history. "What do they eat?"

"Protein cubes, same as us."

"Ah," said Miles, trying not to sound disappointed. He handed the cube back.

The sergeant hovered on, however. "Sir. . ." he began hesitantly.

"Yes?" Miles let his tone be encouraging.

"I've reviewed my procedures—been tested and cleared for light duties—but . . . I haven't been able to remember anything at all about the day I was killed. And the medics wouldn't tell me. It . . . bothers me a bit, sir."

Siembieda's hazel eyes were strange and wary; it bothered him a lot, Miles judged. "I see. Well, the medics couldn't tell you much anyway; they weren't there."

"But you were, sir," said Siembieda suggestively.

Of course, thought Miles. *And if I hadn't been, you wouldn't have died the death intended for me.* "Do you remember our arriving at Mahata Solaris?"

"Yes, sir. Some things, right up to the night before. But that whole day is gone, not just the fight."

"Ah. Well, there's no mystery. Commodore Jesek, myself, you, and your tech team paid a visit to a warehouse for a quality-control check of our resupplies—there'd been a problem with the first shipment—"

"I remember that." Siembieda nodded. "Cracked power cells leaking radiation."

"Right, very good. You spotted the defect, by the way, unloading them into inventory. There are those who might simply have stored them."

"Not on *my* team," muttered Siembieda.

"We were jumped by a Cetagandan hit squad at the warehouse. We never did find out if there was any collusion, though we suspected some in high places when our orbital permits were revoked and we were invited to leave Mahata Solaris local space by the authorities. Or maybe they just didn't like the excitement we'd brought with us. Anyway, a gravitic grenade went off and blew out the end of the warehouse. You were hit in the neck by a freak fragment of something metal, ricocheting from the explosion. You bled to death in seconds." Quite incredible quantities of blood from such a lean young man, once it was spread out and smeared around in the fight—the smell of it, and the burning, came back to Miles as he spoke, but he kept his voice calm and steady. "We had you back to the *Triumph* and iced down in an hour. The surgeon was very optimistic, as you didn't have gross tissue damage." Not like one of the techs, who'd been blown most grossly to bits in that same moment.

"I'd . . . wondered what I'd done. Or not done."

"You scarcely had time to do anything. You were practically the first casualty."

Siembieda looked faintly relieved. *And what goes on in the head of a walking dead man?* Miles wondered. *What personal failure could he possibly fear more than death itself?*

"If it's any consolation," put in Elli, "that sort of memory loss is common in trauma victims of all kinds, not just cryo-revivals. You ask around, you'll find you're not the only one."

"Better strap down," said Miles, as the craft yawed around for takeoff.

Siembieda nodded, looking a little more cheerful, and swung forward to find a seat.

"Do you remember your burn?" Miles asked Elli curiously. "Or is it all a merciful blank?"

Elli's hand drifted across her cheek. "I never quite lost consciousness."

The shuttle shot forward and up. Lieutenant Ptarmigan's hands at the controls, Miles judged dryly. Some hooted commentary from forward passengers confirmed his guess. Miles's hand hesitated over, and fell away from, the control in his seat-arm that would comm link him to the pilot; he would not brass-harass Ptarmigan unless he started flying upside down. Fortunately for Ptarmigan, the craft steadied.

Miles craned his neck for a look out the window as the glittering lights of Greater London and its island fell away beneath them. In another moment he could see the river mouth, with its great dikes and locks running for forty kilometers, defining the coastline to human design, shutting out the sea and protecting the historical treasures and several million souls of the lower Thames watershed. One of the huge channel-spanning bridges gleamed against the leaden dawn water beyond. And so men organized themselves for the sake of their technology as they never had for their principles. The sea's politics were inarguable.

The shuttle wheeled, gaining altitude rapidly, giving Miles a last glimpse of the shrinking maze of London. Somewhere down there in that monstrous city Galen and Mark hid, or ran, or plotted, while Destang's intelligence team quartered and re-quartered Galen's old haunts and the comconsole net looking for traces of them, in a deadly game of hide and seek. Surely Galen had the sense to avoid his friends and stay off the net at all costs. If he cut his losses and ran now, he had a chance of eluding Barrayaran vengeance for another half-lifetime.

But if Galen were running, why had he doubled back to pick up Mark? What possible use was the clone to him now? Did Galen have some dim paternal sense of responsibility to his creation? Somehow, Miles doubted it was love that bound those two together. Could the clone be used—servant, slave, soldier? Could the clone be sold—to the Cetagandans, to a medical laboratory, to a sideshow?

Could the clone be sold to Miles?

Now, there was a proposition that even the hypersuspicious Galen would buy. Let him believe Miles wanted a new body, without the bone dyscrasias that had plagued him since birth . . . let him believe Miles would pay a high price to have the clone for this vile purpose . . . and Miles might gain possession of Mark and slip Galen enough cover and funds to finance his escape without Galen ever realizing he was the object of charity for his son's sake. The idea had only two flaws; one, until he made contact with Galen he couldn't do any deal at all; two, if Galen would make such a diabolical bargain Miles was not so sure he cared to see him elude Barrayar's time-cold vengeance after all. A curious dilemma.

✧   ✧   ✧

It was like coming home, to step aboard the *Triumph* again. Knots Miles had not been conscious of undid themselves in the back of his neck as he inhaled the familiar recycled air and soaked the small subliminal chirps and vibrations of the properly functioning, live ship in through his bones. Things were looking in rather better repair all over than at any time since Dagoola, and Miles made a mental note to find out which aggressive engineering sergeants he had to thank for it. It would be good to be just Naismith again, with no problem more complex than what could be laid out in plain military language by HQ, finite and unambiguous.

He issued orders. Cancel further work contracts by individual Dendarii or their groups. All personnel presently scattered downside on work or leave to go on a six hour recall alert. All ships to begin their twenty-four hour preflight checks. Send Lieutenant Bone to me. It gave him a pleasantly megalomanic sense of drawing all things toward a center, himself, though that humor cooled when he contemplated the unsolved problem waiting for him in his Intelligence division.

Quinn in tow, Miles went to pay Intelligence a visit. He found Bel Thorne manning the security comconsole. If manning was the right term; Thorne was one of Beta Colony's hermaphrodite minority, hapless heirs of a century-past genetic project of dubious merit. It had been one of the lunatic fringe's loonier experiments, in Miles's estimation. Most of the men/women stuck to their own comfortable little subculture on tolerant Beta Colony; that Thorne had ventured out into the wider galactic world bespoke either courage, terminal boredom, or most probably if you knew Thorne, a low taste for unsettling people. Captain Thorne kept soft brown hair cut in a deliberately ambiguous style, but wore hard-earned Dendarii uniform and rank with crisp definition.

"Hi, Bel." Miles pulled up a station chair and hooked it into its clamps; Thorne greeted him with a friendly semi-salute. "Play me back everything the surveillance team picked up from Galen's house after Quinn and I rescued the Barrayaran military attaché and left to deliver him back to their embassy." Quinn kept her face quite straight through this bit of revisionist history.

Thorne obediently fast-forwarded through a half hour of silence, then slowed through the disjointed conversation of the two unhappy Komarran guards awakening from stun. Then the chime of the comconsole; a somewhat degraded image resynthesized from the vid beam; the slow toneless voice and face of

Galen himself, requesting a report on the guard's murderous assignment; the sharp rise in tone, as he heard of the dramatic rescue instead—"Fools!" A pause. "Don't attempt to contact me again." Cut.

"We traced the source of the call, I trust," said Miles.

"Public comconsole at a tube station," said Thorne. "By the time we got someone there, the potential search radius had widened to about a hundred kilometers. Good tube system, that."

"Right. And he never returned to the house after that?"

"Abandoned everything, apparently. He's had previous experience evading security, I take it."

"He was an expert before I was born," sighed Miles. "What about the two guards?"

"They were still at the house when the surveillance guys from the Barrayaran embassy arrived and took over and we packed our kit and went home. Have the Barrayarans paid us for this little job yet, by the way?"

"Handsomely."

"Oh, good. I was afraid they'd hold it up till after we'd delivered Van der Poole too."

"About Van der Poole—Galen," said Miles. "Ah—we're no longer working for the Barrayarans on that one. They've brought in their own team from their Sector headquarters on Tau Ceti."

Throne frowned puzzlement. "But we're still working?"

"For the time being. But you'd better pass the word along to our downside people. From this point on, contact with the Barrayarans is to be avoided."

Thorne's brows rose. "Who are we working for, then?"

"For me."

Thorne paused. "Aren't you playing this one a tad close to your chest, sir?"

"Much too close, if my own Intelligence people are to remain effective." Miles sighed. "All right. An odd and unexpected personal wrinkle has turned up in the middle of this case. Have you ever wondered why I never speak of my family background, or my past?"

"Well—there are a lot of Dendarii who don't. Sir."

"Quite. I was born a clone, Bel."

Thorne looked only mildly sympathetic. "Some of my best friends are clones."

"Perhaps I should say, I was created a clone. In the military laboratory of a galactic power that shall remain nameless. I was created for a covert substitution plot against the son of a certain important man, key of another galactic power—you can figure out who with a very little research, I'm sure—but about seven years ago I declined the honor. I escaped, fled, and set up on my own, creating the Dendarii Mercenaries from, er, materials found ready to hand."

Thorne grinned. "A memorable event."

"But this is where Galen comes in. The galactic power abandoned their plot, and I thought I was free of my unhappy past. But several clones had been run off, so to speak, in the attempt to generate an exact physical duplicate, with certain mental refinements, before the lab finally came up with me. I thought they were all long dead, callously murdered, disposed of. But apparently, one of the earlier, less-successful efforts had been put into cryo-suspension. And somehow, he has fallen into Ser Galen's hands. My sole surviving clone-brother, Bel." Miles's hand closed in a fist. "Enslaved by a fanatic. I want to rescue him." His hand opened in pleading. "Can you understand why?"

Thorne blinked. "Knowing you . . . I guess I do. Is it very important to you, sir?"

"Very."

Thorne straightened slightly. "Then it will be done."

"Thank you." Miles hesitated. "Better have all our downside patrol leaders issued a small medical scanner. Keep it on themselves at all times. As you know, I had my leg bones replaced with synthetics a bit over a year ago. His are normal bone. It's the quickest way to tell the difference between us."

"Your appearance is that close?" said Thorne.

"Our appearances are identical, apparently."

"They are," confirmed Quinn to Thorne. "I've seen him."

"I . . . see. Interesting possibilities for confusion there, sir." Thorne glanced at Quinn, who nodded ruefully.

"Too right. I trust the dissemination of the medical scanners will help keep things dull. Carry on—call me at once if you get a break in the case."

"Right, sir."

In the corridor, Quinn remarked, "Nice save, sir."

Miles sighed. "I had to find some way to warn the Dendarii about Mark. Can't have him playing Admiral Naismith again unimpeded."

"Mark?" said Elli. "Who's Mark, or dare I guess? Miles Mark Two?"

"Lord Mark Pierre Vorkosigan," said Miles calmly. Anyway, he hoped he appeared calm. "My brother."

Elli, alive to the significances of Barrayaran clan claims, frowned. "Is Ivan right, Miles? Has that little sucker hypnotized you?"

"I don't know," said Miles slowly. "If I'm the only one who sees him that way, then maybe, just maybe—"

Elli made an encouraging noise.

A slight smile turned one corner of Miles's mouth. "Then maybe everybody's wrong but me."

Elli snorted.

Miles turned serious again. "I truly don't know. In seven years, I never abused the powers of Admiral Naismith for personal purposes. That's not a record I'm anxious to break. Well, perhaps we'll fail to turn them up, and the question will become moot."

"Wishful thinking," said Elli in disapproval. "If you don't want to turn them up, maybe you'd better stop looking for them."

"Compelling logic."

"So why aren't you compelled? And what do you plan to do with them if you do catch 'em?"

"As for what," said Miles, "it's not too complicated. I want to find Galen and my clone before Destang does, and separate them. And then make sure Destang doesn't find them until I can send a private report home. Eventually, if I vouch for him, I believe a cease-and-desist order will come through countermanding my clone's assassination, without my having to appear directly connected with it."

"What about Galen?" asked Elli skeptically. "No way are you going to get a cease-and-desist order on him."

"Probably not. Galen is—a problem I have not solved."

Miles returned to his cabin, where his fleet accountant caught up with him.

Lieutenant Bone fell on the eighteen-million-mark credit chit with heartfelt and unmilitary glee. "Saved!"

"Disburse it as needed," Miles said. "And get the *Triumph* out of hock. We need to be able to move out at a moment's notice without having to argue about grand theft with the Solar Navy. Ah—hm. D'you think you can create a credit chit, out of petty cash or wherever, in galactic funds, that couldn't in any way be traced back to us?"

A gleam lit her eye. "An interesting challenge, sir. Does this have anything to do with our upcoming contract?"

"Security, Lieutenant," Miles said blandly. "I can't discuss it even with you."

"Security," she sniffed, "doesn't hide as much from Accounting as they think they do."

"Perhaps I should combine your departments. No?" He grinned at her horrified look. "Well, maybe not."

"Who does this chit go to?"

"To the bearer."

Her brows rose. "Very good, sir. How much?"

Miles hesitated. "Half a million marks. However that translates into local credit."

"Half a million marks," she noted wryly, "is not petty."

"Just so long as it's cash."

"I'll do my best, sir."

He sat alone in his cabin after she left, frowning deeply. The impasse was clear. Galen could not be expected to initiate contact unless he saw some way, not to mention some reason, to control the situation or achieve surprise. Letting Galen choreograph his moves seemed fatal, and Miles did not care for the idea of wandering around till Galen chose to surprise him. Still, some sort of feint to create an opening might be better than no move at all, in view of the shrinking time limit. Get off the damned defensive disadvantage, act instead of react . . . A high resolve, but for the minor flaw that until Galen was spotted Miles had no object to act upon. He growled frustration and went wearily to bed.

He woke on his own in the dark of his cabin some twelve hours later, noted the time on the glowing digits of his wall clock, and lay a while luxuriating in the remarkable sensation of finally having gotten enough sleep. His greedy body was just suggesting, in the leaden slowness of his limbs, that *more* would be nice, when his cabin comconsole chimed. Saved from the sin of sloth, he staggered out of bed and answered it.

"Sir." The face of one of the *Triumph's* comm officers appeared. "You have a tight-beam call from the Barrayaran Embassy downside in London. They're asking for you personally, scrambled."

Miles trusted that this was not literally true. It couldn't be Ivan; he would have called on the private comm link. It had to be an official communique. "Unscramble and pipe it in here, then."

"Should I record?"

"Ah—no."

Could the new orders from HQ for the Dendarii fleet have

arrived already? Miles swore silently. If they were forced to break orbit before his Dendarii Intelligence people found Galen and Mark . . .

Destang's grim face appeared over the vid plate. " 'Admiral Naismith.'" Miles could hear the quote marks dropping in around his name. "Are we alone?"

"Entirely, sir."

Destang's face relaxed slightly. "Very well. I have an order for you—Lieutenant Vorkosigan. You are to remain aboard your ship in orbit until I, personally, call again and notify you otherwise."

"Why, sir?" said Miles, though he could damn well guess.

"For my peace of mind. When a simple precaution will prevent the slightest possibility of an accident, it's foolish not to take it. Do you understand?"

"Fully, sir."

"Very well. That's all. Destang out." The commodore's face dissolved in air.

Miles cursed out loud, with feeling. Destang's "precaution" could only mean that his Sector goons had spotted Mark already, before Miles's Dendarii had—and were moving in for the kill. How fast? Was there still a chance . . . ?

Miles slipped on his gray trousers, hung ready to hand, and dug the secured comm link from his pocket and keyed it on. "Ivan?" he spoke into it quietly. "You there?"

"Miles?" It was not Ivan's voice; it was Galeni's.

"Captain Galeni? I found the other half of the comm link . . . ah, are you alone?"

"At present." Galeni's voice was dry, conveying through no more than the tone his opinion of both the misplaced comm link story and those who invented it. "Why?"

"How'd you come by the comm link?"

"Your cousin handed it to me just before he departed on his duties."

"Left for where? What duties?" Was Ivan swept up for Destang's man-hunt? If so, Miles could happily throttle him for divesting Miles's ear on the proceedings just when it might have done the most good—skittish idiot!—if only—

"He's escorting the ambassador's lady to the World Botanical Exhibition and Ornamental Flower Show at the University of London's Horticulture Hall. She goes every year, to glad-hand the local social set. Admittedly, she is also interested in the topic."

Miles's voice rose slightly. "In the middle of a security crisis, you sent Ivan to a *flower show?*"

"Not I," denied Galeni. "Commodore Destang. I, ah—believe he felt Ivan could be most easily spared. He's not thrilled with Ivan."

"What about you?"

"He's not thrilled with me either."

"No, I mean, what are you doing? Are you directly involved with the . . . current operation?"

"Hardly."

"Ah. I'm relieved. I was a little afraid—somebody—might have gotten a short circuit in his head about requiring it of you as proof of loyalty or some damned thing."

"Commodore Destang is neither a sadist nor a fool." Galeni paused. "He's careful, however. I'm confined to quarters."

"You have no direct access to the operation, then. Like where they are, and how close, and when they plan to . . . make a move."

Galeni's voice was carefully neutral, neither offering nor denying help. "Not readily."

"Hm. He just ordered me confined to quarters too. I think he's had some sort of break, and things are coming to a head."

There was a brief silence. Galeni's words drifted out on a sigh. "Sorry to hear that . . ." His voice cracked. "It's so damned useless! The dead hand of the past goes on jerking the strings by galvanic reflex, and we poor puppets dance—nothing is served, not us, not him, not Komarr . . ."

"If I could make contact with your father," began Miles.

"It would be useless. He'll fight, and keep on fighting."

"But he has nothing, now. He blew his last chance. He's an old man, he's tired—he could be ready to change, to quit at last," Miles argued.

"I wish . . . no. He can't quit. Above life itself, he has to prove himself right. To be right redeems his every crime. To have done all that he's done, and be wrong—unbearable!"

"I . . . see. Well, I'll contact you again if I . . . have anything useful to say. There's, ah, no point in turning in the comm link till you have both halves, eh?"

"As you wish." Galeni's tone was not exactly fired with hope. Miles shut down the comm link.

He called Thorne, who reported no visible progress.

"In the meantime," said Miles, "here's another lead for you. An unfortunate one. The team from the Barrayarans has evidently spotted our target within the last hour or so."

"Ha! Maybe we can follow them, and let them lead us to Galen."

"Afraid not. We have to get ahead of them, without treading on their toes. Their hunt is a lethal one."

"Armed and dangerous, eh? I'll pass the word." Thorne whistled thoughtfully. "Your crèche-mate sure is popular."

Miles washed, dressed, ate, made ready: boot knife, scanners, stunners both hip-holstered and concealed, comm links, a wide assortment of tools and toys one might carry through London's shuttleport security checks. It was a far cry from combat gear, alas, though his jacket nearly clanked when he walked. He called the duty officer, made sure a personnel shuttle was fueled, pilot at the ready. He waited without patience.

What was Galen up to? If he wasn't just running—and the fact that the Barrayaran security team had nearly caught up with him suggested he was still hanging around for some reason—why? Mere revenge? Something more arcane? Was Miles's analysis of him too simple, too subtle—what was he missing? What was left in life for the man who had to be right?

His cabin comconsole chimed. Miles sent up a short inarticulate prayer—let it be some break, some chink, some handle—

The comm officer's face appeared. "Sir, I have a call originating from the downside commercial comconsole net. A man who refuses to identify himself says you want to talk to him."

Miles jerked electrically upright. "Trace the call and cut a copy to Captain Thorne in Intelligence. Put it through here."

"Do you want your visual to go out, or just audio?"

"Both."

The comm officer's face faded as another man's appeared, giving an unsettling illusion of transmutation.

"Vorkosigan?" said Galen.

"So?" said Miles.

"I will not repeat myself." Galen spoke low and fast. "I don't give a damn if you're recording or tracing. It's irrelevant. You will meet me in seventy minutes exactly. You will come to the Thames Tidal Barrier, halfway between Towers Six and Seven. You will walk out on the seaward side to the lower lookout. Alone. Then we'll talk. If any condition is not met, we will simply not be there when you arrive. And Ivan Vorpatril will die at 0207."

"You are two. I must be two," Miles began. *Ivan?*

"Your pretty bodyguard? Very well. Two." The vid blinked blank.

"No—"

Silence.

Miles keyed to Thorne. "Did you get that, Bel?"

"Sure did. Sounded threatening. Who's Ivan?"

"A very important person. Where'd this originate?"

"A tubeway nexus, public comconsole. I have a man on the way who can make it in six minutes. Unfortunately—"

"I know. Six minutes gives a search radius of several million people. I think we'll play it his way. Up to a point. Put a patrol in the air over the Tidal Barrier, file a flight plan for my shuttle downside, have an aircar and Dendarii driver and guard meet it. Tell Bone I want that credit chit now. Tell Quinn to meet me in the shuttle hatch corridor, and bring a couple of med scanners. And stand by. I want to check something."

He took a deep breath, and keyed open the comm link. "Galeni?"

A pause. "Yes?"

"You still confined to quarters?"

"Yes."

"I have an urgent request for information. Where's Ivan, really?"

"As far as I know, he's still at—"

"Check it. Check it fast."

There was a long, long pause, which Miles utilized to recheck his gear, find Lieutenant Bone, and walk to the shuttle hatch corridor. Quinn was waiting, intensely curious.

"What's up now?"

"We have our break. Of sorts. Galen wants a meeting, but—"

"Miles?" Galeni's voice came back at last. It sounded rather strained.

"Yes."

"The private we'd sent to be driver/guard called in about ten minutes ago. He'd spelled Ivan, attending on Milady, while Ivan went to piss. When Ivan didn't come back in twenty minutes, the driver went to look for him. Spent thirty minutes hunting—the Horticulture Hall is huge, and mobbed tonight—before he reported back to us. How did you know?"

"I think I've got hold of the other end. Do you recognize whose style of doing business this is?"

Galeni swore.

"Quite. Look. I don't care how you do it, but I want you to meet me in fifty minutes at the Thames Tidal Barrier, Section Six. Pack at least a stunner, and get away preferably without alerting Destang. We have an appointment with your father and my brother."

"If he has Ivan—"

"He had to bring some card to the table, or he wouldn't come play. We've got one last chance to make it come out right. Not a good chance, just the last one. Are you with me?"

A slight pause. "Yes." The tone was decisive.

"See you there."

Pocketing the link, Miles turned to Elli. "Now we move."

They swung through the shuttle hatch. For once, Miles had no objection to Ptarmigan's habit of taking all downside flights at combat-drop speed.

CHAPTER FOURTEEN

The Thames Tidal Barrier, known to local wags as the King Canute Memorial, was a vastly more impressive structure seen from a hundred meters up than it had seemed from the kilometers-high view from the shuttle. The aircar banked, circling. The syntha-crete mountain ran away in both directions farther than Miles's eye could follow, whitened into an illusion of marble by the spotlights that knifed through the faintly misty midnight blackness.

Watchtowers every kilometer housed not soldiers guarding the wall but the night shift of engineers and technicians watching over the sluices and pumping stations. To be sure, if the sea ever broke through, it would raze the city more mercilessly than any army.

But the sea was calm this summer night, dotted with colored navigation lights, red, green, white, and the distant moving twinkle of ships' running lights. The eastern horizon glowed faintly, false dawn from the radiant cities of Europe beyond the waters. On the other side of the white barrier toward ancient London, all the dirt and grime and broken places were swallowed by the night, leaving only the jewelled illusion of something magic, unmarred and immortal.

Miles pressed his face to the aircar's bubble canopy for a last strategic view of the arena they were about to enter before the car dropped toward the near-empty parking area behind the Barrier. Section Six was peripheral to the main channel sections with their enormous navigation locks busy around the clock; it was just dike and auxiliary pumping stations, nearly deserted at this hour. That suited Miles. If the situation devolved into some sort of shooting war, the fewer civilian bystanders wandering through the better. Catwalks and ladders ran to access ports in the structure, geometric black accents on the whiteness; spidery railings marked walkways, some broad and public, some narrow, reserved no doubt to Authorized Personnel. At present they all appeared deserted. No sign of Galen or Mark. No sign of Ivan.

"What's significant about 0207?" Miles wondered aloud. "I have the feeling it should be obvious. It's such an exact time."

Elli the space-born shook her head, but the Dendarii soldier piloting the aircar volunteered, "It's high tide, sir."

"Ah!" said Miles. He sat back, thinking furiously. "How interesting. It suggests two things. They've concealed Ivan around here someplace—and we might do best to concentrate our search below the high waterline. Could they have chained him to a railing down by the rocks or some damned thing?"

"The air patrol could make a pass and check," said Quinn.

"Yes, have them do that."

The aircar settled into a painted circle on the pavement.

Quinn and the second soldier exited first, cautiously, and ran a fast perimeter scan around the area. "There's somebody approaching on foot," the soldier reported.

"Pray it's Captain Galeni," Miles muttered, with a glance at his chrono. Seven minutes remained of his time limit.

It was a man jogging with his dog. The pair stared at the four uniformed Dendarii and arced nervously around them to the far side of the parking lot before disappearing through the bushes softening the north end. Everybody took their hands off their stunners. *Civilized town*, thought Miles. *You wouldn't do that at this hour in some parts of Vorbarr Sultana, unless you had a much bigger dog.*

The soldier checked his infra-red. "Here comes another one."

Not the soft pad of running shoes this time, but the quick ring of boots. Miles recognized the sound of the boots before he could make out the face in the splash of light and shadow. Galeni's uniform turned from dark gray to green as he entered the lot's zone of brighter illumination, walking fast.

"All right," said Miles to Elli, "this is where we split off. Stay back and out of sight at all costs, but if you can find a vantage, good. Wrist comm open?"

Elli keyed her wrist comm. Miles pulled his boot knife and used the point to disengage and extinguish the tiny transmit-indicator light in his own wrist comm, then blew into it; the hiss of it whispered from Elli's wrist. "Sending fine," she confirmed.

"Got your med scanner?"

She displayed it.

"Take a baseline."

She pointed it at him, waved it up and down. "Recorded and ready for auto-comparison."

"Can you think of anything else?"

She shook her head, but still didn't look happy. "What do I do if *he* comes walking back and you don't?"

"Grab him, fast-penta him—got your interrogation kit?"

She flashed open her jacket; a small brown case peeped from an inner pocket.

"Rescue Ivan if you can. Then," Miles took a deep breath, "you can blow the clone's head off or whatever you choose."

"What happened to 'my brother right or wrong'?" said Elli.

Galeni, coming up in the middle of this, cocked his head with interest to hear the answer to that one, but Miles only shook his head. He couldn't think of a simple answer.

"Three minutes left," said Miles to Galeni. "We better move."

They headed up a walk that led to a set of stairs, stepping over the chain that marked them as closed for the night to law-abiding citizens. The stairs climbed the back side of the tidal barrier to a public promenade that ran along the top to allow sightseers a view of the ocean in the daytime. Galeni, who had evidently been moving at speed, was breathing deeply even as they began their climb.

"Have any trouble getting out of the embassy?" asked Miles.

"Not really," said Galeni. "As you know, the trick is getting back in. I think you demonstrated simplest is best. I just walked out the side entrance and took the nearest tubeway. Fortunately, the duty guard had no orders to shoot me."

"Did you know that in advance?"

"No."

"Then Destang knows you left."

"He will know, certainly."

"Think you were followed?" Miles glanced involuntarily over his shoulder. He could see the parking lot and aircar below; Elli and the two soldiers had vanished from view, seeking their vantage no doubt.

"Not immediately. Embassy security," Galeni's teeth flashed in the shadows, "is undermanned at present. I left my wristcomm, and bought cash tokens for the tubeway instead of using my passcard, so they have nothing quick to trace me by."

They panted to the top; the damp air moved cool against Miles's face, smelling of river slime and sea salt, a faintly decayed estuarial tang. Miles crossed the wide promenade and peered down over the railing at the synthacrete outer face of the dike. A narrow railed ledge ran along some twenty meters below, vanishing away out of sight to the right along an outcurving bulge in the Barrier. Not part of the public area; it was reached by keyed extension ladders at intervals along the railing, all folded up and locked for the night of course. They could fuss with trying to break open and decode one of the locked ladder controls—time-consuming, and likely to light up the alarm board of some night-shift supervisor in one of the distant watchtowers—or go down the fast way.

Miles sighed under his breath. Rappelling high over rock-hard surfaces was one of his all-time least favorite activities. He fished the drop-wire spool from its own little pocket on his Dendarii jacket, attached the gravitic grappler carefully and firmly to the railing, and doublechecked it. At a touch, handles telescoped out from the sides of the spool and released the wide ribbon-harness that always looked horribly flimsy despite its phenomenal tensile strength. Miles threaded it round himself, clipped it tight, hopped over the rail, and danced down the wall backwards, not looking down. By the time he reached the bottom his adrenaline was pumping nicely, thank you.

He sent the spool winding itself back up to Galeni, who repeated Miles's performance. Galeni offered no comment about his feelings about heights as he handed back the device, so neither did Miles. Miles touched the control that released the grappler and rewound and pocketed the spool.

"We go right." Miles nodded. He drew his holstered stunner. "What did you bring?"

"I could only get one stunner." Galeni pulled it from his pocket, checked its charge and setting. "And you?"

"Two. And a few other toys. There are severe limits to what you can carry through shuttleport security."

"Considering how crowded this place is, I think they're wise," remarked Galeni.

Stunners in hand, they walked single file along the ledge, Miles first. Sea water swirled and gurgled just below their feet, green-brown transluscence frosted with streaks of foam within the circles of light, silky black beyond. Judging from the discoloration, this walkway was inundated at high tide.

Miles motioned Galeni to pause, and slipped forward. Just beyond the outcurve the walkway widened to a four-meter circle and dead-ended, the railing arcing around to meet the wall. In the wall was a doorway, a sturdy watertight oval hatch.

Standing in front of the hatch were Galen and Mark, stunners in their hands. Mark wore black tee-shirt and Dendarii gray trousers and boots, minus the pocketed jacket—his own clothes, pilfered, Miles wondered, or duplicates? His nostrils flared as he spotted his grandfather's dagger in its lizard-skin sheath at the clone's waist.

"A stand-off," remarked Galen conversationally as Miles halted, with a glance at Miles's stunner and his own. "If we all fire at once, it leaves either me or my Miles on his feet, and the game is mine. But if by some miracle you dropped us both, we could not tell you where your oxlike cousin is. He'd die before you could find him. His death has been automated. I need not get back to him to carry it out. Quite the reverse. Your pretty bodyguard may as well join us."

Galeni stepped around the bend. "Some stand-offs are more curious than others," he said.

Galen's face flickered from its hard irony, lips parting in a breath of deep dismay, then tightening again even as his hand tightened on his weapon. "You were to bring the woman," he hissed.

Miles smiled slightly. "She's around. But you said two, and we are two. Now all the interested parties are here. Now what?"

Galen's eyes shifted, counting weapons, calculating distances, muscle, odds no doubt; Miles was doing the same.

"The stand-off remains," said Galen. "If you're both stunned you lose; if we're both stunned you lose again. It's absurd."

"What would you suggest?" asked Miles.

"I propose we all lay our weapons in the center of the deck. Then we can talk without distraction."

He's got another one concealed, thought Miles. *Same as me.* "An interesting proposition. Who puts his down last?"

Galen's face was a study in unhappy calculation.

He opened his mouth and closed it again, and shook his head slightly.

"I too would like to talk without distraction," said Miles carefully. "I propose this schedule. I'll lay mine down first. Then M—the clone. Then yourself. Captain Galeni last."

"What guarantee . . . ?" Galen glanced sharply at his son. The tension between them was near-sickening, a strange and silent compound of rage, despair, and anguish.

"He'll give you his word," said Miles. He looked for confirmation to Galeni, who nodded slowly.

Silence fell for the space of three breaths, then Galen said, "All right."

Miles stepped forward, knelt, laid his stunner in the center of the deck, stepped back. Mark repeated his performance, staring at him the while. Galen hesitated a long, agonized moment, eyes still full of shifting calculation, then put his weapon down with the others. Galeni followed suit without hesitation. His smile was like a sword-cut. His eyes were unreadable, but for the baseline of dull pain that had lurked in them ever since his father had resurrected himself.

"Your proposition first, then," Galen said to Miles. "If you have one."

"Life," said Miles. "I have concealed—in a place only I know of, and if you'd stunned me you'd never have discovered it in time—a cash-credit chit for a hundred thousand Betan dollars— that's half a million Imperial marks, friends—payable to the bearer. I can give it to you, plus a head start, useful information on how to evade Barrayaran security—which is very close behind you, by the way—"

The clone was looking extremely interested; his eyes had widened when the sum was named, and widened still further at the mention of Barrayaran security.

"—in exchange for my cousin," Miles took a slight breath, "my brother, and your promise to—retire, and refrain from further plots against the Barrayaran Imperium. Which can only result in useless bloodshed and unnecessary pain to your few surviving relations. The war's over, Ser Galen. It's time for someone else to try something else. A different way, maybe a better way—it could scarcely be a worse way, after all."

"The revolt," breathed Galen almost to himself, "must not die."

"Even if everybody in it dies? 'It didn't work, so let's do it some more'? In my line of work they call that military stupidity. I don't know what they call it in civilian life."

"My older sister once surrendered on a Barrayaran's word," Galen remarked. His face was very cold. "Admiral Vorkosigan too was full of soft and logical persuasion, promising peace."

"My father's word was betrayed by an underling," said Miles, "who couldn't recognize when the war was over and it was time to quit. He paid for the error with his life, executed for his crime. My father gave you your revenge then. It was all he could give you; he couldn't bring those dead to life. Neither can I. I can only try to prevent more dying."

Galen smiled sourly. "And you, David. What bribe would you offer me to betray Komarr, to lay alongside your Barrayaran master's money?"

Galeni was regarding his fingernails, a peculiar fey smile playing around his lips as he listened. He buffed them briefly on his trouser seam, crossed his arms, blinked. "Grandchildren?"

Galen seemed taken aback for a bare instant. "You're not even bonded!"

"I might be, someday. Only if I live, of course."

"And they would all be good little Imperial subjects," sneered Galen, recovering his initial balance with an effort.

Galeni shrugged. "Seems to fit in with Vorkosigan's offer of life. I can't give you anything else you want of me."

"You two are more alike than either of you realize, I think," Miles murmured. "So what's your proposition, Ser Galen? Why have you called us all here?"

Galen's right hand went to his jacket, then slowed. He smiled, tilted his head as if asking permission, disarmingly. *Here comes the second stunner,* thought Miles. *Coyly, pretending to the last minute that it's not really a weapon.* Miles didn't flinch, but an involuntary calculation did flash through his mind as to just how fast he could vault the railing, and how far he could swim underwater holding his breath in a strong surf. Wearing boots. Galeni, cool as ever, didn't move either.

Even when the weapon Ser Galen abruptly displayed turned out to be a lethal nerve disruptor.

"Some stand-offs," said Galen, "are more equal than others." His smile tightened to a parody of itself. "Pick up those stunners," he added to the clone, who stooped and gathered them up and stuck them in his belt.

"Now what are you going to do with that?" said Miles lightly, trying not to let his eye be hypnotized, nor his mind paralyzed, by the silver bell-muzzle. Shiny beads, bells and whistles.

"Kill you," Galen explained. His eyes flicked to his son, and away, toward and away; he focused on Miles as if to steady his high resolve.

So why are you still talking instead of firing? Miles didn't speak that thought aloud, lest Galen be struck by its good sense. *Keep him talking, he wants to say more, is driven to say more.* "Why? I don't see how that will serve Komarr at this late hour, except maybe to relieve your feelings. Mere revenge?"

"Nothing mere about it. Complete. My Miles will walk out of here as the only one."

"Oh, come on!" Miles didn't have to call on his acting ability to lend outrage to his tone; it came quite naturally. "You're not still stuck on the bloody substitution plot! Barrayaran Security is all warned, they'll spot you at once now. Can't be done." He glanced at the clone. "You going to let him run you head first into a flash-disposer? You're dead meat the moment you present yourself. It's useless. And it's not *necessary.*"

The clone looked distinctly uneasy, but jerked up his chin and managed a proud smile. "I'm not going to be Lord Vorkosigan. I'm going to be Admiral Naismith. I did it once, so I know I can. Your Dendarii are going to give us a ride out of here—and a new power base."

"Ngh!" Miles made a hair-tearing gesture. "D'you think I'd have walked in here if that were even remotely possible? The Dendarii are warned too. Every patrol leader out there—and you'd better believe I have patrols out there—is carrying a med scanner. First order you give, you'll be scanned. If they find leg bone where my synthetics should be, they'll blow your head off. End plot."

"But my leg bones *are* synthetics," said the clone in a puzzled tone.

Miles froze. "What? You told me your bones didn't break—"

Galen swiveled his head round at the clone. "When did you tell him that?"

"They don't," the clone answered Miles. "But after yours were replaced, so were mine. Otherwise the first cursory med scan I got would have given it all away."

"But you still don't have the pattern of old breaks in your other bones . . . ?"

"No, but that would take a much closer scan. And once the three are eliminated I should be able to avoid that. I'll study your logs—"

"The three what?"

"The three Dendarii who know you are Vorkosigan."

"Your pretty bodyguard, and the other couple," Galen explained vindictively to Miles's look of horror. "I'm sorry you didn't bring her. Now we shall have to hunt her down."

Was that a fleeting queasy look on Mark's face? Galen caught
it too, and frowned faintly.

"You still couldn't bring it off," argued Miles. "There are five
thousand Dendarii. I know hundreds of them by name, on sight.
We've been in combat together. I know things about them their
own mothers don't, not in any log. And they've seen me under
every kind of stress. You wouldn't even know the right jokes to
make. And even if you succeed for a time, become Admiral
Naismith as you once planned to become Emperor—where is Mark
then? Maybe Mark doesn't want to be a space mercenary. Maybe
be wants to be a, a textile designer. Or a doctor—"

"Oh," breathed the clone, with a glance down his twisted body,
"not a doctor . . ."

"—or a holovid programmer, or a star pilot, or an engineer. Or
very far away from *him."* Miles jerked his head at Galen; for a
moment the clone's eyes filled with a passionate longing, as quickly
masked. "How will you ever find out?"

"It's true," said Galen, looking at the clone through suddenly
narrowed eyes, "you must pass for an experienced soldier. And
you've never killed."

The clone shifted uneasily, looking sideways, at his mentor.

Galen's voice had softened. "You must learn to kill if you expect
to survive."

"No, you don't," Miles put in. "Most people go through their
whole lives without killing anybody. False argument."

The nerve disruptor's aim steadied on Miles. "You talk too
much." Galen's eyes fell one last time on his silent, witnessing son,
who raised his chin in defiance, then flicked away as if the sight
burned. "It's time to go."

Galen, face hardening decisively, turned to the clone. "Here."
He handed him the nerve disruptor. "It's time to complete your
education. Shoot them, and let's go."

"What about Ivan?" asked Captain Galeni softly.

"I have as little use for Vorkosigan's nephew as I have for his
son," said Galen. "They can skip down to hell hand in hand." His
head turned to the clone and he added, "Begin!"

Mark swallowed, and raised the weapon in a two-handed firing
stance. "But—what about the credit chit?"

"There is no credit chit. Can't you spot a lie when you hear it,
fool?"

Miles raised his wrist comm, and spoke distinctly into it. "Elli,
do you have all this?"

"Recorded and transmitted to Captain Thorne in I.Q.," Quinn's voice came back cheerily, thin in the damp air. "D'you want company yet?"

"Not yet." He let his hand fall, stood straight, met Galen's furious eyes and clenched teeth: "As I said. End plot. Let's discuss alternatives."

Mark had lowered the nerve disruptor, his face dismayed.

"Alternatives? Revenge will do!" hissed Galen. "Fire!"

"But—" said the clone, agitated.

"As of this moment, you're a free man." Miles spoke low and fast. "He bought and paid for you, but he doesn't own you. But if you kill for him, he'll own you forever. Forever and ever."

Not necessarily, spoke Galeni's silent quirk of the lips, but he did not interfere with Miles's pitch.

"You must kill your enemies," snarled Galen.

Mark's hand and aim sagged, his mouth opening in protest.

"Now, dammit!" yelled Galen, and made to grab back the nerve disruptor.

Galeni stepped in front of Miles. Miles scrabbled in his jacket for his second stunner. The nerve disruptor crackled. Miles drew, too late, too goddamn late—Captain Galeni gasped—*he's dead for my slowness, my one-last-chance stupidity*—face harrowed, mouth open in a silent yell, Miles sprang from behind Galeni and aimed his stunner—

To see Galen crumple, convulsing, back arching in a bone-cracking twist, face writhing—and slump in death.

"Kill your enemies," breathed Mark, his face white as paper. "Right. Ah!" he added, raising the weapon again as Miles started forward, "Stop right there!"

A hiss at Miles's feet—he glanced down to see a thin layer of foam wash past his boots, lose momentum, and recede. In a moment, another. The tide was rising over the ledge. The tide was rising—

"Where's Ivan?" Miles demanded, his hand clenching on his stunner.

"If you fire that you'll never know," said Mark.

His eye hurried nervously, from Miles to Galeni, from Galen's body at his feet to the weapon in his own hand, as if they all added up to some impossibly incorrect sum. His breath was shallow and panicky, his knuckles, wrapped around the nerve disruptor, bone-pale. Galeni was standing very, very still, head cocked, looking down at what lay there, or inward; he did not seem to be conscious of the weapon or its wielder at all.

"Fine," said Miles. "You help us and we'll help you. Take us to Ivan."

Mark backed toward the wall, not lowering the nerve disruptor. "I don't believe you."

"Where are you going to run to? You can't go back to the Komarrans. There's a Barayaran hit squad with murder on its collective mind breathing down your neck. You can't go to the local authorities for protection; you have a body to explain. I'm your only chance."

Mark looked at the body, at the nerve disruptor, at Miles.

The soft whirr of a rappel spool unwinding was barely audible over the hiss of the sea foam underfoot. Miles glanced up. Quinn was flying down in one long swoop, like a falcon stooping, weapon in one hand and rappeling spool controlled by the other.

Mark kicked open the hatch and stumbled backwards into it. "You hunt for Ivan. He's not far. I don't have a body to explain— *you* do. The murder weapon has your fingerprints on it!" He flung down the nerve disruptor and slammed the hatch closed.

Miles leapt for the door, fingers scrabbling, but it was already sealed—he came close to snapping some more finger bones. The slide and clank of a locking mechanism designed to defy the force of the sea itself came muffled through the hatch. Miles hissed through his teeth.

"Should I blow it open?" gasped Quinn, landing.

"Y— good God, no!" The discoloration on the wall marking high water was a good two meters higher than the top of the hatch. "We might drown London. Try to get it open without damaging it. Captain Galeni!" Miles turned. Galeni had not moved. "You in shock?"

"Hm? No . . . no, I don't think so." Galeni came out of himself with an effort. He added in a strangely calm, reflective tone, "Later, perhaps."

Quinn was bent to the hatchway, pulling devices from her pockets and slapping them to the vertical surface, checking readouts. "Electromechanical with a manual override . . . if I use a magnetic . . ."

Miles reached around and pulled the rappeling harness off Quinn. "Go up," he said to Galeni, "and see if you can find another entrance on the other side. We've got to catch that little sucker!"

Galeni nodded and hooked up the rappeling harness.

Miles held out stunner and boot knife. "Want a weapon?"

Mark had taken off with all the spare stunners still stuck in his belt.

"Stunner's useless," Galeni noted. "You'd better keep the knife. If I catch up with him I'll use my bare hands."

With pleasure, Miles added for him silently. He nodded. They had both been through Barrayaran basic unarmed combat school. Three fourths of the moves were barred to Miles in a real fight at full force due to the secret weakness of his bones; the same was not true of Galeni. Galeni ascended into the night air, bounding up the wall on the almost invisible thread as readily as a spider.

"Got it!" cried Quinn. The thick hatch swung wide on a deep, dark hole.

Miles yanked his handlight out of his belt and hopped through. He glanced back at Galen's gray-faced body, lapped by foam, released from obsession and pain. There was no mistaking the stillness of death for the stillness of sleep or anything else; it was the absolute. The nerve-disruptor beam must have hit his head square on. Quinn dragged the hatch shut again behind them, pausing to stuff equipment back into her pockets as the door's mechanism twinkled and beeped, slid and clanked, rendering the lower Thames watershed safe again.

They both scrambled up the corridor. A mere five meters farther on they came to their first check, a T-intersection. This main corridor was lighted, and curved away out of sight in both directions.

"You go left, I'll go right," said Miles.

"You shouldn't be alone," Quinn objected.

"Maybe I should be twins, eh? Go, dammit!"

Quinn threw up her hands in exasperation and ran.

Miles sprinted in the other direction. His footsteps echoed eerily in the corridor, deep in the synthacrete mountain. He paused a moment, listened; heard only Quinn's light fading scuff. He ran on, past hundreds of meters of blank synthacrete, past dark and silent pumping stations, past pumping stations lit up and humming quietly. He was just wondering whether he could have missed an exit—an overhead access port?—when he spotted an object on the corridor floor. One of the stunners, fallen from Mark's belt as he ran in panic. Miles swooped it up with a quick *ah-ha!* of bared teeth, and holstered it as he ran on.

He keyed open his wrist comm. "Quinn?" The corridor curved suddenly into a sort of stark foyer with lift tube. He must be under one of the watchtowers. Beware Authorized Personnel about. "Quinn?"

He stepped into the lift tube and rose. Oh, God, which level had Mark got off at? The third floor he passed opened out onto a glass-walled, lobby-looking area, with doors and the night beyond. Clearly an exit. Miles swung out of the lift tube.

A total stranger, wearing civilian jacket and pants, whirled at the sound of his footstep and dropped to one knee. The silver flash of a parabolic mirror twinkled in his raised hands, a nerve-disruptor muzzle. "There he is!" the man cried, and fired.

Miles recoiled back into the lift tube so fast he rebounded off the far wall. He grabbed for the safety ladder at the side of the tube and began slapping up the rungs faster than the anti-grav field could lift him. He wriggled his facial muscles, shot with pins and needles from the nimbus of the disruptor beam. The man's shoes, Miles realized, gleaming out from the bottom of his trousers, had been Barrayaran regulation Service boots. "Quinn!" he yelped into his wrist comm again.

The next level up opened onto a corridor without gunmen in it. The first three doors Miles tried were locked. The fourth swished open onto a brightly lit office, apparently deserted. On a quick jog around it Miles's eye was caught by a slight movement in the shadows under a console. He bent down to face two women in blue Tidal Authority tech coveralls cowering beneath. One squeaked and covered her eyes; the second hugged her and glared defiantly at Miles.

Miles tried a friendly smile. "Ah . . . hello."

"Who *are* you people?" said the second woman in rising tone.

"Oh, I'm not with them. They're, um . . . hired killers." A just description, after all. "Don't worry, they're not after you. Have you called the police yet?"

She shook her head mutely.

"I suggest you do so immediately. Ah—have you seen me before?"

She nodded.

"Which way did I go?"

She cringed back, clearly terrorized at being cornered by a psychotic. Miles spread his hands in silent apology, and made for the door. "Call the police!" he called back over his shoulder. The faint beep of comconsole keys being pressed drifted down the corridor after him.

Mark was nowhere on this level. The lift tube grav field had now been turned off by someone; the auto safety bar was extended across the opening and the red glow of the warning light filled the corridor. Miles stuck his head cautiously into the lift tube, to spy another head on the level below looking up; he jerked his head back as a nerve disruptor crackled.

A balcony ran right around the outside of the tower. Miles slipped through the door at the seaward end of the corridor and looked around, and up. Only one more floor above. Its balcony was readily reachable by the toss of a grappler. Miles grimaced, pulled out his spool, and made the toss; got a firm hook around the railing above on the first try. A swallow, a brief heart-stopping dangle over the tower, dike, and growling sea forty meters below, and he was clambering onto the next balcony.

He tiptoed to the glass doorway and checked down the corridor. Mark was crouched, silhouetted by the red light, near the entrance to the lift tube, stunner drawn. The—unconscious, Miles trusted—form of a man in tech coveralls lay sprawled on the corridor floor.

"Mark?" Miles called softly, and jerked back. Mark snapped around and let off a stunner burst in his direction. Miles put his back against the wall and called, "Cooperate with me, and I'll get you out of this alive. Where's Ivan?"

This reminder that Mark still held a trump card had the expected calming effect. He did not fire again. "Get me out of this and I'll tell you where he is," he countered.

Miles grinned into the darkness. "All right. I'm coming in." He slipped round the door and joined his image, pausing only to check for a pulse in the neck of the sprawled man. He had one, happily.

"*How* are you going to get me out of this?" demanded Mark.

"Well, now, that's the tricky part," Miles admitted. He paused to listen intently. Someone was on the ladder in the lift tube, trying to climb quietly; not near their level yet. "The police are on their way, and when they arrive I expect the Barrayarans will decamp in a hurry. They won't want to be caught in an embarrassing interplanetary incident which the ambassador would have to explain to the local authorities. This night's operation is already way out of control in that anybody saw 'em at all. Destang will have their blood on the carpet in the morning."

"The police?" Mark's grip tightened on his stunner; competing fears struggled for ascendancy in his face.

"Yes. We could try and play hide and seek in this tower till the police finally get here—whenever. Or we could go up to the roof and have a Dendarii aircar pick us off right now. I know which I'd prefer. How about you?"

"Then I would be your prisoner." Mark's whispering voice blurred with a fear-fueled anger. "Dead now, dead later, what's the difference? I finally figured out what use you had for a clone."

Mark was seeing himself as a walking body-parts bank again, Miles could tell. Miles sighed. He glanced at his chrono. "By Galen's timetable, I have eleven minutes left to find Ivan."

A shifty look stole over Mark's face. "Ivan's not up. He's down. Back the way we came."

"Ah?" Miles risked a flash-peek into the lift tube. The climber had exited at another floor. The hunters were being thorough in their search. By the time they worked their way up here they'd be quite certain of their quarry.

Miles was still wearing the rappelling harness. Very quietly, careful not to clank, he reached out and fastened the grappler to the safety bar and tested it. "So you want to go down, do you? I can arrange that. But you'd better be right about Ivan. Because if he dies I'll dissect you personally. Heart and liver, steaks and chops."

Miles stooped, checked his connections, set the spool's rate of spin and stop-point, and positioned himself under the bar, ready for launch. "Climb on."

"Don't I get straps?"

Miles glanced over his shoulder and grinned. "You bounce better than I do."

Looking extremely dubious, Mark stuffed his stunner back in his belt, sidled up to Miles, and gingerly wrapped his arms and legs around Miles's body.

"You'd better hang on tighter than that. The deceleration at the bottom is going to be severe. And don't scream going down. It would draw attention."

Mark's grip tightened convulsively. Miles checked once more for unwanted company—the tube was still empty—and thrust over the side.

Their doubled weight gathered momentum terrifyingly. They fell unimpeded in near-silence for four stories—Miles's stomach was floating near his back teeth, and the sides of the lift tube were a smear of color—then the rappelling spool began to whine, resisting its blurring spin. The straps bit, and Mark's grip hand-to-hand across Miles's collarbone began to pull apart. Miles's right hand flashed up to clamp around Mark's wrist. They braked to a demure stop a centimeter or two above the lift tube's bottom floor, back in the belly of the synthacrete mountain. Miles's ears popped.

The noise of their descent had seemed thunderous to Miles's exacerbated senses, but no startled heads appeared in the openings above, no weapons crackled. Miles and Mark both nipped back out of the line of sight of the tube, into the little foyer off the tidal barrier's internal access corridor. Miles pressed the control to release his grappler and let the spool rewind; the falling thread made no noise, but the grappler unit clinked hitting bottom, and Miles flinched.

"Back that way," said Mark, pointing right. They jogged down the corridor side by side. A deep, growling vibration began to drown lighter sounds. The pumping station that had been blinking and humming when Miles had first passed that way was now at work, lifting Thames water to high-tide sea level through hidden pipes. The next station down, previously dark and silent, was now lit, preparing to go into action.

Mark stopped. "Here."

"Where?"

Mark pointed, "Each pumping chamber has an access hatch, for cleaning and repairs. We put him in there."

Miles swore.

The pumping chamber was about the size of a large closet. Sealed, it would be dark, cold, slimy, stinking, and utterly silent. Until the rush of rising water, thrumming with immense force, gushed in to turn it into a death chamber. Rushed in to fill the ears, the nose, the dark-staring eyes; rushed in to fill the chamber up, up, not even one little pocket of air for a frantic mouth; rushed through to batter and twist the body ceaselessly, roiling against the thick unyielding walls until the face was pulped beyond recognition, until, with the tide, the dank waters at last receded, leaving—nothing of value. A clog in the line.

"You . . ." breathed Miles, glaring at Mark, "lent yourself to *this* . . . ?"

Mark wiped his palms together nervously, stepping back. "You're here—I brought you here," he began plaintively. "I said I would. . . ."

"Isn't this a rather severe punishment for a man who never did you more harm than to snore and keep you awake? Agh!" Miles turned, his back rigid with disgust, and began punching at the hatch lock controls. The last step was manual, turning the bar that undogged the hatch. As Miles pushed the heavy beveled door inward, an alarm began to beep.

"Ivan?"

"Ah!" The cry from within was nearly voiceless.

Miles thrust his shoulders through, flashed his handlight. The hatch was near the top of the chamber; he found himself looking down at the white smudge of Ivan's face half a meter below, looking up.

"You!" Ivan cried in a voice of loathing, staggering back and slipping in the slime.

"No, not him," Miles corrected. "Me."

"Ah?" Ivan's face was lined, exhausted, almost beyond coherent thought; Miles had seen the same look on men who had been in combat too long.

Miles tossed down his handy-dandy rappelling harness—he shuddered, recalling that he'd almost decided not to include it when he'd been kitting up back in the *Triumph*—and braced the spool. "Ready to come up?"

Ivan's lips moved in a mumble, but he wrapped the harness sufficiently around his arms. Miles hit the spool control, and Ivan lifted. Miles helped him slither through the hatch. Ivan stood, boots planted apart, hands on knees supporting himself, breathing heavily. His green dress uniform was damp, crumpled and beslimed. His hands looked like dog meat. He must have pounded and scratched, scrabbled and screamed in the dark, muffled and unheard . . .

Miles swung the hatch back. It clicked firmly. He twirled the manual locking bar. The alarm stopped beeping. Safety circuits reconnected; the pump immediately began to thrum. No greater noise penetrated from the pumping chamber than a monstrous subliminal hiss. Ivan sat down heavily and pressed his face to his knees.

Miles knelt beside him in worry. Ivan turned his head and managed a sickly grin. "I think," he gulped, "I'm going to take up claustrophobia for a hobby now. . . ."

Miles grinned back and clapped him on the shoulder. He rose and turned. Mark was nowhere in sight.

Miles spat, and lifted his wrist comm to his lips. "Quinn? Quinn!" He stepped out into the corridor, looked up and down it, listened intently. The faintest echo of running footsteps was fading in the distance, in the direction opposite the Barrayaran-infested watchtower. "Little shit," Miles muttered. "To hell with him." He re-keyed his comm for the air patrol. "Sergeant Nim? Naismith here."

"Yes, sir."

"I've lost contact with Commander Quinn. See if you can raise her. If you can't, start looking for her. I last saw her on foot inside the tidal barrier, halfway between Towers Six and Seven, heading south."

"Yes, sir."

Miles turned back and helped pull Ivan to his feet. "Can you walk?" he asked anxiously.

"Yeah . . . sure," said Ivan. He blinked. "I'm just a little . . ." They started down the corridor. Ivan stumbled a bit, leaning on Miles, then steadied. "I never knew my body could pump that much adrenaline. Or for so long. Hours and hours . . . how long was I in there?"

"About," Miles glanced at his chrono, "less than two hours."

"Huh. Seemed longer." Ivan appeared to be regaining his equilibrium somewhat. "Where are we going? Why are you wearing your Naismith-suit? Is M'lady all right? They didn't get her, did they?"

"No, Galen just snatched you. This is an independent Dendarii operation at present. I'm not supposed to be downside just now. Destang ordered me to stay aboard the *Triumph* while his goons were trying to dispose of my double. To prevent confusion."

"Yeah, well, makes sense. That way, any little guy they see they know they can fire at." Ivan blinked again. "*Miles . . .*"

"Right," said Miles. "That's why we're going this way instead of that way."

"Should I walk faster?"

"That would be nice, if you can."

They picked up the pace.

"Why did you come downside?" asked Ivan after a minute or two. "Don't tell me you're still trying to save that graceless little copy's worthless hide."

"Galen sent me an invitation engraved on *your* hide. I don't have too many relatives, Ivan. They're of surprising value to me. If only for their rarity, eh?"

They exchanged a glance; Ivan cleared his throat. "Well. So. But you're on shaky ground, trying to undercut Destang. Say— if his hit squad is that close—where's Galen?" Alarm suffused his face.

"Galen's dead," Miles reported shortly. They were in fact just passing the dark cross corridor to the outer ledge where that body lay.

"Ah? Glad to hear it. Who did the honors? I want to kiss his hand. Or hers."

"I think you'll have the chance in just a moment." The quick tap of running footsteps, as of a person with short legs, was just audible from ahead around the curve of the corridor. Miles drew his stunner. "And this time, I don't have to keep him arguing. Maybe Quinn's spooked him back this way," he added hopefully. He was getting extremely worried about Quinn.

Mark rounded the curve and skidded to a halt before them with a hopeless cry. He turned, stepped, stopped, turned again like an animal in a trap. The right side of his face was streaked red, his ear was edged with oozing yellow-white blisters, and the stench of burnt hair crept faintly through the air.

"*Now* what?" asked Miles.

Mark's voice was high and stretched. "There's some painted lunatic back there after me with a plasma gun! They've taken over the next watchtower—"

"Did you see Quinn anywhere?"

"No."

"Miles," said Ivan in puzzlement, "our guys wouldn't carry plasma arcs on an antipersonnel mission like this, would they? Not in the middle of a critical facility like this—they'd not want to risk damaging the machinery—"

"Painted?" said Miles urgently. "Like how? Not—not face paint like a Chinese opera mask, by chance?"

"I don't know—what a Chinese opera mask looks like," panted Mark, "But they—well, one—had colors solid from ear to ear."

"The ghem-commander, no doubt," Miles breathed. "On formal hunt. They've upped the bid, it seems."

"Cetagandans?" said Ivan sharply.

"Their reinforcements must have finally arrived. They must have picked up my trail at the shuttleport. Oh, God—and Quinn went that way . . . !" Miles too turned in a circle, and swallowed panic back to the pit of his stomach where it belonged. It must not be permitted to rise to the level of his brain. "But you can relax, Mark. They don't want to kill you."

"The hell they don't! He shouted, 'There he is, men!' and tried to blow my head off!"

Miles's lips peeled back on a dirty grin. "No, no," he caroled soothingly. "Merely a case of mistaken identity. Those people want to kill me—Admiral Naismith. It's just the ones on the other end of the tunnel who want to kill you. Of course," he added jovially, "neither of them can tell us apart."

Ivan made a derisive sputter.

"Back this way," said Miles decisively, and led on at a run. He swung into the transverse corridor and skidded to a halt before the outside access hatch. Ivan and Mark galloped up behind.

Miles stood on tiptoe, and gritted his teeth. According to the control readout, the tide had now risen higher than the top of the hatch. This exit was sealed by the sea.

CHAPTER FIFTEEN

Miles slapped his wrist comm channel open. "Nim!" he called.
"Sir!"

"There's a Cetagandan covert ops squad in Tower Seven. Strength unknown, but they have plasma arcs."

"Yes, sir," came Nim's breathless voice. "We just found them."

"Where are you and what can you see?"

"I have a pair of soldiers outside each of the three tower entrances, with a backup in the bushes in the parking area. The— Cetagandans, you say, sir?—just pumped some plasma blasts out the main corridor as we tried to enter."

"Anybody hit?"

"Not yet. We're flat."

"Any sign of Commander Quinn yet?"

"No, sir."

"Can you get a fix on her wrist comm?"

"It's somewhere in the lower levels of this tower. She doesn't respond and it's not moving."

Stunned? Dead? Was her wrist even still in her wrist comm? No telling.

"All right," Miles took a breath, "put in an anonymous call to the local police. Tell them there's armed men in Tower Seven—maybe saboteurs trying to blow up the Barrier. Make it convincing—try to sound scared."

"No problem, sir," said Nim earnestly.

Miles wondered how nearly the plasma beam had parted Nim's

hair. "Until the constables arrive, keep the Cetagandans sealed in the tower. Stun anyone who tries to exit. The locals can sort them out later. Put a couple of point men down in Tower Eight to seal that end, have them work north and drive the Cetagandans back if they try to exit south. But I think they'll head north." He put his hand over the comm and added to Mark, "Chasing you." He lifted his palm and continued to Nim, "As the police arrive, pull back. Avoid contact with 'em. But if you do get cornered, go meekly. We're the good guys. It's those nasty strangers inside the tower with the illegal plasma arcs they should be after. We're just tourists who spotted something peculiar while out for an evening stroll. You copy?"

There was a strained grin in Nim's voice. "Copy, sir."

"Keep an observer in sight of Tower Six. Report when the police arrive. Naismith out."

"Copy, sir. Nim out."

Mark emitted a muffled moan and surged forward to grab Miles by his jacket. "You idiot, what are you doing? Call the Dendarii back—order them to clear the Cetagandans out of Tower Seven! Or I will—" He made to grab at Miles's wrist; Miles held him off and put his left hand behind his back.

"Ah-ah! Calm yourself. There's nothing I'd like more than a game of stunner tag with the Cetagandans, since we outnumber them— but they have plasma arcs. Plasma arcs have more than three times the range of a stunner. I don't ask my people to face that kind of tactical disadvantage without dire need."

"If those bastards catch you they'll kill you. How much more dire does it have to be?"

"But Miles," said Ivan, looking up and down the corridor doubtfully, "didn't you just trap us in the center of a pincers movement?"

"No." Miles grinned, exhilarated. "I did not. Not while we own a cloak of invisibility. Come on!" He trotted back to the T intersection and turned right, back toward the Barrayaran-held Tower Six.

"No!" Mark balked. "The Barrayarans might kill you by accident, but they'll kill me on purpose!"

"The ones back there," Miles jerked his head over his shoulder, "would kill us both just to make sure. The Dagoola operation left the Cetagandans more peeved with Admiral Naismith than I think you have grasped. Come on."

Reluctantly, Mark followed, Ivan bringing up the rear.

Miles's heart pounded. He wished he felt half as confident as his grin to Ivan had suggested. But Mark must not be permitted to sense his doubt. A couple of hundred meters of blank synthacrete jerked past as he ran on tiptoe, trying to make as little noise as possible. If the Barrayarans had already worked their way this far down the tunnel—

They came to the last pumping station, and still no sign of the lethal trouble ahead. Or behind.

This pumping station was quiescent again. It would be another twelve hours to the next high tide. If no unexpected surges came downstream, it should stay shut down till then. Still, Miles was disinclined to leave it to chance, and from the way Ivan was shifting from foot to foot, watching him with growing alarm, he'd better be able to offer a guarantee.

He began looking over the control panels, raising one for a look within. Fortunately, it was much simpler than, say, the control nexus for a jumpship propulsion chamber. A cut here, then there, should disable this pump without lighting up boards in the watchtower. He hoped. Not that anyone in the tower was likely to be paying much attention to their boards just this moment. Miles glanced up at Mark. "I need my knife, please."

Unwillingly, Mark handed the antique dagger over, and, at a look from Miles, its sheath as well. Miles used the point to pop the hair-fine wires. His guess as to which ones were which seemed correct; he tried to look as if he'd known it all along. He did not hand the knife back when he was done.

He went to the pumping chamber hatch and opened it. No beeping this time. His gravitic grappler made an instant handle on the smooth inner surface. Last problem was that damned manual locking bar. If some innocent—or not-so-innocent—came along and gave it a twirl—ah, no. The same model of tensor field lever, ally to the gravitic grappler, that Quinn had used to open the hatch to the ledge worked here. Miles blew a breath of relief through pursed lips. He returned to the control panel facing the corridor and slapped on his fisheye scan at the end of a row of dials. It blended in nicely.

He gestured toward the open hatch to the pumping chamber, as inviting as a coffin. "All right. Everybody in."

Ivan went white. "Oh, God, I was afraid that was what you had in mind." Mark did not look much more thrilled than Ivan.

Miles lowered his voice, softly persuasive. "Look, Ivan, I can't force you. You can head on up the corridor and take the chance that your uniform will keep you from getting your brains fried by somebody's nervous reflex. If you survive contact with Destang's hit squad, you'll get arrested by the locals, which probably won't be fatal. But I'd rather you stuck with me." He lowered his voice still further. "And didn't leave me alone with *him*."

"Oh." Ivan blinked.

As Miles expected, this appeal for help had more impact than logic, demands, or cajolery. He added, "Look, it's just like being in a tactics room."

"It's just like being in a trap!"

"Have you ever been in a tactics room when the power's knocked out? They are traps. All that sense of command and control is an illusion. I'd rather be in the field." He smirked and jerked his head toward his double. "Besides, don't you think Mark ought to get the chance to share your recent experience?"

"When you put it that way," growled Ivan, "it has a certain appeal."

Miles lowered himself into the pumping chamber first. He thought he could just hear distant footsteps scuffing in the corridor. Mark looked as if he wanted to bolt, but with Ivan breathing down his neck he had little choice. Finally Ivan, with a gulp, dropped beside them. Miles keyed on his hand light; Ivan, the only one tall enough, shoved the heavy hatch shut. It was profoundly silent for a moment, but for their breathing, as they squatted knee to knee.

Ivan's swollen, empurpled hands clenched and unclenched, sticky with sweat and blood. "At least y'know they can't hear us."

"Cozy," grunted Miles. "Pray our pursuers are as stupid as I was. I ran past this place twice." He opened the scanner case and set the receiver to project the north-and-south view of the still-empty corridor. There was a very faint draft in the chamber, Miles noted. Anything more would foretell a rush of water through the lines, and it would be time to bail out, Cetagandans or no Cetagandans.

"Now what?" said Mark thinly. He looked as if he felt trapped indeed, sandwiched between the two Barrayarans.

Miles settled back against the slimy wet wall with a false air of ease. "Now we wait. Just like a tactics room. You spend a lot of time waiting in a tactics room. If you have a good imagination, it's—pure hell." He keyed his wrist comm. "Nim?"

"Yo, sir. I was just about to call you." Nim's uneven voice sounded as though he was running, or maybe crawling. "A police aircar just landed at Tower Seven. We're withdrawing through the park strip behind the Barrier. The observer reports the locals just entered Tower Six, too."

"Have you got anything off Quinn's wrist comm?"

"It still hasn't moved, sir."

"Has anyone made contact with Captain Galeni yet?"

"No, sir. Wasn't he with you?"

"He left about the time I lost Quinn. Last seen on the outside of the Tidal Barrier at about the midpoint. I'd sent him to look for another way in. Ah . . . report at once if anyone spots him."

"Yes, sir."

Damn, another worry. Had Galeni run into trouble, Cetagandan, Barrayaran, or local? Had he been betrayed by his own state of mind? Miles now wished he'd kept Galeni by him as heartily as he wished he'd kept Quinn. But they hadn't yet found Ivan then; Miles hardly could have done otherwise. He felt like a man trying to assemble a jigsaw puzzle of live pieces, that moved and changed shape at random intervals with tiny malicious giggles. He unclenched his teeth. Mark was regarding him nervously; Ivan was hunkered down not paying much attention to anything, by the way he was biting his lips locked in an internal struggle with his new-won claustrophobia.

There was a movement in the somewhat distorted 180-degree scanner view of the corridor, a man loping silently around the curvature from the south end. Cetagandan point man, Miles guessed, though he wore civilian clothes. He had a stunner, not a plasma arc in his hand—apparently the Cetagandans were now aware that the locals were on the scene in too great force to silence by a convenient murder, and were now thinking of de-escalating, or at least decapitalizing, the Situation. The Cetagandan scouted up the corridor a few more meters, then vanished back the way he'd come.

A minute later, movement from the north: a pair of men tiptoeing along as quietly as a couple of gorillas of that size could move. One of them was the numbskull who'd managed to appear on a covert op still wearing his regulation Service boots. He too had exchanged his original weapon for a more demure stunner, though his companion still carried a lethal nerve disruptor. It looked as if it really could be shaping up for a round of stunner tag. Ah, the stunner, weapon of choice for all uncertain situations, the one weapon with which you really could shoot first and ask questions later.

"Holster your nerve disruptor, *that's* right, good boy!" Miles murmured, as the second man too switched weapons. "Heads up, Ivan; this could be the best show we'll see all year."

Ivan glanced up, his absorbed uncertain smile transmuting into something genuinely sardonic, more like the old Ivan. "Oh, shit, Miles. Destang will have your nuts for engineering this."

"At present, Destang doesn't even know I'm involved. H'sh. Here we go."

The Cetagandan point man had returned. He made a come-on motion, and was leapfrogged by a second Cetagandan. On the other end of the corridor, beyond their view due to the curve, the remaining three Barrayarans came jogging. That accounted for all the Barrayarans that had been in the tower; any outer-perimeter backup was now cut off from them by the cordon of local police. The Barrayarans had apparently given up on their mysteriously vanished quarry and were in pull-out mode, hoping to exit via Tower Seven as quickly as possible without having to explain themselves to a bunch of unsympathetic Earthmen. The Cetagandans, who had actually witnessed the supposed Admiral Naismith run this way, were still in hunting array, though their rear guard was presumably closing up with the pressure from the locals coming on strong behind.

No sign of the rear guard yet; no sign of Quinn being dragged along as a prisoner. Miles didn't know whether to hope for that or not. It would be very nice to know she was still alive, but fiendishly difficult to extract her from the Cetagandans' clutches before the constables closed in. Least-cost scenario called for letting her be stunned/arrested with the mob of them and reclaiming her from the police at their leisure—but suppose some Cetagandan goon decided in the heat of the final crunch that dead women couldn't talk? Miles jittered like a boiling kettle at the thought.

Perhaps he should have jacked up Ivan and Mark and attacked. The breakable leading the disabled and the unreliable in an assault on the unknown . . . no. But would he have done more, done less, for any other officer in his command? Was he so worried about his command logic being ambushed by his emotions that he was now erring in the opposite direction? That would be a betrayal of both Quinn and the Dendarii. . . .

The lead Cetagandan darted into the line of sight of the lead Barrayaran. They both fired instantly, and dropped each other in a heap.

"Stunner reflexes," muttered Miles. "S' wonderful."

"My God," said Ivan, entranced to the point of wholly forgetting his hermetic enclosure, "it's just like the proton annihilating the antiproton. Poof!"

The remaining Barrayarans, strung out along the corridor, flattened to the wall. The Cetagandan dropped to the floor and crawled to his downed comrade. A Barrayaran popped out into the corridor and blitzed him, the Cetagandan's return shot going wide. Two of the four Barrayarans hurried to the unconscious bodies of their mystery opponents. One prepared to offer covering fire; the other began checking them out, weapons, pockets, clothing. He naturally turned up no IDs. The baffled Barrayaran was just pulling off a shoe to dissect— Miles felt he would continue on to the body itself momentarily—when a distorted amplified voice began booming down the corridor from their rear. Miles could not quite make out the echo-splintered words, but the sense of it was clearly, "Here! Halt! What's all this, then?"

One of the Barrayarans helped another load up the stunned one for a shoulder-carry; it had to have been the biggest man who'd been hit, Boots himself. They were close enough to the fisheye that Miles could make out the carrier's legs shake slightly as he straightened and began staggering south under his burden, two men taking the point before and the remaining one the rear guard behind.

The doomed little army had gone perhaps four steps when another pair of Cetagandans appeared around the south curve. One was firing his stunner back over his shoulder as he ran. His attention was so divided, he did not see his partner go down to the Barrayaran point men's stunner fire until he tripped over the sprawling body and fell headlong. He kept his clutch on his own stunner, turned his fall into a controlled roll, and snapped off return fire. One of the Barrayaran point men went down.

The Barrayaran rear guard leapfrogged forward around the burdened middle man and helped his partner zap the rolling Cetagandan, then ran forward with him, hugging the wall. Unfortunately, they overshot the arc of concealment at the same moment as a blast of massed, unaimed stunner fire from beyond the curvature was clearing the corridor for some forward push from the unknowns—police combat team, Miles deduced both from the tactic and the fact that the Cetagandan had been firing in that direction. Men met energy wave with predictable results.

The remaining Barrayaran stood in the corridor bending under the weight of his unconscious comrade and cursing steadily, his eyes squeezed shut as if to shut out the sheer overwhelming embarrassment of it all. When the police appeared behind him he clumped in a circle to face them and raised his bands in surrender as best he could, flipping his empty palms out and letting his stunner clatter to the floor.

Ivan's voice was choked. "I can just see the vid call to

Commodore Destang now. 'Uh, sir? We ran into this little problem. Will you come get me . . . ?'"

"He may prefer to desert," commented Miles.

The two converging police squads came within a breath of repeating the mutual annihilation of their fleeing suspects, but managed to get their true identities communicated just in time. Miles was almost disappointed. Still, nothing could go on forever; at some point the corridor would have become impassable due to the piles of bodies, and the havoc trail off according to the typical senescence curve of a biological system choked on its own waste. It was probably too much to ask that the police clear themselves, as well as the nine assassins, out of the path to escape. Miles was clearly in for another wait. Blast it.

Creaking, Miles stood, stretched, and leaned against the wall with folded arms. It had better not be too long a wait. As soon as the police combat squad called the all-clear, the bomb squad and Tidal Authority techs would appear and start going over every centimeter of the place. The discovery of Miles's little company was inevitable. But not lethal, as long as—Miles glanced down at Mark, hunkering at his feet—no one panicked.

Miles followed Mark's gaze to the scanner display, where the police were checking over the stunned bodies and scratching their heads. The captured Barrayaran was being properly surly and uninformative. As a covert ops agent he was conditioned to withstand torture and fast-penta too; there was little the London constables were likely to get out of him with the methods at their disposal, and he obviously knew it.

Mark shook his head, watching the chaos in the corridor. "Whose side are you on, anyway?"

"Haven't you been paying attention?" asked Miles. "This is all for you."

Mark looked up at him sharply, scowling. "Why?"

Why, indeed. Miles eyed the object of his fascination. He could see how a clone could get to be an obsession, and vice versa. He jerked up his chin in the habitual tic; apparently unconsciously, Mark did the same. Miles had heard weird tales of strange relationships between people and their clones. But then, anyone who deliberately went out and had a clone made must be kinky to start with. Far more interesting to have a child, preferably with a woman who was smarter, faster, and better-looking than oneself; then there was at least a chance for a bit of evolution in the clan. Miles scratched his wrist. Mark, after a moment, scratched his arm. Miles refrained from deliberately yawning. Better not start anything he couldn't stop.

So. He knew what Mark was. Maybe it was more important to realize what he was not. Mark was not a duplicate of Miles himself, despite Galen's best efforts. Was not even the brother of an only-child's dreams; Ivan, with whom Miles shared clan, friends, Barrayar, private memories of the ever-receding past, was a hundred times more his brother than Mark could ever be. It was just possible he had under-appreciated Ivan's merits. Botched beginnings could never be replayed, though they could be—Miles glanced down at his legs, seeing in his mind's eye the artificial bones within—repaired. Sometimes.

"Yeah, why?" Ivan put in at Miles's lengthening silence.

"What," piped Miles, "don't you like your new cousin? Where's your family feeling?"

"One of you is more than enough, thanks. Your Evil Twin here," Ivan made a horned-finger gesture, "is more than I can take. Besides, you both keep locking me in closets."

"Ah, but at least I called for volunteers."

"Yeah, I know that one. 'I want three volunteers, you, you, and you.' You used to bully me and your bodyguard's daughter around that way even before you were in the military, back when we were little kids. I remember."

"Born to command." Miles grinned briefly. Mark's brows lowered, as the apparently tried to imagine Miles as playground bully to the very large and healthy Ivan. "It's a mental trick," Miles informed him.

He studied Mark, who squatted uncomfortably, drawing his head down into his shoulders like a turtle against his gaze. Was this evil? Confusion, to be sure. Distortion of spirit as well as body—though Galen could have been only a little more awful as a child's mentor than Miles's own grandfather. But to be properly sociopathic one must be self-centered to an extreme degree, which did not seem to describe Mark; he had hardly been permitted to have a self at all. Maybe he was not self-centered enough. "Are you Evil?" Miles asked lightly.

"I'm a murderer, aren't I?" sneered Mark. "What more d'you want?"

"Was that murder? I thought I sensed some element of confusion."

"He grabbed the nerve disruptor. I didn't want to give it up. It went off." Mark's face was pale in memory, white and deeply shadowed in the sharp sideways illumination cast by Miles's handlight stuck to the wall. "I meant it to go off."

Ivan's brows rose, but Miles ruthlessly did not pause to fill him in. "Unpremeditated, perhaps," suggested Miles.

Mark shrugged.

"If you were free . . ." began Miles slowly.

Mark's lips rippled. "Free? Me? What chance? The police will have found the body by now."

"No. The tide was up over the rail. The sea has taken it. Might be three, four days before it surfaces again. If it surfaces again." And a repellent object it would be by then. Would Captain Galeni wish to reclaim it, have it properly buried? Where *was* Galeni? "Suppose you were free. Free of Barrayar and Komarr, free of me too. Free of Galen and the police. Free of obsession. What would you choose? Who are you? Or are you only reaction, never action?"

Mark twitched visibly. "Suck slime."

One corner of Miles's mouth curved up. He scuffed his boot through the gook on the floor, stopped himself before he began doodling with his toe. "I don't suppose you'll ever know as long as I'm standing over you."

Mark spat the dregs of his hatred. "You're the free one!"

"Me?" Miles was almost genuinely startled. "I'll never be as free as you are right now. You were yoked to Galen by fear. His control only equalled his reach, and both were broken together. I'm yoked by—other things. Waking or sleeping, near or far, makes no difference. Yet . . . Barrayar can be an interesting place, seen through other eyes than Galen's. The man's own son saw the possibilities."

Mark smirked sourly, staring at the wall. "You making another play for my body?"

"For what? It's not like you have the height my—our—genes intended or something. And my bones are all on their way to becoming plastic anyway. No advantage there."

"I'd be in reserve, then. A spare in case of accidents."

Miles threw up his hands. "*You* don't even believe that any more. But my original offer still stands. Come with me back to the Dendarii, and I'll hide you. Smuggle you home. Where you can take your time and figure out how to be real Mark, and not imitation anybody."

"I don't want to meet those people," Mark stated flatly.

By which he meant, his mother and father; Miles caught that without difficulty, though Ivan was clearly losing the thread. "I don't think they would behave inappropriately. After all, they're already in you, on a fundamental level. You, ah, can't run away from yourself." He paused, tried again. "If you could do anything, what would it be?"

Mark's scowl deepened. "Bust up the clone business on Jackson's Whole."

"Hm." Miles considered. "It's pretty entrenched. Still, what d'you expect of the descendants of a colony that started as a hijacker base? Naturally they developed into an aristocracy. I'll have to tell you a couple of stories about your ancestors sometime that aren't in the official histories . . ."

So, Mark had picked up that much good from his association with Galen, a thirst for justice that went beyond his own skin even if including it. "As life-goals go, it would certainly keep you occupied. How would you go about it?"

"I don't know." Mark appeared taken aback by this sudden practical turn. "Blow up the labs. Rescue the kids."

"Good tactics, bad strategy. They'd just rebuild. You need more than one level of attack. If you figured out some way to make the business unprofitable, it would die on its own."

"How?" Mark asked in turn.

"Let's see . . . There's the customer base. Unethical rich people. One could hardly expect to persuade them to choose death over life, I suppose. A medical breakthrough offering some other form of personal life extension might divert them."

"Killing them would divert them, too," growled Mark.

"True, but impractical in the mass. People of that class tend to have bodyguards. Sooner or later one would get you, and it would be all over. Look, there must be forty points of attack. Don't get stuck on the first one to come to mind. For example, suppose you returned with me to Barrayar. As Lord Mark Vorkosigan, you could expect in time to amass a personal and financial power base. Complete your education—really fit yourself out to attack the problem strategically, not just, ah, fling yourself off the first wall you come to and go *splat*."

"I will never," said Mark through his teeth, "go to Barrayar."

Yeah, and it seems like all the upper-percentile women in the galaxy are in complete agreement with you . . . you may be smarter than you know. Miles sighed under his breath. *Quinn, Quinn, Quinn, where are you?* In the corridor, the police were now loading the last unconscious assassins onto a float pallet. The break would come soon, or not at all.

Ivan was staring at him, Miles realized. "You're completely loony," Ivan stated with conviction.

"What, don't you think it's time somebody took those Jackson's Whole bastards on?"

"Sure, but . . ."

"I can't be everywhere. But I could support the project," Miles glanced at Mark, "if you're all done trying to be me, that is. Are you?"

Mark watched the last of the assassins get wafted away. "You can have it. It's a wonder you're not trying to switch identities with *me*." His head swiveled toward Miles in suddenly renewed suspicion.

Miles laughed, painfully. What a temptation. Ditch his uniform, walk into a tubeway, and disappear with a credit chit for half a million marks in his pocket. To be a free man . . . His eye fell on Ivan's grimy Imperial dress greens, symbol of their service. *You are what you do—choose again. . . .* No. Barrayar's ugliest child would choose to be her champion still. Not crawl into a hole and be no one at all.

Speaking of holes, it was high time to crawl out of this one. The last of the police combat team was marching away past the curve of the corridor after the float pallet. Tidal techs would be all over the place shortly. Better move fast.

"Time to go," Miles said, shutting down the scanner and retrieving his handlight.

Ivan grunted relief and reached up to pull the hatch open. He boosted Miles through. Miles in turn tossed him a line from his rappelling spool as before. Panic flooded Mark's face for a moment, looking up at Miles framed in the exit, as he realized why he might be last; his expression became closed again as Miles lowered the line. Miles plucked his scanner fisheye and returned it to its case, and keyed his wrist comm. "Nim, status report," he whispered.

"We've got both cars back in the air, sir, about a kilometer inland. The police have cordoned off your area. The place is crawling with 'em."

"All right. Anything from Quinn?"

"No change."

"Give me her exact coordinates inside the tower."

Nim did so.

"Very good. I'm inside the Barrier near Tower Six with Lieutenant Vorpatril of the Barrayaran Embassy and my clone. We're going to attempt to exit via Tower Seven and pick up Quinn on the way. Or at least," Miles swallowed past a stupidly tightened throat, "find out what happened to her. Hold your present station. Naismith out."

They pulled off their boots and padded south down the corridor, hugging the wall. Miles could hear voices, but they were behind them. The T intersection was now lit. Miles held up his hand as they approached, oozed to the corner, and peeked around. A man in Tidal Authority coveralls and a uniformed constable were examining the hatch. Their backs were turned. Miles waved Mark and Ivan forward. They all flitted silently past the tunnel mouth.

There was a police guard stationed in the lift tube foyer at the base of Tower Seven. Miles, boots in one hand and stunner in the other, bared his teeth in frustration. So much for his optimistic hope of exiting without leaving a trace.

No help for it. Maybe they could make up in speed what they were going to lack in finesse. Besides, the man now stood between Miles and Quinn, and thus deserved his fate. Miles aimed his stunner and fired. The constable collapsed.

They floated up the tube. *This level,* Miles pointed silently. The corridor was brightly lit, but there were no subtle people-sounds that Miles could hear. He paced off the meters that Nim had read out to him, and stopped before a closed door marked UTILITY. His stomach was turning over. Suppose the Cetagandans had arranged a slow death for her, suppose the minutes Miles had spent so cool and sensible hiding out had made all the difference. . . .

The door was locked. The control had been buggered. Miles ripped it apart, shorted it out, and heaved the door open manually, nearly snapping his splayed fingers.

She lay in a tumbled heap, too pale and still. Miles fell to his knees beside her. Throat pulse, throat pulse—there was one. Her skin was warm, her chest rose and fell. Stunned, only stunned. Only stunned. He looked up at a blurred Ivan hovering anxiously, swallowed, and steadied his ragged breathing. It had, after all, been the most logical possibility.

CHAPTER SIXTEEN

They paused at the side entrance of Tower Seven to pull their boots back on. The park strip lay between them and the city, spangled with white sparks and green patches along the illuminated walks, dark and mysterious between. Miles estimated the run to the nearest bushes, and triangulated the police vehicles scattered about the parking areas.

"I don't suppose you have your hip flask with you?" Miles whispered to Ivan.

"If I had I'd have emptied it hours ago. Why?"

"I was just wondering how to explain three guys dragging an unconscious woman through the park at this hour of the night. If we sprinkled Quinn with a little brandy, we could at least pretend to be taking her home from a party or something. Stunner hangover's enough like the real thing, it'd be convincing even if she started to wake up groggy."

"I trust she has a sense of humor. Well, what's a little character assassination among friends?"

"Better than the real thing."

"Urgh. Anyway, I don't have my flask. Are we ready?"

"I guess. No, hold it—" Another aircar was dropping down. Civilian, but the police guard at the main tower entrance went to meet it. An older man got out, and they hurried back to the tower together. "Now."

Ivan took Quinn's shoulders and Mark took her feet. Miles stepped carefully over the stunned body of the policeman who had been guarding this exit, and they all double-timed it across the pavement toward cover.

"God, Miles," panted Ivan as they paused in the greenery to scan the next leg, "why don't you go in for little petite women? It'd make more sense . . ."

"Now, now. She only weighs about double a full field pack. You can make it." No shouting from behind, no hurrying pursuers. The area closest to the tower was actually probably the safest. It would have been scanned and swept before now, and pronounced clean of intruders. Police attention would be concentrated at the park's border. Which they would have to cross, to reach the city and escape.

Miles stared into the shadows. With all the artificial lighting about, his eyes were not dark-adapting as well as he'd like.

Ivan stared too. "I can't spot any coppers in the bushes," he muttered.

"I'm not looking for police," Miles whispered back.

"What, then?"

"Mark said a man wearing face paint fired at him. Have you seen anybody wearing face paint yet?"

"Ah . . . maybe the police nabbed him first, before we saw the others." But Ivan looked over his shoulder.

"Maybe. Mark—what color was the face? What pattern?"

"Mostly blue. With white and yellow and black kind of swirling slashes. A ghem-lord of middle rank, right?"

"A century-captain. If you were supposed to be me you should be able to read ghem-markings forward and backward."

"There was so much to learn. . . ."

"Anyway, Ivan—do you really want to just assume a century-captain, highly trained, sent from headquarters, formally sworn to his hunt, really let some London constable sneak up and stun him? The others were just ordinary soldiers. The Cetagandans will bail 'em out later. A ghem-lord'd die before he'd let himself be so embarrassed. He'll be a persistent bugger, too."

Ivan rolled his eyes. "Wonderful."

They wound through a couple hundred meters of trees, shrubbery and shadows. The hiss and hum of traffic on the main coastal highway came faintly now. The pedestrian underpasses were doubtless guarded. The high-speed highway was fenced and strictly forbidden to foot traffic.

A synthacrete kiosk cloaked with bushes and vines hopeful of concealing its blunt utility squatted near the main path to the pedestrian underpass. At first Miles took it for a public latrine, but a closer look revealed only one blank locked door. The spotlights that should have illuminated that side were knocked out. As Miles watched, the door began to slide slowly aside. A weapon in a pale hand glittered faintly in the blackness. Miles aimed his stunner and held his breath. The dark shape of a man slipped out.

Miles exhaled. "Captain Galeni!" he hissed.

Galeni jerked as though shot, crouched, and scurried toward them, joining them in their concealment on hands and knees. He swore under his breath, discovering, as Miles had, that this grouping of ornamental shrubs had thorns. His eyes took instant inventory of the ragged little group, Miles and Mark, Ivan and Elli. "I'll be damned. You're still alive."

"I'd sort of been wondering about you, too," Miles admitted.

Galeni looked—Galeni looked bizarre, Miles decided. Gone was the blank witnessing stillness that had absorbed Ser Galen's death without comment. He was almost grinning, electric with a slightly off-center exhilaration, as if he'd overdone some stimulant drug. He was breathing heavily; his face was bruised, mouth bloody. His swollen hand flexed on his weapon—last seen weaponless, he was now carrying a Cetagandan military-issue plasma arc. A knife hilt stuck out of his boot top.

"Have you, ah, run into a guy wearing blue face paint yet?" Miles inquired.

"Oh yes," said Galeni in a tone of some satisfaction.

"What the hell happened to you? Sir."

Galeni spoke in a rapid whisper. "I couldn't find an entrance in the Barrier near where I'd left you. I spotted that utilities access over there," he jerked his head toward the kiosk, "and thought there might be some power optic or water line tunnels back to the Barrier. I was half-right. There are utility tunnels all under this park. But I got turned around underground, and instead of coming out in the Barrier, I ended up coming out a port in the pedestrian crossing under the Channel Highway. Where I found guess who?"

Miles shook his head. "Police? Cetagandans? Barrayarans?"

"Close. It was my old friend and opposite number from the Cetagandan Embassy, Ghem-lieutenant Tabor. It actually took me a couple of minutes to realize what he was doing there. Playing outer-perimeter backup to the experts from HQ. Same as I would have been doing if I hadn't been," Galeni snickered, "confined to quarters.

"He was not happy to see me," Galeni went on. "He couldn't figure what the hell I was doing there either. We both pretended to be out viewing the moon, while I got a look at the equipment he had packed in his groundcar. He may have actually believed me; I think he thought I was drunk or drugged."

Miles politely refrained from remarking, *I can see why.*

"But then he started getting signals from his team, and had to get rid of me in a hurry. He pulled a stunner on me—I ducked—he didn't hit me square on, but I lay low pretending to be more disabled than I was, listening to his half of the conversation with the squad in the tower and hoping for a chance to reverse the situation.

"The feeling was just coming back to the left half of my body when your blue friend showed up. His arrival distracted Tabor, and I jumped them both."

Miles's brows rose. "How the devil did you manage that?"

Galeni's hands were flexing as he spoke. "I don't . . . quite know," he admitted. "I remember hitting them. . . ." He glanced at Mark. "It was nice to have a clearly defined enemy for a change."

Upon whom, Miles guessed, Galeni had just unloaded all the accumulated tensions of the last impossible week and this mad night. Miles had witnessed berserkers before. "Are they still alive?"

"Oh yes."

Miles decided he would believe that when he'd had a chance to check for himself. Galeni's smile was alarming, all those long teeth gleaming in the darkness.

"Their *car*," said Ivan urgently.

"Their car," agreed Miles. "Is it still there? Can we get to it?"

"Maybe," said Galeni. "There is at least one police squad in the tunnels now. I could hear them."

"We'll have to chance it."

"Easy for you to say," muttered Mark truculently. "You have diplomatic immunity."

Miles stared at him, seized by berserker inspiration. His finger traced over an inner pocket in his gray jacket. "Mark," he breathed, "how would you like to *earn* that hundred-thousand Betan dollar credit chit?"

"There isn't any credit chit."

"That's what Ser Galen said. You might reflect on what else he was wrong about tonight." Miles glanced up to check what effect mention of his father's name had on Galeni. A cooling one, apparently; some of the drawn and inward look returned to his eyes even as Miles watched. "Captain Galeni. Are those two Cetagandans conscious, or can they be brought to consciousness?"

"At least one is. They may both be by now. Why?"

"Witnesses. Two witnesses, ideal."

"I thought the whole point of sneaking off instead of surrendering was to avoid witnesses?" said Ivan plaintively.

"I think," Miles overrode him, "I had better be Admiral Naismith. No offense, Mark, but you don't have your Betan accent quite right. You don't hit your terminal *R*'s quite hard enough or something. Besides, you've practiced Lord Vorkosigan more."

Galeni's eyebrows were going up, as he grasped the idea. He nodded thoughtfully, though his face as he turned his gaze on Mark was unreadable enough to make Mark flinch. "Indeed. You owe us your cooperation, I think." He added even more softly, "You owe me."

This was not the moment to point out how much Galeni owed Mark in return, though a brief meeting of their eyes convinced Miles that Galeni, at least, was perfectly conscious of the two-way flow of that grim debt. But Galeni would not fumble this opportunity.

Sure of his alliance, Admiral Naismith said, "Into the tunnel, then. Lead on, Captain."

The Cetagandan groundcar was parked in a shadowy spot under a tree, a few meters to their left as they rose up out of the lift tube from the pedestrian subway to the Barrier park. Still no police guard on this end; the end toward the park, Galeni had informed them, had a two-man squad, though they had not risked themselves rechecking that fact. The scurry through the tunnels had been hectic enough, barely dodging a police bomb squad.

The spreading plane tree shielded the car from view of most of the (closed, at this hour) shops and apartments lining the other side of the narrow city street. No insomniac peeping out an upper window could have witnessed Galeni's encounter, Miles hoped. The highway above and behind them was walled and blind. Miles still felt exposed.

The groundcar bore no embassy identification, nor any other unusual features to draw attention; bland, neither old nor new, a little dirty. Definitely covert ops. Miles raised his brows and whistled silently at the fresh dents in the side, about the size of a man's head, and the blood spattered on the pavement. In the dimness the red color was fortunately subdued.

"Wasn't that a bit noisy?" Miles inquired of Galeni, pointing to the dents.

"Mm? Not really. Dull thumps. Nobody yelled." Galeni, after a quick look up and down the street and a pause for a lone groundcar to whisper past, raised the mirrored bubble canopy.

Two shapes huddled in the back seat, hitched up with their own equipment. Lieutenant Tabor, in civilian clothes, blinked over his gag. The man with the blue face paint sat slumped next to him. Miles checked one eyelid, and found the eye still rolled back. He rummaged in the front for a medkit. Ivan loaded and settled Elli and took the controls. Mark slid in beside Tabor, and Galeni sandwiched their captives from the other side. At a touch from Ivan the canopy sighed down and locked itself, jamming them all in. Seven was a crowd.

Miles leaned over the back of the front seat and pressed a hypospray of synergine, first aid for shock, against the century-captain's neck. It might bring him around, and certainly would not harm him. At this present peculiar moment, Miles's would-be killer's life and continued health was a most precious commodity. As an afterthought, Miles gave Elli a dose too. She emitted a heartening moan.

The groundcar rose on its skirts and hissed forward. Miles exhaled with relief as they put the coast behind them, turning into the maze of the city. He keyed his wrist comm, and said in his flattest Betan accent, "Nim?"

"Yes, sir."

"Take a fix on my comm. Follow along. We're all done here."

"We have you, sir."

"Naismith out."

He settled Elli's head in his lap and turned to watch Tabor over the seat back. Tabor was staring back and fourth from Miles to Mark, beside him.

"Hello, Tabor," said Mark, carefully coached, in his best Barra-yaran Vor tones—did it really sound that snide?—"How's your bonsai?"

Tabor recoiled slightly. The century-captain stirred, staring through slitted but focusing eyes. He tried to move, discovered his bonds, and settled back—not relaxed, but not wasting energy on futile struggle.

Galeni reached over him and loosed Tabor's gag. "Sorry, Tabor. But you can't have Admiral Naismith. Not here on Earth, anyway. You can pass the word up your chain of command. He's under our protection until his fleet leaves orbit. Part of the agreed price for his helping the Barrayaran Embassy find the Komarrans who had lately kidnapped some of our personnel. So back off."

Tabor's eyes shifted, back and forth, as he spat out his gag, worked his jaw, and swallowed. He croaked, "You're working together?"

"Unfortunately," growled Mark.

"A mercenary," caroled Miles, "gets it where he can."

"You made a mistake," hissed the century-captain, focusing on the admiral, "when you took contract against us at Dagoola."

"You can say that again," agreed Miles cheerily. "After we rescued their damned army, the Underground stiffed us. Did us out of half our promised pay. I don't suppose Cetaganda would like to hire us to go after them in turn, eh? No? Unfortunately, I cannot afford personal vengeance. At present, anyway. Or I would not have taken employment with," he bared his teeth in an unfriendly smile at Mark, who sneered back, "these old friends."

"So you really are a clone," breathed Tabor, staring at the legendary mercenary commander. "We thought . . ." He fell silent.

"We thought he was yours, for years," said Mark-as-Lord-Vorkosigan.

Ours! mouthed Tabor in astonishment.

"But the present operation confirmed his Komarran origin," Mark finished.

"We have an agreement," Miles spoke up as if unsettled by Mark's tone, glaring from Mark to Galeni. "You cover me till I leave Earth."

"We have an agreement," said Mark, "as long as you never come any closer to Barrayar."

"You can have bloody Barrayar. I'll take the rest of the galaxy, thanks."

The century-captain was blurring out again, but fighting it, squeezing his eyes shut and breathing in a controlled pattern. Concussion, Miles judged. In his lap, Elli's eyes popped open. He stroked her curls. She emitted a ladylike burp, saved by the synergine from the more usual post-stun vomiting. She sat up, looked around, saw Mark, the Cetagandans, Ivan, and shut her jaw with a snap, concealing her disorientation. Miles squeezed her hand. *I'll explain later,* his smile promised. She lowered her brows at him in exasperation, *You'd better.* She lifted her chin, poised before the enemy even in the teeth of her own bewilderment.

Ivan turned his head, inquiring out of the side of his mouth of Galeni, "So what do we do with these Cetagandans, sir? Drop them off somewhere? From how high up?"

"There is, I think, no need for an interplanetary incident." Galeni was wolfishly cheerful, taking his tone from Miles. "Is there, Lieutenant Tabor? Or do you wish the local authorities to be told what the ghem-comrade was really trying to do in the Barrier last night? No? I thought not. Very well. They both need medical treatment, Ivan. Lieutenant Tabor unfortunately broke his arm, and I believe his, ah, friend has a concussion. Among other things. Your choice, Tabor. Shall we drop you off at a hospital, or would you prefer treatment at your own embassy?"

"Embassy," croaked Tabor, clearly cognizant of possible legal complications. "Unless you want to try to talk your way out of an attempted murder charge," he counter-threatened.

"Only assault, surely." Galeni's eyes glittered.

Tabor smiled most uneasily, looking as if he'd like to edge away if only there were room. "Whatever. Neither of our ambassadors would be pleased."

"Quite."

It was getting near dawn. Traffic was beginning to increase. Ivan circled a couple of streets before spotting a deserted auto-cab stand that did not have a queue of waiting patrons. This seaside suburb was far from the embassy district. Galeni was quite solicitous, helping unload their passengers—but he didn't toss the code-key to the century-captain's hand and foot bonds to Tabor until Ivan began to accelerate back into the street. "I'll have one of my staff return your car this afternoon," Galeni called back as they sped off. He settled in his seat with a snort as Ivan sealed the canopy and added under his breath, "After we go over it."

"Think that charade'll work?" asked Ivan.

"In the short range—convincing the Cetagandans that Barrayar had nothing to do with Dagoola—maybe, maybe not," sighed Miles. "But for the main security issue—there go two loyal officers who will swear under chemohypnotics that Admiral Naismith and Lord Vorkosigan are without question two separate men. That's going to be worth a great deal to us."

"But will Destang think so?" asked Ivan.

"I do not believe," said Galeni distantly, staring out the canopy, "that I give a good goddamn what Destang thinks."

Miles found himself in mental agreement with that sentiment. But then, they were all very tired. But they were all here: he looked around, savoring the faces, Elli and Ivan, Galeni and

Mark; all alive, all brought through the night to this moment of survival.

Almost all.

"Where do you want to be dropped off, Mark?" Miles asked. He glanced through his lashes at Galeni, expecting an objection, but Galeni offered none. With the jettisoning of the Cetagandans Galeni had lost the hyper-adrenal edge that had been carrying him; he looked drained. He looked old. Miles did not solicit an objection. *Be careful what you ask for, you might get it.*

"A tube station," said Mark. "Any tube station."

"Very well." Miles called up a map on the car's console. "Up three streets and over two, Ivan."

He got out with Mark as the car settled to the pavement in the drop-off zone. "Back in a minute." They walked together to the entrance to the DOWN lift tube. It was still night-quiet here in this district, only a trickle of people flowing past, but morning rush would be starting soon.

Miles opened his jacket and drew out the coded card. From the tense look on Mark's face he was anticipating a nerve disruptor, in the style of Ser Galen, right to the last. Mark took the card and turned it over in wonder and suspicion.

"There you go," said Miles. "If you, with your background and this bankroll, can't disappear on Earth, it can't be done. Good luck."

"But . . . what do you want of me?"

"Nothing. Nothing at all. You're a free man, for as long as you can keep so. We will certainly not be reporting Galen's, ah, semi-accidental death."

Mark slipped the chit into his trouser pocket. "You wanted more."

"When you can't get what you want, you take what you can get. As you are finding." He nodded toward Mark's pocket; Mark's hand closed over it protectively.

"What is it that you want me to do?" Mark demanded. "What are you setting me up for? Did you really take that Jackson's Whole garbage seriously? What do you expect me to do?"

"You can take it and retire to the pleasure domes of Mars, for as long as it lasts. Or buy an education, or two or three. Or stuff it down the first waste chute you pass. I'm not your owner. I'm not your mentor. I'm not your parents. I have no expectations. I have no desires." *Rebel against that—if you can figure out how—little brother. . . .* Miles held his hands palm-out and stepped back.

Mark swung into the lift tube, never turning his back. "WHY NOT?" he yelled suddenly, baffled and furious.

Miles threw back his head and laughed. "You figure it out!" he called.

The tube field took him, and he vanished, swallowed into the earth.

Miles returned to the friends who waited for him.

"Was that smart?" Elli, breaking off a rapid fill-in from Ivan, worried as he settled in beside her. "Just letting him go like that?"

"I don't know," sighed Miles. "'If you can't help, don't hinder.' I can't help him; Galen's made him too crazy. I am his obsession. I suspect I'll always be his obsession. I know all about obsessions. The best I can do is get out of his way. In time he may calm down, without me to react against. In time he may—save himself."

His own weariness flooded in. Elli was warm against him, and he was very, very glad of her. Reminded, he keyed his wrist comm and dismissed Nim and his patrol back to the shuttleport.

"Well," Ivan blinked after a full minute of wiped-out silence from all present, "where now? D'you two want to go back to the shuttleport too?"

"Yeah," breathed Miles, "and flee the planet. . . . Desertion is not practical, I'm afraid. Destang would catch up with me sooner or later anyway. We may as well all go back to the embassy and report. The true report. There's nothing left to lie for, is there?" He squinted, trying to think.

"For all of me, there's not," rumbled Galeni. "I do not care for doctored reports anyway. Eventually, they become history. Embedded sin."

"You . . . know I didn't mean it to work out that way," Miles said to him after a silent moment. "The confrontation last night." A damned sorry weak apology that sounded, for getting the man's father blown away. . . .

"Did you imagine you controlled it? Omniscient and omnipotent? Nobody appointed you God, Vorkosigan." Ghostly faint, one corner of his mouth turned up. "I'm sure it was an oversight." He leaned back and closed his eyes.

Miles cleared his throat. "Back to the embassy then, Ivan. Ah . . . no rush. Drive slowly. I wouldn't mind seeing a last bit of London, eh?" He leaned on Elli and watched the early summer dawn creep over the city, time and all times jumbled and juxtaposed like the light and shadow between one street and the next.

✧   ✧   ✧

When they all lined up in a row in Galeni's Security office at the embassy, Miles was put in mind of the set of Chinese monkeys his Dendarii chief of staff Tung kept on a shelf in his quarters. Ivan was unquestionably See-no-evil. From the tight set of Galeni's jaw, as he returned Commodore Destang's glower, he was a prime candidate for Speak-no-evil. That left Hear-no-evil for Miles, standing between them, but putting his hands over his ears probably wouldn't help much.

Miles had expected Destang to be furious, but he looked more disgusted. The commodore returned their salutes and leaned back in Galeni's station chair. When his eye fell on Miles his lips thinned in a particularly dyspeptic line.

"Vorkosigan." Miles's name hung in the air before them like a visible thing. Destang regarded it without favor, and went on, "When I finished dealing with a certain Investigator Reed of the London Municipal Assizes at 0700 this morning, I was determined that only divine intervention could save you from my wrath. Divine intervention arrived at 0900 in the person of a special courier from Imperial HQ." Destang held up a data disk marked with the Imperial seal between his thumb and forefinger. "Here are the new and urgent orders for your Dendarii irregulars."

Since Miles had passed the courier in the cafeteria, this was not wholly unexpected. He suppressed a surge forward. "Yes, sir?" he said encouragingly.

"It appears that a certain free mercenary fleet operating in the far Sector IV area, supposedly under contract to a subplanetary government, has slipped over the line from guerrilla warfare to outright piracy. Their wormhole blockade has degenerated from stopping and searching ships to confiscations. Three weeks ago they hijacked a Tau Cetan registered passenger vessel to convert into a troop transport. So far so good, but then some bright soul among them hit on the idea of augmenting their payroll by holding the passengers for ransom. Several planetary governments whose citizens are being held have fielded a negotiating team, headed by the Tau Cetans."

"And our involvement, sir?" Sector IV was a long way from Barrayar by any measure, but Miles could guess what was coming. Ivan looked wildly curious.

"Among the passengers happened to be eleven Barrayaran subjects—including the wife of Minister for Heavy Industries Lord Vorvane and her three children. As the Barrayarans are a minority of the two hundred sixteen people being held, Barrayar was of course denied control of the negotiating team. And our fleet has been denied permission by their unfriendly governments to cross three of the necessary wormhole nexuses on the shortest route between Barrayar and Sector IV. The next shortest alternate route would take eighteen weeks to traverse. From Earth, your Dendarii can arrive in that local space area in less than two weeks." Destang frowned thoughtfully; Ivan looked fascinated.

"Your orders, of course, are to rescue alive the Emperor's subjects, and as many other planetary citizens as possible, and to deal such punitive measures as you can compatible with the first goal, sufficient to prevent the perpetrators from ever repeating this performance. Since we ourselves are in the midst of critical treaty negotiations with the Tau Cetans, we don't wish them to become aware of the source of this unilateral rescue effort if, ah, anything goes wrong. Your method of achieving these goals appears to be left totally to your discretion. You'll find all the intelligence details HQ had up to eight days ago in here."

He handed the data disk across at last; Miles's hand closed over it itchily. Ivan now looked envious. Destang produced another object, which he handed to Miles with a little of the air of a man having his liver torn out. "The courier also delivered yet another credit chit for eighteen million marks. For your next six month's operating expenses."

"Thank you, sir!"

"Ha. When you're done you're to report to Commodore Rivik at Sector IV headquarters on Orient Station," Destang finished. "With luck, by the time your irregulars next return to Sector II, I will have retired."

"Yes, sir. Thank you, sir."

Destang turned his eye on Ivan. "Lieutenant Vorpatril."

"Sir?" Ivan stood to attention with his best air of eager enthusiasm. Miles prepared to protest Ivan's complete innocence, ignorance, and victimhood, but it turned out not to be necessary; Destang contemplated Ivan for a moment longer, and sighed, "Never mind."

Destang turned to Galeni, who stood stiff-legged—and stiff-necked, Miles guessed. Having beaten Destang back to the embassy that morning, they had all washed, the two embassy officers had changed to clean uniforms, and they had all filed laconic reports, which Destang had just seen. But no one had slept yet. How much more garbage could Galeni absorb before reaching his explosive limit?

"Captain Galeni," said Destang. "On the military side, you stand charged with disobeying an order to remain confined to your quarters. Since this is identical to the charge that Vorkosigan here has managed to so luckily evade, this presents me with a certain problem of justice. There's also the mitigating factor of Vorpatril's kidnapping. His rescue, and the death of an enemy of Barrayar, are the only two tangible results of last night's . . . activities. All else is speculation, unprovable assertions as to your intentions and state of mind. Unless you choose to submit to a fast-penta interrogation to clear up any lingering doubts."

Galeni looked revulsed. "Is that an order, sir?"

Galeni, Miles realized, was about two seconds away from offering to resign his commission—*now,* when so much had been sacrificed—he wanted to kick him, *No, no!* Wild defenses poured through Miles's mind. *Fast-penta is degrading to the dignity of an officer, sir!* or even, *If you dose him you must dose me too—it's all right, Galeni, I abandoned dignity years ago*—except that Miles's idiosyncratic reaction to fast-penta made that a less than useful offer. He bit his tongue and waited.

Destang looked troubled. After a silence he said simply, "No." He looked up and added, "But it does mean that my reports, and yours, Vorkosigan's, and Vorpatril's, will all be bundled up together and sent to Simon Illyan for review. I will refuse to close the case. I didn't arrive at my rank by shying away from military decisions—nor by involving myself gratuitously with political ones. Your. . . loyalty, like the fate of Vorkosigan's clone, has become too ambiguously political a question. I'm not convinced of the long-range viability of the Komarr integration scheme—but I wouldn't care to go down in history as its saboteur.

"While the case is pending, and in the absence of evidence of treason, you'll resume your routine duties here at the embassy. Don't thank me," he added glumly, as Miles grinned, Ivan choked back an out-loud laugh, and Galeni looked fractionally less black, "it was the ambassador's request.

"You are all dismissed to your duties."

Miles squelched the impulse to run before Destang changed his mind; he returned Destang's salute and walked normally with the others toward the door. As they reached it Destang added, "Captain Galeni?"

Galeni paused. "Sir?"

"My condolences." The words might have been pulled out of Destang with pliers, but his discomfort was perhaps a measure of their sincerity.

"Thank you, sir," Galeni's voice was so devoid of inflection as to be deathly, but in the end he managed a small, acknowledging nod.

The locks and corridors of the *Triumph* were noisy with returning personnel, the final placement of equipment and repairs by tech teams, and the loading of the last supplies. Noisy, but not chaotic; purposeful and energetic but not frantic. The absence of frantic was a good sign, considering how long they'd been on station. Tung's tough cadre of non-coms had not permitted routine preparations to slide till the last minute.

Miles, with Elli at his back, was the center of a hurricane of curiosity from the moment he stepped on board—*What's the new contract, sir?* The speed with which the rumor mill cranked out speculation both shrewd and absurd was amazing. He sent the speculators on their way with a repeated, *Yes, we have a contract— yes, we're breaking orbit. Just as soon as you're ready. Are you ready, Mister? Is the rest of your squad ready? Then maybe you'd better go assist 'em. . . .*

"Tung!" Miles hailed his chief of staff. The squat Eurasian was dressed in civilian gear, carrying luggage. "You just now back?"

"I'm just now leaving. Didn't Auson get hold of you, Admiral? I've been trying to reach you for a week."

"What?" Miles pulled him aside.

"I've turned in my resignation. I'm activating my retirement option."

"*What?* Why?"

Tung grinned. "Congratulate me. I'm getting married."

Stunned, Miles croaked, "Congratulations. Ah—when did this happen?"

"On leave, of course. She's actually my second cousin once removed. A widow. She's been running a tourist boat up the Amazon by herself since her husband died. She's the captain and the cook too. She fries a moo shu pork to kill for. But she's getting a little older—needs some muscle." The bullet-shaped Tung could certainly supply that. "We're going to be partners. Hell," he went on, "when you finish buying out the *Triumph*, we can even afford to dispense with the tourists. You ever want to try water-skiing on the Amazon behind a fifty-meter hoversloop, son, stop by."

And the mutant piranhas could eat what was left, no doubt. The charm of the vision of Tung spending his sunset years watching—

sunsets, from a riverboat deck, with a buxom—Miles was sure she was buxom—Eurasian lady on his lap, a drink in one hand and scarfing down moo shu pork with the other, was a little lost on Miles as he contemplated a) what it was going to cost the fleet to buy out Tung's share of the *Triumph*, and b) the huge Tung-shaped hole this was going to leave in his command structure.

Gibbering, hyperventilating, or running around in small circles were not useful responses. Instead Miles essayed cautiously, "Ah . . . you sure you won't be bored?"

Tung, damn his sharp eyes, lowered his voice and answered the real question. "I wouldn't be leaving if I didn't think you could handle it. You've steadied down a lot, son. Just keep on like you've been." He grinned again and cracked his knuckles. "Besides, you have an advantage not shared by any other mercenary commander in the galaxy."

"What's that?" Miles bit.

Tung lowered his voice still further. "*You* don't have to make a profit."

And that, and his sardonic grin, was as close as cagey Tung was ever likely to admit that he had long ago figured out who their real employer was. He saluted as he left.

Miles swallowed, and turned to Elli. "Well . . . call a meeting of the Intelligence department in half an hour. We'll want to get our pathfinders en route as quickly as possible. Ideally, we want to put a team inside the enemy organization before we arrive."

Miles paused, as he realized he was now looking into the face of the most wily pathfinder in his fleet for people-situations, as versus terrain-situations which called for the talents of a certain Lieutenant Christof. To send her ahead, out of reach, into danger—*No, no!*—was compellingly logical. Quinn's best offensive talents were largely wasted bodyguarding; it was merely an accident of history and security that threw her into that defensive job so often. Miles forced his lips to move on as if never tempted to illogic.

"They're mercenaries; some of our group ought simply to be able to join up. If we can find someone to convincingly simulate the low criminal-psychotic minds of these pirates—"

Private Danio, passing in the corridor, paused to salute. "Thanks for bailing us out, sir. I . . . really wasn't expecting that. You won't regret it, I swear."

Miles and Elli looked at each other as he lumbered on.

"He's all yours," said Miles.

"Right," said Quinn. "Next?"

"Have Thorne pull everything there is off the Earth comm net on this hijacking incident before we quit local space. There might be an odd angle or two not apparent to Imperial HQ." He tapped the data disk in his jacket pocket and sighed, marshaling his concentration for the task ahead. "At least this should be simpler than our late vacation on Earth," he said hopefully. "A purely military operation, no relatives, no politics, no high finance. Straight-up good guys and bad guys."

"Great," said Quinn. "Which are we?"

Miles was still thinking about the answer to that one when the fleet broke orbit.

Mirror Dance

For Patricia Collins Wrede,
for literary midwifery above and beyond
the long-distance call of duty

CHAPTER ONE

The row of comconsole booths lining the passenger concourse of Escobar's largest commercial orbital transfer station had mirrored doors, divided into diagonal sections by rainbow-colored lines of lights. Doubtless someone's idea of decor. The mirror-sections were deliberately set slightly out of alignment, fragmenting their reflections. The short man in the gray and white military uniform scowled at his divided self framed therein.

His image scowled back. The insignia-less mercenary officer's undress kit—pocketed jacket, loose trousers tucked into ankle-topping boots—was correct in every detail. He studied the body under the uniform. A stretched-out dwarf with a twisted spine, short-necked, big-headed. Subtly deformed, and robbed by his short stature of any chance of the disturbing near-rightness passing unnoticed. His dark hair was neatly trimmed. Beneath black brows, the gray eyes' glower deepened. The body, too, was correct in every detail. He hated it.

The mirrored door slid up at last, and a woman exited the booth. She wore a soft wrap tunic and flowing trousers. A fashionable bandolier of expensive electronic equipment hanging decoratively on a jeweled chain across her torso advertised her status. Her beginning stride was arrested at the sight of him, and she recoiled, buffeted by his black and hollow stare, then went carefully around him with a mumbled, "Excuse me ... I'm sorry. ..."

He belatedly twisted up his mouth on an imitation smile, and muttered something half-inaudible conveying enough allegiance to the social proprieties for him to pass by. He hit the keypad to lower the door again, sealing himself from sight. Alone at last, for one last moment, if only in the narrow confines of a commercial comm booth. The woman's perfume lingered cloyingly in the air, along with a *frisson* of station odors: recycled air, food, bodies, stress, plastics and metals and cleaning compounds. He exhaled, and sat, and laid his hands out flat on the small countertop to still their trembling.

Not quite alone. There was another damned mirror in here, for the convenience of patrons wishing to check their appearance before transmitting it by holovid. His dark-ringed eyes flashed back at him malevolently, then he ignored the image. He emptied his pockets out onto the countertop. All his worldly resources fit neatly into a space little larger than his two spread palms. One last inventory. As if counting it again might change the sum . . .

A credit chit with about three hundred Betan dollars remaining upon it: one might live well for a week upon this orbital space station for that much, or for a couple of lean months on the planet turning below, if it were carefully managed. Three false identification chits, none for the man he was now. None for the man he was. Whoever he was. An ordinary plastic pocket comb. A data cube. That was all. He returned all but the credit chit to various pockets upon and in the jacket, gravely sorting them individually. He ran out of objects before he ran out of pockets, and snorted. *You might at least have brought your own toothbrush . . .* too late now.

And getting later. Horrors happened, proceeding unchecked, while he sat struggling for nerve. *Come on. You've done this before. You can do it now.* He jammed the credit card into the slot and keyed in the carefully memorized code number. Compulsively, he glanced one last time into the mirror, trying to smooth his features into something approaching a neutral expression. For all his practice, he did not think he could manage the grin just now. He despised that grin anyway.

The vid plate hissed to life, and a woman's visage formed above it. She wore gray-and-whites like his own, but with proper rank insignia and name patch. She recited crisply, "Comm Officer Hereld, *Triumph*, Dendarii Free . . . Corporation." In Escobaran space, a mercenary fleet sealed its weapons at the Outside jumppoint station under the watchful eyes of the Escobaran military inspectors, and submitted proof of its purely commercial intentions, before it was even allowed to pass. The polite fiction was maintained, apparently, in Escobar orbit.

He moistened his lips and said evenly, "Connect me with the officer of the watch, please."

"Admiral Naismith, sir! You're back!" Even over the holovid a blast of pleasure and excitement washed out from her straightened posture and beaming face. It struck him like a blow. "What's up? Are we going to be moving out soon?"

"In good time, Lieutenant . . . Hereld." An apt name for a communications officer. He managed to twitch a smile. Admiral Naismith would smile, yes. "You'll learn in good time. In the meanwhile, I want a pick-up at the orbital transfer station."

"Yes, sir. I can get that for you. Is Captain Quinn with you?"

"Uh . . . no."

"When will she be following?"

" . . . Later."

"Right, sir. Let me just get clearance for—are we loading any equipment?"

"No. Just myself."

"Clearance from the Escobarans for a personnel pod, then . . ." She turned aside for a few moments. "I can have someone at docking bay E17 in about twenty minutes."

"Very well." It would take him almost that long to get from this concourse to that arm of the station. Ought he to add some personal word for Lieutenant Hereld? She knew him; how well did she know him? Every sentence that fell from his lips from this point on packed risk, risk of the unknown, risk of a mistake. Mistakes were punished. Was his Betan accent really right? He hated this, with a stomach-churning terror. "I want to be transferred directly to the *Ariel*."

"Right, sir. Do you wish me to notify Captain Thorne?"

Was Admiral Naismith often in the habit of springing surprise inspections? Well, not this time. "Yes, do. Tell them to make ready to break orbit."

"Only the *Ariel*?" Her brows rose.

"Yes, Lieutenant." This, in quite a perfect bored Betan drawl. He congratulated himself as she grew palpably prim. The undertone had suggested just the right hint of criticism of a breach of security, or manners, or both, to suppress further dangerous questions.

"Will do, Admiral."

"Naismith out." He cut the comm. She vanished in a haze of sparkles, and he let out a long breath. Admiral Naismith. Miles Naismith. He had to get used to responding to that name again, even in his sleep. Leave the Lord Vorkosigan part completely out of it, for now; it was difficult enough just being the Naismith half of the man. Drill. What is your name? Miles. Miles. Miles.

Lord Vorkosigan pretended to be Admiral Naismith. And so did he. What, after all, was the difference?

But what is your name really?

His vision darkened in a rush of despair, and rage. He blinked it back, controlling his breathing. *My name is what I will. And right now I will it to be Miles Naismith.*

He exited the booth and strode down the concourse, short legs pumping, both riveting and repelling the sideways stares of startled strangers. *See Miles. See Miles run. See Miles get what he deserves.* He marched head-down, and no one got in his way.

He ducked into the personnel pod, a tiny four-man shuttle, as soon as the hatch seal sensors blinked green and the door dilated. He hit the keypad for it to close again behind him immediately. The pod was too little to maintain a grav field. He floated over the seats and pulled himself carefully down into the one beside the lone pilot, a man in Dendarii gray tech coveralls.

"All right. Let's go."

The pilot grinned and sketched him a salute as he strapped in. Otherwise appearing to be a sensible adult male, he had the same look on his face as the comm officer, Hereld: excited, breathless, watching eagerly, as if his passenger were about to pull treats from his pockets.

He glanced over his shoulder as the pod obediently broke free of the docking clamps and turned. They swooped away from the skin of the station into clear space. The traffic control patterns made a maze of colored lights on the navigation console, through which the pilot swiftly threaded them.

"Good to see you back, Admiral," said the pilot as soon as the tangle grew less thick. "What's happening?"

The edge of formality in the pilot's tone was reassuring. Just a comrade in arms, not one of the Dear Old Friends, or worse, Dear Old Lovers. He essayed an evasion. "When you need to know, you'll be told." He made his tone affable, but avoided names or ranks.

The pilot vented an intrigued "*Hm*," and smirked, apparently contented.

He settled back with a tight smile. The huge transfer station fell away silently behind them, shrinking into a mad child's toy, then into a few glints of light. "Excuse me. I'm a little tired." He settled down further into his seat and closed his eyes. "Wake me up when we dock, if I fall asleep."

"Yes, sir," said the pilot respectfully. "You look like you could use it."

He acknowledged this with a tired wave of his hand, and pretended to doze.

He could always tell, instantly, when someone he met thought they were facing "Naismith." They all had that same stupid hyper-alert *glow* in their faces. They weren't all worshipful; he'd met some of Naismith's enemies once, but worshipful or homicidal, they reacted. As if they suddenly switched on, and became ten times more alive than ever before. How the hell did he do it? Make people light up like that? Granted, Naismith was a goddamn hyperactive, but how did he make it so freaking contagious?

Strangers who met him as himself did not greet *him* like that. They were blank and courteous, or blank and rude, or just blank, closed and indifferent. Covertly uncomfortable with his slight deformities, and his obviously abnormal four-foot-nine-inch height. Wary.

His resentment boiled up behind his eyes like sinus pain. All this bloody hero-worship, or whatever it was. All for Naismith. *For Naismith, and not for me ... never for me. ...*

He stifled a twinge of dread, knowing what he was about to face. Bel Thorne, the *Ariel's* captain, would be another one. Friend, officer, fellow Betan, yes, a tough test, well enough. But Thorne also knew of the existence of the clone, from that chaotic encounter two years ago on Earth. They had never met face to face. But a mistake that another Dendarii might dismiss in confusion could trigger in Thorne the suspicion, the wild surmise. ...

Even *that* distinction Naismith had stolen from him. The mercenary admiral, publicly and falsely, now claimed to be a clone himself. A superior cover, concealing his other identity, his other life. *You have two lives,* he thought to his absent enemy. *I have none. I'm the real clone, damn it. Couldn't I have even that uniqueness? Did you have to take it all?*

No. Keep his thoughts positive. He could handle Thorne. As long as he could avoid the terrifying Quinn, the bodyguard, the lover, Quinn. He *had* met Quinn face to face on Earth, and fooled her once, for a whole morning. Not twice, he didn't think. But Quinn was with the real Miles Naismith, stuck like glue; he was safe from her. No old lovers this trip.

He'd never had a lover, not yet. It was perhaps not quite fair to blame Naismith for that as well. For the first twenty years of his life he had been in effect a prisoner, though he hadn't always realized it. For the last two . . . the last two years had been one continuous disaster, he decided bitterly. This was his last chance. He refused to think beyond. No more. This had to be made to work.

The pilot stirred, beside him, and he slitted open his eyes as the deceleration pressed him against his seat straps. They were coming up on the *Ariel*. It grew from a dot to a model to a ship. The Illyrican-built light cruiser carried a crew of twenty, plus room for supercargo and a commando squad. Heavily powered for its size, an energy profile typical of warships. It looked swift, almost rakish. A good courier ship; a good ship to run like hell in. Perfect. Despite his black mood, his lips curled up as he studied that ship. *Now I take, and you give, Naismith.*

The pilot, clearly quite conscious that he was conveying his admiral, brought the personnel pod into its docking clamps with a bare click, neat and smooth as humanly possible. "Shall I wait, sir?"

"No. I shouldn't be needing you again."

The pilot hurried to adjust the tube seals while his passenger was still unbuckling, and saluted him out with another idiot, broad, proud smile. He twitched a returning smile and salute, then grasped the handlebars above the hatch and swung himself into the *Ariel*'s gravity field.

He dropped neatly to his feet in a small loading bay. Behind him, the pod pilot was already re-sealing the hatch to return himself and his pod to its vessel of origin, probably the flagship *Triumph*. He looked up—always, up—into the face of the waiting Dendarii officer, a face he had studied before this only in a holovid.

Captain Bel Thorne was a Betan hermaphrodite, a race that was remnant of an early experiment in human genetic and social engineering that had succeeded only in creating another minority. Thorne's beardless face was framed by soft brown hair in a short, ambiguous cut that either a man or a woman might sport. Its officer's jacket hung open, revealing the black tee shirt underneath curving over modest but distinctly feminine breasts. The gray Dendarii uniform trousers were loose enough to disguise the reciprocal bulge in the crotch. Some people found hermaphodites enormously disturbing. He was relieved to realize he found that aspect of Thorne only slightly disconcerting. *Clones who live in glass houses shouldn't throw . . . what?* It was the radiant I-love-Naismith look on the hermaphrodite's face that really bothered him. His gut knotted, as he returned the *Ariel*'s captain's salute.

"Welcome aboard, sir!" The alto voice was vibrant with enthusiasm.

He was just managing a stiff smile, when the hermaphrodite stepped up and embraced him. His heart lurched, and he barely choked off a cry and a violent, defensive lashing-out. He endured the embrace without going rigid, grasping mentally after shattered composure and his carefully rehearsed speeches. *It's not going to kiss me, is it?!*

The hermaphrodite set him at arm's length, hands familiarly upon his shoulders, without doing so, however. He breathed relief. Thorne cocked its head, its lips twisting in puzzlement. "What's wrong, Miles?"

First names? "Sorry, Bel. I'm just a little tired. Can we get right to the briefing?"

"You look a lot tired. Right. Do you want me to assemble the whole crew?"

"No . . . you can re-brief them as needed." That was the plan, as little direct contact with as few Dendarii as possible.

"Come to my cabin, then, and you can put your feet up and drink tea while we talk."

The hermaphrodite followed him into the corridor. Not knowing which direction to turn, he wheeled and waited as if politely for Thorne to lead on. He trailed the Dendarii officer through a couple of twists and turns and up a level. The ship's internal architecture was not as cramped as he'd expected. He noted directions carefully. Naismith knew this ship well.

The *Ariel*'s captain's cabin was a neat little chamber, soldierly, not revealing much on this side of the latched cupboard doors about the personality of its owner. But Thorne unlatched one to display an antique ceramic tea set and a couple of dozen small canisters of varietal teas of Earth and other planetary origins, all protected from breakage by custom-made foam packing. "What kind?" Thorne called, its hand hovering over the canisters.

"The usual," he replied, easing into a station chair clamped to the floor beside a small table.

"Might have guessed. I swear I'll train you to be more venturesome one of these days." Thorne shot a peculiar grin over its shoulder at him—was that intended to be some sort of double entendre? After a bit more rattling about, Thorne placed a delicately hand-painted porcelain cup and saucer upon the table at his elbow. He picked it up and sipped cautiously as Thorne hooked another chair into its clamps a quarter turn around the table, produced a cup for itself, and sat with a small grunt of satisfaction.

He was relieved to find the hot amber liquid pleasant, if astringent. Sugar? He dared not ask. Thorne hadn't put any out. The Dendarii surely would have, if it expected Naismith to use sugar. Thorne couldn't be making some subtle test already, could it? No sugar, then.

Tea-drinking mercenaries. The beverage didn't seem nearly poisonous enough, somehow, to go with the display, no, working arsenal, of weapons clamped to the wall: a couple of stunners, a needler, a plasma arc, a gleaming metal crossbow with an assortment of grenade-bolts in a bandolier hung with it. Thorne was supposed to be good at its job. If that was true, he didn't care what the creature drank.

"You're in a black study. I take it you've brought us a lovely one this time, eh?" Thorne prodded after another moment's silence.

"The mission assignment, yes." He certainly hoped that was what Thorne meant. The hermaphrodite nodded, and raised its brows in encouraging inquiry. "It's a pick-up. Not the biggest one we've ever attempted, by any means—"

Thorne laughed.

"But with its own complications."

"It can't possibly be any more complicated than Dagoola Four. Say on, oh do."

He rubbed his lips, a patented Naismith gesture. "We're going to knock over House Bharaputra's clone crèche, on Jackson's Whole. Clean it out."

Thorne was just crossing its legs; both feet now hit the floor with a thump. "Kill them?" it said in a startled voice.

"The clones? No, rescue them! Rescue them all."

"Oh. Whew." Thorne looked distinctively relieved. "I had this horrible vision for a second—they *are* children, after all. Even if they are clones."

"Just exactly so." A real smile tugged up the corners of his mouth, surprising him. "I'm . . . glad you see it that way."

"How else?" Thorne shrugged. "The clone brain-transplant business is the most monstrous, obscene practice in Bharaputra's whole catalog of slime services. Unless there's something even worse I haven't heard about yet."

"I think so too." He settled back, concealing his startlement at this instant endorsement of his scheme. Was Thorne sincere? He knew intimately, none better, the hidden horrors behind the clone business on Jackson's Whole. He'd lived through them. He had not expected someone who had not shared his experiences to share his judgment, though.

House Bharaputra's speciality was not, strictly speaking, cloning. It was the immortality business, or at any rate, the life extension business. And a very lucrative business it was, for what price could one put on life itself? All the market would bear. The procedure Bharaputra sold was medically risky, not ideal . . . wagered only against a certainty of imminent death by customers who were wealthy, ruthless, and, he had to admit, possessed of unusual cool foresight.

The arrangement was simple, though the surgical procedure upon which it was based was fiendishly complex. A clone was grown from a customer's somatic cell, gestated in a uterine replicator and then raised to physical maturity in Bharaputra's crèche, a sort of astonishingly-appointed orphanage. The clones were valuable, after all, their physical conditioning and health of supreme importance. Then, when the time was right, they were cannibalized. In an operation that claimed a total success rate of rather less than one hundred percent, the clone's progenitor's brain was transplanted from its aged or damaged body into a duplicate still in the first bloom of youth. The clone's brain was classified as medical waste.

The procedure was illegal on every planet in the wormhole nexus except Jackson's Whole. That was fine with the criminal Houses that ran the place. It gave them a nice monopoly, a steady business with lots of practice upon the stream of wealthy off-worlders to keep their surgical teams at the top of their forms. As far as he had ever been able to tell, the attitude of the rest of the worlds toward it all was "out of sight, out of mind." The spark of sympathetic, righteous anger in Thorne's eyes touched him on a level of pain so numb with use he was scarcely conscious of it any more, and he was appalled to realize he was a heartbeat away from bursting into tears. *It's probably a trick.* He blew out his breath, another Naismith-ism.

Thorne's brows drew down in intense thought. "Are you sure we should be taking the *Ariel*? Last I heard, Baron Ryoval was still alive. It's bound to get his attention."

House Ryoval was one of Bharaputra's minor rivals in the illegal medical end of things. Its specialty was manufacturing genetically-engineered or surgically sculptured humans for any purpose, including sexual, in effect slaves made-to-order; evil, he supposed, but not the killing evil that obsessed him. But what had the *Ariel* to do with Baron Ryoval? He hadn't a clue. Let Thorne worry about it. Perhaps the hermaphrodite would drop more information later. He reminded himself to seize the first opportunity to review the ship's mission logs.

"This mission has nothing to do with House Ryoval. We shall avoid them."

"So I hope," agreed Thorne fervently. It paused, thoughtfully sipping tea. "Now, despite the fact that Jackson's Whole is long overdue for a housecleaning, preferably with atomics, I presume we are not doing this just out of the goodness of our hearts. What's, ah, the mission behind the mission this time?"

He had a rehearsed answer for that one. "In fact, only one of the clones, or rather, one of its progenitors, is of interest to our employer. The rest are to be camouflage. Among them, Bharaputra's customers have a lot of enemies. They won't know which one is attacking who. It makes our employer's identity, which they very much desire to keep secret, all the more secure."

Thorne grinned smugly. "That little refinement was your idea, I take it."

He shrugged. "In a sense."

"Hadn't we better know which clone we're after, to prevent accidents, or in case we have to cut and run? If our employer wants it alive—or does it matter to them if the clone is alive or dead? If the real target is the old bugger who had it grown."

"They care. Alive. But . . . for practical purposes, let us assume that all the clones are the one we're after."

Thorne spread its hands in acquiescence. "It's all right by me." The hermaphrodite's eyes glinted with enthusiasm, and it suddenly smacked its fist into its palm with a crack that made him jump. "It's about time someone took those Jacksonian bastards on! Oh, this is going to be fun!" It bared its teeth in a most alarming grin. "How much help do we have lined up on Jackson's Whole? Safety nets?"

"Don't count on any."

"Hm. How much hindrance? Besides Bharaputra, Ryoval, and Fell, of course."

House Fell dealt mainly in weapons. What had Fell to do with any of this? "Your guess is as good as mine."

Thorne frowned; that was not the usual sort of Naismith answer, apparently.

"I have a great deal of inside information about the crèche, that I can brief you on once we're en route. Look, Bel, you hardly need me to tell you how to do your job at this late date. I trust you. Take over the logistics and planning, and I'll check the finals."

Thorne's spine straightened. "Right. How many kids are we talking about?"

"Bharaputra does about one of these transplants a week, on average. Fifty a year, say, that they have coming along. The last year of the clones' lives they move them to a special facility near House headquarters, for final conditioning. I want to take the whole year's supply from that facility. Fifty or sixty kids."

"All packed aboard the *Ariel*? It'll be tight."

"Speed, Bel, speed."

"Yeah. I think you're right. Timetable?"

"As soon as possible. Every week's delay costs another innocent life." He'd measured out the last two years by that clock. *I have wasted a hundred lives so far.* The journey from Earth to Escobar alone had cost him a thousand Betan dollars and four dead clones.

"I get it," said Thorne grimly, and rose and put away its tea cup. It switched its chair to the clamps in front of its comconsole. "That kid's slated for surgery, isn't it."

"Yes. And if not that one, a crèche-mate."

Thorne began tapping keypads. "What about funds? That *is* your department."

"This mission is cash on delivery. Draw your estimated needs from Fleet funds."

"Right. Put your palm over here and authorize my withdrawal, then." Thorne held out a sensor pad.

Without hesitation, he laid his palm flat upon it. To his horror, the red no-recognition code glinted in the readout. *No! It has to be right, it has to—!*

"Damn machine." Thorne tapped the sensor pad's corner sharply on the table. "Behave. Try again."

This time, he laid his palm down with a very slight twist; the computer digested the new data, and this time pronounced him cleared, accepted, blessed. Funded. His pounding heart slowed in relief.

Thorne keyed in more data, and said over its shoulder, "No question which commando squad you want to requisition for this one, eh?"

"No question," he echoed hollowly. "Go ahead." He had to get out of here, before the strain of the masquerade made him blow away his good start.

"You want your usual cabin?" Thorne inquired.

"Sure." He stood.

"Soon, I gather . . ." The hermaphrodite checked a readout in the glowing complexity of logistics displays above the comconsole vid plate. "The palm lock is still keyed for you. Get off your feet, you look beat. It's under control."

"Good."

"When will Elli Quinn be along?"

"She won't be coming on this mission."

Thorne's eyes widened in surprise. "*Really.*" Its smile broadened, quite inexplicably. "That's too bad." Its voice conveyed not the least disappointment. Some rivalry, there? Over what?

"Have the *Triumph* send over my kit," he ordered. Yes, delegate that thievery too. Delegate it all. "And . . . when you get the chance, have a meal sent to my cabin."

"Will do," promised Thorne with a firm nod. "I'm glad to see you've been eating better, by the way, even if you haven't been sleeping. Good. Keep it up. We worry about you, you know."

Eating better, hell. With his stature, keeping his weight down had become a constant battle. He'd starved for three months just to get back into Naismith's uniform, that he'd stolen two years ago and now wore. Another wave of weary hatred for his progenitor washed over him. He let himself out with a casual salute that he trusted would encourage Thorne to keep working, and managed to keep from snarling under his breath till the cabin door hissed shut behind him.

There was nothing for it but to try every palm lock in the corridor till one opened. He hoped no Dendarii would come along while he was rattling doors. He found his cabin at last, directly across from the hermaphrodite captain's. The door slid open at his touch on the sensor pad without any heart-stopping glitches this time.

The cabin was a little chamber almost identical to Thorne's, only blanker. He checked cupboards. Most were bare, but in one he found a set of gray fatigues and a stained tech coverall just his size. A residue of half-used toiletries in the cabin's tiny washroom included a toothbrush, and his lips twisted in an ironical sneer. The neatly made bed which folded out of the wall looked extremely attractive, and he nearly swooned into it.

I'm on my way. I've done it. The Dendarii had accepted him, accepted his orders with the same stupid blind trust with which they followed Naismith's. Like sheep. All he had to do now was not screw it up. The hardest part was over.

He'd grabbed a quick shower and was just pulling on Naismith's trousers when his meal arrived. His undress state gave him an excuse to wave the attentive tray-bearing Dendarii out again quickly. The dinner under the covers turned out to be real food, not rations. Grilled vat steak, fresh-appearing vegetables, non-synthetic coffee, the hot food hot and the cold food cold, beautifully laid out in little portions finely calculated to Naismith's appetite. Even ice cream. He recognized his progenitor's tastes, and was daunted anew by this rush by unknown people to try to give him exactly what he wanted, even in these tiny details. Rank had its privileges, but this was insane.

Depressed, he ate it all, and was just wondering if the fuzzy green stuff arranged to fill up all the empty space on the plate was edible too, when the cabin buzzer blatted again.

This time, it was a Dendarii non-com and a float pallet with three big crates on it.

"Ah." He blinked. "My kit. Just set it there in the middle of the floor, for now."

"Yes, sir. Don't you want to assign a batman?" The non-com's inviting expression left no doubt about who was first in line to volunteer.

"Not ... this mission. We're going to be cramped for space, later. Just leave it."

"I'd be happy to unpack it for you, sir. I packed it all up."

"Quite all right."

"If I've missed anything, just let me know, and I'll run it right over."

"*Thank* you, corporal." His exasperation leaked into his voice; fortunately, it acted as a brake upon the corporal's enthusiasm. The Dendarii heaved the crates from the float pallet and exited with a sheepish grin, as if to say, *Hey, you can't blame me for trying.*

He smiled back through set teeth, and turned his attention to the crates as soon as the door sealed. He flipped up the latches and hesitated, bemused at his own eagerness. It must be rather like getting a birthday present. He'd never had a birthday present in his life. *So, let's make up for some lost time.*

The first lid folded back to reveal clothes, more clothes than he'd ever owned before. Tech coveralls, undress kit, a dress uniform—

he held up the gray velvet tunic, raising his brows at the shimmer and the silver buttons—boots, shoes, slippers, pajamas, all regulation, all cut down to perfect fit. And civilian clothes, eight or ten sets, in various planetary and galactic styles and social levels. An Escobaran business suit in red silk, a Barrayaran quasi-military tunic and piped trousers, ship knits, a Betan sarong and sandals, a ragged jacket and shirt and pants suitable for a down-on-his-luck dock-worker anywhere. Abundant underwear. Three kinds of chronos with build-in comm units, one Dendarii regulation, one very expensive commercial model, one appearing cheap and battered, which turned out to be finest military surplus underneath. And more.

He moved to the second crate, flipped up the lid, and gaped. *Space armor.* Full-bore attack unit space armor, power and life support packs fully charged, weapons loaded and locked. Just his size. It seemed to gleam with its own dark and wicked glow, nested in its packing. The smell of it hit him, incredibly military, metal and plastic, energy and chemicals . . . old sweat. He drew the helmet out and stared with wonder into the darkened mirror of its visor. He had never worn space armor, though he'd studied it in holovids till his eyes crossed. A sinister, deadly carapace . . .

He unloaded it all, and laid the pieces out in order upon the floor. Strange splashes, scars, and patches deckled the gleaming surfaces here and there. What weapons, what strikes, had been powerful enough to mar that metalloy surface? What enemies had fired them? Every scar, he realized, fingering them, had been intended death. This was not pretend.

It was very disturbing. *No.* He pushed away the cold shiver of doubt. *If he can do it, I can do it.* He tried to ignore the repairs and mysterious stains on the pressure suit and its soft, absorbent underliner as he packed it all away again and stowed the crate. Blood? Shit? Burns? Oil? It was all cleaned and odorless now, anyway.

The third crate, smaller than the second, proved to contain a set of half-armor, lacking built-in weapons and not meant for space, but rather for dirtside combat under normal or near-normal pressure, temperature, and atmospheric conditions. Its most arresting feature was a command headset, a smooth duralloy helmet with built-in telemetry and a vid projector in a flange above the fore-head that placed any data on the net right before the commander's eyes. Data flow was controlled by certain facial movements and voice commands. He left it out on the counter to examine more thoroughly later, and repacked the rest.

By the time he finished arranging all the clothing in the cabin's cupboards and drawers, he'd begun to regret sending the batman away so precipitously. He fell onto the bed and dimmed the lights. When he next woke, he should be on his way to Jackson's Whole. . . .

He'd just begun to doze when the cabin comm buzzed. He lurched up to answer it, mustering a reasonably coherent "Naismith here," in a sleep-blurred voice.

"Miles?" said Thorne's voice. "The commando squad's here."

"Uh . . . good. Break orbit as soon as you're ready, then."

"Don't you want to see them?" Thorne said, sounding surprised.

Inspection. He inhaled. "Right. I'll . . . be along. Naismith out." He hurried back into his uniform trousers, taking a jacket with proper insignia this time, and quickly called up a schematic of the ship's interior layout on the cabin's comconsole. There were two locks for combat-drop shuttles, port and starboard. Which one? He traced a route to both.

The operative shuttle hatch was the first one he tried. He paused a moment in shadow and silence at the curve of the corridor, before he was spotted, to take in the scene.

The loading bay was crowded with a dozen men and women in gray camouflage flight suits, along with piles of equipment and supplies. Hand and heavy weapons were stacked in symmetrical arrays. The mercenaries sat or stood, talking noisily, loud and crude, punctuated with barks of laughter. They were all so big, generating too much energy, knocking into each other in half-horseplay, as if seeking an excuse to shout louder. They bore knives and other personal weapons on belts or in holsters or on bandoliers, an ostentatious display. Their faces were a blur, animal-like. He swallowed, straightened, and stepped among them.

The effect was instantaneous. "Heads up!" someone shouted, and without further orders they arranged themselves at rigid attention in two neat, dead silent rows, each with his or her bundle of equipment at their feet. It was almost more frightening than the previous chaos.

With a thin smile, he walked forward and pretended to look at each one. A last heavy duffel arced out of the shuttle hatch to land with a thump on the deck, and the thirteenth commando squeezed through, stood up, and saluted him.

He stood paralyzed with panic. Whatinhell *was* it? He stared at a flashing belt buckle, then tilted his head back, straining his neck. The freaking thing was *eight feet tall*. The enormous body radiated power that he could feel almost like a wave of heat, and the face—the face was a nightmare. Tawny yellow eyes, like a wolf's, a distorted, outslung mouth with *fangs*, dammit, long white canines locked over the edges of the carmine lips. The huge hands had *claws*, thick, powerful, razor-edged—enamelled with carmine polish. . . . *What?* His gaze traveled back up to the monster's face. The eyes were outlined with shadow and gold tint, echoed by a little gold spangle glued decoratively to one high cheekbone. The mahogany-colored hair was drawn back in an elaborate braid. The belt was cinched in tightly, emphasizing a figure of sorts despite the loose-fitting multi-gray flight suit. The thing was female—?

"Sergeant Taura and the Green Squad, reporting as ordered, sir!" The baritone voice reverberated in the bay.

"Thank you—" It came out a cracked whisper, and he coughed to unlock his throat. "Thank you, that will be all, get your orders from Captain Thorne, you may all stand down." They all strained to hear him, compelling him to repeat, "Dismissed!"

They broke up in disorder, or some order known only to themselves, for the bay was cleared of equipment with astonishing speed. The monster sergeant lingered, looming over him. He locked his knees, to keep himself from sprinting from it—her. . . .

She lowered her voice. "Thanks for picking the Green Squad, Miles. I take it you've got us a real plum."

More first names? "Captain Thorne will brief you en route. It's . . . a challenging mission." And this would be the sergeant in charge of it?

"Captain Quinn have the details, as usual?" She cocked a furry eyebrow at him.

"Captain Quinn . . . will not be coming on this mission."

He swore her gold eyes widened, the pupils dilating. Her lips drew back baring her fangs further in what took him a terrifying moment to realize was a smile. In a weird way, it reminded him of the grin with which Thorne had greeted that same news.

She glanced up; the bay had emptied of other personnel. "Aah?" Her voice rumbled, like a purr. "Well, I'll be your bodyguard any time, lover. Just give me the sign."

What sign, what the hell—

She bent, her lips rippling, carmine clawed hand grasping his shoulder—he had a flashing vision of her tearing off his head, peeling, and eating him—then her mouth closed over his. His breath stopped, and his vision darkened, and he almost passed out before she straightened and gave him a puzzled, hurt look. "Miles, what's the matter?"

That had been a *kiss*. Freaking gods. "Nothing," he gasped. "I've . . . been ill. I probably shouldn't have gotten up, but I had to inspect."

She was looking very alarmed. "I'll say you shouldn't have gotten up—you're shaking all over! You can barely stand up. Here, I'll carry you to sickbay. Crazy man!"

"No! I'm all right. That is, I've been treated. I'm just supposed to rest, and recover for a while, is all."

"Well, you go straight back to bed, then!"

"Yes."

He wheeled. She swatted him on the butt. He bit his tongue. She said, "At least you've been eating better. Take care of yourself, huh?"

He waved over his shoulder, and fled without looking back. Had that been military cameraderie? From a sergeant to an admiral? He didn't think so. That had been *intimacy. Naismith, you bugfuck crazy bastard, what have you been doing in your spare time? I didn't think you had any spare time. You've got to be a freaking suicidal maniac, if you've been screwing that—*

He locked his cabin door behind him and stood against it, trembling, laughing in hysterical disbelief. Dammit, he'd studied everything about Naismith, everything. This couldn't be happening. *With friends like this, who needs enemies?*

He undressed and lay tensely upon his bed, contemplating Naismith/Vorkosigan's complicated life and wondering what other booby-traps it held for him. At last a faint change in the susurrations and creaks of the ship around him, a brief tug of shifting grav fields, made him realize the *Ariel* was breaking free of Escobar orbit. He had actually succeeded in stealing a fully armed and equipped military fast cruiser, and no one even knew it. They were on their way to Jackson's Whole. To his destiny. *His* destiny, not Naismith's. His thoughts spiraled toward sleep at last.

But if you claim your destiny, his demon voice whispered at the last, before the night's oblivion, *why can't you claim your name?*

CHAPTER TWO

They exited the flex tube from the passenger ship in step, arm in arm, Quinn with her duffel swung over her shoulder, Miles with his flight bag gripped in his free hand. In the orbital transfer station's disembarkation lounge, people's heads turned. Miles stole a smug sideways glance at his female companion as they strolled on past the men's half-averted, envious stares. *My Quinn.*

Quinn was looking particularly tough this morning—was it morning? he'd have to check Dendarii fleet time—having half-returned to her normal persona. She'd managed to make her pocketed gray uniform trousers masquerade as a fashion statement by tucking them into red suede boots (the steel caps under the pointed toes eluded notice) and topping them with a skimpy scarlet tank top. Her white skin glowed in contrast to the tank top and to her short dark curls. The surface colors distracted the eye from her athleticism, not apparent unless you knew just how much that bloody duffel weighed.

Liquid brown eyes informed her face with wit. But it was the perfect, sculptured curves and planes of the face itself that stopped men's voices in midsentence. An obviously expensive face, the work of a surgeon-artist of extraordinary genius. The casual observer might guess her face had been paid for by the little ugly man whose arm she linked with her own, and judge the woman, too, to be a purchase. The casual observer never guessed the price she'd really paid: her old face, burned away in combat off Tau Verde. Very nearly the first battle loss in Admiral Naismith's

328

service—ten years ago, now? God. The casual observer was a twit, Miles decided.

The latest representative of the species was a wealthy executive who reminded Miles of a blond, civilian version of his cousin Ivan, and who had spent much of the two-week journey from Sergyar to Escobar under such misapprehensions about Quinn, trying to seduce her. Miles glimpsed him now, loading his luggage onto a float pallet and venting a last frustrated sigh of defeat before sloping off. Except for reminding Miles of Ivan, Miles bore him no ill-will. In fact, Miles felt almost sorry for him, as Quinn's sense of humor was as vile as her reflexes were deadly.

Miles jerked his head toward the retreating Escobaran and murmured, "So what did you finally say to get rid of him, love?"

Quinn's eyes shifted to identify the man, and crinkled, laughing. "If I told you, you'd be embarrassed."

"No, I won't. Tell me."

"I told him you could do push-ups with your tongue. He must have decided he couldn't compete."

Miles reddened.

"I wouldn't have led him on so far, except that I wasn't totally sure at first that he wasn't some kind of agent," she added apologetically.

"You sure now?"

"Yeah. Too bad. It might have been more entertaining."

"Not to me. I was ready for a little vacation."

"Yes, and you look the better for it. Rested."

"I really like this married-couple cover, for travel," he remarked. "It suits me." He took a slightly deeper breath. "So we've had the honeymoon, why don't we have the wedding to go with it?"

"You never give up, do you?" She kept her tone light. Only the slight flinch of her arm, under his, told him his words had given pain, and he silently cursed himself.

"I'm sorry. I promised I'd keep off that subject."

She shrugged her unburdened shoulder, incidentally unlinking elbows, and let her arm swing aggressively as she walked. "Trouble is, you don't want me to be Madame Naismith, Dread of the Dendarii. You want me to be Lady Vorkosigan of Barrayar. That's a downside post. I'm spacer-born. Even if I did marry a dirtsucker, go down into some gravity well and never come up again . . . Barrayar is not the pit I'd pick. Not to insult your home."

Why not? Everyone else does. "My mother likes you," he offered.

"And I admire her. I've met her, what, four times now, and every time I'm more impressed. And yet . . . the more impressed, the more outraged I am at the criminal waste Barrayar makes of her talents. She'd be Surveyor-General of the Betan Astronomical Survey by now, if she'd stayed on Beta Colony. Or any other thing she pleased."

"She's pleased to be Countess Vorkosigan."

"She's pleased to be stunned by your Da, whom I admit is pretty stunning. She doesn't give squat for the rest of the Vor caste." Quinn paused, before they came into the hearing of the Escobaran customs inspectors, and Miles stood with her. They both gazed down the chamber, and not at each other. "For all her flair, she's a tired woman underneath. Barrayar has sucked so much out of her. Barrayar is her cancer. Killing her slowly."

Mutely, Miles shook his head.

"Yours too. Lord Vorkosigan," Quinn added somberly. This time it was his turn to flinch.

She sensed it, and tossed her head. "Anyway, Admiral Naismith is my kind of maniac. Lord Vorkosigan is a dull and dutiful stick by contrast. I've seen you at home on Barrayar, Miles. You're like half yourself there. Damped down, muted somehow. Even your voice is lower. It's extremely weird."

"I can't . . . I have to fit in, there. Scarcely a generation ago, someone with a body as strange as mine would have been killed outright as a suspected mutant. I can't push things too far, too fast. I'm too easy to target."

"Is that why Barrayaran Imperial Security sends you on so many off-planet missions?"

"For my development as an officer. To widen my background, deepen my experience."

"And someday, they're going to hook you out of here permanently, and take you home, and squeeze all that experience back out of you in *their* service. Like a sponge."

"I'm in their service now, Elli," he reminded her softly, in a grave and level voice that she had to bend her head to hear. "Now, then, and always."

Her eyes slid away. "Right-oh . . . so when they do nail your boots to the floor back on Barrayar, I want your job. I want to be Admiral Quinn someday."

"Fine by me," he said affably. The job, yes. Time for Lord Vorkosigan and his personal wants to go back into the bag. He had to stop masochistically rerunning this stupid marriage conversation with Quinn, anyway. Quinn was Quinn; he did not want her to be not-Quinn, not even for . . . Lord Vorkosigan.

Despite this self-inflicted moment of depression, anticipation of his return to the Dendarii quickened his step as they made their way through customs and into the monster transfer station. Quinn was right. He could *feel* Naismith refilling his skin, generated from somewhere deep in his psyche right out to his fingertips. Goodbye, dull Lieutenant Miles Vorkosigan, deep cover operative for Barrayaran Imperial Security (and overdue for a promotion); hello, dashing Admiral Naismith, space mercenary and all-around soldier of fortune.

Or misfortune. He slowed as they came to a row of commercial comconsole booths lining the passenger concourse, and nodded toward their mirrored doors. "Let's see how Red Squad is cooking, first. If they're recovered sufficiently for release, I'd like to go downside personally and spring them."

"Right-oh." Quinn dumped her duffel dangerously close to Miles's sandaled feet, swung into the nearest empty booth, jammed her card into the slot, and tapped out a code on the keypad.

Miles set down his flight bag, sat on the duffel, and watched her from outside the booth. He caught a sliced reflection of himself on the mosaic of mirror on the next booth's lowered door. The dark trousers and loose white shirt that he wore were ambiguously styled as to planetary origin, but, as fit his travel-cover, very civilian. Relaxed, casual. Not bad.

Time was he had worn uniforms like a turtle-shell of high-grade social protection over the vulnerable peculiarities of his body. An armor of belonging that said, *Don't mess with me. I have friends.* When had he stopped needing that so desperately? He was not sure.

For that matter, when had he stopped hating his body? It had been two years since his last serious injury, on the hostage rescue mission that had come right after that incredible mess with his brother on Earth. He'd been fully recovered for quite some time. He flexed his hands, full of plastic replacement bones, and found them as easily his own as before they were last crunched. As before they were ever crunched. He hadn't had an osteo-inflammatory attack in months. *I'm feeling no pain,* he realized with a dark grin. And it wasn't just Quinn's doing, though Quinn had been . . . very therapeutic. *Am I going sane in my old age?*

Enjoy it while you can. He was twenty-eight years old, and surely at some sort of physical peak. He could feel that peak, the exhilarating float of apogee. The descending arc was a fate for some future day.

Voices from the comm booth brought him back to the present moment. Quinn had Sandy Hereld on the other end, and was saying, "Hi, I'm back."

"Hi, Quinnie, I was expecting you. What can I do for you?" Sandy had been doing strange things to her hair, again, Miles noted even from his offsides vantage.

"I just got off the jumpship, here at the transfer station. Planning a little detour. I want transport downside to pick up the Red Squad survivors, then back to the *Triumph*. What's their current status?"

"Hold tight, I'll have it in a second . . ." Lieutenant Hereld punched up data on a display to her left.

In the crowded concourse a man in Dendarii grays walked past. He saw Miles, and gave him a hesitant, cautious nod, perhaps uncertain if the Admiral's civilian gear indicated some sort of cover. Miles returned a reassuring wave, and the man smiled and strode on. Miles's brain kicked up unwanted data. The man's name was Travis Gray, he was a field tech currently assigned to the *Peregrine*, a six-year-man so far, expert in communications equipment, he collected classic pre-jump music of Earth origin . . . how many such personnel files did Miles carry in his head, now? Hundreds? Thousands?

And here came more. Hereld turned back, and rattled off, "Ives was released to downside leave, and Boyd has been returned to the *Triumph* for further therapy. The Beauchene Life Center reports that Durham, Vifian, and Aziz are available for release, but they want to talk to someone in charge, first."

"Right-oh."

"Kee and Zelaski . . . they also want to talk about."

Quinn's lips tightened. "Right," she agreed flatly. Miles's belly knotted, just a little. That was not going to be a happy conversation, he suspected. "Let them know we're on our way, then," Quinn said.

"Yes, Cap'n." Hereld shuffled files on her vid display. "Will do. Which shuttle do you want?"

"The *Triumph*'s smaller personnel shuttle will do, unless you have some cargo to load on at the same time from the Beauchene shuttleport."

"None from there, no."

"All right."

Hereld checked her vid. "According to Escobaran flight control,

I can put Shuttle Two into docking bay J-26 in thirty minutes. You'll be cleared for immediate downside departure."

"Thanks. Pass the word—there'll be a captain and captain-owner's briefing when we get back. What time is it at Beauchene?"

Hereld glanced aside. "0906, out of a 2607 hour day."

"Morning. Great. What's the weather down there?"

"Lovely. Shirtsleeves."

"Good, I won't have to change. We'll advise when we're ready to depart Port Beauchene. Quinn out."

Miles sat on the duffel, staring down at his sandals, awash in unpleasant memories. It had been one of the Dendarii Mercenaries' sweatier smuggling adventures, putting military advisors and material down on Marilac in support of its continuing resistance to a Cetagandan invasion. Combat-drop shuttle A-4 from the *Triumph* had been hit by enemy fire on the last trip up-and-out, with all of Red Squad and several important Marilacans aboard. The pilot, Lieutenant Durham, though mortally injured and in shock himself, had brought his crippled and burning shuttle into a sufficiently low-velocity crunch with the *Triumph*'s docking clamps that the rescue team was able to seal on an emergency flex tube, slice through, and retrieve everyone aboard. They'd managed to jettison the damaged shuttle just before it exploded, and the *Triumph* itself broke orbit barely ahead of serious Cetagandan vengeance. And so a mission that had started out simple, smooth, and covert ended yet again in the sort of heroic chaos that Miles had come to despise. The chaos, not the heroism.

The score, after heartbreaking triage: twelve seriously injured; seven, beyond the *Triumph*'s resources for resuscitation, cryogenically frozen in hope of later help; three permanently and finally dead. Now Miles would find out how many of the second category he must move to the third. The faces, names, hundreds of unwanted facts about them, cascaded through his mind. He had originally planned to be aboard that last shuttle, but instead had gone up on an earlier flight to deal with some other forest fire. . . .

"Maybe they won't be so bad," Quinn said, reading his face. She stuck out her hand, and he pulled himself up off the duffel and gathered up his flight bag.

"I've spent so much time in hospitals myself, I can't help identifying with them," he excused his dark abstraction. One perfect mission. What he wouldn't give for just one perfect mission, where absolutely nothing went wrong. Maybe the one upcoming would finally be it.

✧   ✧   ✧

The hospital smell hit Miles immediately when he and Quinn walked through the front doors of the Beauchene Life Center, the cryotherapy specialty clinic the Dendarii dealt with on Escobar. It wasn't a bad smell, not a stench by any means, just an odd edge to the air-conditioned atmosphere. But it was an odor so deeply associated with pain in his experience, he found his heart beating faster. *Fight or flight.* Not appropriate. He breathed deeply, stroking down the visceral throb, and looked around. The lobby was much in the current style of techno-palaces anywhere on Escobar, clean but cheaply furnished. The real money was all invested upstairs, in the cryo-equipment, regeneration laboratories, and operating theaters.

One of the clinic's senior partners, Dr. Aragones, came down to greet them and escort them upstairs to his office. Miles liked Aragones' office, crammed with the sort of clutter of info disks, charts, and journal-flimsie offprints that indicated a technocrat who thought deeply and continuously about what he was doing. He liked Aragones himself, too, a big bluff fellow with bronze skin, a noble nose, and graying hair, friendly and blunt.

Dr. Aragones was unhappy not to be reporting better results. It hurt his pride, Miles judged.

"You bring us such messes, and want miracles," he complained gently, shifting in his station chair after Miles and Quinn settled themselves. "If you want to assure miracles, you have to start at the very beginning, when my poor patients are first prepared for treatment."

Aragones never called them corpsicles, or any of the other nervous nicknames coined by the soldiers. Always *my patients.* That was another thing Miles liked about the Escobaran physician.

"In general—unfortunately—our casualties don't arrive on a scheduled, orderly, one-by-one basis," Miles half-apologized in turn. "In this case we had twenty-eight people hit sickbay, with every degree and sort of injury—extreme trauma, burns, chemical contamination—all at once. Triage got brutal, for a little while, till things sorted out. My people did their best." He hesitated. "Do you think it would be worth our while to re-certify a few of our medtechs in your latest techniques, and if so, would you be willing to lead the seminar?"

Aragones spread his hands, and looked thoughtful. "Something might be worked out . . . talk with Administrator Margara, before you go."

Quinn caught Miles's nod and made a note on her report panel.

Aragones called up charts on his comconsole. "The worst first. We could do nothing for your Mr. Kee or Ms. Zelaski."

"I . . . saw Kee's head injury. I'm not surprised." *Smashed like a melon.* "But we had the cryo-chamber available, so we tried."

Aragones nodded understanding. "Ms. Zelaski had a similar problem, though less externally obvious. So much of her internal cranial circulation was broken during the trauma, her blood could not be properly drained from her brain, nor the cryo-fluids properly perfused. Between the crystalline freezing and the hematomas, the neural destruction was complete. I'm sorry. Their bodies are presently stored in our morgue, waiting your instructions."

"Kee wished his body to be returned for burial to his family on his homeworld. Have your mortuary department prepare and ship him through the usual channels. We'll give you the address." He jerked his chin at Quinn, who made another note. "Zelaski listed no family or next of kin—some Dendarii just don't, or won't, and we don't insist. But she did once tell some of her squad mates how she wanted her ashes disposed of. Please have her remains cremated and returned to the *Triumph* in care of our medical department."

"Very well." Aragones signed off the charts on his vid display; they disappeared like vanishing spirits. He called up others in their place.

"Your Mr. Durham and Ms. Vifian are both presently only partially healed from their original injuries. Both are suffering from what I would call normal neural-traumatic and cryo-amnesia. Mr. Durham's memory loss is the more profound, partly because of complications due to his pilot's neural implants, which we alas had to remove."

"Will he ever be able to have another headset installed?"

"It's too early to tell. I would call both their long-term prognoses good, but neither will be fit to return to their military duties for at least a year. And then they will need extensive re-training. In both cases I highly recommend they each be returned to their home and family environments, if that is possible. Familiar surroundings will help facilitate and trigger re-establishment of their access to their own surviving memories, over time."

"Lieutenant Durham has family on Earth. We'll see he gets there. Tech Vifian is from Kline Station. We'll see what we can do."

Quinn nodded vigorously, and made more notes.

"I can release them to you today, then. We've done all we can, here, and ordinary convalescent facilities will do for the rest. Now . . . that leaves your Mr. Aziz."

"My trooper Aziz," Miles agreed to the claim. Aziz was three years in the Dendarii, had applied and been accepted for officer's training. Twenty-one years old.

"Mr. Aziz is . . . alive again. That is, his body sustains itself without artificial aids, except for a slight on-going problem with internal temperature regulation that seems to be improving on its own."

"But Aziz didn't have a head wound. What went wrong?" asked Miles. "Are you telling me he's going to be a vegetable?"

"I'm afraid Mr. Aziz was the victim of a bad prep. His blood was apparently drained hastily, and not sufficiently completely. Small freezing hemocysts riddled his brain tissue with necrotic patches. We removed them, and started new growth, which has taken hold successfully. But his personality is permanently lost."

"Everything?"

"He may perhaps retain a few frustrating fragments of memories. Dreams. But he cannot re-access his neural pathways through new routes or sub-routines, because the tissue itself is gone. The new man will start over as a near-infant. He's lost language, among other things."

"Will he recover his intelligence? In time?"

Aragones hesitated for too long before answering. "In a few years, he may be able to do enough simple tasks to be self-supporting."

"I see," Miles sighed.

"What do you want to do with him?"

"He's another one with no next of kin listed." Miles blew out his breath. "Transfer him to a long-term care facility here on Escobar. One with a good therapy department. I'll ask you to recommend one. I'll set up a small trust fund to cover the costs till he's out on his own. However long that takes."

Aragones nodded, and both he and Quinn made notes.

After settling further administrative and financial details, the conference broke up. Miles insisted on stopping to see Aziz, before picking up the other two convalescents.

"He cannot recognize you," Dr. Aragones warned as they entered the hospital room.

"That's all right."

At first glance, Aziz did not look as much like death warmed over as Miles had expected, despite the unflattering hospital gown. There was color and warmth in his face, and his natural melanin level saved him from being hospital-pale. But he lay listlessly, gaunt, twisted in his covers. The bed's sides were up, unpleasantly suggesting a crib or a coffin. Quinn stood against the wall and folded her arms. She had visceral associations about hospitals and clinics too.

"Azzie," Miles called softly bending over him. "Azzie, can you hear me?"

Aziz's eyes tracked momentarily, but then wandered again.

"I know you don't know me, but you might remember this, later. You were a good soldier, smart and strong. You stood by your mates in the crash. You had the sort of self-discipline that saves lives." *Others, not your own.* "Tomorrow, you'll go to another sort of hospital, where they'll help you keep on getting better." *Among strangers. More strangers.* "Don't worry about the money. I'm setting it up so it'll be there as long as you need it." *He doesn't know what money is.* "I'll check back on you from time to time, as I get the opportunity," Miles promised. Promised who? Aziz? Aziz was no more. Himself? His voice softened to inaudibility as he ran down.

The aural stimulation made Aziz thrash around and emit some loud and formless moans; he had no volume control yet, apparently. Even through a filter of desperate hope, Miles could not recognize it as an attempt at communication. Animal reflexes only.

"Take care," he whispered, and withdrew, to stand a moment trembling in the hallway.

"Why do you do that to yourself?" Quinn inquired tartly. Her crossed arms, hugging herself, added silently, *And to me?*

"First, he died for me, literally, and second," he attempted to force his voice to lightness, "don't you find a certain obsessive fascination in looking in the face of what you most fear?"

"Is death what you most fear?" she asked curiously.

"No. Not death." He rubbed his forehead, hesitated. "Loss of mind. My game plan all my life has been to demand acceptance of *this*," a vague wave down the length, or shortness, of his body, "because I was a smart-ass little bastard who could think rings around the opposition, and prove it time after time. Without the brains . . ." *Without the brains I'm nothing.* He straightened against the aching tension in his belly, shrugged, and twitched a smile at her. "March on, Quinn."

After Aziz, Durham and Vifian were not so hard to deal with. They could walk and talk, if haltingly, and Vifian even recognized Quinn. They took them back to the shuttleport in the rented groundcar, and Quinn tempered her usual go-to-hell style of driving in consideration of their half-healed wounds. Upon reaching the shuttle Miles sent Durham forward to sit with the pilot, a comrade, and by the time they reached the *Triumph* Durham had recalled not only the man's name, but some shuttle piloting procedures. Miles turned both convalescents over to the medtech who met them at the shuttle hatch corridor, who escorted them off to sickbay to bed down again after the exhaustion of their short journey. Miles watched them exit, and felt a little better.

"Costly," Quinn observed reflectively.

"Yes," Miles sighed. "Rehabilitation is starting to take an awfully big bite out of the medical department's budget. I may have Fleet Accounting split it off, so Medical doesn't find itself dangerously short-changed. But what would you have? My troops were loyal beyond measure; I cannot betray them. Besides," he grinned briefly, "the Barrayaran Imperium is paying."

"Your ImpSec boss was on about your bills, I thought, at your mission briefing."

"Illyan has to explain why enough cash to fund a private army keeps disappearing in his department budget every year, without ever admitting to the private army's existence. Certain Imperial accountants tend to accuse him of departmental inefficiency, which gives him great pain . . . sh."

The Dendarii shuttle pilot, having shut down his ship, ducked into the corridor and sealed the hatch. He nodded to Miles.

"While I was waiting for you at Port Beauchene, sir, I picked up a minor story on the local news net, that you might be interested in. Minor news here on Escobar, that is." The man was bouncing lightly on his toes.

"Say on, Sergeant LaJoie." Miles cocked an eyebrow up at him.

"The Cetagandans have just announced their withdrawal from Marilac. They're calling it—what was that, now—'Due to great progress in the cultural alliance, we are turning police matters over to local control.'"

Miles's fists clenched, joyously. "In other words, they're abandoning their puppet government! Ha!" He hopped from foot to foot, and pounded Quinn on the back. "You hear that, Elli! We've won! I mean, they've won, the Marilacans." *Our sacrifices are redeemed. . . .*

He regained control of his tightening throat before he burst into tears or some like foolishness. "Do me a favor, LaJoie. Pass the word through the Fleet. Tell them I said, 'You folks do good work.' Eh?"

"Yes, sir. My pleasure." The grinning pilot saluted cheerfully and trod off up the corridor.

Miles's grin stretched his face. "See, Elli! What Simon Illyan just bought would have been cheap at a thousand times the cost. A full-bore Cetagandan planetary invasion—first impeded—then bogged—foundered—failed!" And in a fierce whisper, "*I* did it! I made the difference."

Quinn too was smiling, but one perfect eyebrow curved in a certain dry irony. "It's lovely, but if I was reading between the lines correctly, I thought what Barrayaran Imperial Security really wanted was for the Cetagandan military to be *tied up* in the guerilla war on Marilac. Indefinitely. Draining Cetagandan attention away from Barrayaran borders and jump points."

"They didn't put that in writing." Miles's lips drew back wolfishly. "All Simon said was, 'Help the Marilacans as opportunity presents.' That was the standing order, in so many words."

"But you knew damn well what he really wanted."

"Four bloody years was enough. I have not betrayed Barrayar. Nor anyone else."

"Yeah? So if Simon Illyan is so much more Machiavellian than you are, how is it that your version prevailed? Someday, Miles, you are going to run out of hairs to split with those people. And then what will you do?"

He smiled, and shook his head, evading answer.

His elation over the news from Marilac still made him feel like he was walking in half-gravity when he arrived at his cabin aboard the *Triumph*. After a surreptitious glance to be sure the corridor was unpeopled, he embraced and kissed Quinn, a deep kiss that was going to have to last them for a long while, and she went off to her own quarters. He slipped inside, and echoed the door's closing sigh with his own. Home again.

It *was* home, for half his psyche, he reflected, tossing his flight bag onto his bed and heading directly for the shower. Ten years ago, Lord Miles Vorkosigan had invented the cover identity of Admiral Naismith out of his head in a desperate moment, and frantically faked his way to temporary control of the hastily re-named Dendarii Mercenaries. Barrayaran Imperial Security had discovered the cover to be useful . . . no. Credit where it was due. He had persuaded, schemed, demonstrated, and coerced ImpSec into finding use for this cover. *Be careful what you pretend to be. You might become it.*

When had Admiral Naismith stopped being a pretense? Gradually, surely, but mostly since his mercenary mentor Commodore Tung had retired. Or perhaps the wily Tung had recognized before Miles had that his services in propping Miles up to his prematurely exalted rank were no longer required. Colored vid arrays of Dendarii Free Mercenary Fleet organization bloomed in Miles's head as he showered. Personnel—equipment—administration—logistics—he knew every ship, every trooper, every shuttle and piece of ordnance, now. He knew how they fit together, what had to be done first, second, third, twentieth, to place a precisely calculated force at any point on the tactical fulcrum. *This was expertise*, to be able to look at a ship like the *Triumph* and see with his mind's eye right through the walls to every engineering detail, every strength and vulnerability; to look at a commando squad, or a briefing table ringed with captains and captain-owners and know what each one would do or say before they knew it themselves. *I'm on top. Finally, I'm on top of it all. With this lever, I can move worlds.* He switched the shower to "dry" and turned in the blast of warm air. He left the bathroom still chortling under his breath. *I love it.*

His chortle died away in puzzlement when he unlatched the door to his uniform cupboard and found it bare. Had his batman taken them all off for cleaning or repairs? His bewilderment grew as he tried other drawers, and found only a residue of the wildly assorted civilian togs he wore when he stretched the chain of his identity one link further and played spy for the Dendarii. Plus some of his shabbier underwear. Was this some sort of practical joke? If so, he'd have the last laugh. Naked and irritated, he snapped open the locker where his space armor dwelt. Empty. That was almost shocking. *Somebody's taken it down to Engineering to re-calibrate it, or add tactics programs, or something.* His batman should have returned it by now, though. What if he needed it in a hurry?

Time. His people would be gathering. Quinn had once claimed he could carry on naked, and only make those around him feel overdressed. He was momentarily tempted to test her assertion, but overcame the mordant vision, and put the shirt and trousers and sandals he'd been wearing back on. He didn't need a uniform in order to dominate a briefing room, not any more.

On the way to the meeting, he passed Sandy Hereld in the corridor, coming off duty, and gave her a friendly nod. She wheeled and walked backward in startlement. "You're back, sir! That was quick."

He would hardly describe his several-week journey to Imperial HQ on Barrayar as quick. She must mean the trip downside. "It only took two hours."

"What?" Her nose wrinkled. She was still walking backward, reaching the end of the corridor.

He had a briefing room full of senior officers waiting. He waved and swung down a lift tube.

The briefing room was comfortingly familiar, right down to the array of faces around the darkly shining table. Captain Auson of the *Triumph*. Elena Bothari-Jesek, recently promoted captain of the *Peregrine*. Her husband Commodore Baz Jesek, Fleet engineer and in charge, in Miles's absence, of all the repair and refit activities of the Dendarii Fleet in Escobar orbit. The couple, Barrayarans themselves, were with Quinn among the handful of Dendarii apprised of Miles's double identity. Captain Truzillo of the *Jayhawk*, and a dozen more, all tested and true. His people.

Bel Thorne of the *Ariel* was late. That was unusual. One of Thorne's driving characteristics was an insatiable curiosity; a new mission briefing was like a Winterfair gift to the Betan hermaphrodite. Miles turned to Elena Bothari-Jesek, to make small talk while they waited.

"Did you get a chance to visit your mother, downside on Escobar?"

"Yes, thanks." She smiled. "It was . . . nice, to have a little time. We had a chance to talk about some things we'd never talked about the first time we met."

It had been good for both of them, Miles judged. Some of the permanent strain seemed gone from Elena's dark eyes. Better and better, bit by bit. "Good."

He glanced up as the doors hissed open, but it was only Quinn, blowing in with the secured files in hand. She was back in full officer's undress kit, and looking very comfortable and efficient. She handed the files to Miles, and he loaded them into the comconsole, and waited another minute. Still no Bel Thorne.

Talk died away. His officers were giving him attentive, let's-get-on-with-it looks. He'd better not stand around much longer with his thumb in his ear. Before bringing the console display to life, he inquired, "Is there some reason Captain Thorne is late?"

They looked at him, and then at each other. *There can't be something wrong with Bel, it would have been reported to me first thing.* Still, a small leaden knot materialized in the pit of his stomach. "Where is Bel Thorne?"

By eye, they elected Elena Bothari-Jesek as spokesperson. That was an extremely bad sign. "Miles," she said hesitantly, "was Bel supposed to be back before you?"

"Back? Where did Bel go?"

She was looking at him as though he'd lost his mind. "Bel left with you, in the *Ariel*, three days ago."

Quinn's head snapped up. "That's impossible."

"Three days ago, we were still en route to Escobar," Miles stated. The leaden knot was transmuting into neutron star matter. He was not dominating this room at all well. In fact, it seemed to be tilting.

"You took Green Squad with you. It was the new contract, Bel said," Elena added.

"*This* is the new contract." Miles tapped the comconsole. A hideous explanation was beginning to suggest itself to his mind, rising from the black hole in his stomach. The looks on the faces around the table were also beginning to divide into two uneven camps, appalled surmise from the minority who had been in on that mess on Earth two years ago—oh, they were right with him— total confusion from the majority, who had not been directly involved. . . .

"Where did I say I was going?" Miles inquired. His tone was, he thought, gentle, but several people flinched.

"Jackson's Whole." Elena looked him straight in the eye, with much the steady gaze of a zoologist about to dissect a specimen. A sudden lack of trust . . .

Jackson's Whole. That tears it. "Bel Thorne? The *Ariel*? Taura? Within *ten jumps* of Jackson's Whole?" Miles choked. "Dear God."

"But if you're you," said Truzillo, "who was that three days ago?"

"*If* you're you," said Elena darkly. The initiate crowd were all getting that same frowning look.

"You see," Miles explained in a hollow voice to the *What-the-hell-are-they-talking-about?* portion of the room, "some people have an evil twin. I am not so lucky. What *I* have is an *idiot* twin."

"Your clone," said Elena Bothari-Jesek.

"My brother," he corrected automatically.

"Little Mark Pierre," said Quinn. "Oh . . . *shit.*"

CHAPTER THREE

His stomach seemed to turn inside out, the cabin wavered, and shadow darkened his vision. The bizarre sensations of the wormhole jump were gone almost as soon as they began, but left an unpleasant somatic reverberation, as if he were a struck gong. He took a deep, calming breath. That had been the fourth jump of the voyage. Five jumps to go, on the tortuous zigzag through the wormhole nexus from Escobar to Jackson's Whole. The *Ariel* had been three days en route, almost halfway.

He glanced around Naismith's cabin. He could not continue to hide out in here much longer, pretense of illness or Naismithian black mood or not. Thorne needed every bit of data he could supply to plan the Dendarii raid on the clone-crèche. He had used his hibernation well, scanning the *Ariel*'s mission logs back through time, all the way past his first encounter with the Dendarii two years ago. He now knew a great deal more about the mercenaries, and the thought of casual conversation with the *Ariel*'s crew was far less terrifying.

Unfortunately there was very little in the mission log to help him reconstruct what his first meeting with Naismith on Earth had looked like from the Dendarii point of view. The log had concentrated on rehabilitation and refit reports, dickerings with assorted ship's chandlers, and engineering briefings. He'd found exactly one order pertinent to his own adventures embedded in the data flow, advising all ship masters that Admiral Naismith's clone had been seen on Earth, warning that the clone might attempt to pass himself off as the Admiral, giving the (incorrect) information that the clone's legs would show up on a medical scan as normal bone and not plastic replacements, and ordering use of stunners-only in apprehending the imposter. No explanations, no later revisions or updates. All of Naismith/Vorkosigan's highest-level orders tended to be verbal and undocumented anyway, for security—from the Dendarii, not for them—a habit that had just served him well.

He leaned back in his station chair and glowered at the com-console display. The Dendarii data named him *Mark. That's another thing you don't get to choose,* Miles Naismith Vorkosigan had said. *Mark Pierre. You are Lord Mark Pierre Vorkosigan, in your own right, on Barrayar.*

But he was not on Barrayar, nor ever would be if he could help it. *You are not my brother, and the Butcher of Komarr was never a father to me,* his thought denied for the thousandth time to his absent progenitor. *My mother was a uterine replicator.*

But the power of the suggestion had ridden him ever after, sapping his satisfaction with every pseudonym he'd ever tried, though he'd stared at lists of names till his eyes ached. Dramatic names, plain names, exotic, strange, common, silly . . . Jan Vandermark was the alias he'd used the longest, the closest sideways skittish approach to identity.

Mark! Miles had shouted, being dragged away, for all he knew, to his own death. *Your name is Mark!*

I am not Mark. I am NOT your damned brother, you maniac. The denial was hot and huge, but when its echoes died away, in the hollow chamber left inside his skull he seemed not to be anyone at all.

His head was aching, a grinding tightness that crawled up his spine through his shoulders and neck and spread out under his scalp. He rubbed hard at his neck, but the tension just circulated around through his arms and back into his shoulders.

Not his brother. But to be strictly accurate, Naismith could not be blamed for forcing him to life in the same way as the other House Bharaputran clones' progenitors. Oh, they were genetically identical, yes. It was a matter of . . . intent, perhaps. And where the money came from.

Lord Miles Naismith Vorkosigan had been just six years old when the tissue sample from a biopsy was stolen from some clinical laboratory on Barrayar, during the last gasp of Komarran resistance to Barrayaran imperial conquest. No one, neither

Barrayaran nor Komarran, was intrinsically interested in the crippled child Miles. The focus had all been on his father. Admiral Count Aral Vorkosigan, Regent of Barrayar, Conqueror (or Butcher) of Komarr. Aral Vorkosigan had supplied the will and the wit which had made Komarr into Barrayar's first off-planet conquest. And made himself the target of Komarran resistance and revenge. Hope for successful resistance had faded in time. Hope for revenge lived on in exiled bitterness. Stripped of an army, arms, support, one Komarran hate group plotted a slow, mad vengeance. To strike at the father through the son upon whom he was known to dote . . .

Like a sorcerer in an old tale, the Komarrans dealt with a devil to have a simulacrum made. A bastard clone, he thought with a silent, humorless laugh. But things went wrong. The crippled original boy, poisoned before birth by yet another murderous enemy of his father's, grew strangely, unpredictably; his genetic duplicate grew straight . . . that had been his first clue that he was different from the other clones, he reflected. When the other clones went to the doctors for treatment they came back stronger, healthier, growing ever-faster. Every time he went, and he went often, their painful treatments seemed to make him sicklier, more stunted. The braces they put on his bones, neck, back, never seemed to help much. They had *made* him into this hunchbacked dwarfling as if molding him in a press, die-cut from a cast of his progenitor. *I could have been normal, if Miles Vorkosigan had not been crippled.*

When he first began to suspect the true purpose of his fellow clones, for rumors passed among the children in wild ways even their careful handlers could not totally control, his growing somatic deformations brought him silent suppressed joy. Surely they could not use *this* body for a brain transplant. He might be discarded— he might yet escape his pleasant, smiling jailer-servants. . . .

His real escape, when his Komarran owners came to collect him at age fourteen, was like a miracle. And then the training had begun. The endless harsh tutoring, drill, indoctrination. At first a destiny, any destiny at all, seemed glorious compared to his crèche-mates' end. He determinedly took up the training to replace his progenitor, and strike a blow for dear Komarr, a place he had never seen, against evil Barrayar, a place he had never seen either. But learning to be Miles Vorkosigan turned out to be like running the race in Zeno's paradox. No matter how much he learned, how frantically he drilled, how harshly his mistakes were punished,

Miles learned more, faster; by the time he arrived, his quarry had always moved on, intellectually or otherwise.

The symbolic race became literal once his Komarran tutors actually moved to effect the substitution. They chased the elusive young Lord Vorkosigan halfway around the wormhole nexus, never realizing that when he vanished, he utterly ceased to exist, and Admiral Naismith appeared. The Komarrans had never found out about Admiral Naismith. Not planning but chance had finally brought them together two years ago on Earth, right back where the whole stupid race had started, in pursuit of a vengeance gone twenty years cold.

The time-delay had been critical in a way the Komarrans had not even noticed. When they first began chasing Vorkosigan, their customized clone had been at the peak of his mental conditioning, committed to the goals of the revolt, unreflectingly eager. Had they not saved him from the fate of clones? Eighteen months of watching them screw up, eighteen months of travel, observation, exposure to uncensored news, views, even a few people, had planted secret doubts in his mind. And, bluntly, one could not duplicate even an imitation of a galactic-class education like Vorkosigan's without inadvertently learning something about how to think. In the middle of it all, the surgery to replace his perfectly sound leg bones with synthetics, just because Vorkosigan had smashed his, had been stunningly painful. What if Vorkosigan broke his neck, next time? Realization had crept over him.

Stuffing his head full of Lord Vorkosigan, in bits over time, was just as much of a brain transplant as anything done with vibra-scalpels and living tissue. *He who plots revenge, must dig two graves.* But the Komarrans had dug the second grave for *him.* For the person he never had a chance to become, the man he might have been if he had not been forced at shock-stick point to continually struggle to be someone *else.*

Some days he was not sure who he hated more, House Bhara-putra, the Komarrans, or Miles Naismith Vorkosigan.

He shut off the comconsole with a snort, and rose to pick out his precious data cube from the uniform pocket in which it was still hidden. Upon reflection, he cleaned up and depilated again, before donning fresh Dendarii officer's undress grays. That was as regulation as he could make himself. Let the Dendarii see only the polished surface, and not the man inside the man inside. . . .

He steeled himself, exited the cabin, stepped across the corridor, and pressed the buzzer to the hermaphrodite captain's quarters.

No response. He pressed it again. After a short delay Thorne's blurred alto voice came, "Yes?"

"Naismith here."

"Oh! Come in, Miles." The voice sharpened with interest.

The door slid aside and he stepped within, to realize that the reason for the delay was that he'd woken Thorne from sleep. The hermaphrodite was sitting up on one elbow in bed, brown hair tousled, its free hand falling away from the keypad which had released the door.

"Excuse me," he said, stepping backward, but the door had already sealed again.

"No, it's all right." The hermaphrodite smiled sleepily, curled its body in a C, and patted the bed invitingly in front of its sheeted . . . lap. "For you, anytime. Come sit. Would you like a back rub? You look tense." It was wearing a decidedly frilly night-gown, flowing silk with lace trim edging a plunging vee neckline that revealed the swelling pale flesh of its breasts.

He sidled to a station chair instead. Thorne's smile took on a peculiarly sardonic tinge, even while remaining perfectly relaxed. He cleared his throat. "I . . . thought it was time for that more detailed mission briefing I promised." *I should have checked the duty-roster.* Would Admiral Naismith have known the captain's sleep-cycle?

"Time and past time. I'm glad to see you come up out of the fog. What the hell have you been doing, wherever you went for the past eight weeks, Miles? Who died?"

"No one. Well, eight clones, I suppose."

"Hm." Thorne nodded wry acknowledgment. The seductive sinuosity faded from its posture, and it sat up straight, rubbing the last of the sleep from its eyes. "Tea?"

"Sure. Or, uh, I could come back after your sleep-shift." *Or after you're dressed.*

It swung its silk-swathed legs from the bed. "No way. I'd be up in an hour anyway. I've been waiting for this. Seize the day." It padded across the cabin to do its tea-ritual again. He set up the data cube in the comconsole and paused, both polite and practical, for the captain to take its first sips of the hot black liquid and come fully awake. He wished it would put its uniform on.

He keyed up the display as Thorne wandered close. "I have a detailed holomap of House Bharaputra's main medical complex. This data is not more than four months old. Plus guard sched-ules and patrol patterns—their security is much heavier than a normal civilian hospital, more like a military laboratory, but it's no fortress. Their everyday concern is more against individual local intruders intent on theft. And, of course, in preventing certain of their less voluntary patients from escaping." A significant chunk of his former fortune had gone into that map cube.

The color-coded image spread itself in lines and sheets of light above the vid plate. The complex was truly that, a vast warren of buildings, tunnels, therapy-gardens, labs, mini-manufacturing areas, flyer pads, warehouses, garages, and even two shuttle docks for direct departure to planetary orbit.

Thorne put down its cup, leaned over the comconsole, and stared with interest. It took up the remote control and turned the map-image, shrank and expanded and sliced it. "So do we want to start by capturing the shuttle bays?"

"No. The clones are all kept together over here on the west side, in this sort of hospice area. I figure if we land here in this exercise court we'll be damn near on top of their dormitory. Naturally, I'm not overly concerned about what the drop shuttle damages, coming down."

"Naturally." A brief grin flickered over the captain's face. "Timing?"

"I want to make it a night drop. Not so much for cover, because there's no way we're going to make a combat-drop shuttle inconspicuous, but because that's the one time all the clones are together in a small area. In the day they're all spread out in the exercise and play areas, the swimming pool and what-not."

"And classrooms?"

"No, not exactly. They don't teach 'em much beyond the mini-mum necessary for socialization. If a clone can count to twenty and read signs, that's all they need. Throw-away brains." That had been the other way he'd known he was different from the rest. A real human tutor had introduced him to a vast array of virtual learning programs. He'd lost himself for days at a time in the computer's patient praise. Unlike his Komarran tutors later, they repeated themselves endlessly, and never punished him, never swore or raged or struck or forced him to physical exertion till he grew sick or passed out. . . . "The clones pick up a surprising amount of information despite it all, though. A lot from their holovid games. Bright kids. Damn few of these clones have stupid pro-genitors, or they wouldn't have amassed a sufficient fortune to buy this form of life-extension. Ruthless, maybe, but not stupid."

Thorne's eyes narrowed as it dissected the area on the vid,

taking apart the buildings layer by later, studying the layout. "So a dozen full-kit Dendarii commandos wake fifty or sixty kids out of a sound sleep in the middle of the night . . . do they know we're coming?"

"No. By the way, make sure the troops realize they won't look exactly like kids. We're taking them in their last year of development. They're mostly ten or eleven years old, but due to the growth accelerators they will appear to have the bodies of late teenagers."

"Gawky?"

"Not really. They get great physical conditioning. Healthy as hell. That's the whole point of not just growing them in a vat till transplant time."

"Do they . . . know? Know what's going to happen to them?" Thorne asked with an introspective frown.

"They're not told, no. They're told all kinds of lies, variously. They're told they're in a special school, for security reasons, to save them from some exotic danger. That they're all some kind of prince or princess, or rich man's heir, or military scion, and someday very soon their parents or their aunts or their ambassadors are going to come and take them away to some glamorous future . . . and then, of course, at last some smiling person comes, and calls them away from their playmates, and tells them that today is the day, and they run . . ." he stopped, swallowed, "and snatch up their things, and brag to their friends. . . ."

Thorne was tapping the vid control unconsciously in its palm, and looking pale. "I get the picture."

"And walk out hand-in-hand with their murderers, eagerly."

"You can stop with the scenario-spinning, unless you're trying to make me lose my last meal."

"What, you've known for years that this was going on," he mocked. "Why get all squeamish about it now?" He bit off his bitterness. Naismith. He must be Naismith.

Thorne shot him a sharp glare. "*I* was ready to fry them from orbit the last time, as you may recall. You wouldn't let me."

What last time? No time in the last three years. He'd have to scan the mission logs back even further, dammit. He shrugged, ambiguously.

"So," said Thorne, "are these . . . big kids . . . all going to decide we're their parents' enemies, kidnapping them just before they go home? I see trouble, here."

He clenched, and spread, the fingers of his right hand. "Maybe not. Children . . . have a culture of their own. Passed down from year to year. There are rumors. Boogeyman stories. Doubts. I told you, they aren't stupid. Their adult handlers try to stamp out the stories, or make fun of them, or mix them up with other, obvious lies." And yet . . . they had not fooled him. But then, he had lived in the crèche much longer than the average. He'd had time to see more clones come and go, time to see stories repeated, pseudo-biographies duplicated. Time for their handlers' tiny slips and mistakes to accumulate in his observation. "If it's the same—" *If it's the same as it was in my time*, he almost said, but saved himself, "I should be able to persuade them. Leave that part to me."

"Gladly." Thorne swung a console chair into clamps close beside his, settled down, and rapidly entered some notes on logistics and angle of attack, point-men and back-ups, and traced projected routes through the buildings. "Two dormitories?" It pointed curiously. Thorne's fingernails were cut blunt, undecorated.

"Yes. The boys are kept segregated from the girls, rather carefully. The female—usually female—customers expect to wake up in a body with the seal of virginity still on it."

"I see. So. We get all these kids loaded, by some miracle, before the Bharaputrans arrive in force—"

"Speed is of the essence, yes."

"As usual. But the Bharaputrans will be all over us if there is any little hitch or hold-up. Unlike with the Marilacans at Dagoola you haven't had weeks and weeks to drill these kids on shuttle-loading procedures. What if, then?"

"Once the clones are loaded into the shuttle they become in effect *our* hostages. We'll be safe from lethal fire with them aboard. The Bharaputrans won't risk their investment as long as any chance of recovery remains."

"Once they decide all chance is lost, they'll seek vigorous retribution, to discourage imitators, though."

"True. We must cloud their minds with doubt."

"Then their next move—if we get the shuttle airborne—must be to try to blow up the *Ariel* in orbit before we get there, cutting off our escape."

"Speed," he repeated doggedly.

"Contingencies, Miles dear. Wake up. I don't usually have to re-start your brain in the morning—do you want some more tea? No? I suggest, if we suffer dangerous delay downside, that the *Ariel* take refuge at Fell Station and we rendezvous with it there."

"Fell Station? The orbital one?" He hesitated. "Why?"

"Baron Fell is still in a state of vendetta with Bharaputra and Ryoval, isn't he?"

Jacksonian internecine House politics; he was not as current on them as he should be. He had not even thought of looking for an ally among the other Houses. They were all criminal, all evil, tolerating or sabotaging each other in shifting patterns of power. And here was Ryoval, mentioned again. Why? He took refuge in another wordless shrug. "Getting pinned, trapped on Fell Station with fifty young clones while Bharaputra hustles for control of the jumppoint stations, would not improve our position. No Jacksonian is to be trusted. Run and jump as fast as we can is still the safest strategy."

"Bharaputra won't swing jumpstation Five into line, it's Fell-owned."

"Yes, but I want to return to Escobar. The clones can all get safe asylum there."

"Look, Miles, the jump back on this route is held by the consortium already dominated by Bharaputra. We'll never get back out the way we jump in, unless you've got something up your sleeve—no? Then may I suggest our best escape route is via jumppoint Five."

"Do you really see Fell as so reliable an ally?" he inquired cautiously.

"Not at all. But he is the enemy of our enemies. This trip."

"But the jump from Five leads to the Hegen Hub. We can't jump into Cetagandan territory, and the only other route out of the Hub is to Komarr via Pol."

"Roundabout, but much safer."

Not for me! That's the damned Barrayaran Empire! He swallowed a wordless shriek.

"The Hub to Pol to Komarr to Sergyar and back to Escobar," Thorne recited happily. "You know, this could really work out." It made more notes, leaning across the comconsole, its nightgown shifting and shimmering in the candy lights of the vid display. Then it put its elbows on the console and rested its chin in its hands, breasts compressing, shifting beneath the thin fabric. Its expression grew gently introspective. It glanced up at him at last with an odd, rather sad smile.

"Have any clones ever escaped?" Thorne asked softly.

"No," he answered quickly, automatically.

"Except for your own clone, of course."

A dangerous turn in the conversation. "My clone did not escape either. He was simply removed by his purchasers." He should have tried to escape . . . what life might he have led, had he succeeded?

"Fifty kids," Thorne sighed. "Y'know—I *really approve* of this mission." It waited, watching him with sharp and gleaming eyes.

Acutely uncomfortable, he suppressed an idiocy such as saying *Thank you*, but found himself with no remark to put in its place, resulting in an awkward silence.

"I suppose," said Thorne thoughtfully after the too-long moment, "it would be very difficult for anyone brought up in such an environment to really trust . . . anyone else. Anyone's word. Their good will."

"I . . . suppose." Was this casual conversation, or something more sinister? A trap . . .

Thorne, still with that weird mysterious smile, leaned across their station chairs, caught his chin in one strong, slender hand, and kissed him.

He did not know if he was supposed to recoil or respond, so did neither, in cross-eyed, panicked paralysis. Thorne's mouth was warm, and tasted of tea and bergamot, silky and perfumed. Was Naismith screwing—this—too? If so, who did what to whom? Or did they take turns? *And would it really be that bad?* His terror heightened with an undeniable stirring of arousal. *I believe I would die for a lover's touch.* He had been alone forever.

Thorne withdrew at last, to his intense relief, though only a little way, its hand still trapping his chin. After another moment of dead silence, its smile grew wry. "I shouldn't tease you, I suppose," it sighed. "There is a sort of cruelty in it, all things considered."

It released him, and stood, the sensuous langour abruptly switched off. "Back in a minute." It strode to its cabin washroom, sealing the door behind it.

He sat, unstrung and shaking. *What the hell was that all about?* And from another part of his mind, *You could lose your damned virginity this trip, I bet,* and from another, *No! Not with that!*

Had that been a test? But had he passed, or failed? Thorne had not cried out in accusation, nor called for armed back-up. Perhaps the captain was arranging his arrest right now, by comm link from the washroom. There was no place to run away to, aboard a small ship in deep space. His crossed arms hugged his torso. With effort he uncrossed them, placed his hands on the console, and willed his muscles to uncoil. *They probably won't kill me.* They'd take him back to the fleet and let Naismith kill him.

But no security squad broke down the door, and soon enough

Thorne returned. Nattily dressed in its uniform, at last. It plucked the data cube from the comconsole and closed its palm over it. "I'll sit down with Sergeant Taura and this and do some serious planning, then."

"Ah, yes. It's time." He hated to let the precious cube out of his sight. But it seemed he was still Naismith in Thorne's eyes.

Thorne pursed its lips. "Now that it's time to brief the crew, don't you think it would be a good idea to put the *Ariel* on a communications blackout?"

An outstanding idea, though one he'd been afraid to suggest as too suspicious and strange. Maybe it wasn't so unusual, on these covert ops. He'd had no certain idea as to when the real Naismith was supposed to return to the Dendarii fleet, but from the mercenaries' easy acceptance of him, it had to have been expected soon. He'd lived for the past three days in fear of frantic orders arriving by tight-beam and jump-courier from the real Admiral, telling the *Ariel* to turn around. *Give me a few more days. Just a few more days, and I'll redeem it all.* "Yes. Do so."

"Very good, sir." Thorne hesitated. "How are you feeling, now? Everybody knows these black miasmas of yours can run for weeks. But if only you'll rest properly, I trust you'll be your usual energetic self in time for the drop mission. Shall I pass the word to leave you alone?"

"I . . . would appreciate that, Bel." What luck! "But keep me informed, eh?"

"Oh, yes. You can count on me. It's a straightforward raid, except for handling that herd of kids, in which I defer to your superior expertise."

"Right." With a smile and a cheery salute, he fled across the corridor to the safe isolation of his own cabin. The pulsing combination of elation and his tension headache made him feel as if he were floating. When the door sealed behind him, he fell across his bed and gripped the coverings to hold himself in place. *It's really going to happen!*

Later, diligently scanning ship's logs on his cabin comconsole, he finally found the four-year-old records of the *Ariel*'s previous visit to Jackson's Whole. Such as they were. They started out with utterly boring details about an ordnance deal, inventory entries regarding a cargo of weapons to be loaded from House Fell's orbital transfer station. Completely without preamble, Thorne's breathless voice made a cryptic entry, "Murka's lost the Admiral. He's being held prisoner by Baron Ryoval. I'm going now to make a devil's bargain with Fell."

Then records of an emergency combat-drop shuttle trip downside, followed by the *Ariel*'s abrupt departure from Fell Station with cargo only half loaded. These events were succeeded by two fascinating, unexplained conversations between Admiral Naismith, and Baron Ryoval and Baron Fell, respectively. Ryoval was raving, sputtering exotic death threats. He studied the baron's contorted, handsome face uneasily. Even in a society that prized ruthlessness, Ryoval was a man whom other Jacksonian power-brokers stepped wide around. Admiral Naismith appeared to have stepped right in something.

Fell was more controlled, a cold anger. As usual, all the really essential information, including the reason for the visit in the first place, was lost in Naismith's verbal orders. But he did manage to gather the surprising fact that the eight-foot-tall commando, Sergeant Taura, was a product of House Bharaputra's genetics laboratories, a genetically-engineered prototype super-soldier.

It was like unexpectedly meeting someone from one's old home town. In a weird wash of homesickness, he longed to look her up and compare notes. Naismith had apparently stolen her heart, or at least stolen her away, although that did not seem to be the offense Ryoval was foaming about. It was all rather incomprehensible.

He did garner one other unpleasant fact. Baron Fell was a would-be clone consumer. His old enemy Ryoval in a move of vendetta had apparently arranged to have Fell's clone murdered before the transplant could take place, trapping Fell in his aging body, but the intent was there. Regardless of Bel Thorne's contingency planning, he resolved he would have nothing to do with Baron Fell if he could help it.

He blew out his breath, shut down the comconsole, and went back to practicing simulations with the command headset helmet, a manufacturer's training program that happily had never been deleted from its memory. *I'm going to bring this off. Somehow.*

CHAPTER FOUR

"No reply from the *Ariel* from this courier-hop either, sir," Lieutenant Hereld reported apologetically.

Miles's fists clenched in frustration. He forced his hands flat again along his trouser seams, but the energy only flowed to his feet, and he began to pace from wall to wall in the *Triumph*'s Nav and Com room. "That's the third—third? You have been repeating the message with every courier?"

"Yes, sir."

"The third no-reply. Dammit, what's holding Bel up?"

Lieutenant Hereld shrugged helplessly at this rhetorical question.

Miles re-crossed the room, frowning fiercely. Damn the time-lag. He wanted to know what was happening *right now*. Tight-beam communications crossed a local-space region at the speed of light, but the only way to get information through a wormhole was to physically record it, put it on a jumpship, and jump it through to the next relay station, where it was beamed to the next wormhole and jumped again, if it was economically worthwhile to maintain such a service. In regions of heavy message traffic, such couriers jumped as often as every half-hour or even oftener. Between Escobar and Jackson's Whole, the couriers maintained an every-four-hours schedule. So on top of the delay from the speed of light limitation, was added this other, arbitrary human one. Such a delay could be quite useful sometimes, to people playing complex games with interstellar finances, exchange rates, and futures. Or to independent-minded subordinates wishing to conceal excess

355

information about their activities from their superior officers—
Miles had occasionally used the lag for that purpose himself. A
couple of clarification requests, and their replies, could buy enough
time to bring off all sorts of events. That was why he'd made
certain his recall order to the *Ariel* was personal, forceful, and
crystal-clear. But Bel had not returned some counterfeit-demure
What do you mean by that, sir? Bel had not replied at all.

"It's not some fault in the courier system, is it? Other traffic—
is other traffic on the route getting their messages through?"

"Yes, sir. I checked. Information flow is normal all the way
through to Jackson's Whole."

"They did file a flight plan to Jackson's Whole, they did actually
jump through that exit-point—"

"Yes, sir."

Four bleeding days ago, now. He considered his mental picture
of the wormhole nexus. No mapped jumps leading off this standard
shortest route from Escobar to Jackson's Whole had ever been
discovered to go anywhere of interest. He could not imagine Bel
choosing this moment to play Betan Astronomical Survey and go
exploring. There *was* the very rare ship that jumped through some
perfectly standard route but never materialized on the other
side . . . converted to an unrecoverable smear of quarks in the fabric
of space-time by some subtle malfunction in the ship's Necklin
rods or the pilot's neurological control system. The jump couriers
kept track of traffic on such a heavily commercialized route as this,
though, and would have reported such a disappearance promptly.

He came—was driven—to decision, and that alone heated his
temper a few more degrees. He had grown unaccustomed of late
to being chivvied into any action by events not under his own
control. *This was not in my plans for the day, blast it.* "All right,
Sandy. Call me a staff meeting. Captain Quinn, Captain Bothari-
Jesek, Commodore Jesek, in the *Triumph*'s briefing room, as soon
as they can assemble."

Hereld raised her brows at the list of names even as her hands
moved over the comconsole interface to comply. Inner Circle all.
"Serious shit, sir?"

He managed an edged smile, and tried to lighten his voice.
"Seriously annoying only, Lieutenant."

Not quite. What had his idiot baby brother Mark in mind to
do with that commando squad he'd requisitioned? A dozen fully-
equipped Dendarii troopers were not trivial firepower. Yet, compared to the military resources of, say, House Bharaputra . . . *enough*

force to get into a hell of a lot of trouble, but not enough force to shoot their way back out. The thought of his people—Taura, God!— blindly following the ignorant Mark into some tactical insanity, trustingly thinking it was *him,* drove him wild inside. Klaxons howled and red lights flashed in his head. *Bel, why aren't you answering?*

Miles found himself pacing in the *Triumph's* main briefing room, too, around and around the big main tac display table, until Quinn raised her chin from her hands to growl, "Will you please *sit down?*" Quinn was not as anxious as he; she was not biting her finger-nails yet. The ends remained neat, un-eclipsed half-moons. He found that faintly reassuring. He swung into a station chair. One of his booted feet began tapping on the friction matting. Quinn eyed it, frowned, opened her mouth, closed it, and shook her head. He stilled the foot and bared his teeth at her in a quick false grin. Happily, before his nervous energy could materialize into some even more irritating compulsive twitch, Baz Jesek arrived.

"Elena is podding over from the *Peregrine* right now," Baz reported, seating himself in his usual station chair, and by habit calling up the fleet engineering ops interface from the comconsole. "She should be along in just a few minutes."

"Good, thanks." Miles nodded.

The engineer had been a tall, thin, dark-haired, tensely unhappy man in his late twenties when Miles had first met him, almost a decade ago, at the birth of the Dendarii Mercenaries. The outfit had then consisted only of Miles, his Barrayaran bodyguard, his bodyguard's daughter, one obsolete freighter slated for scrap and its suicidally depressed jump pilot, and an ill-conceived get-rich-quick arms-smuggling scheme. Miles had sworn Baz in as a liege-man to Lord Vorkosigan before Admiral Naismith had even been invented. Now in his late thirties, Baz remained just as thin, with slightly less dark hair, and just as quiet, but possessed of a serene self-confidence. He reminded Miles of a heron, stalking in some reedy lake-margin, all long stillnesses and economical motions.

As promised, Elena Bothari-Jesek entered the chamber shortly thereafter and seated herself beside her engineer-husband. Both being on duty, they limited the demonstration of their reunion to the exchange of a smile and a quick hand-touch under the table. She spared a smile for Miles, too. Secondly.

Of all the Dendarii Inner Circle who knew him as Lieutenant Lord Vorkosigan, Elena was surely the deepest inside. Her father, the late Sergeant Bothari, had been Miles's liege-sworn armsman and personal protector from the day Miles had been born. Age mates, Miles and Elena had been practically raised together, since Countess Vorkosigan had taken a maternal interest in the motherless girl. Elena knew Admiral Naismith, Lord Vorkosigan, and just-plain-Miles as thoroughly—perhaps more thoroughly—as anyone in the universe.

And had chosen to marry Baz Jesek instead . . . Miles found it comforting and useful to think of Elena as his sister. Foster-sister she nearly was in truth. She was as tall as her tall husband, with cropped ebony hair and pale ivory skin. He could still see the echo of borzoi-faced Sergeant Bothari in the aquiline bones of her features, Bothari's leaden ugliness transmuted to her golden beauty by some genetic alchemy. *Elena, I still love you, dammit* . . . he clipped off the thought. He had Quinn now. Or anyway, the Admiral Naismith half of him did.

As a Dendarii officer, Elena was his finest creation. He'd watched her grow from a shy, angry, off-balance girl, barred from military service on Barrayar by her gender, to squad leader to covert operative to staff officer to ship-master. The retired Commodore Tung had once named her his second-best military apprentice ever. Miles sometimes wondered how much of his on-going maintenance of the Dendarii Mercenaries was really service to Imperial Security, how much was the wild self-indulgence of a very questionable aspect of his own faceted—or fractured—personality, and how much was a secret gift to Elena Bothari. Bothari-Jesek. The true springs of history could be murky indeed.

"There's still no word from the *Ariel*," Miles began without preamble; no formalities required with this group. Deep insiders all, he could dare to think out loud in front of them. He could feel his mind relax, re-blending Admiral Naismith and Lord Vorkosigan. He could even let his accent waver from Naismith's strict Betan drawl, and allow a few Barrayaran gutterals to slip in with the swear words. There were going to be swear words, this staff meeting, he was fairly sure. "I want to go after them."

Quinn drummed her nails on the table, once. "I expected you would. Therefore, could little Mark be expecting it too? He's studied you. He's got your number. Could this be a trap? Remember how he diddled you the last time."

Miles winced. "I remember. The possibility that this is some kind of set-up has crossed my mind. That's one reason I didn't take off after them twenty hours ago." Right after the embarrassing, hastily-dismissed full staff meeting. He'd been in the mood for fratricide on the spot. "Assuming, as seems reasonable, that Bel was fooled at first—and I don't see why not, everybody else was— the time-lag might have given Mark a chance to slip up, and Bel to see the light. But in that case the recall order should have brought the *Ariel* back."

"Mark does do an awfully good you," Quinn observed, from personal experience. "Or at least he did two years ago. If you're not expecting the possibility of a double, he seems just like you on one of your off days. His exterior appearance was perfect."

"But Bel does know of the possibility," Elena put in.

"Yes," said Miles. "So maybe Bel hasn't been fooled. Maybe Bel's been spaced."

"Mark would need the crew, or a crew, to run the ship," said Baz. "Though he might have had a new crew waiting, farside."

"If he'd been planning such outright piracy and murder, he'd hardly have taken a Dendarii commando squad along to resist it." Reason could be very reassuring, sometimes. Sometimes. Miles took a breath. "Or maybe Bel has been suborned."

Baz raised his brows; Quinn unconsciously closed her teeth upon, but did not bite through, the little fingernail of her right hand.

"Suborned how?" said Elena. "Not by money." Her smile twisted up. "D'you figure Bel's finally given up trying to seduce you, and is looking for the next best thing?"

"That's not funny," Miles snapped. Baz converted a suspicious snort into a careful cough, and met his glare blandly, but then lost it and sniggered.

"At any rate, it's an old joke," Miles conceded wearily. "But it depends upon what Mark is up to, on Jackson's Whole. The kind of . . . hell, outright slavery, practiced by the various Jacksonian body-sculptors, is a deep offense to Bel's progressive Betan soul. If Mark is thinking of taking some kind of bite out of his old home planet, he just might talk Bel into going along with it."

"At Fleet expense?" Baz inquired.

"That does . . . verge on mutiny," Miles agreed reluctantly. "I'm not accusing, I'm just speculating. Trying to see all the possibilities."

"In that case, is it possible Mark's destination isn't Jackson's Whole at all?" said Baz. "There are four other jumps out of Jacksonian local space. Maybe the *Ariel* is just passing through."

"Physically possible, yes," said Miles. "Psychologically . . . I've studied Mark, too. And while I can't say that I have his number, I know Jackson's Whole looms large in his life. It's only a gut-feeling, but it's a strong gut-feeling." Like a bad case of indigestion.

"How *did* we get blindsided by Mark this time?" Elena asked. "I thought ImpSec was supposed to be keeping track of him for us."

"They are. I get regular reports from Illyan's office," Miles said. "The last report, which I read at ImpSec headquarters not three weeks ago, put Mark still on Earth. But it's the damned time-lag. If he left Earth, say, four or five weeks ago, that report is still in transit from Earth to Illyan on Barrayar and back to me. I'll bet you Betan dollars to anything you please that we get a coded message from HQ in the next few days earnestly warning us that Mark has dropped out of sight. Again."

"Again?" said Elena. "Has he dropped out of sight before?"

"A couple of times. Three, actually." Miles hesitated. "You see, every once in a while—three times in the last two years—I've tried to contact him myself. Invited him to come in, come to Barrayar, or at least to meet with me. Every time, he's panicked, gone underground and changed his identity—he's rather good at it, from all the time he spent as a prisoner of the Komarran terrorists— and it takes Illyan's people weeks or months to locate him again. Illyan's asked me not to try to contact Mark any more without his authorization." He brooded. "Mother wants him to come in so much, but she won't have Illyan order him kidnapped. At first I agreed with her, but now I wonder."

"As your clone, he—" began Baz.

"Brother," Miles corrected, instantly. "Brother. I reject the term 'clone' for Mark. I forbid it. 'Clone' implies something interchangeable. A brother is someone unique. And I assure you, Mark is unique."

"In guessing . . . Mark's next moves," Baz began again, more carefully, "can we even use reason? Is he sane?"

"If he is, it's not the Komarrans' fault." Miles rose and began pacing again around the table, despite Quinn's exasperated look. He avoided her eyes and watched his boots, gray on gray against the friction matting, instead. "After we finally discovered his existence, Illyan had his agents do every kind of background check on him they could. Partly to make up for the acute embarrass- ment of ImpSec's having missed him all these years, I think. I've seen all the reports. Trying and trying to get inside Mark's mind." Around the corner, down the other side, and back.

"His life in Bharaputra's clone-crèche didn't seem too bad—they coddle those bodies—but after the Komarran insurgents picked him up, I gather it got pretty nightmarish. They kept training him to be me, but every time they thought they'd got it, I'd do something unexpected and they had to start over. They kept changing and elaborating their plans. The plot dragged on for years after the time they'd first hoped to bring it off. They were a small group, operating on a shoestring anyway. Their leader, Ser Galen, was half-mad himself, I think." Around and around.

"Part of the time Galen would treat Mark like the great hope for a Komarran uprising, or pet him and set him up with the idea that they were going to make him Emperor of Barrayar in a coup. But part of the time Galen would slip a cog, and see Mark as the personal genetic representative of our father, and make him whipping-boy for all his hatred of the Vorkosigans and Barrayar. Disguising the most ferocious punishments, tortures really—from himself, and maybe even from Mark—as 'training discipline.' Illyan's agent had some of this from a rather illegal fast-penta interrogation of an ex-subordinate of Galen's, so it's flat truth." Around and around.

"For example, apparently Mark's and my metabolisms are not the same. So whenever Mark's weight exceeded my parameters, instead of doing the intelligent thing and having Mark's appetite medically adjusted, Galen would first withhold food for days, then let him gorge, and then force him at shock-stick point to exercise till he vomited. Weird stuff like that, really disturbing. Galen apparently had a hair-trigger temper, at least where Mark was concerned. Or maybe he was deliberately trying to make Mark crazy. Create a Mad Emperor Miles, to replay Mad Emperor Yuri's reign and destroy the Barrayaran government from the top down. Once—this fellow reported—Mark tried to get a night out, just a night out, and actually got away for a while, till Galen's goons brought him back. Galen went nuts, accused him of trying to escape, took his shock-stick and—" his eye caught Elena's paling face, and he hastily edited his nervous outburst, "and did some ugly things." Which couldn't have helped Mark's sexual adjustment any. It had been so bad that Galen's own goons had begged him to stop, according to the informant.

"No wonder he hated Galen," said Quinn softly.

Elena's glance was rather sharper. "There's nothing you could have done. You didn't even know Mark existed, back then."

"We should have known."

"Right. So to what extent is this retroactive guilt distorting your thinking right now, Admiral?"

"Some, I suspect," he admitted. "That's why I called you all here. I feel the need of a cross-check, on this." He paused and forced himself to sit again. "That's not the only reason, however. Before this mess with the *Ariel* leaped out of the wormhole, I had started out to give you a real, bona fide mission assignment."

"Ah, ha," said Baz with satisfaction. "At last."

"The new contract." Despite his distractions, he smiled. "Before Mark showed up, I had it figured for a mission where nothing could possibly go wrong. An all-expenses-paid vacation."

"What, a no-combat-special?" quipped Elena. "I thought you always looked down on old Admiral Oser for those."

"I've changed." He felt, as ever, a brief flash of regret for the late Admiral Oser. "His command philosophy looks better all the time. I'm growing old, I guess."

"Or up," suggested Elena. They exchanged a dry look.

"In any case," Miles continued, "Barrayaran high command wishes to supply a certain independent deep-space transfer station with a better grade of weaponry than they presently own. Vega Station is, not coincidentally, just off one of the Cetagandan Empire's back doors. However, said vacuum-republic is in an awkward junction in the wormhole nexus. Quinn, the map, please."

Quinn keyed up a three-dimensional holovid schematic of Vega Station and its neighbors. The jump routes were represented by sparkling jagged lines between hazy spheres of local space systems.

"Of the three jump points Vega Station commands, one leads into the Cetagandan sphere of influence via its satrapy Ola Three, one is blocked by a sometimes-Cetagandan-ally, sometimes-enemy Toranira, and the other is held by Zoave Twilight, politically neutral with respect to Cetaganda, but wary of its big neighbor." As he spoke of it, Quinn highlighted each system. "Vega Station is outright blockaded through Ola Three and Toranira against the import of any kind of major space-based offensive or defensive weapons systems. Zoave Twilight, under pressure from Cetaganda, is reluctantly cooperating with the arms embargo."

"So where do we come in?" asked Baz.

"Literally, through Toranira. We're smuggling pack-horses."

"What?" said Baz, though Elena caught the reference and suddenly smirked.

"You've never heard that story? From Barrayaran history? It goes, Count Selig Vorkosigan was at war with Lord Vorwyn of Hazelbright, during the First Bloody Century. The town of Vorkosigan Vashnoi was besieged. Twice a week Lord Vorwyn's patrols would stop this crazy, motley fellow with a train of pack horses and search his packs for contraband, food or supplies. But his packs were always filled with rubbish. They poked and prodded and emptied them—he'd always gather it carefully back up—shook him down and searched him, and finally had to let him go. After the war, one of Vorwyn's border guards met Count Selig's liegeman, no longer motley, by chance in a tavern. 'What were you smuggling?' he asked in frustration. 'We know you were smuggling something, what was it?'

"And Count Selig's liegeman replied, 'Horses.'"

"We're smuggling spaceships. To wit, the *Triumph*, the *D-16*, and the *Ariel*, all fleet-owned. We enter Vega Station local space through Toranira, on a through-flight plan, bound for Illyrica. Which we really will be. We exit through Zoave, still with every trooper, but minus three aging ships. We then continue on to Illyrica, and pick up our three brand-new warships, which are being completed even as we speak in the Illyrican orbital shipyards. Our happy Winterfair gift from Emperor Gregor."

Baz blinked. "Will this work?"

"No reason it shouldn't. The spadework—permits, visas, bribes and so on—is all being completed by ImpSec agents on-site. All we have to do is waft through without alarming anybody. There's no war on, not a shot should be fired. The only problem is that one-third of my trade-inventory just left for Jackson's Whole," Miles concluded with a descending snort.

"How much time do we have to recover it?" asked Elena.

"Not as much as we need. The time-window ImpSec has set up for this smuggling scenario is flexible in terms of a few days, but not weeks. The fleet must leave Escobar before the end of this week. I'd originally scheduled it for tomorrow."

"So do we go without *Ariel*?" asked Baz.

"We're going to have to. But not empty handed. I have an idea for a substitution. Quinn, shunt those Illyrican specs to Baz."

Quinn bent her head to the secured data cube in her comconsole interface and released a burst of code to Baz's station. The engineer began keying through advertising displays, descriptions, specifications, and plans from the Illyrican shipbuilders. His thin face lit in a rare smile. "Father Frost is generous this Winterfair," he murmured. His lips parted with delight as the ships' power-plant specs came up, and his eyes moved avidly.

Miles let him wallow for a few minutes more. "Now," he said, when Baz self-consciously came up for air. "The next-up ship in the fleet from the *Ariel* in terms of function and firepower is Truzillo's *Jayhawk*." Unfortunately, Truzillo was a captain-owner under independent contract to the Fleet corporation, not a Fleet employee. "Do you think he could be persuaded to trade? His replacement ship would be newer and faster, but while it's definitely a step up in firepower from the *Ariel*, it's a slight step down from the *Jayhawk*. I'd meant us all to trade up, not even, when we first cooked up this deal."

Elena raised her eyebrows and grinned. "This is one of your scenarios, isn't it?"

He shrugged. "Illyan asked me to solve the arms embargo problem, yes. He accepted my solution."

"Oh," Baz purred, still awash in data, "wait'll Truzillo sees this . . . and *this* . . . and . . ."

"So do you think you can persuade him?" asked Miles.

"Yes," said Baz, with certainty. He glanced up. "So could you."

"Except I'll be headed the other way. Though if things go well, it's not impossible that I might catch up with you later. I'm putting you in charge of this mission, Baz. Quinn will give you the complete orders, all the codes and contact-people—everything Illyan gave me."

Baz nodded. "Very good, sir."

"I'm taking the *Peregrine* to go after the *Ariel*," Miles added.

Baz and Elena exchanged only one quick, sideways glance. "Very good, sir," echoed Elena, with scarcely a pause. "I shifted the *Peregrine* from twenty-four-hour to one-hour alert status yesterday. When shall I schedule our departure with Escorbaran flight control?"

"In one hour." And, though no one had asked for explanations, he added, "The *Peregrine* is the next-fastest thing we have that packs significant firepower, besides the *Jayhawk* and the *Ariel* itself. I think that speed is going to be of the essence. If we can overtake the *Ariel*—well, it's a lot easier to prevent a mess than to try to clean up after one. I'm sorry now I didn't leave yesterday, but I had to give it a chance to be simple. I'm assigning Quinn to myself as floating staff because she's had valuable previous experience with intelligence-gathering on Jackson's Whole."

Quinn rubbed her arm. "House Bharaputra is damn dangerous, if that's where Mark's headed. They have heavy money, heavy shit, and a sharp memory for revenge."

"Why d'you think I avoid the place? That's another danger, that certain Jacksonians will mistake Mark for Admiral Naismith. Baron Ryoval, for example."

Baron Ryoval was a persistent danger. The Dendarii had disposed of the latest bounty-hunter Ryoval had sent seeking Admiral Naismith's scalp only three months ago; he had been the fourth to appear so far. It was shaping up to an annual event. Maybe Ryoval despatched an agent on each anniversary of their first encounter, as a memorial tribute. Ryoval did not command great powers, nor possess a long reach, but he had undergone life-extension treatments; he was patient, and could keep this up for a long, long time.

"Have you considered another possible solution to the problem?" said Quinn slowly. "Send ahead to Jackson's Whole and warn them. Have, say, House Fell arrest Mark and impound the *Ariel* till you arrive to retrieve them. Fell hates Ryoval enough to protect Mark from him for the annoyance-factor alone."

Miles sighed. "I have considered it." He traced a formless pattern on the polished tabletop with his fingertip.

"You asked for a cross-check, Miles," Elena pointed out. "What's wrong with that idea?"

"It might work. But if Mark has really convinced Bel he's me, they might resist arrest. Maybe fatally. Mark is paranoid about Jackson's Whole. Mark is paranoid, period. I don't know what he'd do in a panic."

"You are awfully tender of Mark's sensibilities," said Elena.

"I'm trying to get him to trust me. I can hardly start the process by betraying him."

"Have you considered how much this little side-jaunt is going to cost, once the bill for it arrives on Simon Illyan's desk?" Quinn asked.

"ImpSec will pay. Without question."

Quinn said, "You sure? What's Mark to ImpSec anyway, now that he's only a left-over from the exploded plot? There is no danger any more to Barrayar of him being secretly substituted for you. I thought they only watched him for us as a courtesy. A rather expensive courtesy."

Miles replied carefully, "It is ImpSec's explicit task to guard the Barrayaran Imperium. That includes not only protecting Gregor's person, and running a certain amount of galactic espionage—" a wave of his hand included the Dendarii fleet, and Illyan's far-flung, if thinly stretched, network of agents, military attachés, and informants, "but also keeping watch over Gregor's immediate heirs. Keeping watch not only to protect them, but to protect the Imperium from any little plot got up by them, or by others seeking to use them. I am acutely conscious that the question of just who is Gregor's heir is rather tangled at present. I wish to hell he'd marry and get us all off the hook soon." Miles hesitated for a long moment. "By one interpretation, Lord Mark Pierre Vorkosigan has a place as heir-claimant to the Barrayaran Imperium second only to my own. That makes him not only ImpSec's business, it makes him our *primary* business. My personal pursuit of the *Ariel* is fully justified."

"Justifiable," Quinn corrected dryly.

"Whatever."

"If Barrayar—as you have often claimed—would not accept you as Emperor because of suspicion of mutation, I should think it'd go into spasms at the thought of your clone installed in the Imperial Residence," said Baz. "Twin brother," he amended hastily as Miles opened his mouth.

"It doesn't require the probability of success at gaining the Imperium to make the possibility of an attempt to do so into an ImpSec problem." Miles snorted. "It's funny. All the time the Komarrans thought of their faux-Miles as an imposter-claimant. I don't think either they or Mark realized they'd made a *real* claimant. Well, I'd have to be dead first anyway, so from my point of view the question is moot." He rapped the table and rose. "Let's get moving, people."

On the way out the door, Elena lowered her voice to ask him, "Miles—did your mother see those horrific investigation-reports of Illyan's about Mark, too?"

He smiled bleakly. "Who d'you think ordered them done?"

CHAPTER FIVE

He began donning the half-armor. First, next to his skin, a piece of the hottest new technology on the market: a nerve-disruptor shield-net. The field-generating net was worked into the fabric of a close-fitting gray body-suit and a hood that protected skull, neck, and forehead, leaving only his eyes, nose, and mouth peeping from the hole. And so the threat of one of the most fearsome anti-personnel weapons, the brain-killing nerve disruptor, was rendered null. As an added bonus, the suit stopped stunner-fire, too. Trust Naismith to have the best and newest, and custom-made to fit ... was the elastic fabric supposed to be this bloody tight?

Over the net-suit went a flexible torso-armor that would stop any projectile up to small hand-missiles and down to deadly needler spines. Fortunately for his ability to breathe, its catches were adjustable. He let them out to their fullest extension, rendering the valuable protection merely comfortably and correctly snug. Over it went blessedly loose camouflage-gray fatigues, made of a combat-rated fabric that would neither melt nor burn. Then came belts and bandoliers with stunner, nerve disruptor, plasma arc, grenades, power cells, a rappel-harness and spool, emergency oxygen. On his back he shrugged the harness holding a neat, flat power pack that generated, at the first touch of enemy fire, a one-man-sized plasma arc mirror field, with so miniscule a time lag one barely had time to cook, much. It was good for absorbing thirty or forty direct hits before the power cell, and its porter, died. It seemed almost a misnomer to call it all half-armor: triple armor was more like it.

Over the nerve-disruptor net covering his feet he pulled thick socks, then Naismith's combat boots. At least the boots fit without any embarrassing adjustments. A mere week of inactivity, and his body fought him, thickening... Naismith was a damned anorectic, that was it. A hyperactive anorectic. He straightened. Properly distributed, the formidible array of equipment was surprisingly light.

On the countertop next to his cabin comconsole, the command helmet sat waiting. The empty shadow beneath its forehead flange made him think, for whatever morbid reason, of an empty skull. He raised the helmet in his hands, turning it in the light, and stared hungrily at its elegant curves. His hands could control one weapon, two at most. This, through the people it commanded, controlled dozens; potentially, hundreds or even thousands. This was Naismith's real power.

The cabin buzzer blatted; he jumped, nearly dropping the helmet. He could have pitched it against the wall and not harmed it, but still he set it down carefully.

"Miles?" came Captain Thorne's voice on the intercom. "You about ready?"

"Yes, come in." He touched the keypad to release the door lock.

Thorne entered, attired identically to himself, but with hood temporarily pushed back. The formless fatigues rendered Thorne not bi-sexed, but neuter, a genderless thing, *soldier*. Thorne too bore a command helmet under its arm, of a slightly older and different make.

Thorne walked around him, eyes flicking over every weapon and belt-hook, and checking the readouts of his plasma-shield pack. "Good." Did Captain Thorne normally inspect its Admiral before combat? Was Naismith in the habit of wandering into battle with his boots unfastened, or something? Thorne nodded to the command helmet sitting on the countertop. "That's quite a machine. Sure you can handle it?"

The helmet appeared new, but not that new. He doubted Naismith supplied himself with used military surplus for his personal use, regardless of what economies he practiced in the fleet at large. "Why not?" He shrugged. "I have before."

"These things," Thorne lifted his own, "can be pretty overwhelming at first. It's not a data flow, it's a damned data flood. You have to learn to ignore everything you don't need, otherwise it can be almost better to switch the thing off. You, now . . ." Thorne hesitated, "have that same uncanny ability as old Tung did, of appearing to ignore everything as it goes by, and yet being able to remember and yank it out instantly if it's needed. Of somehow always being on the right channel at the right time. It's like your mind works on two levels. Your command-response time is incredibly fast, when your adrenaline is up. It's kind of addictive. People who work with you a lot come to expect—and rely—on it." Thorne stopped, waited.

What was it expecting him to say? He shrugged again. "I do my best."

"If you're still feeling ill, you know, you can delegate this whole raid to me."

"Do I look ill?"

"You're not yourself. You don't want to make the whole squad sick." Thorne seemed tense, almost urgent.

"I'm *fine*, now, Bel. Back off!"

"Yes, sir," Thorne sighed.

"Is everything ready out there?"

"The shuttle is fueled and armed. Green Squad is kitted up, and is doing the final loading right now. We have it timed so we come into parking orbit just at midnight, downside at Bharaputra's main medical facility. We drop instantly, no waiting around for people to start asking questions. Hit and go. The whole operation should be over in an hour, if things run to plan."

"Good." His heart was beating faster. He disguised a deep breath in a strung-out sigh. "Let's go."

"Let's . . . do our helmet communication checks first, huh?" said Thorne.

That was a good idea, here in the quiet cabin, rather than in the noise and excitement and tension of the drop shuttle. "All right," he said, and added slyly, "Take your time."

There were over a hundred channels in use in the command headset, even for this limited raid. In addition to direct voice contact with the *Ariel*, Thorne, and every trooper, there were battle computers on the ship, in the shuttle, and in the helmet itself. There were telemetry readouts of every sort, weapon power checks, logistics updates. All the troopers' helmets had vid pick-ups so he could see what they were seeing in infra-red, visual, and UV bands; full sound; their medical readouts; holovid map displays. The holomap of the clone-crèche had been specially programmed in, and the plan of attack and several contingencies pre-loaded. There were channels to be dedicated, on the fly, to eavesdropping upon enemy telemetry. Thorne already had Bharaputra's security guards' comm links locked in. They could even pick up commercial entertainment broadcasts from the planet they were approaching. Tinny music filled the air momentarily as he switched past those channels.

They finished, and he found himself and Thorne staring at each other in an awkward silence. Thorne was hollow-faced, apprehensive, as if struggling with some suppressed emotion. *Guilt?* Strange perception, surely not. Thorne couldn't be on to him, or it would have called a halt to this whole operation.

"Pre-combat nerves, Bel?" he said lightly. "I thought you loved your work."

Thorne came out of its lip-sucking abstraction with a start. "Oh, I do." It took a breath. "Let's do it."

"Go!" he agreed, and led the way at last out of his isolated cabin-cave into the light of the corridor and the peopled reality his actions—*his* actions—had created.

The shuttle-hatch corridor resembled his first view of it, reversed; the hulking Dendarii commandos were filing out, not spilling in. They seemed quieter this time, not as much clowning and joking. More businesslike. They had names, now, too, all filed in his command headset, which would keep them straight for him. All wore some variety of half-armor and helmet, with an array of heavier equipment in addition to such hand-weapons as he bore.

He found himself looking at the monster sergeant with new eyes, now that he knew her history. The log had said she was only nineteen years old, though she looked older; she'd been only sixteen, four years ago when Naismith had stolen her away from House Ryoval. He squinted, trying to see her as a girl. He had been taken away at age fourteen, eight years ago. Their mutual time as genetic products and prisoners of House Bharaputra must have overlapped, though he had never met her. The genetic engineering research labs were in a different town from the main surgical facility. House Bharaputra was a vast organization, in its strange Jacksonian way almost a little government. Except Jackson's Whole didn't have governments.

Eight years . . . *No one you knew then is still alive. You know that, don't you?*

If I can't do what I want, I'll at least do what I can.

He stepped up to her. "Sergeant Taura—" She turned, and his brows climbed in startlement. "*What* is that around your neck?" Actually, he could see what it was, a large fluffy pink bow. He supposed his real question was, *why* was it around her neck?

She—smiled, he guessed that repellent grimace was, at him, and fluffed it out a bit more with a huge clawed hand. Her claw-polish was bright pink, tonight. "D'you think it'll work? I wanted something to not scare the kids."

He looked up at eight feet of half-armor, camouflage cloth, boots, bandoliers, muscle and fang. *Somehow, I don't think it'll be enough, Sergeant.* "It's . . . certainly worth a try," he choked. So, she was conscious of her extraordinary appearance. . . . *Fool! How could she not be? Are you not conscious of yours?* He was almost sorry now he had not ventured out of his cabin earlier in the voyage and made her acquaintance. *My home-town girl.*

"What does it feel like, to be going back?" he asked suddenly; a nod in no particular direction indicated the House Bharaputra drop-zone, coming up.

"Strange," she admitted, her thick brows drawing down.

"Do you know this landing-site? Ever been there before?"

"Not that medical complex. I hardly ever left the genetics facility, except for a couple of years that I lived with hired fosterers, which was in the same town." Her head turned, her voice dropped an octave, and she barked an order about loading equipment at one of her men, who gave a half-wave and hustled to obey. She turned back to him and her voice re-softened to conscious, careful lightness. In no other way did she display any inappropriate intimacy while on duty; it seemed she and Naismith were discreet lovers, if lovers they were. The discreetness relieved him. She added, "I didn't get out much."

His own voice lowered. "Do you hate them?" *As I do?* A different kind of intimate question.

Her outslung lips twisted in thought. "I suppose . . . I was terribly manipulated by them when I was growing up, but it didn't seem like abuse to me at the time. There were a lot of uncomfortable tests, but it was all science . . . there wasn't any intent to hurt in it. It didn't really hurt till they sold me to Ryoval's, after the super-soldier project was cancelled. What Ryoval's wanted to do to me was grotesque, but that was just the nature of Ryoval's. It was Bharaputra . . . Bharaputra that didn't care. That threw me away. *That* hurt. But then *you* came . . ." She brightened. "A knight in shining armor and all that."

A familiar, surly wave of resentment washed over him. *Bugger the knight in shining armor, and the horse he rode in on.* And, *I can rescue people too, dammit!* She was looking away, fortunately, and didn't catch the spasm of anger in his face. Or perhaps she took it for anger at their former tormentors.

"But for all that," she murmured, "I would not have even existed, without House Bharaputra. They made me. I am alive, for however long . . . shall I return death for life?" Her strange distorted face grew deeply introspective.

This was not the ideal gung-ho frame of mind to inculcate in a commando on a drop mission, he realized belatedly. "Not . . . necessarily. We're here to rescue clones, not kill Bharaputran employees. We kill only if forced to, eh?"

This was good Naismithery; her head came up, and she grinned at him. "I'm so relieved you're feeling better. I was terribly worried. I wanted to see you, but Captain Thorne wouldn't allow it." Her eyes warmed like bright yellow flames.

"Yes, I was . . . very ill. Thorne did right. But . . . maybe we can talk more on the way home." When this was over. When he'd earned the right . . . *earned the right to what?*

"You got a date, Admiral." She *winked* at him, and straightened, ferociously joyous. *What have I promised?* She bounded forward, happily sergeantly again, to oversee her squad.

He followed her into the combat-drop shuttle. The light level was much lower in here, the air colder, and, of course, there was no gravity. He floated forward from handgrip to handgrip after Captain Thorne, mentally dividing up the floor space for his intended cargo. Twelve or fifteen rows of kids seated four across . . . there was plenty of room. This shuttle was equipped to carry two squads, plus armored hovercars or a whole field hospital. It had a first-aid station at the back, including four fold-down bunks and a portable emergency cryo-chamber. The Dendarii commando-medic was rapidly organizing his area and battening down his supplies. Everything was being fastened down, by quietly-moving fatigue-clad soldiers, with very little fuss or conversation. A place for everything and everything in its place.

The shuttle pilot was at his post. Thorne took the co-pilot's seat. He took a communication station chair just behind them. Out the front window he could see distant hard-edged stars, nearby the winking colored lights of some human activity, and, at the very edge of the field of view, the bright slice of the planet's curvature. Almost home. His belly fluttered, and not just from zero-gee. Bands of tightness throbbed around his head beneath his helmet-straps.

The pilot hit his intercom. "Gimme a body-check back there, Taura. We've got a five-minute thrust to match orbit, then we blow bolts and drop."

After a moment Sergeant Taura's voice returned, "Check. All troops tied down, hatch sealed. We are ready. Go-repeat-go."

Thorne glanced over its shoulder and pointed. Hastily, he fastened his seat straps, and just in time. The straps bit deeply, and he lurched from side to side as the *Ariel* shuddered into its parking orbit, accelerative effects that would have been compensated for and nullified by the artificial gravity generated between the decks of the larger ship.

The pilot poised his hands, and abruptly dropped them, as if he were a musician playing some crescendo. Loud, startling clanks reverberated through the fuselage. Ululating whoops keened in response from the compartment behind the flight deck.

When they say drop, he thought wildly, *they mean it.* Stars and the planet turned, nauseatingly, in the forward window. He closed his eyes; his stomach tried to climb his esophagus. He suddenly realized a hidden advantage to full space armor. If you shit yourself with terror, going down, the suit's plumbing would take care of it, and no one would ever know.

Air began to scream over the outer hull as they hit the ionosphere. His seat straps tried to slice him like an egg. "Fun, huh?" yelled Thorne, grinning like a loon, its face distorted and lips flapping with deceleration. They were pointed straight down, or so the shuttle's nose was aimed, although his seat was attempting to eject him into the cabin ceiling with neck-breaking and skull-smashing force.

"I sure hope there's nothing in our way," the pilot yelled cheerfully. "This hasn't been cleared with anybody's flight control, y'know!"

He pictured a mid-air collision with a large commercial passenger shuttle . . . five hundred women and children aboard . . . vast yellow and black explosions and arcing bodies. . . .

They crossed the terminator into twilight. Then darkness, whipping clouds . . . bigger clouds . . . shuttle vibrating and bellowing like an insane tuba . . . still pointed straight down, he swore, though how the pilot could tell in this screaming fog he did not know.

Then, suddenly, they were level as an airshuttle, clouds above, lights of a town like jewels spilled on a carpet below. An airshuttle that was dropping like a rock. His spine began to compress, harder, harder. More hideous clanks, as the shuttle's feet extended. An array of half-lit building bulked below. A darkened playing-court—*Shit, that's it, that's it!* The buildings loomed up beside them, above them. *Thud-crunch-crunch.* A solid, six-legged landing. The silence stunned him.

"All *right*, let's *go!*" Thorne swung up out of its seat, face flushed, eyes lit, with blood-lust or fear or both he could not tell.

He tramped down the ramp in the wake of a dozen Dendarii. His eyes were about half dark-adapted, and there were enough lights around the complex, diffused by the cool and misty midnight air, that he had no trouble seeing, though the view was drained of color. The shadows were black and sinister. Sergeant Taura, with silent hand signals, divided her squad. No one was making noise. Silent faces were gilded by brief staccato flashes of light as their helmet vids supplied some data bit or another, projected to the side of their vision. One Dendarii, with extra 'scopes on her helmet, rolled out a personal float-bike, mounted it, and rose quietly into the darkness. Air cover.

The pilot stayed aboard, and Taura counted off four other Dendarii. Two vanished into the shadows of the perimeter, two stayed with the shuttle as rear-guard. He and Thorne had argued about that. Thorne had wanted more perimeter. His own gut-feel was that they would need as many troopers as possible at the clone-crèche. The civilian hospital guards were little threat, and it would take time for their better-armed back-up to arrive. By then, the Dendarii would be gone, if they could move the clones along fast enough. He cursed himself, in retrospect, for not ordering two commando squads instead of one, back at Escobar. He could have done so, just as easily, but he'd been caught up in calculations about the *Ariel*'s passenger capacity, and fancied himself conserving life support for the final escape. So many factors to balance.

His own helmet framed his vision with a colored clutter of codes, numbers, and graphs. He'd studied them all, but they flicked by too fast; by the time he'd taken one in, and interpreted it to himself, it was gone, replaced by another. He took Thorne's advice and with a whispered word reduced the light intensity to a bare hallucinatory murmur. The helmet's audio pick-up was not so bad. No one was doing any unnecessary chatter.

He, Thorne, and the other seven Dendarii followed Taura at a trot—her stride—between two adjacent buildings. There was activity on the Bharaputran security guards' comm links, he found by keying his helmet to their audio bands. The first *What the hell. Did you hear that? Joe, check sector four,* stirrings of response. More to follow, he was sure, though he had no intention of waiting around for it.

Around a corner. *There.* A three-story, pleasant white building with lots of plants and landscaping, big windows, balconies. Not quite a hospital, not quite a dormitory, vague, ambiguous, discreet. THE LIFE HOUSE it was labeled in Jacksonian double-speak. *The death house. My dear old home.* It was terribly familiar and terribly strange. Once, it had seemed quite splendid to him. Now it seemed . . . smaller than he remembered.

Taura raised her plasma arc, adjusted its beam to *wide,* and removed the locked glass front doors in an orange, white, and blue spray of flying, spattering cullet. Dendarii bounded through, splitting right and left, before the glow of the spattered globs of glass died. One took up station patrolling the ground floor. Alarms and fire alarms went off: Dendarii killed the noisy speakers they passed with more plasma fire, on the fly, but units in more distant parts of the building kept up a muted clamor. Automatic sprinklers made steam and a mess in their trail.

He ran to catch up. A uniformed Bharaputran security guard in brown trimmed with pink lurched into the corridor ahead. Three Dendarii stunners simultaneously downed him as his own stunner beam was absorbed harmlessly by the ceiling.

Taura and two female Dendarii took the lift tube toward the third floor; another trooper passed them in hope of gaining the roof. He led Thorne and the remaining troopers out into the second floor foyer and to the left. Two unarmed adults, one a night-gowned woman pulling on a robe, were felled the instant they appeared. *There.* Through those double doors. They were locked, and someone was beating on them from the inside.

"We're going to break the door open," Thorne bellowed through it. "Back away, or you'll get hurt!" The pounding stopped. Thorne nodded. A trooper adjusted his plasma arc to narrow beam and sliced through a metal bolt. Thorne kicked the doors wide.

A blond young man fell back a pace, staring at Thorne with bewilderment. "You're not the firemen."

A crowd of other men, tall boys, filled the corridor behind the blond. He did not have to remind himself that these were a bunch of ten-year-olds, but he wasn't sure about the perceptions of the troopers. Every variation of height and racial mix and build was represented, much more motley than the Greek-god look one might have anticipated from their garden-and-fountain setting. Personal wealth, not personal beauty, had been the ticket for their creation. Still, each was as glowingly healthy as the particularities of his genetics permitted. They all wore uniform sleepwear, bronze-brown tunics and shorts.

"Front," Thorne hissed, and shoved him forward. "Start talking."

"Get me a head-count," he ripped out of the corner of his mouth as Thorne pulled him past.

"Right."

He'd practiced the speech for this supreme moment in his mind ten thousand times, every possible variation. The only thing he knew for certain that he was *not* going to start with was, *I'm Miles Naismith.* His heart was racing. He inhaled a huge gulp of air. "We're the Dendarii Mercenaries, and we're here to save you."

The boy's expression was repelled, scared, and scornful all mixed. "You look like a mushroom," he said blankly.

It was so . . . so *off-script.* Of his thousand rehearsed second lines, not one followed this. Actually, with the command helmet and all, he probably did look a bit like a big gray—*not* the heroic image he'd hoped to—

He tore off his helmet, ripped back his hood, and bared his teeth. The boy recoiled.

"Listen up, you clones!" he yelled. "The secret you may have heard whispered is true! Every single one of you is waiting in line to be murdered by House Bharaputra surgeons. They're gonna stick somebody else's brain in your head, and throw your brain away. That's where your friends have been going, one by one, to their deaths. We're here to take you to Escobar, where you'll be given sanctuary—"

Not all the boys had assembled in the corridor in the first place, and now ones at the rear of the mob began to break away and retreat into individual rooms. A babble started to rise from them, and yells and cries. One dark-haired boy tried to dart past them to the corridor beyond the big double doors, and a trooper grabbed him in a standard arm-lock. He screamed in pain and surprise, and the sound and shock seemed to blow the others back in a wave. The boy struggled without effect in the trooper's iron grip. The trooper looked exasperated and uncertain, and stared at him as if expecting some direction or order.

"Get your friends and follow me!" he yelled desperately to the retreating boys. The blond turned on his heel and sprinted.

"I don't think they bought us," said Thorne. The hermaphrodite's face was pale and tense. "It might actually be easier to stun them all and carry them. We can't afford to lose time in here, not with that damned thin perimeter."

"No—"

His helmet was calling him. He jammed it back on. Comm-link babble burst in his ears, but Sergeant Taura's deep voice penetrated, selectively enhanced by her channel. "Sir, we need your help up here."

"What is it?"

Her answer was lost in an override from the woman riding the float-bike. "Sir, there's three or four people climbing down the outside balconies of the building you're in. And there's a group of four Bharaputran security people approaching you from the north."

He sorted frantically through channels till he found the one out-going to the air-guard. "Don't let any get away!"

"How should I stop 'em, sir?" Her voice was edged.

"Stunner," he decided helplessly. "Wait! Don't stun any that are hanging off the balcony, wait'll they reach the ground."

"I may not have a clear shot."

"Do your best." He cut her off and found Taura again. "What do you want, Sergeant?"

"I want you to come talk to this crazy girl. *You* can convince her if anyone can."

"Things are—not quite under control down here."

Thorne rolled its eyes. The captured boy was drumming his bare heels against the Dendarii trooper's shins. Thorne set its stunner to the lightest setting and touched it to the back of the squirming boy's neck. He convulsed and hung more limply. Still conscious, eyes blearing and wild, the boy began to cry.

In a burst of cowardice he said to Throne, "Get them rounded up. Any way you can. I'm going to help Sergeant Taura."

"You do that," growled Thorne in a distinctly insubordinate tone. It wheeled, gathering its men. "You and you, take that side—you, take the other. Get those doors down—"

He retreated ignominiously to the sound of shattering plastic.

Upstairs, things were quieter. There were fewer girls than boys altogether, a disproportion that had also prevailed in his time. He'd often wondered why. He stepped over the stunned body of a heavy-set female security guard and followed his vid map, projected by his helmet, to Sergeant Taura.

A dozen or so girls were seated cross-legged on the floor, their hands clasped behind their necks, under the waving threat of one Dendarii's stunner. Their sleep-tunics and shorts were pink silk, otherwise identical to the boys'. They looked frightened, but at least they sat silent. He stepped into a side room to find Taura and the other trooper confronting a tall Eurasian girl-woman, who sat at a comconsole with her arms aggressively crossed. Where the vid plate should have been was a smoking hole, hot and recent, from plasma fire.

The Eurasian girl's head turned, her long black hair swinging, from Taura to himself and back. "My lady, what a circus!" Her voice was a whip of contempt.

"She refuses to budge," said Taura. Her tone was strangely worried.

"Girl," he nodded curtly. "You are dead meat if you stay here. You are a clone. Your body is destined to be stolen by your progenitor. Your brain will be removed and destroyed. Perhaps very soon."

"*I* know that," she said scornfully, as if he were a babbling idiot.

"What?" His jaw dropped.

"I know it. I am perfectly aligned with my destiny. My lady required it to be so. I serve my lady perfectly." Her chin rose, and her eyes rested in a moment of dreamy, distant worship, of what he could not guess.

"She got a call out to House Security," reported Taura tightly, with a nod at the smoking holovid. "Described us, our gear—even reported an estimate of our numbers."

"You will not keep me from my lady," the girl affirmed with a short, cool nod. "The guards will get you, and save me. I'm very important."

What the hell had the Bharaputrans done to turn this girl's head inside out? And could he undo it in thirty seconds or less? He didn't think so. "Sergeant," he took a deep breath, and said in a high, light voice on the outgoing sigh, "Stun her."

The Eurasian girl started to duck, but the sergeant's reflexes worked at lightning speed. The stunner beam took her precisely between the eyes as she leapt. Taura vaulted the comconsole and caught the girl's head before it could strike the floor.

"Do we have them all?" he asked.

"At least two went down the back stairs before we blocked them," Taura reported with a frown.

"They'll be stunned if they try to escape the building," he reassured her.

"But what if they hide, downstairs? It'll take time to find 'em." Her tawny eyes flicked sideways to take in some chrono display from her helmet. "We should all be on our way back to the shuttle by now."

"Just a second." Laboriously, he keyed through his channels till he found Thorne again. Off in the distance, carried thinly by the audio, someone was yelling, " 'n-of-a-bitch! You little—"

"*What?*" Thorne snapped in a harried voice. "You got those girls rounded up yet?"

"Had to stun one. Taura can carry her. Look, did you get that head-count yet?"

"Yes, took it off a comconsole in a keeper's room—thirty-eight boys and sixteen girls. We're missing four boys who apparently went over the balcony. Trooper Philippi accounted for three of them but says she didn't spot a fourth. How about you?"

"Sergeant Taura says two girls went down the back stairs. Watch for them." He glanced up, peering out of his vid display, which was swirling like an aurora. "Captain Thorne says there should be sixteen bodies here."

Taura stuck her head out into the corridor, lips moving, then returned and eyed the stunned Eurasian girl. "We're still short one. Kesterton, make a pass around this floor, check cupboards and under the beds."

"Right, Sergeant." The Dendarii trooper ran to obey.

He followed her, Thorne's voice urging in his ears, "*Move* it up there! This is a smash-and-grab, remember? We don't have *time* to round up strays!"

"*Wait*, dammit."

In the third room the trooper checked, she bent to look under a bed and said, "Ha! Got her, Sergeant!" She swooped, grabbed a couple of kicking ankles, and yanked. Her prize slid into the light, a short girl-woman in the pink crossover tunic and shorts. She emitted little helpless muted noises, distress with no hope of her cries bringing help. She had a cascade of platinum curls, but her most notable feature was a stunning bustline, huge fat globes that the strained pink silk of her tunic failed to contain. She rolled to her knees, buttocks on heels, her upraised hands vaguely pushing and cradling the heavy flesh as if still shocked and unaccustomed to finding it there.

Ten years old. Shit. She looked twenty. And such monstrous hypertrophy couldn't be natural. The progenitor-customer must have ordered body-sculpture, prior to taking possession. That made sense, let the clone do the surgical and metabolic suffering. Tiny waist, flare of hip . . . from her exaggerated, physically mature femininity, he wondered if she might be one of the change-of-sex transfers. Almost certainly. She must have been slated for surgery very soon.

"No, go away," she was whimpering. "Go away, leave me alone . . . my mother is coming for me. My mother is coming for me *tomorrow*. Go away, leave me alone, I'm going to meet my *mother*. . . ."

Her cries, and her heaving . . . chest, would shortly make him crazy, he thought. "Stun that one too," he croaked. They'd have to carry her, but at least they wouldn't have to listen to her.

The trooper's face was flushed, as transfixed and embarrassed as he by the girl's grotesque build. "Poor doll," she whispered, and put her out of her misery with a light touch of stunner to her neck. She slumped forward, splayed on the floor.

His helmet was calling him, he wasn't sure which trooper's voice. "Sir, we just drove back a crew of House Bharaputra fire-fighters with our stunners. They didn't have anti-stun suits. But the security people who are coming on now do. They're sending new teams, carrying heavier weapons. The stunner-tag game is about over."

He keyed through helmet displays, trying to place the trooper on the map-grid. Before he could, the air-guard's breathless voice cut in. "A Bharaputran heavy-weapons team is circling around your building to the south, sir. You've got to get the hell out of there. It's about to turn real nasty out here."

He waved the Dendarii trooper and her doll-woman burden out of the bedroom ahead of him. "Sergeant Taura," he called. "Did you pick up those outside reports?"

"Yes, sir. Let's move it."

Sergeant Taura slung the Eurasian girl over one broad shoulder and the blonde over the other, apparently without noticing their weight, and they herded the mob of frightened girls down the end stairs. Taura made them walk two-by-two, holding hands, keeping them rather better organized than he would have expected. The girls' hushed voices burbled in shock when they were directed into the boys' dormitory section. "We're not allowed down here," one tried to protest, in tears. "We'll get in *trouble*."

Thorne had six stunned boys laid out face-up on the corridor floor, and another twenty-odd lined up leaning against the wall, legs spread, arms extended, prisoner-control posture, with a couple of nervous troopers yelling at them and keeping them in their places. Some clones looked angry, some were crying, and all looked scared to death.

He looked with dismay at the pile of stunner victims. "How are we going to carry them all?"

"Have some carry the rest," Taura said. "It leaves your hands free and ties up theirs." She gently laid down her own burdens at the end of the row.

"Good," said Thorne, jerking its gaze, with difficulty, from fascinated fixation on the doll-woman. "Worley, Kesterton, let's—" its voice stopped, as the same static-laden emergency message over-rode channels in both their command helmets.

It was the bike-trooper, screaming, "Sonofabitch, the shuttle—watch *out* guys, on your left—" a hot wash of static, and "—oh holy fuckin' shit—" Then a silence, filled only with the hum of an empty channel.

He keyed frantically for a readout, any readout at all, from her helmet. The locator still functioned, plotting her on the ground between two buildings in back of the play-court where the shuttle was parked. Her medical readouts were flatline blanks. Dead? Surely not, there should at least still be blood chemistry . . . the static, empty view being transmitted, upward at an angle into the night fog, at last cued him. Phillipi had lost her helmet. What else she'd lost, he could not tell.

Thorne called the shuttle pilot, over and over, alternated with the rear-guards; no replies. It swore. "*You* try."

He found empty channels too. The other two perimeter Dendarii were tied up in an exchange of fire with the Bharaputran heavy-weapons squad to the south that the bike-trooper had reported earlier.

"We gotta reconnoiter," snarled Thorne under its breath. "Sergeant Taura, take over here, get these kids ready to march. You—" This was to his address, apparently; why did Thorne no longer call him *Admiral*, or *Miles*? "Come with me. Trooper Sumner, cover us."

Thorne departed at a flat-out run; he cursed his short legs as he fell steadily farther behind. Down the lift-tube, out the still-hot front doors, around one dark building, between two others. He caught up with the hermaphrodite, who was flattened against a corner of the building at the edge of the playing-court.

The shuttle was still there, apparently undamaged—surely no hand-weapon could penetrate its combat-hardened shell. The ramp was drawn up, the door closed. A dark shape—downed Dendarii, or enemy?—slumped in the shadow beneath its wing-flanges. Thorne, whispering curses, jabbed codes into a computer control plate bound to its left forearm. The hatch slid aside, and the ramp tongued outward with a whine of servos. Still no human response.

"I'm going in," said Thorne.

"Captain, standard procedure says that's my job," said the trooper

Thorne had detailed to cover them, from his vantage behind a large concrete tree-tub.

"Not this time," said Thorne grimly. Not continuing the argument, it dashed forward in a zigzag, then straight up the ramp, hurtling inside, plasma arc drawn. After a moment its voice came over the comm. "Now, Sumner."

Uninvited, he followed Trooper Sumner. The shuttle's interior was pitch-dark. They all turned on their helmet lights, white fingers darting and touching. Nothing inside appeared disturbed, but the door to the pilot's compartment was sealed.

Silently, Thorne motioned the trooper to take up a firing stance opposite him, bracketing the door in the bulkhead between fuselage and flight deck. He stood behind Thorne. Thorne punched another code into its arm control-pad. The door slid open with a tortured groan, then shuddered and jammed.

A wave of heat boiled out like the breath of a blast furnace. A soft orange explosion followed, as enough oxygen rushed into the searing compartment to re-ignite any flammables that were left. The trooper fastened his emergency oxygen mask, grabbed a chemical fire-extinguisher from a clamp on the wall, and aimed it into the flight deck. After a moment they followed in his wake.

Everything was slagged and burned. The controls were melted, communications equipment charred. The compartment stank, chokingly, of toxic oxidation products from all the synthetic materials. And one organic odor. Carbonized meat. What was left of the pilot—he turned his head, and swallowed. "Bharaputra doesn't have—isn't supposed to have heavy weapons on-site!"

Thorne hissed, beyond swearing. It pointed. "They threw a couple of our own thermal mines in here, closed the door, and ran. Pilot had to have been stunned first. One *smart* goddamn Bharaputran son-of-a-bitch . . . didn't have heavy weapons, so they just used ours. Drew off or ganged up on my guards, got in, and grounded us. Didn't even stick around to ambush us . . . they can do *that* at their leisure, now. This beast won't fly again." Thorne's face looked like a chiseled skull-mask in the white light from their helmets.

Panic clogged his throat. "What do we do now, Bel?"

"Fall back to the building. Set a perimeter. Use our hostages to negotiate some kind of surrender."

"No!"

"You got a better idea—*Miles*?" Thorne's teeth gritted. "I thought not."

The shocked trooper stared at Thorne. "Captain—" he glanced back and forth between them, "the Admiral will pull us through. We've been in tighter spots than this."

"Not this time." Thorne straightened, voice drawn with agony. "My fault—take full responsibility. . . . That's *not* the Admiral. That's his clone-brother, Mark. He set us up, but I've known for days. Tumbled to him before we dropped, before we ever made Jacksonian local space. I thought I could bring this off, and not get caught."

"Eh?" The trooper's brows wavered, disbelieving. A clone, going under anesthetic, might have that same stunned look on his face.

"We can't—we can't betray those children back into Bharaputra's hands," Mark grated. Begged.

Thorne dug its bare hand into the carbonized blob glued to what used to be the pilot's station chair. "Who is betrayed?" It lifted its hand, rubbed a black crumbling smear across his face from cheek to chin. "Who is betrayed?" Thorne whispered. "Do you have. A better. Idea."

He was shaking, his mind a white-out blank. The hot carbon on his face felt like a scar.

"Fall back to the building," said Thorne. "On my command."

CHAPTER SIX

"**N**o subordinates," said Miles firmly. "I want to talk to the head man, once and done. And then get out of here."

"I'll keep trying," said Quinn. She turned back to her comconsole in the *Peregrine*'s tac room, which was presently transmitting the image of a high-ranking Bharaputran security officer, and began the argument again.

Miles sat back in his station chair, his boots flat to the deck, his hands held deliberately still along the control-studded armrests. Calm and control. That was the strategy. That was, at this point, the only strategy left to him. If only he'd been nine hours sooner . . . he'd methodically cursed every delay of the past five days, in four languages, till he'd run out of invective. They'd wasted fuel, profligately, pushing the *Peregrine* at max accelerations, and had nearly made up the *Ariel*'s lead. Nearly. The delays had given Mark just enough time to take a bad idea, and turn it into a disaster. But not Mark alone. Miles was no longer a proponent of the hero-theory of disaster. A mess this complete required the full cooperation of a cast of dozens. He very much wanted to talk privately with Bel Thorne, and very, very soon. He had not counted on Bel proving as much of a loose cannon as Mark himself.

He glanced around the tac room, taking in the latest information from the vid displays. The *Ariel* was out of it, fled under fire to dock at Fell Station under Thorne's second-in-command, Lieutenant Hart. They were now blockaded by half a dozen Bharaputran security vessels, lurking outside Fell's zone. Two more

384

Bharaputran ships presently escorted the *Peregrine* in orbit. A token force, so far; the *Peregrine* outgunned them. That balance of power would shift when all their Bharaputran brethren arrived topside. Unless he could convince Baron Bharaputra it wasn't necessary.

He called up a view of the downside situation on his vid display, insofar as it was presently understood by the *Peregrine*'s battle computers. The exterior layout of the Bharaputran medical complex was plain even from orbit, but he lacked the details of the interiors he'd have liked if he were planning a clever attack. No clever attack. Negotiation, and bribery . . . he winced in anticipation of the upcoming costs. Bel Thorne, Mark, Green Squad, and fifty or so Bharaputran hostages were presently pinned down in a single building, separated from their damaged shuttle, and had been for the last eight hours. The shuttle pilot dead, three troopers injured. *That* would cost Bel its command, Miles swore to himself.

It would be dawn down there soon. The Bharaputrans had evacuated all the civilians from the rest of the complex, thank God, but had also brought in heavy security forces and equipment. Only the threat of harm to their valuable clones held back an overwhelming Bharaputran onslaught. He would not be negotiating from a position of strength, alas. *Cool.*

Quinn, without turning around, raised her hand and flashed him a high sign, *Get ready.* He glanced down, checking his own appearance. His officer's undress grays were borrowed from the next smallest person aboard the *Peregrine*, a five-foot-tall female from Engineering, and fit him sloppily. He only had half his proper insignia. Aggressively messy was a possible command style, but he really needed more props to bring it off. Adrenaline and suppressed rage would have to power his appearance. If not for the biochip on his vagus nerve, his old ulcers would be perforating his stomach about now. He opened his comconsole to Quinn's communications shunt, and waited.

With a sparkle, the image of a frowning man appeared over the vid plate. His dark hair was drawn back in a tight knot held by a gold ring, emphasizing the strong bones of his face. He wore a bronze-brown silk tunic, and no other jewelry. Olive-brown skin; he looked a healthy forty or so. Appearances were deceiving. It took more than one lifetime to scheme and fight one's way to the undisputed leadership of a Jacksonian House. Vasa Luigi, Baron Bharaputra, had been wearing the body of a clone for at least twenty years. He certainly took good care of it. The vulnerable period of another brain transplant would be doubly dangerous for a man whose power so many ruthless subordinates coveted. *This man is not for playing games with,* Miles decided.

"Bharaputra here," the man in brown stated, and waited. Indeed, the man and the House were one, for practical purposes.

"Naismith here," said Miles. "Commanding, Dendarii Free Mercenary Fleet."

"Apparently not completely," said Vasa Luigi blandly.

Miles peeled back his lips on set teeth, and managed not to flush. "Just so. You do understand, this raid was not authorized by me?"

"I understand you claim so. Personally, I should not be so anxious to announce my failure of control over my subordinates."

He's baiting you. Cool. "We need to have our facts straight. I have not yet established if Captain Thorne was actually suborned, or merely taken in by my fellow-clone. In any case, it is your own product, for whatever sentimental reasons, who has returned to attempt to extract some personal revenge upon you. I'm just an innocent bystander, trying to straighten things out."

"You," Baron Bharaputra blinked, like a lizard, "are a curiosity. *We* did not manufacture you. Where did you come from?"

"Does it matter?"

"It might."

"Then it is information for sale or trade, not for free." That was good Jacksonian ettiquette; the Baron nodded, unoffended. They were entering the realm of Deal, if not yet a deal between equals. Good.

The Baron did not immediately pursue Miles's family history, though. "So what is it you want from me, Admiral?"

"I wish to help you. I can, if given a free hand, extract my people from that unfortunate dilemma downside with a minimum of further damage to Bharaputran persons or property. Quiet and clean. I would even consider paying reasonable costs of physical damages thus far incurred."

"I do not require your help, Admiral."

"You do if you wish to keep your costs down."

Vasa Luigi's eyes narrowed, considering this. "Is that a threat?"

Miles shrugged. "Quite the reverse. Both our costs can be very low—or both our costs can be very high. I would prefer low."

The Baron's eyes flicked right, at some thing or person out of range of the vid pick-up. "Excuse me a moment, Admiral." His face was replaced with a holding-pattern.

Quinn drifted over. "Think we'll be able to save any of those poor clones?"

He ran his hands through his hair. "Hell, Elli, I'm still trying to get Green Squad out! I doubt it."

"That's a shame. We've come all this way."

"Look, I have crusades a lot closer to home than Jackson's Whole, if I want 'em. A hell of a lot more than fifty kids are killed each year in the Barrayaran backcountry for suspected mutation, for starters. I can't afford to get . . . quixotic like Mark. I don't know where he picked up those ideas, it couldn't have been from the Bharaputrans. Or the Komarrans."

Quinn's brows rose; she opened her mouth, then shut it as if on some second thought, and smiled dryly. But then she said, "It's Mark I was thinking about. You keep saying you want to get him to trust you."

"Make him a gift of the clones? I wish I could. Right after I finish strangling him with my bare hands, which will be right after I finish hanging Bel Thorne. Mark is Mark, he owes me nothing, but Bel should have known better." His teeth clenched, aching. Her words shook him with galloping visions. Both ships, with every clone aboard, jumping triumphantly from Jacksonian local space . . . thumbing their noses at the bad Bharaputrans . . . Mark stammering gratitude, admiring . . . bring them all home to Mother . . . *madness*. Not possible. If he'd planned it all himself, from beginning to end, maybe. His plans certainly would not have included a midnight frontal assault with no back-up. The vid plate sparkled again, and he waved Quinn out of range. Vasa Luigi reappeared.

"Admiral Naismith." He nodded. "I have decided to allow you to order your mutinous crew to surrender to my security forces."

"I would not wish to put your security to any further trouble, Baron. They've been up all night, after all. Tired, and jumpy. I'll collect all my people myself."

"That will not be possible. But I will guarantee their lives. The individual fines for their criminal acts will be determined later."

Ransoms. He swallowed rage. "This . . . is a possibility. But the fines must be determined in advance."

"You are hardly in a position to add conditions, Admiral."

"I only wish to avoid misunderstandings, Baron."

Vasa Luigi pursed his lips. "Very well. The troopers, ten thousand Betan dollars each. Officers, twenty-five thousand. Your hermaphrodite captain, fifty thousand, unless you wish us to dispose of it ourselves—no? I do not see that you have any use for your, ah, fellow clone, so we'll retain custody of him. In return, I shall waive property damage charges." The Baron nodded in satisfaction at his own generosity.

Upwards of a quarter of a million. Miles cringed inwardly. Well, it could be done. "But I am not without interest in the clone. What . . . price do you put on his head?"

"What possible interest?" Vasa Luigi inquired, surprised.

Miles shrugged. "I'd think it was obvious. My profession is full of hazards. I am the only survivor of my clone-clutch. The one I call Mark was as much a surprise to me as I was to him, I think; neither of us knew there was a second cloning project. Where else would I find such a perfect, ah, organ-donor, and on such short notice?"

Vasa Luigi opened his hands. "We might arrange to keep him safe for you."

"If I needed him at all, I'd need him urgently. In the circumstances, I'd fear a sudden rise in the market price. Besides, accidents happen. Look at the accident that happened to poor Baron Fell's clone, in your keeping."

The temperature seemed to drop twenty degrees, and Miles cursed his tongue. That episode was apparently still classified information in these parts, or at least some kind of hot button. The Baron studied him, if not with more respect, then with increased suspicion. "If you wish another clone made for transplant purposes, Admiral, you've come to the right place. But *this* clone is not for sale."

"*This* clone does not belong to you," Miles snapped out, too quickly. No—steady on. Keep it cool, keep his real thoughts buried deep, maintain that smarmy surface persona that could actually cut a deal with Baron Bharaputra without vomiting. Cool. "Besides, there's that ten-year lead time. It's not some long-anticipated death from old age that concerns me. It's the abrupt surprise sort." After a pause, and with a heroic effort, he choked out, "You need not waive the property damage charges, of course."

"I *need* not do anything at all, Admiral," the Baron pointed out. Coolly.

Don't bet on it, you Jacksonian bastard. "Why do *you* want this particular clone, Baron? Considering how readily you could make yourself another."

"Not that readily. His medical records reveal he was quite a challenge." Vasa Luigi tapped the side of his aquiline nose with one forefinger and smiled without much humor.

"Do you plan punishment? A warning to other malefactors?"

"He will doubtless regard it so."

So, there was a plan for Mark, or at least an idea that smelled of some profit. "Nothing in the direction of our Barrayaran progenitor, I trust. That plot is long dead. They know about us both."

"I admit, his Barrayaran connections interest me. *Your* Barrayaran connections interest me too. It is obvious from the name that you took for yourself that you've long known where you came from. Just what is your relationship with Barrayar, Admiral?"

"Queasy," he admitted. "They tolerate me, I do them a favor now and then. For a price. Beyond that, mutual avoidance. Barrayaran Imperial Security has a longer arm even than House Bharaputra. You don't want to attract their negative attention, I assure you."

Vasa Luigi's brows rose, politely skeptical. "A progenitor and two clones . . . three identical brothers. And all so short. Among you, I suppose you make a whole man."

Not to the point; the Baron was casting for something, information, presumably. "Three, but hardly identical," said Miles. "The original Lord Vorkosigan is a dull stick, I am assured. The limitations of Mark's capacities, he has just demonstrated, I fear. I was the improved model. My creators planned higher things for me, but they did their job too well, and I began planning for myself. A trick neither of my poor siblings seems to have mastered."

"I wish I could talk with your creators."

"I wish you could too. They are deceased."

The Baron favored him with a chill smile. "You're a cocky little fellow, aren't you?"

Miles stretched his lips in return, and said nothing.

The Baron sat back, tenting his fingers. "My offer stands. The clone is not for sale. But every thirty minutes, the fines will double. I advise you to close your deal quickly, Admiral. You will not get a better."

"I must have a brief consultation with my Fleet accountant," Miles temporized. "I will return your call shortly."

"How else?" Vasa Luigi murmured, with a small smile at his own wit.

Miles cut the comm abruptly, and sat. His stomach was shaking, hot red waves of shame and anger radiating outward through his whole body from the pit of his belly.

"But the Fleet accountant isn't here," Quinn pointed out, sounding slightly confused. Lieutenant Bone had indeed departed with Baz and the rest of the Dendarii from Escobar.

"I . . . don't like Baron Bharaputra's deal."

"Can't ImpSec rescue Mark later?"

"*I am* ImpSec."

Quinn could hardly disagree; she fell silent.

"I want my space armor," he growled petulantly, hunching in his station chair.

"Mark has it," said Quinn.

"I know. My half-armor. My command headset."

"Mark has those too."

"I know." His hand slapped down hard on the arm of the chair, the harsh crack in the quiet chamber making Quinn flinch. "A squad leader's helmet, then!"

"What for?" said Quinn in a flat, unencouraging tone. "No crusades here, you said."

"I'm cutting myself a better deal." He swung to his feet. His blood beat in his ears, hotter and hotter. "Come on."

The seat straps bit into his body as the drop shuttle blew its clamps and accelerated away from the side of the *Peregrine*. Miles glanced up over the pilot's shoulder for a quick check of the planet's curvature sliding across the window, and a glimpse of his two fighter-shuttles peeling away from the mothership to cover them. They were followed by the *Peregrine*'s second combat-drop shuttle, the other half of his two pronged attack. His faint feint. Would the Bharaputrans take it seriously? *You hope.* He turned his attention back to the glittering global data-world supplied by his command headset.

He was not stuck with a squad leader's helmet after all. He'd commandeered Elena Bothari-Jesek's downside-team captain's gear, while she rode the tactics room back aboard the *Peregrine*. *Bring it back without any unsightly holes through it, damn you,* she'd told him, her lips pale with unexpressed anxiety. Practically everything he wore was donated. An oversized nerve-disruptor shield-net suit had its cuffs turned up and held with elastic bands at wrists and ankles. Quinn had insisted on it, and as nerve-disruptor damage was his particular nightmare, he hadn't argued. Sloppy fatigues, held ditto. The plasma-mirror field pack straps cinched the extra fabric around his body reasonably well. Two pairs of thick socks kept his borrowed boots from sliding around. It was all very annoying, but hardly his greatest concern while trying to pull together a downside raid on thirty minutes' notice.

His greatest concern was their landing site. On top of Thorne's building would have been his first choice, but the shuttle pilot claimed fears that the whole building would collapse if they tried to set the drop shuttle down on it, and anyway the roof was peaked, not flat. The next closest possible site was occupied by the *Ariel*'s dead and abandoned shuttle. The third-choice site looked as if it was going to be a long walk, especially on the return journey when Bharaputra's security would have had time to set up counter measures. Straight up the slot was not his preferred attack style. Well, maybe Sergeant Kimura and Yellow Squad in the second drop shuttle would give Baron Bharaputra something more urgent to think about. *Take care of your shuttle, Kimura. It's our only back-up, now. I should have brought the whole damned fleet.*

He ignored his own shuttle's clanks and screams of decelera-tion as they hit the atmosphere—it was an excellent hell-drop, but it couldn't go fast enough to suit him—and watched the progress of his high cover in the colored codes and patterns of his helmet data display. The startled Bharaputran fighter-shuttles that had been guarding the *Peregrine* now found their attention suddenly divided. They wasted a few futile shots against the *Peregrine* itself, wavered after Kimura, then turned to pursue Miles's attack formation. One Bharaputran was blown to bits for its attempt almost immediately, and Miles whispered a pithy commendation for his Dendarii fighter pilot into his recorder on the spot. The other Bharaputran, unnerved, broke away to await reinforcements. Well, that had been easy. It was the trip back that was going to be maximum fun. He could feel the adrenaline high starting already, stranger and sweeter than a drug-rush through his body. It would last for hours, then depart abruptly, leaving him a burnt-out husk with hollow eyes and voice. Was it worth it? *It will be if we win.*

We will win.

As they rounded the planet to line-of-sight to their target, he tried contacting Thorne again. The Bharaputrans were jamming the main command channels. He tried dropping down and broad-casting a brief query on commercial bands, but got no response. Someone should have been assigned to monitor those. Well, he'd be able to punch through once they were on-site. He called up the holoview of the medical complex, ghost images dancing before his eyes. Speaking of straight up the slot, he was briefly tempted to order his fighter-shuttles to lay down a line of fire and blast a trench from his proposed landing site to Thorne's refuge, removing those inconvenient buildings from his path. But the trench would take too long to cool, and besides, the cover might benefit his own as much as Bharaputra's forces. Not quite as much;

the Bharaputrans knew the layout better. He considered the probability of tunnels, utility tunnels, and ducts. He snorted at the thought of ducts, and frowned at the thought of Taura, led blindly into this meat grinder by Mark.

The wild, jerking decelerations ended at last as buildings rose around them—*sniper vantage-points*—and the shuttle thumped to the ground. Quinn, who'd been trying to raise communication channels from the station chair opposite his, behind the co-pilot, looked up and said simply, "I've got Thorne. Try setting 6 2 j. Audio only, no vids so far."

With a flick of his eyes and a controlled blink, he keyed in his erstwhile subordinate. "Bel? We're down, and coming for you. Get ready to break out. Is anyone left alive down here?"

He didn't have to see Bel's face to sense the wince. But at least Bel didn't waste time on excuses or apologies. "Two non-walking wounded. Trooper Phillipi died about fifteen minutes ago. We packed her head in ice. If you can bring the portable cryo-chamber, we might save something."

"Will do, but we don't have much time to fool with her. Start prepping her now. We'll be there as fast as we can." He nodded to Quinn, and they both rose and exited the flight-deck. He had the pilots seal the door behind them.

Quinn passed the word to the medic on what he was going to be dealing with, and the first half of Orange Squad swarmed from the shuttle to take up defensive positions. Two small armored hovercars went up immediately behind them, to clear any vantage points of Bharaputran snipers and replace them with Dendarii. When they reported a temporary *Clear!* Miles and Quinn followed Blue Squad down the ramp into the chill, damp dawn. He left the entire second half of Orange Squad to guard the shuttle, lest the Bharaputrans try to repeat their previous successful ploy.

Morning mist roiled faintly around the shuttle's hot skin. The sky was pearly with the slow-growing light, but the medical complex's structures still loomed in blotted shadow. A float-bike soared aloft, two troopers took the point at a dead run, and Blue Squad followed. Miles concentrated, forcing his short legs to pump fast enough to keep up. He wanted no long-legged trooper to temper his stride for his sake, ever. This time at least, none did, and he grunted satisfaction under his remaining breath. A scattered roar of small-arms fire echoing all around told him his Orange Squad perimeter-people were already hard at work.

They streamed around one building, under the cover of a

second's portico, then past a third, the half-squads leap-frogging and covering each other. It was all too easy. The complex reminded Miles of those carnivorous flowers with the nectar-coated spines that all faced inwards. Slipping in was simple, for little bugs like him. It was the attempt to get out that would exhaust and kill. . . .

It was therefore almost a relief when the first sonic grenade went off. The Bharaputrans weren't saving it *all* for dessert. The explosion was a couple of buildings away, and rocked and reverberated strangely around the walkways. Not Dendarii issue, its deafening timbre was a tad off. He keyed his command helmet to follow the fire fight, half-subliminally, as Orange Squad rooted out a nest of Bharaputran security. It wasn't the Bharaputrans his people could smoke out that worried him. It was the ones they overlooked. . . . He wondered if the enemy had brought in more mass-projectile weapons in addition to sonic grenades, and was coldly conscious of the missing element in his borrowed half-armor. Quinn had tried to make him take her torso-armor, but he'd convinced her its oversized loose sliding around as he moved would just make him crazy. *Crazier,* he'd thought he'd heard her mutter, but he hadn't asked for an amplification. He wasn't planning on leading any cavalry charges this trip, that was certain.

He blinked away the distracting ghostly data flow as they rounded a final corner, scared off three or four lurking Bharaputrans, and approached the clone-crèche. Big blocky building, it looked like a hotel. Shattered glass doors led into a foyer where shadowy gray-camouflaged defenders moved among hastily-raised shielding, metal doors torn from hinges and propped up. A quick exchange of countersigns, and they were in. Half of Blue Squad scattered instantly to reinforce the building's weary Green Squad defenders; the other half guarded him.

The medic warped the float pallet containing the portable cryo-chamber through the doors and was hurriedly directed down a hallway by his comrades. Intelligently, they were prepping Phillipi in a side room, out of sight of their clone hostages. Step One was to remove as much as possible of the patient's own blood; under these hasty combat conditions, without any attempt to recover and store it. Rough, ready, and extremely messy; it was not a sight for the faint-hearted, nor the unprepared mind.

"Admiral," said a quiet alto voice.

He wheeled to find himself face to face with Bel Thorne. The hermaphrodite's features were almost as gray as the shield-net hood that framed them, an oval of lined and puffy fatigue. Plus another look, one he hated seeing there despite his anger. *Defeat.* Bel looked beaten, looked like it had lost it all. *And so it has.* They did not exchange a single word of blame or defense. They didn't need to; it was all plain in Bel's face and, he suspected, his own. He nodded in acknowledgment, of Bel, of it all.

Beside Bel stood another soldier, the top of his helmet—*my helmet*—not quite level with the top of Bel's shoulder. He had half-forgotten how startling Mark was. *Do I really look like that?*

"You—" Miles's voice cracked, and he found he had to stop and swallow. "Later, you and I are going to have a long talk. There's a lot you don't seem to understand."

Mark's chin came up, defiantly. *Surely my face is not that round.* It must be an illusion, from the hood. "What about these kids?" said Mark. "These clones."

"What about them?" A couple of young men in brown silk tunics and shorts appeared to be actually helping the Dendarii defenders, scared and excited rather than surly. Another group, boys and girls mixed, sat in a plain-scared bunch on the floor under the watchful eye of a stunner-armed trooper. *Crap, they really are just kids.*

"We've—you've got to take them along. Or I'm not going." Mark's teeth were set, but Miles saw him swallow.

"Don't tempt me," snarled Miles. "Of *course* we're taking them along, how the hell else would we get out of here alive?"

Mark's face lit, torn between hope and hatred. "And then what?" he demanded suspiciously.

"Oh," Miles caroled sarcastically, "we're just going to waltz right over to Bharaputra Station and drop them off, and thank Vasa Luigi kindly for the loan. *Idiot!* What d'you think? We load up and run like hell. The only place to put them would be out the airlock, and I guarantee you'd go first!"

Mark flinched, but took a deep breath and nodded. "All right, then."

"It is not. All. Right," Miles bit out. "It is merely . . . merely . . ." he could not come up with a word to describe what it merely was, aside from the most screwed-up mess he'd ever encountered. "If you were going to try and pull a stupid stunt like this, you might at least have consulted the expert in the family!"

"You? Come to *you* for help? D'you think I'm crazy?" demanded Mark furiously.

"Yes—" They were interrupted by a staring blond clone boy, who'd walked up to them open-mouthed.

"You really *are* clones," he said in wonderment.

"No, we're twins born six years apart," snapped Miles. "Yes, we're just as much clones as you are, that's right, go back and sit down and obey orders, dammit."

The boy retreated hastily, whispering, "It's true!"

"Dammit," Mark howled under his breath, if that squeezed sotto voce could be so described, "how come they believe *you* and not *me*? It's not fair!"

Quinn's voice, through his helmet, derailed the family reunion. "If you and Don Quixote Junior are done greeting each other, Medic Norwood has Phillipi prepped and loaded, and the wounded ready to transport."

"Form up, let's get the first batch out the door, then," he responded. He called up Blue Squad's sergeant. "Framingham, take the first convoy. You ready to roll?"

"Ready. Sergeant Taura has marshaled them for me."

"Go. And don't look back."

Half a dozen Dendarii, about three times that many bewildered and exhausted clones, and the two wounded troopers on float pallets assembled in the foyer and filed out the ruined doors. Framingham did not look too happy to be using a couple of young girls as a projectile-weapon shield; his chocolate-dark face was grim. But any Bharaputran snipers were going to have to take aim very, very carefully. The Dendarii forced the kids forward, if not at a run, then at least at a steady jog. A second group followed the first within a minute. Miles ran both non-coms' helmet transmissions down either side of his periperal vision, while his ears strained for the deadly whine of small-arms fire.

Were they going to bring this off? Sergeant Taura shepherded the final gaggle of clones into the foyer. She greeted him with a demi-salute, without even pausing to puzzle between himself and Mark. "*Glad* to see you, sir," she rumbled.

"You too, Sergeant," he replied, heart-felt. If Mark had managed to get Taura killed, he didn't know how it could ever have been made right between them. At some more convenient moment he urgently wanted to find out how Mark had managed to fool her, and how intimately. Later.

Taura moved closer and lowered her voice. "We lost four kids, escaped back to the Bharaputrans. Makes me kinda sick. Any chance . . . ?"

Regretfully, he shook his head. "No way. No miracles this time. We've got to take what we can get and go, or we'll lose it all."

She nodded, understanding the tactical situation perfectly well. Understanding didn't cure the gut-churning nausea of regret, unfortunately. He offered her a brief *I'm sorry* smile, and her long lips twisted up on one side in wry response.

The Blue Squad medic brought in the big float pallet containing the cryo-chamber, a blanket tossed over the transparent part of the gleaming cylinder to shield his comrade-and-patient's naked and cooling body from uncomprehending or horrified outsiders' eyes. Taura urged the clones to their feet.

Bel Thorne glanced around. "I hate this place," it said levelly.

"Maybe we can bomb it this time, on the way out," Miles returned, equally levelly. "Finally."

Bel nodded.

The mob of them, the fifteen or so last clones, the float pallet, the Dendarii rear-guard, Taura and Quinn, Mark and Bel, oozed out the front door. Miles glanced up, feeling as if he had a bull's-eye painted on the top of his helmet, but the moving shape crossing the roof of the building opposite wore Dendarii grays. Good. The holovid on the right side of his field of view informed him Framingham and his group had made it to the shuttle without incident. Even better. He cut Framingham's helmet transmissions, squelched the second squad leader's to a bare murmur, and concentrated on the present moment.

His concentration was broken by Kimura's voice, the first he'd heard from Yellow Squad across town in their own drop zone. "Sir, resistance is soft. They're not buying us. How far should I go to make them take us seriously?"

"All the way, Kimura. You've got to draw Bharaputran attention off us. Draw them away, but don't risk yourselves, and especially don't risk your shuttle." Miles hoped Lieutenant Kimura was too busy to reflect upon the slightly schizoid logic of that order. If—

The first sign of Bharaputran sharpshooters arrived with a bang, literally; a sonic grenade put down about fifteen meters ahead of them. It blew a hole in the walkway, which returned a few moments later in obedience to gravity as a sharp hot patter of raining fragments, startling but not very dangerous. The clone-childrens' screams were muffled, in his stunned ears.

"Gotta go, Kimura. Use your initiative, huh?"

The miss hadn't been accidental, Miles realized as plasma fire struck a potted tree to the right and a wall to the left of them, exploding both. They were being deliberately bracketed to panic the clones. It was working quite nicely, too—they were ducking, dropping, clutching each other and screaming, and showing every sign of getting ready to bolt off in all directions. There would be no rounding them up after that. A plasma arc beam hit a Dendarii square on, just to prove the Bharaputrans could do it, Miles supposed; the beam was absorbed by his mirror-field and re-emitted with the usual hellish blue snap, further terrifying the nearby kids. The more experienced troopers fired back coolly, while Miles yelled into his headset for his air cover. The Bharaputrans were above them, mostly, judging by the angle of fire.

Taura studied the hysterical clones, glanced around, raised her plasma arc, and blew apart the doors of the nearest building, a big windowless warehouse or garage-looking structure. "Inside!" she bellowed.

It was good, in that if they were going to bolt, at least it had them all bolting in the same direction. As long as they didn't *stop* inside. If they got pinned down and penned up again, there'd be no big brother to rescue *him*.

"Move!" Miles seconded the idea, "but *keep moving.* Out the other side!"

She waved an acknowledgement as the kids stampeded out of the fire-zone into what no doubt looked like safety to them. To him, it looked like a trap. But they needed to stay together. If there was anything worse than being pinned down, it was being *scattered* and pinned down. He waved the squad through and followed. A couple of Blue Squad troopers took rear guard, firing plasma arcs upward at their . . . herders, Miles feared. He figured it for keep-your-heads-down warning shots, but one trooper got lucky. His plasma arc beam hit a Bharaputran who unwisely attempted to dart along the roof-edge on the building opposite. The Bharaputran's shielding absorbed the shot, but then he unbalanced and fell, screaming. Miles tried not to hear the sound when he hit the concrete, but did not quite succeed, even with grenade-stunned ears. The screaming stopped.

Miles turned and dashed down the corridor and through some big double doors, beckoned anxiously onward by Thorne, who waited to help cover him.

"I'll take rear guard," Thorne volunteered.

Was Thorne entertaining thoughts of dying heroically, thus avoiding the inevitable court-martial? For a moment, Miles entertained thoughts of letting it do so. It would be the Vorish thing to do. The Old Vor could be a bunch of assholes, at times. "*You* get those clones to the shuttle," Miles snapped in turn. "Finish the job you took on. If I'm paying this much, I want to get what I'm paying for."

Thorne's teeth bared, but it nodded. They both galloped after the squad.

The double doors opened onto an enormous concrete-floored room, which obviously nearly filled the big building. Red- and green-painted catwalks ran around a girdered ceiling high above, festooned with looping cables of mysterious function. A few harsh pale lights shone down, casting multiple shadows. He blinked in the gloom and almost lowered his infra-red visor. It appeared to be an assembly area for large projects of some kind, though at the moment there seemed to be nothing in progress. Quinn and Mark hesitated, waiting for them to catch up despite Miles's urgent gesture for them to hurry on. "What are you stopping for?" he barked in furious fear. He skidded to a halt beside them.

"Look out!" someone yelled. Quinn spun, raising her plasma arc, seeking aim. Mark's mouth opened, the "o" foolishly echoing the circle of his gray hood around his face.

Miles saw the Bharaputran because they were looking square at each other, in that frozen moment. A team of brown-clad Bharaputran snipers, probably come up through the tunnels. They were scrambling along the girders, barely more prepared than the Dendarii they pursued. The Bharaputran had a hand-sized projectile weapon launcher of some kind pointed straight at him, its muzzle bright with flare.

Miles could not, of course, see the projectile, not even as it entered his chest. Only his chest, bursting outward like a flower, and a sound not heard but only felt, a hammer-blow launching him backward. Dark flowers bloomed too in his eyes, covering everyone.

He was astonished, not by how much he thought, for there was no time for thought, but by how much he felt, in the time it took for his last heartburst of blood to finish flowing through his brain. The chamber careening around him . . . pain beyond measure . . . rage, and outrage . . . and a vast regret, infinitesimal in duration, infinite in depth. *Wait, I haven't—*

CHAPTER SEVEN

Mark was standing so close, the report of the exploding projectile was like a silence, pressing in his ears, obliterating all other sounds. It happened too fast for understanding, too fast to close the eyes and defend the mind against the sight. The little man who had been yelling and gesturing them onward fluttered backward like a gray rag, arms outflung, face contorted. A spray of blood spattered across Mark with stinging force, part of a wide half-circle of blood and tissue-bits. Quinn's whole left side was scarlet.

So. You are not perfect, was his first absurd thought. This sudden absolute vulnerability shocked him unbearably. *I didn't think you could be hurt. Damn you, I didn't think you could be—*

Quinn was screaming, everyone was recoiling, only he stood still, paralyzed in his private, ear-stunned silence. Miles lay on the concrete with his chest blown out, open-mouthed, unmoving. *That's a dead man.* He'd seen a dead man before. There was no mistaking it.

Quinn, her face wild, fired her plasma arc at the Bharaputrans, shot after shot, till hot ceiling fragments started to fall lethally back down around them, and a Dendarii knocked her weapon aside. "Taura, get them!" Quinn pointed upward with her free hand.

The monster sergeant fired a rappel-hook upward, which wrapped around a girder. She rose upon it at full acceleration, like a mad spider. Between the lights and the shadows, Mark could scarcely follow her progress, leaping at inhuman speed along the catwalks, until broken-necked Bharaputran security personnel began raining down. All their high-tech half-armor was no protection at all against those huge, enraged clawed hands. Three men fell in a welter of their own blood, their throats torn out, an insane bombardment; one Dendarii trooper, running across the chamber, was almost smashed beneath an enemy body. Modern warfare wasn't supposed to have this much blood in it. The weapons were supposed to cook everyone neatly, like eggs in their shells.

Quinn paid no attention, scarcely seeming to care about the results of her order. She knelt by Miles's side, her shaking hands outspread, hesitating. Then they dove and pulled off Miles's command helmet. She flung her own squad leader's helmet to the floor and replaced it on her smooth gray hood with Miles's. Her lips moved, establishing contact, checking channels. The helmet was undamaged, apparently. She yelled orders to perimeter-people, queries to the drop shuttle, and one other. "Norwood, get back here, *get back here. Yes*, bring it, bring it *now*. On the double, Norwood!" Her head swiveled away from Miles only long enough to shout, "Taura, get this building secured!" From above, the sergeant in turn bellowed orders to her scurrying troopers.

Quinn pulled a vibra-knife from her belt sheath and began cutting away Miles's fatigues, ripping through belts and the nerve-disruptor shield-suit, tossing the bloody fragments aside. Mark looked up, following her glance, to see the medic with the float-pallet returning, hauling his burden across the concrete. The float-pallet counteracted gravity, but not mass; the inertia of the heavy cryo-chamber fought his attempts to run, and fought him again as he braked and lowered the pallet to the floor near his dead commander. Half a dozen confused clones followed the medic like baby ducks, clustering together and staring around in horror at the ghastly aftermath of the brief sharp firefight.

The medic looked back and forth from Miles's body to the loaded cryo-chamber. "Captain Quinn, it's no good. It won't hold two."

"The hell it's not." Quinn staggered to her feet, her voice grating like gravel. She seemed unaware of the tears running down her face, tracking pinkly through the spatter. "The hell it's not." She stared bleakly at the gleaming cryo-chamber. "Dump her."

"Quinn, I can't!"

"On my order. On my hands."

"*Quinn* . . ." The medic's voice was anguished. "Would *he* have ordered this?"

"*He* just lost his damn vote. All right." She took a deep breath. "I'll do it. You start prepping *him*."

Teeth clenched, the medic moved to obey. He flipped open a door at the end of the chamber and removed a tray of equipment. It was all in disarray, having been used once already and hastily re-packed. He rolled out some big insulated bottles.

Quinn keyed open the chamber. Its lid popped, breaking the seal, and rose. She reached within, unfastening things that Mark could not see. Did not wish to see. She hissed, as instantly-frozen skin tore from her hands, but reached again. With a grunt, she heaved a woman's greenish, empurpled nude body from the chamber and laid it on the floor. It was the smashed-up bike-trooper, Phillipi. Thorne's patrol, daring Bharaputran fire, had finally found her near her downed float-bike some two buildings away from her lost helmet. Broken back, broken limbs; she'd taken hours to die, against all the Green Squad medic's heroic efforts to save her. Quinn looked up and saw Mark staring at her. Her face was ravaged.

"You, you useless . . . *wrap* her." She pointed to Phillipi, then hurried around the cryo-chamber to where the Blue Squad medic now knelt beside Miles.

Mark broke his paralysis at last, to scuttle around and find a thin foil heat wrap among the medical supplies. Frightened of the body, but too terrified by Quinn to disobey, he laid out the silver wrap and rolled the cold dead woman up in it. She was stiff and heavy under his cringing touch.

He rose to hear the medic muttering, with his ungloved hands plunged deep into the gory mess that had been Miles Vorkosigan's chest, "I can't find an *end*. Where the hell's an *end*? At least the damned aorta, *something* . . ."

"It's been over four minutes," snarled Quinn, pulled out her vibra-knife again, and cut Miles's corpse's throat, two neat slashes bracketing but not touching the windpipe. Her fingers scrabbled in the cut.

The medic glanced up only to say, "Be sure you get the carotid and not the jugular."

"I'm *trying*. They're not color-coded." She found something pale and rubbery. She pulled tubing from the top of one of the insulated jugs, and jammed its plastic end-nozzle into the presumed artery. She switched the power on; the tiny pump hummed, pushing lucent greenish cryo-fluid through the transparent tubing. She pulled out a second piece of tubing from the jug and inserted it on the other side of Miles's neck. Blood began to flow from the slashed exit veins, over her hands, over everything; not spurting as from a heart-beat, but in a steady, inhuman, mechanical fashion. It spread on the floor in a shimmering pool, then began to flow away across some subtle drainage-slope, a little carmine creek. An impossible quantity of blood. The clustered clones were weeping. Mark's own head throbbed, pain so bad it darkened his vision.

Quinn kept the pumps going till what came out ran greenish-clear. The medic meanwhile had apparently found the ends he was looking for, and attached two more tubes. More blood, mixed with cryo-fluid, welled up and spilled from the wound. The creek became a river. The medic pulled Miles's boots and socks off, and ran sensors over his paling feet. "Almost there ... damn, we're nearly dry." He hastened to his jug, which had switched itself off and was blinking a red indicator light.

"I used all I had," said Quinn.

"It's probably enough. They were both small people. Clamp those ends—" He tossed her something glittering, which she snatched out of the air. They bent over the little body. "Into the chamber, then," said the medic. Quinn cradled the head, the medic took the torso and hips. The arms and legs dangled down. "He's light . . ." They swung their stripped burden hastily into the cryo-chamber, leaving the blood-soaked uniform on the floor in a sodden heap. Quinn left the medic to make the last connections and turned away blind-eyed, talking to her helmet. She did not look down at the long silver package at her feet.

Thorne appeared, crossing the chamber at a jog. Where had it been? Thorne caught Quinn's eye, and with a jerk of its head at the dead Bharaputrans reported, "They came up through the tunnels, all right. I have the exits secured, for now." Thorne glowered bleakly at the cryo-chamber. The hermaphrodite looked suddenly . . . middle-aged. Old.

Quinn acknowledge this with a nod. "Key to Channel 9-C. We got trouble outside."

A kind of dreary curiosity winkled through Mark's numb shock. He turned his own headset back on. He'd had it help-lessly and hopelessly turned off for hours, ever since Thorne had snatched back its command. He followed the captains' transmissions.

The Blue and Orange Squad perimeter teams were under heavy pressure from beefed-up Bharaputran security forces. Quinn's delay in this building was drawing Bharaputrans like flies to carrion, with a buzzing excitement. With over two-thirds of the clones now packed aboard the shuttle, the enemy had stopped directing heavy fire toward it, but airborne reinforcements were gathering fast, hovering like vultures. Quinn and company were in imminent danger of being surrounded and cut off.

"Got to be another way," muttered Quinn. She switched channels. "Lieutenant Kimura, how's it going with you? Resistance still soft?"

"It's hardened up beautifully. I kinda got my hands full right now, Quinnie." Kimura's thin, weirdly cheerful voice came back cut by a wash of static indicating plasma fire and the activation of his plasma mirror field. "We've achieved our objective and are pulling out now. Trying to. Chat later, huh?" More static.

"Which objective? Take care of your damn shuttle, y'hear, boy? You may yet have to come for us. Report to me the second you're back in the air."

"Right." A slight pause. "Why isn't the Admiral on this channel, Quinnie?"

Quinn's eyes squeezed shut in pain. "He's . . . temporarily out of range. Move it, Kimura!"

Kimura's reply, whatever it was, broke up in another wash of static. No program regarding Kimura and his objective was loaded in Mark's helmet, but the lieutenant seemed to be transmitting from somewhere other than the medical complex. A feint? If so, Kimura wasn't drawing nearly enough enemy troops away from them. Sergeant Framingham's channel, from the drop shuttle, broke in urging Quinn to hurry, almost simultaneously with an Orange Squad perimeter team reporting themselves forced off another vantage point.

"Could the shuttle land on top of this building and pick us up?" Quinn inquired, gazing at the girders overhead.

Thorne frowned, following her eyes. "I think it would cave in the roof."

"Hell. Other ideas?"

"Down," said Mark suddenly. Both Dendarii jerked, catching themselves from flattening to the floor as they realized what he meant. "Through the tunnels. The Bharaputrans got in, we can get back out."

"It's a blind warren," objected Quinn.

"I have a map," said Mark. "All of Green Squad does, loaded programs. Green Squad can lead."

"Why didn't you say so earlier?" snapped Quinn, illogically ignoring the fact that there had hardly been an earlier.

Thorne nodded confirmation and began hastily tracing through its helmet's holovid map. "Can do. There's a route—puts us up inside the building beyond your shuttle, Quinn. Bharaputran defenses are thin, there, and all facing the other way. And their superior numbers won't help them, down below."

Quinn stared down. "I hate dirt. I want vacuum, and elbow room. All right, let's do it. Sergeant Taura!"

A flurry of organization, a few more doors blown away, and the little party was on the march once more, down a lift tube and into the utility tunnels. Troopers scouted ahead of the main group. Taura had half a dozen clones carry Phillipi's wrapped body, laid across three metal bars she'd torn from the catwalk railings. As if the bike-trooper still had some forlorn hope of preservation and revival.

Mark found himself pacing beside the cryo-chamber on its float pallet, tugged along by the anxious medic. He glanced from the corner of his eye through the transparent cover. His progenitor lay open-mouthed, pale and gray-lipped and still. Frost formed feathers along the seals, and a blast of waste heat flowed from the refrigeration unit's radiator. It would burn like a bonfire on an enemy's infra-red sensor 'scope. Mark shivered, and crouched in the heat. He was hungry, and terribly cold. *Damn you, Miles Vorkosigan. There was so much I wanted to say to you, and now you're not listening.*

The straight tunnel they were traversing passed under another building, giving way through double doors to a wide foyer full of multiple cross-connections; several lift tubes, emergency stairs, other tunnels, and utility closets. All the doors were opened or blown open by the point-men looking for Bharaputran resistance. The air was pungent with smoke and the harsh lingering tang from plasma arc fire. Unfortunately, at this juncture the point men found what they were looking for.

The lights went out. Dendarii helmet visors snapped shut all around Mark, as they switched to infra-red. He followed suit and stared disoriented into a world drained of color. His helmet crackled with voice communications stepping on each other as two point-men came running backwards into the foyer from separate corridors, firing plasma arcs that blared blindingly on his heat-enhanced vision. Four half-armored Bharaputran security personnel swung out of a lift tube, cutting Quinn's column in half. So confined was the confusion, they found themselves fighting hand-to-hand. Mark was knocked down by accident by a swinging Dendarii, and crouched near the float-pallet.

"This isn't shielded," the medic groaned, slapping the cryo-chamber as arcs of fire whipped by close overhead. "One square hit, and . . ."

"Into the lift tube, then," yelled Mark at him. The medic nodded and swung the pallet around into the nearest dark opening free of Bharaputrans. The lift-tube was switched off, or the conflicting grav fields might have blown circuits on both tube and pallet. The medic scrambled aboard the cryo-chamber as if it were a horse, and began to sink from sight. Another trooper followed, hand over hand down the emergency ladder on the tube's interior. Plasma arc fire struck Mark three times in rapid succession, as he scrambled to his feet, knocking him down again. His mirror-field shed a roar of blue crackles as he rolled toward the tube through waves of heat. He swung down the ladder after the trooper, out of the line of fire.

But not for long. A Bharaputran helmet flashed above them in the entrance, then plasma arc fire followed them downward with a glare like lightning in the tube. The trooper helped the medic yank and heave the float-pallet out of this sudden shooting gallery and through the lowest entrance, and ducked after. Mark scrambled in their wake, feeling like a human torch, netted and entwined with racketing blue incandescence. How many shots had that been? He'd lost count. How many more could his shielding take before it gave way and burned out?

The trooper took a firing stance aimed back into the lift tube, but no Bharaputran followed them. They stood in a pocket of dark and quiet, shouts and shots echoing faintly down the tube from the battle overhead. This was a much smaller foyer, with only two exits. Dim yellow emergency lighting along the floor gave a falsely cozy sense of warmth.

"Hell," said the medic, staring upward. "I think we've just cut ourselves off."

"Not necessarily," said Mark. Neither the medic nor the trooper were Green Squad, but Mark's helmet of course had Green Squad programming. He called up the holomap, found their current location, and let the helmet's computer sketch a route. "You can get there from this level, too. It's a bit more roundabout, but you're less likely to encounter Bharaputrans for that very reason."

"Let me see," demanded the medic.

Half-reluctant, half-relieved, Mark gave his helmet up to him. The medic jammed it on his head, and studied the red line snaking through the 3-D schematic grid of the medical complex, projected before his eyes. Mark risked a darting glance up the lift tube. No

Bharaputrans loomed overhead, and the sounds of combat were muffled, as if growing more distant. He ducked back to find the trooper staring at him, unsettling glints of his eyes gleaming through his visor. *No. I'm not your damned Admiral. More's the pity, eh?* The trooper clearly was of the opinion that the Bharaputrans had shot the wrong short man. Mark didn't even need words to get that message. He hunched.

"Yeah," the medic decided. His jaw tightened, behind his visor.

"If you hurry, you might even get there ahead of Captain Quinn," said Mark. He still held the medic's helmet. There were no more sounds from overhead. Should he run after Quinn's moving fire-fight, or stay and try to help guide and guard the float-pallet? He was not sure if he was more afraid of Quinn, or of the Bharaputran fire her party drew. Either way he'd probably be safer with the cryo-chamber.

He took a deep breath. "You . . . keep my helmet. I'll take yours." The medic and the trooper were both glowering at him with disfavor, repellingly. "I'll go after Quinn and the clones." His clones. Would Quinn have any regard at all for their lives?

"Go, then," said the medic. He and the trooper aimed the float-pallet out the doors, and didn't look back. They obviously had him pegged as more of a liability than an asset, and felt well-rid of him.

Grimly, he climbed the ladder back up the lift tube. He peeked cautiously across the foyer floor, as it came to his eye level. A lot of property damage. A sprinkler system had added steam to the choking smoke. One brown-clad body lay prone, unmoving. The floor was wet and slippery. He swung out of the tube and darted skittishly out the corridor the Dendarii company must have taken, if they were sticking to their planned route. More plasma arc damage assured him he was on the right track.

He rounded a corner, skidded to a halt, and flung himself backward, out of sight. The Bharaputrans hadn't seen him; they'd been facing the other way. He retreated back down the corridor while awkwardly keying through the channels of the unfamiliar helmet till he made contact with Quinn.

"Captain Quinn? Uh, Mark here."

"Where the hell *are* you, where's *Norwood*?"

"He's got my helmet. He's taking the cryo-chamber through by another route. I'm behind you, but I can't close up. There are at least four Bharaputrans in full space armor between us, coming up on your rear. Watch out."

"Hell, now we're outgunned. That tears it." Quinn paused. "No. I can take care of *them*. Mark, get the hell away, follow Norwood. Run!"

"What are you going to do?"

"Drop the roof on those bastards. Lotta good space armor'll do 'em then. *Run!*"

He ran, realizing what she was planning. At the first lift tube he came to, he took to the ladder, climbing wildly, regardless of where it led. He didn't want to be any further underground than he had to when—

It was like an earthquake. He clung as the tube cracked and buckled, and the *felt* sound beat through his body. It was over in a moment, but for an echoing rumble, and he resumed his climb. Daylight ahead, reflecting silver down a tube entrance.

He came out on the ground floor of a building furnished like a fancy office. Its windows were cracked and starred. He knocked a hole in one and climbed through, and flipped up his infra-red visor. To his right, half of another building had fallen away into an enormous crater. Dust still rose in choking clouds. The Bharaputrans in their sturdy, deadly space armor were possibly still alive, under all that, but it would take an excavation crew hours to dig them out. He grinned despite his terror, panting in the daylight.

The medic's helmet did not have nearly the eavesdropping capacity of the command headset, but he found Quinn again. "All right, Norwood, keep on going," she was saying. "Go like hell! Framingham! Got that? Lock on Norwood. Start pulling in your perimeter people. Lift as soon as Norwood and Tonkin are aboard. Kimura! You in the air?" A pause; Mark could not get Kimura's reply, whoever and wherever he was. But he could fill in the sense of it from Quinn's continuation. "Well, we've just made you a new drop zone. It's a bit lumpy, but it'll do. Follow my signal, come straight down into the crater. You'll just fit. Yes, you will too, I've laser-'scoped it, you do too have clearance. You can risk the shuttle *now*, Kimura. Come on!"

He made for the crater too, scuttling along close to the side of the building, taking advantage of overhangs till the patter of falling concrete chips made him realize that the blast-damaged balcony above his head was losing its structural integrity. Stay under and get smashed, or step out in the open and get shot? Whichever he did would prove the wrong choice, he was certain. What was that line Vorkosigan's military textbooks were so fond of quoting? *No battle plan survives first contact with the enemy.* Quinn's tactics and dispositions shifted with bewildering speed. She was exploiting a quite literal new opening—the roar of a drop shuttle grew in his ears, and he sprinted out from under the balcony as the vibrations weakened it. One end gave way and fell with a crash. He kept on sprinting. Let the Bharaputran snipers try to hit a moving target. . . .

Quinn and her group ventured into the open just as the drop shuttle, feet extended like an enormous insect, felt its way carefully into the crater. A few last Bharaputrans were in position on a roof opposite to offer harrying fire. But they had only plasma arcs, and were still being careful of the clones, though one pink-clad girl screamed, caught in the backwash of a Dendarii plasma mirror field. Light burns, painful but not fatal. She was crying and panicked, but a Dendarii trooper nevertheless caught her and aimed her at the shuttle hatch, now opening and extruding a ramp.

The few Bharaputrans, hopeless of bringing the shuttle down with mere sniper's weapons, changed their tactics. They began concentrating their fire on Quinn, shot after shot pumping into her overloading mirror field. She shimmered in a haze of blue fire, staggering under the impact. Clones and Dendarii pelted up the ramp.

Command helmets draw fire. He could see no other way but to run in front of her. The air around him lit as his mirror field spilled energy, but in the brief respite Quinn regained her balance. She grabbed him by the hand and together they sprinted up the ramp, the last to board. The shuttle was lurching back into the air and the ramp withdrawing even as they fell through the hatch. The hatch sealed behind them. The silence felt like a song.

Mark rolled over on his back and lay gasping for air, lungs on fire. Quinn sat up, her face red in its circle of gray. Just a sunburn. She cried hysterically for three breaths, then clamped her mouth shut. Fearfully, her fingers touched her hot cheeks, and Mark remembered that this was the woman who had had her face burned entirely away by plasma fire, once. But not twice. Not twice.

She scrambled to her knees and began keying through command channels on her almost-fatal headset again. She then yanked herself to her feet and ricocheted forward in the jinking accelerations of the shuttle. Mark sat up and stared around, disoriented. Sergeant Taura, Thorne, the clones, he recognized. The rest were strange Dendarii, Lieutenant Kimura's Yellow Squad presumably, some in the usual gray fatigues, some in full space armor. They looked rather the worse for wear. All four bunks for wounded in the back were folded down and filled, and a fifth man was laid out on the floor. But the attending medic moved smoothly, not frantically. Her patients were clearly stabilized, able to wait for further treatment under more favorable conditions. Yellow Squad's cryo-chamber was recently occupied, though. The prognosis was now so bad for the foil-wrapped Phillipi, Mark wondered if they would even attempt to continue freezing her, once they were back aboard the *Peregrine*. But except for the bike-trooper and the cryo-chamber, there were no more covered forms, no body bags—Kimura's squad seemed to have made it through their mission, whatever it had been, fairly lightly.

The shuttle banked; they were circling, not boosting to orbit yet. Mark moaned under his breath, and rose to follow Quinn and find out what was going on.

When he came in sight of the prisoner he stopped short. The man sat with his hands bound behind him, securely strapped into a seat and guarded by two Yellow Squad troopers, a big fellow and a thin woman who made Mark think of a snake, all sinuous muscle and unblinking beady eyes. The prisoner looked a striking forty or so years of age, and wore a torn brown silk tunic and trousers. Loose strands of dark hair escaped from a gold ring on the back of his head and fell about his face. He did not struggle, but sat calmly, waiting, with a cold patience that quite matched the snake-woman's.

Bharaputra. The Bharaputra, Baron Bharaputra, Vasa Luigi himself. The man hadn't changed a hair in the eight years since Mark had last glimpsed him.

Vasa Luigi's face rose, and his eyes widened slightly, seeing Mark. "So, Admiral," he murmured.

"Just so," Mark responded automatically with a Naismith-phrase. He swayed as the shuttle banked more sharply, concealing weak-kneed terror, concealing exhaustion. He hadn't slept the night before this mission, either. *Bharaputra, here?*

The Baron cocked an eyebrow. "Who is that on your shirt?"

Mark glanced down at himself. The bandolier of blood had not yet turned brown, and was still damp, sticky and cold. He found himself actually wanting to answer, *My brother,* for the shock value. But he wasn't sure the Baron was shockable. He fled forward, avoiding more intimate conversation. *Baron Bharaputra.* Did Quinn and company plan to ride this tiger, and how? But at least he now understood why the shuttle could circle the combat zone without apparent fear of enemy fire.

He found Quinn and Thorne both in the pilot's compartment, along with Kimura the Yellow Squad commander. Quinn had taken over the shuttle's communication station, her gray hood pushed back, sweat-soaked dark curls in disarray.

"Framingham! Report!" she was crying into the comm. "You've got to get into the air. Bharaputran airborne reinforcements are almost on top of you."

Across the flight deck at the station opposite Quinn's, Thorne monitored a tactical holovid. Two Dendarii colored dots, fighter shuttles, dove upon but failed to break up an array of enemy shuttles passing over a ghost city, astral projection of the live city turning below them. Mark glanced out the window past the pilots' shoulders, but could not spot the originals in the sunlit morning smog.

"We have a downed-man recovery in progress, ma'am," Framingham's voice returned. "One minute, till the squad gets back."

"Do you have everyone else? *Do you have Norwood?* I can't raise his helmet!"

There was a short delay. Quinn's fists clenched, opened. Her fingernails were bitten to red stumps.

Framingham's voice at last. "We've got him now, ma'am. Got everyone, the quick and the dead alike, except for Phillipi. I don't want to leave anyone for those bloody bastards if I can help it—"

"We have Phillipi."

"Thank God! Then everyone's accounted for. We have lift-off now, Captain Quinn."

"Precious cargo, Framingham," said Quinn. "We rendezvous in the *Peregrine*'s umbrella of fire. The fighter shuttles will guard your wings." In the tac display, the Dendarii dots peeled away from the lumbering enemy and left them behind.

"What about your wings?"

"We'll be right behind you. Yellow Squad bought us a first-class ticket home free. Home free is Fell Station."

"And then we head out?"

"No. The *Ariel* took some damage, earlier. We're docking. It's arranged."

"Understood. See you there."

The Dendarii formation came together at last and began to boost upward. Mark fell into a station chair, and hung on. The fighter shuttles were more at risk from enemy fire than the drop shuttles, he realized, watching the tac display. One fighter shuttle was distinctly limping. It clung close to the Yellow Squad's craft. The formation paced itself to its wounded member. But for once, things ran to plan. Their Bharaputran harriers dropped reluctantly behind as they broke out of the atmosphere and into orbit.

Quinn rested her elbows for a weary moment on her console, and hid her red-and-white face in her hands, rubbing tender eyelids. Thorne sat pale and silent. Quinn, Thorne, himself, all bore broken segments of that arc of blood. Like a red ribbon, binding them one to another.

Fell Station was coming up at last. It was a huge structure, the largest of the orbital transfer stations circling Jackson's Whole, and House Fell's headquarters and home city. Baron Fell liked holding the high ground. In the delicate interlocking network of the Great Houses, House Fell probably held the most raw power, in terms of capacity for destruction. But raw destruction was seldom profitable, and coup was counted in coins, here. What coin were the Dendarii using to buy Fell Station's help, or at least neutrality? The person of Baron Bharaputra, now secured in the cargo bay? What kind of bargaining chips were the clones, then, small change? And to think he'd despised the *Jacksonians* for being dealers in flesh.

Fell Station was just now passing out of the planet's eclipse, the advancing line of sunlight dramatically unveiling its vast extent. They decelerated toward one arm, giving up direction to Fell's traffic controllers and some heavily armed tugs which appeared out of nowhere to escort them. And there was the *Peregrine*, coasting in. The drop shuttles and the fighter shuttles all gavotted around their mother ship, coming meekly to their docking clamps. The *Peregrine* itself eased delicately toward its assigned mooring.

With a *clank* of the portside clamps and the hiss of flex-tube seals, they were home. In the cargo bay, the Dendarii expedited removal of the wounded to the *Peregrine's* infirmary, then turned much more slowly and wearily to tie-down and clean-up chores. Quinn shot past them, Thorne close on her heels. As if pulled by that mortal red ribbon, Mark followed.

The goal of Quinn's mad dash was the starboard side shuttle hatch, where Framingham's shuttle was coming to dock. They arrived there just as the flex-tube seals were secured, then had to stand out of the way as the wounded were rushed out first. Mark was disturbed to recognize Trooper Tonkin, who had accompanied Norwood the medic, among them. Tonkin had reversed roles, from guard to patient. His face was dark and still, unconscious, as eager hands hustled him past and shifted him onto a float pallet. *Something's very wrong, here.*

Quinn shifted impatiently from foot to foot. Other Dendarii troopers started to exit, herding clones. Quinn frowned, and shouldered upstream past them through the flex tube and into the shuttle.

Thorne and Mark went after her into free fall chaos. There were clone-youths everywhere, some crying, some violently sick— Dendarii were attempting to catch them and get them towed to the exit. One harried trooper with a hand-vac was chasing floating globs of some child's last meal before everyone had to breathe it. The shouts and screams and babble were like a blow to the mind. Framingham's bellows were failing to speed a return to military order any faster than the terrorized clones could be removed from the cargo bay.

"Framingham!" Quinn floated over and grabbed him by the ankle. "Framingham! Where the hell's the cryo-chamber Norwood was escorting?"

He glanced down, frowning. "But you said *you* had it, Captain."
"*What?*"

"You said you *had* Phillipi." His lips stretched in a fierce grimace. "Goddammit, if we've left her behind I'll—"

"We have Phillipi, yes, but she's—she was no longer in the cryo-chamber. Norwood was supposed to be getting it to you, Norwood and Tonkin."

"They didn't have it when my rescue patrol pulled them out. We got them both, what was left of 'em. Norwood was killed. Hit through the eye with one of those frigging projectile spine-grenades. Blew his head apart. But I didn't leave his body, it's in the bag over there."

Command helmets draw fire, oh yes, I knew that. . . . No wonder Quinn hadn't been able to raise Norwood's comm channels.

"The cryo-chamber, Framingham!" Quinn's voice held a high pitch of anguish Mark had never heard before.

"We didn't *see* any goddamn cryo-chamber, Quinn! Norwood and Tonkin didn't have it when we got to them! What's so frigging important about the cryo-chamber if Phillipi wasn't even in it?"

Quinn released his ankle, and floated in a tightening ball, arms and legs drawing in. Her eyes were dark and huge. She bit off a string of inadequate foul words, grinding her teeth so hard her gums went white. Thorne looked like a chalk doll.

"Thorne," Quinn said, when she could speak again. "Get on the comm to Elena. I want both ships on a total security blackout, as of now. No leaves, no passes, no communications with Fell Station or anybody else that isn't cleared by me. Tell her to get Lieutenant Hart over here from the *Ariel*. I want to meet with them both at once, and *not* over comm channels. Go."

Thorne nodded, rotated in air, and launched itself forward toward the flight deck.

"What is this?" demanded Sergeant Framingham.

Quinn took a deep, slow breath. "Framingham, we left the Admiral downside."

"Have you lost your mind, he's right there—" Framingham's finger sagged in mid-point at Mark. His hand closed into a fist. "Oh." He paused. "That's the clone."

Quinn's eyes burned; Mark could feel them boring through to the back of his skull like laser-drills.

"Maybe not," Quinn said heavily. "Not as far as House Bharaputra has to know."

"Ah?" Framingham's eyes narrowed in speculation.

No! Mark screamed inside. Silently. Very silently.

CHAPTER EIGHT

It was like being trapped in a locked room with half a dozen serial killers with hangovers. Mark could hear each one's breathing from where they sat in a ring around the officer's conference table. They were in the briefing chamber off the *Peregrine*'s main tactics room. Quinn's breath was the lightest and fastest; Sergeant Taura's was the deepest and most ominous. Only Elena Bothari-Jesek at her captain's place at the head of the table, and Lieutenant Hart on her right, were shipboard-clean and natty. The rest had come as they were from the drop mission, battered and stinking: Taura, Sergeant Framingham, Lieutenant Kimura, Quinn on Bothari-Jesek's left. And himself, of course, lonely at the far end of the oblong table.

Captain Bothari-Jesek frowned, and wordlessly handed around a bottle of painkiller tablets. Sergeant Taura took six. Only Lieutenant Kimura passed. Taura handed them across to Framingham without offering any to Mark. He longed for the tablets as a thirsty man might yearn after a glass of water, poured out and sinking into desert sand. The bottle went back up the table and disappeared into the captain's pocket. Mark's eyes throbbed in time to his sinuses, and the back of his head felt as tight as drying rawhide.

Bothari-Jesek spoke. "This emergency debriefing is called to deal with just two questions, and as quickly as possible. What the hell happened, and what are we going to do next? Are those helmet recorders on their way?"

414

"Yes, ma'am," said Sergeant Framingham. "Corporal Abromov is bringing them."

"Unfortunately, we are missing the most pertinent one," said Quinn. "Correct, Framingham?"

"I'm afraid so, ma'am. I suppose it's embedded in a wall somewhere at Bharaputra's, along with most of the rest of Norwood's helmet. Friggin' grenades."

"Hells." Quinn hunched in her seat.

The briefing room door slid open, and Corporal Abromov entered at a jog. He carried four small, clear plastic trays, stacked, and labeled "Green Squad," "Yellow Squad," "Orange Squad," and "Blue Squad." Each tray held an array of ten to sixteen tiny buttons. Helmet recorders. Each trooper's personal records of the past hours, tracking every movement, every heartbeat, every scan, shot, hit, and communication. Events that had passed too rapidly for comprehension in real-time could be slowed, analyzed, teased apart, errors of procedure detected and corrected—next time.

Abromov saluted and handed the trays to Captain Bothari-Jesek. She dismissed him with thanks and passed the trays on to Captain Quinn, who in turn inserted them into the simulator's data slot and downloaded them. She also encoded the file top secret. Her raw-tipped fingers darted over the vid control panel.

The now-familiar ghostly three-dimensional holomap of Bharaputra's medical facility formed above the table top. "I'll jump forward to the time we were attacked in the tunnel," Quinn said. "There we are, Blue Squad, part of Green Squad . . ." A spaghetti-tangle of lines of green and blue colored light appeared deep inside a misty building. "Tonkin was Blue Squad Number Six, and kept his helmet throughout what follows." She made Tonkin's Number Six map-track yellow, for contrast. "Norwood was still wearing Blue Squad Number Ten. Mark . . ." her lips pinched, "was wearing Helmet One." That track, of course, was conspicuously missing. She made Norwood's Number Ten track pink. "At what point did you change helmets with Norwood, Mark?" She did not look at him as she asked this question.

Please, let me go. He was sure he was sick, because he was still shivering. A small muscle in the back of his neck spasmed, tiny twitches in a prickling underlayer of pain. "We went to the bottom of that lift tube." His voice came out a dry whisper. "When . . . when Helmet Ten comes back up, I'm wearing it. Norwood and Tonkin went on together, and that's the last I saw of them."

The pink line indeed crawled back up the tube and wormed after the mob of blue and green lines. The yellow track went on alone.

Quinn fast-forwarded voice contacts. Tonkin's baritone came out in a whine like an insect on amphetamines. "When I last contacted them, they were here." Quinn marked the spot with a glowing dot of light, in an interior corridor deep inside another building. She fell silent and let the yellow line snake on. Down a lift tube, through yet another utility tunnel, under a structure, up and through yet another.

"There," said Framingham suddenly, "is the floor they were trapped on. We picked up contact with 'em *there*."

Quinn marked another dot. "Then the cryo-chamber has to be somewhere near the line of march between here and here." She pointed to the two bright dots. "It has to be." She stared, eyes narrowed. "Two buildings. Two and a half, I suppose. But there's not a damned thing on Tonkin's voice transmissions that gives me a clue." The insect-voice described Bharaputran attackers, and cried for help, over and over, but did not mention the cryo-chamber. Mark's throat contracted in synchrony. *Quinn, turn him off, please. . . .*

The program ran to its end. All the Dendarii around the table stared at it, as if willing it to yield up something more. There was no more.

The door slid aside and Captain Thorne entered. Mark had never seen a more exhausted-looking human being. Thorne too was still dressed in dirty fatigues, only the plasma mirror pack discarded from its half armor. Its gray hood was pushed back, brown hair plastered flat to its head. A circle of grime in the middle of Thorne's pale face marked the hood opening, gray twin to the circle of red on Quinn's face from her mirror-field overload burn. Thorne's movements were hurried and jerky, will overriding a fatigue close to collapse. Thorne leaned, hands on the conference table, mouth a grim horizontal line.

"So, could you get anything at all out of Tonkin?" asked Quinn of Thorne. "What the computer has, we just saw. And I don't think it's enough."

"The medics got him waked up, briefly," reported Thorne. "He did talk. I was hoping the recorders would make sense of what he said, but . . ."

"What did he say?"

"He said when they reached this building," Thorne pointed, "they were cut off. Not yet surrounded, but blocked from a line to the shuttle, and the enemy closing the ring fast. Tonkin said, Norwood yelled he had an idea, he'd seen something 'back there.' He had Tonkin create a diversion with a grenade attack, and guard a particular corridor—must be that one there. Norwood took the cryo-chamber and ran back along their route. He returned a few minutes later—not more than six minutes, Tonkin said. And he told Tonkin, 'It's all right now. The Admiral will get out of here even if we don't.' About two minutes later, he was killed by that projectile grenade, and Tonkin was knocked loopy by the concussion."

Framingham nodded. "My crew got there not three minutes after that. They drove off a pack of Bharaputrans who were searching the bodies—looting, looking for intelligence, or both, Corporal Abromov wasn't sure—they picked up Tonkin and Norwood's body and ran like hell. Nobody in the squad reported seeing a cryo-chamber anywhere."

Quinn chewed absently on a fingernail stump. Mark did not think she was even conscious of the gesture. "That's all?"

"Tonkin said Norwood was laughing," Thorne added.

"Laughing." Quinn grimaced. "Hell."

Captain Bothari-Jesek was sunk in her station chair. Everyone around the table appeared to digest this last tid-bit, staring at the holomap. "He did something clever," said Bothari-Jesek. "Or something that he thought was clever."

"He only had about five minutes. How clever could he be in five minutes?" Quinn complained. "Gods *damn* the clever jerk to sixteen hells for not reporting!"

"He was doubtless about to." Bothari-Jesek sighed. "I don't think we need to waste time rationing blame. There's going to be plenty to go around."

Thorne winced, as did Framingham, Quinn, and Taura. Then they all glanced at Mark. He cringed back in his seat.

"It's only been," Quinn glanced at her chrono, "less than two hours. Whatever Norwood did, the cryo-chamber has to still be down there. It has to."

"So what do we do?" Lieutenant Kimura asked dryly. "Mount another drop mission?"

Quinn thinned her lips in non-appreciation of the weary sarcasm. "You volunteering, Kimura?" Kimura flipped up his palms in surrender and subsided.

"In the meantime," Bothari-Jesek said, "Fell Station is calling us, pretty urgently. We have to start dealing. I presume this will involve our hostage." A short nod of thanks in Kimura's direction acknowledged the only wholly successful part of the drop mission, and Kimura nodded back. "Does anyone here know what the Admiral intended to do with Baron Bharaputra?"

A circle of negative headshakes. "Don't *you* know, Quinnie?" asked Kimura, surprised.

"No. There wasn't time to chat. I'm not even sure if the Admiral seriously expected your kidnapping expedition to succeed, Kimura, or whether it was only for the diversionary value. That would be more like his strategizing, not to let the whole mission turn on one unknown outcome. I expect he planned," her voice faded in a sigh, "to use his initiative." She sat up straight. "But I sure as hell know what I intend to do. The deal this time is going to be in *our* favor. Baron Bharaputra could be the ticket out of here for all of us, and the Admiral too, but we have to work it just right."

"In that case," said Bothari-Jesek, "I don't think we should let on to House Bharaputra just how valuable a package we left downside." Bothari-Jesek, Thorne, Quinn, all of them, turned to look at Mark, coldly speculative.

"I've thought of that too," said Quinn.

"No," he whispered. "No!" His scream emerged as a croak. "You can't be serious. You can't make me be him, I don't *want* to be him any more, God! No!" He was shaking, shivering, his stomach turning and knotting. *I'm cold.*

Quinn and Bothari-Jesek glanced at each other. Bothari-Jesek nodded, some unspoken message.

Quinn said, "You are all dismissed to your duties. Except you, Captain Thorne. You are relieved of command of the *Ariel*. Lieutenant Hart will take over."

Thorne nodded, as if this were entirely expected. "Am I under arrest?"

Quinn's eyes narrowed in pain. "Hell, we don't have the time. Or the personnel. And you're not debriefed yet, and besides, I need your experience. This . . . situation could change rapidly at any moment. Consider yourself under house arrest, and assigned to me. You can guard yourself. Take a visiting officer's cabin here on the *Peregrine*, and call it your cell if it makes you feel any better."

Thorne's face went very bleak indeed. "Yes, ma'am," it said woodenly.

Quinn frowned. "Go clean up. We'll continue this later."

Except for Quinn and Bothari-Jesek, they all filed out. Mark tried to follow them. "*Not* you," said Quinn in a voice like a death bell. He sank back into his station chair and huddled there. As the last Dendarii cleared the chamber, Quinn reached over and turned off all recording devices.

Miles's women. Elena-the-childhood-sweetheart, now Captain Bothari-Jesek, Mark had studied back when the Komarrans had tutored him to play Lord Vorkosigan. Yet she was not quite what he had expected. Quinn the Dendarii had taken the Komarran plotters by surprise. The two women had a coincidental resemblance in coloration, both with short dark hair, fine pale skin, liquid brown eyes. Or was it so coincidental? Had Vorkosigan subconsciously chosen Quinn as Bothari-Jesek's substitute, when he couldn't have the real thing? Even their first names were similar, Elli and Elena.

Bothari-Jesek was the taller by a head, with long aristocratic features, and was more cool and reserved, an effect augmented by her clean officer's undress grays. Quinn, fatigue-clad and combat-booted, was shorter, though still a head taller than himself, rounder and hotter. Both were terrifying. Mark's own taste in women, if ever he should live to exercise it, ran more to something like that little blonde clone they'd pulled from under the bed, if only she'd been the age she looked to be. Somebody short, soft, pink, timid, somebody who wouldn't kill and eat him after they mated.

Elena Bothari-Jesek was watching him with a sort of appalled fascination. "So like him. Yet not him. Why are you shivering?"

"I'm cold," muttered Mark.

"*You're* cold!" Quinn echoed in outrage. "*You're* cold! You gods be-damned little sucker—" She turned her station chair abruptly around, and sat with her back to him.

Bothari-Jesek rose and walked around to his end of the table. Willow-wand woman. She touched his forehead, which was clammy; he flinched almost explosively. She bent and stared into his eyes. "Quinnie, back off. He's in psychological shock."

"He doesn't deserve consideration!" Quinn choked.

"He's still in shock, regardless. If you want results, you have to take it into account."

"Hell." Quinn turned back. New clean wet tracks ran down from her eyes across her red-and-white, dirt-and-dried-blood-smudged face. "You didn't see. You didn't see Miles lying there with his heart blown all over the room."

"Quinnie, he's not really dead. Is he? He's just frozen, and . . . and misplaced." Was there the faintest tinge of uncertainty, denial, in her voice?

"Oh, he's really dead all right. Very really frozen dead. And he's going to stay that way forever if we don't get him back!" The blood all over her fatigues, caked in the grooves of her hands, smeared across her face, was finally turning brown.

Bothari-Jesek took a breath. "Let's focus on the business to hand. The immediate question is, can Mark fool Baron Fell? Fell met the real Miles once."

"That's one of the reasons I didn't put Bel Thorne under close arrest. Bel was there, and can advise, I hope."

"Yes. And that's the curious thing . . ." She hitched a hip over the tabletop and let one long booted leg swing. "Shock or no shock, Mark hasn't blown Miles's deep-cover. The name *Vorkosigan* hasn't passed his lips, has it?"

"No," Quinn admitted.

Bothari-Jesek twisted up her mouth, and studied him. "Why not?" she asked suddenly.

He crouched down a little further in his station chair, trying to escape the impact of her stare. "I don't know," he muttered. She waited implacably for more, and he mustered in an only slightly louder voice, "Habit, I guess." Mostly Ser Galen's habit of beating the shit out of him whenever he'd screwed up, back in the bad old days. "When I do the part, I do the part. M-Miles would never have slipped on that one, so I don't either."

"Who are you when you're not doing the part?" Bothari-Jesek's gaze was narrowed, calculating.

"I . . . hardly know." He swallowed, and tried again for more volume in his voice. "What's going to happen to my—to the clones?"

As Quinn began to speak, Bothari-Jesek held up her hand, stopping her. Bothari-Jesek said instead, "What do you want to have happen to them?"

"I want them to go free. To be set free somewhere safe, where House Bharaputra can't kidnap them back."

"A strange altruism. I can't help wondering, why? Why this whole mission in the first place? What did you hope to gain?"

His mouth opened, but no sound came out. He couldn't answer. He was still clammy, weak and shaking. His head ached blackly, as though draining of blood. He shook his head.

"Peh!" snorted Quinn. "What a loser. What a, a damned *anti-*Miles. Snatching defeat from the jaws of victory."

"Quinn," said Bothari-Jesek quietly. There was a profound reproof in her voice, just in that single word, which Quinn heard and acknowledged with a shrug of her shoulder. "I don't think either one of us knows quite what we have hold of, here," Bothari-Jesek continued. "But I know when I'm out of my depth. However, I know someone who wouldn't be."

"Who?"

"Countess Vorkosigan."

"Hm." Quinn sighed. "That's another thing. Who's going to tell *her* about—" A downward jerk of her thumb indicated Jackson's Whole, and the fatal events that had just passed there. "And gods help me, if I'm really in command of this outfit now, I'm gonna have to report all this to Simon Illyan." She paused. "Do you want to be in command, Elena? As senior shipmaster present, now that Bel's under quasi-arrest, and all that. I just grabbed 'cause I had to, under fire."

"You're doing fine," said Bothari-Jesek with a small smile. "I'll support you." She added, "You've been more closely involved with intelligence all along, you're the logical choice."

"Yes, I know." Quinn grimaced. "You'll tell the family, if it comes to that?"

"For that," Bothari-Jesek sighed, "I am the logical choice. I'll tell the Countess, yes."

"It's a deal." But they both looked as if they wondered who had the better, or worse, half of it.

"As for the clones," Bothari-Jesek eyed Mark again, "how would you like to *earn* their freedom?"

"Elena," said Quinn warningly, "don't make promises. We don't know what we're going to have to trade yet, to get out of here. To get—" another gesture downward, "him back."

"No," Mark whispered. "You can't. Can't send them . . . back down there, after all this."

"I traded Phillipi," said Quinn grimly. "I'd trade *you* in a heartbeat, except that *he* . . . Do you know why we came downside on this bloody drop mission in the first place?" she demanded.

Wordlessly, he shook his head.

"It was for you, you little shit. The Admiral had a deal half-cut with Baron Bharaputra. We were going to buy out Green Squad for a quarter of a million Betan dollars. It wouldn't have cost much more than the drop mission, counting all the equipment we lost along with Thorne's shuttle. And the lives. But the Baron refused to throw you into the pot. Why he wouldn't sell you, I don't know. You're worthless to everybody else. But Miles wouldn't leave you!"

Mark stared down at his hands, which plucked at each other.

He glanced up to see Bothari-Jesek studying him again as if he were some vital cryptogram.

"As the Admiral would not leave his brother," said Bothari-Jesek slowly, "so Mark will not leave the clones. Will you? Eh?"

He would have swallowed, but he'd run out of spit.

"You'll do anything to save them, eh? Anything we ask?"

His mouth opened and closed. It might have been a hollow, soundless *yes.*

"You'll play the part of the Admiral for us? We'll coach you, of course."

He half-nodded, but managed to blurt out, "What promise—?"

"We'll take all the clones with us when we go. We'll put them down somewhere House Bharaputra can't reach."

"Elena!" objected Quinn.

"I want," he did swallow this time, "I want the Barrayaran woman's word. Your word," he said to Bothari-Jesek.

Quinn sucked on her lower lip, but did not speak. After a long pause, Bothari-Jesek nodded. "All right. You have my word on it. But you give us your total cooperation, understood?"

"Your word as what?"

"Just my word."

" . . . Yes. All right."

Quinn rose and stared down at him. "But is he even fit to play the part right now?"

Bothari-Jesek followed her look. "Not in that condition, no, I suppose not. Let him clean up, eat, rest. Then we'll see what can be done."

"Baron Fell may not give us time to coddle him."

"We'll tell Baron Fell he's in the shower. That'll be true enough."

A shower. *Food.* He was so ravenous as to be almost beyond hunger, numb in the belly, listless in the flesh. And cold.

"All I can say," said Quinn, "is that he's a damned poor imitation of the real Miles Vorkosigan."

Yes, that's what I've been trying to tell you.

Bothari-Jesek shook her head in, presumably, exasperated agreement. "Come on," she said to him.

She escorted him to an officer's cabin, small but thank-God private. It was disused, blank and clean, military-austere, the air a little stale. He supposed Thorne must now be similarly housed nearby.

"I'll get some clean clothes sent over for you from the *Ariel.* And send some food."

"Food first—please?"

"Sure."

"Why are you being nice to me?" His voice came out plaintive and suspicious, making him sound weak and paranoid, he feared.

Her aquiline face went introspective. "I want to know . . . who you are. What you are."

"You know. I'm a manufactured clone. Manufactured right here on Jackson's Whole."

"I don't mean your body."

He hunched in an automatic defensive posture, though he knew it emphasized his deformities.

"You are very closed," she observed. "Very alone. That's not at all like Miles. Usually."

"He's not a man, he's a mob. He's got a whole damned army trailing around after him." *Not to mention the harrowing harem.* "I suppose he likes it like that."

Her lips curved in an unexpected smile. It was the first time he'd seen her smile. It changed her face. "He does, I think." Her smile faded. "Did."

"You're doing this for him, aren't you. Treating me like this because you think he'd want it." Not in his own right, no, never, but all for Miles and his damned brother-obsession.

"Partly."

Right.

"But mostly," she said, "because someday Countess Vorkosigan will ask me what I did for her son."

"You're planning to trade Baron Bharaputra for him, aren't you?"

"Mark . . ." her eyes were dark with a strange . . . pity? irony? He could not read her eyes. "She'll mean you."

She turned on her heel and left him by himself, sealed in the cabin.

He showered in the hottest water the tiny unit would yield, and stood for long minutes in the heat of the dryer-blast, till his skin flushed red, before he stopped shivering. He was dizzy with exhaustion. When he finally emerged, he found someone had been and gone and left clothes and food. He hastily pulled on underwear, a black Dendarii tee-shirt, and a pair of his progenitor's ship-knit gray trousers, and fell upon the dinner. It wasn't a dainty Naismith-special-diet this time, but rather a tray of standard ready-to-eat rations designed to keep a large and physically active trooper going strong. It was far from gourmet fare, but it was the first time he'd had enough food on his plate for weeks. He devoured it all, as if whatever fairy had delivered it might reappear and snatch it away again. Stomach aching, he rolled into bed and lay on his side. He no longer shivered as if from cold, nor felt drained and sweating and shaky from low blood sugar. Yet a kind of psychic reverberation still rolled like a black tide through his body.

At least you got the clones out.

No. Miles *got the clones out.*

Dammit, dammit, dammit . . .

This half-baked disaster was not the glorious redemption of which he'd dreamed. Yet what had he expected the aftermath to be? In all his desperate plotting, he'd planned almost nothing past his projected return to Escobar with the *Ariel.* To Escobar, grinning, with the clones under his wing. He'd imagined himself dealing with an enraged Miles then, but then it would have been too late for Miles to stop him, too late to take his victory from him. He'd half-expected to be arrested, but to go willingly, whistling. What *had* he wanted?

To be free of survivor guilt? To break that old curse? *Nobody you knew back then is still alive. . . .* That was the motive he'd thought was driving him, when he thought at all. Maybe it wasn't so simple. He'd wanted to free himself from something. . . . In the last two years, freed of Ser Galen and the Komarrans by the actions of Miles Vorkosigan, freed again altogether by Miles on a London street at dawn, he had not found the happiness he'd dreamed of during his slavery to the terrorists. Miles had broken only the physical chains that bound him; others, invisible, had cut so deep that flesh had grown around them.

What did you think? That if you were as heroic as Miles, they'd have to treat you like Miles? That they would have to love you?

And who were *they*? The Dendarii? Miles himself? Or behind Miles, those sinister, fascinating shadows, Count and Countess Vorkosigan?

His image of Miles's parents was blurred, uncertain. The unbalanced Galen had presented them, his hated enemies, as black villains, the Butcher of Komarr and his virago wife. Yet with his other hand he'd required Mark to study them, using unedited source materials, their writings, their public speeches, private vids. Miles's parents were clearly complex people, hardly saints, but just as clearly not the foaming sadistic sodomite and murderous bitch of Galen's raving paranoias. In the vids Count Aral Vorkosigan appeared merely a gray-haired, thick-set man with oddly intent eyes in his rather heavy face, with a rich, raspy, level voice. Countess Cordelia Vorkosigan spoke less often, a tall woman with red-roan hair and notable gray eyes, too powerful to be called pretty, yet so centered and balanced as to seem beautiful even though, strictly speaking, she was not.

And now Bothari-Jesek threatened to deliver him to them. . . .

He sat up and turned on the light. A quick tour of the cabin revealed nothing to commit suicide with. No weapons or blades— the Dendarii had disarmed him when he'd come aboard. Nothing to hang a belt or rope from. Boiling himself to death in the shower was not an option; a sealed fail-safe sensor turned it off automatically when it exceeded physiological tolerances. He went back to bed.

The image of a little, urgent, shouting man with his chest exploding outward in a carmine spray replayed in slow motion in his head. He was surprised when he began to cry. Shock, it had to be the shock that Bothari-Jesek had diagnosed. *I hated the little bugger when he was alive, why am I crying?* It was absurd. Maybe he was going insane.

Two nights without sleep had left him ringingly numb, yet he could not sleep now. He only dozed, drifting in and out of near-dreams and recent, searing memories. He half-hallucinated about being in a rubber raft on a river of blood, bailing frantically in the red torrent, so that when Quinn came to get him after only an hour's rest, it was actually a relief.

CHAPTER NINE

"Whatever you do," said Captain Thorne, "don't mention the Betan rejuvenation treatment.

Mark frowned. "What Betan rejuvenation treatment? Is there one?"

"No."

"Then why the hell would I mention it?"

"Never mind, just don't."

Mark gritted his teeth, swung around in his station chair square to the vid plate, and pressed the keypad to lower his seat till his booted feet were flat to the floor. He was fully kitted in Naismith's officer's grays. Quinn had dressed him as though he were a doll, or an idiot child. Quinn, Bothari-Jesek, and Thorne had then proceded to fill his head with a mass of sometimes-conflicting instructions on how to play Miles in the upcoming interview. *As if I didn't know.* The three captains now each sat in station chairs out of range of the vid pick-up in the *Peregrine's* tac room, ready to prompt him through an ear-bug. And he'd thought *Galen* was a puppet master. His ear itched, and he wriggled the bug in irritation, earning a frown from Bothari-Jesek. Quinn had never stopped scowling.

Quinn had never stopped. She still wore her blood-soaked fatigues. Her sudden inheritance of command of this debacle had allowed her no rest. Thorne had cleaned up and changed to ship grays, but obviously had not slept yet. Both their faces stood out pale in the shadows, too sharply lined. Quinn had made Mark take a stimulant when, getting him dressed, she'd found him too muzzy-mouthed for her taste, and he did not quite like its effects. His head and eyes were almost too clear, but his body felt beaten. All the edges and surfaces of the tac room seemed to stand out with unnatural clarity. Sounds and voices in his ears seemed to have a painful serrated quality, sharp and blurred at once. Quinn was on the stuff too, he realized, watching her wince at a high electronic squeal from the comm equipment.

("All right, you're on,") said Quinn through the ear-bug as the vid plate in front of him began to sparkle. They all shut up at last.

The image of Baron Fell materialized, and frowned at him too. Georish Stauber, Baron Fell of House Fell, was unusual for the leader of a Jacksonian Great House in that he still wore his original body. An old man's body. The Baron was stout, pink of face, with a shiny liver-spotted scalp fringed by white hair trimmed short. The silk tunic he wore in his House's particular shade of green made him look like a hypothyroid elf. But there was nothing elfin about his cold and penetrating eyes. Miles was not intimidated by a Jacksonian Baron's power, Mark reminded himself. Miles was not intimidated by any power backed by less than three entire planets. His father the Butcher of Komarr could eat Jacksonian Great Houses for breakfast.

He, of course, was not Miles.

Screw that. I'm Miles for the next fifteen minutes, anyway.

"So, Admiral," rumbled the Baron. "We meet again after all."

"Quite." Mark managed not to let his voice crack.

"I see you are as presumptuous as ever. And as ill-informed."

"Quite."

("Start talking, dammit,") Quinn's voice hissed in his ear.

Mark swallowed. "Baron Fell, it was not a part of my original battle plan to involve Fell Station in this raid. I am as anxious to decamp with my forces as you are to have us leave. To that end, I request your help as a go-between. You . . . know that we've kidnapped Baron Bharaputra, I trust?"

"So I'm told." One of Fell's eyelids tic'd. "You've rather over-reached your available back-up, have you not?"

"Have I?" Mark shrugged. "House Fell is in a state of vendetta with House Bharaputra, are you not?"

"Not exactly. House Fell was on the verge of *ending* the vendetta with House Bharaputra. We've found it mutually unprofitable, of late. I'm now suspected of collusion in your raid." The Baron's frown deepened.

"Uh . . ." his thought was interrupted by Thorne whispering, ("Tell him Bharaputra's alive and well.")

"Baron Bharaputra is alive and well," said Mark, "and can remain so, for all I care. As a go-between, it seems to me you would be well-placed to demonstrate your good faith to House Bharaputra by helping to get him back. I only wish to trade him—intact—for one item, and then we'll be gone."

"You are optimistic," Fell said dryly.

Mark plowed on. "A simple, advantageous trade. The Baron for my clone."

("Brother,") Thorne, Quinn, and Bothari-Jesek all corrected in unison in his ear-bug.

"—brother," Mark continued, edged. He unset his teeth. "Unfortunately, my . . . brother, was shot in the mêlée downside. Fortunately, he was successfully frozen in one of our emergency cryo-chambers. Um, unfortunately, the cryo-chamber was accidently left behind in the scramble to get off. A live man for a dead one; I fail to see the difficulty."

The Baron barked a laugh, which he muffled in a cough. The three Dendarii faces across from Mark in the shadows were chill and stiff and not amused. "You've been having an interesting visit, Admiral. What do you want with a dead clone?"

("Brother,") Quinn said again. ("Miles insists, always.")

("Yes,") seconded Thorne. ("That's how I first knew you weren't Miles, back on the *Ariel*, when I called you a clone and you didn't jump down my throat.")

"Brother," Mark repeated wearily. "There was no head-wound, and the cryo-treatment was begun almost instantly. He has good hope of revival, as such things go."

("Only if we get him back,") Quinn growled.

"I have a brother," remarked Baron Fell. "He inspires no such emotions in me."

I'm right with you, Baron, Mark thought.

Thorne piped up in Mark's ear, ("He's talking about his half-brother, Baron Ryoval of House Ryoval. The original axis of this vendetta was between Fell and Ryoval. Bharaputra got dragged in later.")

I know who Ryoval is, Mark wanted to snap, but could not.

"In fact," Baron Fell went on, "my brother will be quite excited to learn you are here. After you so reduced his resources on your last visit, he is alas limited to small-scale attacks. But I suggest you watch your back."

"Oh? Do Ryoval's agents operate so freely on Fell Station?" Mark purred.

Thorne approved, ("Good one! Just like Miles.")

Fell stiffened. "Hardly."

Thorne whispered, ("Yes, remind him you helped him with his brother.")

What the hell had Miles done here, four years ago? "Baron. I helped you with your brother. You help me with mine, and we can call it square."

"Hardly that. The apples of discord you threw among us on your last departure took far too much time to sort out. Still . . . it's true you dealt Ry a better blow that I could have." Was there a tiny glint of approval in Fell's eye? He rubbed his round chin. "Therefore, I will give you one day to complete your business and depart."

"You'll act as go-between?"

"The better to keep an eye on both parties, yes."

Mark explained the Dendarii's best guess as to the approximate location of the cryo-chamber, and gave its description and serial numbers. "Tell the Bharaputrans, we think it may have been hidden or disguised in some way. Please emphasize, we wish it returned in good condition. And their Baron will be too."

("Good,") Bothari-Jesek encouraged. ("Let 'em know it's too valuable to destroy, without letting 'em guess they could hold us up for more ransom.")

Fell's lips thinned. "Admiral, you are an acute man, but I don't think you altogether understand how we do things on Jackson's Whole."

"But you do, Baron. That's why we'd like to have you on our side."

"I am not on your side. That is perhaps the first thing you don't understand."

Mark nodded, slowly; Miles would have, he thought. Fell's attitude was strange. Faintly hostile. *Yet he acts as if he respects me.*

No. He respected *Miles.* Hell. "Your neutrality is all I ask."

Fell shot him a narrow glance from under his white eyebrows. "What about the other clones?"

"What about them?"

"House Bharaputra will be inquiring."

"They do not enter into this transaction. Vasa Luigi's life should be sufficient and more."

"Yes, the trade seems uneven. What is so valuable about your late clone?"

Three voices chorused in his ear, ("Brother!") Mark yanked the ear-bug out and slapped it to the counter beside the vid plate. Quinn nearly choked.

"I cannot trade back fractions of Baron Bharaputra," snapped Mark. "Tempted as I am to start doing so."

Baron Fell raised a placating plump palm. "Calm, Admiral. I doubt it will be necessary to go so far."

"I hope not." Mark trembled. "It'd be a shame if I had to send him back without his brain. Like the clones."

Baron Fell apparently read the absolute personal sincerity of his threat, for he opened both palms. "I'll see what I can do, Admiral."

"Thank you," whispered Mark.

The Baron nodded; his image dissolved. By some trick of the holovid or the stimulant, Fell's eyes seemed to linger for one last unsettling stare. Mark sat frozen for several seconds till he was certain they were gone.

"Huh," said Bothari-Jesek, sounding surprised. "You did that rather well."

He did not bother to answer that one.

"Interesting," said Thorne. "Why didn't Fell ask for a fee or a cut?"

"Dare we trust him?" asked Bothari-Jesek.

"Not trust, exactly." Quinn ran the edge of her index finger along her white teeth, nibbling. "But we must have Fell's cooperation to exit jumppoint Five. We dare not offend him, not for any money. I thought he would be more pleased with our bite out of Bharaputra, but the strategic situation seems to have changed since your last visit here, Bel."

Thorne sighed agreement.

Quinn continued, "I want you to see what you can find out about the current balance of power here. Anything that may affect our operations, anything we can use to help. Houses Fell, Bharaputra and Ryoval, and anything coming up on the blindside. There's something about all this that's making me feel paranoid as hell, though it may be just the drugs I'm on. But I'm too damned tired to see it right now."

"I'll see what I can do." Thorne nodded and withdrew.

When the door hissed shut behind Thorne, Bothari-Jesek asked Quinn, "Have you reported all this to Barrayar yet?"

"No."

"*Any* of it?"

"No. I don't want to send this one over any commercial comm channel, not even in code. Illyan may have a few deep cover agents here, but I don't know who they are or how to access them. Miles would have known. And . . ."

"And?" Bothari-Jesek raised an eyebrow.

"And I'd really like to have the cryo-chamber back first."

"To shove under the door along with the report? Quinnie, it wouldn't fit."

Quinn shrugged one defensive shoulder.

After a moment Bothari-Jesek offered, "I agree with you about not sending anything through the Jacksonian jump-courier system, though."

"Yes, from what Illyan's said, it's riddled with spies, and not just the Great Houses checking up on each other, either. There's nothing Barrayar could do to help us in the next day-cycle anyway."

"How long," Mark swallowed, "is that how long I have to go on playing Miles?"

"I don't know!" said Quinn sharply. She gulped back control of her voice. "A day, a week, two weeks—at least till we can deliver you and the cryo-chamber to ImpSec's galactic affairs HQ on Komarr. Then it will be out of my hands."

"How the hell do you think you're going to keep all this under wraps?" Mark asked scornfully. "Dozens of people know what really happened."

" 'Two can keep a secret, if one of them is dead'?" Quinn grimaced. "I don't know. The troops will be all right, they have the discipline. The clones I can keep incommunicado. Anyway, we're all going to be bottled up on this ship till we reach Komarr. Later . . . I'll deal with it later."

"I want to see my . . . the . . . my clones. What you've done with them," Mark demanded suddenly.

Quinn looked as if she was about to explode, but Bothari-Jesek cut in, "I'll take him down, Quinnie. I want to check on my passengers too."

"Well . . . as long as you escort him back to his cabin when you're done. And put a guard on his door. We can't have him wandering around the ship."

"Will do." Bothari-Jesek chivvied him out quickly, before Quinn decided to have him bound and gagged as well.

The clones had been housed in three hastily-cleared freight storage chambers aboard the *Peregrine*, two assigned to the boys and one to the girls. Mark ducked through a door behind Bothari-Jesek into one of the boys' chambers, and looked around. Three rows of bedrolls, which must have been podded over from the *Ariel*, filled the floor space. A self-contained field latrine was strapped into one corner, and a field shower hastily connected in the other, to keep any need for the clones to move about the ship to a minimum. Half jail, half refugee camp, crowded—as he walked down a row between bedrolls the boys glowered up at him with the hollow faces of prisoners.

I freed you all, dammit. Don't you know I freed you?

It had been a rough rescue, true. During that hideous night of siege the Dendarii had been liberal with the most dire threats, to keep their charges under control. Some clones now slept, exhausted. The stunned ones were waking up sick and disoriented; a female Dendarii medic moved among them administering synergine and soothing words. Things were . . . under control. Suppressed. Silent. Not jubilant; not grateful. *If they believed our threats, why don't they believe our promises?* Even the active boys who had cooperated enthusiastically in the excitement of siege and firefight now stared at him with renewed doubt.

The blond boy was one of them. Mark stopped by his bedroll and hunkered down. Bothari-Jesek waited, watching them. "All this," Mark waved vaguely at the chamber, "is temporary, you know. It's going to get better later. We're going to get you out of here."

The boy, propped on his elbow, shrank slightly away. He chewed on his lip. "Which one are you?" he asked suspiciously.

The live one, he thought of answering, but did not dare in front of Bothari-Jesek. She might mistake it for flippancy. "It doesn't matter. We're going to get you out of here just the same." Truth or not? He had no control over the Dendarii now, still less over the Barrayarans, if indeed as Quinn threatened that was their new destination. Dreary depression washed over him as he stood and followed Bothari-Jesek into the girls' chamber across the corridor.

The physical set-up was identical, with bedrolls and sanitary facilities, though with only fifteen girls it was slightly less crowded. A Dendarii was passing out a stack of packaged meals, which lent the chamber a moment of positive activity and interest. The trooper was Sergeant Taura, unmistakable even from the back and dressed in clean gray ship-knits and friction-slippers. She sat cross-legged to reduce her intimidating height. The girls, overcoming fear, crept up to her and even touched her with apparent fascination. Of all the Dendarii Taura had never, even in the most frantic moments, addressed the clones with anything but politely-worded requests. She now had all the air of a fairy-tale heroine trying to make pets of wild animals.

And succeeding. As Mark came up, two of the clone girls actually skittered around behind the seated sergeant, to peek at him over the protection of her broad shoulders. Taura frowned at him and looked at Bothari-Jesek, who returned a short nod, *It's all right. He's with me.*

"S-surprised to see you here, Sergeant," Mark managed.

"I volunteered to baby-sit," rumbled Taura. "I didn't want anybody bothering them."

"Is . . . that likely to be a problem?" Fifteen beautiful virgins . . . well, maybe. *Sixteen, counting yourself,* came a tiny jeer from the back of his brain.

"Not now," said Bothari-Jesek firmly.

"Good," he said faintly.

He waffled up the row of mats for a moment. It was all as comfortable and secure as possible, under the circumstances, he supposed. He found the short platinum blonde clone asleep on her side, the soft masses of her body sculpture spilling out of her pink tunic. Embarrassed by his own arrested eye, he knelt and drew her cover up to her chin. His hand, half-unwilled, stole a touch of her fine hair in passing. Guiltily, he glanced up at Taura. "Has she had a dose of synergine?"

"Yes. We're letting her sleep it off. She should feel all right when she wakes up."

He took one of the sealed meal trays and set it down by the blonde's head, for when she did wake. Her breathing was slow and steady. There seemed not much else he could do for her. He looked up to catch the Eurasian girl watching him with knowing, malicious eyes, and he turned hastily away.

Bothari-Jesek completed her inspection and exited, and he followed in her trail. She paused to speak with the stunner-armed guard in the corridor.

"—wide dispersal," she was saying. "Shoot first and ask questions later. They're all young and healthy, you don't have to worry about hidden heart conditions with this lot, I don't think. But I doubt they'll give you much trouble."

"With one exception," Mark put in. "There's this dark-haired girl, slim, very striking—she appears to have undergone some special mental conditioning. Not . . . quite sane. Watch out for her."

"Yes, sir," said the trooper automatically, then caught himself, glancing at Bothari-Jesek, " . . . uh . . ."

"Sergeant Taura confirms the report on that one," said Bothari-Jesek. "Anyway, I don't want any of them loose on my ship. They're totally untrained. Their ignorance could be as dangerous as any hostility. This is not an ornamental guard post. Stay awake."

They exchanged parting salutes. The trooper, overcoming reflex, managed not to include Mark in his directed courtesy. Mark trotted after Bothari-Jesek's long stride.

"So," she said after a moment, "does our treatment of your clones meet with your approval?" He could not quite tell if her tone was ironic.

"It's as good as anyone could do for them, for now." He bit his tongue, but the too self-revealing outburst escaped it anyway. "Dammit, it's not fair!"

Bothari-Jesek's brows rose, as she paced along the corridor. "What's not fair?"

"I *saved* these kids—or we did, you did—and they act like we're some kind of villains, kidnappers, monsters. They're not happy at all."

"Perhaps . . . it will have to be enough for you just to have saved them. To demand that they be happy about it too may exceed your mandate . . . little hero." Her tone was unmistakably ironic now, though oddly devoid of scorn.

"You'd think there'd be a little gratitude. Belief. Acknowledgement. Something."

"Trust?" she said in a quiet voice.

"Yes, trust! At least from some of them. Can't any of them tell we're on the level?"

"They've been rather traumatized. I wouldn't expect too much if I were you, till they get a chance to see more evidence." She paused, in speech and stride, and swung to face him. "But if you ever figure it out—figure out how to make an ignorant, traumatized, paranoid stupid kid trust you—tell Miles. He urgently wants to know."

Mark stood, nonplused. "Was that . . . directed to me?" he demanded, dry-mouthed.

She glanced over his head, around the empty corridor, and smiled a bitter, maddening smile. "You're home." She nodded pointedly toward his cabin door. "Stay there."

✧   ✧   ✧

He slept at last, for a long time, though when Quinn came to wake him it seemed like not long enough. Mark wasn't sure if Quinn had slept at all, though she had finally cleaned up and changed back into her officer's undress grays. He'd been starting to imagine her planning to wear the bloodstained fatigues till they retrieved the cryo-chamber, as some sort of vow. Even without the fatigues she radiated an unsettling edginess, red-eyed and strained.

"Come on," she growled. "I need you to talk to Fell again. He's been giving me a run-around. I'm starting to wonder if he could be in collusion with Bharaputra. I don't understand. It doesn't add up."

She hauled him off to the tac room again, though this time she did not rely on the ear-bug, but stood aggressively at his elbow. To the outside eye, she'd ranged herself as bodyguard and chief assistant; all Mark could think of was how conveniently placed she was to grab him by the hair and slit his throat.

Captain Bothari-Jesek sat in, occupying a spare station chair as before, watching quietly. She eyed Quinn's frazzled demeanor with a look of concern, but said nothing.

When Fell's face appeared above the vid plate again, its pinkness was decidedly more irate than jolly. "Admiral Naismith, I told Captain Quinn that when I had firm information, *I* would contact *you*."

"Baron, Captain Quinn . . . serves me. Please forgive any importunity on her part. She only, ah, faithfully reflects my own anxieties." Miles's typical overflowing vocabulary filled his mouth like flour. Quinn's fingers bit into his shoulder, silent painful warning that he had better not let his invention carry him too far. "What, shall we say, less-than-firm information can you give us?"

Fell settled back, frowning but placated. "To put it bluntly, the Bharaputrans say they cannot find your cryo-chamber."

"It has to be there," hissed Quinn.

"Now, now, Quinnie." Mark patted her hand. It clamped like a vise. Her nostrils flared murderously, but she achieved a faint false smile for the holovid. Mark turned back to Fell. "Baron— in your best judgment—are the Bharaputrans lying?"

"I don't think so."

"Do you have some independent corroboration for your opinion? Agents on site, or anything of the sort?"

The Baron's lips twisted. "Really, Admiral, I cannot say."

Naturally not. He rubbed his face, a Naismith-thoughtful gesture.

"Can you say anything specific about what the Bharaputrans are doing?"

"They are in fact turning their medical complex inside out right now. All the employees, and all the security forces they brought in to contain your raid, have been engaged in the search."

"Could it be an elaborate charade, to mislead us?"

The Baron paused. "No," he said flatly at last. "They're really scrambling. On all levels. Are you aware . . ." he took a decisive breath, "of what your kidnapping of Baron Bharaputra, if it should prove more than a brief interlude, could do to the balance of power among the Great Houses of Jackson's Whole?"

"No, what?"

The Baron's chin went up, and he checked Mark sharply for signs of sarcasm. The vertical lines between his eyes deepened, but he answered seriously. "You should realize, the value of your hostage may go down with time. No power-vacuum at the top of a Great House, or even a House Minor, can last long. There are always factions of younger men waiting, perhaps in secret, to rush in and fill it. Even supposing Lotus manages to get Vasa Luigi's chief loyalist lieutenant to fill and retain his place—as time goes on, it can only dawn on him that the return of his master will involve demotion as well as reward. Think of a Great House as the hydra of mythology. Chop off its head, and seven more arise on the stump of neck—and begin biting each other. Eventually, only one will survive. In the meantime, the House is weakened, and all its old alliances and deals are thrown into doubt. The turmoil expands in a widening ring to associate Houses . . . such abrupt changes are not welcomed, here. Not by anyone." Least of all by Baron Fell himself, Mark gathered.

"Except maybe by your younger colleagues," Mark suggested.

A wave of Fell's hand dismissed the concerns of his younger colleagues. If they wanted power, the wave implied, let them plot and scramble and kill for it as he had.

"Well, I have no desire to keep Baron Bharaputra till he grows old and moldy," said Mark. "I have no personal use for him at all, out of this context. Please urge House Bharaputra to speed in finding my brother, eh?"

"They need no urging." Fell regarded him coldly. "Be aware, Admiral, if this . . . situation is not brought to a satisfactory conclusion quickly, Fell Station will not be able to harbor you."

"Uh . . . define quickly."

"Very soon. Within another day-cycle."

Fell Station surely had enough force to evict the two small Dendarii ships whenever it willed. Or worse than evict. "Understood. Uh . . . what about unimpeded passage out at jumppoint Five?" If things did not go well . . .

"That . . . you may have to deal for separately."

"Deal how?"

"If you still had your hostage . . . I would not desire that you carry Vasa Luigi out of Jacksonian local space. And I am positioned to see that you do not."

Quinn's fist slammed down beside the vid plate. "No!" she cried. "No way! Baron Bharaputra is the only card we have to get muh, get the cryo-chamber back. We will not give him up!"

Fell recoiled slightly. "Captain!" he reproved.

"We *will* take him with us if we're forced out," Quinn threatened, "and you can all hang out to dry. Or he can walk back from jumppoint Five without a pressure suit. If we don't get that cryo-chamber—well, we have better allies than you. And with fewer inhibitions. They won't care about your profits, or your deals, or your balances. The only question they'll be asking is whether to start at the north pole, and burn down, or at the south pole, and burn up!"

Fell grimaced angrily. "Don't be absurd, Captain Quinn. You speak of a planetary force."

Quinn leaned into the vid pick-up and snarled, "Baron, I speak of a *multi*-planetary force!"

Bothari-Jesek, startled, made an urgent throat-slicing gesture across her neck, *Cut it, Quinn!*

Fell's eyes went hard and bright as glass glints. "You're bluffing," he said at last.

"I am not. You'd best believe I am not!"

"No one would do all that for one man. Still less for one corpse."

Quinn hesitated. Mark's hand closed on hers upon his shoulder and squeezed hard to say, *Control yourself, dammit.* She was on the verge of giving away what she'd practically threatened him with death not to reveal. "You may be right, Baron," she said finally. "You'd better pray you're right."

After a long moment of silence, Fell inquired mildly, "And just who is this uninhibited ally of yours, Admiral?"

After an equally long pause, Mark looked up and said sweetly, "Captain Quinn was bluffing, Baron."

Fell's lips drew back on an extremely dry smile. "All Cretans are liars," he said softly. His hand moved to cut the comm; his image faded in the usual haze of sparkles. This time it was his cold smile that seemed to linger, bodiless.

"Good job, Quinn," Mark snarled into the silence. "You've just let Baron Fell know how much he could really get for that cryo-chamber. And maybe even who from. Now we have two enemies."

Quinn was breathing hard, as though she'd been running. "He's not our enemy; he's not our friend. Fell serves Fell. Remember that, 'cause he will."

"But was Fell lying, or was he merely passing on House Bhara-putra's lies?" Bothari-Jesek asked slowly. "What independent line of profit could Fell possibly have on all this?"

"Or are they both lying?" said Quinn.

"What if neither of them are?" asked Mark in irritation. "Have you thought of that? Remember what Norwood—"

A comm beeper interrupted him. Quinn leaned on her hands on the comconsole to listen.

"Quinn, this is Bel. That contact I found agrees to meet us at the *Ariel*'s docking bay. If you want to be in on the interrogation, you need to pod over now."

"Yes, right, I'll be there, Quinn out." She turned, haggard, and started for the door. "Elena, see that *he*," a jerk of her thumb, "is confined to quarters."

"Yeah, well, after you talk with whatever Bel dragged in, get yourself some rest, huh, Quinnie? You're unstrung. You almost lost it back there."

Quinn's ambiguous parting wave acknowledged the truth of this, without making any promises. As Quinn exited, Bothari-Jesek turned to her station console, to order up a personnel pod to be ready for Quinn by the time she arrived at the hatch.

Mark rose and wandered around the tactics room, his hands thrust carefully into his pockets. A dozen real-time and holo-schematic display consoles sat dark and still; communication and encoding systems lay silent. He pictured the tactics nerve center fully staffed, alive and bright and chaotic, heading into battle. He imagined enemy fire peeling the ship open like a meal tray, all that life smashed and burned and spilled into the hard radiation and vacuum of space. Fire from House Fell's station at jumppoint Five, say, as the *Peregrine* fought for escape. He shuddered, nauseated.

He paused before the sealed door to the briefing chamber. Bothari-Jesek was now engaged in some other communication, some decision having to do with the security of their Fell Station moorings. Curious, he laid his palm upon the lock-pad. Somewhat to his surprise, the door slid demurely open. Somebody had some re-programming to do, if all top-secured Dendarii facilities were keyed to admit a dead man's palm print. A lot of reprogramming—Miles doubtless had it fixed so he could just waft right through anywhere in the fleet. That would be his style.

Bothari-Jesek glanced up, but said nothing. Taking that as tacit permission, Mark walked into the briefing room and circled the table. Lights came up for him as he paced. Thorne's words, spoken here, echoed in his head. *Norwood said, The Admiral will get out of here even if we don't.* How carefully had the Dendarii examined their recordings of the drop mission? Surely someone had been over them all several times by now. What could he possibly see that they hadn't? They knew their people, their equipment. *But I know the medical complex. I know Jackson's Whole.*

He wondered how far his palm would take him. He slipped into Quinn's station chair; sure enough, files bloomed for him, opened at his touch as no woman ever had. He found the downloaded records of the drop mission. Norwood's data was lost, but Tonkin had been with him part of the time. What had Tonkin seen? Not colored lines on the map, but real-time, real-eye, real-ear? Was there such a record? The command helmet had kept such, he knew, if trooper-helmets did too then—ah, ha. Tonkin's visuals and audio came up on the console before his fascinated eyes.

Trying to follow them gave him an almost instant headache. This was no ballasted and gimballed vid pick-up, no steady pan, but rather the jerky, snatching glances of real head movements. He slowed the replay to watch himself in the lift-tube foyer, a short, agitated fellow in gray camouflage, glittering eyes in a set face. *Do I really look like that?* The deformities of his body were not so apparent as he'd imagined, under the loose uniform.

He sat behind Tonkin's eyes and walked with him through the hurried maze of Bharaputra's buildings, tunnels, and corridors, all the way to the last firefight at the end. Thorne had quoted Norwood correctly; it was right there on the vid. Though he'd been wrong on the time; Norwood was gone eleven minutes by the helmet's unsubjective clock. Norwood's flushed face reappeared, panting, the urgent laugh sounded—and, moments later, the grenade-strike, the explosion—almost ducking, Mark hastily shut off the vid, and glanced down at himself as if half-expecting to be branded with another mortal splattering of blood and brains.

If there's any clue, it has to be earlier. He started the program again from the parting in the foyer. The third time through, he slowed it down and took it step by step, examining each. The patient, finicky, self-forgetful absorption was almost pleasurable. Tiny details—you could lose yourself in tiny details, an anesthetic for brain-pain.

"*Got you*," he whispered. It had flashed past so fast as to be subliminal, if you were running the vid in real-time. The briefest glimpse of a sign on the wall, an arrow on a cross-corridor labeled *Shipping and Receiving.*

He looked up to find Bothari-Jesek watching him. How long had she been sitting there? She slumped relaxed, long legs crossed at booted ankles, long fingers tented together. "What have you got?" she asked quietly.

He called up the holomap of the ghostly buildings with Norwood and Tonkin's line of march glowing inside. "Not here," he pointed, "but *there.*" He marked a complex well off-sides from the route the Dendarii had traveled with the cryo-chamber. "*That's* where Norwood went. Through that tunnel. I'm sure of it! I've seen that facility—been all over that building. Hell, I used to play hide and seek in it with my friends, till the babysitters made us stop. I can see it in my head as surely as if I had Norwood's helmet vid playing right here on the table. He took that cryo-chamber down to Shipping and Receiving, and he *shipped* it!"

Bothari-Jesek sat up. "Is that possible? He had so little time!"

"Not just possible. Easy! The packing equipment is fully automated. All he had to do was put the cryo-chamber in the casing machine and hit the keypad. The robots would even have delivered it to the loading dock. It's a busy place—receives supplies for the whole complex, ships everything from data disks to frozen body parts for transplants to genetically engineered fetuses to emergency equipment for search and rescue teams. Such as reconditioned cryo-chambers. All sorts of stuff! It operates around the clock, and it would have had to be evacuated in a hurry when our raid hit. While the packing equipment was running, Norwood could have been generating the shipping label on the computer. Slapped 'em together, gave it to the transport robot—and then, if he was as smart as I think, erased the file record. Then he ran like hell back to Tonkin."

"So the cryo-chamber is sitting packed on a loading dock downside! Wait'll I tell Quinn! I suppose we'd better tell the Bharaputrans where to look—"

"I . . ." He held up a restraining hand. "I think . . ."

She looked at him and sank back into the station chair, eyes narrowing. "Think what?"

"It's been almost a full day since we lifted. It's been a half-day and more since we told the Bharaputrans to look for the cryo-chamber. If that cryo-chamber was still sitting on a loading dock, I think the Bharaputrans would have found it by now. The automated shipping system is *efficient*. I think the cryo-chamber already went out, maybe within the first hour. I think the Bharaputrans and Fell are telling the truth. They must be going insane right now. Not only is there no cryo-chamber down there, they haven't got a clue in hell where it went!"

Bothari-Jesek sat stiff. "Do we?" she asked. "My God. If you're right—it could be on its way *anywhere*. Freighted out from any of two dozen orbital transfer stations—it could have been *jumped* by now! Simon Illyan is going to have a stroke when we report this."

"No. Not anywhere," Mark corrected intently. "It could only have been addressed to somewhere that Medic Norwood knew. Someplace he could remember, even when he was surrounded and cut off and under fire."

She licked her lips, considering this. "Right," she said at last. "Almost anywhere. But at least we can start guessing by studying Norwood's personnel files." She sat back and looked up at him with grave eyes. "You know, you do all right, alone in a quiet room. You're not stupid. I didn't see how you could be. You're just not the field-officer type."

"I'm not any kind of officer-type. I hate the military."

"Miles loves field work. He's addicted to adrenaline rushes."

"I hate them. I hate being afraid. I can't think when I'm scared. I freeze when people shout at me."

"Yet you *can* think. . . . How much of the time are you scared?"

"Most of it," he admitted grimly.

"Then why do you . . ." she hesitated, as if choosing her words very cautiously, "why do you keep trying to be Miles?"

"I'm not, you're making me play him!"

"I didn't mean now. I mean generally."

"I don't know what the hell you mean."

CHAPTER TEN

Twenty hours later, the two Dendarii ships undocked from Fell Station and manuevered to boost toward jumppoint Five. They were not alone. An escort of half a dozen House Fell security vessels paced and policed them. The Fell vessels were dedicated local space warships, lacking Necklin rods and wormhole jump capacity; the power thus saved was shunted into a formidible array of weapons and shielding. Muscle-ships.

The convoy was trailed at a discreet distance by a Bharaputran cruiser, more yacht than warship, prepared to accept the final transfer of Baron Bharaputra, as arranged, in space near Fell's jumppoint Five station. Unfortunately, Miles's cryo-chamber was not aboard it.

Quinn had come close to a breakdown, before accepting the inevitable. Bothari-Jesek had literally backed her against the wall, at their last private conference in the briefing room.

"I won't leave Miles!" Quinn howled. "I'll space that Bharaputran bastard first!"

"Look," Bothari-Jesek hissed, Quinn's jacket bunched in her fist. If she'd been an animal, Mark thought, her ears would have been flat to her head. He huddled in a station chair and tried to make himself small. Smaller. "I don't like this any better than you do, but the situation has gone way beyond our capacity. Miles is clearly out of Bharaputran hands, heading God knows where. We need reinforcements: not warships, but trained intelligence agents. A pile of 'em. We need Illyan, and ImpSec, we need them bad, and we

442

need them as fast as possible. It's time to cut and run. The faster we get out of here, the faster we can return."

"I *will* be back," Quinn swore.

"That'll be between you and Simon Illyan. I promise you, he'll be just as interested as we are in retrieving that cryo-chamber."

"Illyan's just a Barrayaran," Quinn sputtered for a word, "*bureaucrat*. He can't care the way we do."

"Don't bet on that," whispered Bothari-Jesek.

In the end, Bothari-Jesek, Quinn's downward duty to the rest of the Dendarii, and the logic of the situation had prevailed. And so Mark found himself dressing in officer's grays for what he earnestly prayed would be his last public appearance ever as Admiral Miles Naismith, observing the transfer of their hostage onto a House Fell shuttle. Whatever happened to Vasa Luigi after that would be up to Baron Fell. Mark could only hope it would be something unpleasant.

Bothari-Jesek came to escort Mark personally from his cabin-prison to the shuttle hatch corridor where the Fell ship was scheduled to clamp on. She looked cool as ever, if weary, and unlike Quinn she limited her critique of the fit of his uniform to a pass of her hand to straighten his collar insignia. The pocketed jacket was roomy, and came down far enough to cover and so disguise the tight bite of the trouser waistband, and the way his flesh was beginning to burgeon over the belt. He yanked the jacket down firmly, and followed the *Peregrine*'s captain through her ship.

"Why do I have to do this?" he asked her plaintively.

"It's our last chance to prove—for certain—to Vasa Luigi that you are Miles Naismith, and that . . . thing in the cryo-chamber is just a clone. Just in case the cryo-chamber didn't go off-planet, and just in case, by whatever chance, wherever it went, Bharaputra finds it again before we do."

They arrived at the shuttle hatch corridor at the same time as a couple of heavily-armed Dendarii techs, who took up station at the docking clamp controls. Baron Bharaputra appeared shortly thereafter, escorted by a wary Captain Quinn and two edgy Dendarii guards. The guards, Mark decided, were mainly ornamental. The real power, and the real threat, the heavy pieces on this chessboard, were jumppoint Station Five and the House Fell ships that supported it. He pictured them, arrayed in space around the Dendarii ships. Check. Was Baron Bharaputra king? Mark felt like a pawn masquerading as a knight. Vasa Luigi ignored the guards, kept half an eye on Quinn the Red Queen, but mostly watched the shuttle hatch.

Quinn saluted Mark. "Admiral."

He returned the salute. "Captain." He stood at parade rest, as if overseeing his operation. Was he supposed to bandy words with the Baron? He waited for Vasa Luigi to open the conversation. The Baron merely waited, with a disturbingly controlled patience, as if he did not even perceive time the same way Mark did.

Regardless of how outgunned they were, the Dendarii were only minutes from escape. As soon as the transfer was complete, the *Peregrine* and the *Ariel* could jump, and the clones would be beyond House Bharaputra's lethal reach. That much he had accomplished, ass-backwards and screwed up beyond repair, but done. Small victories.

At last came the clanking of the shuttle hatch clamps grasping and positioning their prey, and the hiss of the flex-tube sealing. The Dendarii oversaw the dilation of the hatch portal and stood to attention. On the other side of the portal a man dressed in House Fell green with captain's insignia, and flanked by two ornamental guards of his own, nodded sharply and identified himself and his vessel of origin.

He spotted Mark as the highest ranking officer present, and saluted. "Baron Fell's compliments, Admiral Naismith sir, and he is returning to you something you accidentally left behind."

Quinn went pale with hope; Mark could swear her heart stopped beating. The Fell captain stepped back from the hatch. But through it swung not the ardently-desired cryo-chamber on a float pallet, but a file of three men and two women, civilian-clothed, looking variously sheepish, angry, and grim. One man was limping, and supported by another.

Quinn's spies. The group of Dendarii volunteers she had attempted to slip onto Fell Station to continue the search. Quinn's face flushed red with chagrin. But she raised her chin and said clearly, "Tell Baron Fell we thank him for his care."

The Fell captain acknowledged the message with a salute and a sour smirk.

"Meet you all in debriefing, soonest," she breathed, and dismissed the unhappy mob with a nod. They clattered off. Bothari-Jesek went with them.

The Fell captain announced, "We are ready to board our passenger." Punctiliously, he did not set foot aboard the *Peregrine*, but waited. Equally punctiliously, the Dendarii guards and Quinn stood away from Baron Bharaputra, who raised his square chin and began to stride forward.

"My lord! Wait for me!"

The high cry from behind them made Mark's head snap around. The Baron's eyes too widened in surprise.

The Eurasian girl, her hair swinging, slipped out of a cross-corridor and ran forward. She held hands with the platinum blonde clone. She darted like an eel around the Dendarii guards, who had better sense than to draw weapons in this dicey moment, but not quite enough speed of reflex to catch her. The small-footed blonde was not so athletic, half out-of-balance with her other arm crossed under her breasts, and she was pulled along gasping for breath, blue eyes wide with fear.

Mark saw her, in his mind's eye, laid out on some operating table, light-crowned scalp peeled carefully back—the whine of a surgical saw cutting through bone, the slow teasing apart of living neurons in the brain stem, then at last the lifting-out of brain, like a gift, mind, memory, person, an offering to some dark god in the masked monster's gloved hands—

He tackled her around the knees. Her fine-boned hand jerked out of the dark-haired girl's grip, and she fell forward on the deck. She cried out, then just cried, and kicked at him, rocking and bucking and twisting onto her back. Terrified he would lose his clutch, he worked upward till he lay across her with his full weight. She squirmed beneath him, ineffectually; she didn't even know enough to try to knee him in the groin. "Stop. Stop, for God's sake, I don't want to hurt you," he mumbled in her ear around a mouthful of sweet-smelling hair.

The other girl meanwhile had succeeded in diving through the shuttle hatch. The House Fell guard captain was confused by her arrival, but not by the Dendarii; he'd drawn a nerve disruptor instantly, repelling the first reflexive lurch of Quinn's men. "Stop right there. Baron Bharaputra, what is this?"

"My lord!" the Eurasian girl cried. "Take me with you, please! I will be united with my lady. I will!"

"Stay on that side," the Baron advised her calmly. "They cannot touch you there."

"You try me—" began Quinn, starting forward, but the Baron raised a hand, fingers delicately crooked, neither fist nor obscenity yet somehow faintly insulting.

"Captain Quinn. Surely you do not wish to create an incident and delay your departure, do you? Clearly, this girl chooses of her own free will."

Quinn hesitated.

"No!" screamed Mark. He scrambled to his feet, hauled the blonde girl up, and jammed her into the grip of the biggest Dendarii guard. "*Hold* her." He wheeled to pass Baron Bharaputra.

"Admiral?" The Baron raised a faintly ironic brow.

"You're wearing a corpse," Mark snarled. "Don't talk to me." He staggered forward, hands out, to face the dark-haired girl across that little, dreadful, politically significant gap. "Girl . . ." He did not know her name. He did not know what to say. "Don't go. You don't have to go. They'll kill you."

Growing more certain of her security, though still positioned behind the Fell captain and well out of reach of any Dendarii lunge, she smiled triumphantly at Mark and tossed back her hair. Her eyes were alight. "I've saved my honor. All by myself. My honor is my lady. *You* have no honor. Pig! My life is an offering . . . greater than you can imagine being. I am a flower on her altar."

"You are frigging crazy, Flowerpot," Quinn opined bluntly.

Her chin rose, and her lips thinned. "Baron, come," she ordered coolly. She held out a theatric hand.

Baron Bharaputra shrugged as if to say, *What would you?*, and walked toward the hatch. No Dendarii raised a weapon; Quinn had not ordered them to. Mark had no weapon. He turned to her, anguished. "*Quinn . . .*"

She was breathing hard. "If we don't jump now, we could lose it all. *Stand still.*"

Vasa Luigi paused in the hatchway, hand on the seal, one foot still on the *Peregrine*'s deck, and turned back to face Mark. "In case you are wondering, Admiral—she is my wife's clone," he purred. He raised his right hand, licked his index finger, and touched it to Mark's forehead. It left a cool spot. Counting coup. "One for me. Forty-nine for you. If you ever dare to return here, I promise you I'll even up that score in ways that will make your death something you'll beg for." He slipped the rest of the way through the shuttle hatch. "Hello, Captain, thank you for your patience . . ." The hatch seals closed on the rest of his greeting to his rival's, or ally's, guards.

The silence was broken only by the releasing clank of the clamps and the blonde clone's hopeless, abandoned weeping. The spot on Mark's forehead itched like ice. He rubbed at it with the back of his hand as if half-expecting it to shatter.

Friction-slippered footsteps were nearly silent, but these were heavy enough to vibrate the deck. Sergeant Taura pelted into the shuttle hatch corridor. She saw the blonde clone and yelled over her shoulder, "Here's another one! Just two to go." Another trooper came panting in her wake.

"What happened, Taura?" sighed Quinn.

"That girl, that ringleader. The really smart one," said Taura, skidding to a halt. Her eyes checked the cross-corridors as she spoke. "She told all the girls some bullshit story about how we were a slave ship. She persuaded ten of them to try for a break-out at once. Stunner guard got three, the other seven scattered. We've recaptured four. Mostly just hiding, but I think that long-haired girl actually had a coherent plan to try to get to the personnel pods before we jumped from local space. I've put a guard on them to cut her off."

Quinn swore, bleakly. "Good thinking, Sergeant. Your cut-off must have succeeded, because she came up here. Unfortunately, she ran smack into Baron Bharaputra's exchange. She got out with him. We were able to grab the other one before she made it across." Quinn nodded at the blonde, whose weeping had choked down to snivels. "So you're only looking for one more."

"How did—" the sergeant's eyes flicked over the shuttle hatch corridor, puzzled. "How did you let that happen, ma'am?"

Quinn's face was set in an expressionless mask. "I chose not to start a fire-fight over her."

The sergeant's big clawed hands twitched in bewilderment, but no verbal criticism of her superior escaped those outslung lips. "We'd better find the last one, then, before something worse happens."

"Carry on, Sergeant. You four, help her." Quinn gestured to her now-unemployed guards. "Report to me in the briefing room when you have them all re-secured, Taura."

Taura nodded, motioned the troopers down the various cross-corridors, and herself loped toward the nearest lift tube. Her nostrils flared; she seemed to be almost sniffing for her quarry.

Quinn turned on her heel, muttering, "I've got to get to the debriefing. Find out what happened to—"

"I'll . . . take her back to the clone quarters, Quinn," Mark volunteered, with a nod at the blonde.

Quinn looked doubtfully at him.

"Please. I want to."

She glanced at the hatch where the Eurasian girl had gone, and back at his face. He didn't know what his face looked like, but she inhaled. "You know, I've been over the drop records a couple of times, since we left Fell Station. I hadn't . . . had a chance to tell you. Did you realize, when you stepped in front of me when we were scrambling to board Kimura's drop shuttle, just what your plasma mirror field power was down to?"

"No. I mean, I knew I'd taken a lot of hits, in the tunnels."

"One hit. If it had absorbed one more hit, it would have failed. Two more hits and you'd have fried."

"Oh."

She frowned at him, as if still trying to decide whether to credit him with courage or simply with stupidity. "Well. I thought it was interesting. Something you'd want to know." She hesitated longer. "My power pack was down to zero. So if you're really comparing scores with Baron Bharaputra, you can raise yours back to fifty."

He didn't know what she expected him to say. At last Quinn sighed, "All right. You can escort her. If it'll make you feel better." She strode off toward the debriefing, her own face very anxious.

He turned and took the blonde by the arm, very gently; she flinched, blinking through big tear-sheened blue eyes. Even though he knew very well—none better—how intentionally her features and body were sculptured and designed, the effect was still overwhelming: beauty and innocence, sexuality and fear mixed in an intoxicating draught. She looked a ripe twenty, at fresh physical peak, a perfect match to his own age. And only a few centimeters taller than himself. She might have been designed to be the heroine in his drama, except that his life had dissolved into some sub-heroic puddle, chaotic and beyond control. No rewards, only more punishments.

"What's your name?" he asked with false brightness.

She looked at him suspiciously. "Maree."

Clones had no surnames. "That's pretty. Come on, Maree. I'll take you back to your, uh, dormitory. You'll feel better, when you're back with your friends."

She perforce began to walk with him.

"Sergeant Taura is all right, you know. She really wants to take care of you. You just scared her, running off like that. She was worried you'd get hurt. You're not really afraid of the sergeant, are you?"

Her lovely lips pressed closed in confusion. "I'm . . . not sure." Her walk was a dainty, swaying thing, though her steps made her breasts wobble most distractingly, half-bagged in the pink tunic. She ought to be offered reduction treatment, though he was not sure such was in the *Peregrine's* ship's surgeon's range of expertise. And if her somatic experiences at Bharaputra's were anything like his had been, she was probably sick of surgery right now. He certainly had been, after all the bodily distortions they'd laid on him.

"We're not a slave ship," he began again earnestly. "We're taking you—" The news that their destination was the Barrayaran Empire might not be so reassuring, at that. "Our first stop will probably be Komarr. But you might not have to stay there." He had no power to make promises about her ultimate destination. None. One prisoner could not rescue another.

She coughed and rubbed her eyes.

"Are you . . . all right?"

"I want a drink of water." Her voice was hoarse from the running and the crying.

"I'll get you one," he promised. His own cabin was just a corridor away; he led her there.

The door hissed open at the touch of his palm upon the pad. "Come in. I never had a chance to talk with you. Maybe if I had . . . that girl wouldn't have fooled you." He guided her within and settled her on the bed. She was trembling slightly. So was he. "Did she fool you?"

"I . . . don't know, Admiral."

He snorted bitterly. "I'm not the Admiral. I'm a clone, like you. I was raised at Bharaputra's, one floor down from where you live. Lived." He went to his washroom, drew a cup of water, and carried it to her. He had half an impulse to offer it to her on his knees. She had to be made to—"I have to make you understand. Understand who you are, what's happened to you. So you won't be fooled again. You have a lot to learn, for your own protection." Indeed—in *that* body. "You'll have to go to school."

She swallowed water. "Don't want to go to school," she said, muffled into the cup.

"Didn't the Bharaputrans ever let you into the virtual learning programs? When I was there, it was the best part. Better even than the games. Though I liked the games, of course. Did you play Zylec?"

She nodded.

"That was fun. But the history, the astrography shows—the virtual instructor was the funniest program. A white-haired old geezer in twentieth-century clothes, this jacket with patches on the elbows—I always wondered if he was based on a real person, or was a composite."

"I never saw them."

"What did you do all day?"

"We talked among ourselves. We did our hair. Swam. The proctors made us do calesthenics every day—"

"Us, too."

"—till they did this to me." She touched a breast. "Then they only made me swim."

He could see the logic of that. "Your last body-sculpture was pretty recent, I take it."

"About a month ago." She paused. "You really don't . . . think my mother was coming for me?"

"I'm sorry. You don't have a mother. Neither do I. What was coming for you . . . was a horror. Almost beyond imagining." Except he could imagine it all too vividly.

She frowned at him, obviously reluctant to part with her beloved dream-future. "We're all beautiful. If you're really a clone, why aren't you?"

"I'm glad to see you're beginning to think," he said carefully. "My body was sculpted to match my progenitor's. He was crippled."

"But if it's true—about the brain transplants—why not you?"

"I was . . . part of another plot. My purchasers took me away whole. It was only later that I learned all the truth, for sure, about Bharaputra's." He sat beside her on the bed. The smell of her—had they genetically engineered some subtle perfume into her skin? It was intoxicating. The memory of her soft body, squirming under his on the hatch corridor deck, perturbed him. He could have dissolved into it. . . . "I had friends—don't you?"

She nodded mutely.

"By the time I could do anything for them—long before I could do anything for them—they were gone. All killed. So I rescued you instead."

She stared doubtfully at him. He could not tell what she was thinking.

The cabin wavered, and a flash of nausea that had nothing to do with suppressed eroticism twisted his stomach.

"What was that?" Maree gasped, her eyes widening. Unconsciously, she grasped his hand. His hand burned at her touch.

"It's all right. It's more than all right. That was your first wormhole jump." From his vantage of, well, several wormhole jumps, he made his tone heartily reassuring. "We're away. The Jacksonians can't get us now." *Much* better than the double-cross he'd been half-anticipating, in some reserved part of his mind, from Baron Fell's forces the moment he had Vasa Luigi hostage in his own fat hands. Not the roar and rock of enemy fire. Just a nice little tame jump. "You're safe. We're all safe now." He thought of the mad Eurasian girl. *Almost all.*

He so wanted Maree to believe. The Dendarii, the Barrayarans—he'd scarcely expected them to understand. But this girl—if only he could shine in her eyes. He wanted no reward but a kiss. He swallowed. *You sure it's only a kiss you want?* There was an uncomfortable hot knot growing in his belly, beneath that ghastly constricted waistband. An embarrassing stiffening in his loins. Maybe she wouldn't notice. Understand. Judge.

"Will you . . . kiss me?" he asked humbly, very dry-mouthed. He took the cup from her, and tossed back the last trickle of water. It was not enough to unlock the tension in his throat.

"Why?" she asked, brow wrinkling.

"For . . . pretend."

That was an appeal she understood. She blinked, but, willingly enough, leaned forward and touched her lips to his. Her tunic shifted. . . .

"Oh," he breathed. His hand went round her neck, and stopped its retreat. "Please, again . . ." He drew her face to his. She neither resisted nor responded, but her mouth was amazing nonetheless. *I want, I want . . .* It couldn't hurt to touch her, just to touch her. Her hands went around his neck, automatically. He could feel each cool finger, tipped by a tiny bite of nail. Her lips parted. He melted. His head was pounding. Hot, he shrugged off his jacket.

Stop. Stop now, dammit. But she *should* have been his heroine. Miles had a damned harem full of them, he was certain. Might she let him . . . do more than kiss her? Not penetration, definitely not. Nothing to hurt her, nothing invasive. A rub between those vast breasts could not hurt her, though it would doubtless bewilder her. He might bury himself in that soft flesh and find release as effectively, more effectively, than between her thighs. She might think he was crazy, but it wouldn't hurt her. His mouth sought hers again, hungrily. He touched her skin. *More.* He slipped her tunic down off her shoulders, freeing her body to his starving hand. Her skin was velvet soft. His other hand, shaking, dove to release the strangling-tight waistband of his trousers. That was a relief.

He was dreadfully, excruciatingly aroused. But he would not touch her below the waist, no. . . .

He rolled her backwards on the bed, pinning her, kissing frantically down her body. She emitted a startled gasp. His breath deepened, then, suddenly, stopped. A spasm reached deep into his lungs, as if all his bronchia had constricted at once with a snap like a trap closing.

No! Not again! It was happening again, just like the time he'd tried last year—

He rolled off her, icy sweat breaking out all over his body. He fought his locked throat. He managed one asthmatic, shuddering, indrawn breath. The flashbacks of memory were almost hallucinatory in their clarity.

Galen's angry shouting. Lars and Mok, pinning him at Galen's command, pulling off his clothes, as if the beating he'd just taken at their hands was not punishment enough. They'd sent the girl away before they'd started; she'd run like a rabbit. He spat salt-and-iron blood. The shock-stick pointing, touching, there, *there,* pop and crackle. Galen going even more red-faced, accusing him of treason, worse, raving on about Aral Vorkosigan's alleged sexual proclivities, turning up the power far too high. "Flip him." Knotting terror deep in his gut, the visceral memory of pain, humiliation, burning and cramps, a weird short-circuited arousal and horribly shameful release despite it all, the stink of searing flesh. . . .

He pushed back the visions, and almost passed out before he managed to inhale and exhale one more time. Somehow he was sitting not on the bed but on the floor beside it, arms and legs spasmodically drawn up. The astonished blonde girl crouched half-naked on the rumpled mattress, staring down at him. "What's the matter with you? Why did you stop? Are you dying?"

No, just wishing I were. It wasn't *fair.* He knew exactly where this conditioned reflex came from. It wasn't a memory buried in his subconscious, more's the pity, nor from some distant, blurred childhood. It was barely four years ago. Wasn't that sort of clear insight supposed to free one from such demons of the past? Was he going to go into self-induced spasms every time he tried to have sex with a real girl? Or was it just the extreme tension of the occasion? If ever the situation was less tense, less conscience-thwarted, if ever he really had time to make love instead of a hasty, sweaty scramble, then maybe he might overcome memory and madness—*or maybe I won't* . . . he fought for another shuddering inhalation. Another. His lungs began to work again. Was he really in danger of choking to death? Presumably once he actually passed out his autonomic nervous system would take over again.

His cabin door slid open. Taura and Bothari-Jesek stood silhouetted in the aperture, peering into the dimness. What they saw made Bothari-Jesek swear, and Sergeant Taura shoulder forward.

Now, he wanted to pass out *now*. But his single-minded demon did not cooperate. He continued to breathe, curled up with his trousers around his knees.

"What are you doing?" Sergeant Taura growled. A dangerous, truly wolflike timbre; her fangs gleamed at the corners of her mouth in the soft light. He'd seen her tear men's throats out with one hand.

The little clone sat up on her knees on the bed, looking terribly worried, her hands as usual trying to cover and support her most notable features, as usual only drawing more attention to them. "I only asked for a drink of water," she whimpered. "I'm sorry."

Sergeant Taura hastily dropped her eight-foot height to one knee and turned out her palms, to indicate to the girl that she wasn't angry with *her*. Mark wasn't sure if Maree caught that subtlety.

"Then what happened?" Bothari-Jesek asked sternly.

"He made me kiss him."

Bothari-Jesek's eye raked his huddled disarray and glinted furiously. She was stiff and tense as a drawn bow. She wheeled to face him. Her voice went very low. "Did you just try to rape her?"

"No! I don't know. I only—"

Sergeant Taura rose, grasped him by the shirt and some skin, pulled him to his feet and beyond, and pinned him against the nearest wall. The floor was a meter beyond his stretching toes. "Answer straight, damn you," the sergeant snarled.

He closed his eyes, and took a deep breath. Not for any threat from Miles's women, no. Not for them. But for the second half of Galen's humiliation of him, in its own way a more excruciating rape than the first. When Lars and Mok, alarmed, had finally persuaded Galen to stop, Mark had been in shock so deep as to be skirting cardiac arrest. Galen had been forced to take his valuable clone to his pet physician in the middle of the night, the one he'd somehow strong-armed into supplying him with the drugs and hormones to keep Mark's body growth on track, matching Miles's. Galen had explained the burns by telling the physician that Mark had been secretly masturbating with the shock-stick, accidentally powered it up, and been unable to turn it off for the muscle spasms it caused, till his screams brought help. The doctor had actually barked a shocked laugh. Thin-voiced, Mark had concurred, too afraid to gainsay Galen even when he was alone with the physician. Yet the doctor saw his bruises, must have known there was more to the story. But said nothing. Did nothing. It was his own weak concurrence that he regretted most, in hindsight, the black laugh that burned the deepest. He could not, would not, let Maree exit bearing any such burden of proof.

In short, blunt phrases, he described exactly what he had just tried to do. It all came out sounding terribly ugly, though it had been her beauty that had overwhelmed him. He kept his eyes shut. He did not mention his panic attack, or try to explain Galen. He writhed inside, but spoke flat truth. Slowly, as he spoke, the wall bumped up his spine till his feet were on the deck again. The pressure on his shirt released, and he dared to open his eyes.

He almost closed them again, scorched by the open contempt in Bothari-Jesek's face. He'd done it now. She who had been almost sympathetic, almost kind, almost his only friend here, stood rigidly enraged, and he knew he had alienated the one person who might have spoken for him. It hurt, a killing hurt, to have so little and then lose it.

"When Taura reported she was one clone short," Bothari-Jesek bit out, "Quinn said you'd insisted on taking her. Now we know why."

"*No.* I didn't intend . . . anything. She really only wanted a drink of water." He pointed to the cup, lying on its side on the deck.

Taura turned her back on him, and knelt on one knee by the bed, and addressed the blonde in a deliberately gentle voice. "Are you hurt?"

"I'm all right," she quavered. She pulled her tunic back up over her shoulders with a shrug. "But that man was real sick." She stared at him in puzzled concern.

"Obviously," muttered Bothari-Jesek. Her chin went up, and her eyes nailed Mark, still clinging to the wall. "You're confined to quarters, mister. I'm putting the guard back on your door. Don't even try to come out."

I won't, I won't.

They marched Maree away. The door seals hissed closed like a falling guillotine blade. He rolled onto his narrow bed, shaking.

Two weeks to Komarr. He very seriously wished he were dead.

CHAPTER ELEVEN

Mark spent the first three days of his solitary confinement lying in a depressed huddle. He had meant his heroic mission to save lives, not destroy them. He added up the body count, one by one. The shuttle pilot. Phillipi. Norwood. Kimura's trooper. And the eight seriously wounded. All those people hadn't had names, back when he had first been planning this. And all the anonymous Bharaputrans, too. The average Jacksonian security guard was just a joe scrambling for a living. He wondered bleakly if any of the dead Bharaputrans were people he had once met or joked with when he'd lived in the clone crèche. As ever, the little people were ground up like meat, while those with enough power to really be held responsible escaped, walking out free like Baron Bharaputra.

Did the lives of forty-nine clones outweigh four dead Dendarii? The Dendarii did not seem to think so. *Those people were not volunteers. You tricked them to their deaths.*

He was shaken by an unwelcome insight. Lives did not add as integers. They added as infinities.

I didn't mean it to come out this way.

And the clones. The blonde girl. He of all men knew she was not the mature woman her general physique and particular augmentations so stunningly advertised her as being. The sixty-year-old brain that had been planning to move in doubtless would have known how to handle such a body. But Mark had seen her so clearly, in his mind, that ten-year-old on the inside. He hadn't wanted to hurt or frighten her, yet he'd managed to do both. He'd

455

wanted to please her, make her face light. *The way they all lit up for Miles?*, the internal voice mocked.

None of the clones could possibly respond as he so ached to have them do. He must let that fantasy go. Ten years from now, twenty years from now, they might thank him for their lives. Or not. *I did all I could. I'm sorry.*

Somewhere around the second day he became obsessed with the thought of himself as brain-transplant bait for Miles. Oddly enough, or perhaps logically enough, he did not fear it from Miles. But Miles was hardly in a position to veto the plan. What if it occurred to someone that it would be easier to transplant Miles's brain into Mark's warm and living body than to attempt the tedious repair of that gaping mortal chest wound, and all the cryo-trauma on top of it? It was so frightening a possibility that he half-wanted to volunteer, just to get it over with.

The only thing that kept him from total gibbering breakdown was the reflection that with the cryo-chamber lost, the threat was moot. Until it was found again. In the dark of his cabin, his head buried in his pillow, it came to him that the face he'd most desired to see transformed with respect for him by his daring clone-rescue was Miles's.

You've rather eliminated that possibility, haven't you?

The only surcease from his mental treadmill came with food, and sleep. Forcing down an entire field-ration tray left him blood-stunned enough to actually doze, in inadequate snatches. Desiring unconsciousness above all things, he cajoled the glowering Dendarii who shoved the trays through his door three times a day to bring him extras. Since the Dendarii apparently did not regard their disposable-container field rations as treats, they were willing enough to do so.

Another Dendarii brought, and shoved through the door, a selection of Miles's clean clothing from the stores on the *Ariel*. This time all the insignia were carefully removed. On the third day he gave up even attempting to fasten Naismith's uniform trousers, and switched to loose ship knits. At this point the inspiration struck him.

They can't make me play Miles if I don't look like Miles.

After that, things grew a little foggy, in his head. One of the Dendarii became so irritated by his repeated requests for extra rations that he lugged in a whole case, dumped it in a corner, and told Mark roughly not to pester him again. Mark was left alone with his self-rescue and cunning calculation. He had heard of prisoners tunneling out of their cells with a spoon; might not he?

Still, loony as it was, and on some level he knew that it was, it gave his life a focus. From too much time, endless hours on the multi-jump boost through to Komarr, suddenly there seemed to be not enough. He read the nutrition labels. If he maintained maximum inactivity, a single tray provided all the daily fuel he required. Everything he consumed after that must be converted directly into Not-Miles. Every four trays ought to produce a kilo of extra body mass, if he had the numbers right. Too bad they were all the same menu. . . .

There were scarcely enough days to make the project work. Still, on his body, any extra kilos had no place to hide. Toward the end, panicked at the thought of time running out, he ate continuously, till the sheer gasping pain forced him to stop, thus combining pleasure, rebellion, and punishment into one weirdly satisfying experience.

Quinn entered without knocking, flipping up the lights with brutal efficiency from pitch-dark to full illumination.

"Agh." Mark recoiled, and held his hands over his eyes. Ripped from his uncomfortable doze, he rolled over in bed. He blinked at the chrono on the wall. Quinn had come for him a half day-cycle earlier than he'd expected. The Dendarii ships must have been putting on maximum accelerations, if this meant they were about to arrive in Komarr orbit. *Oh, help.*

"Get up," said Quinn. She wrinkled her nose. "Get washed. Put on this uniform." She laid something forest-green with gold gleams across the foot of the bed. From her general air he'd have expected her to fling things; from the reverent care she bestowed, Mark deduced the uniform must be one of Miles's.

"I'll get up," said Mark. "And I'll get washed. But I won't put on the uniform, or any uniform."

"You'll do as you're told, mister."

"That's a Barrayaran officer's uniform. It represents real power, and they guard it accordingly. They *hang* people who wear fake uniforms." He tossed off the covers and sat up. He was a little dizzy.

"My *gods*," said Quinn in a choked voice. "What have you done to yourself?"

"I suppose," he allowed, "you can still try to stuff me into the uniform. But you might want to consider the effect." He staggered to the washroom.

While washing and depiliating, he inventoried the results of his escape attempt. There just hadn't been enough time. True, he'd regained the kilos he'd had to lose to play Admiral Naismith at Escobar, plus maybe a slight bonus, and in a mere fourteen days instead of the year it had taken them to creep on in the first place. A hint of a double chin. His torso was notably thickened, though, his abdomen—he moved carefully—achingly distended. *Not enough, not enough to be safe yet.*

Quinn being Quinn, she had to convince herself, and she tried the Barrayaran uniform on him anyway. He made sure to slump. The effect was . . . very unmilitary. She gave up, snarling, and let him dress himself. He chose clean ship-knit pants, soft friction-slippers, and a loose Barrayaran civilian-style tunic of Miles's with big sleeves and an embroidered sash. It took him a moment of careful consideration to decide whether it would annoy Quinn more to see the sash positioned across his rounding belly, equatorially, or under the bulge like a sling. Judging from the lemon-sucking look on her face, under it was, and he left it that way.

She sensed his fey mood. "Enjoying yourself?" she inquired sarcastically.

"It's the last fun I'll get today. Isn't it?"

Her hand opened in dry acquiescence.

"Where are you taking me? For that matter, where are we?"

"Komarr orbit. We are about to pod over, secretly, to one of the Barrayaran military space stations. There we are going to have a very private meeting with Chief of Imperial Security Captain Simon Illyan. He came by fast courier all the way from ImpSec headquarters on Barrayar on the basis of a rather ambiguous coded message I sent him, and he's going to be extremely hot to know why I've interrupted his routine. He's going to demand to know what the hell was so important. And," her voice wavered in a sigh, "I'm going to have to tell him."

She led him out of his cabin-cell through the *Peregrine*. She had evidently dismissed his door guard when she'd first come in, but in fact all the corridors seemed deserted. No, not deserted. Cleared.

They came to a personnel pod hatch and ducked through to find Captain Bothari-Jesek herself at the controls. Bothari-Jesek and no one else. A very private party indeed.

Bothari-Jesek's usual coolness seemed particularly frigid today. When she glanced over her shoulder at him, her eyes widened, and her dark winged brows drew down in startled disapproval of his pasty, bloated appearance.

"Hell, Mark. You look like a drowned corpse that's floated to the surface after a week."

I feel like one. "Thank you," he intoned blandly.

She snorted, whether with amusement, disgust, or derision he was not sure, and turned her attention back to the pod control interface. Hatches sealed, clamps retracted, and they sped silently away from the side of the *Peregrine*. Between the zero-gee and the accelerations, he found his attention centered on his stretched stomach again, and he swallowed against the nausea.

"Why is the ImpSec head man only ranked as captain?" Mark inquired, to take his mind off his queasiness. "It can't be for secrecy, everybody knows who he is."

"Another Barrayaran tradition," Bothari-Jesek said. Her tone put a slightly bitter spin on the term *tradition*. At least she was speaking to him. "Illyan's predecesor in the post, the late great Captain Negri, never took a promotion beyond captain. That kind of ambition was apparently irrelevant to Emperor Ezar's Familiar. Everybody knew Negri spoke with the Emperor's Voice, and his orders cut across all ranks. Illyan . . . was always a little shy of promoting himself over the rank of his former boss, I guess. He's paid a vice-admiral's salary, though. Whatever poor sucker heads ImpSec next after Illyan retires is probably going to be stuck with the rank of captain forever."

They approached a mid-sized high orbital space station. Mark finally glimpsed Komarr, turning far below, shrunken by the distance to a half-moon. Bothari-Jesek kept strictly to the flight path assigned to her by an extremely laconic station traffic control. After a nervous pause while they exchanged codes and countersigns, they locked onto a docking hatch.

They were met by two silent, expressionless armed guards, very neat and trim in Barrayaran green, who ushered them through the station and into a small windowless chamber set up as an office, with a comconsole desk, three chairs, and no other decoration.

"Thank you. Leave us," said the man behind the desk. The guards exited as silently as they had done everything else.

Alone, the man seemed to relax slightly. He nodded to Bothari-Jesek. "Hullo, Elena. It's good to see you." His light voice had an unexpected warm timbre, like an uncle greeting a favorite niece.

The rest of him seemed exactly as Mark had studied in Galen's vids. Simon Illyan was a slight, aging man, gray rising in a tide from his temples into his brown hair. A rounded face with a snub nose was too etched with faint lines to look quite youthful. He wore, on this military installation, correct officer's undress greens and insignia like the ones Quinn had tried to foist on Mark, with the Horus-eye badge of Imperial Security winking from his collar.

Mark realized Illyan was staring back at him with the most peculiar look on his face. "My God, Miles, you—" he began in a strangled voice, then his eye lit with comprehension. He sat back in his chair. "Ah." His mouth twisted up on one side. "Lord Mark. Greetings from your lady mother. And I am most pleased to meet you at last." He sounded perfectly sincere.

Not for long, thought Mark hopelessly. And, *Lord Mark? He can't be serious.*

"Also pleased to know where you are again. I take it, Captain Quinn, that my department's message about Lord Mark's disappearance from Earth finally caught up with you?"

"Not yet. It's probably still chasing us from . . . our last stop."

Illyan's brows rose. "So did Lord Mark come in from the cold on his own, or did my erstwhile subordinate send him to me?"

"Neither, sir." Quinn seemed to have trouble speaking. Bothari-Jesek wasn't even trying to.

Illyan leaned forward, growing more serious, though still tinged with a slight irony. "So what half-cocked, insubordinate, I-thought-you-wanted-me-to-use-my-initiative-sir scam has he sent you to try to con me into paying for this time?"

"No scam, sir," muttered Quinn. "But the bill is going to be huge."

The coolly amused air faded altogether as he studied her gray face. "Yes?" he said after a moment.

Quinn leaned on the desk with both hands, not for emphasis, Mark fancied, but for support. "Illyan, we have a problem. Miles is dead."

Illyan took this in with a waxen stillness. Abruptly, he turned his chair around. Mark could see only the back of his head. His hair was thin. When he turned back, the lines had sprung out on his set face like a figure-ground reversal; like scars. "That's not a problem, Quinn," he whispered. "That's a *disaster.*" He laid his hands down flat, very carefully, across the smooth black surface of the desk. *So that's where Miles picked up that gesture,* Mark, who had studied it, thought irrelevantly.

"He's frozen in a cryo-chamber." Quinn licked her dry lips.

Illyan's eyes closed; his mouth moved, whether on prayers or curses Mark could not tell. But he only said, mildly, "You might have said that first. The rest would have followed as a logical supposition." His eyes opened, intent. "So what happened? How bad were his wounds—not a head wound, pray God? How well-prepped was he?"

"I helped do the prep myself. Under combat conditions. I . . . I *think* it was good. You can't know until . . . well. He took a very bad chest wound. As far as I could tell he was untouched from the neck up."

Illyan breathed, carefully. "You're right, Captain Quinn. Not a disaster. Only a problem. I'll alert the Imperial Military Hospital at Vorbarr Sultana to expect their star patient. We can transfer the cryo-chamber from your ship to my fast courier immediately." Was the man babbling, just a little, with relief?

"Uh . . ." said Quinn. "No."

Illyan rested his forehead gingerly in his hand, as if a headache was starting just behind his eyes. "Finish, Quinn," he said in a tone of muffled dread.

"We lost the cryo-chamber."

"How could you lose a cryo-chamber?!"

"It was a portable." She intercepted his burning stare, and hurried up her report. "It was left downside in the scramble to get off. Each of the combat-drop shuttles thought the other one had it. It was a mis-communication—I *checked*, I swear. It turned out the medic in charge of the cryo-chamber had been cut off from his shuttle by enemy forces. He found himself with access to a commercial shipping facility. We think he shipped the cryo-chamber from there."

"You *think*? I will ask—*what* combat drop mission, in a moment. Where did he ship it?"

"That's just it, we don't know. He was killed before he could report. The cryo-chamber could be on its way literally anywhere • by now."

Illyan sat back and rubbed his lips, which were set in a thin, ghastly smile. "I see. And all this happened when? And where?"

"Two weeks and three days ago, on Jackson's Whole."

"*I* sent you all to Illyrica, via Vega Station. How the hell did you end up on Jackson's Whole?"

Quinn stood at parade rest and took it from the top, a stiff, clipped synopsis of the events of the last four weeks from Escobar onward. "I have a complete report with all our vid records and Miles's personal log here, sir." She laid a data cube on his comconsole.

Illyan eyed it like a snake; his hand did not move toward it. "And the forty-nine clones?"

"Still aboard the *Peregrine*, sir. We'd like to off-load them."

My clones. What would Illyan do with them? Mark dared not ask.

"Miles's personal log tends to be a fairly useless document, in my experience," observed Illyan distantly. "He is quite canny about what to leave out." He grew introspective, and fell silent for a time. Then he rose and walked from side to side across the little office. The cool facade cracked without warning; face contorted, he turned and slammed his fist into the wall with bone-crunching force, shouting, "*Damn* the boy for making a fucking farce out of his own funeral!"

He stood with his back to them; when he turned again and sat down his face was stiff and blank. When he looked up, he addressed Bothari-Jesek.

"Elena. It's clear I'm going to have to stay here at Komarr, for the moment, to coordinate the search from ImpSec's galactic affairs HQ. I can't afford to put an extra five days of travel time between myself and the action. I will, of course . . . compose the formal missing-in-action report on Lieutenant Lord Vorkosigan and forward it immediately to Count and Countess Vorkosigan. I hate to think of it delivered by some subordinate, but it will have to be. But will you, as a personal favor to me, escort Lord Mark to Vorbarr Sultana, and deliver him to their custody?"

No, no, no, Mark screamed inside.

"I . . . would rather not go to Barrayar, sir."

"The Prime Minister will have questions that only one who was on the spot can answer. You are the most ideal courier I can imagine for a matter of such . . . complex delicacy. I grant you the task will be painful."

Bothari-Jesek was looking trapped. "Sir, I'm a senior shipmaster. I'm not free to leave the *Peregrine*. And—frankly—I do not care to escort Lord Mark."

"I'll give you anything you ask, in return."

She hesitated. "Anything?"

He nodded.

She glanced at Mark. "I gave my word that all the House Bharaputra clones would be taken somewhere safe, somewhere humane, where the Jacksonians can't reach. Will you redeem my word for me?"

Illyan chewed his lip. "ImpSec can launder their identities readily enough, of course. No difficulty there. Appropriate placement might be trickier. But yes. We'll take them on."

Take them on. What did Illyan mean? For all their other flaws, the Barrayarans at least did not practice slavery.

"They're children," Mark blurted. "You have to remember they're only children." *It's hard to remember*, he wanted to add, but couldn't, under Bothari-Jesek's cold eyes.

Illyan averted his glance from Mark. "I shall seek Countess Vorkosigan's advice, then. Anything else?"

"The *Peregrine* and the *Ariel*—"

"Must remain, for the moment, in Komarr orbit and communications quarantine. My apologies to your troops, but they'll have to tough it out."

"You'll cover the costs for this mess?"

Illyan grimaced. "Alas, yes."

"And . . . and look *hard* for Miles!"

"Oh, yes," he breathed.

"Then I'll go." Her voice was faint, her face pale.

"Thank you," said Illyan quietly. "My fast courier will be at your disposal as quickly as you can make ready to depart." His eye fell reluctantly on Mark. He had been avoiding looking at Mark for the whole last half of this interview. "How many personal guards do you wish?" he asked Bothari-Jesek. "I'll make it clear to them that they are under your command till they see you safe to the Count."

"I don't want any, but I suppose I have to sleep sometime. Two," Bothari-Jesek decided.

And so he was officially made a prisoner of the Barrayaran Imperial government, Mark thought. *The end of the line.*

Bothari-Jesek rose and motioned Mark to his feet. "Come on. I want to get a few personal items from the *Peregrine.* And tell my exec he's got the command, and explain to the troops about being confined to quarters. Thirty minutes."

"Good. Captain Quinn, please remain."

"Yes, sir."

Illyan stood, to see Bothari-Jesek out. "Tell Aral and Cordelia," he began, and paused. Time stretched.

"I will," said Bothari-Jesek quietly. Mutely, Illyan nodded.

The door seals hissed open for her stride. She didn't even look back to see if Mark was following. He had to break into a run every five steps to keep up.

His cabin aboard the ImpSec fast courier proved to be even tinier and more cell-like than the one he'd occupied aboard the *Peregrine.* Bothari-Jesek locked him in and left him alone. There was not even the time marker and limited human contact of three-times-a-day ration delivery; the cabin had its own computer-controlled food dispensing system, pneumatically connected to some central store. He over-ate compulsively, no longer sure why or what it could do for him, besides provide a combination of comfort and self-destruction. But death from the complications of obesity took years, and he only had five days.

On the last day his body switched strategies, and he became violently ill. He managed to keep this fact secret until the trip downside in the personnel shuttle, where it was mistaken for zero-gravity and motion sickness by a surprisingly sympathetic ImpSec guard, who apparently suffered from some such slight weakness himself. The man promptly and cheerfully slapped an anti-nausea patch from the med kit on the wall onto the side of Mark's neck.

The patch also had some sedative power. Mark's heart rate slowed, an effect which lasted till they landed and transferred to a sealed groundcar. A guard and a driver took the front compartment, and Mark sat across from Bothari-Jesek in the rear compartment for the last leg of his nightmare journey, from the military shuttleport outside the capital into the heart of Vorbarr Sultana. The center of the Barrayaran Empire.

It wasn't until he found himself having something resembling an asthma attack that Bothari-Jesek looked up from her own glum self-absorption and noticed.

"What the hell's the matter with you?" She leaned forward and took his pulse, which was racing. He was clammy all over.

"Sick," he gasped, and then at her irritated I-could-have-figured-that-out-for-myself look, admitted, "Scared." He thought he'd been as frightened as a human being could be, under Bharaputran fire, but that was as nothing compared to this slow, trapped terror, this drawn-out suffocating helplessness to affect his destiny.

"What do you have to be afraid of?" she asked scornfully. "Nobody's going to hurt you."

"Captain, they're going to kill me."

"Who? Lord Aral and Lady Cordelia? Hardly. If for any reason we fail to get Miles back, you could be the next Count Vorkosigan. Surely you've figured on that."

At this point he satisfied a long-held curiosity. When he passed out, his breathing did indeed begin again automatically. He blinked away black fog, and fended off Bothari-Jesek's alarmed attempt to loosen his clothes and check his tongue to be sure he hadn't swallowed it. She had pocketed a couple of anti-nausea patches from the shuttle medkit, just in case, and she held one uncertainly. He motioned urgently for her to apply it. It helped.

"Who do you think these people are?" she demanded angrily, when his breathing grew less irregular.

"I don't know. But they're sure as hell going to be pissed at me."

The worst was the knowledge that it need not have been this bad. Any time before the Jackson's Whole debacle he could in theory have walked right in and said hello. But he'd wanted to meet Barrayar on his own terms. Like trying to storm heaven. His attempt to make it better had made it infinitely worse.

She sat back and regarded him with slow bemusement. "You really are scared to death, aren't you?" she said, in a tone of revelation that made him want to howl. "Mark, Lord Aral and Lady Cordelia are going to give you the benefit of every doubt. I know they will. But you have to do your part."

"What is my part?"

"I'm . . . not sure," she admitted.

"Thanks. You're such a help."

And then they were there. The groundcar swung through a set of gates and into the narrow grounds of a huge stone residence. It was the pre-electric Time-of-Isolation design that gave it such an air of fabulous age, Mark decided. The architecture he'd seen like it in London all dated back well over a millenium, though this pile was only a hundred and fifty standard years old. Vorkosigan House.

The canopy swung up, and he struggled out of the groundcar after Bothari-Jesek. This time she waited for him. She grasped him firmly by the upper arm, either worried he would collapse or fearing he would bolt. They stepped through a pleasantly-hued sunlight into the cool dimness of a large entry foyer paved in black and white stone and featuring a remarkable wide curving staircase. How many times had Miles stepped across this threshold?

Bothari-Jesek seemed an agent of some evil fairy, which had snatched away the beloved Miles and replaced him with this pallid, pudgy changeling. He choked down an hysterical giggle as the sardonic mocker in the back of his brain called out, *Hi, Mom and Dad, I'm home. . . .* Surely the evil fairy was himself.

CHAPTER TWELVE

They were met in the entry hall by a pair of liveried servants wearing Vorkosigan brown and silver. In a high Vor household even the staff played soldier. One of them directed Bothari-Jesek away to the right. Mark could have wept. She despised him, but at least she was familiar. Stripped of all support and feeling more utterly alone than when locked in the darkness of his cabin, he turned to follow the other manservant through a short arched hallway and a set of doors on the left.

He had memorized the layout of Vorkosigan House under Galen's tutelage, long ago, so he knew they were entering a room dubbed the First Parlor, an antechamber to the great library that ran from the front of the house to the back. By the standards of Vorkosigan House's public rooms he supposed it was relatively intimate, though its high ceiling seemed to lend it a cool, disapproving austerity. His consciousness of the architectural detail was instantly obliterated when he saw the woman sitting on a padded sofa, quietly awaiting him.

She was tall, neither thin nor stout, a sort of middle-aged solid in build. Red hair streaked with natural gray wound in a complex knot on the back of her head, leaving her face free to make its own statement of cheekbone, line of jaw, and clear gray eye. Her posture was contained, poised rather than resting. She wore a soft silky beige blouse, a hand-embroidered sash that he suddenly realized matched the pattern on his own stolen one, and a calf-length tan skirt and buskins. No jewelry. He had expected something more ostentatious, elaborate, intimidating, the formal icon of Countess Vorkosigan from the vids of reviewing stands and receptions. Or was her sense of power so fully encompassed that she didn't need to wear it, she *was* it? He could see no physical similarity whatsoever between her and himself. Well, maybe eye color. And the paleness of their skins. And the bridge of the nose, perhaps. The line of the jaw had a certain congruence not apparent from vids—

"Lord Mark Vorkosigan, milady," the manservant announced portentously, making Mark flinch.

"Thank you, Pym," she nodded to the middle-aged retainer, dismissing him. The armsman's disappointed curiosity was well-concealed, except for one quick glance back before closing the doors after himself.

"Hello, Mark." Countess Vorkosigan's voice was a soft alto. "Please sit." She waved at an armchair set at a slight angle opposite her sofa. It did not appear to be hinged and sprung to snap closed upon him, and it was not too close to her; he lowered himself into it, gingerly, as instructed. Unusually, it was not too high for his feet to touch the floor. Had it been cut down for Miles?

"I am glad to meet you at last," she stated, "though I'm sorry the circumstances are so awkward."

"So am I," he mumbled. Glad, or sorry? And who were these *I*'s sitting here, lying politely to each other about their gladness and sorrow? *Who are we, lady?* He looked around fearfully for the Butcher of Komarr. "Where is . . . your husband?"

"Ostensibly, greeting Elena. Actually, he funked out and sent me into the front line first. Most unlike him."

"I . . . don't understand. Ma'am." He didn't know what to call her.

"He's been drinking stomach medicine in beverage quantities for the past two days . . . you have to understand how the information has been trickling in, from our point of view. Our first hint that there was anything amiss came four days ago in the form of a courier officer from ImpSec HQ, with a brief standard message from Illyan that Miles was missing in action, details to follow. We were not at first inclined to panic. Miles has been missing before, sometimes for quite extended periods. It was not until Illyan's full transmission was relayed and decoded, several hours later, together with the news that you were on your way, that it all came clear. We've had three days to think it through."

He sat silent, struggling with the concept of the great Admiral

Count Vorkosigan, the feared Butcher of Komarr, that massive, shadowy monster, even having a point of view, let alone one that low mortals such as himself were casually expected to understand.

"Illyan never uses weasel-words," the Countess continued, "but he made it through that whole report without once using the term 'dead,' 'killed,' or any of their synonyms. The medical records suggest otherwise. Correct?"

"Um . . . the cryo-treatment appeared successful." What did she want from him?

"And so we are mired in an emotional and legal limbo," she sighed. "It would be almost easier if he . . ." She frowned fiercely down into her lap. Her hands clenched, for the first time. "You understand, we're going to be talking about a lot of possible contingencies. Much revolves around you. But I won't count Miles as dead till he's dead and *rotted*."

He remembered that tide of blood on the concrete. "Um," he said helplessly.

"The fact that you could potentially play Miles has been a great distraction to some people." She looked him over bemusedly. "You say the Dendarii accepted you . . . ?"

He cringed into the chair, body-conscious under her sharp gray gaze, feeling the flesh of his torso roll and bunch under Miles's shirt and sash, the tightness of the trousers. "I've . . . put on some weight since then."

"All that? In just three weeks?"

"Yes," he muttered, flushing.

One brow rose. "On purpose?"

"Sort of."

"Huh." She sat back, looking surprised. "That was *extremely* clever of you."

He gaped, realized it emphasized his doubling chin, and closed his mouth quickly.

"Your status has been the subject of much debate. I voted against any security ploy to conceal Miles's situation by having you pose as him. In the first place, it's redundant. Lieutenant Lord Vorkosigan is often gone for months at a time; his absence is more normal than not, these days. It's strategically more important to establish you as yourself, Lord Mark, if Lord Mark is indeed who you are to be."

He swallowed in a dry throat. "Do I have a choice?"

"You will, but a reasoned one, after you've had time to assimilate it all."

"You can't be serious. I'm a *clone*."

"I'm from Beta Colony, kiddo," she said tartly. "Betan law is very sensible and clear on the topic of clones. It's only Barrayaran custom that finds itself at a loss. Barrayarans!" She pronounced it like a swear word. "Barrayar lacks a long experience of dealing with all the technological variants on human reproduction. No legal precedents. And if it's not a *tradition*," she put the same sour spin on the word as had Bothari-Jesek, "they don't know how to cope."

"What am I, to you as a Betan?" he asked, nervously fascinated.

"Either my son or my son once removed," she answered promptly. "Unlicensed, but claimed by me as an heir."

"Those are actual legal categories, on your homeworld?"

"You bet. Now, if *I* had ordered you cloned from Miles, after getting an approved child-license first of course, you would be my son pure and simple. If Miles as a legal adult had done the same, he would be your legal parent and I would be your mother-once-removed, and bear claims upon you and obligations to you approximately the equivalent of a grandparent. Miles was not, of course, a legal adult at the time you were cloned, nor was your birth licensed. If you were still a minor, he and I could go before an Adjudicator, and your guardianship would be assigned according to the Adjudicator's best judgment of your welfare. You are no longer, of course, a minor in either Betan or Barrayaran law." She sighed. "The time for legal guardianship is past. Lost. The inheritance of property will mostly be tangled in the Barrayaran legal confusions. Aral will discuss Barrayaran customary law, or the lack of it, with you when the time comes. That leaves our emotional relationship."

"Do we have one?" he asked cautiously. His two greatest fears, that she would either pull out a weapon and shoot him, or else throw herself upon him in some totally inappropriate paroxysm of maternal affection, both seemed to be fading. He was left facing a level-voiced mystery.

"We do, though exactly what it is remains to be discovered. Realize this, though. Half my genes run through your body, and my selfish genome is heavily evolutionarily pre-programmed to look out for its copies. The other half is copied from the man I admire most in all the worlds and time, so my interest is doubly riveted. The artistic combination of the two, shall we say, arrests my attention."

Put like that, it actually seemed to make sense, logically and without threat. He found his stomach un-knotting, his throat relaxing. He promptly felt hungry again, for the first time since planetary orbit.

"Now, what's between you and me has nothing to do with what's between you and Barrayar. That's Aral's department, and he'll have to speak for his own views. It's all so undecided, except for one thing. While you are here, you are yourself, Mark, Miles's six-years-younger twin brother. And not an imitation or a substitute for Miles. So the more you can establish yourself as distinct from Miles, from the very beginning, the better."

"Oh," he breathed, "please, yes."

"I suspected you'd already grasped that. Good, we agree. But just not-being-Miles is no more than the inverse of being an imitation Miles. I want to know, who is Mark?"

"Lady ... I don't know." His prodded honesty had an edge of anguish.

She watched him, sapiently. "There is time," she said calmly. "Miles ... wanted you to be here, you know. He talked about showing you around. Imagined teaching you to ride horseback." She gave a furtive shudder.

"Galen tried to have me taught, in London," Mark recalled. "It was terrifically expensive, and I wasn't very good at it, so he finally told me just to avoid horses, when I got here."

"Ah?" She brightened slightly. "Hm. Miles, you see, has ... had ... has these only-child romantic notions about siblings. Now, I have a brother, so I have no such illusions." She paused, glanced around the room, and leaned forward with a suddenly confidential air, lowering her voice. "You have an uncle, a grandmother, and two cousins on Beta Colony who are just as much your relatives as Aral and myself and your cousin Ivan here on Barrayar. Remember, you have more than one choice. I've given one son to Barrayar. And watched for twenty-eight years while Barrayar tried to destroy him. Maybe Barrayar has had its turn, eh?"

"Ivan's not here *now*, is he?" Mark asked, diverted and horrified.

"He's not staying at Vorkosigan House, no, if that's what you mean. He is in Vorbarr Sultana, assigned to Imperial Service Headquarters. Perhaps," her eye lit in speculation, "he could take you out and show you some of the things Miles wanted you to see."

"Ivan may still be angry for what I did to him in London," Mark jittered.

"He'll get over it," the Countess predicted confidently. "I have to admit, Miles would have positively enjoyed unsettling people with you."

A quirk Miles inherited from his mother, clearly.

"I've lived almost three decades on Barrayar," she mused. "We've come such a long way. And yet there is still so terribly far to go. Even Aral's will grows weary. Maybe we can't do it all in one generation. Time for the changing of the guard, in my opinion . . . ah, well."

He sat back in his chair for the first time, letting it support him, starting to watch and listen instead of just cower. An ally. It seemed he had an ally, though he was still not sure just why. Galen had not spent much time on Countess Cordelia Vorkosigan, being totally obsessed with his old enemy the Butcher. Galen, it appeared, had seriously underestimated her. She had survived twenty-nine years here . . . might he? For the first time, it seemed something humanly possible.

A brief knock sounded on the hinged double doors to the hallway. At Countess Vorkosigan's "Yes?", they swung open partway, and a man poked his head around the frame and favored her with a strained smile.

"Is it all right for me to come in now, dear Captain?"

"Yes, I think so," said Countess Vorkosigan.

He let himself through and closed the doors again. Mark's throat locked; he swallowed and breathed, swallowed and breathed, with frighteningly fragile control. He would *not* pass out in front of this man. Or vomit. He hadn't more than a teaspoon of bile left in his belly by now anyway. It was him, unmistakably him, Prime Minister Admiral Count Aral Vorkosigan, formerly Regent of the Barrayaran Empire and de facto dictator of three worlds, conqueror of Komarr, military genius, political mastermind—accused murderer, torturer, madman, too many impossible things to be contained in that stocky form now striding toward Mark.

Mark had studied vids of him taken at every age; perhaps it was not so odd that his first coherent thought was, *He looks older than I expected.* Count Vorkosigan was ten standard years older than his Betan wife, but he looked twenty or thirty years older. His hair was a whiter shade of gray than in the vids from even two years ago. He was short for a Barrayaran, eye to eye with the Countess. His face was heavy, intense, weathered. He wore green uniform trousers but no jacket, just the cream shirt with the long sleeves rolled up and open at the round collar which, if it was an attempt at a casual look, was failing utterly. The tension in the room had risen to choking levels with his entrance.

"Elena is settled," Count Vorkosigan reported, seating himself beside the Countess. His posture was open, hands on knees, but he did not lean back comfortably. "The visit seems to be stirring up more old memories than she was ready for. She's rather disturbed."

"I'll go talk to her in a bit," promised the Countess.

"Good." The Count's eyes inventoried Mark. Puzzled? Repelled? "Well." The practiced diplomat whose job it was to talk three planets down the road to progress sat speechless, at a loss, as if unable to address Mark directly. He turned instead to his wife. "*He* passed as Miles?"

A tinge of dark amusement flashed in Countess Vorkosigan's eyes. "He's put on weight since then," she said blandly.

"I see."

The silence stretched for excruciating seconds.

Mark blurted out, "The first thing I was supposed to do when I met you was try to kill you."

"Yes. I know." Count Vorkosigan settled back on the sofa, eyes on Mark's face at last.

"They made me practice about twenty different back-up methods, till I could do them in my sleep, but the primary was to have been a skin patch with a paralyzing toxin that left evidence on autopsy pointing to heart failure. I was to get alone with you, touch it to any part of your body I could reach. It was strangely slow, for an assassination drug. I was to wait, in your sight, for twenty minutes while you died, and never let on that I was not Miles."

The Count smiled grimly. "I see. A good revenge. Very artistic. It would have worked."

"As the new Count Vorkosigan, I was then to go on and spearhead a drive for the Imperium."

"*That* would have failed. Ser Galen expected it to. It was merely the chaos of its failure, during which Komarr was supposed to rise, that he desired. You were to be another Vorkosigan sacrifice then." He actually seemed to grow more at ease, professional, discussing these grotesque plots.

"Killing you was the entire reason for my existence. Two years ago I was all primed to do it. I endured all those years of Galen for no other purpose."

"Take heart," advised the Countess. "Most people exist for no reason at all."

The Count remarked, "ImpSec assembled a huge pile of documentation on you, after the plot came to light. It covers the time from when you were a mere mad gleam in Galen's eye, to the latest addition about your disappearance from Earth two months ago. But there's nothing in the documentation that suggests your, er, late adventure on Jackson's Whole was some sort of latent programming along the lines of my projected assassination. Was it?" A faint doubt colored his voice.

"No," said Mark firmly. "I've been programmed enough to know. It's not something you can fail to notice. Not the way Galen did it, anyway."

"I disagree," said Countess Vorkosigan unexpectedly. "You were set up for it, Mark. But not by Galen."

The Count raised his brows in startled inquiry.

"By Miles, I'm afraid," she explained. "Quite inadvertently."

"I don't see it," said the Count.

Mark felt the same way. "I was only in contact with Miles for a few days, on Earth."

"I'm not sure you're ready for this, but here goes. You had exactly three role models to learn how to be a human being from. The Jacksonian body-slavers, the Komarran terrorists—and Miles. You were *steeped* in Miles. And I'm sorry, but Miles thinks he's a knight-errant. A rational government wouldn't allow him possession of a pocket-knife, let alone a space fleet. And so, Mark, when you were finally forced to choose between two palpable evils and a lunatic—you upped and ran after the lunatic."

"I think Miles does very well," objected the Count.

"Agh." The Countess buried her face in her hands, briefly. "Love, we are discussing a young man upon whom Barrayar laid so much unbearable stress, so much pain, he created an entire other personality to escape into. He then persuaded several thousand galactic mercenaries to support his psychosis, and on top of that conned the Barrayaran Imperium into paying for it all. Admiral Naismith is one hell of a lot more than just an ImpSec cover identity, and you know it. I grant you he's a genius, but don't you dare try to tell me he's sane." She paused. "No. That's not fair. Miles's safety valve works. I won't really begin to fear for his sanity till he's cut off from the little admiral. It's an extraordinary balancing act, in all." She glanced at Mark. "And a nearly impossible act to follow, I should think."

Mark had never thought of Miles as seriously crazed; he'd only thought of him as perfect. This was all highly unsettling.

"The Dendarii truly function as a covert operations arm of ImpSec," said the Count, looking a bit unsettled himself. "Spectacularly well, on occasion."

"Of course they do. You wouldn't let Miles keep them if they didn't, so he makes sure of it. I merely point out that their official function is not their only function. And—if Miles ever ceases to need them, it won't be a year before ImpSec finds reason to cut that tie. And you'll all earnestly believe you are acting perfectly logically."

Why weren't they blaming him . . . ? He mustered the courage to ask it aloud. "Why aren't you blaming me for killing Miles?"

With a glance, the Countess fielded the question to her husband, who nodded and answered. For them both? "Illyan's report stated Miles was shot by a Bharaputran security trooper."

"But he wouldn't have been in the line of fire if I hadn't—"

Count Vorkosigan held up an interrupting hand. "If he hadn't foolishly chosen to be. Don't attempt to camouflage your real blame by taking more than your share. I've made too many lethal errors myself to be fooled by that one." He glanced at his boots. "We have also considered the long view. While your personality and persona are clearly distinct from Miles's, any children you sire would be genetically indistinguishable. Not you, but your son, may be what Barrayar needs."

"Only to continue the Vor system," Countess Vorkosigan put in dryly. "A dubious goal, love. Or are you picturing yourself as a grand-fatherly mentor to Mark's theoretical children, as your father was to Miles?"

"God forbid," muttered the Count fervently.

"Beware your own conditioning." She turned to Mark. "The trouble is . . ." she looked away, looked back, "if we fail to recover Miles, what you will be facing is not just a relationship. It's a job. At a minimum, you'd be responsible for the welfare of a couple of million people in your District; you would be their Voice in the Council of Counts. It's a job Miles was trained for literally from birth; I'm not sure it's possible to send in a last-minute substitute."

Surely not, oh, surely not.

"I don't know," said the Count thoughtfully. "*I* was such a substitute. Until I was eleven years old I was the spare, not the heir. I admit, after my older brother was murdered, the rush of events made the shift in destinies easy for me. We were all so intent on revenge, in Mad Yuri's War. By the time I looked up and drew breath again, I'd fully assimilated the fact I would be Count some-day. Though I scarcely imagined that someday would be another fifty years. It's possible you too, Mark, could have many years to study and train. But it's also possible my Countship could land in your lap tomorrow."

The man was seventy-two standard years old, middle-aged for a galactic, old for harsh Barrayar. Count Aral had used himself hard; had he used himself nearly up? His father Count Piotr had lived twenty years more than that, a whole other lifetime. "Would Barrayar even accept a clone as your heir?" he asked doubtfully.

"Well, it's past time to start developing laws one way or the other. Yours would be a major test case. With enough concentrated will, I could probably ram it down their throats—"

Mark didn't doubt that.

"But starting a legal war is premature, till things sort themselves out with the missing cryo-chamber. For now, the public story is that Miles is away on duty, and you are visiting for the first time. All true enough. I need scarcely emphasize that the details are classified."

Mark shook his head and nodded in agreement, feeling dizzy. "But—is this necessary? Suppose I'd never been created, and Miles was killed in the line of duty somewhere. Ivan Vorpatril would be your heir."

"Yes," said the Count, "and House Vorkosigan would come to an end, after eleven generations of direct descent."

"What's the problem with that?"

"The problem is that it is not the case. You do exist. The problem is . . . that I have always wanted Cordelia's son to be my heir. Note, we're discussing rather a lot of property, by ordinary standards."

"I thought most of your ancestral lands glowed in the dark, after the destruction of Vorkosigan Vashnoi."

The Count shrugged. "Some remain. This residence, for example. But my estate is not just property; as Cordelia puts it, it comes with a full-time job. If we allow your claim upon it, you must allow its claim upon you."

"You can keep it all," said Mark sincerely. "I'll sign anything."

The Count winced.

"Consider it orientation, Mark," said the Countess. "Some of the people you may encounter will be thinking much about these questions. You simply need to be aware of the unspoken agendas."

The Count acquired an abstracted look; he let out his breath in a slow trickle. When he looked up again his face was frighteningly serious. "That's true. And there's one agenda that is not only unspoken, it's unspeakable. You must be warned."

So unspeakable Count Vorkosigan was having trouble spitting it out himself, apparently. "What now?" asked Mark warily.

"There is a . . . false theory of descent, one of six possible lines, that puts me next in line to inherit the Barrayaran Imperium, should Emperor Gregor die without issue."

"Yes," said Mark impatiently, "of course I knew. Galen's plot turned on exploiting that legal argument. You, then Miles, then Ivan."

"Yes, well now it's me, then Miles, then you, then Ivan. And Miles is—technically—dead at the moment. That leaves only me between you, and being targeted. Not as an imitation Miles, but in your own right."

"That's *rubbish*," exploded Mark. "That's even crazier than the idea of my becoming Count Vorkosigan!"

"Hold that thought," advised the Countess. "Hold it hard, and never even hint that you could think otherwise."

I am fallen among madmen.

"If anyone approaches you with a conversation on the subject, report it to me, Cordelia, or Simon Illyan as soon as possible," the Count added.

Mark had retreated as far back into his chair as he could go. "All right. . . ."

"You're scaring him, dear," the Countess remarked.

"On *that* topic, paranoia is the key to good health," said the Count ruefully. He watched Mark silently for a moment. "You look tired. We'll show you to your room. You can wash up and rest a bit."

They all rose. Mark followed them out to the paved hallway. The Countess nodded to an archway leading straight back under the curved stairway. "I'm going to take the lift tube up and see Elena."

"Right," the Count agreed. Mark perforce followed him up the stairs. Two flights let him know how out of shape he was. By the time they reached the second landing he was breathing as heavily as the old man. The Count turned down a third floor hallway.

Mark asked in some dread, "You're not putting me in Miles's room, are you?"

"No. Though the one you're getting was mine, once, when I was a child."

Before the death of his older brother, presumably. The second son's room. That was almost as unnerving.

"It's just a guest room, now." The Count swung open another blank wooden door on hinges. Beyond it lay a sunny chamber.

Obviously hand-made wooden furniture of uncertain age and enormous value included a bed and chests; a domestic console to control lighting and the mechanized windows sat incongruously beside the carved headboard.

Mark glanced back, and collided with the Count's deeply questioning stare. It was a thousand times worse than even the Dendarii's I-love-Naismith look. He clenched his hands to his head, and grated, "Miles isn't in here!"

"I know," said the Count quietly. "I was looking for . . . myself, I suppose. And Cordelia. And you."

Uncomfortably compelled, Mark looked for himself in the Count, reciprocally. He wasn't sure. Hair color, formerly; he and Miles shared the same dark hair he had seen on vids of the younger Admiral Vorkosigan. Intellectually, he'd known Aral Vorkosigan was the old General Count Piotr Vorkosigan's younger son, but that lost older brother had been dead for sixty years. He was astonished the present Count remembered with such immediacy, or made of it a connection with himself. Strange, and frightening. *I was to kill this man. I still could. He's not guarding himself at all.*

"Your ImpSec people didn't even fast-penta me. Aren't you at all worried that I might still be programmed to assassinate you?" *Or did he seem so little threat?*

"I thought you shot your father-figure once already. Catharsis enough." A bemused grimace curved the Count's mouth.

Mark remembered Galen's surprised look, when the nerve-disruptor beam had taken him full in the face. Whatever Aral Vorkosigan would look like, dying, Mark fancied it would not be surprised.

"You saved Miles's life then, according to his description of the affray," the Count said. "You chose your side two years ago, on Earth. Very effectively. I have many fears for you, Mark, but my death at your hand is not one of them. You're not as one-down with respect to your brother as you imagine. Even-all, by my count."

"Progenitor. Not brother," said Mark, stiff and congealed.

"Cordelia and I are your progenitors," said the Count firmly. Denial flashed in Mark's face.

The Count shrugged. "Whatever Miles is, we made him. You are perhaps wise to approach us with caution. We may not be good for you, either."

His belly shivered with a terrible longing, restrained by a terrible fear. Progenitors. *Parents.* He was not sure he wanted parents, at this late date. They were such enormous figures. He felt obliterated in their shadow, shattered like glass, annihilated. He felt a sudden weird wish to have Miles back. Somebody his own size and age, somebody he could talk to.

The Count glanced again into the bedchamber. "Pym should have arranged your things."

"I don't have any things. Just the clothes I'm wearing . . . sir." It was impossible to keep his tongue from adding that honorific.

"You must have had something more to wear!"

"What I brought from Earth, I left in a storage locker on Escobar. The rent's up by now. It's probably confiscated."

The Count looked him over. "I'll send someone to take your measurements, and supply you with a kit. If you were visiting under more normal circumstances, we would be showing you around. Introducing you to friends and relatives. A tour of the city. Getting you aptitude tests, making arrangements for furthering your education. We'll do some of that, in any case."

A school? What kind? Assignment to a Barrayaran military academy was very close to Mark's idea of a descent into hell. Could they make him . . . ? There were ways to resist. He had successfully resisted being lent Miles's wardrobe.

"If you want anything, ring for Pym on your console," the Count instructed.

Human servants. So very strange. The physical fear that had turned him inside out was fading, to be replaced by a more formless general anxiety. "Can I get something to eat?"

"Ah. Please join Cordelia and me for lunch in one hour. Pym will show you to the Yellow Parlor."

"I can find it. Down one floor, one corridor south, third door on the right."

The Count raised an eyebrow. "Correct."

"I've studied you, you see."

"That's all right. We've studied you, too. We've all done our homework."

"So what's the test?"

"Ah, that's the trick of it. It's not a test. It's real life."

And real death. "I'm sorry," Mark blurted. For Miles? For himself? He scarcely knew.

The Count looked as if he was wondering too; a brief ironic smile twitched one corner of his mouth. "Well . . . in a strange way, it's almost a relief to know that it's as bad as it can be. Before, when Miles was missing, one didn't know where he was, what he might be doing to, er, magnify the chaos. At least this time we know he can't possibly get into any worse trouble."

With a brief wave, the Count walked away, not entering the room after Mark, not crowding him in any way. Three ways to kill him flashed through Mark's mind. But that training seemed ages stale. He was too out of shape now anyway. Climbing the stairs had exhausted him. He pulled the door shut and fell onto the carved bed, shivering with reaction.

CHAPTER THIRTEEN

Ostensibly to allow Mark to recover from jump-lag, the Count and Countess set no tasks for him the first two days. Indeed, except for the rather formal mealtimes, Mark did not see Count Vorkosigan at all. He wandered the house and grounds at will, with no apparent guard but the Countess's discreet observation of him. There were uniformed guards at the gates; he did not yet have the nerve to test and discover if they were charged to keep him in as well as unauthorized persons out.

He had studied Vorkosigan House, yes, but the immediacy of actually being here took some getting used to. It all seemed subtly askew from his expectations. The place was a warren. But despite all the antiques with which Vorkosigan House was cluttered, every original window had been replaced with modern high-grade armor-glass and automatic shutters, even the ones high up on the wall in the basement kitchen. It was like a shell, if a vast one, of protection, palace/fortress/prison. Could he slide into this shell?

I've been a prisoner all my life. I want to be a free man.

On the third day, his new clothing arrived. The Countess came to help him unpack it all. The morning light and cool air of early autumn streamed into his bedchamber through the window which he had, mulishly, opened wide to the mysterious, dangerous, unknown world.

He opened one bag on a hanger to reveal a garment in a disturbingly military style, a high-necked tunic and side-piped trousers in Vorkosigan brown and silver, very like the Count's armsmen's liveries, but with more glitter on the collar and epaulettes. "What's this?" he asked suspiciously.

"Ah," said the Countess. "Gaudy, isn't it? It's your uniform as a cadet lord of House Vorkosigan."

His, not Miles's. All the new clothes were computer-cut to generous fit; his heart sank as he calculated how much he'd have to eat to escape *this* one.

The Countess's lips curved up at the dismayed expression on his face. "The only two places you actually have to wear it are if you attend a session of the Council of Counts, or if you go to the Emperor's birthday ceremonies. Which you might; they're coming up in a few weeks." She hesitated, her finger tracing over the Vorkosigan logo embroidered on the tunic's collar. "Miles's birthday isn't very long after that."

Well, Miles wasn't aging at the moment, wherever he was. "Birthdays are sort of a non-concept, for me. What do you call it when you take someone out of a uterine replicator?"

"When I was taken out of *my* uterine replicator, my parents called it my birthday," she said dryly.

She was Betan. Right. "I don't even know when mine is."

"You don't? It's in your records."

"What records?"

"Your Bharaputran medical file. Haven't you ever seen it? I'll have to get you a copy. It's, um, fascinating reading, in a sort of horrifying way. Your birthday was the seventeenth of last month, in point of fact."

"I missed it anyway, then." He closed the bag and stuffed the uniform far back in his closet. "Not important."

"It's important that someone celebrate our existence," she objected amiably. "People are the only mirror we have to see ourselves in. The domain of all meaning. All virtue, all evil, are contained only in people. There is none in the universe at large. Solitary confinement is a punishment in every human culture."

"That's . . . true," he admitted, remembering his own recent imprisonment. "Hm." The next garment he shook out suited his mood: solid black. Though on closer examination it proved to be almost the same design as the cadet lord's uniform, the logos and piping muted in black silk instead of glowing in silver thread, almost invisible against the black cloth.

"That's for funerals," commented the Countess. Her voice was suddenly rather flat.

"Oh." Taking the hint, he tucked it away behind the Vor cadet's uniform. He finally chose the least military-flavored outfit avail-able, soft loose trousers, low boots without buckles, steel toe caps, or any other aggressive decorations, and a shirt and vest, in dark colors, blues, greens, red-browns. It felt like a costume, but it was all extremely well-made. Camouflage? Did the clothes represent the man inside, or disguise him? "Is it me?" he asked the Countess, upon emerging from the bathroom for inspection.

She half-laughed. "A profound question, to ask of one's clothing. Even I can't answer that one."

On the fourth day, Ivan Vorpatril turned up at breakfast. He wore an Imperial lieutenant's undress greens, neatly setting off his tall, physically-fit frame; with his arrival the Yellow Parlor seemed suddenly crowded. Mark shrank down guiltily as his putative cousin greeted his aunt with a decorous kiss on the cheek and his uncle with a formal nod. Ivan nailed a plate from the sideboard and piled it precariously with eggs, meat, and sugared breads, juggled a mug of coffee, hooked back a chair with his foot, and slid into a place at the table opposite Mark.

"Hello, Mark," Ivan acknowledged his existence at last. "You look like hell. When did you get so bloated?" He shoved a forkful of fried meat into his mouth and started chewing.

"Thank you, Ivan," Mark took what refuge he could in faint sarcasm. "You haven't changed, I see." Implying *no improvement*, he hoped.

Ivan's brown eyes glinted; he started to speak, but was stopped by his aunt's "Ivan" in a tone of cool reproof.

Mark didn't think it was for trying to talk with his mouth full, but Ivan swallowed before replying, not to Mark but to the Count-ess, "My apologies, Aunt Cordelia. But I still have a problem with closets and other small, unvented dark areas because of him."

"Sorry," muttered Mark, hunching. But something in him resisted being cowed by Ivan, and he added, "I only had Galen kidnap you to fetch Miles."

"So that was *your* idea."

"It worked, too. He came right along and stuck his head in the noose for you."

Ivan's jaw tightened. "A habit he has failed to break, I under-stand," he returned, in a tone halfway between a purr and a snarl.

It was Mark's turn to be silent. Yet in a way, it was almost comforting. Ivan at least treated him as he deserved. A little welcome punishment. He felt himself reviving under the rain of scorn like a parched plant. Ivan's challenge almost brightened his day. "Why are you here?"

"It wasn't my idea, believe me," said Ivan. "I am to take you Out. For an airing."

Mark glanced at the Countess, but she was focused on her husband. "Already?" she asked.

"It is by request," said Count Vorkosigan.

"Ah ha," she said, as if enlightened. No light dawned for Mark; it wasn't *his* request. "Good. Perhaps Ivan can show him a bit of the city on the way."

"That's the idea," said the Count. "Since Ivan is an officer, it eliminates the need for a bodyguard."

Why, so they could talk frankly? A terrible idea. And who would protect him from Ivan?

"There will be an outer perimeter, I trust," said the Countess. "Oh, yes."

The outer perimeter was the guard no one was supposed to see, not even the principals. Mark wondered what prevented the outer perimeter people from just taking the day off, and claiming they'd been there, invisible men. You could get away with the scam for quite a long time, between crises, he suspected.

Lieutenant Lord Vorpatril had his own groundcar, Mark discovered after breakfast, a sporty model featuring lots of red enamel. Reluctantly, Mark slid in beside Ivan. "So," he said, in an uncertain voice. "Do you still want to scrag me?"

Ivan whipped the car through the residence's gates and out into Vorbarr Sultana city traffic. "Personally, yes. Practically, no. I need all the bodies I can get to stand between me, and Uncle Aral's job. I wish Miles had a dozen children. He could have, by now, if only he'd started—in a way, you are a godsend. They'd have me clamped in as heir apparent right now if not for you." He hesitated, in speech only; the groundcar he accelerated through an intersection, weaving narrowly past four other vehicles bearing down in collision courses. "How dead is Miles really? Uncle Aral was pretty vague, on the vid telling me about it. I wasn't sure if it was for security, or—I've never seen him so stiff."

The traffic was worse than London's and, if possible, even more disorderly, or ordered according to some rule involving survival of the fittest. Mark gripped the edges of his seat and replied, "I don't know. He took a needle-grenade in the chest. Almost as bad as it could be without actually blowing him in half."

Did Ivan's lips ripple in suppressed horror? If so, the breezy facade re-closed again almost instantly. "It will take a top-notch revival facility to put his torso back together right," Mark continued. "For the brain . . . you never know till revival's over." *And then it's too late.* "But that's not the problem. Or not the problem yet."

"Yeah." Ivan grimaced. "That was a real screw-up, y'know? How could you *lose* . . ." He turned so sharply he trailed an edge, which struck sparks from the pavement, and swore cheerfully at a very large hovertruck which nearly lunged through Mark's side of the groundcar. Mark crouched down and shut his mouth. Better the conversation should die than him; his life could depend on not distracting the driver. His first impression of the city of Miles's birth was that half the population was going to be killed in traffic before nightfall. Or maybe just the ones in Ivan's path. Ivan did a violent U-turn and skidded sideways into a parking space, cutting off two other groundcars maneuvering toward it, and coming to a halt so abruptly Mark was nearly launched into the front panel.

"Vorhartung Castle," Ivan announced with a nod and a wave as the engine's whine died away. "The Council of Counts is not in session today, so the museum is open to the public. Though *we* are not the public."

"How . . . cultural," said Mark warily, peering out through the canopy. Vorhartung Castle really looked like a castle, a rambling, antiquated pile of featureless stone rising out of the trees. It perched on a bluff above the river rapids that divided Vorbarr Sultana. Its grounds were now a park; beds of cultivated flowers grew where men and horses had once dragged siege engines through icy mud in vain assaults. "What is this really?"

"You are to meet a man. And I am not to pre-discuss it." Ivan popped the canopy and clambered out. Mark followed.

Ivan, whether by plan or perversity, really did take him to the museum, which occupied one whole wing of the castle and was devoted to the arms and armor of the Vor from the Time of Isolation. As a soldier in uniform, Ivan was admitted free, though he dutifully paid Mark's way in with a few coins. For a cover, Mark guessed, for members of the Vor caste were also admitted free, Ivan explained in a whisper. There was no sign to that effect. If you were Vor you were presumed to know.

Or maybe it was Ivan's subtle slur on Mark's Vor-ness, or lack of same. Ivan played the upper-class lout with the same cultivated thoroughness with which he played the Imperial lieutenant, or any other role his world demanded of him. The real Ivan was rather more elusive, Mark gauged; it would not do to underestimate his subtlety, or mistake him for a simpleton.

So he was to meet a man. What man? If it was another ImpSec debriefing, why couldn't he have met the man at Vorkosigan House? Was it someone in government, or Prime Minister Count Aral's Centrist Coalition party? Again, why not come to him? Ivan couldn't be setting him up for an assassination; the Vorkosigans could have had him killed in secret anytime these past two years. Maybe he was being set up to be *accused* of some staged crime? Even more arcane plot ideas twisted through his mind, all sharing the same fatal flaw of being totally lacking in motivation or logic.

He stared at a crammed array of dual sword sets in a chronological row on a wall, displaying the evolution of the Barrayaran smiths' art over two centuries, then hurried to join Ivan in front of a case of chemical-explosive-propelled projectile weapons: highly decorated large-bore muzzle loaders that had once, the card proclaimed, belonged to Emperor Vlad Vorbarra. The bullets were peculiar in being solid gold, massive spheres the size of Mark's thumbtip. At short range, it must have been like being hit by a terminal-velocity brick. At long range, they probably missed. So what poor peasant or squire had been stuck with the job of going around retrieving the misses? Or worse, the hits? Several of the bright balls in display were flattened or misshapen, and to Mark's intense bemusement, one card informed the museum patron that this very distorted blob had killed Lord Vor So-and-so during the battle of Such-and-such... "taken from his brain," after death, Mark presumed. Hoped. Yech. He was only surprised someone had cleaned the ancient gore from the spent bullet before mounting it, given the blood-thirsty gruesomeness of some of the other displays. The tanned and cured scalp of Mad Emperor Yuri, for instance, on loan from some Vor clan's private collection.

"Lord Vorpatril." It was not a question. The man speaking had appeared so quietly Mark was not even sure from what direction he had come. He was dressed as quietly, middle-aged, intelligent-looking; he might have been a museum administrator. "Come with me, please."

Without question or comment, Ivan fell in behind the man, gesturing Mark ahead of him. Thus sandwiched, Mark trod in his wake, torn between curiosity and nerves.

They went through a door marked "No Admittance," which the

man unlocked with a mechanical key and then locked again behind them, went up two staircases, and down an echoing wood-floored corridor to a room occupying the top floor of a round tower at the building's corner. Once a guard post, it was now furnished as an office, with ordinary windows cut into the stone walls in place of arrow slits. A man waited within, perched on a stool, gazing pensively down at the grounds falling away to the river, and the sprinkling of brightly-dressed people strolling or climbing the paths.

He was a thin, dark-haired fellow in his thirties, pale skin set off by loose dark clothing entirely lacking in pseudo-military detailing. He looked up with a quick smile at their guide. "Thank you, Kevi." Both greeting and dismissal seemed combined, for the guide nodded and exited.

It wasn't until Ivan nodded and said, "Sire," that recognition clicked.

Emperor Gregor Vorbarra. Shit. The door behind Mark was blocked by Ivan. Mark controlled his surge of panic. Gregor was only a man, alone, apparently unarmed. All the rest was . . . prop-aganda. Hype. Illusion. His heart beat faster anyway.

"Hullo, Ivan," said the Emperor. "Thank you for coming. Why don't you go study the exhibits for a while."

"Seen 'em before," said Ivan laconically.

"Nevertheless." Gregor jerked his head doorward.

"Not to put too fine a point on it," said Ivan, "but this is not Miles, not even on a good day. And despite appearances, he *was* trained as an assassin, once. Isn't this a touch premature?"

"Well," said Gregor softly, "we'll find out, won't we? Do you want to assassinate me, Mark?"

"No," Mark croaked.

"There you have it. Take a hike, Ivan. I'll send Kevi for you in a bit."

Ivan grimaced in frustration, and, Mark sensed, not a little frus-trated curiosity. He departed with an ironic salaam that seemed to say, *On your head be it.*

"So, Lord Mark," said Gregor. "What do you think of Vorbarr Sultana so far?"

"It went by pretty fast," Mark said cautiously.

"Dear God, don't tell me you let *Ivan* drive."

"I didn't know I had a choice."

The Emperor laughed. "Sit down." He waved Mark into the station chair behind the comconsole desk; the little room was otherwise sparsely furnished, though the antique military prints and maps cluttering the walls might be spill-over from the nearby museum.

The Emperor's smile faded back into his initial pensive look as he studied Mark. It reminded Mark a little of the way Count Vorkosigan looked at him, that *Who are you?* look, only without the Count's ravenous intensity. A bearable wonder.

"Is this your office?" asked Mark, cautiously settling himself in the Imperial swivel-chair. The room seemed small and austere for the purpose.

"One of them. This whole complex is crammed with various offices, in some of the oddest niches. Count Vorvolk has one in the old dungeons. No head room. I use this as a private retreat when attending the Council of Counts meetings, or when I have other business here."

"Why do I qualify as business? Besides not being pleasure. Is this personal or official?"

"I can't spit without being official. On Barrayar, the two are not very separable. Miles . . . was . . ." Gregor's tongue tripped over that past tense too, "in no particular order, a peer of my caste; an officer in my service; the son of an extremely, if not supremely, important official; and a personal friend of lifelong standing. And the heir to the Countship of a District. And the Counts are the mechanism whereby one man," he touched his chest, "multiplies to sixty, and then to a multitude. The Counts are the first officers of the Imperium; I am its captain. You do understand, that *I* am not the Imperium? An empire is mere geography. The Imperium is a society. The multitude, the whole body—ultimately, down to every subject—*that* is the Imperium. Of which I am only a piece. An interchangeable part, at that—did you notice my great-uncle's scalp, downstairs?"

"Um . . . yes. It was, uh, prominently displayed."

"This *is* the home of the Council of Counts. The fulcrum of the lever may fancy itself supreme, but it is nothing without the lever. Mad Yuri forgot that. I don't. The Count of the Vorkosigans' District is another such living piece. Also interchangeable." He paused.

"A . . . link in a chain," Mark offered carefully, to prove he was paying attention.

"A link in a chain-mail. In a web. So that one weak link is not fatal. Many must fail at once, to achieve a real disaster. Still . . . one wants as many sound, reliable links as possible, obviously."

"Obviously." *Why are you looking at me?*

"So. Tell me what happened on Jackson's Whole. As you saw it." Gregor sat up on his perch, hooking one heel and crossing his booted ankles, apparently centered and comfortable, like a raven on a branch.

"I'd have to start the story back on Earth."

"Feel free." His easy brief smile implied Mark had all the time in the world, and one hundred percent of his attention.

Haltingly, Mark began to stammer out his tale. Gregor's questions were few, only interjected when Mark hung up on the difficult bits; few but searching. Gregor was not in pursuit of mere facts, Mark quickly realized. He had obviously already seen Illyan's report. The Emperor was after something else.

"I cannot argue with your good intentions," said Gregor at one point. "The brain transplant business is a loathsome enterprise. But you do realize—your effort, your raid, is hardly going to put a dent in it. House Bharaputra will just clean up the broken glass and go on."

"It will make a permanent difference to the forty-nine clones," Mark asserted doggedly. "Everybody makes that same damned argument. 'I can't do it all, so I'm not going to do any.' And they don't. And it goes on, and on. And anyway, if I had been able to go back via Escobar as I'd planned in the first place—there would have been a big news splash. House Bharaputra might even have tried to reclaim the clones legally, and then there would *really* have been a public stink. I'd have made sure of it. Even if I'd been in Escobaran detention. Where, by the way, the House Bharaputra enforcers would have had a hard time getting at me. And maybe . . . maybe it would have interested some more people in the problem."

"Ah!" said Gregor. "A publicity stunt."

"It was not a stunt," Mark grated.

"Excuse me. I did not mean to imply your effort was trivial. Quite the reverse. But you *did* have a coherent long-range strategy after all."

"Yeah, but it went down the waste disintegrator as soon as I lost control of the Dendarii. As soon as they knew who I really was." He brooded on the memory of that helplessness.

At Gregor's prodding, Mark went on to recount Miles's death, the screw-up with the lost cryo-chamber, their aborted efforts to retrieve it, and their humiliating ejection from Jacksonian local space. He found himself revealing far more of his real thoughts than he was comfortable doing, yet . . . Gregor almost put him at his ease. How did the man do it? The soft, almost self-effacing demeanor camouflaged a consummately skillful people-handler. In a garbled rush, Mark described the incident with Maree and his half-insane time in solitary confinement, then trailed off into inarticulate silence.

Gregor frowned introspectively, and was quiet for a time. Hell, the man was quiet all the time. "It seems to me, Mark, that you devalue your strengths. You have been battle-tested, and proved your physical courage. You can take an initiative, and dare much. You do not lack brains, though sometimes . . . information. It's not a bad start on the qualities needed for a countship. Someday."

"Not any day. I don't want to be a Count of Barrayar," Mark denied emphatically.

"It could be the first step to my job," Gregor said suggestively, with a slight smile.

"No! That's even worse. They'd eat me alive. My scalp would join the collection downstairs."

"Very possibly." Gregor's smile faded. "Yes, I've often wondered where all my body parts are going to end up. And yet—I understand you were set to try it, just two years ago. Including Aral's countship."

"Fake it, yes. Now you're talking about the real thing. Not an imitation." *I'm just an imitation, don't you know?* "I've only studied the outsides. The inner surface I can barely imagine."

"But you see," said Gregor, "we all start out that way. Faking it. The role is a simulacrum, into which we slowly grow real flesh."

"Become the machine?"

"Some do. That's the pathological version of a Count, and there are a few. Others become . . . more human. The machine, the role, then becomes a handily-worked prosthetic, which serves the man. Both types have their uses, for my goals. One must simply be sure where on the range of self-delusion the man you're talking to falls."

Yes, Countess Cordelia had surely had a hand in training this man. Mark sensed her trail, like phosphorescent footsteps in the dark. "What are your goals?"

Gregor shrugged. "Keep the peace. Keep the various factions from trying to kill each other. Make bloody sure that no galactic invader ever puts a boot on Barrayaran soil again. Foster economic progress. Lady Peace is the first hostage taken when economic discomfort rises. Here my reign is unusually blessed, with the terraforming of the second continent, and the opening of Sergyar for full colonization.

Finally, now that that vile subcutaneous worm plague is under control. Settling Sergyar should absorb everyone's excess energies for several generations. I've been studying various colonial histories lately, wondering how many of the mistakes we can avoid . . . well, so."

"I still don't want to be Count Vorkosigan."

"Without Miles, you don't exactly have a choice."

"Rubbish." At least, he hoped it was rubbish. "You just said it's an interchangeable part. They could find someone else just fine if they had to. Ivan, I guess."

Gregor smiled bleakly. "I confess, I've often used the same argument. Though in my case the topic is progeny. Bad dreams about the destiny of my body parts are nothing compared to the ones I have about my theoretical future children's. And I'm not going to marry some high Vor bud whose family tree crosses mine sixteen times in the last six generations." He contained himself abruptly, with an apologetic grimace. And yet . . . the man was so controlled, Mark fancied even this glimpse of the inner Gregor served a purpose, or could be made to.

Mark was getting a headache. Without Miles . . . *With* Miles, all these Barrayaran dilemmas would be Miles's. And Mark would be free to face . . . his own dilemmas, anyway. His own demons, not these adopted ones. "This is not my . . . gift. Talent. Interest. Destiny. Something, I don't know." He rubbed his neck.

"Passion?" said Gregor.

"Yes, that'll do. A countship is not my passion."

After a moment, Gregor asked curiously, "What is your passion, Mark? If not government, or power, or wealth—you have not even mentioned wealth."

"Enough wealth to destroy House Bharaputra is so far beyond my reach, it just . . . doesn't apply. It's not a solution I can have. I . . . I . . . some men are cannibals. House Bharaputra, its customers—I want to stop the cannibals. *That* would be worth getting out of bed for." He became aware his voice had grown louder, and slumped down again in the soft chair.

"In other words . . . you have a passion for justice. Or dare I say it, Security. A curious echo of your, um, progenitor."

"No, no!" *Well . . . maybe, in a sense.* "I suppose there are cannibals on Barayar too, but they haven't riveted my close personal interest. I don't think in terms of law enforcement, because the transplant business isn't illegal on Jackson's Whole. So a policeman isn't the solution either. Or . . . it would have to be a damned unusual policeman." Like an ImpSec covert ops agent? Mark tried to imagine a detective-inspector bearing a letter of marque and reprisal. For some reason a vision of his progenitor kept coming up. Damn Gregor's unsettling suggestion. *Not a policeman. A knight-errant. The Countess had it dead-on.* But there was no place for knights-errant any more; the police would have to arrest them.

Gregor sat back with a faintly satisfied air. "That's very interesting." His abstracted look resembled that of a man assimilating the code-key to a safe. He slid from his stool to wander along the windows and gaze down from another angle. Face to the light, he remarked, "It seems to me your future access to your . . . passion, depends rather heavily on getting Miles back."

Mark sighed in frustration. "It's out of my hands. They'll never let me . . . what can I do that ImpSec can't? Maybe they'll turn him up. Any day now."

"In other words," said Gregor slowly, "the most important thing in your life at this moment is something you are powerless to affect. You have my profound sympathies."

Mark slipped, unwilled, into frankness. "I'm a virtual prisoner here. I can't do anything, and I can't leave!"

Gregor cocked his head. "Have you tried?"

Mark paused. "Well . . . no, not yet, actually."

"Ah." Gregor turned away from the window, taking a small plastic card from his inner jacket pocket. He handed it across the desk to Mark. "My Voice carries only to the borders of Barrayar's interests," he said. "Nevertheless . . . here is my private vidcom number. Your calls will be screened by only one person. You'll be on their list. Simply state your name, and you will be passed through."

"Uh . . . thank you," said Mark, in cautious confusion. The card bore only the code-strip: no other identification. He put it away very carefully.

Gregor touched an audiocom pin on his jacket, and spoke to Kevi. In a few moments there came a knock, and the door swung open to admit Ivan again. Mark, who had started to rock in Gregor's station chair—it did not squeak—self-consciously climbed out of it.

Gregor and Ivan exchanged farewells as laconically as they had exchanged greetings, and Ivan led Mark out of the tower room. As they rounded the corner Mark looked back at the sound of footsteps. Kevi was already ushering in the next man for his Imperial appointment.

"So how did it go?" Ivan inquired.

"I feel drained," Mark admitted.

Ivan smiled grimly. "Gregor can do that to you, when he's being Emperor."

"Being? Or playing?"

"Oh, not playing."

"He gave me his number." *And I think he got mine.*

Ivan's brows rose. "Welcome to the club. I can count the number of people who have that access without even taking both boots off."

"Was . . . Miles one of them?"

"Of course."

CHAPTER FOURTEEN

Ivan, apparently acting under orders—from the Countess, was Mark's first guess—took him out to lunch. Ivan followed a lot of orders, Mark noticed with a slight twinge of sympathy. They went to a place called the caravanserai, a stretched walking distance from Vorhartung Castle. Mark escaped another groundcar ride with Ivan by virtue of the narrowness of the streets—alleys—in the ancient district.

The caravanserai itself was a curious study in Barrayaran social evolution. Its oldest core was cleaned up, renovated, and converted into a pleasant maze of shops, cafes, and small museums, frequented by a mixture of city workers seeking lunch and obvious provincial tourists, come up to the capital to do the historic shrines.

This transformation had spread from the clusters of old government buildings like Vorhartung Castle along the river, toward the district's center; on the fringes to the south, the renovation petered out into the kind of shabby, faintly dangerous areas that had given the caravanserai its original risky reputation. On the way, Ivan proudly pointed out a building in which he claimed to have been born, during the war of Vordarian's Pretendership. It was now a shop selling overpriced hand-woven carpets and other antique crafts supposedly preserved from the Time of Isolation. From the way Ivan carried on Mark half-expected there to be a plaque on the wall commemorating the event, but there wasn't; he checked.

After lunch in one of the small cafes, Ivan, his mind now running on his family history, was seized with the notion of taking

493

Mark to view the spot on the pavement where his father Lord Padma Vorpatril had been murdered by Vordarian's security forces during that same war. Feeling it fit in with the general gruesome historic tenor of the rest of the morning, Mark agreed, and they set out again on foot to the south. A shift in the architecture, from the low tan stucco of the first century of the Time of Isolation to the high red brick of its last century, marked the marches of the caravanserai proper, or improper.

This time, by God, there *was* a plaque, a cast bronze square set right in the pavement; groundcars ran past and over it as Ivan gazed down.

"You'd think they'd at least have put it on the sidewalk," said Mark.

"Accuracy," said Ivan. "M'mother insisted."

Mark waited a respectful interval to allow Ivan who-knew-what inward meditations. Eventually Ivan looked up and said brightly, "Dessert? I know this great little Keroslav District bakery around the corner. Mother always took me there after, when we came here to burn the offering each year. It's sort of a hole in the wall, but good."

Mark had not yet walked down lunch, but the place proved as delectable on the inside as it was derelict on the outside, and he somehow ended up possessed of a bag of nut rolls and traditional brillberry tarts, for later. While Ivan lingered over a selection of delicacies to be delivered to Lady Vorpatril, and possibly some sweeter negotiation with the pretty counter-girl—it was hard to tell if Ivan was serious, or just running on spinal reflex—Mark stepped outside.

Galen had placed a couple of Komarran underground spy contacts in this area once, Mark remembered. Doubtless picked up two years ago in the post-plot sweep by Barrayaran Imperial Security. Still, he wondered if he could have found them, if Galen's dreams of revenge had ever come real. Should be one street down and two over . . . Ivan was still chatting up the bakery girl. Mark took a walk.

He found the address in a couple of minutes, to his sufficient satisfaction; he decided he didn't need to check inside. He turned back and took what looked like a short cut toward the main street and the bakery. It proved to be a cul-de-sac. He turned again and started for the alley's mouth.

An old woman and a skinny youth, who had been sitting on a stoop and watched him go in, now watched him coming out. The old woman's dull eye lit with a faint hostility as he came again into her short-sighted focus.

"That's no boy. That's a *mutie*," she hissed to the youth. Grandson? She nudged him pointedly. "A mutie come on *our* street."

Thus prodded, the youth slouched to his feet and stepped in front of Mark. Mark stopped. The kid was taller than he—who wasn't?—but not much heavier, greasy-haired and pale. He spread his legs aggressively, blocking Mark's dodge. Oh, God. Natives. In all their surly glory.

"Shouldn't ought to be here, mutie." He spat, in imitation-bully-mode; Mark almost laughed.

"You're right," he agreed easily. He let his accent go mid-Atlantic Earth, non-Barrayaran. "This place is a pit."

"Offworlder!" the old woman whined in even sharper disapproval. "You can take a wormhole jump to hell, offworlder!"

"I seem to have already," Mark said dryly. Bad manners, but he was in a bad mood. If these slum-louts wanted to bait him, he would bait them right back. "Barrayarans. If there's anything worse than the Vor it's the fools under 'em. No wonder galactics despise this place for a hole." He was surprised at how easily the suppressed rage vented, and how good it felt. Better not go too far.

"Gonna get you, mutie," the boy promised, hovering on the balls of his feet in nervous threat. The hag urged her bravo on with a rude gesture at Mark. A peculiar set-up; little old ladies and punks were normally natural enemies, but these two seemed in it together. Comrades of the Imperium, no doubt, uniting against a common foe.

"Better a mutie than a moron," Mark intoned with false cordiality.

The lout's brows wrinkled. "Hey! Is that back-chat to me? Huh?"

"Do you see any *other* morons around here?" At the boy's eye-flicker, Mark looked over his shoulder. "Oh. Excuse me. There *are* two more. I understand your confusion." His adrenaline pumped, turning his late lunch into a lump of regret in his belly. Two more youths, taller, heavier, older, but only adolescents. Possibly vicious, but untrained. Still . . . where was Ivan now? Where was that bloody invisible supposed outer perimeter guard? On break? "Aren't you late for school? Your remedial drooling class, perhaps?"

"*Funny* mutie," said one of the older ones. He wasn't laughing.

The attack was sudden, and almost took Mark by surprise; he thought etiquette demanded they exchange a few more insults first, and he was just working up some good ones. Exhilaration mixed strangely with the anticipation of pain. Or maybe it was the anticipation of pain that was exhilarating. The biggest punk tried to kick him in the groin. He caught the foot with one hand and boosted it skyward, flipping the kid onto his back on the stones with a wham that knocked the wind out of him. The second one launched a blow with his fist; Mark caught his arm. They whirled, and the punk found himself stumbling into his skinny companion. Unfortunately, now they both were between Mark and the exit.

They scrambled to their feet, looking astonished and outraged; what kind of easy pickings had they expected, for God's sake? *Easy enough.* His reflexes were two years stale, and he was already getting winded. Yet the extra weight made him harder to knock off his feet. *Three to one on a crippled-looking fat little lost stranger, eh? You like those odds? Come to me, baby cannibals.* The bakery bag was still clutched absurdly in his fist as he grinned and opened his arms in invitation.

They jumped him both together, telegraphing every move. The purely defensive *katas* continued to work charmingly; they flowed into, and out of, his momentum-gate to end up both on the ground, shaking their heads dizzily, victims of their own aggression. Mark wriggled his jaw, which had taken a clumsy blow, hard enough to sting and wake him up. The next round was not so successful; he ended up rolling out of reach, finally losing his grip on the bakery bag, which promptly got stomped. And then one of them caught up with him in a grapple, and they took some of their own back, pounding unscientific blows of clenched fists. He was getting seriously out of breath. He planned an arm-bar and a sprint to the street. It might have ended there, a good time having been had by all, if one of the idiot punks, crouching, hadn't pulled out a battered old shock-stick and jabbed it toward him.

Mark almost killed him instantly with a kick to the neck; he pulled his punch barely in time, and the blow landed slightly off-center. Even through his boot he could feel the tissues crush, a sickening sensation richoceting up through his body. Mark recoiled in horror as the kid lay gurgling on the ground. *No, I wasn't trained to fight. I was trained to kill. Oh, shit.* He'd managed not to quite smash the larynx. He prayed the kick hadn't snapped a major internal blood vessel. The other two assailants paused in shock.

Ivan pounded around the corner. "What the hell are you doing?" he cried hoarsely.

"I don't know," Mark gasped, bent over with his hands on his knees. His nose was bleeding all over his new shirt. In delayed reaction, he was beginning to shake. "They jumped me." *I baited them. Why* the hell was he doing this? It had all happened so fast. . . .

"Is the mutie with *you*, soldier?" the skinny kid demanded in a mixture of surprise and dread.

Mark could see the struggle in Ivan's face with the urge to disavow all connection with him. "Yes," Ivan choked out at last. The big punk who was still on his feet faded backward, turned, and ran. The skinny kid was glued to the scene by the presence of the injured man and the old woman, though he looked as if he wanted to run too. The hag, who had risen and hobbled over to her downed champion, screamed accusations and threats at Mark. She was the only one present who seemed undismayed by the sight of Ivan's officer's greens. Then the municipal guards arrived.

Once he was sure the injured punk was going to be taken care of, Mark shut up and let Ivan handle it. Ivan lied like a . . . trooper, to keep the name of *Vorkosigan* from ever coming up; the municipal guards in turn, realizing who Ivan was, dampened the old woman's hysteria and extricated them with speed. Mark declined to press assault charges even without Ivan's urgent advice to that effect. Thirty minutes later they were back in Ivan's groundcar. This time Ivan drove much more slowly; residual terror, Mark judged, from having almost lost his charge.

"Where the hell was that outer perimeter guy who was supposed to be my guardian angel?" Mark asked, gingerly probing the contusions on his face. His nose had finally stopped bleeding. Ivan hadn't let him in his groundcar until it had, and he'd made sure Mark wasn't going to throw up.

"Who d'you think called the municipal guards? The outer perimeter's *supposed* to be discreet."

"Oh." His ribs hurt, but nothing was broken, Mark decided. Unlike his progenitor, he'd never had a broken bone. *Mutie.* "Was . . . did *Miles* have to deal with this kind of crap?" All he'd done to those people was walk past them. If Miles had been dressed as he was, been alone as he was, would they have attacked *him*?

"*Miles* wouldn't have been stupid enough to wander in there by himself in the first place!"

Mark frowned. He'd gained the impression from Galen that Miles's rank made him immune to Barrayar's mutagenic prejudices. Did Miles actually have to run a constant safety-calculation in his head, editing where he could go, what he could do?

"And if he had," Ivan continued, "he'd have talked his way out of it. Slid on by. Why the hell did you mix in with three guys? If you just want somebody to beat the shit out of you, come to me. I'd be glad to."

Mark shrugged uncomfortably. Is that what he'd been secretly seeking? Punishment? Was that why things went so bad, so fast? "I thought you all were the great Vor. Why should you have to slide on by? Can't you just stomp the scum?"

Ivan groaned. "No. And am I ever glad I'm not going to be *your* permanent bodyguard."

"I'm glad too, if this is a sample of your work," Mark snarled in return. He checked his left canine tooth; his gum and lips were puffy, but it wasn't actually loose.

Ivan merely growled. Mark settled back, wondering how the kid with the damaged throat was doing. The municipal guards had taken him away for treatment. Mark should not have fought him; he'd come within a centimeter of killing him. He might have killed all three. The punks were only *little* cannibals, after all. Which was why, Mark realized, Miles would have talked and slid away; not fear, and not *noblesse oblige*, but because those people weren't up to his ... weight class. Mark felt ill. *Barrayarans. God help me.*

Ivan swung by his apartment, which was in a tower in one of the city's better districts, not far from the entirely modern government buildings housing the Imperial Service Command headquarters. There he allowed Mark to wash up and remove the bloodstains from his clothing before his return to Vorkosigan House. Tossing Mark's shirt back to him from the dryer, Ivan remarked, "Your torso is going to be piebald, tomorrow. Miles would have been in hospital for the next three weeks over that. I'd have had to cart him out of there on a board."

Mark glanced down at the red blotches, just starting to turn purple. He was stiffening up all over. Half a dozen pulled muscles protested their abuse. All that, he could conceal, but his face bore marks that were going to have to be explained. Telling the Count and Countess that he'd been in a groundcar wreck with Ivan would be perfectly believable, but he doubted they'd get away with the lie for long.

In the event, Ivan did the talking again, delivering him back to the Countess with a true but absolutely minimized account of Mark's adventure: "Aw, he wandered off and got pushed around a little by the local residents, but I caught up with him before anything much could happen. 'Bye, Aunt Cordelia ..." Mark let him escape without impediment.

The whole report had certainly caught up with the Count and Countess by dinner. Mark sensed the cool faint tension even as he slid into his place at the table opposite Elena Bothari-Jesek, who was back at last from her lengthy and presumably grueling debriefing at ImpSec HQ.

The Count waited until the first course had been served and the human servant had departed the dining room before remarking, "I'm glad your learning experience today was not lethal, Mark."

Mark managed to swallow without gagging, and said in a subdued voice, "For him, or me?"

"Either. Do you wish a report on your, ah, victim?"

No. "Yes. Please."

"The physicians at the municipal hospital expect to release him in two days. He will be on a liquid diet for a week. He will recover his voice."

"Oh. Good." *I didn't mean to . . .* What was the point of excuses, apologies, protests? None, surely.

"I looked into picking up his medical bill, privately, only to discover that Ivan had been in ahead of me. Upon reflection, I decided to let him stand for it."

"Oh." Ought he to offer to repay Ivan, then? Did he have any money, or any right to any? Legally? Morally?

"Tomorrow," stated the Countess, "Elena will be your native guide. And Pym will accompany you."

Elena looked very much less than thrilled.

"I spoke with Gregor," Count Vorkosigan continued. "You apparently impressed him enough, somehow, that he has given his approval for my formal presentation of you as my heir, House Vorkosigan's cadet member of the Council of Counts. At a time of my discretion, if and when Miles's death is confirmed. Obviously, this step is still premature. I'm not sure myself whether it would be better to get your confirmation pushed through before the Counts get to know you, or after they have had time to get used to the idea. A swift maneuver, hit and run, or a long tedious siege. For once, I think a siege would be better. If we won, your victory would be far more secure."

"Can they reject me?" Mark asked. *Is that a light I see at the end of this tunnel?*

"They must accept and approve you by a simple majority vote for you to inherit the Countship. My personal property is a separate matter. Normally, such approval is routine for the eldest son, or, lacking a son, whatever competent male relative a count may put forward. It doesn't even have to be a relative, technically, though it almost always is. There was the famous case of one of the Counts Vortala, back in the Time of Isolation, who had fallen out with his son. Young Lord Vortala had allied with his father-in-law in the Zidiarch Trade War. Vortala disinherited his son and somehow managed to maneuver a rump session of the counts into approving his horse, Midnight, as his heir. Claimed the horse was just as bright and had never betrayed him."

"What . . . a hopeful precedent for me," Mark choked. "How did Count Midnight do? Compared to the average Count."

"Lord Midnight. Alas, no one found out. The horse pre-deceased the Vortala, the war petered out, and the son eventually inherited after all. But it was one of the zoological high points of the Council's varied political history, right up there with the infamous Incendiary Cat Plot." Count Vorkosigan's eye glinted with a certain skewed enthusiasm, relating all this. His eye fell on Mark and his momentary animation faded. "We've had several centuries to accumulate any precedent you please, from absurdities to horrors. And a few sound saving graces."

The Count did not make further inquiries into Mark's day, and Mark did not volunteer further details. The dinner went down like lead, and Mark escaped as soon as he decently could.

He slunk off to the library, the long room at the end of one wing of the oldest part of the house. The Countess had encouraged him to browse there. In addition to a reader accessing public data banks and a code-locked and secured government comconsole with its own dedicated comm links, the room was lined with bound books printed and even hand-calligraphed on paper from the Time of Isolation. The library reminded Mark of Vorhartung Castle, with its modern equipment and functions awkwardly stuffed into odd corners of an antique architecture that had never envisioned nor provided place for them.

As he was thinking about the museum, a large folio volume of woodcuts of arms and armor caught his eye, and he carefully pulled it from its slipcase and carried it to one of a pair of alcoves flanking the long glass doors to the back garden. The alcoves were luxuriously furnished, and a little table pulled up to a vast wing-chair provided support for the, in both senses, heavy volume. Bemused, Mark leafed through it. Fifty kinds of swords and knives, with every slight variation possessing its own name, and names for all the parts as well . . . what an absolutely fractal knowledge-base, the kind created by, and in turn creating, a closed in-group such as the Vor. . . .

The library's door swung open, and footsteps sounded across the marble and carpeting. It was Count Vorkosigan. Mark shrank back in the chair in the alcove, drawing his legs up out of sight. Maybe the man would just take something and go out again. Mark did not want to get trapped into some intimate chat, which this comfortable room so invited. He had conquered his initial terror of the Count, yet the man managed still to make him excruciatingly uncomfortable, even without saying a word.

Unfortunately, Count Vorkosigan seated himself at one of the comconsoles. Reflections of the colored lights of its display flickered on the glass of the windows Mark's chair faced. The longer he waited, Mark realized, lurking like an assassin, the more awkward it was going to be to reveal himself. *So say hello. Drop the book. Blow your nose, something.* He was just working up the courage to try a little throat-clearing and page-rustling, when the door hinges squeaked again, and lighter footsteps sounded. The Countess. Mark huddled into a ball in the wing-chair.

"Ah," said the Count. The lights reflecting in the window died away as he shut down the machine in favor of this new diversion, and swung around in his station chair. Did she lean over for some quick embrace? Fabric whispered as she seated herself.

"Well, Mark is certainly getting a crash-course about Barrayar," she remarked, effectively spiking Mark's last frantic impulse to make his presence known.

"It's what he needs," sighed the Count. "He has twenty years of catching up to do, if he is to function."

"Must he function? I mean, instantly?"

"No. Not instantly."

"Good. I thought you might be setting him an impossible task. And as we all know, the impossible takes a little longer."

The Count vented a short laugh, which faded quickly. "At least he's had a glimpse of one of our worst social traits. We must be sure he gets a thorough grounding in the history of the mutagen disasters, so he'll understand where the violence is coming from. How deeply the agony and the fear are embedded, which drive the visible anxieties and, ah, as you Betans would see it, bad manners."

"I'm not sure he'll ever be able to duplicate Miles's native ability to dance through that particular minefield."

"He seems more inclined to plow through it," murmured the

Count dryly, and hesitated. "His appearance . . . Miles took enormous pains to move, act, dress, so as to draw attention away from his appearance. To make his personality overpower the evidence of the eye. A kind of whole-body sleight-of-hand, if you will. Mark . . . almost seems to be willfully exaggerating it."

"What, the surly slump?"

"That, and . . . I confess, I find his weight gain disturbing. Particularly, judging from Elena's report, its rapidity. Perhaps we ought to have him medically checked. It can't be good for him."

The Countess snorted. "He's only twenty-two. It's not an immediate health problem. That's not what's bothering you, love."

"Perhaps . . . not entirely."

"He embarrasses you. My body-conscious Barrayaran friend."

"Mm." The Count did not deny this, Mark noticed.

"Score one for his side."

"Would you care to clarify that?"

"Mark's actions are a language. A language of desperation, mostly. They're not always easy to interpret. *That* one is obvious, though."

"Not to me. Analyze, please."

"It's a three-part problem. In the first place, there's the purely physical side. I take it you did not read the medical reports as carefully as I did."

"I read the ImpSec synopsis."

"I read the raw data. All of it. When the Jacksonian body-sculptors were cutting Mark down to match Miles's height, they did not genetically retrofit his metabolism. Instead they brewed up a concoction of time-release hormones and stimulants which they injected monthly, tinkering with the formula as needed. Cheaper, simpler, more controlled in result. Now, take Ivan as a phenotypic sample of what Miles's genotype should have resulted in, without the soltoxin poisoning. What we have in Mark is a man physically reduced to Miles's height who is genetically programmed for Ivan's weight. And when the Komarrans' treatments stopped, his body again began to try to carry out its genetic destiny. If you ever bring yourself to look at him square on, you'll notice it's not just fat. His bones and muscles are heavier too, compared to Miles or even to himself two years ago. When he finally reaches his new equilibrium, he's probably going to look rather low-slung."

You mean spherical, Mark thought, listening with horror, and intensely conscious of having overeaten at dinner. Heroically, he smothered an incipient belch.

"Like a small tank," suggested the Count, evidently entertaining a somewhat more hopeful vision.

"Perhaps. It depends on the other two aspects of his, um, body-language."

"Which are?"

"Rebellion, and fear. As for rebellion—all his life, *other* people have made free with his somatic integrity. Forcibly chosen his body-shape. Now at last it's his turn. And fear. Of Barrayar, of us, but most of all fear, frankly, of being overwhelmed by Miles, who can be pretty overwhelming even if you're not his little brother. And Mark's right. It's actually been something of a boon. The armsmen and servants are having no trouble distinguishing him, taking him as Lord Mark. The weight ploy has that sort of half-cocked half-conscious brilliance that . . . reminds me of someone else we both know."

"But where does it stop?" The Count was now picturing something spherical too, Mark decided.

"The metabolism—when he chooses. He can march himself to a physician and have it adjusted to maintain any weight he wants. He'll choose a more average body-type when he no longer needs rebellion or feels fear."

The Count snorted. "I know Barrayar, and its paranoias. You can never be safe enough. What do we do if he decides he can never be fat enough?"

"Then we can buy him a float pallet and a couple of muscular body-servants. *Or*—we can help him conquer his fears. Eh?"

"If Miles is dead," he began.

"If Miles is not recovered and revived," she corrected sharply.

"Then Mark is all we have left of Miles."

"No!" Her skirts rustled as she rose, stepped, turned, paced. *God, don't let her walk over this way!* "That's where you take the wrong turn, Aral. Mark is all we have left of *Mark*."

The Count hesitated. "All right. I concede the point. But if Mark is all we have—do we have the next Count Vorkosigan?"

"Can you accept him as your son even if he *isn't* the next Count Vorkosigan? Or is that the test he has to pass to get in?"

The Count was silent. The Countess's voice went low. "Do I hear an echo of your father's voice in yours? Is that him I see, looking out from behind your eyes?"

"It is . . . impossible . . . that he not be there." The Count's voice was equally low, disturbed, but defiant of apology. "On some level. Despite it all."

"I . . . yes. I understand. I'm sorry." She sat again, to Mark's frozen relief. "Although surely it isn't that hard to qualify as a count of Barrayar. Look at some of the odd ducks who sit on the Council now. Or fail to show up, in some cases. How long did you say it's been since Count Vortienne cast a vote?"

"His son is old enough to hold down his desk now," said the Count. "To the great relief of the rest of us. The last time we had to have a unanimous vote, the Chamber's Sergeant-at-Arms had to go collect him bodily from his Residence, out of the most extraordinary scene of . . . well, he finds some unique uses for his personal guard."

"Unique qualifications, too, I understand." There was a grin in Countess Cordelia's voice.

"Where did you learn *that?*"

"Alys Vorpatril."

"I'm . . . not even going to ask how she knows."

"Wise of you. But the point is, Mark would really have to work at it to be the worst count on the Council. They are not so elite as they pretend."

"Vortienne is an unfairly horrible example. It's only because of the extraordinary dedication of so many of the counts that the Council functions at all. It consumes men. But—the counts are only half the battle. The sharper edge of the sword is the District itself. Would the people accept him? The disturbed clone of the deformed original?"

"They came to accept Miles. They've even grown rather proud of him, I think. But—Miles creates that himself. He radiates enough loyalty, they can't help but reflect some of it back."

"I'm not sure what Mark radiates," mused the Count. "He seems more of a human black hole. Light goes in, nothing comes out."

"Give him time. He's still afraid of you. Guilt projection, I think, from having been your intended assassin all these years."

Mark, breathing through his mouth for silence, cringed. Did the damned woman have x-ray vision? She was a most unnerving ally, if ally she was.

"Ivan," said the Count slowly, "would certainly have no trouble with popularity in the District. And, however reluctantly, I think he would rise to the challenge of the Countship. Neither the worst nor the best, but at least average."

"That's exactly the system he's used to slide through his schooling, the Imperial Service Academy, and his career so far. The invisible average man," said the Countess.

"It's frustrating to watch. He's capable of so much more."

"Standing as close to the Imperium as he does, how brightly does he dare shine? He'd attract would-be conspirators the way a searchlight attracts bugs, looking for a figurehead for their faction. And a handsome figurehead he'd make. He only plays the fool. He may in fact be the least foolish one among us."

"It's an optimistic theory, but if Ivan is so calculating, how can he have been like this since he could walk?" the Count asked plaintively. "You'd make of him a fiendishly Machiavellian five-year-old, dear Captain."

"I don't insist on the interpretation," said the Countess comfortably. "The point is, if Mark were to choose a life on, say, Beta Colony, Barrayar would contrive to limp along somehow. Even your District would probably survive. And Mark would not be one iota less our son."

"But I wanted to leave so much more. . . . You keep coming back to that idea. Beta Colony."

"Yes. Do you wonder why?"

"No." His voice grew smaller. "But if you take him away to Beta Colony, I'll never get a chance to know him."

The Countess was silent, then her voice grew firmer. "I'd be more impressed by that complaint if you showed any signs of wanting to get to know him *now*. You've been avoiding him almost as assiduously as he's been ducking you."

"I cannot stop all government business for this personal crisis," said the Count stiffly. "As much as I might like to."

"You did for Miles, as I recall. Think back on all the time you spent with him, here, at Vorkosigan Surleau . . . you stole time like a thief to give to him, snatches here and there, an hour, a morning, a day, whatever you could arrange, all the while carrying the Regency at a dead run through about six major political and military crises. You cannot deny Mark the advantages you gave Miles, and then turn around and decry his failure to outperform Miles."

"Oh, Cordelia," the Count sighed. "I was younger then. I'm not the Da Miles had twenty years ago. That man is gone, burned up."

"I don't ask that you try to be the Da you were then; that would be ludicrous. Mark is no child. I only ask that you try to be the father you are now."

"Dear Captain . . ." His voice trailed off in exhaustion.

After a thoughtful silence, the Countess said pointedly, "You'd have more time and energy if you *retired*. Gave up the Prime Ministership, at long last."

"Now? Cordelia, think! I dare not lose control now. As Prime Minister, Illyan and ImpSec still report to me. If I step down to a mere Countship, I am out of that chain of command. I'll lose the very power to prosecute the search."

"Nonsense. Miles is an ImpSec officer. Son of the Prime Minister or not, they'll hunt for him just the same. Loyalty to their own is one of ImpSec's few charms."

"They'll search to the limits of reason. Only as Prime Minister can I compel them to go beyond reason."

"I think not. I think Simon Illyan would still turn himself inside out for you after you were dead and buried, love."

When the Count spoke again at last his voice was weary. "I was ready to step down three years ago and hand it off to Quintillan."

"Yes. I was all excited."

"If only he hadn't been killed in that stupid flyer accident. Such a pointless tragedy. It wasn't even an assassination!"

The Countess laughed blackly at him. "A *truly* wasted death, by Barrayaran standards. But seriously. It's time to stop."

"Past time," the Count agreed.

"Let *go*."

"As soon as it's safe."

She paused. "You will never be fat enough, love. Let go anyway."

Mark sat bent over, paralyzed, one leg gone pins and needles. He felt plowed and harrowed, more thoroughly worked over than by the three thugs in the alley. The Countess was a scientific fighter, there was no doubt.

The Count half-laughed. But this time he made no reply. To Mark's enormous relief, they both rose and exited the library together. As soon as the door shut he rolled out of the wing-chair onto the floor, moving his aching arms and legs and trying to restore circulation. He was shaking and shivering. His throat was clogged, and he coughed at last, over and over, blessedly, to clear his breathing. He didn't know whether to laugh or cry, felt like doing both at once, and settled for wheezing, watching his belly rise and fall. He felt obese. He felt insane. He felt as if his skin had gone transparent, and passers-by could look and point to every private organ.

What he did not feel, he realized as he caught his breath again after the coughing jag, was afraid. Not of the Count and Countess, anyway. Their public faces and their privates ones were . . . unexpectedly congruent. It seemed he could trust them, not so much not to hurt him, but to be what they were, what they appeared. He could not at first put a word to it, this sense of personal unity. Then it came to him. *Oh. So that's what integrity looks like. I didn't know.*

CHAPTER FIFTEEN

The Countess kept her promise, or threat, to send Mark touring with Elena. The ensuing few weeks were punctuated by frequent excursions all over Vorbarr Sultana and the neighboring Districts, slanted heavily to the cultural and historical, including a private tour of the Imperial Residence. Gregor was not at home that day, to Mark's relief. They must have hit every museum in town. Elena, presumably acting under orders, also dragged him over what must have been two dozen colleges, academies, and technical schools. Mark was heartened to learn that not every institution on the planet trained military officers; indeed, the largest and busiest school in the capital was the Vorbarra District Agricultural and Engineering Institute.

Elena remained a formal and impersonal factotum in Mark's presence. Whatever her own feelings upon seeing her old home for the first time in a decade, they seldom escaped the ivory mask, except for an occasional exclamation of surprise at some unexpected change: new buildings sprouted, old blocks leveled, streets re-routed. Mark suspected that the frenetic pace of the tours was just so she wouldn't have to actually talk to him; she filled the silences instead with lectures. Mark began to wish he'd buttered up Ivan more. Maybe his cousin could have sneaked him out to go pub-crawling, just for a change.

Change came one evening when the Count returned abruptly to Vorkosigan House and announced that they were all going to Vorkosigan Surleau. Within an hour Mark found himself and his

508

things packed into a lightflyer, along with Elena, Count Vorkosigan, and Armsman Pym, arrowing south in the dark to the Vorkosigans' summer residence. The Countess did not accompany them. The conversation en route ranged from stilted to non-existent, except for an occasional laconic code between the Count and Pym, all half-sentences. The Dendarii mountain range loomed up at last, a dark blot against cloud shadows and stars. They circled a dimly glimmering lake to land halfway up a hill in front of a rambling stone house, lit up and made welcoming by yet more human servants. The Prime Minister's ImpSec guards were discreet shapes exiting a second lightflyer in their wake.

Since it was nearing midnight, the Count limited himself to giving Mark a brief orienting tour of the interior of the house and depositing him in a second-floor guest bedroom with a view downslope to the lake. Mark, alone at last, leaned on the windowsill and stared into the darkness. Lights shimmered across the black silken waters, from the village at the end of the lake and from a few isolated estates on the farther shore. *Why have you brought me here?* he thought to the Count. Vorkosigan Surleau was the most private of the Vorkosigans' several residences, the guarded emotional heart of the Count's scattered personal realm. Had he passed some test, to be let in here? Or was Vorkosigan Surleau itself to be a test? He went to bed and fell asleep still wondering.

He woke blinking with morning sun slanting through the window he'd failed to re-shutter the night before. Some servant last night had arranged a selection of his more casual clothing in the room's closet. He found a bathroom down the hall, washed, dressed, and went in cautious search of humanity. A housekeeper in the kitchen directed him outside to find the Count, without, alas, offering to feed him breakfast.

He walked along a path paved with stone chips toward a grove of carefully-planted Earth-import trees, their distinctive green leaves mottled and gilded by the beginnings of autumn color change. Big trees, very old. The Count and Elena were near the grove in a walled garden that served now as the Vorkosigan family cemetery. The stone residence had originally been a guard barracks serving the now-ruined castle at the lake's foot; its cemetery had once received the guardsmen's last stand-downs.

Mark's brows rose. The Count was a violent splash of color in his most formal military uniform, Imperial parade red-and-blues. Elena was equally, if more quietly, decorous in Dendarii dress-gray velvet set off with silver buttons and white piping. She squatted beside a shallow bronze brazier on a tripod. Little pale orange flames flickered in it, and smoke rose to wisp away in the gold-misted morning air. They were burning a death-offering, Mark realized, and paused uncertainly by the wrought-iron gate in the low stone wall. Whose? Nobody had invited him.

Elena rose; she and the Count spoke quietly together while the offering, whatever it was, burned to ash. After a moment Elena folded a cloth into a pad, picked the brazier off its tripod, and tapped out the gray and white flakes over the grave. She wiped out the bronze basin and returned it and its folding tripod to an embroidered brown and silver bag. The Count gazed over the lake, noticed Mark standing by the gate, and gave him an acknowledging nod; it did not exactly invite him in, but neither did it rebuff him.

With another word to the Count, Elena exited the walled garden. The Count saluted her. She favored Mark with a courteous nod in passing. Her face was solemn, but, Mark fancied, less tense and mask-like than he had seen since their coming to Barrayar. Now the Count definitely waved Mark inside. Feeling awkward, but curious, Mark let himself in through the gate and crunched over the gravel walks to his side.

"What's . . . up?" Mark finally managed to ask. It came out sounding too flippant, but the Count did not seem to take it in bad part.

Count Vorkosigan nodded to the grave at their feet: *Sergeant Constantine Bothari*, and the dates. *Fidelis.* "I found that Elena had never burned a death-offering for her father. He was my armsman for eighteen years, and had served under me in the space forces before that."

"Miles's bodyguard. I knew that. But he was killed before Galen started training me. Galen didn't spend much time on him."

"He should have. Sergeant Bothari was very important to Miles. And to us all. Bothari was . . . a difficult man. I don't think Elena ever was quite reconciled to that. She's needed to come to some acceptance of him, to be easy with herself."

"Difficult? Criminal, I'd heard."

"That is very . . ." The Count hesitated. *Unjust*, Mark expected him to add, or *untrue*, but the word he finally chose was " . . . incomplete."

They walked around among the graves, the Count giving Mark a tour. Relatives and retainers . . . who was Major Amor Klyeuvi? It reminded Mark of all those museums. The Vorkosigan family history since the Time of Isolation encapsulated the history of Barrayar. The Count pointed out his father, mother, brother, sister, and his Vorkosigan grandparents. Presumably anyone dying prior to their dates had been buried at the old District capital of Vorkosigan Vashnoi, and been melted down along with the city by the Cetagandan invaders.

"I mean to be buried here," commented the Count, looking over the peaceful lake and the hills beyond. The morning mist was clearing off the surface, sun-sparkle starting to glitter through. "Avoid that crowd at the Imperial Cemetery in Vorbarr Sultana. They wanted to bury my poor father there. I actually had to argue with them over that, despite the declaration of his will." He nodded to the stone, *General Count Piotr Pierre Vorkosigan*, and the dates. The Count had won the argument, apparently. The Counts.

"Some of the happiest periods of my life were spent here, when I was small. And later, my wedding and honeymoon." A twisted smile flitted across his features. "Miles was conceived here. Therefore, in a sense, so were you. Look around. This is where you came from. After breakfast, and I change clothes, I'll show you more."

"Ah. So, uh, no one's eaten yet."

"You fast, before burning a death-offering. They often tend to be dawn events for just that reason, I suspect." The Count half-smiled.

The Count could have had no other use for the glorious parade uniform here, nor Elena her Dendarii grays. They'd packed them along for that dedicated purpose. Mark glanced at the dark distorted reflection of himself in the Count's mirror-polished boots. The convex surface widened him to grotesque proportions. His future self? "Is that what we all came down here for, then? So that Elena could do this ceremony?"

"Among other things."

Ominous. Mark followed the Count back to the big stone house, feeling obscurely unsettled.

Breakfast was served by the housekeeper on a sunny patio off the end of the house, made private by landscaping and flowering bushes except for a view cut through to the lake. The Count re-appeared wearing old black fatigue trousers and a backcountry style tunic, loose-cut and belted. Elena did not join them. "She wanted to take a long walk," explained the Count briefly. "So shall we." Prudently, Mark returned a third sweet roll to its covered basket.

He was glad for his restraint very shortly, as the Count led him directly up the hill. They crested it and paused to recover. The view of the long lake, winding between the hills, was very fine and worth the breath. On the other side a little valley flattened out, cradling old stone stables and pastures cultivated to Earth-green grasses. Some unemployed-looking horses idled around the pasture. The Count led Mark down to the fence and leaned on it, looking pensive.

"That big roan over there is Miles's horse. He's been rather neglected, of late years. Miles didn't always get time to ride even when he was home. He used to come running, when Miles called. It was the damndest thing, to see that big lazy horse get up and come running." The Count paused. "You might try it."

"What? Call the horse?"

"I'd be curious to see. If the horse can tell the difference. Your voices are . . . very like, to my ear."

"I was drilled on that."

"His name is, uh, Ninny." At Mark's look he added, "A sort of pet or stable name."

Its name is Fat Ninny. You edited it. Ha. "So what do I do? Stand here and yell 'Here, Ninny, Ninny'?" He felt a fool already.

"Three times."

"What?"

"Miles always repeated the name three times."

The horse was standing across the pasture, its ears up, looking at them. Mark took a deep breath, and in his best Barrayaran accent called, "Here, Ninny, Ninny, Ninny. Here, Ninny, Ninny, Ninny!"

The horse snorted and trotted over to the fence. It didn't exactly run, though it did kick up its heels once, bouncing, en route. It arrived with a huff that sprayed horse moisture across both Mark and the Count. It leaned against the fence, which groaned and bent. Up close, it was bloody huge. It stuck its big head over the fence. Mark ducked back hastily.

"Hello, old boy." The Count patted its neck. "Miles always gives him sugar," he advised Mark over his shoulder.

"No wonder it comes running, then!" said Mark indignantly. And he'd thought it was the I-love-Naismith effect.

"Yes, but Cordelia and I give him sugar too, and he doesn't come running for us. He just sort of ambles around in his own good time."

The horse was staring at him in, Mark swore, utter bewilderment.

Yet another soul he had betrayed by not being Miles. The other two horses, in some sort of sibling rivalry, now arrived also, a massive jostling crowd determined not to miss out. Intimidated, Mark asked plaintively, "Did you bring any sugar?"

"Well, yes," said the Count. He drew half a dozen white cubes from his pocket and handed them to Mark. Cautiously, Mark put a couple into his palm and held it out as far as his arm would reach. With a squeal, Ninny laid his ears back and snapped from side to side, driving off his equine rivals, then demurely pricked them forward again and grubbed up the sugar with big rubbery lips, leaving a trail of grass-green slime in Mark's palm. Mark wiped some of it off on the fence, considered his trouser seam, and wiped the rest off on the horse's glossy neck. An old ridged scar spoiled the fur, bumpy under his hand. Ninny butted him again, and Mark retreated out of range. The Count restored order in the mob with a couple of shouts and slaps—*Ah, just like Barrayaran politics*, Mark thought irreverently—and made sure the two laggards received a share of sugar as well. He did wipe his palms on his trouser seams afterward, quite unself-consciously.

"Would you like to try riding him?" the Count offered. "Though he hasn't been worked lately, he's probably a bit fresh."

"No, thank you," choked Mark. "Some other time, maybe."

"Ah."

They walked along the fence, Ninny trailing them on the other side till its hopes were stopped by the corner. It whinnied as they walked away, a staggeringly mournful noise. Mark's shoulders hunched as from a blow. The Count smiled, but the attempt must have felt as ghastly as it looked, for the smile fell off again immediately. He looked back over his shoulder. "The old fellow is over twenty, now. Getting up there, for a horse. I'm beginning to identify with him."

They were heading toward the woods. "There's a riding trail . . . it circles around to a spot with a view back toward the house. We used to picnic there. Would you like to see it?"

A hike. Mark had no heart for a hike, but he'd already turned down the Count's obvious overture about riding the horse. He didn't dare refuse him twice, the Count would think him . . . surly. "All right." No armsmen or ImpSec bodyguards in sight. The Count had gone out of his way to create this private time. Mark cringed in anticipation. Intimate chat, incoming.

When they reached the woods' edge the first fallen leaves rustled and crackled underfoot, releasing an organic but pleasant tang. But the noise of their feet did not exactly fill the silence. The Count, for all his feigned country-casualness, was stiff and tense. Off-balance. Unnerved by him, Mark blurted, "The Countess is making you do this. Isn't she."

"Not really," said the Count, " . . . yes."

A thoroughly mixed reply and probably true.

"Will you ever forgive the Bharaputrans for shooting the wrong Admiral Naismith?"

"Probably not." The Count's tone was equable, unoffended.

"If it had been reversed—if that Bharaputran had aimed one short guy to the left—would ImpSec be hunting my cryo-chamber now?" Would Miles even have dumped Trooper Phillipi, to put Mark in her place?

"Since Miles would in that case be ImpSec in the area—I fancy the answer is yes," murmured the Count. "As I had never met you, my own interest would probably have been a little . . . academic. Your mother would have pushed all the same, though," he added thoughtfully.

"Let us by all means be honest with each other," Mark said bitterly.

"We cannot possibly build anything that will last on any other basis," said the Count dryly. Mark flushed, and grunted assent.

The trail ran first along a stream, then cut up over a rise through what was almost a gully or wash, paved with loose and sliding rock. Thankfully it then ran level for a time, branching and re-branching through the trees. A few little horse jumps made of cut logs and brush were set up deliberately here and there; the trails ran around as well as over them, optionally. Why was he certain Miles chose to ride over them? He had to admit, there was something prime-vally restful about the woods, with its patterns of sun and shade, tall Earth trees and native and imported brush creating an illusion of endless privacy. One could imagine that the whole planet was such a people-less wilderness, if one didn't know anything about terraforming. They turned onto a wider double track, where they could walk side by side.

The Count moistened his lips. "About that cryo-chamber."

Mark's head came up like the horse's had, sensing sugar. ImpSec wasn't talking to him, the Count hadn't been talking to him; driven half-crazy by the information vacuum, he'd finally broken down and badgered the Countess, though it made him feel ill to do so. But even she could only report negatives. ImpSec now knew over four hundred places the cryo-chamber was not. It was a start. Four hundred down, the rest of the universe to go . . . it was impossible, useless, futile—

"ImpSec has found it." The Count rubbed his face.

"What!" Mark stopped short. "They got it back? Hot damn! It's over! Where did they—why didn't you—" He bit off his words as it came to him that there was probably a very good reason the Count hadn't told him at once. And he wasn't sure he wanted to hear it. The Count's face was bleak.

"It was empty."

"Oh." What a stupid thing to say, *Oh.* Mark felt incredibly stupid, just now. "How—I don't understand." Of all the scenarios he'd pictured, he'd never pictured that. *Empty?* "Where?"

"The ImpSec agent found it in the sales inventory of a medical supply company in the Hegen Hub. Cleaned and re-conditioned."

"Are they sure it's the right one?"

"If the identifications Captain Quinn and the Dendarii gave us are correct, it is. The agent, who is one of our brighter boys, simply quietly purchased it. It's being shipped back by fast courier to ImpSec headquarters on Komarr for a thorough forensic analysis right now. Not that, apparently, there is much to analyze."

"But it's a lead, a break at last! The supply company must have records—ImpSec should be able to trace it back to—to—" To what?

"Yes, and no. The record trail breaks one step back from the supply company. The independent carrier they bought it from appears to be guilty of receiving stolen property."

"From Jackson's Whole? Surely that narrows down the search area!"

"Mm. One must remember that the Hegen Hub is a *hub.* The possibility that the cryo-chamber was routed into the Cetagandan Empire from Jackson's Whole, and back out again via the Hegen Hub, is . . . remote but real."

"No. The timing."

"The timing would be tight, but possible. Illyan has calculated it. The timing limits the search area to a mere . . . nine planets, seventeen stations, and all the ships en route between them." The Count grimaced. "I almost wish I was sure we were dealing with a Cetagandan plot. The Ghem-lords at least I could trust to know or guess the value of the package. The nightmare that makes me despair is that the cryo-chamber somehow fell into the hands of some Jacksonian petty thief, who simply dumped the contents in order to re-sell the equipment. We would have paid a ransom . . . a dozen times the value of the cryo-chamber for the dead body alone.

For Miles preserved and potentially revivable—whatever they asked. It drives me mad to think that Miles is rotting somewhere by *mistake.*"

Mark pressed his hands to his forehead, which was throbbing. His neck was so tight it felt like a piece of solid wood. "No . . . it's crazy, it's too crazy. We have both ends of the rope now, we're only missing the middle. It has to be connectable. Norwood—Norwood was loyal to Admiral Naismith. And smart. I met him, briefly. Of course, he hadn't planned to be killed, but he wouldn't have sent the cryo-chamber into danger, or off at random." Was he so sure? Norwood had expected to be able to pick up the cryo-chamber from its destination within a day at most. If it had arrived . . . wherever . . . with some sort of cryptic hold-till-called-for note attached, and then no one had called for it . . . "Was it re-conditioned before or after the Hub supply company purchased it?"

"Before."

"Then there has to be some sort of medical facility hidden in the gap somewhere. Maybe a cryo-facility. Maybe . . . maybe Miles was shifted into somebody's permanent storage banks." Unidentified, and destitute? On Escobar such a charity might be possible, but on Jackson's Whole? A most forlorn hope.

"I pray so. There are only a finite number of such facilities. It's checkable. ImpSec is on it now. Yet only the . . . frozen dead require that much expertise. The mere mechanics of cleaning an emptied chamber could be done by any ship's sickbay. Or engineering section. An unmarked grave could be harder to locate. Or maybe no grave, just disintegrated like garbage. . . ." The Count stared off into the trees.

Mark bet he wasn't seeing trees. Mark bet he was seeing the same vision Mark was, a frozen little body, chest blown out—you wouldn't even need a hand-tractor to lift it—shoved carelessly, mindlessly, into some disposal unit. Would they even wonder who the little man had been? Or would it just be a repellent *thing* to them? Who was *them*, dammit?

And how long had the Count's mind been running on this same wheel of thought, and how the devil was it that he could still walk and talk at the same time? "How long have you known this?"

"The report came in yesterday afternoon. So you see . . . it becomes measurably more important that I know where you stand. In relation to Barrayar." He started again up the trail, then took a side branch that narrowed and began to rise steeply through an area of taller trees and thinner brush.

Mark toiled on his heels. "Nobody in their right mind would stand in relation to Barrayar. They would run in relation to Barrayar. Away."

The Count grinned over his shoulder. "You've been talking too much to Cordelia, I fear."

"Yes, well, she's about the only person here who will talk to me." He caught up with the Count, who had slowed.

The Count grimaced painfully. "That's been true." He paced up the steep stony trail. "I'm sorry." After a few more steps he added, with a flash of dark humor, "I wonder if the risks I used to take did this to my father. He is nobly avenged, if so." More darkness than humor, Mark gauged. "But it's more than ever necessary . . . to know . . ."

The Count stopped and sat down abruptly by the side of the trail, his back to a tree. "That's strange," he murmured. His face, which had been flushed and moist with the hill-climb and the morning's growing warmth, was suddenly pale and moist.

"What?" said Mark cautiously, panting. He rested his hands on his knees and stared at the man, so oddly reduced to his eye level. The Count had a distracted, absorbed look on his face.

"I think . . . I had better rest a moment."

"Suits me." Mark sat too, on a nearby rock. The Count did not continue the conversation at once. Extreme unease tightened Mark's stomach. *What's wrong with him? There's something wrong with him. Oh, shit. . . .* The sky had grown blue and fine. A little breeze made the trees sigh, and a few more golden leaves flutter down. The cold chill up Mark's spine had nothing to do with the weather.

"It is not," said the Count in a distant, academic tone, "a perforated ulcer. I've had one of those, and this isn't the same." He crossed his arms over his chest. His breath was becoming shallow and rapid, not recovering its rhythm with sitting as Mark's was.

Something very wrong. A brave man trying hard not to look scared was, Mark decided, one of the most frightening sights he'd ever seen. Brave, but not stupid: the Count did not, for example, choose to pretend that nothing was the matter and go charging up the trail to prove it.

"You don't look well."

"I don't feel well."

"What do you feel?"

"Er . . . chest pain, I'm afraid," he admitted in obvious

embarrassment. "More of an ache, really. A very . . . odd . . . sensation. Came up between one step and the next."

"It couldn't be indigestion, could it?" Like the kind that was boiling up acidly in Mark's belly right now?

"I'm afraid not."

"Maybe you had better call for help on your comm link," Mark suggested diffidently. There sure as hell wasn't anything *he* could do, if this was the medical emergency it looked like.

The Count laughed, a dry wheeze. It was not a comforting sound. "I left it."

"What? You're the frigging Prime Minister, you can't go around without—"

"I wanted to assure an uninterrupted, private conversation. For a change. Unpunctuated by half the under-ministers in Vorbarr Sultana calling up to ask me where they left their agendas. I used to . . . do that for Miles. Sometimes, when it got too thick. Drove everyone crazy but eventually . . . they became . . . reconciled." His voice went high and light on the last word. He lay back altogether, in the detritus and fallen leaves. "No . . . that's no improvement. . . ." He extended a hand and Mark, his own heart lumping with terror, pulled him back into the sitting position.

A paralyzing toxin . . . heart failure . . . I was to get alone with you . . . I was to wait, in your sight, for twenty minutes while you died. . . . How had he made this happen? Black magic? Maybe he *was* programmed, and part of him was doing things the rest of him didn't know anything about, like one of those split personalities. *Did I do this? Oh, God. Oh shit.*

The Count managed a pallid grin. "Don't look so scared, boy," he whispered. "Just go back to the house and get my guardsmen. It's not that far. I promise I won't move." A hoarse chuckle.

I wasn't paying any attention to the paths on the way up. I was following you. Could he possibly carry . . . ? No. Mark was no medtech, but he had a clear cold feeling that it would be a very bad idea to try to move this man. Even with his new girth he was heavily outweighed by the Count. "All right." There hadn't been that many possible wrong turns, had there? "You . . . you . . ." *Don't you dare die on me, godammit. Not now!*

Mark turned, and trotted, skidded, and flat ran back down the path. Right or left? Left, down the double track. Where the hell had they turned on to it, though? They'd pushed through some brush—there was brush all along it, and half a dozen openings. There was one of those horse-jumps they'd passed. Or was it? A lot of them looked alike. *I'm going to get lost in this frigging woods, and run around in circles for . . . twenty minutes, till he's brain-dead and rigor-stiff, and they're all going to think I did it on purpose . . .* He tripped, and bounced off a tree, and scrambled for balance and direction. He felt like a dog in a drama, running for help; when he arrived, all he'd be able to do would be bark and whine and roll on his back, and no one would understand. . . . He clung to a tree, gasping and staring around. Wasn't moss supposed to grow on the north side of trees, or was that only on Earth? These were Earth trees, mostly. On Jackson's Whole a sort of slimy lichen grew on the south sides of everything, including buildings, and you had to scrape it out of the door grooves . . . ah! there was the creek. But had they walked up or down stream? *Stupid, stupid, stupid.* A stitch had started in his side. He turned left and ran.

Hallelujah! A tall female shape was striding down the path ahead of him. Elena, heading back to the barn. Not only was he on the right path, he'd found help. He tried to shout. It came out a croak, but it caught her attention; she looked over her shoulder, saw him, and stopped. He staggered up to her.

"What the hell's got into you?" Her initial coldness and irritation gave way to curiosity and nascent alarm.

Mark gasped out, "The Count . . . took sick . . . in the woods. Can you get . . . his guardsmen . . . up there?"

Her brows drew down in deep suspicion. "Sick? How? He was just fine an hour ago."

"*Real* sick, pleasedammit, hurry!"

"What did you *do*—" she began, but his palpable agony overcame her wariness. "There's a comm link in the stable, it's closest. Where did you leave him?"

Mark waved vaguely backward. "Somewhere . . . I don't know what you call it. On the path to your picnic spot. Does that make sense? Don't the bloody ImpSec guards have scanners?" He found he was practically stamping his feet in frustration at her slowness. "You have longer legs. Go!"

She believed at last, and ran, with a blazing look back at him that practically flayed his skin.

I didn't do— He turned and began to leg it back to where he'd left the Count. He wondered if he ought to be running for cover instead. If he stole a lightflyer and made it back to the capital, could he get one of the galactic embassies there to give him political asylum? *She thinks I . . . they're all going to think I . . .* hell, even *he* didn't trust himself, why should the Barrayarans? Maybe he ought to save steps and just kill himself right now, here in these stupid woods. But he had no weapon, and rough as the terrain was, there hadn't been any cliffs high and steep enough to fling himself over and be sure of death on impact.

At first Mark thought he'd taken another wrong turn. Surely the Count couldn't have risen and walked on—no. There he was, lying down on his back beside a fallen log. He was breathing in short labored gasps, with too-long pauses in between, arms clutched in, clearly in much greater pain than when Mark had left him. But not dead. Not dead yet.

"Hello. Boy," he huffed in greeting.

"Elena's bringing help," Mark promised anxiously. He looked up and around, and listened. *But they're not here yet.*

"Good."

"Don't . . . try to talk."

This made the Count snort a laugh, an even more horrible effect against the disrupted breathing. "Only Cordelia . . . has ever succeeded . . . in shutting me up." But he fell silent after that. Mark prudently allowed him the last word, lest he try to go another round.

Live, damn you. Don't leave me here like this.

A familiar whooshing sound made Mark look up. Elena had solved the problem of getting transport through the trees with a float-bike. A green-uniformed ImpSec man rode behind her, clutching her around the waist. Elena swiftly dropped the bike through the thinner branches, which crackled. She ignored the whipping backlash that left red lines across her face. The ImpSec man dismounted while the bike was still half a meter in the air. "Get back," he snarled to Mark. At least he carried a medkit. "What did you do to him?"

Mark retreated to Elena's side. "Is he a doctor?"

"No, just a medic." Elena was out of breath too.

The medic looked up and reported, "It's the heart, but I don't know what or why. Don't have the Prime Minister's doctor come here, have him meet us in Hassadar. Without delay. I think we're going to need the facilities."

"Right." Elena snapped orders into a comm link.

Mark tried to help them get the Count temporarily positioned on the float bike, propped between Elena and the corpsman. The medic glared at Mark. "Don't touch him!"

The Count, whom Mark had thought half-conscious, opened his eyes and whispered, "Hey. The boy's all right, Jasi." Jasi the medic wilted. "'S all right, Mark."

He's frigging dying, yet he's still thinking ahead. He's trying to clear me of suspicion.

"The aircar's meeting us in the nearest clearing," Elena pointed downslope. "Get there if you want to ride along." The bike rose slowly and carefully.

Mark took the hint and galloped off down the hill, intensely conscious of the moving shadow just above the trees. It left him behind. He slammed faster, using tree trunks to make turns, and arrived at the double trail with palms scraped raw just as the ImpSec medic, Elena, and Armsman Pym finished laying Count Vorkosigan across the backseat of the rear compartment of a sleek black aircar. Mark tumbled in and sat next to Elena on the rear-facing seat as the canopy closed and sealed. Pym took the controls in the front compartment, and they spiraled into the air and shot away. The medic crouched on the floor by his patient and did logical things like attaching oxygen and administering a hypospray of synergine to stabilize against shock.

Mark was puffing louder than the Count, to the point that the absorbed corpsman actually glanced up at him with a medical frown, but unlike the Count, Mark caught his breath after a time. He was sweating, and shaking inside. The last time he'd felt this bad Bharaputran security troops had been firing lethal weapons at him. *Are aircars supposed to fly this fast?* Mark prayed they wouldn't suck anything bigger than a bug into the thruster intakes.

Despite the synergine the Count's eyes were going shocked and vague. He pawed at the little plastic oxygen mask, batted away the medic's worried attempt to control his hands, and motioned urgently to Mark. He so clearly wanted to say something, it was less traumatic to let him than to try and stop him. Mark slid onto his knees by the Count's head.

The Count whispered to Mark in a tone of earnest confidence, "All . . . true wealth . . . is biological."

The medic glanced wildly at Mark for interpretation; Mark could only shrug helplessly. "I think he's going out of it."

The Count only tried to speak once more, on the hurtling trip; he clawed his mask away to say, "Spit," which the medic held his head to do, a nasty hacking which cleared his throat only temporarily.

The Great Man's last words, thought Mark blackly. All that monstrous, amazing life dwindled down at the end to *Spit.* Biological indeed. He wrapped his arms around himself and sat in a huddled ball on the floor, gnawing absently on his knuckles.

When they arrived at the landing pad at Hassadar District Hospital, what seemed a small army of medical personnel descended instantly upon them and whisked the Count away. The corpsman and the armsman were swept up; Mark and Elena were shuttled into a private waiting area, where they perforce waited.

At one point a woman with a report panel in her hand popped in to ask Mark, "Are you the next-of-kin?"

Mark's mouth opened, and stopped. He literally could not reply. He was rescued by Elena, who said, "Countess Vorkosigan is flying down from Vorbarr Sultana. She should be here in just a few more minutes." It seemed to satisfy the woman, who popped out again.

Elena had it right. It wasn't another ten minutes before the corridor was enlivened by the clatter of boots. The Countess swung in trailed by two double-timing liveried armsmen. She flashed past, giving Mark and Elena a quick reassuring smile, but blasted on through the double doors without pausing. Some clueless passing doctor on the other side actually tried to stop her: "Excuse me, ma'am, no visitors beyond this point—"

Her voice overrode his: "Don't give me that crap, kid, I *own* you." His protests ended in an apologetic gurgle as he saw the armsmen's uniforms and made the correct deduction; with a "Right this way, m'lady," their voices faded into the distance.

"She meant that," Elena commented to Mark with a faint sardonic curl to her lip. "The medical network in the Vorkosigan's District has been one of her pet projects. Half the personnel here are oath-sworn to her to serve in exchange for their schooling."

Time ticked by. Mark wandered to the window and stared out over the Vorkosigan's District capital. Hassadar was a New City, heir of destroyed Vorkosigan Vashnoi; almost all its building had taken place after the end of the Time of Isolation, mostly in the last thirty years. Designed around newer methods of transportation than horse carts, it was spread out like a city on any other developed galactic world, accented by a few sky-piercing towers gleaming in the morning sun. Still only morning? It seemed a century since dawn. This hospital was indistinguishable from a similar modest one on, say, Escobar. The Count's official residence here was one of the few entirely modern villas in the Vorkosigans' household inventory. The Countess claimed to like it, yet they used it only when in Hassadar on District business; more of a hotel than a home. Curious.

The shadows of Hassadar's towers had shortened toward noon before the Countess returned to collect them. Mark searched her face anxiously as she entered. Her steps were slow, her eyes tired and strained, but her mouth was not distorted with grief. He knew the Count still lived even before she spoke.

She embraced Elena and nodded to Mark. "Aral is stabilized. They're going to transfer him to the Imperial Military Hospital in Vorbarr Sultana. His heart is badly damaged. Our man says a transplant or a mechanical is definitely indicated."

"Where were you earlier this morning?" Mark asked her.

"ImpSec Headquarters." That was logical. She eyed him. "We divided up the work load. It didn't take the both of us to ride the tight-beam decoding room. Aral did tell you the news, didn't he? He swore to me he would."

"Yes, just before he collapsed."

"What were you doing?"

Slightly better than the usual, *What did you do to him?* Haltingly, Mark tried to describe his morning.

"Stress, breakfast, running up hills," the Countess mused. "He set the pace, I'll bet."

"Militarily," Mark confirmed.

"Ha," she said darkly.

"Was it an occlusion?" asked Elena. "That's what it looked like."

"No. That's why this took me so by surprise. I knew his arteries were clean—he takes a medication for that, or his awful diet would have killed him years ago. It was an arterial aneurism, within the heart muscle. Burst blood vessel."

"Stress, eh?" said Mark, dry-mouthed. "Was his blood pressure up?"

Her eyes narrowed. "Yes, considerably, but the vessel was weakened. It would have happened sometime soon anyway."

"Was there . . . any more word come in from ImpSec?" he asked timidly. "While you were there."

"No." She paced to the window, and stared unseeing at the web and towers of Hassadar. Mark followed her. "Finding the cryochamber that way . . . was pretty shattering to our hopes. At least it finally goaded Aral into trying to connect with you." Pause. "Did he?"

"No . . . I don't know. He took me around, showed me things. He tried. He was trying so hard, it hurt to watch." It hurt still, a knotted ache somewhere behind his solar plexus. The soul dwelt there, according to somebody-or-other's mythology.

"Did it," she breathed.

It was all too much. The window was safely shatterproof, but his hand was not; his soul-driven fist bunched, drew back, and struck.

The Countess caught it with a quick open hand; his self-directed violence smacked into her palm and was deflected.

"Save that," she advised him coolly.

CHAPTER SIXTEEN

A large mirror in a hand-carved frame hung on the wall of the antechamber to the library. Mark, nervous, detoured to stand in front of it for one last check before his inspection by the Countess.

The brown and silver Vorkosigan cadet's uniform did little to conceal the shape of his body, old distortions or new, though when he stood up very straight he fancied it lent him a certain blunt blockiness. Unfortunately, when he slumped, so did the tunic. It fit well, which was ominous, as when it had been delivered eight weeks ago it had been a little loose. Had some ImpSec analyst calculated his weight gain against this date? He wouldn't put it past them.

Only eight weeks ago? It felt as if he'd been a prisoner here forever. A gently held prisoner, true, like one of those ancient officers who, upon giving his oath of parole, was allowed the run of the fortress. Though no one had demanded his word on anything. Perhaps his word had no currency. He abandoned his repellent reflection and trudged on into the library.

The Countess was seated on the silk sofa, careful of her long dress, which was a high-necked thing in cloud-soft beige netted with ornate copper and silver embroidery. It echoed the color of her hair, done up in loops on the back of her head. Not a speck of black or gray or anything that could suggest anticipation of mourning anywhere: almost arrogantly elegant. *We're just fine here,* the ensemble seemed to say, *and very Vorkosigan.* Her head turned at Mark's entry, and her absorbed look melted into a brief spontaneous smile. It drew an answering smile from him despite himself.

"You look well," she said approvingly.

"So do you," he replied, and then, because it seemed too familiar, added, "ma'am."

Her brow quirked at the addition, but she made no comment. He paced to a nearby chair but, too keyed-up to sit, only leaned on its back. He suppressed a tendency for his right boot to tap on the marble floor. "So how do you think they're going to take this tonight? Your Vor friends."

"Well, you will certainly rivet their attention," she sighed. "You can count on it." She lifted a small brown silk bag with the Vorkosigan logo embroidered in silver on it, and handed it across to Mark. It clinked interestingly from the heavy gold coins it held. "When you present this to Gregor in the taxation ceremony tonight as proxy for Aral, it will serve formal notice to all that we claim you as a legitimate son—and that you accept that claim. Step One. Many others to follow."

And at the end of that path—the countship? Mark frowned deeply.

"Whatever your own feelings—whatever the final outcome of the present crisis—don't let them see you shake," the Countess advised. "It's all in the mind, this Vor system. Conviction is contagious. So is doubt."

"You consider the Vor system an illusion?" Mark asked.

"I used to. Now I would call it a creation, which, like any living thing, must be continually re-created. I've seen the Barrayaran system be awkward, beautiful, corrupt, stupid, honorable, frustrating, insane and breathtaking. Its gets most of the work of government done most of the time, which is about average for any system."

"So . . . do you approve of it, or not?" he asked, puzzled.

"I'm not sure my approval matters. The Imperium is like a very large and disjointed symphony, composed by a committee. Over a three-hundred year period. Played by a gang of amateur volunteers. It has enormous inertia, and is fundamentally fragile. It is neither unchanging nor unchangeable. It can crush you like a blind elephant."

"What a heartening thought."

She smiled. "We aren't plunging you into total strangeness, tonight. Ivan and your Aunt Alys will be there, and young Lord and Lady Vortala. And the others you've met here in the past few weeks."

Fruit of the excruciating private dinner parties. From before the Count's collapse, there had been a select parade of visitors to Vorkosigan House to meet him. Countess Cordelia had determinedly continued the process despite the week-old medical crisis, in preparation for this night.

"I expect everyone will be trolling for inside information on Aral's condition," she added.

"What should I tell 'em?"

"Flat truth is always easiest to keep track of. Aral is at ImpMil awaiting a heart to be grown for transplant, and being a very bad patient. His physician is threatening alternately to tie him to his bed or resign if he doesn't behave. You don't need to go into all the medical details."

Details that would reveal just how badly damaged the Prime Minister was. Quite. ". . . What if they ask me about Miles?"

"Sooner or later," she took a breath, "if ImpSec doesn't find the body, sooner or later there must be a formal declaration of death. While Aral lives, I would rather it be later. No one outside of the highest echelons of ImpSec, Emperor Gregor, and a few government officials knows Miles is anything but an ImpSec courier officer of modest rank. It is a perfectly true statement that he is away on duty. Most who inquire after him will be willing to accept that ImpSec hasn't confided to you where they sent him or for how long."

"Galen once said," Mark began, and stopped.

The Countess gave him a level look. "Is Galen much on your mind, tonight?"

"Somewhat," Mark admitted. "He trained me for this, too. We did all the major ceremonies of the Imperium, because he didn't know in advance just what time of year he'd drop me in. The Emperor's Birthday, the Midsummer Review, Winterfair—all of 'em. I can't do this and not think of him, and how much he hated the Imperium."

"He had his reasons."

"He said . . . Admiral Vorkosigan was a murderer."

The Countess sighed, and sat back. "Yes?"

"Was he?"

"You've had a chance to observe him for yourself. What do you think?"

"Lady . . . *I'm* a murderer. And I can't tell."

Her eyes narrowed. "Justly put. Well. His military career was long and complex—and bloody—and a matter of public record. But I imagine Galen's main focus was the Solstice Massacre, in which his sister Rebecca died."

Mark nodded mutely.

"The Barrayaran expedition's Political Officer, not Aral, ordered that atrocious event. Aral executed him for it with his own hands, when he found out. Without the formality of a court martial, unfortunately. So he evades one charge, but not the other. So yes. He is a murderer."

"Galen said it was to cover up the evidence. There'd been a verbal order, and only the Political Officer knew it."

"So how could Galen know it? Aral says otherwise. I believe Aral."

"Galen said he was a torturer."

"No," said the Countess flatly. "*That* was Ges Vorrutyer, and Prince Serg. Their faction is now extinct." She smiled a thin, sharp smile.

"A madman."

"No one on Barrayar is sane, by Betan standards." She gave him an amused look. "Not even you and me."

Especially not me. He took a small breath. "A sodomite."

She tilted her head. "Does that matter, to you?"

"It was . . . prominent, in Galen's conditioning of me."

"I know."

"You do? Dammit . . ." Was he glass, to these people? A feelie-drama for their amusement? Except the Countess didn't seem amused. "An ImpSec report, no doubt," he said bitterly.

"They fast-penta'd one of Galen's surviving subordinates. A man named Lars, if that means anything to you."

"It does." He gritted his teeth. Not a chance at human dignity, not one shred left to him.

"Aside from Galen, does Aral's private orientation matter? To you?"

"I don't know. Truth matters."

"So it does. Well, in truth . . . I judge him to be bisexual, but subconsciously more attracted to men than to women. Or rather—to soldiers. Not to men generally, I don't think. I am, by Barrayaran standards, a rather extreme, er, tomboy, and thus became the solution to his dilemmas. The first time he met me I was in uniform, in the middle of a nasty armed encounter. He thought it was love at first sight. I've never bothered explaining to him that it was his compulsions leaping up." Her lips twitched.

"Why not? Or were your compulsions leaping up too?"

"No, it took me, oh, four or five more days to come completely unglued. Well, three days, anyway." Her eyes were alight with memory. "I wish you could have seen him then, in his forties. At the top of his form."

Mark had overheard himself verbally dissected by the Countess too, in this very library. There was something weirdly consoling in the knowledge that her scalpel was not reserved for him alone. *It's not just me. She does this to everybody. Argh.*

"You're . . . very blunt, ma'am. What did Miles think of this?"

She frowned thoughtfully. "He's never asked me anything. It's possible that unhappy period in Aral's youth has come to Miles's ears only as the garbled slander of Aral's political enemies, and been discounted."

"Why tell me?"

"You asked. You are an adult. And . . . you have a greater need to know. Because of Galen. If things are ever to be square between you and Aral, your view of him should be neither falsely exalted nor falsely low. Aral is a great man. I, a Betan, say this; but I don't confuse greatness with perfection. To be great anyhow is . . . the higher achievement." She gave him a crooked smile. "It should give you hope, eh?"

"Huh. Block me from escape, you mean. Are you saying that no matter how screwed up I was, you'd still expect me to work wonders?" *Appalling.*

She considered this. "Yes," she said serenely. "In fact, since no one is perfect, it follows that all great deeds have been accomplished out of imperfection. Yet they were accomplished, somehow, all the same."

It wasn't just his *father* who had made Miles crazy, Mark decided. "I've never heard you analyze yourself, ma'am," he said sourly. Yes, who shaved the barber?

"Me?" She smiled bleakly. "I'm a fool, boy."

She evaded the question. Or did she? "A fool for love?" he said lightly, in an effort to escape the sudden awkwardness his question had created.

"And other things." Her eyes were wintry.

A wet, foggy dusk was gathering to cloak the city as the Countess and Mark were conveyed to the Imperial Residence. The splendidly liveried and painfully neat Pym drove the groundcar. Another half-dozen of the Count's armsmen accompanied them in another vehicle, more as honor guards than bodyguards, Mark sensed; they seemed to be looking forward to the party. At some comment of his to the Countess she remarked, "Yes, this is more of a night off for them than usual. ImpSec will have the Residence sewn up. There is a whole parallel sub-society of servants at these things—and it's not been totally unknown for an armsman of address to catch the eye of some junior Vor bud, and marry upward, if his military background is good enough."

They arrived at the Imperial pile, which was architecturally reminiscent of Vorkosigan House multipled by a factor of eight. They hurried out of the clinging fog into the warm, brilliantly-lit interior. Mark found the Countess formally attached to his left arm, which was both alarming and reassuring. Was he escort, or appendage? In either case, he sucked in his stomach and straightened his spine as much as he could.

Mark was startled when the first person they met in the vestibule was Simon Illyan. The security chief was dressed for the occasion in Imperial parade red-and-blues, which did not exactly render his slight form inconspicuous, though perhaps there were enough other red-and-blues present for him to blend in. Except that Illyan wore real lethal weapons at his hip, a plasma arc and a nerve disruptor in used-looking holsters, and not the blunted dual dress sword sets of the Vor officers. An oversized earbug glittered in his right ear.

"Milady." Illyan nodded and drew them aside. "When you saw him this afternoon," he said in a low voice to the Countess, "how was he?"

No need to specify who *he* was, in this context. The Countess glanced around, to be sure they were out of earshot of casual passers-by. "Not good, Simon. His color's bad, he's very edemic, and he tends to drift in and out of focus, which I find more frightening than all the rest put together. The surgeon wants to spare him the double stress of having a mechanical heart installed while they're waiting to bring the organic one up to size, but they may not be able to wait. He could end up in surgery for that at any moment."

"Should I see him, or not, in your estimation?"

"Not. The minute you walk in the door he'll sit up and try to do business. And the stress of trying will be as nothing compared to the stress of failing. That would agitate the hell out of him." She paused. "Unless you just popped in for a moment to, say, convey a bit of good news."

Illyan shook his head in frustration. "Sorry."

Since the Countess did not speak again immediately into the silence that followed, Mark dared to say, "I thought you were on Komarr, sir."

"I had to come back for this. The Emperor's Birthday Dinner is the security nightmare of the year. One bomb could take out practically the whole damned government. As you well know. I was en route when the news of Aral's . . . illness, reached me. If it would have made my fast courier go any faster, I would have gotten out and pushed."

"So . . . what's happening on Komarr? Who's supervising the, uh, search?"

"A trusted subordinate. Now that it appears we may be searching only for a body—" Illyan glanced at the Countess and cut himself off. She frowned grayly.

They're dropping the priority of the search. Mark took a disturbed breath. "So how many agents do you have searching Jackson's Whole?"

"As many as can be spared. This new crisis," a jerk of Illyan's head indicated Count Vorkosigan's dangerous illness, "is straining my resources. Do you have any idea how much unhealthy excitement the Prime Minister's condition is going to create on Cetaganda alone?"

"How many?" His voice went sharp, and too loud, but the Countess at least made no motion to quiet him. She watched with cool interest.

"Lord Mark, you are not yet in a position to request and require an audit of ImpSec's most secret dispositions!"

Not yet? Not ever, surely. "Request only, sir. But you can't pretend that this operation is not my business."

Illyan gave him an ambiguous, noncommittal nod. He touched his earbug, looked abstracted for a moment, and gave the Countess a parting salute. "You must excuse me, Milady."

"Have fun."

"You too." His grimace echoed the irony of her smile.

Mark found himself escorting the Countess up a wide staircase and into a long reception room lined with mirrors on one side and tall windows on the other. A major domo at the wide-flung doors announced them by title and name in an amplified voice.

Mark's first impression was of a faceless, ominous blur of colorful forms, like a garden of carnivorous flowers. A rainbow of Vor house uniforms, heavily sprinkled with parade red-and-blues, actually outshone the splendid dresses of the ladies. Most of the people stood in small, changing groups, talking in a babble; a few sat in spindly chairs along the walls, creating their own little courts. Servants moved smoothly among them, offering trays of food and drink. Mostly servants. All those extremely physically-fit young men in the uniform of the Residence's staff were surely ImpSec agents. The tough-looking older men in the Vorbarra livery who manned the exits were the Emperor's personal armsmen.

It was only his paranoia, Mark decided, that made it seem as if all heads turned toward him and a wave of silence crossed the crowd at their entry; but a few heads did turn, and a few nearby conversations did stop. One was Ivan Vorpatril and his mother, Lady Alys Vorpatril; she waved Countess Vorkosigan over to them at once.

"Cordelia, dear." Lady Vorpatril gave her a worried smile. "You must bring me up to date. People are asking."

"Yes, well, you know the drill," the Countess sighed.

Lady Vorpatril nodded wryly. She turned her head to direct Ivan, evidently continuing the conversation the Vorkosigan entrance had interrupted, "Do make yourself pleasant to the Vorsoisson girl this evening, if the opportunity arises. She's Violetta Vorsoisson's younger sister, perhaps you'll like her better. And Cassia Vorgorov is here. This is her first time at the Emperor's Birthday. And Irene Vortashpula, do get in at least one dance with her, later. I promised her mother. Really, Ivan, there are so many suitable girls here tonight. If only you would apply yourself a little . . ." The two older women linked arms to step away, effectively shedding Mark and Ivan from their private conversation. A firm nod from Countess Vorkosigan to Ivan placed him on notice that he was on guard duty again. Recalling the last time, Mark thought he might prefer the more formidible social protection of the Countess.

"What was that all about?" Mark asked Ivan. A servant passed with a tray of drinks; following Ivan's example, Mark snagged one too. It turned out to be a dry white wine flavored with citrus, reasonably pleasant.

"The biennial cattle drive." Ivan grimaced. "This and the Winterfair Ball are where all the high Vor heifers are trotted out for inspection."

This was an aspect of the Emperor's Birthday ceremonies Galen had never mentioned. Mark took a slightly larger gulp of his drink. He was beginning to damn Galen more for what he'd left out than for what and how he'd forced Mark to learn. "They won't be looking back at me, will they?"

"Considering some of the toads they do kiss, I don't see why not," shrugged Ivan.

Thank you, Ivan. Standing next to Ivan's tall red-and-blue glitter, he probably did look rather like a squat brown toad. He certainly felt like one. "I'm out of the running," he said firmly.

"Don't bet on it. There are only sixty Counts' heirs, but a lot more daughters to place. Hundreds, seems like. Once it gets out what happened to poor damned Miles, anything could happen."

"You mean . . . I wouldn't have to chase women? If I just stood still, they'd come to me?" Or at any rate, to his name, position, and money. A certain glum cheer came with the thought, if that wasn't a contradiction in terms. Better to be loved for his rank than not to be loved at all; the proud fools who proclaimed otherwise had never come so close to starving to death for a human touch as he had.

"It seemed to work that way for Miles," said Ivan, an inexplicable tincture of envy in his voice. "I could never get him to take advantage of it. Of course, he couldn't stand rejection. *Try again*, was my motto, but he'd just get all shattered and retreat into his shell for days. He wasn't adventurous. Or maybe he just wasn't greedy. Tended to stop at the first safe woman he came to. First Elena, and then when that fell through, Quinn. Though I suppose I can see why he might stop at Quinn." Ivan knocked back the rest of his wine and exchanged the glass for a full one from a passing tray.

Admiral Naismith, Mark reminded himself, was Miles's *alternate* personality. Very possibly Ivan did not know everything about his cousin.

"Aw, hell," Ivan remarked, glancing over his glass rim. "There's one of the ones on Mamere's short list, being aimed our way."

"So are you chasing women, or not?" asked Mark, confused.

"There's no point in chasing the ones *here*. It's all look-don't-touch. No chance."

By *chance* in this context, Mark gathered Ivan meant sex. Like many backward cultures still dependent on biological reproduction instead of the technology of uterine replicators, the Barrayarans divided sex into two categories: licit, inside a formal contract where any resultant progeny must be claimed, and illicit, i.e., all the rest. Mark brightened still further. Was this event, then, a sexual safety-zone? No tension, no terror?

The young woman Ivan had spotted was approaching them. She wore a long, soft pastel-green dress. Dark brown hair was wound up on her head in braids and curls, with some live flowers woven in. "So what's wrong with that one?" whispered Mark.

"Are you kidding?" murmured Ivan in return. "Cassia Vorgorov? Little shrimp kid with a face like a horse and a figure like a board . . . ?" He broke off as she came within earshot, and gave her a polite nod. "Hi, Cass." He kept almost all of the pained boredom out of his voice.

"Hello, Lord Ivan," she said breathlessly. She gave him a starry-eyed smile. True, her face was a little long, and her figure slight, but Mark decided Ivan was too picky. She had nice skin, and pretty eyes. Well, all of the women here had pretty eyes, it was the make-up. And the heady perfumes. She couldn't be more than eighteen. Her shy smile almost made him want to cry, so uselessly focused was it on Ivan. *Nobody has ever looked at me like that. Ivan, you are a filthy ingrate!*

"Are you looking forward to the dance?" she inquired of Ivan, transparently encouraging.

"Not particularly," shrugged Ivan. "It's the same every year."

She wilted. Her first time here, Mark bet. If there had been stairs, Mark would have been tempted to kick Ivan down them. He cleared his throat. Ivan's eye fell on him and lit with inspiration.

"Cassie," Ivan purred, "have you met my new cousin, Lord Mark Vorkosigan, yet?"

She seemed to notice him for the first time. Mark gave her a tentative smile. She stared back dubiously. "No . . . I'd heard . . . I guess he doesn't look exactly like Miles, does he."

"No." said Mark. "I'm not Miles. How do you do, Lady Cassia."

Belatedly recovering her manners, she replied, "How do you do, um, Lord Mark." A nervous bob of her head made the flowers shiver.

"Why don't you two get acquainted. Excuse me, I have to see a man—" Ivan waved to a red-and-blue uniformed comrade across the room and slithered away.

"Are you looking forward to the dance?" Mark tried. He'd been so concentrated on remembering all the formal moves of the taxation ceremony and the dinner, not to mention a Who's Who approximately three hundred names long all starting with "Vor," he'd hardly given the ensuing dance a thought.

"Um . . . sort of." Her eyes reluctantly abandoned Ivan's successful retreat, touched Mark, and flicked away.

Do you come here often? he managed not to blurt. What to say? *How do you like Barrayar?* No, that wouldn't do. *Nice fog we're having outside tonight.* Inside, too. *Give me a cue, girl! Say something, anything!*

"Are you really a *clone?*"

Anything but that. "Yes."

"Oh. My."

More silence.

"A lot of people are," he observed.

"Not here."

"True."

"Uh . . . oh!" Her face melted with relief. "Excuse me, Lord Mark. I see my mother is calling me—" She handed off a spasmodic smile like a ransom, and turned to hurry toward a Vorish dowager on the other side of the room. Mark had not seen her beckon.

Mark sighed. So much for the hopeful theory of the overpowering attraction of rank. Lady Cassia was clearly not anxious to kiss a toad. *If I were Ivan I'd do handstands for a girl who looked at me like that.*

"You look thoughtful," observed Countess Vorkosigan at his elbow. He jumped slightly.

"Ah, hello again. Yes. Ivan just introduced me to that girl. Not a girlfriend, I gather."

"Yes, I was watching the little playlet past Alys Vorpatril's shoulder. I stood so as to keep her back to it, for charity's sake."

"I . . . don't understand Ivan. She seemed like a nice enough girl to me."

Countess Vorkosigan smiled. "They're all nice girls. That's not the point."

"What is the point?"

"You don't see it? Well, maybe when you've had more time to observe. Alys Vorpatril is a truly doting mother, but she just can't overcome the temptation to try to micro-manage Ivan's future. Ivan is too agreeable, or too lazy, to resist openly. So he does whatever she begs of him—except the one thing she wants above all others, which is to settle into a marriage and give her grandchildren. Personally, I think his strategy is wrong. If he really wants to take the heat off himself, grandchildren would absolutely divert poor Alys's attention. Meanwhile her heart is in her mouth every time he takes a drive."

"I can see that," allowed Mark.

"I could slap him sometimes for his little game, except I'm

not sure he's conscious of it, and anyway it's three-quarters Alys's fault."

Mark watched Lady Vorpatril catch up with Ivan, down the room. Checking his evening's progress down the short list already, Mark feared. "You seem able to maintain a reasonably hands-off maternal attitude yourself," he observed idly.

"That . . . may have been a mistake," she murmured.

He glanced up and quailed inwardly at the deathly desolation he surprised, momentarily, in the Countess's eyes. *My mouth. Shit.* The look twitched away so instantly, he didn't even dare apologize.

"Not altogether hands-off," she said lightly, attaching herself to his elbow again. "Come on, and I'll show you how they cross-net, Barrayaran style."

She steered him down the long room. "There are, as you have just seen, two agendas being pursued here tonight," the Countess lectured amiably. "The political one of the old men—an annual renewal of the forms of the Vor—and the genetic agenda of the old women. The men imagine theirs is the only one, but that's just an ego-serving self-delusion. The whole Vor system is founded on the women's game, underneath. The old men in government councils spend their lives arguing against or scheming to fund this or that bit of off-planet military hardware. Meanwhile, the uterine replicator is creeping in past their guard, and they aren't even conscious that the debate that will fundamentally alter Barrayar's future is being carried on right now among their wives and daughters. To use it, or not to use it? Too late to keep it out, it's already here. The middle classes are picking it up in droves. Every mother who loves her daughter is pressing for it, to spare her the physical dangers of biological childbearing. They're fighting not the old men, who haven't got a clue, but an old guard of their sisters who say to their daughters, in effect, *We* had to suffer, so must you! Look around tonight, Mark. You're witnessing the last generation of men and women on Barrayar who will dance this dance in the old way. The Vor system is about to change on its blindest side, the side that looks to—or fails to look to—its foundation. Another half generation from now, it's not going to know what hit it."

Mark almost swore her calm, academic voice concealed a savagely vengeful satisfaction. But her expression was as detached as ever.

A young man in a captain's uniform approached them, and split a nod of greeting between the Countess and Mark. "The Major of Protocol requests your presence, my lord," he murmured. The statement too seemed to hang indeterminately in the air between them. "This way, please."

They followed him out of the long reception room and up an ornately carved white marble staircase, down a corridor, and into an antechamber where half a dozen Counts or their official representatives were marshaled. Beyond a wide archway in the main chamber, Gregor was surrounded by a small constellation of men, mostly in red-and-blues, but three in dark Minister's robes.

The Emperor was seated on a plain folding stool, even less than a chair. "I was expecting a throne, somehow," Mark whispered to the Countess.

"It's a symbol," she whispered back. "And like most symbols, inherited. It's a standard-issue military officer's camp stool."

"Huh." Then he had to part from her, as the Major of Protocol herded him into his appointed place in line. The Vorkosigan's place. *This is it.* He had a moment of utter panic, thinking he'd somehow mislaid or dropped the bag of gold along the way, but it was still looped safely to his tunic. He undid the silken cords with sweaty fingers. *This is a stupid little ceremony. Why should I be nervous now?*

Turn, walk forward—his concentration was nearly shattered by an anonymous whisper from somewhere in the antechamber behind him, "My God, the Vorkosigans are really going to do it . . . !"—step up, salute, kneel on his left knee; he proffered the bag right-handed, palm correctly up, and stuttered out the formal words, feeling as if plasma arc beams were boring into his back from the gazes of the waiting witnesses behind him. Only then did he look up to meet the Emperor's eyes.

Gregor smiled, took the bag, and spoke the equally formal words of acceptance. He handed the bag aside to the Minister of Finance in his black velvet robe, but then waved the man away.

"So here you are after all—Lord Vorkosigan," murmured Gregor.

"Just Lord Mark," Mark pleaded hastily. "I'm not Lord Vorkosigan till Miles is, is . . ." the Countess's searing phrase came back to him, "dead and *rotted*. This doesn't mean anything. The Count and Countess wanted it. It didn't seem like the time to give them static."

"That's so." Gregor smiled sadly. "Thank you for that. How are you doing yourself?"

Gregor was the first person ever to ask after him instead of the

Count. Mark blinked. But then, Gregor could get the real medical bulletins on his Prime Minister's condition hourly, if he wanted them. "All right, I guess." He shrugged. "Compared to everybody else, anyway."

"Mm," said Gregor. "You haven't used your comm card." At Mark's bewildered look he added gently, "I didn't give it to you for a souvenir."

"I . . . I haven't done you any favors that would allow me to presume upon you, sir."

"Your family has established a credit account with the Imperium of nearly infinite depth. You can draw on it, you know."

"I haven't asked for anything."

"I know. Honorable, but stupid. You may fit right in here yet."

"I don't want any favors."

"Many new businesses start with borrowed capital. They pay it back later, with interest."

"I tried that once," said Mark bitterly. "I borrowed the Dendarii Mercenaries, and bankrupted myself."

"Hm." Gregor's smile twisted. He glanced up, beyond Mark, at the throng no-doubt backing up in the antechamber. "We'll talk again. Enjoy your dinner." His nod became the Emperor's formal dismissal.

Mark creaked to his feet, saluted properly, and withdrew back to where the Countess waited for him.

CHAPTER SEVENTEEN

At the conclusion of the lengthy and tedious taxation ceremony, the Residence's staff served a banquet to a thousand people, spread through several chambers according to rank. Mark found himself dining just downstream from Gregor's own table. The wine and elaborate food gave him an excuse not to chat much with his neighbors. He chewed and sipped as slowly as possible. He still managed to end up uncomfortably overfed and dizzy from alcohol poisoning, till he noticed the Countess was making it through all the toasts by merely wetting her lips. He copied her strategy. He wished he'd noticed sooner, but at least he was able to walk and not crawl from the table afterwards, and the room only spun a little.

It could have been worse. I could have had to make it through all this while simultaneously pretending to be Miles Vorkosigan.

The Countess led him to a ballroom with a polished marquetry floor, which had been cleared for dancing, though no one was dancing yet. A live human orchestra, all men in Imperial Service uniforms, was arrayed in one corner. At the moment only a half dozen of its musicians were playing, a sort of preliminary chamber music. Long doors on one side of the room opened to the cool night air of a promenade. Mark noted them for future escape purposes. It would be an unutterable relief to be alone in the dark right now. He was even beginning to miss his cabin back aboard the *Peregrine*.

"Do you dance?" he asked the Countess.

"Only once tonight."

The explanation unfolded shortly when Emperor Gregor appeared, and with his usual serious smile led Countess Vorkosigan out onto the floor to officially open the dance. On the music's first repeat other couples began to join them. The Vor dances seemed to tend to the formal and slow, with couples arranged in complex groups rather than couples alone, and with far too many precise moves to memorize. Mark found it vaguely allegorical of how things were done here.

Thus stripped of his escort and protectress, Mark fled to a side chamber where the volume of the music was filtered to background level. Buffet tables with yet more food and drink lined one wall. For a moment, he longingly considered the attraction of anesthetic drinking. Blurred oblivion . . . *Right, sure. Get publicly drunk, and then, no doubt, get publicly sick.* Just what the Countess needed. He was halfway there already.

Instead he retreated to a window embrasure. His surly presence seemed enough to claim it against all comers. He leaned against the wall in the shadows, folded his arms, and set himself grimly to endure. Maybe he could persuade the Countess to take him home early, after her one dance. But she seemed to be working the crowd. For all that she appeared relaxed, social, cheerful, he hadn't heard a single word out of her mouth tonight that didn't serve her goals. So much self-control in one so secretly strained was almost disturbing.

His grim mood darkened further, as he brooded on the meaning of that empty cryo-chamber. *ImpSec can't be everywhere,* the Countess had once said. Dammit . . . ImpSec was supposed to be all-seeing. That was the intended implication of the sinister silver Horus-eye insignia on Illyan's collar. Was ImpSec's reputation just propaganda?

One thing was certain. Miles hadn't removed *himself* from that cryo-chamber. Whether or not Miles was rotted, disintegrated, or still frozen, a witness or witnesses must exist, somewhere. A thread, a string, a hook, a connection, a trail of bloody breadcrumbs, *something. I believe it's going to kill me if there isn't.* There had to be something.

"Lord Mark?" said a light voice.

He raised his eyes from blind contemplation of his boots to find himself facing a lovely cleavage, framed in raspberry pink gauze with white lace trim. Delicate line of collarbone, smooth swelling curves, and ivory skin made an almost abstract sculpture, a tilted topological landscape. He imagined himself shrunk to insect size, marching across those soft hills and valleys, barefoot—

"Lord Mark?" she repeated, less certainly.

He tilted his head back, hoping the shadows concealed the embarrassed flush in his cheeks, and managed at least the courtesy of eye contact. *I can't help it, it's my height. Sorry.* Her face was equally rewarding to the eye: electric blue eyes, curving lips. Short loose ash-blonde curls wreathed her head. As seemed the custom for young women, tiny pink flowers were braided into it, sacrificing their little vegetable lives for her evening's brief glory. However, her hair was too short to hold them successfully, and several were on the verge of falling out.

"Yes?" It came out sounding too abrupt. Surly. He tried again with a more encouraging, "Lady—?"

"Oh." She smiled. "I'm not Lady anything. I'm Kareen Koudelka."

His brow wrinkled. "Are you any relation to Commodore Clement Koudelka?" A name high on the list of Aral Vorkosigan's senior staff officers. Galen's list, of further assassinations if opportunity had presented.

"He's my father," she said proudly.

"Uh . . . is he here?" Mark asked nervously.

The smile disappeared in a momentary sigh. "No. He had to go to HQ tonight, at the last minute."

"Ah." To be sure. It would be a revealing study, to count the men who should have been here tonight but weren't because of the Prime Minister's condition. If Mark were actually the enemy agent he'd trained to be, in that other lifetime, it would be a fast way for him to discover who were the real key men in Aral Vorkosigan's support constellation, regardless of what the rosters said.

"You really don't look quite like Miles," she said, studying him with a critical eye—he stiffened, but decided sucking in his gut would only draw more attention to it—"your bones are heavier. It would be a treat to see you two together. Will he be back soon?"

She does not know, he realized with a kind of horror. *Doesn't know Miles is dead, doesn't know I killed him.* "No," he muttered. And then, masochistically, asked, "Were you in love with him too?"

"Me?" She laughed. "I haven't a chance. I have three older sisters, and they're *all* taller than I am. They call me the dwarf."

The top of his head was not quite level with the top of her shoulder, which meant that she was about average height for a Barrayaran woman. Her sisters must be valkyries. Just Miles's style. The perfume of her flowers, or her skin, rocked him in faint, delicate waves.

An agony of despair twisted all the way from his gut to behind his eyes. *This could have been mine. If I hadn't screwed it up, this could have been my moment.* She was friendly, open, smiling, only because she did not know what he had done. And suppose he lied, suppose he tried, suppose he found himself contrary to all reason walking in Ivan's most drunken dream with this girl, and she invited him mountain-climbing, like Miles—what then? How entertaining would it be for her, to watch him choke half to death in all his naked impotence? Hopeless, helpless, hapless—the mere anticipation of that pain and humiliation, again, made his vision darken. His shoulders hunched. "Oh, for God's sake go away," he moaned.

Her blue eyes widened in startled doubt. "Pym warned me you were moody . . . well, all right." She shrugged and turned, tossing her head.

A couple of the little pink flowers lost their moorings and bounced down. Spasmodically, Mark clutched at them. "Wait—!"

She turned back, still frowning. "What?"

"You dropped some of your flowers." He held them out to her in his two cupped hands, crushed pink blobs, and attempted a smile. He was afraid it came out as squashed as the blossoms.

"Oh." She took them back—long clean steady fingers, short undecorated nails, not an idle woman's hands—stared down at the blooms, and rolled up her eyes as if unsure how to reattach them. She finally stuffed them unceremoniously through a few curls on top of her head, out of order of their mates and more precarious than before. She began to turn away again.

Say something, or you'll lose your chance! "You don't wear your hair long, like the others," he blurted. Oh, no, she'd think he was criticizing—

"I don't have time to fool with it." Unconsciously compelled, her fingers raked a couple of curls, scattering more luckless vegetation.

"What do you do with your time?"

"Study, mostly." The vivacity his rebuff had so brutally suppressed began to leak back into her face. "Countess Vorkosigan has promised me, if I keep my class standing she'll send me to school on

Beta Colony next year!" The light in her eyes focused to a laser-scalpel's edge. "And I can. I'll show them. If Miles can do what he does, I can do this."

"What do you know about what Miles does?" he asked, alarmed.

"He made it through the Imperial Service Academy, didn't he?" Her chin rose, inspired. "When everyone said he was too puny and sickly, and it was a waste, and he'd just die young. And then after he succeeded they said it was only his father's favor. But he graduated near the top of his class, and I don't think his father had anything to do with *that*." She nodded firmly, satisfied.

But they had the die-young part right. Clearly, she was not apprised of Miles's little private army.

"How old are you?" he asked her.

"Eighteen-standard."

"I'm, um, twenty-two."

"I know." She observed him, still interested, but more cautious. Her eye lit with sudden understanding. She lowered her voice. "You're very worried about Count Aral, aren't you?"

A most charitable explanation for his rudeness. "The Count my father," he echoed. That was Miles's one-breath phrase. "Among other things."

"Have you made any friends here?"

"I . . . don't quite know." Ivan? Gregor? His mother? Were any of them friends, exactly? "I've been too busy making relatives. I never had any relatives before, either."

Her brows went up. "Nor any friends?"

"No." It was an odd realization, strange and late. "I can't say as I missed friends. I always had more immediate problems." *Still do.*

"Miles always seems to have a lot of friends."

"I'm not Miles," Mark snapped, stung on the raw spot. No, it wasn't her fault, he was raw all over.

"I can see that . . ." She paused, as the music began again in the adjoining ballroom. "Would you like to dance?"

"I don't know any of your dances."

"That's a mirror dance. Anybody can do the mirror dance, it's not hard. You just copy everything your partner does."

He glanced through the archway, and thought of the tall doors to the promenade. "Maybe—maybe outside?"

"Why outside? You wouldn't be able to see me."

"Nobody would be able to see me, either." A suspicious thought struck him. "Did my mother ask you to do this?"

"No . . ."

"Lady Vorpatril?"

"No!" She laughed. "Why ever should they? Come on, or the music will be over!" She took him by the hand and towed him determinedly through the archway, dribbling a few more flowers in her wake. He caught a couple of buds against his tunic with his free hand, and slipped them surreptitiously into his trouser pocket. *Help, I'm being kidnapped by an enthusiast . . . !* There were worse fates. A wry half-smile twitched his lips. "You don't mind dancing with a toad?"

"What?"

"Something Ivan said."

"Oh, Ivan." She shrugged a dismissive white shoulder. "Ignore Ivan, we all do."

Lady Cassia, you are avenged. Mark brightened still further, to medium-gloomy.

The mirror dance was going on as described, with partners facing each other, dipping and swaying and moving along in time to the music. The tempo was brisker and less stately than the large group dances, and had brought more younger couples out onto the floor.

Feeling hideously conspicuous, Mark plunged in with Kareen and began copying her motions, about half a beat behind. Just as she had promised, it took about fifteen seconds to get the hang of it. He began to smile, a little. The older couples were quite grave and elegant, but some of the younger ones were more creative. One young Vor took advantage of a hand-pass to bait his lady by briefly sticking one finger up his nose and wriggling the rest at her; she broke the rule and didn't follow, but he mirrored her look of outrage perfectly. Mark laughed.

"You look quite different when you laugh," Kareen said, sounding startled. She cocked her head in bemusement.

He cocked his head back at her. "Different from what?"

"I don't know. Not so . . . funereal. You looked as if you'd lost your best friend, when you were hiding back there in the corner."

If only you knew. She pirouetted; he pirouetted. He swept her an exaggerated bow; looking surprised but pleased, she swept one back at him. The view was charming.

"I'll just have to make you laugh again," she decided firmly. So, perfectly deadpan, she proceeded to tell him three dirty jokes in rapid succession; he ended up laughing at the absurdity of their juxtaposition with her maidenly airs as much as anything else.

"Where did you learn those?"

"From my big sisters, of course." She shrugged.

He was actually sorry when the music came to an end. This time he took the lead and urged her back into the next room for something to drink, and then out onto the promenade. After the concentration of the dance was over he'd become uncomfortably conscious of just how many people were looking at him, and it wasn't paranoid dementia this time. They'd made a conspicuous couple, the beautiful Kareen and her Vorkosigan toad.

It was not as dark outside as he'd hoped. In addition to the lights spilling from the Residence windows, colored spotlights in the landscaping were diffused by the fog to a gentle general illumination. Below the stone balustrade the slope was almost woods-like with old-growth bushes and trees. Stone-paved walkways zig-zagged down, with granite benches inviting lingerers. Still, the night was chilly enough to keep most people inside, which helped.

It was a highly romantic setting, to be wasted on him. *Why am I doing this?* What good was it to bait a hunger that could not feed? Just looking at her hurt. He moved closer anyway, more dizzy with her scent than with the wine and the dancing. Her skin was radiantly warm with the exercise; she'd light up a sniperscope like a torch. Morbid thought. Sex and death seemed too close-connected, somewhere in the bottom of his brain. He was afraid. *Everything I touch, I destroy. I will not touch her.* He set his glass on the stone railing and shoved his hands deep into his trouser pockets. His left fingertips compulsively rotated the little flowers he'd secreted there.

"Lord Mark," she said, after a sip of wine, "you're almost a galactic. If you were married, and going to have children, would you want your wife to use a uterine replicator, or not?"

"Why would any couple not choose to use a replicator?" he asked, his head spinning with this sudden new tack in conversation.

"To, like, prove her love for him."

"Good God, how barbaric! Of course not. I'd think it would prove just the opposite, that he didn't love *her*." He paused. "That was a strictly theoretical question, wasn't it?"

"Sort of."

"I mean, you don't know anyone who's seriously having this debate—not your sisters or anything?" he asked in worry. *Not you, surely?* Some barbarian needed his head stuck in a bucket of ice water, if so. And held under for a good long time, like till he stopped wriggling.

"Oh, none of my sisters are married yet. Though it's not for lack of offers. But Mama and Da are holding out. It's a strategy," she confided.

"Oh?"

"Lady Cordelia encouraged them, after the second of us girls came along. There was a period soon after she immigrated here, when galactic medicine was really spreading out, and there was this pill you could take to choose the sex of your child. Everyone went crazy for boys, for a while. The ratio's evened up again lately. But my sisters and I are right in the middle of the girl-drought. Any man who won't agree in the marriage contract to let his wife use a uterine replicator is having a real hard time getting married, right now. The go-betweens won't even bother dealing for him." She giggled. "Lady Cordelia's told Mama if she plays the game well, every one of her grandchildren could be born with a Vor in front of their names."

"I see." Mark blinked. "Is that an ambition of your parents?"

"Not necessarily." Kareen shrugged. "But all else being equal, that prefix does give a fellow an edge."

"That's . . . good to know. I guess." He considered his wine, and did not drink.

Ivan came out of one of the ballroom doors, saw them both, and gave them a friendly wave, but kept on going. He had not a glass but an entire bottle swinging from his hand, and he cast a slightly hunted look back over his shoulder before disappearing down the walkway. Glancing over the balustrade a few minutes later, Mark saw the top of his head pass by on a descending path.

Mark took a gulp of his drink then. "Kareen . . . am I *possible?*"

"Possible for what?" She tilted her head and smiled.

"For—for women. I mean, look at me. Square on. I really do look like a toad. All twisted up, and if I don't do something about it soon, I'm going to end up as wide as I am . . . short. And on top of it all, I'm a clone." Not to mention the little breathing problem. Summed up that way, hurling himself head-first over the balustrade seemed a completely logical act. It would save so much pain in the long run.

"Well, that's all true," she allowed judiciously.

Dammit, woman, you're supposed to deny it all, to be polite.

"But you're *Miles's* clone. You have to have his intelligence, too."

"Do brains make up for all the rest? In the female view?"

"Not to every woman, I suppose. Just to the smart ones."

"*You're* smart."

"Yes, but it would be rude of me to say so." She raked her curls and grinned.

How the hell was he to construe that? "Maybe I don't have Miles's brains," he said gloomily. "Maybe the Jacksonian body-sculptors stupified me, when they were doing all the rest, to keep me under control. That would explain a *lot* about my life." Now there was a morbid new thought to wallow in.

Kareen giggled. "I don't think so, Mark."

He smiled wryly back at her. "No excuses. No quarter."

"Now you sound like Miles."

A young woman emerged from the ballroom. Dressed in some pale blue silky stuff, she was athletically trim, glowingly blonde, and nearly as tall as Ivan. "Kareen!" She waved. "Mama wants us all."

"*Now*, Delia?" said Kareen, sounding quite put-out.

"Yes." She eyed Mark with alarmingly keen interest, but drawn by whatever daughterly duty, swung back inside.

Kareen sighed, pushed away from the stonework upon which she had been leaning, dusted futilely at a snag in her raspberry gauze, and smiled farewell. "It was nice meeting you, Lord Mark."

"It was nice talking with you too. And dancing with you." It was true. He waved, more casually than he felt, as she vanished into the warm light of the Residence. When he was sure she was out of sight, he knelt and surreptitiously collected the last of the tiny flowers she had shed and stuffed them into his pocket with the rest.

She smiled at me. Not at Miles. Not at Admiral Naismith. Me, myself, Mark. This was how it could have been, if he hadn't bankrupted himself at Bharaputra's.

Now that he was alone in the dark as he had wished, he discovered he didn't much care for it. He decided to go find Ivan, and struck off down the garden walkways. Unfortunately, the paths divided and re-divided, presumably to more than one destination. He passed couples who had taken to the sheltered benches despite the chill, and a few other men and women who'd just wandered down here for private talks, or to cool off. Which way had Ivan gone? Not this way, obviously; a little round balcony made a dead-end. He turned back.

Someone was following him, a tall man in red-and-blues. His face was in shadow. "Ivan?" said Mark uncertainly. He didn't think it was Ivan.

"So you're Vorkosigan's *clowne*." Not Ivan's voice. But his skewed pronunciation made the intended insult very clear.

Mark stood square. "You've got that straight, all right," he growled. "So who in this circus are you, the dancing bear?"

"A Vor."

"I can tell that by the low, sloping forehead. Which Vor?" The hairs were rising on the back of his neck. The last time he'd felt such exhilaration combined with intense sickness to his stomach had been in the alley in the caravanserai. His heart began to pound. *But he's made no threat yet, and he's alone. Wait.*

"Offworlder. You have no concept of the honor of the Vor," the man grated.

"None whatsoever," Mark agreed cheerfully. "I think you're all insane."

"You are no soldier."

"Right again. My, we are quick tonight. I was trained strictly as a lone assassin. Death in the shadows is a sort of speciality of mine." He began counting seconds in his head.

The man, who had started to move forward, sagged back again. "So it seems," he hissed. "You've wasted no time, promoting yourself to a countship. Not very subtle, for a trained assassin."

"I'm not a subtle man." He centered his balance, but did not move. No sudden moves. Keep bluffing.

"I can tell you this, little *clowne*." He gave it the same insulting slur as before. "If Aral Vorkosigan dies, it won't be *you* who steps into his place."

"Well, that's just exactly right," purred Mark. "So what are you all hot about, Vor bore?" *Shit. This one knows that Miles is dead. How the hell does he know? Is he an ImpSec insider?* But no Horus-eye stared from his collar; he bore a ship insignia of some kind, which Mark could not quite make out. Active-duty type. "What, to you, is one more little spare Vor drone living off a family pension in Vorbarr Sultana? I saw a herd of them up there tonight, swilling away."

"You're very cocky."

"Consider the venue," said Mark in exasperation. "You're not going to carry out any death threats here. It would embarrass ImpSec. And I don't think you want to annoy Simon Illyan, whoever the hell you are." He kept on counting.

"I don't know what hold you think you have on ImpSec," the man began furiously.

But he was interrupted. A smiling servant in the Residence's livery walked down the path carrying a tray of glasses. He was a very physically-fit young man.

"Drinks, gentlemen?" he offered.

The anonymous Vor glowered at him. "No, thank you." He turned on his heel and strode off. Shrubbery whipped in his wake, scattering droplets of dew.

"I'll take one, thanks," said Mark brightly. The servant proffered the tray with a slight bow. For his abused stomach's sake Mark stuck with the same light wine he'd been drinking most of the evening. "Eighty-five seconds. Your timing is lousy. He could have killed me three times over, but you interrupted just as the talk was getting interesting. How do you fellows pick this stuff out, real-time? You can't possibly have enough people upstairs to be following every conversation in the building. Automated key-word searches?"

"Canapé, sir?" Blandly, the servant turned the tray and offered the other side.

"Thank you again. Who was that proud Vor?"

The servant glanced down the now-empty pathway. "Captain Edwin Vorventa. He's on personal leave while his ship is in orbital dock."

"He's not in ImpSec?"

"No, my lord."

"Oh? Well, tell your boss I'd like to talk to him, at his earliest convenience."

"That would be Lord Voraronberg, the castellan's food and beverage manager."

Mark grinned. "Oh, sure. Go away, I'm drunk enough."

"Very good, my lord."

"Not come morning. Ah! One more thing. You wouldn't know where I could find Ivan Vorpatril right now, would you?"

The young man stared absently over the balcony a moment, as though listening, though no earbug showed. "There is a sort of gazebo at the bottom of the next left-hand turn, my lord, near a fountain. You might try there."

"Thank you."

Mark followed his directions, through the cool night mist. In a stray ray of light, fog droplets on his uniform sleeve shone like a cloud across the little silver rivers of the embroidery. He soon heard the plash of the fountain. A petite stone building, no walls, just deeply shadowed arches, overlooked it.

It was so quiet in this pocket of the garden, he could hear the breathing of the person inside. Only one person; good, he wasn't about to diminish his already low popularity still further by interrupting a tryst. But it was strangely hoarse. "Ivan?"

There was a long pause. He was trying to decide whether to call again or tiptoe off when Ivan's voice returned an uninviting growl of, "What?"

"I just . . . wondered what you were doing."

"Nothing."

"Hiding from your mother?"

" . . . Yeah."

"I, ah, won't tell her where you are."

"Good for you," was the sour reply.

"Well . . . see you later." He turned to go.

"Wait."

He waited, puzzled.

"Want a drink?" Ivan offered after a long pause.

"Uh . . . sure."

"So, come get it."

Mark ducked inside and waited for his eyes to adjust. The usual stone bench, and Ivan a seated shadow. Ivan proffered the gleaming bottle, and Mark topped up his glass, only to find too late that Ivan wasn't drinking wine, but rather some sort of brandy. The accidental cocktail tasted vile. He sat down by the steps with his back to a stone post and set his glass aside. Ivan had dispensed with the formality of a glass.

"Are you going to be able to make it back to your groundcar?" asked Mark doubtfully.

"Don't plan to. The Residence's staff will cart me out in the morning, when they pick up the rest of the trash."

"Oh." His night vision continued to improve. He could pick out the glittery bits on Ivan's uniform, and the polished glow of his boots. The reflections of his eyes. The gleam of wet tracks down his cheeks. "Ivan, are you—" Mark bit his tongue on *crying,* and changed it in mid-sentence to, "all right?"

"I," Ivan stated firmly, "have decided to get very drunk."

"I can see that. Why?"

"Never have, at the Emperor's Birthday. It's a traditional challenge, like getting laid here."

"Do people do that?"

"Sometimes. On a dare."

"How entertaining for ImpSec."

Ivan snorted a laugh. "Yeah, there is that."

"So who dared you?"

"Nobody."

Mark felt he was running out of probing questions faster than Ivan was running out of monosyllabic replies.

But, "Miles and I," Ivan said in the dark, "used to work this party together, most every year. I was surprised . . . how much I missed the little bugger's slanderous political commentary, this time around. Used to make me laugh." Ivan laughed. It was a hollow and un-funny noise. He stopped abruptly.

"They told you about finding the empty cryo-chamber, didn't they," said Mark.

"Yeah."

"When?"

"Couple of days ago. I've been thinking about it, since. Not good."

"No." Mark hesitated. Ivan was shivering, in the dark. "Do you . . . want to go home and go to bed?" *I sure do.*

"Never make it up the hill, now," shrugged Ivan.

"I'll give you a hand. Or a shoulder."

" . . . All right."

It took some doing, but he hoisted Ivan to his unsteady feet, and they navigated back up the steep garden. Mark didn't know what charitable ImpSec guardian angel passed the word, but they were met at the top not by Ivan's mother, but by his aunt.

"He's, ah . . ." Mark was not sure what to say. Ivan peered around blearily.

"So I see," said the Countess.

"Can we spare an armsman, to drive him home?" Ivan sagged, and Mark's knees buckled. "Better make it two armsmen."

"Yes." The Countess touched a decorative comm pin on her bodice. "Pym . . . ?"

Ivan was thus taken off his hands, and Mark breathed a sigh of relief. His relief grew to outright gratitude when the Countess commented that it was time for them to quit, too. In a few minutes Pym brought the Count's groundcar around to the entrance, and the night's ordeal was over.

The Countess didn't talk much, for a change, in the groundcar going back to Vorkosigan House. She leaned back against her seat and closed her eyes in exhaustion. She didn't even ask him anything.

In the black-and-white paved foyer the Countess handed off her cloak to a maid, and headed left, toward the library.

"You'll excuse me, Mark. I'm going to call ImpMil."

She looked so tired. "Surely they'd have called you, ma'am, if there was any change in the Count's condition."

"I'm going to call ImpMil," she said flatly. Her eyes were puffy slits. "Go to bed, Mark."

He didn't argue with her. He trudged wearily up the stairs to his bedroom corridor.

He paused outside the door to his room. It was very late at night. The hallway was deserted. The silence of the great house pressed on his ears. On an impulse, he turned back and stepped down the hall to Miles's room. There he paused again. In all his weeks on Barrayar, he had not ventured in here. He had not been invited. He tried the antique knob. The door was not locked.

Hesitantly, he entered, and keyed up the lights with a word. It was a spacious bedchamber, given the limits of the house's old architecture. An adjoining antechamber once meant for personal servants had long ago been converted to a private bathroom. At first glance the room seemed almost stripped, bare and neat and clean. All the clutter of childhood must have been boxed and put away in an attic, in some spasm of maturity. He suspected Vorkosigan House's attics were astonishing.

Yet a trace of the owner's personality remained. He walked slowly around the room, hands in his pockets like a patron at a museum.

Reasonably enough, the few mementos that had been retained tended heavily to reminders of successes. Miles's diploma from the Imperial Service Academy, and his officer's commission, were normal enough, though Mark wondered why a battered old Service issue weather manual was also framed and placed exactly between them. A box of old gymkhana awards going back to youth looked as if they might be heading for an attic very soon. Half a wall was devoted to a massive book-disk and vid collection, thousands of titles. How many had Miles actually read? Curious, he took the hand-viewer off its hook on the wall nearby and tried three disks at random. All had at least a few notes or glosses entered in the margin-boxes, tracks of Miles's thought. Mark gave up the survey, and passed on.

One object he knew personally; a cloissoné-hilted dagger, which Miles had inherited from old General Piotr. He dared to take it down and test its heft and edge. So when in the past two years had Miles stopped carting it around, and sensibly begun leaving it safely at home? He replaced it carefully on the shelf in its sheath.

One wall-hanging was ironic, personal, and obvious: an old metal leg-brace, crossed, military-museum fashion, with a Vor sword. Half joke, half defiance. Both obsolete. A cheap photonic reproduction of a page from an ancient book was matted and mounted in a wildly expensive silver frame. The text was all out of context, but appeared to be some sort of pre-jump religious gibberish, all about pilgrims, and a hill, and a city in the clouds. Mark wasn't sure what that was all about; nobody had ever accused Miles of being the religious type. Yet it was clearly important to him.

Some of these things aren't prizes, Mark realized. *They are lessons.*

A holovid portfolio box rested on the bedside table. Mark sat down and activated it. He expected Elli Quinn's face, but the first videoportrait to come up was of a tall, glowering, extraordinarily ugly man in Vorkosigan armsmen's livery. Sergeant Bothari, Elena's father. He keyed through the contents. Quinn was next, then Bothari-Jesek. His parents, of course. Miles's horse, Ivan, Gregor: after that, a parade of faces and forms. He keyed through faster and faster, not recognizing even a third of the people. After the fiftieth face, he stopped clicking.

He rubbed his face wearily. *He's not a man, he's a mob.* Right. He sat bent and aching, face in his hands, elbows on his knees. *No. I am not Miles.*

Miles's comconsole was the secured type, in no way junior to the one in the Count's library. Mark walked over and examined it only by eye; his hands he shoved back deep into his trouser pockets. His fingertips encountered Kareen Koudelka's crumpled flowerlets.

He drew them out and spread them on his palm. In a spasm of frustration, he smashed the blooms with his other hand, and threw them to the floor. Less than a minute later he was on his hands and knees frantically scraping the scattered bits up off the carpet again. *I think I must be insane.* He sat on his knees on the floor and began to cry.

Unlike poor Ivan, no one interrupted his misery, for which he was profoundly grateful. He sent a mental apology after his Vorpatril cousin, *Sorry, sorry* ... though odds were even whether Ivan would remember anything about his intrusion come the morning. He gulped for control of his breath, his head aching fiercely.

Ten minutes delay downside at Bharaputra's had been all the

difference. If they'd been ten minutes faster, the Dendarii would have made it back to their drop shuttle before the Bharaputrans had a chance to blow it up, and all would have unfolded into another future. Thousands of ten-minute intervals had passed in his life, unmarked and without effect. But *that* ten minutes had been all it took to transform him from would-be hero to permanent scum. And he could never recover the moment.

Was that, then, the commander's gift: to recognize those critical minutes, out of the mass of like moments, even in the chaos of their midst? To risk all to grab the golden ones? Miles had possessed that gift of timing to an extraordinary degree. Men and women followed him, laid all their trust at his feet, just for that.

Except once, Miles's timing had failed. . . .

No. He'd been screaming his lungs out for them to keep moving. *Miles's* timing had been shrewd. His feet had been fatally slowed by others' delays.

Mark climbed up off the floor, washed his face in the bathroom, and returned and sat in the comconsole's station chair. The first layer of secured functions was entered by a palm-lock. The machine did not quite like his palm-print; bone growth and subcutaneous fat deposits were beginning to distort the pattern out of the range of recognition. But not wholly, not yet; on the fourth try it took a reading that pleased it, and opened files to him. The next layer of functions required codes and accesses he did not know, but the top layer had all he needed for now: a private, if not secured, comm channel to ImpSec.

ImpSec's machine bounced him to a human receptionist almost immediately. "My name is Lord Mark Vorkosigan," he told the corporal on night duty, whose face appeared above the vid plate. "I want to speak with Simon Illyan. I suppose he's still at the Imperial Residence."

"Is this an emergency, my lord?" the corporal asked.

"It is to me," growled Mark.

Whatever the corporal thought of that, he patched Mark on through. Mark insisted his way past two more layers of subordinates before the ImpSec chief's tired face materialized.

Mark swallowed. "Captain Illyan."

"Yes, Lord Mark, what is it?" Illyan said wearily. It had been a long night for ImpSec, too.

"I had an interesting conversation with a certain Captain Vorventa, earlier this evening."

"I am aware. You offered him some not-too-oblique threats."

And Mark had assumed that ImpSec guard/servant had been sent to protect *him* . . . ah, well.

"So I have a question for you, sir. Is Captain Vorventa on the list of people who are supposed to know about Miles?"

Illyan's eyes narrowed. "No."

"Well, he does."

"That's . . . very interesting."

"Is that helpful for you to know?"

Illyan sighed. "It gives me a new problem to worry about. Where is the internal leak? Now I'll have to find out."

"But—better to know than not."

"Oh, yes."

"Can I ask a favor in return?"

"Maybe." Illyan looked extremely non-committal. "What kind of favor?"

"I want in."

"What?"

"I want in. On ImpSec's search for Miles. I want to start by reviewing your reports, I suppose. After that, I don't know. But I can't stand being kept alone in the dark any more."

Illyan regarded him suspiciously. "No," he said at last. "I'm not turning you loose to romp through my top-secret files, thank you. Good night, Lord Mark."

"Wait, sir! You complained you were understaffed. You can't turn down a volunteer."

"What do you imagine you can do that ImpSec hasn't?" Illyan snapped.

"The point is, sir—ImpSec hasn't. You haven't found Miles. I can hardly do *less*."

He hadn't put that quite as diplomatically as he should have, Mark realized, as Illyan's face darkened with anger. "Good *night*, Lord Mark," Illyan repeated through his teeth, and cut the link with a swipe of his hand.

Mark sat frozen in Miles's station chair. The house was so quiet the loudest sound he could hear was his own blood in his ears. He should have pointed out to Illyan how clever he'd been, how quick on the uptake; Vorventa had revealed what he knew, but in no way had Mark cross-revealed that he knew Vorventa knew. Illyan's investigation must now take the leak, whatever it was, by surprise. *Isn't that worth something? I'm not as stupid as you think I am.*

You're not as smart as I thought you were, either, Illyan. You are not . . . perfect. That was disturbing. He had expected ImpSec to be perfect, somehow; it had anchored his world to think so. And Miles, perfect. And the Count and Countess. All perfect, all unkillable. All made out of rubber. The only real pain, his own.

He thought of Ivan, crying in the shadows. Of the Count, dying in the woods. The Countess had kept her mask up better than any of them. She had to. She had more to hide. Miles himself, the man who had created a whole other personality just to escape into. . . .

The trouble, Mark decided, was that he had been trying to be Miles Vorkosigan all by himself. Even *Miles* didn't do Miles that way. He had co-opted an entire supporting cast. A cast of thousands. *No wonder I can never catch up with him.*

Slowly, curiously, Mark opened his tunic and removed Gregor's comm card from his inner breast pocket, and set it on the comconsole desk. He stared hard at the anonymous plastic chip, as if it bore some coded message for his eyes only. He rather fancied it did.

You knew. You knew, didn't you, Gregor you bastard. You've just been waiting for me to figure it out for myself.

With spasmodic decision, Mark jammed the card into the comconsole's read-slot.

No machines this time. A man in ordinary civilian clothing answered immediately, though without identifying himself. "Yes?"

"I'm Lord Mark Vorkosigan. I should be on your list. I want to talk to Gregor."

"Right now, my lord?" said the man mildly. His hand danced over a keypad array to one side.

"Yes. Now. Please."

"You are cleared." He vanished.

The vid plate remained dark, but the audio transmitted a melodious chime. It chimed for quite a long time. Mark began to panic. What if—but then it stopped. There was a mysterious clanking sound, and Gregor's voice said, "Yes?" in a bleary tone. No visuals.

"It's me. Mark Vorkosigan. Lord Mark."

"Yeah?"

"You told me to call you."

"Yes, but it's . . ." a short pause, "five in the bleeding *morning,* Mark!"

"Oh. Were you asleep?" he caroled frantically. He leaned forward and beat his head gently on the hard cool plastic of the desk. *Timing. My timing.*

"*God*, you sound just like Miles when you say that," muttered the Emperor. The vid plate activated; Gregor's image came up as he turned on a light. He was in some sort of bedroom, dim in the background, and was wearing nothing but loose black silky pajama pants. He peered at Mark, as if making sure he wasn't talking to a ghost. But the *corpus* was too corpulant to be anyone but Mark. The Emperor heaved an oxygenating sigh and blinked himself to focus. "What do you need?"

How wonderfully succinct. If he answered in full, it could take him the next six hours.

"I need to be in on ImpSec's search for Miles. Illyan won't let me. You can override him."

Gregor sat still for a minute, then barked a brief laugh. He swiped a hand through sleep-bent black hair. "Have you asked him?"

"Yes. Just now. He turned me down."

"Mm, well . . . it's his job to be cautious for me. So that my judgment may remain untrammeled."

"In your untrammeled judgment, sir. Sire. Let me in!"

Gregor studied him thoughtfully, rubbing his face. "Yes . . ." he drawled slowly after a moment. "Let's . . . see what happens." His eyes were not bleary now.

"Can you call Illyan right now, sire?"

"What is this, pent-up demand? The dam breaks?"

I am poured out like water . . . where did that quote come from? It sounded like something of the Countess's. "He's still up. Please. Sire. And have him call me back at this console to confirm. I'll wait."

"Very well," Gregor's lips twisted up in a peculiar smile, "Lord Mark."

"Thank you, sire. Uh . . . good night."

"Good morning." Gregor cut the comm.

Mark waited. The seconds ticked by, stretched out of all recognition. His hangover was starting, but he was still slightly drunk. The worst of both worlds. He had started to doze when the comconsole chimed at last, and he nearly spasmed out of his chair.

He slapped urgently at the controls. "Yes. Sir?"

Illyan's saturnine face appeared over the vid plate. "Lord Mark." He gave Mark the barest nod. "If you come to ImpSec headquarters at the beginning of normal business hours tomorrow morning, you will be permitted to review the files we discussed."

"Thank you, sir," said Mark sincerely.

"That's two-and-one-half hours from now," Illyan mentioned with, Mark thought, an understandable hint of sadism. Illyan hadn't slept either.

"I'll be there."

Illyan acknowledged this with a shiver of his eyelids, and vanished.

Damnation through good works, or grace alone? Mark meditated on Gregor's grace. *He knew. He knew it before I did.* Lord Mark Vorkosigan was a real person.

CHAPTER EIGHTEEN

The level light of dawn turned the night's lingering mist to gold, a smoky autumnal haze that gave the city of Vorbarr Sultana an almost magical air. The Imperial Security Headquarters building stood windowless, foursquare against the light, a vast utilitarian concrete block with enormous gates and doors certainly designed to diminish any human supplicant fool enough to approach it. In his case, a redundant effect, Mark decided.

"What awful architecture," he said to Pym, beside him, chauffeuring him in the Count's groundcar.

"Ugliest building in town," the armsman agreed cheerfully. "It dates back to Mad Emperor Yuri's Imperial architect, Lord Dono Vorrutyer. An uncle to the later vice-admiral. He managed to get up five major structures before Yuri was killed, and they stopped him. The Municipal Stadium runs this a close second, but we've never been able to afford to tear it down. Still stuck with it, sixty years later."

"It looks like the sort of place that has dungeons in the basement. Painted institutional green. Run by ethics-free physicians."

"It did," said Pym. The armsman negotiated their way past the gate guards and slowed in front of a vast flight of steps.

"Pym . . . aren't those steps a bit oversized?"

"Yep," grinned the armsman. "You'd have a cramp in your leg by the time you reached the top, if you tried to take it in one go." Pym eased the groundcar forward and stopped to let Mark off. "But if you go around the left end, here, you'll find a little door

559

at ground level, and a lift tube foyer. That's where everybody actually goes in."

"Thank you." Pym popped the front canopy, and Mark climbed out. "Whatever happened to Lord Dono, after Mad Yuri's reign? Assassinated by the Architectural Defense League, I hope?"

"No, he retired to the country, lived off his daughter and son-in-law, and died stark mad. There's a bizarre set of towers he built on their estate, that they charge admission to see, now." With a wave, Pym lowered the canopy and pulled away.

Mark trod around to the left, as directed. So here he was, bright and early . . . or at least, early. He'd taken a long shower, donned comfortable dark civilian clothes, and tanked himself on enough painkillers, vitamins, hangover remedies, and stimulants to leave him feeling artificially normal. More artificial than normal, but he was determined not to let Illyan bully him out of his chance.

He presented himself to the ImpSec guards in the foyer. "I'm Lord Mark Vorkosigan. I'm expected."

"Hardly that," growled a voice from the lift tube. Illyan himself swung out. The guards braced; Illyan put them back at ease with an unmilitary wave. Illyan too had showered, and changed back into his usual undress greens. Mark suspected Illyan had eaten pills for breakfast too. "Thank you, Sergeant, I'll take him up."

"What a depressing building to work in," Mark commented, as he rose in the lift tube beside the ImpSec chief.

"Yes," sighed Illyan. "I visited the Investigatif Federale building on Escobar, once. Forty-five stories, all glass . . . I was never closer to emigrating. Dono Vorrutyer should have been strangled at birth. But . . . it's mine now." Illyan glanced around with a dubious possessiveness.

Illyan led him deep into the—yes, this building definitely had bowels, Mark decided. The bowels of ImpSec. Their footsteps echoed down a bare corridor lined with tiny, cubicle-like rooms. Mark glanced through a few half-open doors at highly-secured comconsoles manned by green-uniformed men. One man at least had a bank of non-regulation full spectrum lights blazing away, aimed at his station chair. There was a large coffee dispenser at the end of the corridor. He didn't think it was random chance that Illyan led him to the cubicle numbered thirteen.

"This comconsole has been loaded with every report I've received pertaining to the search for Lieutenant Vorkosigan," said Illyan coolly. "If you think you can do better with it than my trained analysts have, I invite you to try."

"Thank you, sir." Mark slid into the station chair and powered up the vid plate. "This is unexpectedly generous."

"You should have no complaint, my lord," Illyan stated, in the tone of a directive. Gregor must have lit quite a fire under him, earlier this morning, Mark reflected, as Illyan bowed himself out with a distinctly ironic nod. Hostile? No. That was unjust. Illyan was not nearly as hostile as he had a right to be. *It's not only obedience to his Emperor*, Mark realized with a shiver. Illyan could have stood up to Gregor on a security issue like this if he'd really wanted to. *He's getting desperate.*

He took a deep breath and plunged into the files, reading, listening, and viewing. Illyan hadn't been joking about the *everything* part. There were literally hundreds of reports, generated by fifty or sixty different agents scattered throughout the near wormhole nexus. Some were brief and negative. Others were long and negative. But somebody seemed to have visited, at least once, every possible cryo-facility on Jackson's Whole, its orbital and jump point stations, and several adjoining local space systems. There were even recently-received reports tracing as far away as Escobar.

What was missing, Mark realized after quite a while, were any synopses or finished analyses. He had received raw data only, in all its mass. On the whole, he decided he preferred it that way.

Mark read till his eyes were dry and aching, and his stomach gurgled with festering coffee. *Time to break for lunch*, he thought, when a guard knocked at his door.

"Lord Mark, your driver is here," the guard informed him politely.

Hell—it was time to break for *dinner.* The guard escorted him back through the building and delivered him to Pym. It was dark outside. *My head hurts.*

Doggedly, Mark returned the next morning and started again. And the next. And the next. More reports arrived. In fact, they were arriving faster than he could read them. The harder he worked, the more he was falling behind. Halfway through the fifth day he leaned back in his station chair and thought, *This is crazy.* Illyan was burying him. From the paralysis of ignorance, he had segued with surprising speed to the paralysis of information-glut. *I've got to triage this crap, or I'll never get out of this repulsive building.*

"Lies, lies, all lies," he muttered wildly to his comconsole. It seemed to blink and hum back at him, sly and demure.

With a decisive punch, he turned off the comconsole with its endless babble of voices and fountains of data, and sat for a while in darkness and silence, till his ears stopped ringing.

ImpSec hasn't. Hasn't found Miles. He didn't need all this data. Nobody did. He just needed one piece. *Let's cut this down to size.*

Start with a few explicit assumptions. One. Miles is recoverable.

Let ImpSec look for a rotted body, unmarked grave, or disintegration record all they wanted. Such a search was no use to *him*, even if successful. Especially if successful.

Only cryo-chambers, whether permanent storage banks or other portables, were of interest. Or—less likely, and notably less common—cryo-revival facilities. But logic put an upper cap on his optimism. If Miles had been successfully revived by friendly hands, the first thing he would do would be to report in. He hadn't, ergo: he was still frozen. Or, if revived, in too bad a shape to function. Or not in friendly hands. So. Where?

The Dendarii cryo-chamber had been found in the Hegen Hub. Well . . . so what? It had been sent there after it was emptied. Sinking down into his station chair with slitted eyes, Mark thought instead about the opposite end of the trail. Were his particular obsessions luring him into believing what he wanted to believe? *No, dammit. To hell with the Hegen Hub. Miles never got off the planet.* In one stroke, that eliminated over three-fourths of the trash-data clogging his view.

We look at Jackson's Whole reports only, then. Good. Then what?

How had ImpSec checked all the remaining possible destinations? Places without known motivations or connections with House Bharaputra? For the most part, ImpSec had simply asked, concealing their own identity but offering a substantial reward. All at least four weeks after the raid. A cold trail, so to speak. Quite a lot of time for someone to think about their surprise package. Time to hide it, if they were so inclined. So that, in those cases where ImpSec did a second and more complete pass, they were even more likely to come up empty.

Miles is in a place that ImpSec has already checked off, in the hands of someone with hidden motivations to be interested in him.

There were still hundreds of possibilities.

I need a connection. There has to be a connection.

ImpSec had torn apart Norwood's available Dendarii records down to the level of a word-by-word analysis. Nothing. But Norwood was medically trained. And he hadn't sent his beloved

Admiral's cryo-chamber off at random. He'd sent it *someplace* to *someone.*

If there's a hell, Norwood, I hope you're roasting in it right now.

Mark sighed, leaned forward, and turned the comconsole back on.

A couple of hours later, Illyan stopped by Mark's cubicle, closing the soundproof door behind him. He leaned, falsely casual, on the wall and remarked, "How is it going?"

Mark ran his hands through his hair. "Despite your amiable attempt to bury me, I think I'm actually making some progress."

"Oh? What kind?" Illyan did not deny the charge, Mark noticed.

"I am absolutely convinced Miles never left Jackson's Whole."

"So how do you explain our finding the cryo-chamber in the Hegen Hub?"

"I don't. It's a diversion."

"Hm," said Illyan, non-committally.

"And it worked," Mark added cruelly.

Illyan's lips thinned.

Diplomacy, Mark reminded himself. Diplomacy, or he'd never get what he needed. "I accept that your resources are finite, sir. So put them to the point. Everything that you do have available for this, you ought to send to Jackson's Whole."

The sardonic expression on Illyan's face said it all. The man had been running ImpSec for nearly thirty years. It was going to take a lot more than diplomacy for him to accept Mark telling him how to do his job.

"What did you find out about Captain Vorventa?" Mark tried another line.

"The link was short, and not too sinister. His younger brother was my Galactic Operations supervisor's adjutant. These are not disloyal men, you understand."

"So . . . what have you done?"

"About Captain Edwin, nothing. It's too late. The information about Miles is now out on the Vorish net, as whispers and gossip. Beyond damage control. Young Vorventa has been transferred and demoted. Leaving an ugly hole in my staffing. He was good at his job." Illyan did not sound very grateful to Mark.

"Oh." Mark paused. "Vorventa thought I did something to the Count. Is that out on the gossip net too?"

"Yes."

Mark winced. "Well . . . at least *you* know better," he sighed. He glanced up at Illyan's stony face, and felt a nauseated alarm. "Don't you, sir?"

"Perhaps. Perhaps not."

"How not?! You have the medical reports!"

"Mm. The cardiac rupture certainly appeared natural. But it could have been artificially created, using a surgical hand-tractor. The subsequent damage to the cardiac region would have masked its traces."

Mark shuddered in helpless outrage. "Tricky work," he choked. "Extremely precise. How did I make the Count hold still, and not notice, while I was doing this?"

"That is one problem with the scenario," Illyan agreed.

"And what did I do with the hand tractor? And the medical scanner, I'd have needed one of those, too. Two or three kilos of equipment."

"Ditched them in the woods. Or somewhere."

"Have you found them?"

"No."

"Have you looked?"

"Yes."

Mark rubbed his face, hard, and clenched and unclenched his teeth. "So. You have all the men you need to quarter and re-quarter several square kilometers of woods looking for a hand tractor that isn't there, but not enough to send to Jackson's Whole to look for Miles, who is. *I* see." No. He had to keep his temper, or he'd lose everything. He wanted to howl. He wanted to beat Illyan's face in.

"A galactic operative is a highly-trained specialist with rare personal qualities," said Illyan stiffly. "Area-searches for known objects can be conducted by low-level troopers, who are more abundant."

"Yes. I'm sorry." *He* was apologizing? *Your goals. Remember your goals.* He thought of the Countess, and drew a deep, calming breath. He drew several.

"I do not hold this as a conviction," Illyan said, watching his face. "I hold it merely as a doubt."

"Thank-you-I-think," Mark snarled.

He sat for a full minute, trying to marshal his scattered thoughts, his best arguments. "Look," he said at last. "You are wasting your resources, and one of the resources you are wasting is me. Send *me* back to Jackson's Whole. I know more about the entire situation than any other agent you have. I have some training, an assassin's training only maybe, but some. Enough to lose your spies

three or four times on Earth! Enough to get this far. I know
Jackson's Whole, visceral stuff you can only acquire growing up
there. And you wouldn't even have to pay me!" He waited, holding his breath in the courage of his terror. *Go back?* Blood sprayed
through his memory. *Going to give the Bharaputrans a chance to
correct their aim?*

Illyan's cool expression did not change. "Your track record so
far in covert ops is not notably impressive for its successes, Lord
Mark."

"So, I'm not a brilliant combat field commander. I am not Miles.
We all know that by now. How many of your other agents are?"

"If you are as, ah, incompetent as you have appeared, sending
you would be a further waste. But suppose you are more sly than
even I think. All your thrashing around here, a mere smokescreen."
Illyan could deliver the veiled insults too. Stiletto-sharp, right
between the ribs. "And suppose you get to Miles before we do.
What happens then?"

"What do you mean, what happens then?"

"If you return him to us as a room-temperature corpse, fit only
for burying, instead of a cryo-stat hopeful—how will we know that
was the way you found him? And you will inherit his name, his
rank, his wealth, and his future. Tempting, Mark, to a man without
an identity. Very tempting."

Mark buried his face in his hands. He sat crushed, infuriated,
and wildly frustrated. "Look," he said through his fingers, "look.
Either I'm the man who, by your theory, succeeded in half-
assassinating Aral Vorkosigan and was so good I left no trace of
proof—or I'm not. You can argue that I'm not competent enough
to send. Or you can argue that I'm not trustworthy enough to
send. But you can't use both arguments at once. Pick one!"

"I await more evidence." Illyan's eyes were like stones.

"I swear," Mark whispered, "excess suspicion makes us bigger
fools than excess trust does." It had certainly been true in his case.
He sat up suddenly. "So fast-penta me."

Illyan raised his brows. "Mm?"

"Fast-penta me. You never have. Relieve your suspicions." Fast-
penta interrogations could be excruciatingly humiliating experiences,
by all reports. So what. What was one more humiliation in *his* life?
Warm and familiar, that was what.

"I have longed to, Lord Mark," Illyan admitted, "but your, ah,
progenitor has a known idiosyncratic response to fast-penta that
I assume you share. Not the usual allergy, exactly. It creates an

appalling hyperactivity, a great deal of babble, but alas, no over-whelming compulsion to tell the truth. It is useless."

"In Miles." Mark seized the hope. "You assume? You don't know! My metabolism is demonstrably not like Miles's. Can't you at least check?"

"Yes," said Illyan slowly, "I can do that." He pushed himself off from the wall, and exited the cubicle, saying, "Carry on. I'll be back shortly."

Tense, Mark rose and paced the little room, two steps each way. Fear and desire pulsed in his brain. The memory of the inhuman chill of Baron Bharaputra's eyes clashed with hot rage in his throat. *If you want to find something, look where you lost it.* He'd lost it all on Jackson's Whole.

Illyan returned at last. "Sit down and roll up your left sleeve."

Mark did so. "What's that?"

"Patch test."

Mark felt a burr-like prickle, as Illyan pressed the tiny med-pad onto the underside of his forearm, then peeled it away. Illyan glanced at his chrono and leaned on the comconsole, watching Mark's arm.

Within a minute, there was a pink spot. Within two, it was a hive. Within five, it had grown to a hard white welt surrounded by angry red streaks that ran from his wrist to his elbow.

Illyan sighed disappointment. "Lord Mark. I highly recommend that you avoid fast-penta at all costs, in your future."

"That was an allergic reaction?"

"That was a highly allergic reaction."

"Shit." Mark sat and brooded. And scratched. He rolled down his sleeve before he drew blood. "If Miles had been sitting here, reading these files, making these same arguments, would you have listened to him?"

"Lieutenant Vorkosigan has a sustained record of successes that compels my attention. Results speak for themselves. And, as you yourself have *repeatedly* pointed out, you are not Miles. You can't use both arguments at once," he added icily. "Pick one."

"Why did you even bother letting me in here, if nothing I say or do can make any difference?" Mark exploded.

Illyan shrugged. "Aside from Gregor's direct order—at least I know where you are and what you are doing."

"Like a detention cell, except that I enter it voluntarily. If you could lock me in a cell without a comconsole, you'd be even happier."

"Frankly, yes."

"Just. So." Blackly, Mark switched the comconsole back on. Illyan left him to it.

Mark jumped out of his chair, stumbled to the door, and stuck his head out. Illyan's retreating back was halfway down the corridor.

"I have my own name now, Illyan!" Mark shouted furiously.

Illyan glanced back over his shoulder, raised his brows, and walked on.

Mark tried reading another report, but it seemed to turn to gibberish somewhere between his eyes and his brain. He was too rattled to continue his analysis today. He gave up at last, and called Pym for a pick-up. It was still light out. He stared into the sunset, glimpsed between the buildings on the way home to Vorkosigan House, till his eyes burned.

It was the first time that week he had returned from ImpSec in time to join the Countess for dinner. He found her and Bothari-Jesek dining casually in a ground-floor nook that looked onto a sheltered corner of the garden, densely arranged with autumn flowers and plants. Spot lighting kept the display colorful in the gathering dusk. The Countess wore a fancy green jacket and long skirt, a Vor matron's town wear; Bothari-Jesek wore a similar costume in blue obviously borrowed from the Countess's wardrobe. A place was set for him at the table despite the fact that he hadn't shown up for the meal for four straight days. Obscurely touched, he slid into his seat.

"How was the Count today?" he asked diffidently.

"Unchanged," the Countess sighed.

As was the Countess's custom, there was a minute of silence before they plowed in, which the Countess used for an inward prayer that Mark suspected involved more this day than calling blessings upon the bread. Bothari-Jesek and he waited politely, Bothari-Jesek meditating God-knew-what, Mark rerunning his conversation with Illyan in his head and evolving all the smarter things he should have said, too late. A servant brought food in covered dishes and departed to leave them in privacy, which was the way the Countess preferred it when not dining formally with official guests. *Family style. Huh.*

In truth, Bothari-Jesek had been lending the Countess the support of a daughter in the days since the Count's collapse, accompanying her on her frequent trips to the Imperial Military

Hospital, running personal errands, acting as confidant; Mark suspected the Countess had revealed more of her real thoughts to Bothari-Jesek than to anyone else, and felt a little inexplicable envy. As their favorite armsman's only child, Elena Bothari had been practically the Vorkosigans' foster-daughter; Vorkosigan House had been the home in which she had grown up. So if he was really Miles's brother, did that make Elena his foster-sister too? He would have to try the idea on her. And prepare to duck. Some other time.

"Captain Bothari-Jesek," Mark began, after he'd swallowed the first couple of bites, "what's going on with the Dendarii at Komarr? Or does Illyan keep you in the dark too?"

"He'd better not," said Bothari-Jesek. To be sure, Elena had allies that outranked even the ImpSec commander. "We've done a little re-shuffling. Quinn retained the chief eyewitnesses to your, um, raid—" kind of her, not to use some more forthright term, like *debacle*, "Green Squad, part of Orange and Blue Squads. She's sent everyone else off in the *Peregrine* under my second, to rejoin the fleet. People were getting itchy, cooped up in orbit with no down-side leave and no duties." She looked distinctly unhappy at this temporary loss of her command.

"Is the *Ariel* still at Komarr, then?"

"Yes."

"Quinn of course . . . Captain Thorne? Sergeant Taura?"

"All still waiting."

"They must be pretty itchy themselves, by now."

"Yes," said Bothari-Jesek, and stabbed her fork so hard into a chunk of vat protein that it skittered across her plate. Itchy. Yes.

"So what have you learned this week, Mark?" the Countess asked him.

"Nothing you don't already know, I'm afraid. Doesn't Illyan pass you reports?"

"Yes, but due to the press of events I've only had time to glance at his analysts' synopses. In any case, there's only one piece of news I really want to hear."

Right. Encouraged, Mark began to detail his survey to her, including his data-triage and his growing convictions.

"You seem to have been quite thorough," she remarked.

He shrugged. "I now know roughly what ImpSec knows, if Illyan has been honest with me. But since ImpSec frankly doesn't know where Miles is, it's all futile. I swear . . ."

"Yes?" said the Countess.

"I *swear* Miles is still on Jackson's Whole. But I can't get Illyan to focus down. His attention is spread all over hell and gone. He has Cetagandans on the brain."

"There are sound historical reasons for that," said the Countess. "And current ones too, I'm afraid, though I'm sure Illyan has been cagey about confiding to you any of ImpSec's troubles not directly connected to Miles's situation. To say he's had a bad month would be a gross understatement." She hesitated too, for rather a long time. "Mark . . . you are, after all, Miles's clone-twin. As close as one human being can be to another. This conviction of yours has a passionate edge. You seem to *know*. Do you suppose . . . you really do know? On some level?"

"Do you mean, like, a psychic link?" he said. What an awful idea.

She nodded, faintly flushed. Bothari-Jesek looked appalled, and gave him a strange beseeching look, *Don't you dare mess with her mind, you—!*

This is the true measure of her desperation. "I'm sorry. I'm not psychic. Only psychotic." Bothari-Jesek relaxed. He slumped, then brightened slightly with an idea. "Though it might not hurt to let *Illyan* think that you think so."

"Illyan is too sturdy a rationalist." The Countess smiled sadly.

"The passion is only frustration, ma'am. No one will let me do anything."

"What is it that you wish to do?"

I want to run away to Beta Colony. The Countess would probably help him to.

. . . No. I am never running away again.

He took a breath, in place of a courage he did not feel. "I want to go back to Jackson's Whole and look for him. I could do as good a job as Illyan's other agents, I know I could! I tried the idea on him. He wouldn't bite. If he could, he'd like to lock me in a security cell."

"It's days like these poor Simon would sell his soul to make the world hold still for a while," the Countess admitted. "His attention isn't just spread right now, it's splintered. I have a certain sympathy for him."

"I don't. I wouldn't ask Simon Illyan for the time of day. Nor would he give it to me." Mark brooded. "Gregor would hint obliquely where I might look for a crono. You . . ." his metaphor extended itself, unbidden, "would give me a clock."

"If I had one, son, I'd give you a clock factory," the Countess sighed.

Mark chewed, swallowed, stopped, looked up. "Really?"

"R—" she began positively, then caution caught up with her. "Really what?"

"Is Lord Mark a free man? I mean, I've committed no crime within the Barrayaran Empire, have I? There being no law against stupidity. I'm not under arrest."

"No . . ."

"I could go to Jackson's Whole myself! Screw Illyan and his precious resources. If—" ah, the catch—he deflated slightly, "if I had a ticket," he ran down. His whole wealth, as far as he knew, was seventeen Imperial marks left from a twenty-five note the Countess had given him for spending money earlier in the week, now wadded up in his trouser pocket.

The Countess pushed her plate away and sat back, her face drained. "This does not strike me as a very safe idea. Speaking of stupidity."

"Bharaputra's probably got an execution contract out on you now, after what you did," Bothari-Jesek put in helpfully.

"No—it's on Admiral Naismith," Mark argued. "And I wouldn't be going back to Bharaputra's." Not that he didn't agree with the Countess. The spot on his forehead where Baron Bharaputra had counted coup burned in secret. He stared urgently at her. "Ma'am . . ."

"Are you seriously asking me to finance your risking your life?" she said.

"No—my saving it! I can't"—he waved around helplessly, at Vorkosigan House, at his whole situation—"go on like this. I'm all out of balance here, I'm all wrong."

"Balance will come to you, in time. It's just too soon," she said earnestly. "You're still very new."

"I have to go back. I have to try to undo what I did. If I can."

"And if you can't, what will you do then?" asked Bothari-Jesek coldly. "Take off, with a nice head start?"

Had the woman read his mind? Mark's shoulders bowed with the weight of her scorn. And his doubt. "I," he breathed, "don't . . ." *know.* He could not finish the sentence aloud.

The Countess laced her long fingers. "I don't doubt your heart," she said, looking at him steadily.

Hell, and she could break that heart more thoroughly with her trust than Illyan ever could with his suspicion. He crouched in his seat.

"But—you are my second chance. My new hope, all unlooked-for. I never thought I could have another child, on Barrayar. Now

Jackson's Whole has eaten Miles, and you want to go down there after him? You, too?"

"Ma'am," he said desperately, "Mother—I cannot be your consolation prize."

She crossed her arms and rested her chin in one hand, cupped over her mouth. Her eyes were gray as a winter sea.

"You of all people, have to see," Mark pleaded, "how important a second chance can be."

She pushed back her chair and stood up. "I'll . . . have to think about this." She exited the little dining room. She'd left half her meal on her plate, Mark saw with dismay.

Bothari-Jesek saw it too. "Good job," she snarled.

I'm sorry, I'm sorry. . . .

She rose to run after the Countess.

Mark sat, abandoned and alone. And, blindly and half-consciously, proceeded to eat himself sick. He stumbled up to his room's level by the lift tube, afterward, and lay wishing for sleep more than for breath. Neither came to him.

After an interminable time his stunned headache and hot abdominal pain were just starting to recede, when there came a knock on his door. He rolled over with a muffled groan. "Who is it?"

"Elena."

He keyed on the light and sat up in bed against the carved headboard, stuffing a pillow under his spine against some killer solid walnut acanthus leaves in high relief. He didn't want to talk to Bothari-Jesek. Or to any other human being. He refastened his shirt as loosely as it would go. "Enter," he muttered.

She came cautiously around the doorframe, her face serious and pale. "Hello. Are you feeling all right?"

"No," he admitted.

"I came to apologize," she said.

"You? Apologize to me? Why?"

"The Countess told me . . . something of what was going on with you. I'm sorry. I didn't understand."

He'd been dissected again, *in absentia*. He could tell by the horrified way Bothari-Jesek was looking at him, as if his swollen belly were laid open and spread wide in an autopsy with a cut from *here* to *there*. "Aw, hell. What did she say now?" He struggled, with difficulty, to sit up straighter.

"Miles had talked around it. But I hadn't understood how bad it really was. The Countess told me exactly. What Galen did to you. The shock-stick rape, and the, um, eating disorders. And the other disorder." She kept her eyes away from his body, onto his face, a dead give-away of the unwelcome depth of her new knowledge. She and the Countess must have been talking for two hours. "And it was all so deliberately *calculated*. That was the most diabolical part."

"I'm not so sure about the shock-stick incident being calculated," Mark said carefully. "Galen seemed out of his head, to me. Over the top. Nobody's that good an actor. Or maybe it started out calculated, and got out of hand." And then burst out, helplessly, *"Dammit!"* Bothari-Jesek jumped a foot in the air. "She has no *right* to talk about that with you! Or with anybody! What the hell am I, the best show in town?"

"No, no." Bothari-Jesek opened her hands. "You have to understand. I told her about Maree, that little blonde clone we found you with. What I thought was going on. I accused you to the Countess."

He froze, flushed with shame, and a new dismay. "I didn't realize you hadn't told her at the first." Was everything he thought he'd built with the Countess on a rotten foundation, collapsing now in ruins?

"She wanted you for a son so badly, I couldn't bring myself to. But I was so furious with you tonight, I blurted it all out."

"And then what happened?"

Bothari-Jesek shook her head in wonderment. "She's so Betan. She's so strange. She's never where you think she is, mentally. She wasn't the least surprised. And then she explained it all to me— I felt as though my head was being turned inside out, and given a good wash-and-brush."

He almost laughed. "That sounds like a typical conversation with the Countess." His choking fear began to recede. *She doesn't despise me . . . ?*

"I was wrong about you," Bothari-Jesek said sturdily.

His hands spread in exasperation. "It's nice to know I have such a defender, but you weren't wrong. What you thought was exactly what *was* going on. I would have if I could have," he said bitterly. "It wasn't my virtue that stopped me, it was my high-voltage conditioning."

"Oh, I don't mean wrong about the facts. But I was projecting a lot of my own anger, into the way I was explaining you to myself. I had no idea how much you were a product of systematic torture. And how incredibly you resisted. I think I would have gone catatonic, in your place."

"It wasn't that bad *all* the time," he said uncomfortably.

"But you have to understand," she repeated doggedly, "what was going on with *me*. About my father."

"Huh?" He felt as if his head had just been given a sharp half-twist to the left. "I know what my father has to do with this, why the hell is yours in on it?"

She walked around the room. Working up to something. When she did speak, it came out all in a rush. "My father raped my mother. That's where I came from, during the Barrayaran invasion of Escobar. I've known for some years. It's made me allergically sensitive on the subject. I can't stand it," her hands clenched, "yet it's *in* me. I can't escape it. It made it very hard for me to see you clearly. I feel as if I've been looking at you through a fog for the last ten weeks. The Countess has dispelled it." Indeed, her eyes did not freeze him any more. "The Count helped me too, more than I can say."

"Oh." What was he to say? So, it hadn't been just him they'd been talking about for the past two hours. There was clearly more to her story, but *he* sure wasn't going to ask. For once, it wasn't his place to apologize. "I'm . . . not sorry you exist. However you got here."

She smiled, crookedly. "Actually, neither am I."

He felt very strange. His fury at the violation of his privacy was fading, to be replaced by a light-heartedness that astonished him. He was greatly relieved, to be unburdened of his secrets. His dread was shrunken, as if giving it away had literally diminished it. *I swear if I tell four more people, I'll be altogether free.*

He swung his legs out of the bed, grabbed her by the hand, led her to a wooden chair beside his window, climbed up and stood on it, and kissed her. "Thank you!"

She looked quite startled. "What for?" she asked on the breath of a laugh. Firmly, she repossessed her hand.

"For existing. For letting me live. *I* don't know." He grinned, exhilarated, but the grin faded in dizziness, and he climbed down more carefully, and sat.

She stared down at him, and bit her lip. "Why do you do that to yourself?"

No use to pretend he didn't know what *that* was; the physical manifestations of his compulsive gorge were obvious enough. He felt monstrous. He swiped a hand over his sweaty face. "I don't know. I do think, half of what we call madness is just some poor slob dealing with pain by a strategy that annoys the people around him."

"How is it dealing with pain to give yourself more pain?" she asked plaintively.

He half-smiled, hands on his knees, staring at the floor. "There is a kind of riveting fascination to it. Takes your mind off the real thing. Consider what a toothache does to your attention span."

She shook her head. "I'd rather not, thank you."

"Galen was only trying to screw up my relation with my father," he sighed, "but he managed to screw up my relation with everything. He knew he wouldn't be able to control me directly once he turned me loose on Barrayar, so he had to build in motivations that would last." He added lowly, "It ricocheted back on him. Because in a sense, Galen was my father too. My foster-father. First one I ever had." The Count had been alive to that one. "I was so hungry for identity, when the Komarrans picked me up on Jackson's Whole. I think I must have been like one of those baby birds that imprints on a watering pot or something, because it's the first parent-bird-sized thing it sees."

"You have a surprising talent for information analysis," she remarked. "I noticed it even back at Jackson's Whole."

"Me?" he blinked. "Certainly not!" Not a talent, surely, or he'd be getting better results. But despite all his frustrations, he had felt a kind of contentment, in his little cubicle at ImpSec this past week. The serenity of a monk's cell, combined with the absorbing challenge of that universe of data . . . in an odd way it reminded him of the peaceful times with the virtual learning programs, in his childhood back at the clone-crèche. The times when no one had been hurting him.

"The Countess thinks so too. She wants to see you."

"What, now?"

"She sent me to get you. But I had to get my word in first. Before it got any later, and I lost my chance. Or my nerve."

"All right. Let me pull myself together." He was intensely grateful wine had not been served tonight. He retreated to his bathroom, washed his face in the coldest water, forced down a couple of painkiller tabs, and combed his hair. He slipped one of the back-country-style vests over his dark shirt, and followed Bothari-Jesek into the hall.

She took him to the Countess's own study, which was a serene and austere chamber overlooking the back garden, just off her bedroom. Her and her husband's bedroom. Mark glimpsed the dark interior, down a step and through an archway. The Count's absence seemed an almost palpable thing.

The Countess was at her comconsole, not a secured government model, just a very expensive commercial one. Shell flowers inlaid on black wood framed the vid plate, which was generating the image of a harried-looking man. The Countess was saying sharply, "Well, find out the arrangements, then! Yes, tonight, now. And then get back to me. Thank you." She batted the off-key and swung around to face Mark and Bothari-Jesek.

"Are you checking on a ticket to Jackson's Whole?" he asked tremulously, hoping against hope.

"No."

"Oh." Of course not. How could she let him go? He was a fool. It was useless to suppose—

"I was checking on getting you a ship. If you're going, you'll need a lot more independent mobility than scheduled commercial transport will allow."

"*Buy* a ship?" he said, stunned. And he'd thought that line about the clock factory had been a *joke.* "Isn't that pretty expensive?"

"Lease, if I can. Buy if I have to. There seem to be three or four possibilities, in Barrayar or Komarr orbit."

"Still—how?" He didn't think even the Vorkosigans could buy a jump-ship out of pocket change.

"I can mortgage something," the Countess said rather vaguely, looking around.

"Since synthetics came in, you can't hock the family jewels any more." He followed her gaze. "Not Vorkosigan House!"

"No, it's entailed. Same problem with the District Residence at Hassadar. I can pledge Vorkosigan Surleau on my bare word, though."

The heart of the realm, oh shit . . .

"All these houses and history are all very well," she complained, raising her eyebrows at his dismayed expression, "but a bloody museum doesn't make a very liquid asset. In any case, the finances are my problem. You'll have your own worries."

"A crew?" was the first thought that popped into his head, and out of his mouth.

"A jump-pilot and engineer will come with the ship, at a minimum. As for supercargo, well, there are all those idle Dendarii, hanging in Komarr orbit. I imagine you could find a volunteer or two among them. It's obvious they can't take the *Ariel* back into Jacksonian local space."

"Quinnie has bleeding fingers by now, from scratching at the doors," Bothari-Jesek said. "Even Illyan won't be able to hold her much longer, if ImpSec doesn't get a break soon."

"Will Illyan try to hold me?" asked Mark anxiously.

"If it weren't for Aral, I'd be going myself," said the Countess. "And I sure as hell wouldn't let Illyan stop *me*. You are my proxy. I'll deal with ImpSec."

Mark bet she would. "The Dendarii I'm thinking of are highly motivated, but—I foresee problems, getting them to follow my orders. Who will be in command of this little private excursion?"

"It's the golden rule, boy. He who has the gold, makes the rules. The ship will be yours. The choice of companions will be yours. If they want a ride, they have to cooperate."

"That would last past the first wormhole jump. Then Quinn would lock me in a closet."

The Countess puffed a laugh despite herself. "Hm. That is a point." She leaned back in her station chair, steepling her fingers together, her eyes half-closed for a minute or two. They opened wide again. "Elena," she said. "Will you take oath to Lord Vorkosigan?" The fingers of her right hand fanned at Mark.

"I'm already sworn to Lord Vorkosigan," Elena said stiffly. Meaning, to Miles.

The gray eyes went flinty. "Death releases all vows." And then glinted. "The Vor system never has been very good at catching the curve balls thrown at it by galactic technologies. Do you know, I don't think there has ever been a ruling as to the status of a voice-oath when one of the respondents is in cryo-stasis? Your word can't be your breath when you don't have any breath, after all. We shall just have to set our own precedent."

Elena paced to the window, and stared out into nothing. The reflecting lights of the room obscured any view of the night. At last, she turned decisively on her heel, went down on both knees in front of Mark, and raised her hands pressed palm to palm. Automatically, Mark enclosed her hands with his own.

"My lord," she said, "I pledge you the obedience of a liege-woman."

"Um . . ." said Mark. "Um . . . I think I may need more than that. Try this one. 'I, Elena Bothari-Jesek, do testify I am a freewoman of the District Vorkosigan. I hereby take service under Lord Mark Pierre Vorkosigan, as an Armsman—Armswoman?—simple, and will hold him as my liege commander until my death or his releases me.'"

Shocked, Bothari-Jesek stared up at him. Not very far up, true. "You can't do that! Can you?"

"Well," said the Countess, watching this playlet with her eyes alight, "there isn't actually a law saying a Count's heir can't take a female Armsman. It's just never been done. You know— *tradition.*"

Elena and the Countess exchanged a long look. Hesitantly, as if half-hypnotized, Bothari-Jesek repeated the oath.

Mark said, "I, Lord Mark Pierre Vorkosigan, vassal secundus to Emperor Gregor Vorbarra, do accept your oath, and pledge you the protection of a liege commander; this by my word as Vorkosigan." He paused. "Actually," he said aside to the Countess, "I haven't made my oath to Gregor yet, either. Would that invalidate this?"

"Details," said the Countess, waving her fingers. "You can work out the details later."

Bothari-Jesek stood up again. She looked at him like a woman waking up in bed with a hangover and a strange partner she didn't remember meeting the night before. She rubbed the backs of her hands where his skin had touched hers.

Power. Just how much Vor-power did this little charade give him? Just as much as Bothari-Jesek allowed, Mark decided, eyeing her athletic frame and shrewd face. No danger she would permit him to abuse his position. The uncertainty in her face was giving way to a suppressed pleasure that delighted his eye. *Yes. That was the right move.* No question but that he had pleased the Countess, who was grinning outright at her subversive son.

"Now," said the Countess, "how fast can we pull this together? How soon can you be ready to travel?"

"Immediately," said Bothari-Jesek.

"At your command, ma'am," said Mark. "I do feel—it's nothing psychic, you understand. It's not even the general itch. It's only logic. But I do think we could be running out of time."

"How so?" asked Bothari-Jesek. "There's nothing more static than cryo-stasis. We're all going crazy from uncertainty, sure, but that's our problem. Miles may have more time than we do."

Mark shook his head. "If Miles had fallen frozen into friendly or even neutral hands, they ought to have responded to the rumors of reward by now. But if . . . someone . . . wanted to revive him, they'd have to do the prep first. We're all very conscious right now of how long it takes to grow organs for transplant."

The Countess nodded wryly.

"If—wherever Miles is—committed to the project soon after they got him, they could be nearly ready to attempt a revival by now."

"They might botch it," said the Countess. "They might not be careful enough." Her fingers drummed on the pretty shell inlay.

"I don't follow that," objected Bothari-Jesek. "Why would an enemy bother to revive him? What fate could be worse than death?"

"I don't know," sighed Mark. *But if there is one, I bet the Jacksonians can arrange it.*

CHAPTER NINETEEN

With breath, came pain.

He was in a hospital bed. That much he knew even before opening his eyes, from the discomfort, the chill, and the smell. That seemed right. Vaguely, if unpleasantly, familiar. He blinked, to discover that his eyes were plastered with goo. Scented, translucent, medical goo. It was like trying to see through a pane of glass covered with grease. He blinked some more, and achieved a limited focus, then had to stop and catch his breath from the effort.

There was something terribly wrong with his breathing, labored panting that didn't provide enough air at all. And it whistled. The whistling came from a plastic tube down his throat, he realized, trying to swallow. His lips were dry and cracked; the tube blocking his mouth prevented him from moistening them. He tried to move. His body sent back shooting aches and pains, burning through every bone. There were tubes going into, or perhaps out of, his arms. And his ears. And his nose.

There were too damned many tubes. That was bad, he realized dimly, though how he knew he could not have said. With a heroic effort, he tried to raise his head and see down his body. The tube in his throat shifted painfully.

Ridges of ribs. Belly gaunt and sunken. Red welts radiated all over his chest, like a long-legged spider crouched just beneath his skin, its body over his sternum. Surgical glue held together jagged incisions, multiple scarlet scars looking like a map of a major river

579

drainage delta. He was pocked with monitor-pads. More tubes ran from places orifices ought not to be. He caught a glimpse of his genitalia, lying in a limp discolored lump; there was a tube from there, too. Pain from there would be subtly reassuring, but he couldn't feel anything at all. He couldn't feel his legs or feet, either, though he could see them. His whole body was covered thickly with the scented goo. His skin was peeling in nasty big pale flakes, stuck in the stuff. His head fell back on a pad, and black clouds boiled in his eyes. *Too many damn tubes. Bad . . .*

He was in a muzzy, half-awake state, floating between confusing dream-fragments and pain, when the woman came.

She leaned into his blurred vision. "We're taking the pacer out, now." Her voice was clear and low. The tubes had gone away from his ears, or maybe he'd dreamed them. "Your new heart will be beating and your lungs working all on their own."

She bent over his aching chest. Pretty woman, of the elegantly intellectual type. He was sorry he was dressed only in goo, in front of her, though it seemed to him that he had carried on with even less to wear, once. He could not remember where or how. She did something to the spider-body lump; he saw his skin part in a thin red slit and then be sealed again. She seemed to be cutting out his heart, like an antique priestess making sacrifice, but that could not be, for his labored breathing continued. She'd definitely taken out something, for she placed it on a tray held by her male assistant.

"There." She watched him closely.

He watched her in return, blinking away the distortions of the ointment. She had straight, silky black hair, bound in a knot— more of a wad, actually—on the back of her head. A few fine strands escaped to float around her face. Golden skin. Brown eyes with a hint of an epicanthic fold. Stubby, stubborn black lashes. The bridge of her nose was coolly arched. A pleasant, original face, not surgically altered to a mathematically perfect beauty, but enlivened by an alert tension. Not an empty face. Somebody interesting was in there. But not, alas, somebody familiar.

She was tall and slim, dressed in a pale green lab smock over other clothes. "Doc-tor," he tried to guess, but it came out a formless gurgle around the plastic in his mouth.

"I'm going to take that tube out now," she told him. She pulled something sticky from around his lips and cheeks—tape? More dead skin came with it. Gently, she drew out the throat-tube. He

gagged. It was like un-swallowing a snake. The relief of being rid
of it almost made him pass out again. There was still some sort
of tube—oxygen?—blocking his nostrils.

He moved his jaw, and swallowed for the first time in . . .
in . . . Anyway, his tongue felt thick and swollen. His chest hurt
terribly. But saliva flowed; his dry mouth re-hydrated. One did not
really appreciate saliva till one was forced to do without it. His
heart beat fast and light, like bird wings fluttering. It did not feel
right, but at least he felt something.

"What's your name?" she asked him.

The subliminal terror he had been studiously ignoring yawned
black beneath him. His breath quickened in his panic. Despite the
oxygen, he could not get enough air. And he could not answer
her question. "Ah," he whispered. "Ag . . ." He did not know who
he was, nor how he had come by this huge burden of hurt. The
not-knowing frightened him far more than the hurt.

The young man in the pale-blue medical jacket snorted, "I think
I'm going to win my bet. That one's coagulated behind the eyeballs. All short circuits back there." He tapped his forehead.

The woman frowned in annoyance. "Patients don't come popping up out of cryo-stasis like a meal out of a microwave. It takes
just as much healing as if the original injury hadn't killed them,
and more. It will be a couple of days before I can even begin to
evaluate his higher neural functions."

Still, she pulled something sharp and shiny from the lapel of
her jacket and moved around him, touching him and watching a
monitor readout on the wall above his head. When his right hand
jerked back at a prick, she smiled. *Yeah, and when my prick jerks
up at a right hand, I'll smile,* he thought dizzily.

He wanted to speak. He wanted to tell that blue fellow to take
a wormhole jump to hell, and take his bet with him. All that came
out of his mouth was a hollow hiss. He shuddered with frustration. He had to function, or die. That, he was bone-sure of. Be
the best or be destroyed.

He didn't know where this certainty came from. Who was going
to kill him? He didn't know. Them, some faceless them. No time
to rest. March or die.

The medical duo left. Driven by the obscure fear, he began
to try to exercise, isometrics in his bed. All he could move was
his right arm. Attracted by his thrashing as reported by his
monitor pads, the youth came back and sedated him. When the
darkness closed in again, he wanted to howl. He had very bad

dreams, after that; any content would have been welcome to his bewildered brain, but all he could remember when he woke was the badness.

An interminable time later, the doctor returned to feed him. Sort of.

She touched a control to raise the head of his bed, saying chattily, "Let's try out your new stomach, my friend."

Friend? Was he? He needed a friend, no question.

"Sixty milliliters of glucose solution—sugar water. The first meal of your life, so to speak. I wonder if you have enough basic muscle control to suck on a straw yet?"

He did, once she touched a few drops of liquid to his lips to get him started. Suck and swallow, you couldn't get much more basic than that. Except that he couldn't drink it all.

"That's all right," she rippled on. "Your stomach's not fully grown yet, you see. Neither were your heart or lungs. Lilly was in a hurry to have you awake. All your replacement organs are a bit under-sized for your body, which means they're going to be working hard, and won't grow as fast as they did in the vat. You're going to be short of breath for quite a while. Still, it made it all easier to install. More elbow room for me, which I appreciated."

He wasn't quite sure if she was talking to him, or just to her-self, as a lonely person might talk to a pet. She took the cup away and came back with a basin, sponges, and towels, and began washing him, section by section. Why was a surgeon doing nurs-ing care? DR. R. DURONA, read the name on the breast pocket of her green coat. But she seemed to be doing a neurophysiological examination at the same time. Checking her work?

"You were quite a little mystery, you know. Delivered to me in a crate. Raven said you were too small to be a soldier, but I picked out enough camouflage cloth and nerve disruptor shield-netting, along with the forty-six grenade fragments, to be quite sure you weren't just a bystander. Whatever you were, that needle-grenade had your name on it. Unfortunately, not in writing." She sighed half to herself. "Who *are* you?"

She did not pause for an answer, which was just as well. The effort of swallowing the sugar water had exhausted him again. An equally pertinent question was, *Where* was he, and he was peeved that she, who must surely know, didn't think to tell him. The room was an anonymous high-tech medical locale, without windows. On a planet, not a ship.

How do I know that? A vague picture of a ship, in his head, seemed to shatter at his touch. *What ship?* For that matter, what planet?

There ought to be a window. A big window, framing a high hazy city-scape with a rapid river cutting through it. And people. There were people missing, who ought by rights to be here, though he could not picture them. The mix of generic medical familiarity and particular strangeness tied his guts in knots.

The cleaning-cloths were icy, grating, but he was glad to be rid of the goo, not to mention all the disgusting crud stuck in it. He felt like a lizard, shedding his skin. When she was done, all the dead white flakes were gone. The new skin looked very raw.

She rubbed depilatory cream over his face, which seemed redundant and stung like hell. He decided he liked the sting. He was starting to relax and enjoy her ministrations, embarrassingly intimate though they were. She was returning him at least to the dignity of being clean, and she did not feel like an enemy. Some sort of ally, at least on the somatic level. She cleaned his face of cream, beard, and a good deal of skin, and also combed his hair, though unfortunately, like his skin, his hair too seemed to be coming out in alarming clumps.

"There," she said, sounding satisfied. She held a large hand-mirror up to his face. "See anybody you recognize?" She was watching him closely, he realized, noting his eyes focus and track.

That's me? Well . . . I suppose I can get used to it. Red skin stretched over its frame of bones. Jutting nose, a sharp chin . . . the gray eyes looked bizarrely hung-over, their whites solid scarlet. His dark hair was patchy, like a bad case of mange. He'd really been hoping for something much better-looking.

He tried to speak, to ask. His mouth moved but, like his thoughts, too disconnectedly for coherence. He puffed air and spittle. He couldn't even swear, which made him want to swear even more, which rapidly degenerated into a gurgling snarl. She hastily took the mirror away and stood staring at him in worry.

Steady on. If he kept thrashing around, they'd probably hit him with another dose of sedative, and he didn't want that. He lay back panting helplessly. She lowered the bed again, dimmed the lights, and made to leave. He managed a moan. It worked; she came back.

"Lilly called your cryo-chamber Pandora's box," she murmured reflectively. "But I thought of it as the enchanted knight's crystal coffin. I wish it *were* as easy as waking you with a kiss."

She bent over, eyelids fluttering half-closed, and touched her lips to his. He lay very still, half-pleased, half-panicked. She straightened, watched him another moment, and sighed. "Didn't think it would work. Maybe I'm just not the right princess."

You have a very strange taste in men, milady, he thought dizzily. *How fortunate for me. . . .*

Feeling hopeful of his future for the first time since recovering consciousness, he lay quietly and let her go. Surely she would come back. Before, he had passed out, or been knocked out; this time natural sleep came to him. He didn't exactly like it—*if I should die before I wake*—but it served his body's craving, and blotted out the pain.

Slowly, he gained control of his left arm. Then he made his right leg twitch. His beautiful lady came back and fed him more sugar water, but with no more sweet kisses for dessert. By the time he compelled his left leg to twitch, she came back again, but this time there was something terribly wrong.

Dr. Durona looked ten years older, and had grown cool. Cold. Her hair was parted in the middle and hung down in two smooth wings, chopped off at jaw-length, with threads of silver gleaming in the ebony. Her hands on his body, helping him to sit up, were dryer, colder, more severe. Not caressing.

I've gone into a time-warp. No. I've been frozen again. No. I'm taking too long to recover, and she's pissed at me for making her wait. No . . . Confusion clogged his throat. He'd just lost the only friend he had, and he didn't know why. *I have destroyed our joy. . . .*

She massaged his legs, very professionally, provided him with a loose patient gown, and made him stand up. He almost passed out. She put him back to bed and left.

When she came back the next time, she'd changed her hair yet again. This time it was grown long, held back tightly bound in a silver ring on the back of her head, and flowing down in a blunt-ended horse-tail with wide silver streaks running through it. She'd aged another ten years, he swore. *What's happening to me?* Her manner was a little softened, but nothing so happy as at first. She walked him across the room and back, which drained him totally, after which he slept again.

He was deeply distressed when she returned once more in her cold, short-haired incarnation. He had to admit, she was efficient getting him up and moving. She barked at him like a drill sergeant, but he walked, and then he walked unassisted. She steered him outside of his room for the first time, to where a short hallway ended in a sliding door, and then back.

They'd just turned for another circuit when the door at the end hissed open, and Dr. Durona came through. She was in her horse-tail morph. He stared at the wing-haired Dr. Durona beside him, and almost burst into tears. *It's not fair. You're confusing me.* Dr. Durona strode up to Dr. Durona. He blinked back the water in his eyes, and focused on their name tags. Wing-hair was Dr. C. Durona. Horse-tail was Dr. P. Durona. *But where's my Dr. Durona? I want Dr. R.*

"Hi, Chrys, how's he doing?" asked Dr. P.

Dr. C. answered, "Not too badly. I've just about worn him out for this therapy-session, though."

"I should say so—" Dr. P. moved to help catch him as he collapsed. He could not make his mouth form words; they came out choked sobs. "Over-done it, I'd say."

"Not at all," said Dr. C., supporting his other side. Together they steered him back to bed. "But it looks like mental recovery is going to come after physical recovery, in this one. Which is not good. The pressure's on. Lilly's getting impatient. He has to start making connections soon, or he'll be no use to us."

"Lilly is never impatient," chided Dr. P.

"She is this time," said Dr. C. grimly.

"Will the mental recovery really follow?" She helped him lie back without falling.

"Anyone's guess. Rowan has guaranteed us the physical. Tremendous job, that. There's plenty of electrical activity in his brain; something has to be healing."

"Yes, but not instantly," came a warmly amused voice from the hallway. "What are you two doing to my poor patient?"

It was Dr. Durona. Again. She had long fine hair bunched in a messy wad on the back of her head, pure ebony dark. He peered worriedly at her name tag as she approached, smiling. *Dr. R. Durona. His Dr. Durona.* He whimpered in relief. He wasn't sure he could take much more confusion; it hurt more than the physical pain. His nerves seemed more shattered than his body. It was like being in one of his bad dreams, except that his dreams were much nastier, with more blood and dismemberment, not just a green-coated woman standing all around a room arguing with herself.

"P.T. stands for Physical Torture," Dr. C. quipped.

That explained it. . . .

"Come back and torture him again later," Dr. R. invited. "But—gently."

"How hard dare I push?" Dr. C. was intent, serious, standing with her head cocked, making notes on a report panel. "Urgent queries are coming down from above, you know."

"I know. Physical therapy no oftener than every four hours, till I give you the go-ahead. And don't run his heart rate above one-forty."

"That high?"

"An unavoidable consequence of its still being undersized."

"You have it, love." Dr. C. snapped her report panel closed and tossed it to Dr. R., then marched out; Dr. P. wafted after her.

His Dr. Durona, Dr. R., came to his side, smiled, and brushed his hair out of his eyes. "You're going to need a haircut soon. And new growth is starting on the bare patches. That's a very good sign. With all that happening on the outside of your head, I think there has to be something happening on the inside, hey?"

Only if you counted spasms of hysteria as activity . . . a tear left over from his earlier burst of terror escaped his eye at a nervous blink. She touched its track. "Oh," she murmured in sympathetic worry, which he found suddenly embarrassing. *I am not . . . I am not . . . I am not a mutant.* What?

She leaned closer. "What's your name?"

He tried. "Whzz . . . d'buh . . ." His tongue would not obey him. He knew the words, he just couldn't make them come out. "Whzz . . . yr nme?"

"Did you repeat me?" She brightened. "It's a start—"

"Ngh! Whzz *yr* nme?" He touched her jacket pocket, hoping she wouldn't think he was trying to grope her.

"What . . . ?" She glanced down. "Are you asking what's *my* name?"

"Gh! Gh!"

"My name is Dr. Durona."

He groaned, and rolled his eyes.

" . . . My name is Rowan."

He fell back onto his head-pad, sighing with relief. *Rowan.* Lovely name. He wanted to tell her it was a lovely name. But what if they were all named Rowan—no, the sergeantly one had been called Chrys. It was all right. He could cut his Dr. Durona out of the herd if he had to; she was unique. His wavering hand touched her lips, then his own, but she didn't take the hint and kiss him again.

Reluctantly, only because he didn't have the strength to hold her, he let her pull her hand from his. Maybe he had dreamed that kiss. Maybe he was dreaming all of this.

A long, uncertain time passed after she left, but for a change he did not doze off. He lay awake, awash in disquieting, disconnected thought. The thought-stream carried odd bits of jetsam, an image here, what might be a memory there, but as soon as his attention turned inward to examine it the flow of thoughts froze, and the tide of panic rose again. Well, and so. Let him occupy himself otherwise, only watching his thoughts at an angle, obliquely; let him observe himself reflected in what he knew, and play detective to his own identity. *If you can't do what you want, do what you can.* And if he couldn't answer the question, Who was he?, he might at least take a crack at *Where* was he? His monitor pads were gone; he was no longer radio-tagged.

It was very silent. He slipped out of bed and navigated to the door. It opened automatically onto the short hallway, which was dimly lit by night-strips at floor level.

Including his own, there were only four rooms off the little corridor. None had windows. Or other patients. A tiny office or monitor-station was empty—no. A beverage cup steamed on the countertop next to a switched-on console, its program on *hold*. Somebody would be back soon. He nipped past and tried the only exit door, at the corridor's end; it too opened automatically.

Another short corridor. Two well-equipped surgeries lined it. Both were shut down, cleaned up, night-silent. And windowless. A couple of storage rooms, one locked, one not. Two palm-locked laboratories; one had a bank of small animal cages at one end, that he could glimpse dimly through the glass. It was all crammed with equipment of the medical/biochemical sort, far more than a mere treatment clinic would require. The place fairly reeked of research.

How do I know—no. Don't ask. Just keep going. A lift-tube beckoned at the corridor's end. His body ached, breathing hurt, but he had to grab his chance. *Go, go, go.*

Wherever he was, he was at the very bottom of it. The tube's floor was at his feet. It rose into dimness, lit by panels reading S-3, S-2, S-1. The tube was switched off, its safety door locked across the opening. He slid it open manually, and considered his options. He could switch the tube on, and risk lighting up some security monitor panel somewhere (why could he picture such a thing?); or he could leave it off and climb the safety-ladder in secret. He tried one rung of the ladder; his vision blackened. He backed down carefully and switched on the tube.

He rose gently to level S-1, and swung out. A tiny foyer had one door, solid and blank. It opened before him, and closed behind him. He stared around what was obviously a junk-storage chamber, and turned back. His door had vanished into a blank wall.

It took him a full minute of frightened examination to convince himself his sputtering brain wasn't playing tricks on him. The door was disguised as the wall. And he'd just locked himself out. He patted it frantically all over, but it would not re-admit him. His bare feet were freezing on the polished concrete floor, and he was dizzy and dreadfully tired. He wanted to go back to bed. The frustration and fear were almost overwhelming, not that they were so vast, but that he was so weak.

You only want it 'cause you can't have it. Perverse. Go on, he told himself sternly. He made his way from support to support to the outer door of the storage chamber. It too was locked from the outside, he found out the hard way when it sealed behind him. *Go on.*

The storage room had opened onto another short corridor, centered around an ordinary lift-tube foyer. This level pretended to be the end of the line, Level B-2; openings marked B-1, G, 1, 2, and so on ascended out of sight. He went for the zero-point, G. G for Ground? Yes. He exited into a darkened lobby.

It was a neat little place, elegantly furnished but in the manner of a business rather than a home, with potted plants and a reception or security desk. No one around. No signs. But there were windows at last, and transparent doors. They reflected a dim replica of the interior; it was night outside. He leaned on the comconsole desk. Jackpot. Here was not only a place to sit down, but data in abundance . . . hell. It was palm-locked, and would not even turn on for him. There were ways to overcome palm-locks—how did he . . . ?—the fragmentary visions exploded like a school of minnows, eluding his grasp. He nearly cried with the uselessness of it, sitting in the station chair with his too-heavy head laid in his arms, across the blank unyielding vid plate.

He shivered. *God, I hate cold.* He wobbled over to the glass door. It was snowing outside, tiny scintillant dots whipping by slantwise through the white arc of a floodlight. They would be hard, and hiss and sting on bare skin. A weird vision of a dozen naked men standing shivering in a midnight blizzard flitted across his mind's eye, but he could attach no names to the scene, only a sensation of deep disaster. Was that how he had died, freezing in the wind and snow? Recently, nearby?

I was dead. The realization came to him for the first time, a burst of shock radiating outward from his belly. He traced the aching scars on his torso through the thin fabric of his gown. *And I'm not feeling too good now, either.* He giggled, an off-balance noise disturbing even to his own ears. He stifled his mouth with his fist. He must not have had time to be afraid, before, because the retroactive wash of terror knocked him to his knees. Then to his hands and knees. The shivering cold was making his hands shake uncontrollably. He began to crawl.

He must have triggered some sensor, because the transparent door hissed open. Oh, no, he wasn't going to make that error again, and get exiled to the outer darkness. He began to crawl away. His vision blurred, and he got turned around somehow; icy concrete instead of smooth tile beneath his hand warned him of his mistake. Something seemed to seize his head, half-shock, half-blow, with a nasty buzzing sound. Violently rebuffed, he smelled singed hair. Fluorescent patterns spun on his retinas. He tried to withdraw, but collapsed across the door-groove in a puddle of ice water and some slimy orange glop like gritty mold. *No, damn it no, I don't want to freeze again . . . !* He curled up in desperate revulsion.

Voices; shouts of alarm. Footsteps, babble, warm, oh blessed warm hands pulled him away from the deadly portal. A couple of women's voices, and one man's: "How did he get up here?" "—shouldn't have gotten out." "Call Rowan. Wake her up—" "He looks terrible." "No," a hand held his face to the light by his hair, "that's the way he looks anyway. You can't tell."

The face belonging to the hand loomed over his, harsh and worried. It was Rowan's assistant, the young man who'd sedated him. He was a lean fellow with Eurasian features, with a definite bridge to his nose. His blue jacket said *R. Durona,* insanely enough. But it wasn't *Dr. R. So call him . . . Brother Durona.* The young man was saying, "—dangerous. It's incredible that he penetrated our security in that condition!"

"Na' sec'rty." Words! His mouth was making words! "Fire saf'ty." He added reflectively, "Dolt."

The young man's face jerked back in bewildered offense. "Are you talking to me, Short Circuit?"

"He's talking!" *His* Dr. Durona's face circled overhead, her voice thrilled. He recognized her even with her fine hair loose, falling all around her face in a dark cloud. *Rowan, my love.* "Raven, what did he say?"

The youth's dark brows wrinkled. "I'd swear he just said 'fire safety.' " Gibberish, I guess."

Rowan smiled wildly. "Raven, all the secured doors open outward without code-locks. For escape in case of fire or chemical accident or—do you realize the level of understanding that reveals?"

"No," said Raven coldly.

That *dolt* must have stung, considering its source . . . he grinned darkly up at the hovering faces and the lobby ceiling wavering beyond them.

An older, alto voice came in from the left, restoring order, disbanding the crowd. "If you don't have a function here, get back to bed." A Dr. Durona whose short-cut hair was almost pure white, the owner of the alto voice, shuffled into his field of view and stared thoughtfully down at him. "Dear heart, Rowan, he almost escaped, disabled as he is!"

"Hardly an escape," said Brother Raven. "Even if he'd somehow gotten through the force screen, he'd have frozen to death in twenty minutes out there tonight, dressed like that."

"How did he get out?"

An upset Dr. Durona confessed, "He must have gone past the monitor station while I was in the lav. I'm sorry!"

"Suppose he had made it this far in the daytime?" speculated the alto. "Suppose he had been seen? It could have been disastrous."

"I'll palm-lock the door to the private wing after this," the flustered Dr. Durona promised.

"I'm not sure that will be enough, considering this remarkable performance. Yesterday he couldn't even walk. Still, this fills me with hope as much as alarm. I think we have something here. We had better set a closer guard."

"Who can be spared?" asked Rowan.

Several Dr. Duronas, clad variously in robes and nightgowns, looked at the young man.

"Aw, no," Raven protested.

"Rowan may watch him in the daytime, and continue her work. You will take the night shift," the white-haired woman instructed firmly.

"Yes, ma'am," the youth sighed.

She gestured imperiously. "Take him back to his room now. You had better check him for damages, Rowan."

"I'll get a float pallet," said Rowan.

"You don't need a float pallet for him," scoffed Raven. He knelt, gathered the wanderer up in his arms, and grunted to his feet. Showing off his strength? Well . . . no. "He weighs about as much as a wet coat. Come on, Short Circuit, back to bed with you."

Muzzily indignant, he suffered himself to be carried off. Rowan hovered apprehensively at his side across the lobby, down the tube, through the storage chamber, and back into the peculiar building-under-a-building. At least, in response to his continued shivering, she set the bed's heat-bubble zone to a higher temperature this time.

Rowan examined him, with particular attention to his aching scars. "He hasn't managed to rip anything apart inside. But he seems physiologically upset. It may be from the pain."

"Do you want me to give him another two cc's of sedative?" asked Raven.

"No. Just keep the room dim and quiet. He's exhausted himself. Once he warms up I think he'll sleep on his own." She touched his cheek, then his lips, tenderly. "That was the second time today that he spoke, do you know?"

She wanted him to speak to her. But he was too tired now. And too rattled. There had been a tension among those people tonight, all those Dr. Duronas, that was more than medical fear for a patient's safety. They were very worried about something. Something to do with him? He might be a blank to himself, but they knew more and they weren't telling him.

Rowan eventually pulled her night robe more closely about herself, and left. Raven arranged two chairs, one for a seat and one for his feet, settled down, and began reading from a hand-viewer. Studying, for he occasionally re-ran screens or made notes. Learning to be a doctor, no doubt.

He lay back, drained beyond measure. His excursion tonight had nearly killed him, and what had he learned for all his pains? Not much, except this: *I am come to a very strange place.*

And I am a prisoner here.

CHAPTER TWENTY

Mark, Bothari-Jesek, and the Countess were in the library of Vorkosigan House going over ship specs the day before the scheduled departure.

"Do you think I would have time to stop and see my clones on Komarr?" Mark asked the Countess a little wistfully. "Would Illyan let me?"

ImpSec had settled on a Komarran private boarding school as the clones' initial depository, after consultation with the Countess, who had in turn kept Mark informed. ImpSec liked it because it meant they had only one location to guard. The clones liked it because they were together with their friends, the only familiarity in their sudden new situation. The teachers liked it because the clones could all be treated as one remedial class, and brought up to academic speed together. At the same time the young refugees had a chance to mingle with youths from normal, if mostly upper-class, families, and begin to get a handle on socialization. Later, when it was safer, the Countess was pushing for placement in foster-families despite the clones' awkward age and size. *How will they learn to form families themselves, later, if they have no models?* she'd argued with Illyan. Mark had listened in on that conversation with the most intense imaginable fascination, and kept his mouth tightly shut.

"Certainly, if you wish," the Countess now said to Mark. "Illyan will kick, but that's pure reflex. Except . . . I can think of one proper complaint he might have, because of your destination. If you encounter House Bharaputra again, God forbid, it might be better if you don't know everything about ImpSec's arrangements. Stopping on your way back might be more prudent." The Countess looked as if she didn't care for the flavor of her own words, but years of living with security concerns made her reasoning automatic.

If I encounter Vasa Luigi again, the clones will be the least of my worries, Mark thought wryly. What did he want of a personal visit anyway? Was he still trying to pass himself off as a hero? A hero should be more self-contained and austere. Not so desperate for praise as to pursue his—victims—begging for it. Surely he'd played the fool enough. "No," he sighed at last. "If any of them ever want to talk to me, they can find me, I guess." No heroine was going to kiss him anyway.

The Countess raised her brows at his tone, but shrugged agreement.

Led by Bothari-Jesek, they turned to more practical matters involving fuel costs and life-support system repairs. Bothari-Jesek and the Countess—who, Mark was reminded, had been a ship captain herself once—were deep into a startlingly technical discussion involving Necklin rod adjustments, when the comconsole image split, and Simon Illyan's face appeared.

"Hello, Elena." He nodded to her, in the comconsole's station chair. "I wish to speak with Cordelia, please."

Bothari-Jesek smiled, nodded, muted the outgoing audio, and slid aside. She beckoned urgently to the Countess, whispering, "Do we have trouble?"

"He's going to block us," worried Mark, agitated, as the Countess settled into the comconsole's station chair. "He's going to nail me to the floor, I know he is."

"Hush," reproved the Countess, smiling slightly. "Both of you sit over there and resist the temptation to talk. Simon is my meat." She re-opened her audio transmission mode. "Yes, Simon, what can I do for you?"

"Milady," Illyan gave her a short nod, "in a word, you can desist. This scheme you are putting forward is unacceptable."

"To whom, Simon? Not to me. Who else gets a vote?"

"Security," Illyan growled.

"You are Security. I'll thank you to take responsibility for your own emotional responses, and not try to shift them onto some vague abstraction. Or get off the line and let me talk to Captain Security, then."

"All right. It's unacceptable to me."

"In a word—tough."

"I *request* you to desist."

"I refuse. If you want to stop me, ultimately, you'll have to generate an order for Mark's and my arrest."

"I will speak to the Count," said Illyan stiffly, with the air of a man driven to a last resort.

"He's much too ill. And I've spoken with him already."

Illyan swallowed his bluff without gagging, much. "I don't know what you think this unauthorized venture can do, besides muddy the waters, maybe risk lives, and cost you a small fortune."

"Well, that's just the point, Simon. I *don't* know what Mark will be able to do. And neither do you. The trouble with ImpSec is that you've had no competition lately. You take your monopoly for granted. A bit of hustle will be good for you."

Illyan sat with his teeth clenched for a short time. "You put House Vorkosigan at triple risk, with this," he said at last. "You are endangering your last possible back-up."

"I am aware. And I choose the risk."

"Do you have that right?"

"I have more right than you."

"The government is in the biggest uproar behind closed doors that I've seen in years," said Illyan. "The Centrist Coalition is scrambling to find a man to replace Aral. And so are three other parties."

"Excellent. I hope one of them may succeed before Aral gets back on his feet, or I'll never get him to retire."

"Is that what you see in this?" Illyan demanded. "A chance to end your husband's career? Is this *loyal*, milady?"

"I see a chance to get him out of Vorbarr Sultana alive," she said icily, "an end I have often despaired of, over the years. You pick your loyalties, I'll pick mine."

"Who is capable of succeeding him?" asked Illyan plaintively.

"A number of men. Racozy, Vorhalas, or Sendorf, to name three. If not, there was something terribly wrong with Aral's leadership. One mark of a great man is the legacy of men he leaves behind him, to whom he's passed on his skills. If you think Aral so small as to have stifled all possible others around him, spreading small-ness like a plague, then perhaps Barrayar is better off without him."

"You know I don't think that!"

"Good. Then your argument annihilates itself."

"You tie me in knots." Illyan rubbed his neck. "Milady," he said at last, "I didn't want to have to say this to you. But have you considered the possible *dangers* of letting Lord Mark get to Lord Miles before anyone else?"

She leaned back in her chair, smiling, her fingers lightly drumming. "No, Simon. What dangers are you thinking of?"

"The temptation to promote himself," Illyan bit out.

"Murder Miles. Say what you damn mean." Her eyes glinted dangerously. "So you'll just have to make sure your people get to Miles first. Won't you. I've no objection."

"Damn it, Cordelia," he cried, harried, "you realize, that if they get into trouble, the first thing they're going to do is cry to ImpSec for rescue!"

The Countess grinned. "You live to serve, I believe you fellows say in your oath. Don't you?"

"We'll see," snapped Illyan, and cut the comm.

"What's he going to do?" asked Mark anxiously.

"At a guess, go over my head. Since I've already cut him out with Aral, that leaves only one choice. I don't think I'll bother getting up. I expect I'll get another call here shortly."

Distracted, Mark and Bothari-Jesek attempted to carry on with the ship specs. Mark jumped when the comm chimed again.

An anonymous young man appeared, nodded to the Countess, stated, "Lady Vorkosigan. Emperor Gregor," and vanished. Gregor's face appeared in his place, looking bemused.

"Good morning, Lady Cordelia. You really ought not to stir up poor Simon that way, you know."

"He deserved it," she said equably. "I admit, he has far too much on his mind at the moment. Suppressed panic turns him into a prick every time; it's what he does instead of running in circles screaming. A way of coping, I suppose."

"While others of us cope by becoming over-analytical," Gregor murmured. The Countess's lip twitched, and Mark suddenly thought he knew who might shave the barber.

"His security concerns are legitimate," Gregor continued. "Is this Jackson's Whole venture *wise*?"

"A question that can only be answered by empirical testing. So to speak. I grant you, Simon argues sincerely. But—how do you consider *Barrayar's* concerns will best be served, Sire? That's the question you must answer."

"I'm divided in mind."

"Are you divided in heart?" Her question was a challenge. She opened her hands, half-placation, half-pleading. "One way or another, you're going to be dealing with Lord Mark Vorkosigan for a long time to come. This excursion, if it does nothing else, will test the validity of all doubts. If they are not tested, they will always remain with you, an unanswered itch. And that's not fair to Mark."

"How very scientific," he breathed. They regarded each other with equal dryness.

"I thought it might appeal to you."

"Is Lord Mark with you?"

"Yes." The Countess gestured him to her side.

Mark entered the range of the vid pick-up. "Sire."

"So, Lord Mark." Gregor studied him gravely. "It seems your mother wants me to give you enough rope to hang yourself."

Mark swallowed. "Yes, Sire."

"Or save yourself . . ." Gregor nodded. "So be it. Good luck and good hunting."

"Thank you, Sire."

Gregor smiled and cut the comm.

They did not hear from Illyan again.

In the afternoon, the Countess took Mark with her to the Imperial Military Hospital on her daily visit to her husband. Mark had made that journey in her company twice before, since the Count's collapse. He didn't much care for it. For one thing, the place smelled entirely too much like the clinics that had helped make a torment of his Jacksonian youth; he found himself remembering details of early surgeries and treatments that he thought he'd altogether forgotten. For another, the Count himself still terrified Mark. Even laid low, his personality was as powerful as his life was precarious, and Mark wasn't sure which teetering aspect scared him more.

His feet slowed to a halt in the hospital corridor outside the Prime Minister's guarded room, and he stood in indecisive misery. The Countess glanced back, and stopped. "Yes?"

"I . . . really don't want to go in there."

She frowned thoughtfully. "I won't force you. But I'll predict you a prediction."

"Say on, oh seeress."

"You will never regret having done so. But you may deeply regret not having done so."

Mark digested that. "All right," he said faintly, and followed her.

They tiptoed in quietly on the deep carpeting. The drapes were open on a wide view of the Vorbarr Sultana city-scape, sweeping down to the ancient buildings and the river that bisected the capital's heart. It was a cloudy, chilly, rainy afternoon, and gray and white mists swirled around the tops of the highest modern towers. The Count's face was turned to the silver light. He looked abstracted, bored, and ill, his face puffy and greenish, only partly a reflection of the light and the green uniform pajamas that reminded all forcibly of his patient-status. He was peppered with monitor pads, and had an oxygen tube to his nostrils.

"Ah." His head turned at their entry, and he smiled. He keyed up a light at his bedside, which cast a warmer pool of illumination that nonetheless failed to improve his color. "Dear Captain. Mark." The Countess bent to his bedside, and they exchanged a longer-than-formal kiss. The Countess swung herself up on the end of his bed and perched there cross-legged, arranging her long skirt. Casually, she began to rub his bare feet, and he sighed contentedly.

Mark advanced to about a meter distance. "Good afternoon, sir. How are you feeling?"

"Hell of a deal, when you can't kiss your own wife without running out of breath," he complained. He lay back, panting heavily.

"They let me into the lab to see your new heart," the Countess commented. "It's chicken-heart sized already, and beating away cheerfully in its little vat."

The Count laughed weakly. "How grotesque."

"*I* thought it was cute."

"*You* would."

"If you really want grotesque, consider what you want to do with the old one, after," the Countess advised with a wicked grin. "The opportunities for tasteless jokes are almost irresistible."

"The mind reels," murmured the Count. He glanced up at Mark, still smiling.

Mark took a breath. "Lady Cordelia has explained to you what I intend to do, hasn't she, sir?"

"Mm." The Count's smile faded. "Yes. Watch out for your back. Nasty place, Jackson's Whole."

"Yes, I . . . know."

"So you do." He turned his head to stare out the gray window. "I wish I could send Bothari with you."

The Countess looked startled. Mark could read her thought right off her face, *Has he forgotten Bothari is dead?* But she was afraid to ask. She pasted a brighter smile on her mouth instead.

"I'm taking Bothari-Jesek, sir."

"History repeats itself." He struggled to sit up on one elbow, and added sternly, "It had better not, boy, y'hear?" He relaxed back into his pillows before the Countess could respond and make him. Her face lost its tension; he was clearly a little fogged, but he wasn't so far out of it as to have forgotten his armsman's violent death. "Elena's smarter than her father was, I'll give her that," he sighed. The Countess finished with his feet.

He lay back, brows drawn down, apparently struggling to think of more useful advice. "I once thought—I only found this out when I grew old, understand—that there is no more terrible fate than to become the mentor. To be able to tell how, yet not to do. To send your protégé out, all bright and beautiful, to stand your fire . . . I think I've found a worse fate. To send your student out knowing damn well you haven't had a chance to teach *enough*. . . . Be smart, boy. Duck fast. Don't sell yourself to your enemy in advance, in your mind. You can only be defeated *here*." He touched his hands to his temples.

"I don't even know who the enemy is, yet," said Mark ruefully.

"They'll find you, I suppose," sighed the Count. "People give themselves to you, in their talking, and in other ways, if you are quiet and patient and let them, and not in such a damned rush to give yourself to *them* you go bat-blind and deaf. Eh?"

"I guess so. Sir," said Mark, baffled.

"Huh." The Count had run himself completely out of breath. "You'll see," he wheezed. The Countess eyed him, swung herself off the bed, and stood up.

"Well," said Mark, and nodded briefly, "goodbye." His word hung in the air, insufficient. *Cardiac conditions are not contagious, dammit. What are you scared of?* He swallowed, and cautiously went nearer the Count. He had never touched the man except the once when trying to help load him onto the float bike. Afraid, emboldened, he held out his hand.

The Count grasped it, a brief, strong grip. His hand was big and square and blunt-fingered, a hand fit for shovels and picks, swords and guns. Mark's own hand seemed small and child-like, plump and pale by contrast. They had nothing in common but the grip.

"Confusion to the enemy, boy," whispered the Count.

"Turn-about is fair play, sir."

His father snorted a laugh.

✧   ✧   ✧

Mark made one final vid-call that evening, his last night on Barrayar. He sneaked off to use the console in Miles's room, not in secret, exactly, but in private. He stared at the blank machine for ten minutes before spasmodically punching in the code he had obtained.

A middle-aged blonde woman's image appeared over the vid plate when the chime stopped. The remains of a striking beauty made her face strong and confident. Her eyes were blue and humorous. "Commodore Koudelka's residence," she answered formally.

It's her mother. Mark choked down panic to quaver, "May I speak with Kareen Koudelka, please—ma'am?"

A blonde brow twitched. "I believe I know which one you are, but—who may I say is calling?"

"Lord Mark Vorkosigan," he got out.

"Just a moment, my lord." She left the range of the vid pick-up; he could hear her voice fading in the distance, calling "Kareen!"

There was a muffled bumping in the background, garbled voices, a shriek, and Kareen's laughing voice crying, "No, Delia, it's for me! Mother, make her go away! Mine, all mine! Out!" The sound of a door thumping closed on, presumably, flesh, a yelp, then a firmer and more final slam.

Panting and tousled, Kareen Koudelka arrived in range, and gave him a starry-eyed "Hi!"

If not *just* like the look Lady Cassia had given Ivan, it was a robust and blue near-cousin. Mark felt faint. "Hello," he said breathlessly. "I called to say goodbye." No, dammit, that was much too short—

"What?"

"Um, excuse me, that's not quite what I meant. But I'm going to be traveling off-planet soon, and I didn't want to leave without speaking to you again."

"Oh." Her smile drooped. "When will you come back?"

"I'm not sure. But when I do, I'd like to see you again."

"Well . . . sure."

Sure, she said. What a lot of joyful assumptions were embedded in that *sure.*

Her eyes narrowed. "Is there something wrong, Lord Mark?"

"No," he said hastily. "Um . . . was that your sister I heard in the background just now?"

"Yes. I had to lock her out, or she'd stand out of range and make faces at me while we talked." Her earnest air of injury was immediately spoiled when she added, "That's what I do to her, when fellows call."

He was a *fellow*. How ... how *normal*. He led her on with one question after another, to talk about her sisters, her parents, and her life. Private schools and cherished children ... The Commodore's family was well-to-do, but with some sort of Barrayaran-style work ethic driving a passion for education and accomplishment, an ideal of service running like an undercurrent, towing them all into their future. He went awash in her words, dreamily sharing. She was so peaceable and real. No shadow of torment, nothing spoiled or deformed. He felt as if he was feeding, not his belly but his head. His brain felt warm and distended and happy, a sensation near-erotic but less threatening. Alas, after a time she became conscious of the disproportion in the conversation.

"Good heavens, I'm babbling. I'm sorry."

"No! I like listening to you talk."

"That's a first. In this family, I'm lucky to get a word in edgewise. I didn't talk till I was three. They had me tested. It turned out it was just because my sisters were answering everything for me!"

Mark laughed.

"Now they say I'm making up for lost time."

"I know about lost time," Mark said ruefully.

"Yes, I've ... heard a little. I guess your life has been quite an adventure."

"Not an adventure," he corrected. "A disaster, maybe." He wondered what his life would look like, reflected in her eyes. Something shinier. ... "Maybe when I get back I can tell you a bit about it." If he got back. If he brought this off.

I'm not a nice person. You should know that, before. Before what? The more over-extended their acquaintance became, the harder it would be to tell her his repellent secrets.

"Look, I ... you have to understand." God, he sounded just like Bothari-Jesek, working up to her confession. "I'm kind of a mess, and I'm not just talking about my outsides." Hell, hell, and what had this nice young virgin to do with the arcane subtleties of psycho-programming tortures, and their erratic results? What right had he to put horrors in her head? "I don't even know what I should tell you!"

Now was too soon, he could feel that clearly. But *later* might be too late, leaving her feeling betrayed and tricked. And if he continued this conversation one more minute, he'd drift into abject-blurting mode, and lose the one bright, un-poisoned thing he'd found.

Kareen tilted her head in puzzlement. "Maybe you ought to ask the Countess."

"Do you know her well? To talk to?"

"Oh, yes. She and my mother are best friends. My mother used to be her personal bodyguard, before she retired to have us."

Mark sensed the shadowy league of grandmothers again. Powerful old women with genetic agendas. . . . He felt obscurely that there were some things a man ought to do for himself. But on Barrayar, they used go-betweens. He had in his camp an ambassadoress-extraordinary to the whole female gender. The Countess would act for his good. Yeah, like a woman holding down a screaming child to get it a painful vaccination that would save it from a deadly disease.

How much did he trust the Countess? Did he dare trust her in this?

"Kareen . . . before I come back, do me a favor. If you get a chance to talk privately to the Countess, ask her what she thinks you ought to know about me, before we get better acquainted. Tell her I asked you to."

"All right. I like to talk with Lady Cordelia. She's sort of been my mentor. She makes me think I can do anything." Kareen hesitated. "If you're back by Winterfair, will you dance with me again at the Imperial Residence Ball? And not hide in the corner this time," she added sternly.

"If I'm back by Winterfair, I won't have to hide in the corner. Yes."

"Good. I'll hold you to your word."

"My word as Vorkosigan," he said lightly.

Her blue eyes widened. "Oh. My." Her soft lips parted in a blinding smile.

He felt like a man who'd gone to spit, and had a diamond pop accidently from his lips instead. And he couldn't call it back and re-swallow it. There must be a Vorish streak in the girl, to take a man's word so seriously.

"I have to go now," he said.

"All right. Lord Mark—be careful?"

"I—why do you say that?" He hadn't said a word about where he was going or why, he swore.

"My father is a soldier. You have that same look in your eyes that he gets, when he's lying through his teeth about some difficulty he's heading into. He can never fool my mother, either."

No girl had ever told him to *be careful*, as though she meant it. He was touched beyond measure. "Thank you, Kareen." Reluctantly, he cut the comm, with a gesture that was nearly a caress.

CHAPTER TWENTY-ONE

Mark and Bothari-Jesek hitched a ride from Barrayar back to Komarr on an ImpSec courier vessel very like the one they'd ridden before, the last favor, Mark swore, that he would ever ask of Simon Illyan. This resolve lasted till they arrived at Komarr orbit, where Mark found that the Dendarii had given him his Winterfair gift early. All of Medic Norwood's personal effects had finally arrived, shipped from the main Dendarii fleet.

ImpSec being ImpSec, they had opened it first. So much the better; they would hardly have let Mark touch it if they had not convinced themselves they'd already emptied it of all its secrets. With Bothari-Jesek's backing, Mark begged, bluffed, bullied and whined his way to access to it. With obvious reluctance, ImpSec admitted him under supervision to a locked room in their orbital HQ. But they admitted him.

Mark turned Bothari-Jesek loose to oversee the arrangements for the ship the Countess's agent had located. As a Dendarii shipmaster Bothari-Jesek was not only the most logical person for the logistical tasks, she was probably overkill. With barely a pang of conscience Mark dismissed her from his thoughts to plunge into his examination of his new treasure box. Alone in an empty room. Heavenly.

After his first excited pass through the material—which included old clothing, a disk library, letters, and souvenir knickknacks from Norwood's four years of Dendarii service—Mark, depressed, was inclined to allow ImpSec was right. There was nothing here of value. Nothing up any of the sleeves—ImpSec had checked; Mark set aside clothing, boots, mementos, and all the physical effects. It gave him a queer feeling to handle the old clothes, marked with the wear of a body that was gone forever. Too damned much mortality around here. He turned his attention instead to the more intellectual detritus of the medic's life and career: his library and technical notes. ImpSec had gone through this same focusing before him, he noted glumly.

He sighed, settling back in his station chair for a long slog. He desperately wanted Norwood to yield him the clue, if only so that a man he had inadvertently led to his death might not have died so in vain. *I never want to be a combat commander again. Ever.*

He hadn't expected it to be obvious. But his connector, when he finally ran across it hours later, was just about as subliminal as they came. It was a note hand-jotted on a plastic flimsy stuck in a pile of similar notes, interspersed in a cryo-prep training manual for emergency medical technicians. All it said was, *See Dr. Durona at 0900 for laboratory materials.*

Not *the* Durona . . . ?

Mark back-pedaled to Norwood's certifications and transcripts, part of the medic's computerized records he'd already seen in the ImpSec files on Barrayar. Norwood had taken his Dendarii cryonics training at a certain Beauchene Life Center, a respected commercial cryo-revival facility on Escobar. The name "Dr. Durona" did not appear anywhere among his immediate instructors. It did not appear on a listing of the Life Center's staff. It did not, in fact, appear anywhere at all. Mark checked it all again, to be sure.

There are probably lots of people named Durona on Escobar. It's not that rare a name. He clutched the flimsy anyway. It itched in his palm.

He called Quinn, aboard the *Ariel* moored nearby.

"Ah," she said, eyeing him without favor in the vid. "You're back. Elena said you were. What do you think you're doing?"

"Never mind that. Look, is there anyone here among the Dendarii, any medics or medtechs, who were trained at the Beauchene Life Center? Preferably at the same time as Norwood? Or near his time?"

She sighed. "There were three in his group. Red Squad's medic, Norwood, and Orange Squad's medic. ImpSec has already asked us about that, Mark."

"Where are they now?"

"Red Squad's medic was killed in a shuttle crash several months ago—"

"Agh!" He ran his hands through his hair.

"Orange Squad's man is here on the *Ariel*."

"Right!" Mark crowed happily. "I have to talk to him." He almost said, *Put him on,* then remembered he was on ImpSec's private line and certainly being monitored. "Send a personnel pod to pick me up."

"One, ImpSec has already interrogated him, at great length, and two, who the hell are you to give orders?"

"Elena hasn't told you much, I see." Curious. Did Bothari-Jesek's dubious Armsman's oath then outrank her loyalties to the Dendarii? Or was she just too busy to chat? How much time had he been— he glanced at his chrono. *My God.* "I happen to be on my way to Jackson's Whole. Very soon. And if you are *very* nice to me, I *might* ask ImpSec to release you to me, and let you ride along as my guest. Maybe." He grinned breathlessly at her.

The smoldering look she gave him in return was more eloquent than the bluest string of swear words he'd ever heard. Her lips moved—counting to ten?—but no sound came out. When she did speak, her tone was clipped to a burr. "I'll have your pod at the station's hatch ring in eleven minutes."

"Thank you."

The medic was surly.

"Look, I've been through this. For hours on end. We're *done.*"

"I promise I'll keep it brief," Mark assured him. "Just one question."

The medic eyed Mark malignantly, perhaps correctly identifying him as the reason why he'd been stuck ship-bound in Komarr orbit for the last dozen weeks.

"When you and Norwood were taking your cryonics training at Beauchene Life Center, do you ever remember meeting a Dr. Durona? Handing out lab supplies, maybe?"

"The place was knee-deep in doctors. No. Can I go now?" The medic made to rise.

"Wait!"

"That was your one question. And the ImpSec goons asked it before you."

"And that was the answer you gave them? Wait. Let me think." Mark bit his lip anxiously. The name alone was not enough to hare off on, not even for him. There had to be more. "Do you ever remember . . . Norwood being in contact with a tall, striking woman with Eurasian features, straight black hair, brown eyes . . . extremely smart." He didn't dare to suggest an age. It could be anywhere between twenty and sixty.

The medic stared at him in astonishment. "Yeah! How did you know?"

"What was she? What was her relation with Norwood?"

"She was a student too, I think. He was chasing her for a time, playing off his military glamour to the hilt, but I don't think he caught her."

"Do you remember her name?"

"Roberta, or something like that. Rowanna. I don't remember."

"Was she from Jackson's Whole?"

"Escobaran, I thought." The medic shrugged. "The clinic had post-doc trainees from all over the planet to take residencies in cryo-revival. I never talked to her. I saw her with Norwood a couple of times. He might have figured we'd try to cut him out with her."

"So the clinic is a top place. With a wide reputation."

"We thought so."

"Wait here." Mark left the medic sitting in the *Ariel*'s little briefing room, and rushed out to find Quinn. He hadn't far to rush. She was waiting in the corridor, her boot tapping.

"Quinn, quick! I need a visual off Sergeant Taura's helmet recorder from the drop mission. Just one still."

"ImpSec confiscated the originals."

"You kept copies, surely."

She smiled sourly. "Maybe."

"*Please*, Quinn!"

"Wait here." She returned promptly, and handed him a data disk. This time she followed him into the briefing room. Since the secured console wouldn't take his palm-print any more no matter how he wriggled it, Mark perforce let her power it up. He fast-forwarded Taura's visuals to the image he wanted. A close-up of a tall, dark-haired girl, her head turning, eyes wide. Mark blurred the background of the clone-crèche, in the view.

Only then did he motion the medic to look.

"Hey!"

"Is it her?"

"It's . . ." the medic peered. "She's younger. But it's her. Where did you get that?"

"Never mind. Thank you. I won't take any more of your time. You've been a great help."

The medic exited as reluctantly as he had entered, staring back over his shoulder.

"What's this all about, Mark?" Quinn demanded.

"When we're on my ship and on our way, I'll tell you. Not before." He had a head-start on ImpSec, and he wasn't going to give it up. If they were anything less than desperate, they'd never let him go, Countess or no Countess. It was quite fair; he didn't have any information ImpSec didn't, potentially. He'd just put it together a little differently.

"Where the hell did you get a ship?"

"My mother gave it to me." He tried not to smirk.

"The Countess? Rats! She's turning *you* loose?"

"Don't begrudge me my little ship, Quinn. After all, my parents gave my big brother a whole *fleet* of ships." His eyes gleamed. "I'll see you on board, as soon as Captain Bothari-Jesek reports it ready."

His ship. Not stolen, nothing faked or false. His by right of legitimate gift. He who'd never had a birthday present, had one now. Twenty-two years' worth.

The little yacht was a generation old, formerly owned by a Komarran oligarch in the palmy days before the Barrayaran conquest. It had been quite luxurious, once, but obviously had been neglected for the past ten years or so. This did not represent hard times for the Komarran clan, Mark understood; they were in process of replacing it, hence the sale. The Komarrans understood business, and the Vor understood the relation between business and taxation. Business under the new regime had recovered much of its former vigor.

Mark had declared the yacht's lounge to be the mission-briefing room. He glanced around now at his invitees, draped variously over the furniture secured to the carpeted deck around a fake fireplace that ran a vid program of atavistic dancing flames, complete with infra-red radiance.

Quinn was there, of course, still in her Dendarii uniform. She had entirely overgrazed her fingernails and had taken to cheek-biting instead. Bel Thorne sat silent and reserved, a permanent bleakness emphasizing the fine lines around its eyes. Sergeant Taura loomed next to Thorne, big and puzzled and wary.

It was no strike-group. Mark wondered if he ought to have packed along more muscle . . . no. If there was one thing his first mission had taught him, it was that if you didn't have enough force to win, it was better not to engage force at all. What he *had* done was cream off the maximum expertise the Dendarii could supply on the subject of Jackson's Whole.

Captain Bothari-Jesek entered and gave him a nod. "We're on our way. We've broken orbit, and your pilot has the comm. Twenty hours to the first jump point."

"Thank you, Captain."

Quinn made a place beside her for Bothari-Jesek; Mark sat on the fake fieldstone hearth with his back to the crackling flames, his hands clasped loosely between his knees. He took a deep breath. "Welcome aboard, and thank you all for coming. You all understand, this is not an official Dendarii expedition, and is neither authorized nor funded by ImpSec. Our expenses are being privately paid by Countess Vorkosigan. You are all listed as being on unpaid personal leave. With one exception, I have no formal authority over any of you. Nor you over me. We do have an urgent mutual interest, which demands we pool our skills and information. The first piece is the proper identity of Admiral Naismith. You've brought Captain Thorne and Sergeant Taura up to speed on that, haven't you, Quinn?"

Bel Thorne nodded. "Old Tung and I had it figured out a long time ago. Miles's secret identity isn't as secret as he hoped, I'm afraid."

"It was news to me," rumbled Sergeant Taura. "It sure explained a lot I'd wondered about, though."

"Welcome to the Inner Circle anyway," said Quinn. "Officially." She turned to Mark. "All right, what do you have? A connection, finally?"

"Oh, Quinn. I'm up to my ass in connections. It's motive I'm missing now."

"You're ahead of ImpSec, then."

"Maybe not for long. They've sent an agent to Escobar for more details on the Beauchene Life Center—they're bound to make the same connection I did. Eventually. But I planned this expedition with a primary list of twenty sites on Jackson's Whole to re-check in depth. As a result of something I found in Norwood's personal effects, I've altered the order of the list. If Miles gets revived—which is part of my hypothesis—how long d'you think it would be till he did something to draw attention to himself?"

"Not long," said Bothari-Jesek reluctantly.

Quinn nodded wryly. "Though he could well wake amnesic, for a time." *Or forever,* she did not add aloud, though Mark could see the fear in her face. "It's almost more normal than not, in cryo-revivals."

"The thing is—ImpSec and we are not the only ones looking for him. I'm getting a timing-itch. Whose attention will he draw first?"

"Mm," said Quinn glumly. Thorne and Taura exchanged a worried look.

"All right." Mark rubbed his hands through his hair. He did not rise and pace, Miles-fashion; for one thing, Quinn's disapproving glances made him feel as if he was starting to waddle. "Here's what I found and here's what I think. When Norwood was on Escobar for his cryo-prep training, he met a certain Dr. Roberta or Rowanna Durona, from Jackson's Whole, who was there also taking a residency in cryo-revival. They had some positive relationship; enough, anyway, that when Norwood was cornered at Bharaputra's, he remembered her. And trusted her enough to ship her the cryo-chamber. Remember, Norwood was also under the impression at this time that House Fell was our ally. Because the Durona Group works for House Fell."

"Wait a minute," said Quinn instantly. "House Fell claims not to have the cryo-chamber!"

Mark held up a restraining hand. "Let me give you a little Jacksonian history, as far as I know it. About ninety or a hundred years ago—"

"My God, Lord Mark, how long is this story going to be?" asked Bothari-Jesek. Quinn glanced up sharply at her use of the Barrayaran honorific.

"Bear with me. You have to understand who the Durona Group is. About ninety years ago, the present Baron Ryoval's father was setting up his arcane little genetic slave-trade, the manufacture of humans to order. At some point it occurred to him: Why hire genius from outside? Grow your own. Mental properties are the most elusive to create genetically, but the old Ryoval was a genius himself. He started a project that culminated in the creation of a woman he named Lilly Durona. She was to be his medical research muse, his slave-doctor. In both senses.

"She grew, was trained, and put to work. And she was brilliant. About this time the old Baron Ryoval died, not too mysteriously, during an early attempt at a brain transplant.

"I say not too mysteriously because of the character his son and successor, the present Baron Ryoval, immediately revealed. His first project was to get rid of all his potential sibling-rivals. The old man had sired a lot of children. Ryoval's early career is something of a Jacksonian legend. The eldest and most dangerous males, he simply had assassinated. The females and some of the younger males he sent to his body-modification laboratories, and thence to his very-private bordellos, to service the customers on that side of the business. I suppose they're all dead by now. If they're lucky.

"Ryoval also, apparently, used this direct management approach on the staff he had inherited. His father had handled Lilly Durona as a cherished treasure, but the new Baron Ryoval threatened to send her after his sisters, to satisfy the biological fantasies of his customers directly, if she didn't cooperate. She began to plot her escape with a despised young half-brother of Ryoval's by the name of Georish Stauber."

"Ah! Baron Fell!" said Thorne. Thorne was looking enlightened, Taura fascinated, Quinn and Bothari-Jesek horrified.

"The same, but not yet. Lilly and young Georish escaped to the protection of House Fell. In fact, I gather that Lilly was Georish's ticket in. They both set up in service to their new masters, with considerable negotiated autonomy, at least on Lilly's part. It was the Deal. Deals are as semi-sacred as anything can be, on Jackson's Whole.

"Georish began to rise through the ranks of House Fell. And Lilly began the Durona Research Group by cloning herself. Again and again. The Durona Group, which is now up to thirty or forty cloned sisters, serves House Fell in several ways. It's sort of a family doctor for upper level Fell executives who don't want to entrust their health to outside specialist houses like Bharaputra. And since House Fell's stock in trade is weapons, they've done R&D military poisons and biologicals. And their antidotes. The Durona Group made House Fell a small fortune on Peritaint, and a few years later made it a huge fortune on Peritaint's antidote. The Durona Group is kind of quietly famous, if you follow that sort of thing. Which ImpSec does. There was a pile of stuff on 'em even in the stripped-down files they let me see. Though most of this is common knowledge on Jackson's Whole.

"Georish, not least owing to the coup he brought House Fell in the person of Lilly, ascended to the pinnacle a few years back when he became Baron Fell. Now, enter the Dendarii Mercenaries. And now you have to tell *me* what happened." Mark nodded to Bel Thorne. "I've only caught garbled bits."

Bel whistled. "I knew some of this, but I don't think I'd ever heard the whole story. No wonder Fell and Ryoval hate each other."

It glanced at Quinn: she nodded permission to proceed. "Well, about four years ago, Miles brought the Dendarii a little contract. It was for a pick-up. Our Employer—excuse me, Barrayar, I've been calling them Our Employer for so long it's a reflex."

"Keep that reflex," Mark advised.

Bel nodded. "The Imperium wanted to import a galactic geneticist. I don't quite know why." It glanced at Quinn.

"Nor do you need to," said she.

"But a certain Dr. Canaba, who was then one of House Bharaputra's top genetics people, wanted to defect. House Bharaputra takes a lethally dim view of employees departing with a head full of trade secrets, so Canaba needed help. He struck a deal with the Barrayaran Imperium to take him in."

"That's where I come from," Taura put in.

"Yes," said Thorne. "Taura was one of his pet projects. He, um, insisted on taking her along. Unfortunately, the super-soldier project had recently been cancelled, and Taura sold to Baron Ryoval, who collects genetic, excuse me Sergeant, oddities. So we had to break her out of House Ryoval, in addition to breaking Canaba out of House Bharaputra. Um, Taura, you'd better say what happened next."

"The Admiral came and rescued me from Ryoval's main biologicals facility," the big woman rumbled. She heaved a large sigh, as if at some sweet memory. "In the process of escaping, we totally destroyed House Ryoval's main gene banks. A hundred-year-old tissue collection went up in smoke. Literally." She smiled, baring her fangs.

"House Ryoval lost about fifty percent of its assets that night, Baron Fell estimated," Thorne added. "At least."

Mark hooted, then sobered. "*That* explains why you all think Baron Ryoval's people will be hunting for Admiral Naismith."

"Mark," said Thorne desperately, "if Ryoval finds Miles first, he'll have him revived just so he can kill him again. And again. And again. That's why we were all so insistent that you play Miles, when we were pulling out of Jackson's Whole. Ryoval has no motive to take revenge on the clone, just on the Admiral."

"I see. Gee. Thanks. Ah, whatever happened to Dr. Canaba? If I may ask."

"He was delivered safely," said Quinn. "He has a new name, a new face, a new laboratory, and a salary that ought to keep him happy. A loyal new subject for the Imperium."

"Hm. Well, that brings me to the other cross-connection. It's not a new or secret one, though I don't know yet what to make of it. Neither does ImpSec, incidently, though as a result of it they've sent agents to check the Durona Group twice. Baronne Lotus Bharaputra, the Baron's wife, is a Durona clone."

Taura's clawed hand flew to her lips. "That girl!"

"Yes, *that* girl. I wondered why she gave me the cold chills. I'd seen her before, in another incarnation. The clone of a clone.

"The Baronne is one of the oldest of Lilly Durona's clone daughters, or sisters, or whatever you want to call the tribe. Hive. She didn't sell herself cheaply. Lotus went renegade for one of the biggest bribes in Jacksonian history—co-control, or nearly so, of House Bharaputra. She's been Baron Bharaputra's mate for twenty years. And now it seems she's getting one other thing. The Durona Group among them have an astonishing range of bio-expertise, but they refuse to do clone-brain transplants. It was written right into Lilly Durona's foundation-deal with House Fell. But Baronne Bharaputra, who must be over sixty-standard, apparently plans to embark on her second youth very shortly. Judging from what we witnessed."

"Rats," muttered Quinn.

"So that's another cross-connection," said Mark. "In fact, it's a damned cat's cradle of cross-connections, once you get hold of the right thread. But it doesn't explain, to me at least, why the Durona Group would conceal Miles *from their own House Fell bosses.* Yet they must have done so."

"If they have him," Quinn said, gnawing on her cheek.

"If," Mark conceded. "Although," he brightened slightly, "it would explain why that incriminating cryo-chamber ended up in the Hegen Hub. The Durona Group wasn't trying to hide it from ImpSec. They were trying to hide it from other Jacksonians."

"It almost all fits," said Thorne.

Mark opened his hands and held them apart palm to palm, as if invisible threads ran back and forth between them. "Yeah. Almost." He closed his hands together. "So here we are. And there we're going. Our first trick will be to re-enter Jacksonian space past Fell's jump point station. Captain Quinn has brought along quite a kit for doctoring our identities. Coordinate your ideas with her on that one. We have ten days to play with it."

The group broke up to study the new problems each in his, her, or its own way. Bothari-Jesek and Quinn lingered as Mark rose and stretched his aching back. His aching brain.

"That was quite a pretty piece of analysis, Mark," said Quinn grudgingly. "If it's not all hot air."

She ought to know. "Thank you, Quinn," he said sincerely. He too prayed it wouldn't all turn out to be hallucinatory, an elaborate mistake.

"Yes . . . he's changed a bit, I think," Bothari-Jesek observed judiciously. "Grown."

"Yeah?" Quinn's gaze swept him, up and down. "True . . ."

Mark's heart warmed in hungry anticipation of a crumb of approval.

"—he's fatter."

"Let's get to work," Mark growled.

CHAPTER TWENTY-TWO

He could remember studying tongue-twisters, once. He could even picture a whole screen-list of them, black words on pale blue. Had it been for some sort of rhetoric course? Unfortunately, though he could picture the screen, he could only remember one of the actual lines. He struggled to sit upright in bed and try it. "Sheshells . . . shsh . . . she shells she *shit!*" He took a breath, and started over. Again. Again. His tongue seemed thick as an old sock. It felt staggeringly important to recover control of his speech. As long as he kept talking like an idiot, they were going to keep treating him like one.

It could be worse. He was eating real food now, not sugar-water or soft sludge. He'd been showering and dressing on his own for two whole days. No more patient gowns. They'd given him a shirt and pants, instead. *Like ship knits.* Their gray color at first pleased him, then worried him because he could not think why it pleased him. "She. Sells. Sea. Shells. By. The. Sea. Shore. Ha!" He lay back, wheezing in triumph. He glanced up to see Dr. Rowan leaning in the doorway, watching him with a slight smile.

Still catching his breath, he waved his fingers at her in greeting. She pushed off and came to sit at his side on his bed. She wore her usual concealing green smock, and carried a sack.

"Raven said you were babbling half the night," she remarked, "but you weren't, were you. You were practicing."

"Yuh," he nodded. "Gotta talk. C'mand—" he touched his lips, and waved vaguely around the room, "obey."

"You think so, do you?" Her brows arched in amusement but

614

her eyes, beneath them, regarded him sharply. She shifted and swung his tray table across between them. "Sit up, my authoritarian little friend. I brought you some toys."

"Sec'on chil'hd," he muttered glumly, and shoved himself upright again. His chest only ached. At least he seemed done with the more repulsive aspects of his second infancy. A second adolescence still to come? God forbid. Maybe he could skip over that part. *Why do I dread an adolescence I cannot remember?*

He laughed briefly as she upended the bag and spread about two dozen parts from some disassembled hand weapons across the table. "Test, huh?" He began to pick them up and fit them together. Stunner, nerve disruptor, plasma arc, and a projectile gun . . . slide, twist, click, knock home . . . one, two, three, four, he laid them in a row. "Pow'r cells dea'. Not armin' me, eh? These—extras." He swept half a dozen spare or odd parts aside into a pile. "Ha. Trick." He grinned smugly at her.

"You never pointed those at me or yourself while you were handling them," she observed curiously.

"Mm? Didn' notice." She was right, he realized. He fingered the plasma arc doubtfully.

"Did anything come up for you while you were doing that?" she asked.

He shook his head in renewed frustration, then brightened. "'Membered som'thin s'mornin, tho'. Inna shar." At speed, his speech slurred into unintelligibility again, a logjam of the lips.

"In the shower," she translated encouragingly. "Tell me. Slow down as much as you need."

"Slow. Is. Death," he enunciated clearly.

She blinked. "Still. Tell me."

"Ah. Well. Think I wuzza boy. Ridin' onna horse. Old man on 'nother horse. Uppa hill. 'S chilly. Horses . . . puffin' lak I 'm." His deep breaths were not deep enough to satisfy. "Trees. Mountain, two, three mountain, covered w' trees, all strung tog'ther wi' new plastic tubes. Runnin' down to a shack a' t' bottom. Gran'da *happy* . . . 'cause tubes are *efficient.*" He struggled to get that last word out intact, and succeeded. "Men'r 'appy too."

"What are they doing, in this scene?" she asked, sounding baffled. "These men."

He could see it again in his head, the memory of a memory. "Burnin' wood. Makin' sugar."

"That makes no sense. Sugar comes from biological production vats, not from burning trees," said Rowan.

"Trees," he asserted. "Brown sug'r trees." Another memory wavered up: the old man breaking off a chunk of something that looked like tan sandstone and giving him a taste by popping it in his mouth. The feel of the gnarled old stained fingers cool against his cheek, sweetness tinged with leather and horses. He shivered at the overwhelming sensory blast. *This was real.* But he still could name no names. *Gran'da.*

"Mountains mine," he added. The thought made him sad, and he didn't know why.

"What?"

"Own 'em." He frowned glumly.

"Anything else?"

"No. 'S all there is." His fists clenched. He straightened them, spreading his fingers carefully on the tray table.

"Are you sure this wasn't a dream from last night?"

"*No.* Inna *shar*," he insisted.

"It's very strange. This, I expected." She nodded to the reassembled weapons, and began putting them back in the cloth bag. "*That*," a toss of her head indicated his little story, "doesn't fit. Trees made out of sugar sound pretty dream-like to me."

Doesn't fit what? A desperate excitement surged through him. He grabbed her around one slim wrist, trapping her hand with a stunner still in it. "Doesn' fi' wha'? *Wha' d' you know?*"

"Nothing."

"Na' nothin'!"

"That hurts," she said levelly.

He let go of her instantly. "Na' nothin'," he insisted again. "*Som*'thin. *Wha*'?"

She sighed, finished bagging the weapons, and sat back and studied him. "It was a true statement that we did not know who you were. It is now a truer statement that we are not sure which *one* you are."

"I gotta choice? Tell me!"

"You are at a . . . tricky stage of your recovery. Cryo-revival amnesics seldom recover all of their memories at once. It comes in little cascades. A typical bell-curve. A few at first, then a growing mass. Then it trails off. A few last holes may linger for years. Since you had no other gross cranial injuries, my prognosis is that you will eventually recover your whole personality. But."

A most sinister *but*. He stared at her beseechingly.

"At this stage, on the verge of cascading, a cryo-amnesic can be so hungry for identity, he'll pick up a mistaken one, and start assembling evidence to support it. It can take weeks or months to get it straightened out again. In your case, for special reasons, I think this is not only more than usually possible, it could be more than usually difficult to detangle again. I have to be very, very careful not to suggest anything to you that I am not absolutely certain about. And it's hard, because I'm theorizing in my head probably just as urgently as you are. I have to be sure that anything you give me really comes from you, and is not a reflection of some suggestion on my part."

"Oh." He sagged back in bed, horribly disappointed.

"There is a possible short-cut," she added.

He surged back up again. "Wha'? Gimme!"

"There is a drug called fast-penta. One of its derivatives is a psychiatric sedative, but its usual use is as an interrogation drug. It's actually a misnomer to call it a truth serum, though laymen insist on doing so."

"I . . . know fas'pent'." His brows drew down. He knew something important about fast-penta. What was it?

"It has some extremely relaxing effects, and sometimes, in cryo-revival patients, it can trigger memory cascades."

"Ah!"

"However, it can also be embarrassing. Under its influence people will happily talk about whatever crosses their minds, even their most intimate and private thoughts. Good medical ethics requires me to warn you about that. Also, some people are allergic to the drug."

"Where'd . . . you learn . . . goo' med'cal ethics?" he asked curiously.

Strangely, she flinched. "Escobar," she said, and eyed him.

"Where we *now*?"

"I'd rather not say, just yet."

"How could that contam'nate m' mem'ry?" he demanded indignantly.

"I can tell you soon, I think," she soothed. "Soon."

"Mm," he growled.

She pulled a little white packet from her coat pocket, opened it, and peeled off a plastic-backed dot. "Hold out your arm." He obeyed, and she pressed the dot against the underside of his forearm. "Patch test," she explained. "Because of what I theorize about your line of work, I think you have a higher than normal chance of allergy. Artificially-induced allergy."

She peeled the dot away again—it prickled—and gazed closely at his arm. A pink spot appeared. She frowned at it. "Does that itch?" she asked suspiciously.

"No," he lied, and clenched his right hand to keep from scratching at the spot. A drug to give him his mind back—he had to have it. *Turn white again, blast you*, he thought to the pink splotch.

"You seem to be a little sensitive," she mused. "Marginally."

"*Pleassse . . .*"

Her lips twisted in doubt. "Well . . . what do we have to lose? I'll be right back."

She exited, returning shortly with two hyposprays, which she laid on the tray table. "This is the fast-penta," she pointed, "and this is the fast-penta antagonist. You let me know right away if you start to feel strange, itch, tingle, have trouble breathing or swallowing, or if your tongue starts to feel thick."

"Feels th'ck now," he objected, as she pushed up both his sleeves on his thin white arms and pressed the first spray to the inside of his elbow. "How d'I tell?"

"You'll be able to tell. Now just lie back and relax. You should start to feel dreamy, like you're floating, by the time you count backward from ten. Try it."

"Te'. Nan. Ei'. Seben. Si', fav, fo', tree-two-wun." He did not feel dreamy. He felt tense and nervous and miserable. "You sure yo' go' rat one?" His fingers began to drum on the tray table. The sound was unnaturally loud in his ears. Objects in the room were taking on hard, bright outlines with colored fringes. Rowan's face seemed suddenly drained of personality, an ivory mask.

The mask loomed threateningly toward him. "What's your name?" it hissed.

"I . . . I . . . yiyi . . ." His mouth clogged with stutters. He was the invisible eye, nameless. . . .

"Strange," the mask murmured. "Your blood pressure should be going down, not up."

Abruptly, he remembered what was so important about fast-penta. "Fas'pent'—maksmeyper." She shook her head in non-comprehension. "*Yiper*," he reiterated, out of a mouth that seemed to be seizing up in spasms. He wanted to talk. A thousand words rushed to his tongue, a chain-collision along his nerves. "Ya. Ya. Ya."

"This isn't usual." She frowned at the hypospray, still in her hand.

"No sh't." His arms and legs drew up like coiled springs. Rowan's face grew charming, like a doll's. His heart raced. The room wavered, as if he were swimming underwater. With an effort, he uncoiled. He had to relax. He had to relax *right now*.

"Do you remember anything?" she asked. Her dark eyes were

like pools, liquid and beautiful. He wanted to swim in those eyes, to shine in them. He wanted to please her. He wanted to coax her out of that green cloth armor, to dance naked with him in the starlight, to . . . His mumbles to this effect suddenly found voice in poetry, of a sort. Actually, it was a very dirty limerick playing on some obvious symbolism involving wormholes and jumpships. Fortunately, it came out rather garbled.

To his relief, she smiled. But there was some un-funny association. . . . "Las' time I recited that, som'bod' beat shit outta me. Wuz on fas'pent' then, too."

Alertness coursed through her lovely long body. "You've been given fast-penta before? What else do you remember about it?"

"'Is name wuz Galen. Angry wi' me. Doan' know why." He remembered a reddening face wavering over him, radiating an implacable, murderous hatred. Blows raining on him. He searched himself for remembered fear, and found it oddly mixed with pity. "I doan' unnerstan'."

"What else did he ask you about?"

"Doan' know. Told 'im 'nother poem."

"You recited poetry at him, under fast-penta interrogation?"

"Fer *hours*. Made 'im mad as hell."

Her brows rose; one finger touched her soft lips, which parted in delight. "You *beat* a fast-penta interrogation? Remarkable! Let's not talk about poetry, then. But you remember Ser Galen. Huh!"

"Galen fit?" He cocked his head anxiously. *Ser* Galen, yes! The name was important; she recognized it. "*Tell me.*"

"I'm . . . not sure. Every time I think I'm taking a step forward with you, we seem to go two sideways and one back."

"Lak to step out wi' *you*," he confided, and listened to himself in horror as he went on to describe, briefly and crudely, what else he would like to do with her. "Ah. Ah. Sorry, m'lady." He stuffed his fingers into his mouth, and bit them.

"It's all right," she soothed. "It's the fast-penta."

"No—izza *testost'rone*."

She laughed outright. It was most encouraging, but his momentary elation was drowned again in a new wash of tension. His hands plucked and twisted at his clothing, and his feet twitched.

She frowned at a medical monitor on the wall. "Your blood pressure is still going up. Charming as you are under fast-penta, this is not a normal reaction." She picked up the second hypospray. "I think we'd better stop now."

"M' not a normal man," he said sadly. "Mutant." A wave of

anxiety rushed over him. "You gonna tak' my brain out?" he asked in sudden suspicion, eyeing the hypospray. And then, in a mind-blinding blast of realization, "*Hey!* I know where I am! I'm on *Jackson's Whole!*" He stared at her in terror, jumped to his feet, and bolted for the door, dodging her lunge.

"No, wait, wait!" she called, running after him with the glittering hypospray still in her hand. "You're having a drug reaction, stop! Let me get rid of it! Poppy, grab him!"

He dodged the horse-tail-haired Dr. Durona in the lab corridor, and flung himself into the lift tube, boosting himself up with yanks on the safety ladder that sent bolts of searing pain through his half-healed chest muscles. A whirling chaos of corridors and floors, shouts and running footsteps, resolved at last into the lobby he had found before.

He shot past some workmen maneuvering a float-pallet stacked with cases through the transparent doors. No force screen shocked him backward this time. A green-parka'd guard turned in slow motion, drawing a stunner, mouth open on a shout that emerged as thickly as cold oil.

He blinked in blinding gray daylight at a ramp, a paved lot for vehicles, and dirty snow. Ice and gravel bit his bare feet as he ran, gasping, across the lot. A wall enclosed the compound. There was a gate in the wall, open, and more guards in green parkas. "Don't stun him!" a woman yelled from behind him.

He ran into a grimy street, and barely dodged a groundcar. The piercing gray-whiteness alternated with bursts of color in his eyes. A broad open space across the street was dotted with bare black trees with branches like clutching claws, straining at the sky. He glimpsed other buildings, behind walls, farther down the street, looming and strange. Nothing was familiar in this landscape. He made for the open space and the trees. Black and magenta dizziness clouded his eyes. The cold air seared his lungs. He staggered and fell, rolling onto his back, unable to breathe.

Half a dozen Dr. Duronas pounced on him like wolves upon their kill. They took his arms and legs, and pulled him up off the snow. Rowan dashed up, her face strained. A hypospray hissed. They hustled him back across the roadway like a trussed sheep, and hurried him inside the big white building. His head began to clear, but his chest was racked with pain, as if it were clamped in a squeezing vise. By the time they put him back in his bed in the underground clinic, the drug-induced false paranoia had washed out of his system. To be replaced by real paranoia. . . .

"Do you think anyone saw him?" an alto voice asked anxiously.

"Gate guards," another voice bit out. "Delivery crew."

"Anybody else?"

"I don't know," Rowan panted, her hair escaping in snow-dampened wisps. "Half a dozen groundcars went by while we were chasing him. I didn't see anyone in the park."

"I saw a couple of people walking," volunteered another Dr. Durona. "At a distance, across the pond. They were looking at us, but I doubt they could see much."

"We were a hell of a show, for a few minutes."

"What happened this time, Rowan?" the white-haired alto Dr. Durona demanded wearily. She shuffled closer and stared at him, leaning on a carved walking stick. She did not seem to carry it as an affectation, but as a real prop. All deferred to her. Was this the mysterious Lilly?

"I gave him a dose of fast-penta," Rowan reported stiffly, "to try and jog his memory. It works sometimes, for cryo-revivals. But he had a reaction. His blood pressure shot up, he went paranoid, and he took off like a whippet. We didn't run him down till he collapsed in the park." She was still catching her own breath, he saw as his agony started to recede.

The old Dr. Durona sniffed. "Did it work?"

Rowan hesitated. "Some odd things came up. I need to talk with Lilly."

"Immediately," said the old Dr. Durona—not-Lilly, apparently. "I—" but she was cut off when his shivering, stuttering attempt to talk blended into a convulsion.

The world turned to confetti for a moment. He came back to focus with two of the women holding him down, Rowan hovering over him snapping orders, and the rest of the Duronas scattering. "I'll come up as soon as I can," said Rowan desperately over her shoulder. "I can't leave him now."

The old Dr. Durona nodded understanding, and withdrew. Rowan waved away a proffered hypospray of some anti-convulsant. "I'm writing a standing order. This man gets nothing without a sensitivity scan first." She ran off most of her helpers, and made the room dim and quiet and warm again. Slowly, he recovered the rhythm of his breath, though he was still very sick to his stomach.

"I'm sorry," she told him. "I didn't realize fast-penta could do that to you."

He tried to say, *It's not your fault,* but his powers of speech seemed to have relapsed. "D-d-d-i, diddi, do. Bad. Thing?"

She took far too long to reply. "Maybe it will be all right."

Two hours later, they came with a float-pallet and moved him.

"We're getting some other patients," Dr. Chrys of the wing-hair told him blandly. "We need your room." Lies? Half-truths?

Where they moved him to puzzled him most of all. He had visions of a locked cell, but instead they took him upstairs via a freight lift tube and deposited him on a camp-bed set up in Rowan's personal suite. It was one of a row of similar chambers, presumably the Duronas' residence-floor. Her suite consisted of a sitting room/study and a bedroom, plus a private bath. It was reasonably spacious, though cluttered. He felt less like a prisoner than like a pet, being smuggled against the rules into some women's dormitory. Though he had seen another male-morph Dr. Durona besides Raven, a man of about thirty Dr. Chrys had addressed as "Hawk." Birds and flowers, they were all birds and flowers in this concrete cage.

Later still, a young Durona brought dinner on a tray, and he ate together with Rowan at a little table in her sitting room as the gray day outside faded to dusk. He supposed there was no real change in his prisoner/patient status, but it felt good to be out of the hospital-style room, free of the monitors and sinister medical equipment. To be doing something so prosaic as having dinner with a friend.

He walked around the sitting room, after they ate. "Mind 'f I look at your things?"

"Go ahead. Let me know if anything comes up for you."

She still would not tell him anything directly about himself, but she now seemed willing at least to talk about herself. His internal picture of the world *shifted* as they spoke. *Why do I have wormhole maps in my head?* Maybe he was going to have to recover himself the hard way. Learn everything that existed in the universe, and whatever was left, that dwarfish-man-shaped hole in the center, would be him by process of elimination. A daunting task.

He stared out the polarized window at the faint glitter hanging in the air, as if fairy dust were falling all around. He recognized the force screen for what it was, now, an improvement in cognition over his initial head-first encounter with it. The shield was military-grade, he realized, impermeable down to viruses and gas molecules, and up to . . . what? Projectiles and plasma, certainly. Must be a powerful generator around here somewhere. The protection was a late add-on to the building's architecture, not incorporated into its design. Some history inherent there. . . . "We *are* on Jackson's Whole, aren' we?" he asked.

"Yes. What does that mean to you?"

"Danger. Bad things happenin'. What *is* this pla'?" He waved around.

"The Durona Clinic."

"Ya, so? What you do? Why'm I here?"

"We are the personal clinic of House Fell. We do all sorts of medical tasks for them, as needed."

"House Fell. Weapons." The associations fell into place quite automatically. "Biological weapons." He eyed her accusingly.

"Sometimes," she admitted. "And biological defenses, too."

Was he a House Fell trooper? A captured enemy trooper? Hell, what army would employ a half-crippled dwarf as any kind of trooper? "House Fell give me to you to do?"

"No."

"No? S—why'm I here?"

"That's been a great puzzle for us, too. You arrived frozen in a cryo-chamber, with every sign of having been prepped in great haste. In a crate addressed to me, via common carrier, with no return address. We hoped if we revived you, you could tell us."

" 'S more goin' on than that."

"Yes," she said frankly.

"Bu' you won' tell me."

"Not yet."

"Wha' happens if I walk outta here?"

She looked alarmed. "Please don't. That could get you killed."

"Again."

"Again." She nodded.

"By who?"

"That . . . depends on who you are."

He veered off the subject, then ran the conversation around to it three more times, but could not lull or trick her into telling him any more about himself. Exhausted, he gave up for the night, only to lie awake on his cot worrying the problem as a predator might worry a carcass. But all his bone-tossing did no good but to freeze his mind with frustration. *Sleep on it,* he told himself. Tomorrow must bring him something new. Whatever else this situation was, it wasn't stable. He felt that, felt balanced as though on a knife-edge; below him lay darkness, concealing feathers or sharpened stakes or maybe nothing at all, an endless fall.

He wasn't quite sure of the rationale behind the hot bath and the therapeutic massage. Exercise, now, he could see that; Dr. Chrys had lugged in an exercise bicycle to Rowan's study, and let him sweat himself near to passing out. Anything that painful must be good for him. No push-ups yet, though. He'd tried one, and collapsed with a wide-eyed, muffled squeak of agony, and been yelled at quite firmly by an irate Dr. Chrys for attempting unauthorized bodily motions.

Dr. Chrys had made notes and gone off again, leaving him to Rowan's tenderer mercies. He lay now steaming gently in Rowan's bed, dressed in a towel, while she reviewed skeleto-muscular structure all up and down his back. Dr. Chrys's fingers, doing massage, had been like probes. Rowan's hands caressed. Not anatomically equipped to purr, he did manage a small, encouraging moan of appreciation now and then. She worked down to his feet and toes, and started back up.

Face down, mashed comfortably into her pillows, he became gradually aware that a very important bodily system was reporting for duty, for the first time since his revival. Res-erection indeed. His face flushed in a mixture of embarrassment and delight, and he flung an arm up as-if-casually to conceal his expression. *She's your doctor. She'll want to know.* It wasn't as if she weren't intimately familiar with every part of his body, inside and out, already. She'd been up to her bloody elbows in him, literally. He stayed hidden in his arm-cave anyway.

"Roll over," Rowan said, "and I'll do your other side."

"Er . . . d'rather not," he mumbled into the pillow.

"Why not?"

"Um . . . 'member how you keep askin' if somethin' has come up for me?"

"Yes . . ."

"Well . . . somethin' has."

There was a brief silence, then, "Oh! In that case, definitely roll over. I need to examine you."

He took a breath. "Things we do fer science."

He rolled over, and she took away his towel. "Has this happened before?" she inquired.

"No. Firs' time in my life. This life."

Her long cool fingers probed quickly, medically. "That looks good," she said with enthusiasm.

"*Thank* you," he caroled cheerfully.

She laughed. He didn't need a memory to tell him it was a very good sign when a woman laughed at his jokes at this point. Experimentally, gently, he pulled her down to face him. *Hooray for science. Let's see what happens.* He kissed her. She kissed him back. He melted.

Speech and science were both put aside for a time, after that. Not to mention the green coat and all the layers underneath. Her body was as lovely as he'd imagined, a pure aesthetic of line and curve, softness and floral, hidden places. His own body contrasted vividly, a little rack of bones scored with shocking red scars.

An intense consciousness of his recent death welled up in him, and he found himself kissing her frantically, passionately, as if she were life itself and he could so consume and possess her. He didn't know if she was enemy or friend, if this was a right or wrong thing. But it was warm and liquid and moving, not icy and still, surely the most opposite thing imaginable to cryo-stasis. *Seize the day.* Because the night waited, coldly implacable. This lesson burned from his center outward, like radiation. Her eyes widened. Only his shortness of breath forced him to slow down to a more decorous, reasonable pace.

His ugliness ought to have bothered him, but it didn't, and he wondered why. *We make love with our eyes closed.* Who had told him that? The same woman who'd told him, *It's not the meat, it's the motion?* Opening Rowan's body was like facing that pile of field-stripped weaponry. He knew what to do, what parts counted and which were camouflage, but could not remember how he'd learned it all. The training was there, yet the trainer was erased. It was a more deeply disturbing coupling of the familiar with the strange than any he'd yet experienced here.

She shivered, sighed, and relaxed, and he kissed his way back up her body to murmur in her ear, "Um . . . doan' think I can do push-ups, jus' yet."

"Oh." Her glazed eyes opened, and focused. "My. Yes." A few moments of experiment found a medically-approved position, flat on his back in great comfort with no pressure or strain on his chest, arms, or abdomen, and then it was his turn. That felt right, ladies first and then he wouldn't have pillows thrown at him for falling asleep immediately afterwards. A terribly familiar pattern, with all the details wrong. Rowan had done this before too, he judged, though perhaps not often. But great expertise on her part was scarcely required. His body worked just fine. . . .

"Dr. D," he sighed up at her, "yr a gen'ius. Aes . . . Asku . . . Aesch . . . that Greek guy coul' tak' lessons in resurr'ction from you."

She laughed, and oozed down beside him, body to body. *My height doesn't matter when we're lying down.* He'd known that, too. They exchanged less-hurried, exploratory kisses, savored slowly like after-dinner mints.

"You're *very* good at that," she murmured wheezily, nibbling on his ear.

"Yea . . ." His grin faded, and he stared at the ceiling, brows drawing down in a combination of gentle, post-coital melancholy, and renewed, if purely mental, frustration. " . . . wonder if I was married?" Her head drew back, and he could have bitten his tongue at her stricken look. "Doan' think so," he added quickly.

"No . . . no." She settled back again. "You're not married."

"Which ever one I am?"

"That's right."

"Huh." He hesitated, winding her long hair in his fingers, spreading it idly out in a fan across the burst of red lines on his torso. "So who d'you think you were makin' love to, jus' now?"

She touched a long index finger gently to his forehead. "You. Just you."

This was most pleasing, but . . . "Wuzzat love, or therapy?"

She smiled quizzically, tracing his face. "A little of both, I think. And curiosity. And opportunity. I've been pretty immersed in you, for the past three months."

It felt like an honest answer. "Seems t'me you made t' opportunity."

A small smirk escaped her lips. "Well . . . maybe."

Three months. Interesting. So he'd been dead a bit over two months. He must have absorbed a lot of the Durona Group's resources, in that time. To begin with, three months of this woman's labor were not cheap.

"Why you doin' this?" he asked, frowning at the ceiling as she snuggled carefully around his shoulder. "I mean t'whole thing. What d'you expect me to do for you?" Half-crippled, tongue-tied, blank and stupid, not a dollar to his non-existent name. "You're all hangin' on m'recovery like I'm your hope 'f heaven." Even the brutally efficient physical therapist Chrys he'd come to see as pushing him for his good. He almost liked her best, for her merciless drive. He resonated to it. "Who else wants me, tha' you should hide me? Enemies?" *Or friends?*

"Enemies for certain," Rowan sighed.

"Mm." He lay back in lassitude; she dozed, he didn't. He touched her net of hair and wondered. What did she see in him? *I thought of it as the enchanted knight's crystal coffin . . . I picked out enough grenade fragments to be certain you weren't a bystander. . . .*

So, there was work to be done. Nor did the Durona Group want an ordinary mercenary. If this was Jackson's Whole, they could hire ordinary thugs by the boatload.

But then, he'd never thought he was an ordinary man. Not even for a minute.

Oh, milady. Who do you need me to be?

CHAPTER TWENTY-THREE

The re-discovery of sex fairly immobilized him for the next three days, but his instinct for escape surfaced one afternoon when Rowan left him sleeping, but he wasn't. He unlidded his eyes, and traced the pattern of scars on his chest, and thought it over. *Out* was clearly a wrong direction. *In* was one he hadn't tried yet. Everybody here seemed to go to Lilly with their problems. Very well. He would go to Lilly too.

Up, or down? As a Jacksonian leader, she ought traditionally to lodge in either a penthouse or a bunker. Baron Ryoval lived in a bunker, or at least there was a dim image in his head associated with that name, involving shadowy sub-basements. Baron Fell took the penthouse at apogee, looking down on it all from his orbital station. He seemed to have a lot of pictures in his head of Jackson's Whole. Was it his home? The thought confused him. Up. Up and in.

He dressed in his gray knits, borrowed some of Rowan's socks, and slipped into the corridor. He found a lift tube and took it to the top floor, just one above Rowan's. It was another floor of residence suites. At its center he found another lift tube, palm-locked. Any Durona could use it. A spiral staircase wound around it. He climbed the stairs very slowly, and waited, near the top, till he had all his breath back. He knocked on the door.

It slid aside, and a slim Eurasian boy of about ten regarded him gravely. "What do you want?" The boy frowned.

"I want to see your . . . grandmother."

"Bring him in, Robin," a soft voice called.

The boy ducked his head and motioned him inside. His sock feet trod noiselessly across a deep carpet. The windows were polarized against the dark gray afternoon, and pools of warmer, yellower lamplight fought the gloom. Beyond the window, the force field revealed itself with tiny scintillations, as water droplets or particulate matter were detected and repelled or annihilated.

A shrunken woman sat in a wide chair, and watched him approach her through dark eyes set in a face of old ivory. She wore a high-necked black silk tunic and loose trousers. Her hair was pure white, and very long; a slim girl, most literally twin to the boy, was brushing it over the back of the chair, in long, long strokes. The room was very warm. Regarding her regarding him, he wondered how he could ever have thought that worried old woman with the cane might be Lilly. Hundred-year-old eyes looked at you differently.

"Ma'am," he said. His mouth felt suddenly dry.

"Sit down." She nodded to a short sofa set around the corner of the low table in front of her. "Violet, dear," a thin hand, all white wrinkles and blue ropy veins, touched the girl's hand which had paused protectively on her black silk shoulder. "Bring tea now. Three cups. Robin, please go downstairs and get Rowan."

The girl arranged the hair in a falling fan around the woman's upright torso, and the two children vanished in un-childlike silence. Clearly, the Durona Group did not employ outsiders. No chance of a mole ever penetrating their organization. With equal obedience, he sank into the seat she'd indicated.

Her vowels had a vibrato of age, but her diction, containing them, was perfect. "Have you come to yourself, sir?" she inquired.

"No, ma'am," he said sadly. "Only to you." He thought carefully about how to phrase his question. Lilly would not be any less medically careful than Rowan about yielding him clues. "Why can't you identify me?"

Her white brows rose. "Well-put. You are ready for an answer, I think. Ah."

The lift tube hummed, and Rowan's alarmed face appeared. She hurried out. "Lilly, I'm sorry. I thought he was asleep—"

"It's all right, child. Sit down. Pour the tea," for Violet reappeared around the corner bearing a large tray. Lilly whispered to the girl behind a faintly trembling hand, and she nodded and scampered off. Rowan knelt in what appeared to be a precise old

ritual—had she once held Violet's place? he rather thought so—
and poured green tea into thin white cups, and handed it round.
She sat at Lilly's knees, stealing a brief, reassuring touch of the
white hair coiled there.

The tea was very hot. Since he'd lately taken a deep dislike to
cold, this pleased him, and he sipped carefully. "Answers, ma'am?"
he reminded her cautiously.

Rowan's lips parted in a negative, alarmed breath; Lilly crooked
up one finger, and quelled her.

"Background," said the old woman. "I believe the time has come
to tell you a story."

He nodded, and settled back with his tea.

"Once upon a time," she smiled briefly, "there were three brothers. A proper fairy tale, ai? The eldest and original, and two young
clones. The eldest—as happens in these tales—was born to a
magnificent patrimony. Title—wealth—comfort—his father, if not
exactly a king, commanded more power than any king in pre-
jump history. And thus he became the target of many enemies.
Since he was known to dote upon his son, it occurred to more
than one of his enemies to try and strike at him through his
only child. Hence this peculiar multiplication." She nodded at
him. It made his belly shiver. He sipped more tea, to cover his
confusion.

She paused. "Can you name any names yet?"

"No, ma'am."

"Mm." She abandoned the fairy tale; her voice grew more
clipped. "Lord Miles Vorkosigan of Barrayar was the original. He
is now about twenty-eight standard years old. His first clone was
made right here on Jackson's Whole, twenty-two years ago, a
purchase by a Komarran resistance group from House Bharaputra.
We do not know what this clone names himself, but the Komarrans'
elaborate substitution plot failed about two years ago, and the clone
escaped."

"Galen," he whispered.

She glanced sharply at him. "He was the chief of those
Komarrans, yes. The second clone . . . is a puzzle. The best guess
is that he was manufactured by the Cetagandans, but no one
knows. He first appeared about ten years ago as a full-blown and
exceptionally brilliant mercenary commander, claiming the quite
legal Betan name of Miles Naismith, in his maternal line. He has
shown himself no friend to the Cetagandans, so the theory that
he is a Cetagandan renegade has a certain compelling logic. No

one knows his age, though obviously he can be no more than twenty-eight." She took a sip of her tea. "It is our belief that you are one of those two clones."

"Shipped to you like a crate of frozen meat? With my chest blown out?"

"Yes."

"So what? Clones—even frozen ones—can't be a novelty here." He glanced at Rowan.

"Let me go on. About three months ago, Bharaputra's manu-factured clone returned home—with a crew of mercenary soldiers at his back that he had apparently stolen from the Dendarii Fleet by the simple expedient of pretending to be his clone-twin, Admiral Naismith. He attacked Bharaputra's clone-crèche in an attempt to either steal, or possibly free, a group of clones slated to be the bodies for brain transplants, a business which I personally loathe."

He touched his chest. "He . . . failed?"

"No. But Admiral Naismith followed in hot pursuit of his stolen ship and troops. In the mêlée that ensued downside at Bharaputra's main surgical facilities, one of the two was killed. The other escaped, along with the mercenaries and most of Bharaputra's very valuable clone-cattle. They made a fool of Vasa Luigi—I laughed myself sick when I first heard about it." She sipped tea demurely.

He could actually almost picture her doing so, though it made his eyes cross slightly.

"Before they jumped, the Dendarii Mercenaries posted a reward for the return of a cryo-chamber containing the remains of a man they claim to have been the Bharaputran-made clone."

His eyes widened. "Me?"

She held up a hand. "Vasa Luigi, Baron Bharaputra, is absolutely convinced that they were lying, and that the man in the box was really their Admiral Naismith."

"Me?" he said less certainly.

"Georish Stauber, Baron Fell, refuses to even guess. And Baron Ryoval would tear a town apart for even a fifty percent chance of laying hands on Admiral Naismith, who injured him four years ago as no one has in a century." Her lips curved in a scalpel-smile.

It all made sense, which made no sense at all. It was like a story heard long ago, in childhood, and re-encountered. *In another life-time.* Familiarity under glass. He touched his head, which ached. Rowan watched the gesture with concern.

"Don't you have medical records? Something?"

"At some risk, we obtained the developmental records of Bharaputra's clone. Unfortunately, they only go up to age fourteen. We have nothing on Admiral Naismith. Alas, one cannot run a triangulation on one data point."

He turned toward Rowan. "You know me, inside and out. Can't you tell?"

"You're *strange*." Rowan shook her head. "Half your bones are plastic replacement parts, do you know? The real ones that are left show old breaks, old traumas.... I'd guess you not only older than Bharaputra's clone ought to be, I'd guess you older than the original Lord Vorkosigan, and that makes no sense. If we could just get one solid, certain clue. The memories you've reported so far are terribly ambiguous. You know weapons, as the Admiral might—but Bharaputra's clone was trained as an assassin. You remember Ser Galen, and only Bharaputra's clone should do that. I found out about those sugar trees. They're called maple trees, and they originate on Earth—where Bharaputra's clone was taken for training. And so on." She flung up her hands in frustration.

"If you're not getting the right answer," he said slowly, "maybe you're not asking the right question."

"So what is the right question?"

He shook his head, mutely. "Why . . ." His hands spread. "Why not turn my frozen body over to the Dendarii and collect the reward? Why not sell me to Baron Ryoval, if he wants me so much? Why revive me?"

"I wouldn't sell a laboratory rat to Baron Ryoval," Lilly stated flatly. She twitched a brief smile. "Old business, between us."

How old? Older than he, whoever he was.

"As for the Dendarii—we may deal with them yet. Depending on who you are."

They were approaching the heart of the matter; he could sense it. "Yes?"

"Four years ago, Admiral Naismith visited Jackson's Whole, and besides counting a most spectacular coup on Ry Ryoval, left with a certain Dr. Hugh Canaba, one of Bharaputra's top genetics people. Now, I knew Canaba. More to the point, I know what Vasa Luigi and Lotus paid to get him here, and how many House secrets he was privy to. They would never have let him go alive. Yet he's gone, and no one on Jackson's Whole has ever been able to trace him."

She leaned forward intently. "Assuming Canaba was not just

disposed of out an airlock—Admiral Naismith has shown he can get people out. In fact, it's a speciality he's famous for. *That* is our interest in him."

"You want off-planet?" He glanced around at Lilly Durona's comfortable, self-contained little empire. "Why?"

"I have a Deal with Georish Stauber—Baron Fell. It's a very old Deal, as we are very old dealers. My time is surely running out, and Georish is growing," she grimaced, "unreliable. If I die—or if he dies—or if he succeeds in having his brain transplanted to a younger body, as he has attempted at least once to arrange— our old Deal will be broken. The Durona Group might be offered less admirable deals than the one we have enjoyed so long with House Fell. It might be broken up—sold—weakened so as to invite attack from old enemies like Ry, who remembers an insult or an injury *forever*. It might be forced to work it does not choose. I've been looking for a way out for the last couple of years. Admiral Naismith knows one."

She wanted him to be Admiral Naismith, obviously the most valuable of the two clones. "What if I'm the other one?" He stared at his hands. They were just his hands. No hints there.

"You might be ransomed."

By whom? Was he savior, or commodity? What a choice. Rowan looked uneasy.

"What am I to you if I can't remember who I am?"

"No one at all, little man." Her dark eyes glinted, momentarily, like obsidian chips.

This woman had survived nearly a century on Jackson's Whole. It would not do to underestimate her ruthlessness on the basis of one quirky prejudice about clone-brain transplants.

They finished their tea, and retreated to Rowan's room.

"What in all that seemed familiar to you?" Rowan asked him anxiously when they were alone on her little sofa.

"All of it," he said, in deep perplexity. "And yet—Lilly seems to think I can spirit you all away like some kind of magician. But even if I am Admiral Naismith, I can't remember how I did it!"

"Sh," she tried to calm him. "You're ripe for memory-cascade, I swear. I can almost see it starting. Your speech has improved vastly in just the last few days."

"All that therapuetic kissing." He smiled, a suggestive compli- ment that won him, as he'd hoped, some more therapy. But when he came up for air he said, "It won't come back to me if I'm the other one. I remember Galen. Earth. A house in London . . . what's the clone's name?"

"We don't know," she said, and at his exasperated grasp of her hands added, "No, we *really* don't."

"Admiral Naismith . . . shouldn't be Miles Naismith. He should be Mark Pierre Vorkosigan." How the hell did he know that? Mark Pierre. *Piotr Pierre. Peter, Peter, pumpkin eater, had a wife and couldn't keep her,* a taunt from out of a crowd that had put an old man into a terrifying murderous rage, he'd had to be restrained by—the image escaped him. *Gran'da?* "If the Bharaputra-made clone is the third son, he could be named anything." Something wasn't right.

He tried to imagine Admiral Naismith's childhood as a Cetagandan secret covert ops project. His childhood? It must have been extraordinary, if he'd not only escaped at the age of eighteen or less, but evaded Cetagandan Intelligence and established his fortune within a year. But he could think of nothing from such a youth. A complete blank.

"What are you going to do with me if I'm not Naismith? Keep me as a pet? For how long?"

Rowan pursed her lips in worry. "If you are the Bharaputran-made clone—you're going to need to get off Jackson's Whole yourself. The Dendarii raid made an awful mess out of Vasa Luigi's headquarters. He has blood to avenge, as well as property. And pride. If it's the case—I'll try to get you out."

"You? Or you all?"

"I've never gone against the group." She rose and paced across her sitting room. "Yet I lived a year, on Escobar, alone, when I was taking my cryo-revival training. I've often wondered . . . what it would be like to be half of a couple. Instead of one-fortieth of a group. Would I feel bigger?"

"Were you bigger when you were all of one, on Escobar?"

"I don't know. It's a silly conceit. Still—one can't help thinking of Lotus."

"Lotus. Baronne Bharaputra? The one who left your group?"

"Yes. Lilly's oldest daughter after Rose. Lilly says . . . if we don't hang together, we'll all hang separately. It's a reference to an ancient method of execution that—"

"I know what hanging is," he said hastily, before she could go into the medical details.

Rowan stared out her window. "Jackson's Whole is no place to be alone. You can't trust anybody."

"An interesting paradox. Makes for quite a dilemma."

She searched his face for irony, found it, and frowned. "It's no joke."

Indeed. Even Lilly Durona's self-referential maternal strategy hadn't quite solved the problem, as Lotus had proved.

He eyed her. "Were you ordered to sleep with me?" he asked suddenly.

She flinched. "No." She paced again. "But I did ask permission. Lilly said to go ahead, it might help attach you to our interests." She paused. "Does that seem terribly cold, to you?"

"On Jackson's Whole—merely prudent." And attachments surely ran two ways. Jackson's Whole was no place to be alone. *But you can't trust anyone.*

If anyone was sane here, he swore it was by accident.

Reading, an exercise that had at first given him a stabbing sensation in the eyes and instant excruciating headaches, was getting easier. He could go for up to ten minutes at a time now before it became too blinding to bear. Holed up in Rowan's study, he pushed himself to the limits of pain, an information-bite, a few minutes' rest, and try again. Beginning at the center outward, he read up first on Jackson's Whole, its unique history, non-governmental structure, and the one hundred and sixteen Great Houses and countless Houses Minor, with their interlocking alliances and vendettas, roiling deals and betrayals. The Durona Group was well on its way to growing into a House Minor in its own right, he judged, budding from House Fell like a hydra, also like a hydra reproducing asexually. Mentions of Houses Bharaputra, Hargraves, Dyne, Ryoval and Fell triggered images in his head that did not come from the vid display. A few of them were even starting to cross-connect. Too few. He wondered if it was significant that the Houses that seemed most familiar were also the ones most famous for dealing in off-planet illegalities.

Whoever I am, I know this place. And yet . . . his visions tasted small in scope, too shallow to represent a formative lifetime. Maybe he'd been a small person. Still, it was more than he could dredge up from his subconscious regarding the youth of the putative Admiral Naismith, the Cetagandan-produced clone.

Gran'da. Those had been memories with mass, an almost stunning sensory weight. Who was Gran'da? Jacksonian fosterer? Komarran mentor? Cetagandan trainer? Someone huge and fascinating, mysterious and old and dangerous. Gran'da had no source. He seemed to come with the universe.

Sources. Perhaps a study of his progenitor, the crippled Barrayaran lordling Vorkosigan, might yield up something. He'd been made in Vorkosigan's image, after all, which was a hell of a thing to do to any poor sod. He pulled up a listing of references to Barrayar from Rowan's comconsole library. There were some hundreds of non-fiction books, vids, documents and documentaries. For the sake of a frame, he began with a general history, scanning rapidly. The Fifty-thousand Firsters. Wormhole collapse. The Time of Isolation, the Bloody Centuries . . . the Rediscovery . . . the words blurred. His head felt full to bursting. Familiar, so achingly familiar . . . he had to stop.

Panting, he darkened the room and lay down on the little sofa till his eyes stopped throbbing. But then, if he'd ever been trained to replace Vorkosigan, it all ought to be very familiar indeed. He'd have had to study Barrayar forward and backward. *I have.* He wanted to beg Rowan to shackle him to a wall and give him another dose of fast-penta, regardless of what it did to his blood pressure. The stuff had almost worked. Maybe another try . . .

The door hissed. "Hello?" The lights came up. Rowan stood in the doorway. "Are you all right?"

"Headache. Reading."

"You shouldn't try to . . ."

Take it so fast, he supplied silently, Rowan's constant refrain of the last few days, since his interview with Lilly. But this time, she cut herself off. He pushed up; she came and sat by him. "Lilly wants me to bring you upstairs."

"All right—" He made to rise, but she stopped him.

She kissed him. It was a long, long kiss, which at first delighted and then worried him. He broke away to ask, "Rowan, what's the matter?"

" . . . I think I love you."

"This is a problem?"

"Only my problem." She managed a brief, unhappy smile. "I'll handle it."

He captured her hands, traced tendon and vein. She had brilliant hands. He did not know what to say.

She drew him to his feet. "Come on." They held hands all the way to the entrance to the penthouse lift-tube. When she disengaged to press the palm lock, she did not take his hand again. They rose together, and exited around the chromium railing into Lilly's living room.

Lilly sat upright and formal in her wide padded chair, her white hair braided today in a single thick rope that wound down over her shoulder to her lap. She was attended by Hawk, who stood silently behind her and to her right. *Not an attendant. A guard.* Three strangers dressed in gray quasi-military uniforms with white trim were ranged around her, two women seated and a man standing. One of the women had dark curls, and brown eyes that turned on him with a gaze that scorched him. The other, older woman had short light-brown hair barely touched with gray. But it was the man who riveted him.

My God. It's the other me.

Or . . . not-me. They stood eye to eye. This one was painfully neat, boots clean, uniform pressed and formal, his mere appearance a salute to Lilly. Insignia glinted on his collar. *Admiral . . . Naismith? Naismith* was the name stitched over the left breast of his officer's pocketed undress jacket. A sharp intake of breath, an electric snap of the gray eyes, and a half-suppressed smile made the short man's face wonderfully alive. But if he was a bony shadow of himself, this one was him doubled. Stocky, squared-off, muscular and intense, heavy-jowled and with a notable gut. He *looked* like a senior officer, body-mass balanced over stout legs spread in an aggressive parade rest like an overweight bulldog. So this was Naismith, the famous rescuer so desired by Lilly. He could believe it.

His utter fascination with his clone-twin was penetrated by a growing, dreadful realization. *I'm the wrong one.* Lilly had just spent a fortune reviving the wrong clone. How angry was she going to be? For a Jacksonian leader, such a vast mistake must feel like counting coup on *yourself.* Indeed, Lilly's face was set and stern, as she glanced toward Rowan.

"It's him, all right," breathed the woman with the burning eyes. Her hands were clenched in tight fists, in her lap.

"Do I . . . know you, ma'am?" he said politely, carefully. Her torch-like heat perturbed him. Half-consciously, he moved closer to Rowan.

Her expression was like marble. Only a slight widening of her eyes, like a woman drilled neatly through the solar plexus by a laser beam, revealed a depth of . . . what feeling? Love, hate? Tension . . . His headache worsened.

"As you see," said Lilly. "Alive and well. Let us return to the discussion of the price." The round table was littered with cups and crumbs—how long had this conference been going on?

"Whatever you want," said Admiral Naismith, breathing heavily. "We pay and go."

"Any price within reason." The brown-haired older woman gave her commander an oddly quelling look. "We came for a man, not an animated body. A botched revival suggests a discount for damaged goods, to my mind." That voice, that ironic alto voice . . . *I know you.*

"His revival is not botched," said Rowan sharply. "If there was a problem, it was in the prep—"

The hot woman jerked, and frowned fiercely.

"—but in fact, he's making a good recovery. Measurable progress every day. It's just too soon. You're pushing too hard." A glance at Lilly? "The stress and pressure slow down the very results they seek to hurry. He pushes *himself* too hard, he winds himself in knots so bad—"

Lilly held up a placating hand. "So speaks my cryo-revival specialist," she said to the Admiral. "Your clone-brother is in a recovering state, and may be expected to improve. If that is in fact what you desire."

Rowan bit her lip. The hot woman chewed on her fingertip.

"Now we come to what *I* desire," Lilly continued. "And, you may be pleased to learn, it isn't money. Let us discuss a little recent history. Recent in my view, that is."

Admiral Naismith glanced out the big square windows, framing another dark Jacksonian winter afternoon, with low scudding clouds starting to spit snow. The force screen sparkled, silently eating the ice spicules. "Recent history is much on my mind, ma'am," he said to Lilly. "If you know it, you know why I don't wish to linger here. Get to your point."

Not nearly oblique enough for Jacksonian business etiquette, but Lilly nodded. "How is Dr. Canaba these days, Admiral?"

"What?"

Succinctly, for a Jacksonian, Lilly again described her interest in the fate of the absconded geneticist. "Yours is the organization that made Hugh Canaba completely disappear. Yours is the organization that lifted ten thousand Marilacan prisoners of war from under the noses of their Cetagandan captors on Dagoola Four, though I admit they have spectacularly not-disappeared. Somewhere between those two proven extremes lies the fate of my little family. You will pardon my tiny joke if I say you appear to me to be just what the doctor ordered."

Naismith's eyes widened; he rubbed his face, sucked air through his teeth, and managed a strained-looking grin. "I see. Ma'am. Well. In fact, such a project as you suggest might be quite negotiable, particularly if you think you might like to join Dr. Canaba. I'm not prepared to pull it out of my pockets this afternoon, you understand—"

Lilly nodded.

"But as soon as I make contact with my back-up, I think something might be arranged."

"Then as soon as you make contact with your back-up, return to us, Admiral, and your clone-twin will be made available to you."

"No—!" began the hot woman, half-rising; her comrade caught her arm and shook her head, and she sank back into her seat. "Right, Bel," she muttered.

"We'd hoped to take him today," said the mercenary, glancing at him. Their eyes intersected joltingly. The Admiral looked away, as if guarding himself from some too-intense stimulus.

"But as you can see, that would strip me of what seems to be my main bargaining chip," Lilly murmured. "And the usual arrangement of half in advance and half on delivery is obviously impractical. Perhaps a modest monetary retainer would reassure you."

"They seem to have taken good care of him so far," said the brown-haired officer in an uncertain voice.

"But it would also," the Admiral frowned, "give you an opportunity to auction him to other interested parties. I would caution you against starting a bidding war in this matter, ma'am. It could become the real thing."

"Your interests are protected by your uniqueness, Admiral. No one else on Jackson's Whole has what I want. You do. And, I think, vice versa. We are very well suited to deal."

For a Jacksonian, this was bending over backward to encourage. *Take it, close the deal!* he thought, then wondered why. What did these people want him for? Outside, a gust of wind whipped the snowfall to a blinding, whirling curtain. It ticked on the windows.

It ticked on the windows. . . .

Lilly was the next to be aware, her dark eyes widening. No one else had noticed yet, the cessation of that silent glitter. Her startled gaze met his, as his head turned back from his first stare outward, and her lips parted for speech.

The window burst inward.

It was a safety-glass; instead of slicing shards, they were all bombarded by a hail of hot pellets. The two mercenary women shot to their feet, Lilly cried out, and Hawk leaped in front of her, a stunner appearing in his hand. Some kind of big aircar was hovering at the window: one, two . . . three, four huge troopers leaped through. Transparent biotainer gear covered nerve-disruptor shield-suits; their faces were fully hooded and goggled. Hawk's repeated stunner fire crackled harmlessly over them.

You'd get farther if you threw the damned stunner at them! He looked around wildly for a projectile weapon, knife, chair, table-leg, anything to attack with. Over one of the mercenary women's pocket comm links a tinny voice was crying, "Quinn, this is Elena. Something just dropped the building's force screen. I'm reading energy discharges—what the hell is going on in there? You want back-up?"

"Yes!" screamed the hot woman, rolling aside from a stunner beam, which followed her, crackling, across the carpet. *Stunner-tag.* The assault was a snatch, not an assassination, then. Hawk finally recovered the wit to pick up the round table and swing with it. He hit one trooper but was stunner-dropped by another. Lilly stood utterly still, watching grimly. A gust of cold wind fluttered her silk pant legs. Nobody aimed at her.

"Which one's Naismith?" boomed an amplified voice from one of the biotainered troopers. The Dendarii must have disarmed for the parley; the brown-haired merc closed hand-to-hand on an intruder. Not an option open to him. He grabbed Rowan's hand and dodged behind a chair, trying to get a clear run toward the exit tube.

"Take 'em both," the leader shouted over the din. A trooper leaped toward the lift tube to cut them off; the rectangular facet of his stunner discharger winked in the light as he found near-point-blank aim.

"Like hell!" yelled the Admiral, cannoning into the trooper. The trooper stumbled and his aim went wild. The last thing he saw as he and Rowan dove for the lift tube was a stunner beam from the leader taking Naismith in the head. Both the other Dendarii were down.

They descended with agonizing slowness. If he and Rowan could get to the force screen generator, could they get it turned back on and trap the attackers inside? Stunner fire sizzled after them, starry bursts on the walls. They twisted in air, somehow landed on their feet, and stumbled backward into the corridor. No time to explain—he grabbed Rowan's hand and slapped it flat to the

Durona-keyed lock-pad, and hit the power-off square with his elbow. The trooper pursuing them yelped and fell three meters, not quite head-first.

He winced at the thud, and towed Rowan down the corridor. "Where are the generators?" he yelled over his shoulder at her. Other Duronas, alarmed, were appearing from all directions. A pair of green-clad Fell guards burst into the corridor's far end and pelted toward the penthouse lift-tube. But what side were they on? He pulled Rowan into the nearest open doorway.

"Lock it!" he gasped. She keyed the door shut. They were in some Durona's residence suite. A cul-de-sac made a poor bolt-hole, but help seemed to be on the way. He just wasn't sure for whom. *Something just dropped your force screen. . . .* From the inside. It could only have been dropped from the inside. He half-bent, mouth wide for air, lungs on fire, heart racing and chest aching, a dizzy darkness clouding his vision. He stumbled to the dangerous window anyway, trying to get a handle on the tactical situation. Muffled shouts and thumps penetrated from the wall by the corridor.

"How t'hell'd those bastards get your screen down?" he wheezed to Rowan, clutching the windowsill. "Didn't hear an explosion— traitor?"

"I don't know," Rowan replied anxiously. "That's outer-perimeter security. Fell's men are supposed to be in charge of it."

He stared out over the icy parking lot of the compound. A couple more green-clad men were running across it, shouting, pointing upward, taking cover behind a parked vehicle, and struggling to get a projectile weapon aimed. Another guard made urgent negative gestures at them; a miss could take out the penthouse and everyone in it. They nodded and waited.

He craned his neck, face to the glass, trying to see upward and to the left. The armored aircar loomed, still hovering at the penthouse window.

The assailants were withdrawing already. Damn! No chance with the force-screen. *I'm too slow.* The aircar rocked as the troopers hastily re-boarded. Hands flashed, and a thick little gray-clad figure was dragged across the gap, six heart-stopping flights above the concrete. A limp trooper was dragged across too. They were leaving no wounded for questioning. Rowan, teeth clenched, pulled him back. "Get out of the line of fire!"

He resisted her. "They're getting away!" he protested. "We should fight them *now*, on our own turf—"

Another aircar rose from the street, beyond the old and obsolete compound wall. A small civilian model, unarmed and unarmored, it fought for altitude. Through its canopy he could see a blurred gray-clad figure at the controls, a white flash of teeth set in a grimace. The assailants' armored car yawed away from the window. The Dendarii aircar tried to ram it, to force it down. Sparks sprayed, plastic cracked, and metal screeched, but the armored car shook it off; it pinwheeled to the pavement and landed with a terminal crunch.

"Rented, I bet," he groaned, watching. "Gonna have to pay for it. Good try, it almost worked—Rowan! Are any of those aircars down there yours?"

"You mean the group's? Yes, but—"

"Come on. We've got to get down there." But the building was crawling with security by now. They'd be nailing everyone to the wall till identified and cleared. He could scarcely leap out the window and fly down the five flights, though he longed to. Oh, for a cloak of invisibility.

Oh. Yes!

"Carry me! Can you carry me?"

"I suppose, but—"

He raced to the door, and fell backwards into her arms as it opened again.

"Why?" she asked.

"Do it, do it, do it!" he hissed through his teeth. She dragged him back out into the corridor. He studied the chaos through slitted eyes, gasping realistically. Assorted agitated Duronas milled behind a cordon of Fell security now blocking the entry to the penthouse. "Get Dr. Chrys to take my feet," he muttered out of the corner of his mouth.

Temporarily too overwhelmed to argue, Rowan cried, "Chrys, help me! We have to get him downstairs."

"Oh—" Given the impression that this was some kind of medical emergency, Dr. Chrys asked no questions. She grabbed his ankles, and within seconds they were forcing their way through the mob. Two Doctors Durona carrying a white-faced, injured-looking fellow at a run—green-clad armed men stepped hastily aside and waved them on.

As they reached the ground floor Chris tried to gallop toward the clinic area. For a moment he was yanked two ways, then he freed his feet from the astonished Dr. Chrys, and pulled away from Rowan. She gave chase, and they arrived at the outer door together.

The guards' attention was focused on the efforts of the two men with the projectile launcher; his eyes followed their aim to the shadowy form of their retreating target, being swallowed by the snowy clouds. *No, no, don't shoot . . . !* The launcher burped; the bright explosion rocked the car but did not bring it down.

"Take me to the biggest, fastest thing you can make go," he gasped to Rowan. "We can't let them get away." *We can't let Fell's men blow it up, either.* "Hurry!"

"*Why?*"

"Those goons just kidnapped my, my . . . brother," he panted. "Gotta follow. Bring 'em down if we can, follow if we can't. The Dendarii must have reinforcements of some kind, if we don't lose them. Or Fell. Lilly's his, his liegewoman, isn't she? He has to respond. Or *someone* does." He was shivering violently. "Lose 'em and we'll never get 'em back. They're figuring on it."

"What the hell would we do if we caught them?" Rowan objected. "They just tried to kidnap you, and you want to run after them? That's a job for security!"

"I am—I am . . ." *What? What am I?* His frustrated stutters segued into a confetti-scramble of perception. *No, not again—*

His vision cleared with the hiss of a hypospray, biting cold on his arm. Dr. Chrys was supporting him, and Rowan had one thumb pressed against his eyelid, holding it up while she stared into his eye, while her other hand slipped the hypospray back into her pocket. A kind of glassy bemusement descended upon him, as if he were wrapped in cellophane. "That should help," said Rowan.

"No, it doesn't," he complained, or tried to. His words came out a mumble.

They had dragged him out of the lobby, out of sight near one of the lift tubes to the underground part of the clinic. He had only lost moments to the convulsion, then. There was still a chance— he struggled in Chrys's grip, which tightened.

The snap of women's steps, not a guard's boots, rounded the corner. Lilly appeared, her face set and her nostrils flaring, flanked by Dr. Poppy.

"Rowan. Get him out of here," Lilly said, in a voice dead-level in tone despite its breathlessness. "Georish will be downside himself to investigate this one. *He* has to never have been here. Our attackers seem to have been one of Naismith's enemies. The story will be that the Dendarii came here looking for Naismith's clone, but didn't find him. Chrys, get rid of the physical evidence in Rowan's room, and hide those files. Go!"

Chrys nodded and ran. Rowan took over holding him on his feet. He had an odd tendency to slump, as if he were melting. He blinked against the drug. *No, we have to go after—*

Lilly tossed Rowan a credit chit, and Dr. Poppy handed her a couple of coats and a medical bag. "Take him out the back door and disappear. Use the evacuation codes. Pick a place at random and go to ground, *not* one of our properties. Report in on a secured line from a separate location. By then I should know what I can salvage from this mess." Her wrinkled lips peeled back on ivory teeth set in anger. "Move, girl."

Rowan nodded obediently, and didn't argue at all, he noticed indignantly. Holding him firmly by the arm, she guided his stumbling feet down a freight lift-tube, through the sub-basement, and into the underground clinic. A concealed doorway on its second level opened onto a narrow tunnel. He felt like a rat scurrying through a maze. Rowan stopped three times to key through some security device.

They came out in some other building's under-level, and the door disappeared behind them, indistinguishable from the wall. They continued on through ordinary utility tunnels. "You use this route often?" he panted.

"No. But every once in a while we want to get something in or out not recorded by our gate guards, who are Baron Fell's men."

They emerged finally in a small underground parking garage. She led him to a little blue lightflyer, elderly and inconspicuous, and bundled him into the passenger seat. "This isn' righ'," he complained, thick-tongued. "Admiral Naismith—someone should go after Admiral Naismith."

"Naismith owns a whole mercenary fleet." Rowan strapped herself into the pilot's seat. "Let them tangle with his enemies. Try to calm down and catch your breath. I don't want to have to dose you again."

The flyer rose into the swirling snow and rocked uncertainly in the gusts. The city sprawling below them disappeared quickly into the murk as Rowan powered them up. She glanced aside at his agitated profile. "Lilly will do something," she reassured him. "She wants Naismith too."

"It's wrong," he muttered. "It's all wrong." He huddled in the jacket Rowan had wrapped around him. She turned up the heat.

I'm the wrong one. It seemed he had no intrinsic value but his mysterious hold on Admiral Naismith. And if Admiral Naismith was removed from the Deal, the only person still interested in him would be Vasa Luigi, wanting vengeance upon him for crimes he couldn't even remember committing. Worthless, unwanted, lonely and scared ... His stomach churned in pain, and his head throbbed. His muscles ached, tense as wire.

All he had was Rowan. And, apparently, the Admiral, who had come searching for him. Who had very possibly risked his life to recover him. Why? *I have to do ... something.*

"The Dendarii Mercenaries. Are they all here? Does the Admiral have ships in orbit, or what? How much back-up does he have? He said it would take time for him to contact his back-up. How much time? Where did the Dendarii come in from, a commercial shuttleport? Can they call down air support? How many—how much—where—" His brain tried madly to assemble data that wasn't there into patterns for attack.

"Relax!" Rowan begged. "There's nothing we can do. We're only little people. And you're in no condition. You'll drive yourself into another convulsion if you keep on like this."

"Screw my condition! I have to—I have to—"

Rowan raised wry eyebrows. He lay back in his seat with a sick sigh, drained. *I should have been able to do this ... to do something. ...* He listened to nothing, half-hypnotized by the sound of his own shallow breathing. Defeated. Again. He didn't like the taste. He brooded at his pale and distorted reflection on the inside of the canopy. Time seemed to have become viscous.

The lights on the control panel died. They were suddenly weightless. His seat straps bit him. Fog began to stream up around them, faster and faster.

Rowan screamed, fought and banged the control panel. It flickered; momentarily, they had thrust again. Then lost it again. They descended in stutters. "What's wrong with it, damn it!" Rowan cried.

He looked upward. Nothing but icy fog—they dropped below cloud level. Then above them, a dark shape loomed. Big lift van, heavy. ...

"It's not a systems failure. We're being intermittently field-drained," he said dreamily. "We're being forced down."

Rowan gulped, concentrated, trying to keep the flyer level in the brief bursts of control. "My God, is it them again?"

"No. I don't know ... maybe they had some back-up." With adrenaline and determination, he forced his wits to function through the sedative-haze. "Make a noise!" he said. "Make a splash!"

"What?"

She didn't understand. She didn't catch it. She should have—somebody should have—"Crash this sucker!" She didn't *obey*.

"Are you crazy?" They lurched to ground right-side-up and intact in a barren valley, all snow and crackling scrub.

"Somebody wants to make a snatch. We've got to leave a mark, or we'll just disappear off the map without a trace. No comm link," he nodded toward the dead panel. "We have to make footprints, set fire to something, something!" He fought his seat straps for escape.

Too late. Four or five big men surrounded them in the gloom, stunners at ready. One reached up and unlatched his door, and dragged him out. "Be careful, don't hurt him!" Rowan cried fearfully, and scrambled after. "He's my patient!"

"We won't, ma'am," one of the big parka-clad men nodded politely, "but you mustn't struggle." Rowan stood still.

He stared around wildly. If he made a sprint for their van, could he—? His few steps forward were interrupted when one of the goons grabbed him by his shirt and hoisted him into the air. Pain shot through his scarred torso as the man twisted his hands behind his back. Something coldly metallic clicked around his wrists. They were not the same men who'd broken into the Durona Clinic, no resemblance in features, uniforms, or equipment.

Another big man crunched through the snow. He pushed back his hood, and shone a hand light upon the captives. He appeared about forty-standard, with a craggy face, olive brown skin, and dark hair stripped back in a simple knot. His eyes were bright and very alert. His black brows bent in puzzlement, as he stared at his prey.

"Open his shirt," he told one of the guards.

The guard did so; the craggy man shone the hand-light on the spray of scars. His lips drew back in a white grin. Suddenly, he threw back his head and laughed out loud. The echoes of his voice lost themselves in the empty winter twilight. "Ry, you fool! I wonder how long it will take you to figure it out?"

"Baron Bharaputra," Rowan said in a thin voice. She lifted her chin in a quick defiant jerk of greeting.

"Dr. Durona," said Vasa Luigi in return, polite and amused. "Your patient, is he? Then you won't refuse my invitation to join us. Please be our guest. You'll make it quite the little family reunion."

"What do you want from him? He has no memory."

"The question is not what I want from him. The question is . . . what someone else may want from him. And what I may want from *them*. Ha! Even better!" He motioned to his men, and turned away. They chivvied their captives into the closed lift van.

One of the men split off to pilot the blue lightflyer. "Where should I leave this, sir?"

"Take it back to the city and park it on a side street. Anywhere. See you home."

"Yes, sir."

The van doors closed. The van lifted.

CHAPTER TWENTY-FOUR

Mark groaned. Bright prickles of pain shot through a dark nausea.

"You gonna give him a dose of synergine?" said a voice, surprised. "I didn't get the idea the Baron wanted this one handled gently."

"You want to clean up the flyer if he vomits his breakfast?" rumbled another voice.

"Ah."

"The Baron will do his own handling. He just specified he wanted him alive. Which he is."

A hypospray hissed.

"Poor sod," said the first voice reflectively.

Thanks to the synergine, Mark began to recover from the stunner hit. He didn't know how much time and space lay between him and the Durona Clinic; they'd changed vehicles at least three times after he'd regained consciousness, once to something bigger and faster than an aircar. They stopped at some location, and he and the troopers all went through a decontamination chamber. The anonymously-dressed troopers went their way, and he was given over to two other guards, big flat-faced men in black trousers and red tunics.

House Ryoval's colors. *Oh.*

They laid him face down, hands and feet bound, in the back of a lightflyer. The gray clouds, darkening toward evening, gave no clue as to the direction they were heading.

Miles is alive. The relief of that fact was so intense, he smiled in elation even with his face squashed into the sticky plastic seat. What a joyful sight the skinny little bugger had been! Upright and breathing. He'd almost wept. What he'd done, was undone. He could really be Lord Mark, now. *All my sins are taken from me.*

Almost. He prayed that Durona doctor had spoken straight about Miles still recovering. Miles's eyes had been frighteningly bewildered. And he hadn't recognized Quinn, which must have nearly slain her. *You'll get better. We'll get you home, and you'll get better.* He'd haul Miles home and everything would be all right again, better than all right. It would be wonderful.

As soon as that idiot Ryoval had his delusions straightened around. Mark was ready to gut the man outright for screwing up his family reunion. *ImpSec will handle him.*

They entered an underground parking garage without his getting a glimpse of the exterior of their destination. The two guards hauled him roughly to his feet, and released his legs, which twitched and tingled. They passed through an electronic security chamber, after which his clothing was taken from him. They marched him through the . . . facility. It wasn't a prison. It wasn't one of House Ryoval's famous bordellos. The air bore a faint, unsettling medical tang. The place was far too utilitarian to be where surgical body-sculpture was done on patrons. It was too secret and secure to be where slaves were done to order, where humans were made into things not humanly possible. It wasn't very large. There were no windows. Underground? *Where the hell am I?*

He would not panic. He entertained himself with a brief vision of what Ryoval might do to his own troopers, once he discovered they'd snatched the wrong twin. If Ryoval did not realize the mistake at the very first sight of him, he toyed with the idea of concealing his identity for a while. Let Miles and the Dendarii get a bigger head-start. They had not been taken; they were free. *I found him!* They must come for him. And if not them, ImpSec. ImpSec could not be more than a week behind him, and closing fast. *I've won, goddammit, I've won!*

His head was still spinning with a bizarre mixture of elation and terror when the guards delivered him to Ryoval's presence. It was a luxurious office, or study; the Baron evidently kept private quarters here, for he glimpsed a living room beyond an archway. Mark had no trouble recognizing Ryoval. He'd seen him in the vid recording from the *Ariel*'s first mission here. The conversation where he'd threatened to have Admiral Naismith's severed head encased in plastic for a wall-hanging. In another man, this might be dismissed as hyperbole, but Mark had the uneasy feeling Ryoval had meant it literally. Ryoval was leaning half-seated on his comconsole desk. He had shining dark hair arranged in elaborate bands, a high-bridged nose, and smooth skin. Strong and youthful, for a centenarian.

He's wearing a clone. Mark's smile became vulpine. He hoped Ryoval would not mistake his post-stun tremula for fear.

The guards sat him in a chair and fastened him down with metal bands to his wrists. "Wait outside," the Baron instructed them. "It won't be long." They exited.

Ryoval's hands were trembling slightly. The skin of his bronzed face was faintly moist. When he looked up and smiled back at Mark, his eyes seemed alight with some internal glow, the look of a man so filled with the visions inside his head, he scarcely saw the present reality. Mark was almost too enraged to care. *Clone-consumer!*

"Admiral," Ryoval breathed happily. "I promised you we would meet again. As inevitably as fate." He looked Mark up and down; his dark brows rose. "You've put weight on, the last four years."

"Good living," Mark snarled, uncomfortably reminded of his nakedness. For all he'd loathed the Dendarii uniform, it had actually made him look rather good. Quinn had personally re-tailored it for this masquerade, and he wished for it back. Presumably it had been what had fooled Ryoval's troopers, though, in that moment of heroic temporary insanity.

"I'm so glad you are alive. At first I'd hoped for your unpleasant death in one of your little combats, but upon reflection I actually began to pray for your survival. I've had four years to plan this meeting. Revising and refining. I'd have hated for you to miss your appointment."

Ryoval did not recognize him as not-Naismith. Ryoval was barely seeing him at all. He seemed to be looking through him. The Baron began to stride up and down in front of him, pouring out his plans like a nervous lover, elaborate plans for vengeance that ranged from the obscene to the insane to the impossible.

It could be worse. Ryoval could be making these threats right now to that thin little, vague-eyed, bewildered cryo-amnesic, who would not know even who he was, let alone why these things should be happening to him. The thought sickened Mark. *Yeah. Better me than him, right now. No shit.*

He means to terrorize you. It's only words. What was it the Count had said? *Don't sell yourself to your enemy in advance, in your mind. . . .*

Hell, Ryoval wasn't even *his* enemy. All these gaudy scenarios had been tailored for Miles. No, not even for Miles. For Admiral Naismith, a man who didn't exist. Ryoval chased a ghost, a chimera.

Ryoval stopped beside him, interrupting his whispered tirade. Curiously, he ran a moist hand down Mark's body, fingers curving in precise anatomical tracing of the muscles hidden beneath the layer of fat. "Do you know," he breathed, "I'd planned to have you starved. But I think I've changed my mind. I believe I'll have you force-fed, instead. The results could be even more amusing, in the long run."

Mark shivered sickly for the first time. Ryoval felt it, beneath his probing fingers, and grinned. The man had an appalling instinct for the target. Better he should keep Ryoval focused on the chimera? *Better we should get the hell out of here.*

He took a breath. "I hate to burst your bubble, Baron, but I have some bad news for you."

"Now, did I ask you to speak?" Ryoval's fingers traced back up, to pinch the flesh around his jaw. "This isn't an interrogation. This isn't an inquisition. Confession will gain you nothing. Not even death."

It was that damned contagious hyperactivity. Even Miles's enemies caught it.

"I'm not Admiral Naismith. I'm the clone the Bharaputrans made. Your goons grabbed the wrong guy."

Ryoval merely smiled. "Nice try, Admiral. But we've been watching the Bharaputran clone at the Durona Clinic for days. I knew you would come for him, after what you did to try and get him back the first time. I don't know what passion he inspires in you— were you lovers? You'd be amazed how many people have clones made for that purpose."

So. When Quinn had sworn no one could possibly be following them, she'd been right. Ryoval hadn't been following them. He'd been *waiting* for them. Swell. It had been his actions, not his words or his uniform, which had convicted him of being Naismith.

"But I will obtain him too." Ryoval shrugged. "Very soon."

No, you won't. "Baron, I really am the other clone. Prove it to yourself. Have me examined."

Ryoval chuckled. "What do you suggest? A DNA scan? Even the Duronas couldn't decide." He sighed deeply. "There's so much I want to do to you, I scarcely know where to begin. I must take it slowly. And in logical order. One cannot torture body parts that have already been removed, for example. I wonder how many years I can make you last? Decades?"

Mark felt his self-control cracking. "*I'm not Naismith,*" he said, his voice going high with strain.

Ryoval grasped Mark's chin and tilted it up, his lips twisting in ironic disbelief. "Then I will practice on you. A dry run. And Naismith will be along. In time."

You're going to be astonished at what will be along, in time. ImpSec would have no hesitation whatsoever about taking Ryoval's House apart around him, no inhibitions even by Jacksonian standards.

To rescue Miles.

He, of course, wasn't Miles.

He reflected worriedly on that, as the guards entered again at Ryoval's summons.

The first beating was unpleasant enough. It wasn't the pain. It was pain without escape, fear without release, that worked upon the mind, tensed the body. Ryoval watched. Mark screamed without restraint. No silent, suffering, manly pride here, thank you. Maybe that would convince Ryoval he was not Naismith. This was crazy. Still, the guards broke no bones, and ended the exercise perfunctorily. They left him locked naked in a very cold, tiny room or closet, without windows. The air vent was perhaps five centimeters across. He couldn't get his fist, let alone his body, though it.

He tried to prepare, to steel himself. To give himself hope. Time was on his side. Ryoval was a supremely practiced sadist, but of a psychological bent. Ryoval would keep him alive, and relatively undamaged, at least at first. After all, nerves must be intact to report pain. A mind must be relatively unclouded, to experience all the nuances of agony. Elaborate humiliations, rather than immediate flaying to death, must be first on the menu. All he had to do was survive. Later—there wouldn't be a later. The Countess had said Mark's going to Jackson's Whole would force Illyan to assign more agents here whether he wanted to or not, that alone being a sure benefit of Mark's journey even if he accomplished nothing personally at all.

And what, after all, were a few more humiliations to him? Miles's immense pride could be shattered. He had none. Torture was old news to him. *Oh, Ryoval. Have you ever got the wrong man.*

Now, if Ryoval were half the psychologist he clearly imagined himself to be, he would have grabbed a few of Miles's friends, to torment in front of him. That would work beautifully, on Miles. But not, of course, on him. He had no friends. *Hell, Ryoval. I can think of worse things than you can.*

No matter. His friends would rescue him. Any time now.

Now.

He kept up his mental defiance till the technicians came for him.

They returned him to his little cell, afterward, presumably to give him some solitude to think about it. He didn't think for quite some time. He lay on his side breathing in tiny gasps, half-conscious, arms and legs slowly starfishing in rhythm to the pain inside that didn't stop.

At length, the clouds lifted a little from his vision, and the pain eased fractionally, to be replaced by a black, black rage. The techs had secured him, shoved a tube down his throat, and pumped him full of some repulsive high-calorie sludge. Laced with an anti-emetic, they told him, to prevent him getting rid of it later, and a cocktail of metabolic aids to speed digestion and deposition. It was far too subtly complex to have been designed on the spot; it must be something House Ryoval kept in stock. And he'd imagined this was his own private and unique perversion. He thought he'd done himself harm before, but Ryoval's people took it far beyond the limits of merely toying with pain, under the eye of their master, who'd come to watch. And study him, with a growing smile. Ryoval *knew*. He'd seen it in the man's sly, pleased eyes.

Ryoval had stripped his very own rebellion of all its secret pleasure. The one somatic power that had been his call, his control, taken from him. Ryoval had hooked him, gotten under his skin. Way under.

They could do *to* you all day long, and you could just not-be-there, but it was as nothing compared to getting you to do to yourself. The difference between mere torture and true humiliation was in the participation of the victim. Galen, whose torments were physically much milder than anything Ryoval contemplated, had known this; Galen had always had him doing to himself, or thinking he was.

That Ryoval knew this too, he demonstrated later, when he administered a violent aphrodisiac to Mark by hypospray, before giving him to his—guards? or were they employees borrowed from one of the bordellos? So that he became a glazed-eyed participant in his own degradation. It doubtless made a great show for the hovering holovids, recording it all from every angle.

They brought him back to his little cell to digest this new experience much as they'd brought him back to digest the first force-feeding. It took a long time for the shock and drug-fog to clear away. He oscillated slowly between a drained lassitude and horror. Curious. The drug had short-circuited his shock-stick conditioning, reducing it to something like a case of the hiccups, or the show would have been much duller and shorter. Ryoval had watched.

No. Ryoval had *studied.*

His consciousness of the man's eyes had become an obsession. Ryoval's interest had not been erotic. Mark felt the Baron must have become bored with the stereotyped banality of every possible physical act decades ago. Ryoval had been watching him for . . . reflexes? Small betrayals of interest, fear, despair. The exercise had not been arranged for the sake of pain. There had been plenty of pain, but it had been incidental. Discomfort from the force-feeding, and running out of neurotransmitters, mostly.

That wasn't the torture, Mark realized. *That was only the pre-testing. My torture is still being designed.*

Suddenly, he saw what was coming, all whole. First, Ryoval would condition him to this, addict him by repeated doses. Only then would he add pain, and pin him, vibrating, between pain and pleasure; require him to torture himself, to win through to the dark reward. And then he would withdraw the drug and let Mark, conditioned to the scenarios, continue. And he would. And then Ryoval would offer him his freedom. And he would weep and beg to stay, plead to remain a slave. Destruction by seduction. End-game. Revenge complete.

You see me, Ryoval, but I see you. I see you.

The force-feedings turned out to be on a schedule of every three hours. It was the only clock he had, or he would have thought time had stopped. He had surely entered eternity.

He'd always thought being skinned alive was something done with sharp knives. Or dull ones. Ryoval's technicians did it chemically, spraying carefully selected areas of his body with an aerosol. They wore gloves, masks, protective clothing; he tried, but failed, to grab off a mask and let one share what they administered. He cursed his littleness, and cried, and watched his skin bubble up and drip away. The chemical was not a caustic, but rather some strange enzyme; his nerves were left horribly intact, exposed. Touching anything, or being touched, was agony after that, especially the pressure of sitting or lying down. He stood in the little closet-cell, shifting from foot to foot, touching nothing, for hours, till his shaking legs finally gave way.

It was all happening so fast. Where the hell was everybody? How long had he been here? A day?

So. I have survived one day. Therefore, I can survive another one-day. It couldn't be worse. It could only be more.

He sat, and rocked, mind half whited-out with pain. And rage. Especially rage. From the moment of the first force-feeding, it hadn't been Naismith's war any more. This was personal now, between Ryoval and him. But not personal enough. He'd never been alone with Ryoval. He'd always been outnumbered, outweighed, passed from one set of bindings to another. Admiral Naismith was being treated as a fairly dangerous little prick, even now. That wouldn't do.

He would have told them everything, all about Lord Mark, and Miles, and the Count, and the Countess, and Barrayar. And Kareen. But the force-feedings had stopped his mouth, and the drug had stripped him of language, and the other things had kept him too busy screaming. It was all Ryoval's fault. The man watched. But he didn't *listen*.

I wanted to be Lord Mark. I just wanted to be Lord Mark. Was that so bad? He still wanted to be Lord Mark. He'd almost had it, brushing his grasp. Ripped away. He wept for it, hot tears splashing like molten lead on his not-skin. He could feel Lord Mark slipping from him, racked apart, buried alive. Disintegrating. *I just wanted to be human. Screwed up again.*

CHAPTER TWENTY-FIVE

He circled the room for the hundreth time, tapping on the walls. "If we could figure out which one is the exterior," he said to Rowan, "maybe we could break through it somehow."

"With what, our fingernails? What if we're three floors up? Will you please *sit down*," Rowan gritted. "You're driving me crazy!"

"We have to get out."

"We have to wait. Lilly will miss us. And something will be done."

"By who? And how?" He glared around their little bedroom. It wasn't designed as a prison. It was only a guest room, with its own bath attached. No windows, which suggested it was underground or in an interior section of the house. If it was underground, breaking through a wall might not be much use, but if they could bore into another room, the possibilities bloomed. One door, and two stunner-armed guards outside of it. They'd tried enticing the guards into opening the door last night, once with faked illness, and once for real when his frantic agitation had resulted in another convulsion. The guards had handed in Rowan's medical bag, which was no help, because then the exhausted woman had started responding to his demands for action by threatening to sedate him.

"Survive, escape, sabotage," he recited. It had become a litany, running through his head in an endless loop. "It's a soldier's duty."

"I'm not a soldier," said Rowan, rubbing her dark-ringed eyes. "And Vasa Luigi isn't going to kill me, and if he was going to kill you he'd have done it last night. He doesn't play with his prey like

656

Ryoval does." She bit her lip, perhaps regretting that last sentence. "Or maybe he's going to leave us in here together till *I* kill you." She rolled over in bed, and pulled her pillow over her head.

"You should have crashed that lightflyer."

A noise from under the pillow might have been either a groan or a curse. He had probably mentioned that regret a few too many times.

When the door clicked open he spun as if scalded.

A guard half-saluted, politely. "Baron Bharaputra's compliments, ma'am, sir, and would you prepare to join him and the Baronne for dinner. We will escort you upstairs when you're ready."

The Bharaputras' dining room had large glass doors giving a view onto an enclosed, winter-frosted garden, and a big guard by every exit. The garden glimmered in the gathering gloom; they had been here a full Jacksonian day, then, twenty-six hours and some odd minutes. Vasa Luigi rose at their entry, and at his gesture the guards faded back to positions outside the doors, giving an illusion of privacy.

The dining room was arranged stylishly, with individual couches and little tables set in a tiered semi-circle around the view of the garden. A very familiar-looking woman sat on one of the couches.

Her hair was white streaked with black, and wound up in elaborate braids around her head. Dark eyes, thin ivory skin softening with tiny wrinkles, a high-bridged nose—Dr. Durona. Again. She was dressed in a fine flowing silk shirt in a pale green perhaps accidentally reminiscent of the color of the Durona lab coats, and soft trousers the color of cream. Dr. Lotus Durona, Baronne Bharaputra, had elegant tastes. And the means to indulge them.

"Rowan, dear." She held out a hand as if Rowan might give it a courtier's kiss.

"Lotus," said Rowan flatly, and compressed her lips. Lotus smiled and turned her hand over, converting it into an invitation to sit, which they all did.

Lotus touched a control pad at her place. A girl wearing Bharaputra brown and pink silks entered, and served drinks, to the Baron first, curtseying with lowered eyes before him. A very familiar-looking girl, tall and willowy, with a high-bridged nose, fine straight black hair bound at her nape and flowing in a horse-tail down her back. . . . When she made her offering to the Baronne, her eyes flicked up, opening like flowers to the sun, bright with joy. When she bowed before Rowan, her up-turning gaze grew startled, and her dark brows drew down in puzzlement. Rowan gazed back equally startled, a look that changed to dawning horror as the girl turned away.

When she bowed before him, her frown deepened. "You . . . !" she whispered, as if amazed.

"Run along, Lilly dear, don't gawk," said the Baronne kindly.

As she left the room, with a swaying walk, she glanced covertly back over her shoulder at them.

"Lilly?" Rowan choked. "You named her Lilly?"

"A small revenge."

Rowan's hands clenched in deep offense. "How can you? Knowing what you are? Knowing what we are?"

"How can you choose death over life?" The Baronne shrugged. "Or worse—let Lilly choose it for you? Your time of temptation is not yet, Rowan my dear sister. Ask yourself again in twenty or thirty years, when you can feel your body rotting around you, and see if the answer comes so easily then."

"Lilly loved you as a daughter."

"Lilly used me as her servant. Love?" The Baronne chuckled. "It's not love that keeps the Durona herd together. It's predator pressure. If all the exterior economic and other dangers were removed, the far corners of the wormhole nexus would not be far enough for us to get away from our dear sibs. Most families are like that, actually."

Rowan assimilated the point. She looked unhappy. But she didn't disagree.

Vasa Luigi cleared his throat. "Actually, Dr. Durona, you wouldn't have to travel to the far reaches of the galaxy for a place of your own. House Bharaputra could find a use for your talents and training. And perhaps even a little autonomy. Head of a department, for example. And later, who knows?—maybe even a division."

"No. Thank you." Rowan bit out.

The Baron shrugged. Did the Baronne look faintly relieved?

He interrupted urgently, "Baron—was it really Ryoval's squad who took Admiral Naismith? Do you know where?"

"Well, now, that's an interesting question," Vasa Luigi murmured, eyeing him. "I've been trying to contact Ry all day, without success. I suspect that wherever Ry is, your clone-twin is also— Admiral."

He took a deep breath. "Why do you think I am the Admiral, sir?"

"Because I met the other one. Under telling circumstances. I don't think the real Admiral Naismith would permit his bodyguard to give him orders—do you?"

His head was aching. "What's Ryoval doing to him?"

"Really, Vasa, this is not dinner conversation," reproved the Baronne. She glanced curiously at him. "Besides—why should you care?"

" 'Miles, what have you done with your baby brother?' " The quote came from nowhere, fell out of his mouth. He touched his lips uncertainly. Rowan stared at him. So did Lotus.

Vasa Luigi said, "As to your question, Admiral, it turns on whether Ry has come to the same conclusions as I did. If he has—likely he's not doing much. If he hasn't, his methods will depend upon your clone-twin."

"I . . . don't understand."

"Ryoval will study him. Experiment. His choice of actions will flow from his analysis of his subject's personality."

That didn't sound so bad. He pictured multiple-choice tests. He frowned, bewildered.

"Ry is an artist, in his way," continued the Baron. "He can create the most extraordinary psychological effects. I've seen him turn an enemy into a slave utterly devoted to his person, who will obey any order. The last man who attempted to assassinate him and had the misfortune to live ended up serving drinks at Ryoval's private parties, and begging to offer gratification of any kind to any guest on request."

"What did you ask for?" the Baronne inquired dryly.

"White wine. It was before your time, love. I watched, though. The man had the most haunted eyes."

"Are you considering selling me to Ryoval?" he asked slowly.

"If he's the highest bidder, Admiral. Your and your clone-twin's raid upon my property—and I am still not certain you did not plan it together from first to last—was very costly to my House. And," his eyes glinted, "personally annoying. I'll not bother avenging myself upon a cryo-amnesic, but I do wish to shave my losses. If I sell you to Ry, you'll be better punished than even I care to think about. Ry would be delighted to own a matched pair." Vasa Luigi sighed. "House Ryoval will always be a minor house, I fear, as long as Ry allows his personal gratification to outweigh its profits. It's a shame. I could do so much more with his resources."

The girl returned, served little plates of hors d'ouvers, refreshed their drinks, some wine-and-fruit concoction, and wafted out again. Slowly. Vasa Luigi's eyes followed her. The Baronne's eyes narrowed, noting his gaze. Her lashes swept down, focusing on her drink, as his head turned back.

"What about . . . the Dendarii Mercenaries, as a bidder?" *Yes!* Just let Bharaputra make that offer, and the Dendarii would come knocking on his door. With a plasma cannon. High bid indeed. This game must be a short one. Bharaputra could not put him up for auction without revealing that he had him, and then, and then . . . *what?* "If nothing else, you could use their competition to force Ryoval's bid up," he added slyly.

"Their resources are too finite, I fear. And not here."

"We saw them. Yesterday."

"A mere covert ops team. No ships. No back-up. I understand they only revealed their identity at all in order to get Lilly to talk with them. But . . . I have reason to believe there is another player in this game. My instincts twitch, looking at you. I have the oddest urge to take a modest middleman's profit, and let the negative bidders apply to House Ryoval." The Baron chuckled.

Negative bidders? Oh. People with plasma cannons. He tried not to react.

Vasa Luigi continued, "Which brings us back to the original question—what *is* Lilly's interest in all this? Why did Lilly set you to revive this man, Rowan? For that matter, how did Lilly obtain him, when some hundreds of other earnest searchers could not?"

"She didn't say," said Rowan blandly. "But I was glad for a chance to sharpen my skills. Thanks to your security guard's excellent aim, he was quite a medical challenge."

The conversation became medical-technical, between Lotus and Rowan, and then more desultory, as the clone-girl served them an elaborate meal. Rowan evaded as smoothly as the Baron questioned, and no one expected him to know anything. But Baron Bharaputra seemed not to be in a hurry. Clearly, he was setting up to play some kind of waiting game. Afterwards the guards escorted them back to their room, which he realized at last was part of a corridor of identical chambers designed, perhaps, to house the servants of important visitors.

"Where are we?" he hissed at Rowan as soon as the door shut behind them. "Could you tell? Is this Bharaputra's headquarters?"

"No," said Rowan. "His main residence is still under renovation. Something about a commando raid blowing out several rooms," she added snappishly.

He walked slowly around their chamber, but he did not take up banging on the walls again, to Rowan's obvious relief. "It occurs

to me . . . that there's another way to escape besides breaking from
the inside out. That's to get someone else to break from the outside
in. Tell me . . . would it be harder to break in and take someone
held prisoner by House Bharaputra, House Fell, or House Ryoval?"

"Well . . . Fell would be the hardest, I suppose. He has more
troops and heavy weapons. Ryoval would be the easiest. Ryoval's
really a House Minor, except he's so old, he gets the honors of a
House Major by habit."

"So . . . if one wanted someone bigger and badder than Bharaputra, one might go to Fell."

"One might."

"And . . . if one knew help were on the way . . . it might be
tactically brighter to leave said prisoner at Ryoval's, rather than
to have him shifted to some more formidible location."

"It might," she conceded.

"We have to get to Fell."

"How? We can't even get out of this room!"

"Out of the room, yes, we must get out of the room. But we
might not have to get out of the house. If one of us could just
get to a comconsole for a few uninterrupted minutes. Call Fell,
call *someone*, let the world know Vasa Luigi has us. *That* would
start things moving."

"Call Lilly," said Rowan sturdily. "Not Fell."

I need Fell. Lilly can't break into Ryoval's. He considered the
uneasy possibility that he and the Durona Group might be starting
to move at cross-purposes. He wanted a favor from Fell, whom
Lilly wished to escape. Still—one would not have to offer very
much to interest Fell in a raid on Ryoval. A break-even in materials,
and the profit in old hatred. Yeah.

He wandered into the bathroom and stared at himself in the
mirror. *Who am I?* A skinny, haggard, pale, odd-looking little man
with desperate eyes and a tendency to convulsions. If he could even
decide which one his clone-twin was, glimpsed so painfully yesterday, he could dub himself the other by process of elimination.
The fellow had looked like Naismith to him. But Vasa Luigi was
no fool, and Vasa Luigi was convinced of the reverse. He had to
be one or the other. Why couldn't he decide? *If I am Naismith,
why did my brother claim my place?*

At that moment, he discovered why it was called a *cascade*.

The sensation was of being under a waterfall, of some river that
emptied a continent, tons of water battering him to his knees. He
emitted a tiny mewl, crouching down with his arms wrapping his

head, shooting pains behind his eyes and terror locking his throat. He pressed his lips together to prevent any other sound escaping, that would attract Rowan in all her concern. He needed to be alone for this, oh yes.

No wonder I couldn't guess. I was trying to choose between two wrong answers. Oh, Mother. Oh, Da. Oh, Sergeant. Your boy has screwed up this one, bad. Real bad. Lieutenant Lord Miles Naismith Vorkosigan crawled on the tiled floor and screamed in silence, just a faint hiss. *No, no, no, oh, shit. . . .*

Elli . . .

Bel, Elena, Taura . . .

Mark . . . Mark? That stout, glowering, controlled, determined fellow had been *Mark?*

He could not remember anything about his death. He touched his chest, fearfully, tracing the evidence of . . . what event? He squeezed his eyes shut, trying to remember the last that he could. The raid downside at Bharaputra's surgical facility, yes. Mark had engineered a disaster, Mark and Bel between them, and he'd come flying down to try and pull all their nuts out of the fire. Some megalomanic inspiration to top Mark, show him how the experts did it, to take those clone-children from Vasa Luigi, who had offended him . . . take 'em home to Mother. *Crap, what does my mother know about all this by now?* Nothing, he prayed. They were all still here on Jackson's Whole, somehow. *How* long had he been dead . . . ?

Where the hell is ImpSec?

Besides rolling around here on this bathroom floor, of course.

Ow, ow, ow. . . .

And Elli. *Do I know you, ma'am?* he'd asked. He should have bitten his tongue out.

Rowan . . . Elli. It made sense, in a weird way. His lover was a tall, brown-eyed, dark-haired, tough-minded, smart woman. The first thing presented to his confused awakening senses had been a tall, brown-eyed, dark-haired, tough-minded, smart woman. It was a very natural mistake.

He wondered if Elli was going to buy that explanation. His taste for heavily-armed girlfriends did have potential drawbacks. He inhaled a hopeless laugh.

It clogged in his throat. *Taura, here?* Did Ryoval know it? Did he know what a lovely big clawed hand she'd had in the destruction of his gene banks, four years ago, or did he just blame "Admiral Naismith"? True, all of Ryoval's bounty hunters he'd encountered subsequently had seemed focused obsessively and exclusively upon himself. But Ryoval's troopers had mistaken Mark for the Admiral; had Ryoval? Surely Mark would tell him he was the clone. *Hell, I'd tell him the same if it were me, on the off-chance of confusing the issue.* What was happening to Mark? Why had Mark offered himself as Miles's . . . ransom? Mark couldn't possibly be cryo-amnesic too, could he? No—Lilly had said the Dendarii, and the clones, and "Admiral Naismith" had all escaped. So how did they come to be *back*?

They came looking for you, Admiral Dipshit.

And had run headlong into Ryoval, looking for the same thing. He was a damned rendezvous.

What a *merciful* state cryo-amnesia was. He wished for it back.

"Are you all right?" Rowan called doubtfully. She stepped to the bathroom door, and saw him on the floor. "Oh, no! Another convulsion?" She dropped to her knees beside him, long fingers checking for damages. "Did you hit yourself on anything?"

"Ah . . . ah . . ." *I'll not bother avenging myself upon a cryo-amnesic,* Vasa Luigi had said. He had better remain a cryo-amnesic then, for the moment, till he had a better grip on things. And on himself. "I think I'm all right."

He suffered her to anxiously put him to bed. She stroked his hair. He stared at her in dismay through half-lidded, pretend-post-convulsion-sleepy eyes. *What have I done?*

What am I going to do?

CHAPTER TWENTY-SIX

He had forgotten why he was here. His skin was beginning to grow back.

He wondered where Mark had gone.

People came, and tormented a nameless thing without boundaries, and went away again. He met them variously. His emerging aspects became personas, and eventually, he named them, as well as he could identify them. There was Gorge, and Grunt, and Howl, and another, quiet one that lurked on the fringes, waiting.

He let Gorge go out to handle the force-feedings, because Gorge was the only one who actually enjoyed them. Gorge, after all, would never have been permitted to do all that Ryoval's techs did. Grunt he sent forth when Ryoval came again with the hypospray of aphrodisiac. Grunt had also been responsible for the attack on Maree, the body-sculptured clone, he rather thought, though Grunt, when not all excited, was very shy and ashamed and didn't talk much.

Howl handled the rest. He began to suspect Howl had been obscurely responsible for delivering them all to Ryoval in the first place. Finally, he'd come to a place where he could be punished *enough. Never give aversion therapy to a masochist. The results are unpredictable.* So Howl deserved what Howl got. The elusive fourth one just waited, and said that someday, they would all love him best.

They did not always stay within their lines. Howl had a tendency to eavesdrop on Gorge's sessions, which came regularly while Howl's did not; and more than once Gorge turned up riding along with Grunt on his adventures, which then became exceptionally peculiar. Nobody joined Howl by choice.

Having named them all, he finally found Mark by process of elimination. Gorge and Grunt and Howl and the Other had sent Lord Mark deep inside, to sleep through it all. Poor, fragile Lord Mark, barely twelve weeks old.

Ryoval could not even see Lord Mark down in there. Could not reach him. Could not touch him. Gorge and Grunt and Howl and the Other were all very careful not to wake the baby. Tender and protective, they defended him. They were *equipped* to. An ugly, grotty, hard-bitten bunch, these psychic mercenaries of his. Unlovely. But they got the job done.

He began to hum little marching tunes to them, from time to time.

CHAPTER TWENTY-SEVEN

*A*bsence *makes the heart grow fonder.* And, Miles feared, the converse. Rowan had pulled her pillow over her head again. He continued to pace. And talk. He couldn't seem to stop himself. In the time that had passed since his concealed memory cascade, he had evolved a multitude of plans for their escape, all with some fatal flaw. Unable to put any of them into effect, he had re-ordered and refined them out loud. Over and over. Rowan had stopped critiquing them . . . yesterday? In fact, she'd stopped talking to him at all. She'd given up trying to pet him and relax him, and instead tended to stay on the far side of the room, or hide for long periods in the bathroom. He couldn't blame her. His returning nervous energy seemed to be building to something like a frenzy.

This forced confinement was stressing her affection for him to the limit. And, he had to admit, he had not been able to conceal his slight new hesitation toward her. A coolness in his touch, an increased resistance to her medical authority. He loved and admired her, no question, and would be delighted to have her in charge of any sickbay he owned. Under his command. But guilt and the sense of no privacy had combined to cripple his interest in intimacy. He had other passions at the moment. And they were consuming him.

Dinner was due soon. Assuming three meals per long Jacksonian day, they'd been here four days. The Baron had not spoken with them again. What schemes was Vasa Luigi evolving, out there?

666

Had he been auctioned yet? What if the next person through the door was his buyer? What if nobody bid at all, what if they left him in here forever?

Meals were usually brought on a tray by a servant, under the watchful eye of a couple of stunner-armed guards. He'd tried everything he could think of short of breaking his cover to sub-orn them, in their brief snatches of conversation. They'd just smiled at him. He was dubious of his ability to outrun a stunner-beam, but at the next opportunity, he resolved to try. He hadn't had a chance to try anything clever. He was ready to try something stupid. Surprise sometimes worked. . . .

The lock clicked. He spun, poised to dart forward. "Rowan, get up!" he hissed. "I'm going to try for it."

"Oh, hell," she moaned, emerging. Without faith, brow-beaten, she rose and trudged around the bed to stand by his side. "Stunning hurts, you know. And then you throw up. *You'll* probably have convulsions."

"Yes. I know."

"But at least it'll shut you up for a while," she muttered under her breath.

He rose on the balls of his feet. Then sank back again as the servant entered. *Oh, my. What's this?* There was suddenly a new player in the game, and his mind locked into over-drive. Rowan, watching him for his announced bolt, looked up too, and her eyes widened.

It was the clone-girl Lilly—Lilly Junior, he supposed he must think of her—in her brown-and-pink silk house-servant's uniform, a long wrap skirt and spangled jacket. Straight-backed, she carried their meal tray, and set it down on the table across the room. Incomprehensibly, the guard nodded at her and withdrew, closing the door behind him.

She began to lay out their meal, servant-fashion; Rowan approached her, lips parted.

He saw a dozen possibilities, instantly; also that this chance might never come again. There was no way, in his debilitated state, that he could overpower the girl himself. What about that seda-tive Rowan had threatened him with? Could Rowan get the drop on her? Rowan was not good at catching oblique hints, and terrible at following cryptic orders. She'd want explanations. She'd want to *argue*. He could only try.

"*Goodness* you two look alike," he chirped brightly, glaring at Rowan. She gave him a look of exasperated bafflement, which she converted to a smile as the girl turned toward them. "How is it that we rate, uh, such a high-born servant, milady?"

Lilly's smooth hand touched her chest. "*I* am not my lady," she said, in a tone that suggested he must be a complete fool. Not without reason. "But you . . ." She looked searchingly at Rowan. "I don't understand you."

"Did the Baronne send you?" Miles asked.

"No. But I told the guards your food was drugged, and the Baronne sent me to stay and watch you eat it," she added, somewhat off-the-cuff.

"Is that, uh, true?" he asked.

"No." She tossed her head, making her long hair swing, and dropped him from her attention to focus hungrily upon Rowan. "Who *are* you?"

"She is the Baronne's sister," he said instantly. "Daughter to your lady's mother. Did you know you were named after your, uh, grandmother?"

". . . Grandmother?"

"Tell her about the Durona Group, Rowan," he said urgently.

"Give me a chance to speak, then, why don't you," Rowan said through her teeth, smiling.

"Does she know what she is? Ask her if she knows what she is," he demanded, then stuffed his knuckle into his mouth and bit it. The girl hadn't come for him. She'd come for Rowan. He had to let Rowan take this one.

"Well," Rowan glanced at the closed door, and back to the girl, "The Duronas are a group of thirty-six cloned siblings. We live under the protection of House Fell. Our mother—the first Durona—is named Lilly, too. She was very sad when Lotus—the Baronne—left us. Lotus used to be my . . . older sister, you see. You must be my sister too, then. Has Lotus told you why she had you? Are you to be her daughter? Her heir?"

"I am to be united with my lady," said the girl. There was a faint defiance in her tone, but her fascination with Rowan was obvious. "I wondered . . . if you were to take my place." Jealousy? *Madness.*

Rowan's eyes darkened in muted horror. "Do you understand just what that means? What a clone-brain transplant is? She will take your body, Lilly, and you will be nowhere."

"Yes. I know. It's my destiny." She tossed her head again, flipping her hair back from her face. Her tone was one of conviction. But her eyes . . . was there the faintest question, in her eyes?

"So much alike, you two," he murmured, circling them in

suppressed anxiety. Smiling. "I'll bet you could exchange clothes with each other, and no one could tell the difference." Rowan's quick glance told him yes, she'd caught it, but thought he was pushing it too hard. "Naw," he went on, pursing his lips and tilting his head, "I don't think so. The girl's too fat. Don't you think she's too fat, Rowan?"

"I am not fat!" said Lilly Junior indignantly.

"Rowan's clothes would never fit you."

"You're wrong," said Rowan, giving up and letting herself be pushed into fast-forward. "He's an idiot. Let's prove it, Lilly." She began to peel out of her jacket, blouse, trousers.

Slowly, very curiously, the girl took off her jacket and skirt, and took up Rowan's outfit. Rowan did not yet touch Lilly's silks, laid out neatly on the bed.

"Oh, that looks nice," said Rowan. She nodded toward the bathroom. "You should go look at yourself."

"I was wrong," Miles admitted nobly, steering the girl toward the bathroom. No time to plot, no way to give orders. He'd have to utterly rely on Rowan's . . . initiative. "Actually, Rowan's clothes look quite good on you. Imagine yourself as a Durona surgeon. They're all doctors there, did you know? You could be a doctor too. . . ." Out of the corner of his eye, he saw Rowan tear the bands from her hair and shake it loose, and grab for the silks. He let the door shut behind him and Lilly, aiming her at the mirror. He turned on the water, to mask the sound of Rowan's knock on the outer door, of the guard opening it, of her retreat, hair swinging down across her face. . . .

Lilly stared into the long mirror. She glanced at him by her side in it, waving his hand as if to introduce her to herself, then down at the top of his head by her shoulder. He grabbed a cup and took a gulp of water, to clear his throat for action. How long could he keep the girl distracted in here? He didn't think he could successfully sap her on the skull, and he was not completely certain which item in Rowan's medical satchel, sitting on the countertop, was the threatened sedative.

To his surprise, she spoke first. "You're the one who came for me, aren't you. For all us clones."

"Uh . . ." The disasterous Dendarii raid on Bharaputra's? Had she been one of the rescuees? What was she doing back here, then? "Excuse me. I've been dead, lately, and my brain isn't working too well. Cryo-amnesia. It might have been me, but you might have met my clone-twin."

"You have clone-sibs too?"

"At least one. My . . . brother."

"You were really dead?" She sounded faintly disbelieving.

He pulled up his gray knit shirt and displayed his scars.

"Oh," she said, impressed. "I guess you were."

"Rowan put me back together. She's very good." No, don't draw her attention to the missing Rowan. "You could be just as good, I'll bet, if you tried. If you were trained."

"What was it like? Being dead?" Her eyes were suddenly intent upon his face.

He shrugged his shirt back down. "Dull. Really boring. A blank. I don't remember anything. I don't remember dying—" His breath caught. . . . *the projectile weapon's muzzle, bright with flame . . . his chest bursting outward, terrible pain* . . . He inhaled and leaned against the counter, legs suddenly weak. "Lonely. You wouldn't like it. I guarantee." He took her warm hand. "Being alive is much better. Being alive is, is . . ." He needed something to stand on. He scrambled up on the counter instead, crouching eye to eye with her at last. He twined her hair in his hand, tilted his head, and kissed her, just a brief press of the lips. "You can tell you're alive when somebody touches you back."

She drew back, shocked and interested. "You kiss differently from the Baron."

His brain seemed to hiccup. "The Baron has kissed you?"

"Yes . . ."

Sampling his wife's new body early? How soon was that transplant scheduled? "Have you always lived with, uh, your lady?"

"No. I was brought here after the clone-crèche was wrecked. The repairs are almost complete. I'll be moving back soon."

"But . . . not for long."

"No."

The temptations to the Baron must be . . . interesting. After all, she would have her brain destroyed soon, and be unable to accuse. Vasa Luigi could do anything but damage her virginity. What was this doing to her apparent mental conditioning, her allegiance to her destiny? Something, obviously, or she wouldn't be here.

She glanced at the closed door, and her mouth went round in sudden suspicion. She pulled her hand from his grip, and raced back to the empty bedroom. "Oh, no!"

"Sh! Sh!" He ran after her, grabbed her hand again, lunged up to stand on the bed to turn her face to his and regain eye contact. "Don't shout!" he hissed. "If you run out and tell the guards, you'll be in terrible trouble, but if you just wait until she comes back, no one will ever know." He felt quite vile, to be playing so on her obvious panic, but it had to be done. "Be quiet, and no one will ever know." He had no idea if Rowan intended to come back, for that matter. By this point maybe she had just wanted to escape from *him*. None of his plans had assumed a piece of luck like this.

Lilly Junior could physically overpower him with ease, though he was not sure if she realized it. One good punch to his chest would drop him to the floor. She wouldn't even have to hit him very hard.

"Sit down," he told her. "Here, next to me. Don't be afraid. Actually, I can't imagine what you could possibly be afraid of, if your destiny doesn't make you blink. You must be a courageous girl. Woman. Sit . . ." He drew her down; she glanced from him to the door in great uncertainty, but allowed herself to be settled, temporarily. Her muscles were tight as springs. "Tell me . . . tell me about yourself. Tell me about your life. You are a most interesting person, do you know?"

"Me?"

"I can't remember much about my life, right now, which is why I ask. It's a terror to me, not to be able to remember. It's killing me. What's the very earliest thing about yourself that you can remember?"

"Why . . . I suppose . . . the place I lived before I came to the crèche. There was a woman who took care of me. I have—this is silly—but I remember she had some purple flowers, as tall as I was, that grew out of this little square of a garden, hardly a meter square, and they smelled like grapes."

"Yes? Tell me more about those flowers . . ."

They were in for a long conversation, he feared. And then what? That Rowan had not yet been *brought* back was a very good sign. That she might not be *coming* back left an unsettling dilemma for Lilly Junior. *So what could the Baron and Baronne possibly do to her?* his mind mocked savagely. *Kill her?*

They talked of her life in the crèche. He teased out an account of the Dendarii raid from her point of view. How she had managed to re-join the Baron. Sharp, sharp kid. What a mess for Mark. The pauses grew longer. He was going to end up talking about himself soon, just to keep things going, and that was incredibly dangerous. She was running out of conversation, her eyes turning more and more often toward the door.

"Rowan's not coming back," said Lilly Junior at last. "Is she."

"I think not," he said frankly. "I think she's escaped clean."

"How can you tell?"

"If they had caught her, they would have come for you, even if they didn't bring her back here. From their point of view, Rowan is still in here. It's you who's missing."

"You don't think they could have mistaken her for me, do you?" she gasped in alarm. "Taken her to be united with my lady?"

He wasn't sure if she was afraid for Rowan, or afraid that Rowan would steal her place. What a ghastly, hideous new paranoia. "How soon are you . . . no," he reassured her. Himself. "No. At a glance in the hallway, sure, you'd look quite alike, but someone would have to take a closer look for that. She's years older than you. It's just not possible."

"What should I do?" She tried to get to her feet; he held her arm, pulled her back to his side on the bed.

"Nothing," he advised. "It's all right. Tell them—tell them I made you stay in here."

She looked askance at his littleness. "How?"

"Trickery. Threats. Psychological coercion," he said truthfully. "You can blame it on me."

She looked most dubious.

How old was she? He'd spent the last two hours teasing out her whole life story, and there didn't seem to be very much of it. Her talk was an odd mixture of sharpness and naivete. The greatest adventure of her life had been her brief kidnapping by the Dendarii Mercenaries.

Rowan. *She's made it out. Then what?* Would she come back for him? How? This was Jackson's Whole. You couldn't trust anyone. People were meat, here. Like this girl in front of him. He had a sudden nightmarish picture of her, empty-skulled, blank-eyed.

"I'm sorry," he whispered. "You are so beautiful . . . on the *inside*. You deserve to live. Not be eaten by that old woman."

"My lady is a great woman," she said sturdily. "She deserves to live more."

What kind of twisted ethics drove Lotus Durona, to make of this girl an imitation-willing sacrifice? Who did Lotus think she was fooling? Only herself, apparently.

"Besides," said Lilly Junior. "I thought you liked that fat blonde. You were squirming all over her."

"Who?"

"Oh, that's right. That must have been your clone-twin."

"My brother," he corrected automatically. What was *this* story, Mark?

She was getting relaxed, now, reconciled to her strange captivity. And bored. She looked at him speculatively. "Would you like to kiss me again?" she inquired.

It was his height. It brought out the beast in women. Unthreatened, they became bold. He normally considered it a quite delightful effect, but this girl worried him. She was not his . . . equal. But he had to kill time, keep her in here, keep her entertained for as long as possible. "Well . . . all right. . . ."

After about twenty minutes of tame and decorous necking, she drew back and remarked, "That's not the way the Baron does it."

"What do you do for Vasa Luigi?"

She unfastened his trouser-strings and started to show him. After about a minute, he choked, "Stop!"

"Don't you like it? The Baron does."

"I'm sure." Dreadfully aroused, he fled to the chair by the little dining table, and scrunched himself up in it. "That's, um, very nice, Lilly, but it's too serious for you and me."

"I don't understand."

"Just exactly so." She was a *child*, despite her grown-up body, he was increasingly certain of it. "When you are older . . . you will find your own boundaries. And you can invite people across them as you choose. Right now you scarcely know where you leave off and the world begins. Desire should flow from within, not be imposed from without." He tried to choke off his own flow by sheer will-power, half-successfully. *Vasa Luigi, you scum.*

She frowned thoughtfully. "I'm not going to be older."

He wrapped his arms around his drawn-up knees and shuddered. *Hell.*

He suddenly remembered how he'd met Sergeant Taura. How they had become lovers, in that desperate hour. Ah, ambushed again by the pot-holes in his memory. There were certain obvious parallels with his current situation; it must be why his subconscious was trying to apply the old successful solution. But Taura was a bioengineered mutation, short-lived. The Dendarii medicos had stolen her a little more time with metabolic adjustments, but not much. Every day was a gift, each year a miracle. She was living her whole life as a smash-and-grab, and he heartily approved. Lilly Junior could live a century, if she wasn't . . . cannibalized. She needed to be seduced to life, not sex.

Like integrity, love of life was not a subject to be studied, it was

a contagion to be caught. And you had to catch it from someone who had it. "Don't you want to live?" he asked her.

"I . . . don't know."

"I do. I want to live. And believe me, I have considered the
alternative *deeply*."

"You are . . . a funny, little, ugly man. What can you get from
life?"

"*Everything*. And I mean to get more." *I want, I want.* Wealth,
power, love. Victories, splendid, brilliant victories, shining reflected
in the eyes of comrades. Someday, a wife, children. A herd of
children, tall and healthy, to rock those who whispered *Mutant!*
right back on their heels and over on their pointed heads. *And I
mean to have a brother.*

Mark. Yeah. The surly little fellow that Baron Ryoval was, quite
possibly, taking apart strand by strand right now. In Miles's place.
His nerves stretched to the screaming point, with no release. *I've
got to make time.*

He finally persuaded Lilly Junior to go to sleep, wrapped up in
the covers on Rowan's side of the bed. Chivalrously, he took the
chair. A couple of hours into the night and he was in agony. He
tried the floor. It was cold. His chest ached. He dreaded the thought
of waking with a cough. He finally crept into the bed on top of
the covers, and curled up facing away from her. He was intensely
conscious of her body. The reverse was obviously not so. His
anxiety was the more enormous for being so formless. He didn't
have control of *anything*. Near morning, he at last warmed up
enough to doze.

"Rowan, m'love," he muttered muzzily, nuzzling into her scented
hair and wrapping himself around her warm, long body. "M'lady."
A Barrayaran turn of phrase; he knew where that *milady* came
from, at long last. She flinched; he recoiled. Consciousness returned.
"Ak! Sorry."

Lilly Junior sat up, shaking off his ugly-little-man grasp. Grope,
actually. "I am not my lady!"

"Sorry, wrong referent. I think of Rowan as milady, inside my
head. She is milady, and I'm her . . ." *court fool* "knight. I really
am a soldier, you know. Despite being short."

At the second knock on the door, he realized what had awakened him. "Breakfast. Quick! Into the bathroom. Rattle around in
there. I swear we can keep this going another round."

For once he did not try to engage the guards in conversation leading to bribery. Lilly Junior came back out when the door closed again behind the servant. She ate slowly, dubiously, as if she doubted her right to food. He watched her, increasingly fascinated. "Here. Have this other roll. You can put sugar on it, you know."

"I'm not allowed to eat sugar."

"You should have sugar." He paused. "You should have everything. You should have friends. You should have . . . sisters. You should have education to the limits of your mind's powers, and work to challenge your spirit. Work makes you bigger. More real. You eat it up, and grow. You should have love. A knight of your own. Much taller. You should have . . . ice cream."

"I mustn't get fat. My lady is my destiny."

"Destiny! What do you know about destiny?" He rose and began to pace, zig-zagging around bed and table. "I'm a frigging *expert* on destiny. Your lady is a false destiny, and do you know how I know? She takes everything, but she doesn't give anything back.

"*Real* destiny takes everything—the last drop of blood, and strip out your veins to be sure—and gives it back doubled. Quadrupled. A thousand-fold! But you can't give halves. You have to give it all. I *know*. I *swear*. I've come back from the dead to speak the truth to you. Real destiny gives you a *mountain* of life, and puts you on top of it."

His conviction felt utterly megalomanic. He adored moments like this.

"You're insane," she said, staring at him warily.

"How would you know? You've never met a sane person in your life. *Have you?* Think about it."

Her rising interest fell. "It's no use. I'm a prisoner anyway. Where would I go?"

"Lilly Durona would take you in," he said promptly. "The Durona Group is under House Fell's protection, you know. If you could get to your grandmother, you'd be safe."

Her brows drew down just like Rowan's had, when she was knocking holes in his escape plans. "How?"

"They can't leave us in here forever. Suppose . . ." he walked behind her, gathered up her hair, and held it in a messy wad on the back of her head. "I didn't get the impression Vasa Luigi meant to keep Rowan past the point of need for secrecy. When I go, so should she. If they thought you were Rowan, I bet you could just walk right out."

"What . . . would I say?"

"As little as possible. Hello, Dr. Durona, your ride is here. Pick up your bag, and go."

"I couldn't."

"You could try. If you fail, you'll lose nothing. If you win, you'll win *everything*. And—if you got away—you could tell people where I've gone. Who took me, and when. All it takes is a few minutes of nerve, and that's free. We make it ourselves, out of ourselves. Nerve can't be taken away from you like a purse or something. Hell, why am I telling you that? You escaped the Dendarii Mercenaries on nerve and wit alone."

She looked utterly boggled. "I was doing it for my lady. I've never done anything for . . . for *myself*."

He felt like crying, strung up to the point of pure nervous collapse. This was the sort of all-out exalted eloquence he usually reserved for persuading people to *risk* their lives, not save them. He leaned across to whisper demonically in her ear. "Do it for yourself. The universe will be around to collect its cut later."

After breakfast, he tried to help her fix her hair Rowan-fashion. He was terrible at hair. Since Rowan was too, the final result was quite convincing, he fancied. They survived the delivery and removal of lunch.

He knew it wasn't dinner when they didn't knock before entering.

There were three guards, and a man in House livery. Two of the guards took him, wordlessly, and fastened his hands in front of him. He was grateful for that small favor. Behind his back would have been excruciating, after the first half-hour. They prodded him into the hall. No sign of Vasa and Lotus. Out looking for their lost clone, he hoped? He glanced back over his shoulder.

"Dr. Durona," the House man nodded at Lilly Junior. "I am to be your driver. Where to?"

She brushed a loose wisp of hair from her eyes, picked up Rowan's bag, stepped forward, and said, "Home."

"Rowan," Miles said. She turned.

"Take all, for it will all be taken back in time. That's a grave truth." He moistened dry lips. "Kiss me goodbye?"

She tilted her head, wheeled, bent. Pressed her lips to his, briefly. Followed the driver.

Well, it was enough to impress the guards. "How'd you rate that?" one inquired, amiably amused, as he was led in the opposite direction.

"I'm an acquired taste," he informed them smugly.

"Cut the chat," sighed the senior man.

He made two attempted breaks on the way to the groundcar; after the second, the biggest guard simply slung him over his shoulder, head-down, and threatened to drop him if he wriggled. They'd used enough force tackling him the second time that Miles didn't think he was joking. They bundled him into the back of the vehicle between two of them.

"Where are you taking me?"

"To a transfer point," one said.

"What transfer point?"

"That's all you need to know."

He kept up a steady stream of commentary, bribes, threats, insults, and at last, invective, but they never rose to the bait again. He wondered if any of them could be the man who'd killed him. No. No one involved in that mess at the surgical facility could be so calm about it all. These guys had been far away, that day. His voice went hoarse. It was a long ride. Groundcars were hardly used outside the cities, the roads were so bad. And they were far outside any city. It was past dusk when they pulled over beside a lonely intersection.

They handed him off to two humorless, flat-faced men in red and black House livery, who were waiting patiently as oxen. Ryoval's colors. These men fastened his hands behind his back, and his ankles too, before slinging him into the back of a lightflyer. It rose silently into darkness.

Looks like Vasa Luigi got his price.

Rowan, if she'd made it, must send anyone looking for him to Bharaputra's. Where Miles would not be. Not that he was so sure Vasa Luigi wouldn't just cheerfully sic them right on to Ryoval.

But if Ryoval's location was easy to find, they would have found it by now.

By God. I could be the first ImpSec agent on-site. He'd have to be sure and point that out, in his report to Illyan. He had looked forward to making posthumous reports to Illyan. Now he wondered if he was going to live long enough.

CHAPTER TWENTY-EIGHT

"**I** hate to be the one to tell you this, Baron," said the technician, "but your torture victim appears to be having a wonderful time."

Gorge grinned around the tube gagging his mouth as Baron Ryoval walked around him and stared. Admiring his amazing stomach, perhaps.

"There are a number of possible psychological defenses in these situations," Ryoval said. "Split personalities and identification with the captor included. I expected Naismith to work through them all, eventually, but—so soon?"

"I didn't believe it either, sir, so I took a series of brain scans. The results were unusual."

"If his personality is indeed splitting, it should show up on the scan."

"*Something* shows up on the scan. He seems to be shielding portions of his mind from our stimuli, and his surface responses certainly suggest a split, but . . . the pattern is abnormally abnormal, if that makes sense, sir."

"Not really." Ryoval pursed his lips with interest. "I'll take a look at them."

"Whatever is going on, he's not faking it. That I am sure of."

"So impossibly fast . . ." murmured Ryoval. "When do you think he snapped? How could I have missed it?"

"I'm not sure. Early. The first day—maybe the first hour. But if he keeps it up, he's going to be very elusive, to bring much force to bear upon. He can keep . . . changing shifts."

"So can I," stated Ryoval coldly.

The pressure in his stomach was growing into pain. Howl prodded anxiously, but Gorge would not give way. It was still his turn. The Other listened attentively. The fourth one always listened, when Baron Ryoval was present. Rarely slept, almost never spoke.

"I didn't expect him to reach this stage of disintegration for months. It throws off my time-table," the Baron complained.

Yes, Baron. Aren't we fascinating? Don't we intrigue you?

"I must consider how best to re-focus him," Ryoval mused. "Bring him to my quarters later. I'll see what a little quiet conversation and a few experiments will yield, in the way of new directions."

Beneath his flattened affect, the Other shivered in anticipation.

Two guards delivered him/them to Baron Ryoval's pleasant living room. There were no windows, though a large holovid display took up most of one wall, presently running a view of some tropical beach. But Ryoval's quarters were surely underground. Nobody would break through windows here.

His skin was still patchy. The techs had sprayed the raw areas with some kind of coating, to keep him from oozing on Ryoval's fine furniture, and dressed the other wounds with plastic bandage, so they wouldn't break open and bleed and stain.

"Think this'll do any good?" the tech with the sprayer had asked.

"Probably not," his comrade had sighed. "I suppose I'd better go ahead and put a cleaning crew on call. Wish he'd put down a tarp or something."

The guards sat him now in a low, wide chair. It was just a chair, no spikes or razors or impalements. His hands were fastened behind him, which meant he could not settle back. He spread his knees and sat uncomfortably upright, panting.

The senior guard asked Ryoval, "Do you wish us to secure him, sir?"

Ryoval raised an eyebrow. "Can he stand up without help?"

"Not readily, from that position."

Ryoval's lips crooked up in amused contempt, as he gazed down at his prisoner. "Ah, we're getting there. Slowly. Leave us. I'll call you. Don't interrupt. It may become noisy."

"Your soundproofing is very effective, sir." The flat-faced guards saluted and withdrew. There was something wrong with those guards. When not following orders, they tended to just sit, or stand, wordless and blank. Constructed that way, no doubt.

Gorge and Grunt and Howl and the Other stared around with interest, wondering whose turn it was going to be next.

You just had your turn, said Howl to Gorge. *It'll be me.*

Don't bet on it, said Grunt. *Could be me.*

If it weren't for Gorge, said the Other, grimly, *I'd take my turn right now. Now I have to wait.*

You've never taken a turn, said Gorge curiously. But the Other was silent again.

"Let's watch a show," said Ryoval, and touched a remote. The tropic display changed to a life-sized vid recording of one of Grunt's sessions with the . . . creatures, from the bordello. Grunt watched himself with great interest and delight, from all these new angles. Gorge's work was gradually threatening to put many interesting events out of sight, below his equator.

"I am thinking of sending a copy of this to the Dendarii mercenary fleet," Ryoval murmured, watching him. "Imagine all your senior staff officers, viewing this. I think it would fetch a few to me, no?"

No. Ryoval was lying. His presence here was still secret, or he wouldn't *be* present here. And Ryoval could be in no rush to give that secret away. The Other muttered dryly, *Send a copy to Simon Illyan, why don't you, and see what that fetches you.* But Illyan belonged to Lord Mark, and Mark wasn't here, and anyway, the Other never, ever, ever spoke aloud.

"Imagine that pretty bodyguard of yours, joining you here . . ." Ryoval went on, in detail. Grunt was perfectly willing to imagine some parts of it, though other parts offended even him. *Howl?*

Not me! said Howl. *That's not my job.*

We'll just have to make a new recruit, they all said. He could make a thousand of them, at need. He was an army, flowing like water, parting around obstacles, impossible to destroy with any one cut.

The vid display changed to one of Howl's finest moments, the one which had given him his name. Shortly after he'd been chemically skinned, the techs had painted sticky stuff on him that made him itch unbearably. The techs hadn't had to touch him. He'd almost killed himself. They'd given him a transfusion afterwards, to replace the blood lost in the raking wounds.

He stared impassively at the convulsing creature in the vid. The show that Ryoval wanted to see was himself. Looking at him right now must have all the drama and excitement of watching a test-pattern. Boring. Ryoval looked as if he wanted to aim the remote at him, and switch programs.

The Other waited with growing impatience. He was beginning to get his breath back, but there was still the damned low chair to contend with. It had to be tonight. By the next opportunity, if any ever came, Gorge might have immobilized them all. Yes. He waited.

Ryoval's lips puffed with disappointment, watching his serene profile. He shut the vid off and rose, and walked around the chair, studying him through narrowed eyes. "You're not even with me, are you? You've gone up around some bend. I must think what will bring you back to me. Or should I say, you all."

Ryoval was much too perceptive.

I don't trust you, said Gorge to the Other, doubtfully. *What will happen to me, after?*

And me, added Grunt. Only Howl said nothing. Howl was very tired.

I promise Mark will still feed you, Gorge, the Other whispered, from deep inside. *At least now and then. And Grunt. Mark could take you to Beta Colony. There are people there who could help you clean up enough to come out in the daylight, I think. You wouldn't need Ryoval's hypospray. Poor Howl is all exhausted anyway, he's worked the hardest, covering for the rest of you lot. Anyway, Grunt, what if Ryoval decides on castration next? Maybe you and Howl can get together, and Mark could rent you a squad of beautiful women— wouldn't women be a lovely change?—with whips and chains. This is Jackson's Whole, I bet you could find some in the vid directory. You don't need Ryoval. We save Mark, and he'll save us. I promise.*

Who are you, to pledge Mark's word? said Gorge grumpily.

I am the closest to him.

You've certainly hidden out the best, said Howl, with a hint of resentment.

It was necessary. But we will all perish, one by one, as Ryoval hunts us down. He's terribly sharp. We are the originals. The new recruits would only be distorted shadows of us anyway.

This was true, they all could see.

"I'm bringing you a friend to play with," Ryoval commented, walking around him. Having Ryoval behind him had some odd effects on his internal topography. Gorge flattened, Howl emerged, then sank again as Ryoval came back in view. Grunt watched alertly for his cues, rocking just slightly. "Your clone-twin. The one my stupid squad failed to take along."

Deep down inside, Lord Mark came wide awake, screaming. The Other smothered him up. *He lies. He lies.*

"Their fumble proved to be a costly error, for which they will pay. Your double vanished, then somehow turned up with Vasa Luigi. A typically smooth bit of sleight of hand on Vasa's part. I'm still not convinced dear Lotus doesn't have a private line of some kind into the Durona Group."

Ryoval circled him again. It was very disorienting. "Vasa is quite convinced his twin is the Admiral, and you are the clone. He has infected me with his doubts, though if as he claims the man is indeed cryo-amnesic, it could prove most disappointing even if he's right. But it doesn't matter now. I have you both. Just as I predicted. Can you guess what is the first thing I shall have you two do to each other?"

Grunt could. Spot-on, though not with the whispered refinements Ryoval added.

Lord Mark raged, wept with terror and dismay. Not a vibration rippled Grunt's slack-mouthed surface, nor marred the flat glisten of his eyes with any inner purpose. *Wait,* begged the Other.

The Baron walked to a counter or bar, made of some zebra-grained, polished wood, and unwrapped an array of glittering tools, which no one could quite see, though Howl stretched his neck. Meditatively, Ryoval looked his kit over.

You have to stay out of my way. And not sabotage me, said the Other. *I know Ryoval gives you what you hunger for—but it's a trick.*

Ryoval doesn't feed you, said Gorge.

Ryoval is my food, whispered the Other.

You'll only get one chance, said Howl nervously. *And then they'll come after me.*

I only need one chance.

Ryoval turned back. A surgical hand-tractor gleamed in his grip. Grunt, frightened, gave way to the Other.

"I believe," said Ryoval, "that I will pull out one of your eyes, next. Just one. That should have some interesting psychological focusing effects, when I threaten the remaining one."

Smoothly, Howl gave way. Last of all, reluctantly, Gorge gave way, as Ryoval walked toward them.

Killer's first attempt to struggle to his feet failed, and he fell back. *Damn you, Gorge.* He tried again, shifted his weight forward, heaved up, stepped once, half-unbalanced without the use of his arms to save himself. Ryoval watched, highly amused, unalarmed by the waddling little monster he doubtless thought he had created.

Trying to work around Gorge's new belly was something like being the Blind Zen Archer. But his alignment was absolute.

His first kick took Ryoval in the crotch. This folded him neatly over, and put his upper body within practical range. He flowed instantly into the second kick, striking Ryoval squarely in the throat. He could feel cartilage and tissue crunch all the way back to Ryoval's spine. Since he was not wearing steel-capped boots this time, it also broke several of his toes, smashed up and down at right angles. He felt no pain. That was Howl's job.

He fell over. Getting up again wasn't easy, with his hands still shackled behind him. Wallowing around on the floor trying to get his legs under himself, he saw with disappointment that Ryoval wasn't dead yet. The man writhed and gurgled and clutched his throat, on the carpet next to him. But the room's computer control did not recognize the Baron's voice commands now. They had a little time yet.

He rolled near to Ryoval's ear. "I am *too* a Vorkosigan. The one who was trained as a deep-penetration mole and assassin. It really pisses me off when people underestimate me, y'know?"

He managed to get back on his feet, and studied the problem, which was, Ryoval was still alive. He sighed, swallowed, stepped forward, and pounded the man with repeated blows of his feet till Ryoval stopped vomiting blood, convulsing, and breathing. It was a nauseating process, but in all, he was very relieved that there seemed no part of himself who actually enjoyed it. Even Killer had to muster a determined professionalism, to see it through to the end.

He considered the Other, whom he now recognized as Killer. *Galen made you, mostly, didn't he?*

Yes. But he didn't make me out of nothing.

You did very well. Hiding out. Stalking. I'd wondered if any of us possessed any sense of timing at all. I'm glad at least one of us does.

It was what the Count our Father said, Killer admitted, pleased and embarrassed to be praised. *That people would give themselves to you, if you waited them out, and didn't rush to give yourself to them. And I did. And Ryoval did.* He added shyly, *The Count's a killer too, you know. Like me.*

Hm.

He pulled his wrists against the shackles, and limped over to the zebra-wood counter to study Ryoval's kit. The selection included a laser-drill, as well as a sickening assortment of knives, scapels, tongs, and probes. The drill was a short-focal-range surgical type suitable for cutting bone, a dubious weapon, but a most suitable tool.

He wobbled around and tried to pick it up, behind his back. He almost wept when he dropped it. He was going to have to get down on the floor again. Awkwardly, he did so, and lumbered around till he managed to grub up the drill. It took many minutes of fiddling, but at last he got it turned around and aimed in such a way as to cut through his shackles without either slicing his hand off, or burning himself in the butt. Released, he flung his arms around his swollen torso, and rocked himself like someone rocking a weary child. His foot was starting to throb. The assorted mass vectors had apparently also combined to wrench his back, when he'd kicked Ryoval in the throat.

He stared, aside, at his victim/tormentor/prey. *Clone-consumer.* He felt apologetic toward the body he had pummeled underfoot. *It wasn't your fault. You died, what, ten years ago?* It was the one up top, inside the skull, who had been his enemy.

An illogical fear possessed him that Ryoval's guards would break in, and save their master even in death. He crawled over, much easier now that he had his hands free, took the laser-drill, and made certain that no one would be transplanting that brain again, ever. No one, no way.

He sagged back into the low chair, and sat in utter exhaustion, waiting to die. Ryoval's men surely had orders to avenge their fallen lord.

No one came.

. . . Right. The boss had locked himself in his quarters with a prisoner and a surgical kit, and told his goons not to bother him. How long before one worked up the courage to interrupt his little hobby? Could be . . . quite a long time.

The weight of hope returning was an almost intolerable burden, like walking on a broken bone. *I don't want to move.* He was very angry with ImpSec for abandoning him here, but thought he might forgive them everything if only they would charge in *now*, and waft him away without any further exertion or effort on his part. *Haven't I earned a break?* The room grew very silent.

That was over-kill, he thought, staring down at Ryoval's body. *A trifle unbalanced, that. And you've made a mess on the carpet. I don't know what to do next.*

Who was speaking? Killer? Gorge, Grunt? Howl? All of them? *You're good troops, and loyal, but not too bright.*

Bright is not our job.

It was time for Lord Mark to wake up. Had he ever really been asleep?

"All right, gang," he muttered aloud, enfolding himself. "Everybody up." The low chair was a torture-device in its own right. Ryoval's last snide dig. With a groan, he regained his feet.

It was impossible that an old fox like Ryoval would have only one entrance to his den. He poked around the underground suite. Office, living room, small kitchen, big bedroom, and a rather oddly equipped bathroom. He gazed longingly at the shower. He had not been allowed to bathe since he'd been brought here. But he was afraid it might wash off the plastic skin. He did brush his teeth. His gums were bleeding, but that was all right. He drank a little cold water. *At least I'm not hungry.* He vented a small cackle.

He found the emergency exit at last in the back of the bedroom closet.

If it's not guarded, stated Killer, *it must be booby-trapped.*

Ryoval's main defenses will work from the outside in, said Lord Mark slowly. *From the inside out, it will be set up to facilitate a quick escape. For Ryoval. And Ryoval alone.*

It was palm-locked. Palm-lock pads read pulse, temperature, and the electrical conductivity of the skin, as well as the whorls of fingerprints and grooves of life-lines. Dead hands didn't open palm-locks.

There are ways around palm locks, murmured Killer. Killer had been trained in such things once, in a previous incarnation. Lord Mark let go, and floated, watching.

The surgical array was almost as useful as an electronics kit, in Killer's hands. Given abundant time, and as long as the palm lock was never going to be required to work again. Lord Mark gazed dreamily as Killer loosened the sensor-pad from the wall, touched here, cut there.

The control virtual on the wall lit at last. *Ah,* murmured Killer proudly.

Oh, said the rest. The display projected a small glowing square.

It wants a code-key, said Killer in dismay. His panic at being trapped quickened their heart rate. Howl's tenuous containment loosened, and electrical twinges of pain coursed through them.

Wait, said Lord Mark. If they needed a code-key, so must Ryoval.

Baron Ryoval has no successor. Ryoval had no second-in-command, no trained replacement. He kept all his oppressed subordinates in separate channels of communication. House Ryoval consisted of

Baron Ryoval, and slaves, period. That's why House Ryoval failed to grow. Ryoval didn't delegate authority, ever.

Therefore, Ryoval had no place nor trusted subordinates with whom to leave his private code-keys. He had to carry them on his person. At all times.

The black gang whimpered as Lord Mark turned around and returned to the living room. Mark ignored them. *This is my job, now.*

He turned Ryoval's body over on its back and searched it methodically from head to toe, down to the skin and farther. He missed no possibility, not even hollow teeth. He sat back uncomfortably, distended belly aching, sprained back on fire. His level of pain was rising as he re-integrated, which made it a very tentative process. *It has to be here. It has to be here somewhere.*

Run, run, run, the black gang gibbered, in a remarkably unified chorus.

Shut up and let me think. He turned Ryoval's right hand over in his own. A ring with a flat black stone gleamed in the light. . . .

He laughed out loud.

He swallowed the laugh fearfully, looking around. The Baron's soundproofing held, apparently. The ring would not slide off. Stuck? Riveted to the bone? He cut off Ryoval's right hand with the laser drill. The laser also cauterized the wrist, so it wasn't too drippy. Nice. He limped slowly and painfully back to the bedroom closet and stared at the little glowing square, just the size of the ring's stone.

Which way up? Would the wrong rotation trigger an alarm?

Lord Mark pantomimed Baron Ryoval in a hurry. Slap the palm lock, turn his hand over and jam the ring into the code slot— "This way," he whispered.

The door slid open on a personal lift tube. It extended upward some twenty meters. Its antigrav control pads glowed, green for up, red for down. Lord Mark and Killer gazed around. No obvious defenses, such as a tanglefield generator. . . .

A faint draft brought a scent of fresh air from above. *Let's go!* screamed Gorge and Grunt and Howl.

Lord Mark stood spraddle-legged and stodgy, staring, refusing to be rushed. *It has no safety ladder,* he said at last.

So what?

So. What?

Killer sagged back, and muffled the rest of them, and waited respectfully.

I want a safety ladder, muttered Lord Mark querulously. He turned away, and wandered back through Ryoval's quarters. While he was at it, he looked for clothes. There wasn't much to choose from; this clearly was not Ryoval's main residence. Just a private suite. The garments were all too long and not wide enough. The trousers were impossible. A soft knit shirt stretched over his raw skin, though. A loose jacket, left open, provided some more protection. A Betan-style sarong, bath-wear, wrapped his loins. A pair of slippers were sloppy on his left foot, tight on his swollen, broken right foot. He searched for cash, keys, anything else of use. But there was no handy climbing gear.

I'll just have to make my own safety ladder. He hung the laser drill around his neck on a tie made from a couple of Ryoval's belts, stepped into the bottom of the lift tube, and systematically began to burn holes in the plastic side.

Too slow! the black gang wailed. Howl howled inside, and even Killer screamed, *Run, dammit!*

Lord Mark ignored them. He turned on the "up" field, but did not let it take them. Clinging to his hot hand and foot holds, he pocked his way upward. It was not difficult to climb, buoyed in the flowing grav field, only hard to remember to keep his three points of contact. His right foot was nearly useless. The black gang gibbered in fear. Mulish and methodical, Mark ascended. Melt a hole. Wait. Move a hand, foot, hand, foot. Melt another hole. Wait. . . .

Three meters from the top, his head came level with a small audio pick-up, flush to the wall, and a shielded motion sensor.

I imagine it wants a code word. In Ryoval's voice, Lord Mark remarked blandly, observing. *Can't oblige.*

It doesn't have to be what you guess, Killer said. *It could be anything. Plasma arcs. Poison gas.*

No. Ryoval saw me, but I saw Ryoval. It will be simple. And elegant. And you will do it to yourself. Watch.

He gripped his handhold, and extended the laser drill up past the motion sensor for the next burn.

The lift tube's grav field switched off.

Even half-expecting it, he was nearly ripped from his perch by his own weight. Howl could not contain it all. Mark screamed silently, flooded in pain. But he clung, and did not let them fall.

The last three meters of ascent could have been called a nightmare, but he had new standards for nightmares now. It was merely tedious.

There was a tanglefield trap at the top entrance, but it faced outward. The laser drill disarmed its controls. He managed a crippled, shuffling, crabwise walk into a private underground garage. It contained the Baron's lightflyer. The canopy opened at the touch of Ryoval's ring.

He slid into the lightflyer, adjusted the seat and controls as best he could around his distorted and aching contours, powered it up, eased it forward. That button on the control panel—there? The garage door slid aside. Once through, he shot up, and up, and up, through the dark, the acceleration pummeling him. Nobody even fired on him. There were no lights below. A rocky winter waste. The whole little installation must be underground.

He checked the flyer's map display, and picked his direction— *East.* Toward the light. That seemed right.

He kept accelerating.

CHAPTER TWENTY-NINE

The lightflyer banked. Miles craned his neck, catching a glimpse of what was below. Or what wasn't below. Dawn was creeping over a wintry desert. There appeared to be nothing of interest for kilometers around.

"'S funny," said the guard who was piloting the lightflyer. "Door's open." He touched his comm, and transmitted some sort of code-burst. The other guard shifted uneasily, watching his comrade. Miles twisted around, trying to watch them both.

They descended. Rocks rose around them, then a concrete shaft. Ah. Concealed entrance. They came to the bottom, and moved forward into an underground garage.

"Huh," said the other guard. "Where's all the vehicles?"

The flyer came to rest, and the bigger guard dragged Miles out of the backseat, and unfastened his ankles, and stood him upright. He almost fell down again. The scars on his chest ached with the strain from his hands bound behind his back. He got his feet under himself and stared around much as the guards were doing. Just a utilitarian garage, badly-lit, echoing and cavernous. And empty.

The guards marched him toward an entrance. They coded through some automatic doors, and walked to an electronic security chamber. It was up and running, humming blankly. "Vaj?" one guard called. "We're here. Scan us."

No answer. One of the guards went forward, looked around. Tapped a code into a wall pad. "Bring him through anyway."

The security chamber passed him. He was still wearing the gray knits the Duronas had given him; no interesting devices woven into the fabric, it seemed, alas.

The senior guard tried an intercom. Several times. "Nobody answers."

"What should we do?" asked his comrade.

The senior man frowned. "Strip him and take him to the boss, I guess. Those were the orders."

They pulled his ship-knits off him; he was far too out-massed to fight them, but he regretted the loss deeply. It was too damned cold. Even the ox-like guards stared a moment at his raked and scored chest. They re-fastened his hands behind him and marched him through the facility, their eyes shifting warily at every intersection.

It was very quiet. Lights burned, but no people appeared anywhere. A strange structure, not very large, plain and—he sniffed—decidedly medical in odor. Research, he decided. Ryoval's private biological research facility. Evidently, after the Dendarii raid of four years ago, Ryoval had decided his main facility wasn't secure enough. Miles could see that. This place did not have the business-air of the other locale. It felt military-paranoid. The sort of place where if you went there to work, you didn't come out again for years at a time. Or, considering Ryoval, ever. He glimpsed a few lab-like rooms, in passing. But no techs. The guards called out, a couple of times. No one answered.

They came to an open door, beyond which lay some sort of study or office. "Baron, sir?" the senior guard ventured. "We have your prisoner."

The other guard rubbed his neck. "If he's not here, should we go ahead and work him like the other one?"

"He hasn't ordered it yet. Better wait."

Quite. Ryoval was not the sort to reward initiative in subordinates, Miles suspected.

With a deep, nervous sigh, the senior man stepped across the threshold and looked around. The junior man prodded Miles forward in his wake. The study was finely furnished, with a real wood desk, and an odd chair in front of it with metal wrist-locks for the person who sat in it. Nobody ran out on a conversation with Baron Ryoval till Baron Ryoval was ready, apparently. They waited.

"What do we do now?"

"Don't know. This is as far as my orders went." The senior man paused. "Could be a test. . . ."

They waited about five more minutes.

"If you don't want to look around," said Miles brightly, "I will."

They looked at each other. The senior man, his forehead creased, drew a stunner and sidled cautiously through an archway into the next room. His voice came back after a moment. "*Shit.*" And, after another moment, an odd mewling wail, cut off and swallowed.

This was too much even for the dim bulb who held Miles. With his ham hand still locked firmly around Miles's upper arm, the second guard followed the first into a large chamber arranged as a living room. A wall-sized holovid was blank and silent. A zebra-grained wood bar divided the room. An extremely low chair faced an open area. Baron Ryoval's very dead body lay there face-up, naked, staring at the ceiling with dry eyes.

There were no obvious signs of a struggle—no overturned furniture, nor plasma arc burns in the walls—except upon the body. There the marks of violence were focused, utterly concentrated: throat crushed, torso pulped, dried blood smeared around his mouth. A double line of fingertip-sized black dots were stitched neatly across the Baron's forehead. They looked like burns. His right hand was missing, cut away, the wrist a cauterized stump.

The guards twitched in something like horror, an all-too-temporary paralysis of astonishment. "What happened?" whispered the junior man.

Which way will they jump?

How did Ryoval control his employee/slaves, anyway? The lesser folk, through terror, of course; the middle-management and tech layer, through some subtle combination of fear and self-interest. But these, his personal bodyguards, must be the innermost cadre, the ultimate instrument by which their master's will was forced upon all the rest.

They could not be as mentally stunted as their stolidity suggested, or they would be useless in an emergency. But if their narrow minds were intact, it followed that they must be controlled through their emotions. Men whom Ryoval let stand behind him with activated weapons must be programmed to the max, probably from birth. Ryoval must be father, mother, family and all to them. Ryoval must be their god.

But now their god was dead.

What would they do? Was *I am free* even an intelligible concept to them? Without its focal object, how fast would their programming start to break down? *Not fast enough.* An ugly light, compounded of rage and fear, was growing in their eyes.

"I didn't do it," Miles pointed out with quick prudence. "I was with you."

"Stay here," growled the senior man. "I'll reconnoiter." He loped off through the Baron's apartment, to return in a few minutes with a laconic, "His flyer's gone. Lift tube defenses buggered all to hell, too."

They hesitated. Ah, the downside of perfect obedience: crippled initiative.

"Hadn't you better check around the facility?" Miles suggested. "There might be survivors. Witnesses. Maybe . . . maybe the assassin is still hiding somewhere." *Where is Mark?*

"What do we do with *him*?" asked the junior man, with a jerk of his head at Miles.

The senior man scowled in indecision. "Take him along. Or lock him up. Or kill him."

"You don't know what the Baron wanted me for," Miles interrupted instantly. "Better take me along till you find out."

"He wanted you for the other one," said the senior man, with an indifferent glance down at him. Little, naked, half-healed, with his hands bound behind him, the guards clearly did not perceive him as a threat. *Too right. Hell.*

After a brief muttered conference, the junior man pushed him along, and they began as rapid and methodical a tour of the facility as Miles would have wished to make himself. They found two of their red-and-black uniformed comrades, dead. A mysterious pool of blood snaked across a corridor from wall to wall. They found another body, fully dressed as a senior tech, in a shower, the back of his head crushed with some blunt object. On descending levels they found more signs of struggle, of looting, and of by-no-means-random destruction, comconsoles and equipment smashed.

Had it been a slave revolt? Some power struggle among factions? Revenge? All three simultaneously? Was the murder of Ryoval its cause, or its goal? Had there been a mass evacuation, or a mass killing? At every corner, Miles braced himself for a scene of carnage.

The lowest level had a laboratory with half a dozen glass-walled cells lining one end. From the smell, some experiment had been left cooking far too long. He glanced into the cells and swallowed.

They had been human, once, those lumps of flesh, scar tissue, and growths. They were now . . . culture-dishes of some kind. Four had been female, two male. Some departing tech, as an act of mercy, had neatly cut each one's throat. He eyed them desperately, his face pressed to the glass. Surely they were all too large to have been Mark. Surely such effects could not have been achieved in a mere five days. Surely. He did not want to enter the cells for a closer examination.

At least it explained why more of Ryoval's slaves did not try to resist. There was an air of awful ecomony about it. Don't like your work in the bordello, girl? Sick of the boredom and brutality of being a guard, man? How would you like to go into scientific research? The last stop for any would-be Spartacus among Ryoval's human possessions. *Bel was right. We should have nuked this place the last time we were here.*

The guards gave the cells a brief glance, and pressed on. Miles hung back, seized by inspiration. It was worth a try. . . .

"*Shit!*" Miles hissed, and jumped.

The guards spun around.

"That . . . that man in there. He moved. I think I'm going to vomit."

"Can't have." The senior guard stared through the transparent wall at a body which lay with its back to them.

"He couldn't possibly have witnessed anything from in there, could he?" said Miles. "For God's sake, don't open the door."

"Shut up." The senior guard chewed his lip, stared at the control virtual, and after an irresolute moment, coded open the door and trod cautiously within.

"Gah!" said Miles.

"What?" snapped the junior guard.

"He moved again. He, he, sort of spasmed."

The junior man drew his stunner and followed his comrade inside, covering him. The senior man extended his hand, faltered, and on second thought pulled his shock stick from his belt and prodded it warily toward the body.

Miles smacked the door control with a duck of his forehead. The glass seal slid shut, barely in time. The guards smashed into the door and up it like rabid dogs. It barely transmitted the vibration. Their mouths were open, howling curses and threats at him, but no sound passed. The transparent walls must be space-grade material; it stopped stunner fire, too.

The senior man pulled out a plasma arc and began burning.

The wall started to glow slightly. Not good. Miles studied the control panel . . . there. He pushed at menu blocks with his tongue till it brought up *oxygen*, and re-set it down as far as it would go. Would the guards pass out before the wall gave way to the plasma arc?

Yes. Good environmental system, that. Ryoval's dogs crumpled against the glass, clawed hands relaxing in unconsciousness. The plasma arc fell from nerveless fingers, and shut off.

Miles left them sealed in their victim's tomb.

It was a lab. There had to be cutters, and tools of all sorts . . . right. It took several minutes of contortions, working behind his back, during which he nearly passed out, but his shackles gave way at last. He whimpered with relief as his hands came free.

Weapons? All weapons *per se* had been taken, apparently, by the departing inhabitants, and without a biotainer suit he was disinclined to re-open the glass cell and retrieve the guards' gear. But a laser-scalpel from the lab made him feel less vulnerable.

He wanted his clothing. Shivering from the cold, he trotted back through the eerie corridors to the security entrance, and donned his knits again. He turned back into the facility, and began to seriously search. He tried every comconsole he came to that wasn't smashed. All were internally dedicated, no way to tap an outside channel.

Where is Mark? It occured to him suddenly that if there could be anything worse than being held prisoner in some cell here, waiting for his tormentors to come again, it would be to be locked in a cell here waiting for tormentors who *never* came again. In what was perhaps the most frantic half-hour he'd ever experienced in his life, he opened or broke open every door in the facility. Behind every one he expected to find a sodden little body, its throat mercifully cut . . . He was wheezing and fearing another convulsion when, with great relief, he found the cell—closet—near Ryoval's quarters. Empty. It stank of recent occupation, though. And the bloodstains and other stains on the walls and floor turned his stomach cold and sick. But wherever Mark was, and in whatever condition, he was not here. He had to get out of here too.

He caught his breath, and found a plastic basket, and went shopping in the labs for useful electronic equipment. Cutters and wires, circuit-diagnostics, readers and relays, whatever he could find. When he thought he had enough, he returned to the Baron's study, and proceeded to dissect the damaged comconsole. He finally managed to jump the palm-lock, only to have a little bright square patch come up on-view and demand, *Insert code-key.* He cursed, and stretched his aching back, and sat again. This was going to be tedious.

It took another pass through the facility for equipment before he was able to jump the code-key block. And the comconsole would never be the same. But at last, finally, he punched through to the planetary communications net. There was another short glitch while he figured out how to charge the call to House Ryoval's account; all fees were collected in advance, here on Jackson's Whole.

He paused a moment, wondering who to call. Barrayar kept a consulate on the Hargraves-Dyne Consortium Station. Some of the staff were actually diplomatic and/or economic personnel, but even they doubled as ImpSec analysts. The rest were agents-proper, running a thin network of informants scattered across the planet and its satellites and stations. Admiral Naismith had a contact there. But had ImpSec been here already? Was this their work, rescuing Mark? No, he decided. It was ruthless, but not nearly methodical enough. In fact, it was utter chaos.

So why didn't you guys come looking for Mark? A bothersome question, and one to which he had no answer. He punched through the consulate's code. *Let the circus begin.*

They were down on him in half an hour, a tense ImpSec lieutenant named Iverson with a rented squad of local muscle from House Dyne in paramilitary uniforms and with decent military equipment. They'd dropped straight from orbit in a shuttle; heat wavered off its skin in the watery morning light. Miles sat on a rock outside the pedestrian entrance, or more properly speaking, emergency exit he'd found, and watched sardonically as they all galloped out, weapons at the ready, and spread out as if to take the installation by assault.

The officer hurried up to him, and half-saluted. "Admiral Naismith?"

Iverson was no one he knew; at this level of the echelon the man must take him for a valued, but non-Barrayaran, ImpSec hireling. "The one and only. You can tell your men to relax. The installation is secured."

"You secured it yourself?" Iverson asked in faint disbelief.

"More or less."

"We've been looking for this place for two years!"

Miles suppressed an irate remark about people who couldn't find their own prick with a map and a hand-light. "Where is, ah, Mark? The other clone. My double."

"We don't know, sir. Acting on a tip from an informant, we were about to make an assault on a House Bharaputra location to retrieve you, when you called."

"I was there last night. Your informant did not know I was moved." Had to be Rowan—she'd got out, hooray! "You would have been embarrassingly late."

Iverson's lips thinned. "This has been an incredibly fouled-up operation from first to last. The orders kept changing."

"Tell me," Miles sighed. "Have you heard anything from the Dendarii Mercenaries?"

"A covert ops team from your outfit is supposed to be on its way, sir." Iverson's "sirs" were tinged with uncertainty, the dubious regard of a Barrayaran regular for a self-promoted mercenary. "I . . . wish to ascertain for myself if the installation is fully secure, if you don't mind."

"Go ahead," Miles said. "You'll find it an interesting tour. If you have a strong stomach." Iverson marched his troopers indoors. Miles would have laughed, if he weren't screaming inside. He sighed, slipped from his perch, and followed them.

Miles's people came in a small personnel shuttle, swooping right into the concealed garage. He watched them on the monitor from Ryoval's study, and gave them directions how to find him. Quinn, Elena, Taura and Bel, all in half-armor. They came clanking into the study double-time, almost as impressively useless as the ImpSec crowd.

"Why the party clothes?" was his first weary question as they heaved into view. He should stand, and receive and return salutes and things, but Ryoval's station chair was incredibly comfortable and he was incredibly tired.

"Miles!" Quinn cried passionately.

With the sight of her concerned face he realized just how very angry he was, and guilty for it. Furiously angry because furiously afraid. *Where is Mark, damn you all?* "Captain Quinn," he put her on notice that this was duty-time before she could fling herself on him. She skidded to a halt in mid-fling, and came to a species of attention. The others piled up behind her.

"We were just coordinating with ImpSec for a raid on House

Bharaputra," Quinn said breathlessly. "You've come back to yourself! You were cryo-amnesic—have you recovered? That Durona doctor said you would—"

"About ninety percent, I think. I'm still finding holes in my memory. Quinn—what *happened*?"

She looked slightly overwhelmed. "Since when? When you were killed—"

"Start from five days ago. When you came to the Durona Group."

"We came looking for you. *Found* you, after nearly four bleeding months!"

"You were stunned, Mark was taken, and Lilly Durona hustled me and my surgeon off to what she thought was going to be safety," Miles cued her to the focus he wanted.

"Oh, she was your *doctor*. I thought—never mind." Quinn bit back her emotions, pulled off her helmet and pushed back her hood, raked red-tipped fingers through her smashed curls, and began organizing the information into its essentials, combat-style. "We lost hours at the start. By the time Elena and Taura got another aircar, the snatchers were long gone. They searched, but no luck. When they got back to the Durona Group, Bel and I were just waking up. Lilly Durona insisted you were safe. I didn't believe her. We pulled out, and I contacted ImpSec. They started to pull in their people, who were scattered all over the planet looking for clues as to your whereabouts, and sent them to focus on Mark. More delays, while they worked through their pet theory that the kidnappers were Cetagandan bounty-hunters. And House Ryoval had about fifty different sites and facilities to check on, not including this one, which really was secret.

"Then Lilly Durona decided you were missing after all. Since it seemed more important to find you, we diverted all available forces to that. But we had fewer leads. We didn't even find the abandoned lightflyer for two days. And it yielded up *no* clues."

"Right. But you suspected Ryoval had Mark."

"But Ryoval wanted Admiral Naismith. We thought Ryoval would figure out he had the wrong man."

He ran his hands over his face. His head was aching. And so was his stomach. "Did you ever figure that Ryoval wouldn't *care*? In a few minutes, I want you to go down the corridor and look at the cell they kept him in. And smell it. I want you to look *closely*. In fact, go now. Sergeant Taura, stay."

Reluctantly, Quinn led Elena and Bel out. Miles leaned forward; Taura bent to hear.

"Taura, what happened? You're a Jacksonian. You know what Ryoval is, what this place is. How did you all lose sight of that?"

She shook her big head. "Captain Quinn thought Mark was a complete screw-up. After your death, she was so angry she could barely give him the time of day. And at first I agreed with her. But . . . I don't know. He tried so hard. The crèche raid only failed by a hair. If we'd been faster, or if the shuttle defense perimeter had done their job, we would have brought it off, I think."

He grimaced in agreement. "There's no mercy for failures of timing in no-margin operations like that one was. Commanders can have no mercy either, or you might as well stay in orbit and feed your troops directly into the ship's waste disintegrators, and save steps." He paused. "Quinn will be a good commander someday."

"I think so, sir." Taura pulled off her helmet and hood, and stared around. "I kind of came to like the little schmuck, though. He *tried*. He tried and failed, but no one else tried at all. And he was so alone."

"Alone. Yes. Here. For five days."

"We really did think Ryoval would figure out he wasn't you."

"Maybe . . . maybe so." Some part of his mind clung to that hope himself. Maybe it hadn't been as bad as it looked, as bad as his galloping imagination supplied.

Quinn and company returned, looking universally grim.

"So," he said, "you've found me. Now maybe we can all focus on Mark. I've been all over this place in the last hours, and I haven't found a clue. Did the absconding staff take him along? Is he out wandering around in the desert somewhere, freezing? I've got six of Iverson's men looking outside with 'scopes, and another one checking the facility's disintegration records for fifty-plus kilo lumps of protein. And other bright ideas, folks?"

Elena came back from a peek in the next room. "Who do you figure did the honors on Ryoval?"

Miles opened his hands. "Don't know. He had hundreds of mortal enemies, after his career."

"He was killed by an unarmed person. A kick to the throat, then beaten to death somehow after he was down."

"I noticed that."

"You notice the tool kit?"

"Yeah."

"Miles, it was Mark."

"How could it have been? It had to have happened sometime

last night. After what, five days of being worked over—and Mark's a little guy like me. I don't think it's physically possible."

"Mark's a little guy, but not like you," said Elena. "And he almost killed a man in Vorbarr Sultana with a kick to the throat."

"*What?*"

"He was *trained*, Miles. He was trained to take out your father, who is an even bigger man than Ryoval, and has years of combat experience."

"Yes, but I never believed—*when* was Mark in Vorbarr Sultana?" *Amazing, how being dead for two or three months will put you out of touch.* For the first time, his impulse to fling himself directly back into active-duty command status was checked. *A maniac with three-quarters of a memory and a habit of going into convulsions is just what we want in charge, sure. Not to mention the shortness of breath.*

"Oh, and about your father, I should mention—no, maybe that had better wait." Elena eyed him in worry.

"What about—" He was interrupted by a buzz from the comm link Iverson had given him as a courtesy. "Yes, Lieutenant?"

"Admiral Naismith, Baron Fell is here at the entrance. With a double-squad. He, ah . . . says he's here to collect his deceased half-brother's body, as next-of-kin."

Miles whistled soundlessly, and grinned. "Is he, now? Well. Tell you what. Let him come inside, with one bodyguard. And we'll talk. He may know something. Don't let his squad in yet, though."

"Do you think that's wise?"

How the hell should I know? "Sure."

In a few minutes, Baron Fell himself puffed in, escorted by one of Iverson's rental troopers and flanked by a big green-clad guard. Baron's Fell's round face was slightly pinker than usual with the exertion, otherwise he was the same plump, grandfatherly figure as ever, exuding the usual dangerously deceptive good cheer.

"Baron Fell." Miles nodded. "How good to see you again."

Fell nodded back. "Admiral. Yes, I imagine everything looks good to you just now. So, it really was you the Bharaputran sniper shot. Your clone-twin did an excellent job of pretending to be you, afterward, I must say, much to the confusion of an already very confused situation."

Argh! "Yes. And, ah, what brings you here?"

"Trade," stated Fell, Jacksonian short-hand for, *You first.*

Miles nodded. "The late Baron Ryoval had me brought me here in a lightflyer by two of his erstwhile bodyguards. We found things much as you see them. I, um, neutralized them at my first opportunity. How I came to be in their hands is a more complicated story." Meaning, *That's all you get till I get some.*

"There are some extraordinary rumors starting to circulate about my dear departed—he is departed, I trust?"

"Oh, yes. You can see in a moment."

"Thank you. My dear departed half-brother's death. I had one first-hand."

A former Ryoval employee from here fled directly to him as an informant. Right. "I hope his virtue was rewarded."

"It will be, as soon as I ascertain he was telling the truth."

"Well. Why don't you come look." He had to get up out of the station chair. He marshaled the effort with difficulty, and led the Baron into the living room, the House Fell bodyguard and the Dendarii following.

The big bodyguard shot a worried glance at Sergeant Taura, looming over him; she smiled back, her fangs gleaming. "Hi, there. You're kinda cute, you know?" she told him. He recoiled, and sidled closer to his master.

Fell hurried to the body, knelt by its right side, and held up the severed wrist. He hissed with disappointment. "Who has done this?"

"We don't know yet," said Miles. "That's how I found him."

"Exactly?" Fell shot him a sharp glance.

"Yes."

Fell traced the black holes across the corpse's forehead. "Whoever did this, knew what he was doing. I want to find the assassin."

"To . . . avenge your brother's death?" Elena asked cautiously.

"No. To offer him a *job!*" Fell laughed, a booming, jolly sound. "Do you realize how many people have been trying, for how many years, to accomplish this?"

"I've an idea," said Miles. "If you can help—"

In the next room, Ryoval's half-butchered comconsole chimed.

Fell looked up, eyes intent. "No one can call in here without the code-key," he stated, and heaved to his feet. Miles barely beat him back into the study, and slid into the station chair.

He activated the vid plate. "Yes?" And almost fell out of his seat again.

Mark's puffy face formed above the vid plate. He looked as if he'd just come out of a shower, face scrubbed, hair wet and slicked back. He was wearing gray knits like Miles's. Blue bruises, going greenish-yellow around the edges, made what skin Miles could see look like a patch-work quilt, but both eyes were open and very bright. His ears were still on. "Ah," he said cheerfully, "there you are. I thought you might be. Have you figured out who you are yet?"

"Mark!" Miles almost tried to crawl through the vid image. "Are you all right? *Where are you?*"

"You have, I see. Good. I'm at Lilly Durona's. God, Miles. What a place. What a woman. She let me have a *bath*. She put my *skin* back on. She fixed my foot. She gave me a hypo of muscle-relaxant for my back. With her own hands, she performed medical services too intimate and disgusting to describe, but very badly needed, I assure you, and held my head while I screamed. Did I mention the bath? I love her, and I want to marry her."

All this was delivered with such dead-pan enthusiasm, Miles could not tell if Mark was joking. "What are you *on?*" he asked suspiciously.

"Pain killers. Lots and lots of pain killers. Oh, it's wonderful!" He favored Miles with a weird broad grin. "But don't worry, my head is perfectly clear. It's just the bath. I was holding it together till she gave me the bath. It unmanned me. Do you know what a wonderful thing a bath is, when you're washing off—never mind."

"How did you get out of here, and back to the Durona Clinic?" Miles asked urgently.

"In Ryoval's lightflyer, of course. The code-key worked."

Behind Miles, Baron Fell drew in his breath. "Mark." He leaned into the vid pick up with a smile. "Would you put Lilly on a moment, please?"

"Ah, Baron Fell!" said Mark. "Good. I was going to call you next. I want to invite you to tea, here at Lilly's. We have a lot to talk about. You too, Miles. And bring *all* your friends." Mark gave him a sharply meaningful glance.

Quietly, Miles reached down and pressed the "alert" button on Iverson's comm link. "Why, Mark?"

"Because I need them. My own troops are much too tired for any more work today."

"Your troops?"

"Please do as I ask. Because I ask it. Because you *owe* me," Mark added, in a voice so low Miles had to strain to hear. Mark's eyes burned, a brief spark.

Fell muttered, "He used it. He has to know—" He leaned in again, and said to Mark, "Do you know what you have in ah, hand, Mark?"

"Oh, Baron. I know what I'm doing. I don't know why so many people have so much trouble believing that," Mark added in a tone of hurt complaint. "I know *exactly* what I'm doing." Then he laughed. It was a very disturbing laugh, edgy and too loud.

"Let me talk to Lilly," said Fell.

"No. You come here and talk to Lilly," said Mark petulantly. "Anyway, you want to talk to me." He nailed Fell's eye with a direct look. "I promise you will find it profitable."

"I believe I do want to talk with you," murmured Fell. "Very well."

"Miles. You're there in Ryoval's study, where I was." Mark searched his face, for what Miles could not guess, but then Mark nodded quietly to himself, as if satisfied. "Is Elena there?"

"Yes . . ."

Elena leaned forward on Miles's other side. "What do you need, Mark?"

"I want to talk to you a moment. Armswoman. Privately. Would you clear the room of everyone else, please? Everyone."

"You can't," Miles began. " . . . Armswoman? Not—not liege-sworn? You can't be."

"Technically, I suppose she's not, now that you're alive again," said Mark. He smiled sadly. "But I want a service. My first and last request, Elena. *Privately.*"

Elena looked around. "Everybody out. Please, Miles. This is between Mark and me."

"Armswoman?" Miles muttered, allowing himself to be thrust back out into the corridor. "How can—" Elena shut the door on them all. Miles called Iverson to arrange transport, and other things. It was still a polite race with Fell, but it was clearly a race.

Elena emerged after a few minutes. Her face was strained. "You go on to Durona's. Mark has asked me to find something for him here. I'll catch up."

"Collect all the data you can for ImpSec while you're at it, then," said Miles, feeling bewildered by the pace of events. Somehow, he seemed not to be in charge here. "I'll tell Iverson to give you a free hand. But—Armswoman? Does that mean what I think it does? How can—"

"It means nothing, now. But I owe Mark. We all do. He killed Ryoval, you know."

"I was beginning to realize it had to be so. I just didn't see how."

"With both hands tied behind his back, he says. I believe him." She turned again toward Ryoval's suite.

"That was Mark?" Miles muttered, heading reluctantly in the opposite direction. He couldn't have acquired some other clone-brother while he was dead, could he? "It didn't sound like Mark. For one thing, he sounded like he was glad to see me. That's *Mark*?"

"Oh, yes," said Quinn. "That was Mark all right."

He quickened his pace. Even Taura had to lengthen her stride to keep up.

CHAPTER THIRTY

The Dendarii's little personnel shuttle kept pace with Baron Fell's larger drop shuttle; they arrived at the Durona Group's clinic almost simultaneously. A House Dyne shuttle belonging temporarily to ImpSec was waiting politely across the street from the entrance, by the little park. Just waiting.

As they were circling for a landing, Miles asked Quinn, who was piloting, "Elli—if we were flying along, in a lightflyer or an aircar or something, and I suddenly ordered you to crash it, would you?"

"Now?" asked Quinn, startled. The shuttle lurched.

"No! Not now. I mean theoretically. Obey, instantly, no questions asked."

"Well, sure, I suppose so. I'd ask questions afterward though. Probably with my hands wrapped around your neck."

"That's what I thought." Miles sat back, satisfied.

They rendezvoused with Baron Fell at the front entrance, where the gate guards prepared to code open a portal in the force screen. Fell frowned at the three Dendarii in their half-armor, Quinn and Bel and Taura, trailing Miles in his gray knits.

"This is my facility," Fell pointed out. His own pair of green-clad men eyed them without favor.

"These are my bodyguards," said Miles, "for whom I have a demonstrated need. Your force screen appears to have a malfunction."

"*He* was taken care of," said Fell grimly. "That won't happen again."

"Nevertheless." By way of concession, Miles jerked his thumb at the shuttle by the park. "My other friends can wait outside."

Fell frowned, thinking it over. "All right," he said at last. They followed him inside. Hawk met them, bowed to the Baron, and escorted them formally up through the series of lift tubes to Lilly Durona's penthouse.

The word for it, Miles thought, rising past the chromium railing, was "tableau." It was all arranged as perfectly as any stage setting.

Mark was the centerpiece. He sat back comfortably in Lilly Durona's own chair, his bandaged right foot propped on a silk pillow on the low round tea table. Surrounded by Duronas. Lilly herself, her white hair braided today like a crown wreathing her head, stood at Mark's right hand, leaning bemusedly on the upholstered chair back, smiling down beneficently upon the top of his head. Hawk took up position on Mark's left side. Dr. Chrys, Dr. Poppy, and Dr. Rose clustered admiringly around them. Dr. Chrys had a large fire-extinguisher by her knee. Rowan was not here. The window had been repaired.

On the center of the table sat a transparent cold-box. Within it lay a severed hand wearing a big silver ring set with what appeared to be a square black onyx.

Mark's physical appearance disturbed Miles. He had been braced to witness traumas of unnamed tortures, but Mark was covered neck to ankle in concealing gray knits like his own. Only the bruises on his face and the bandage on his foot hinted at the past five days' activities. But his face and body were strangely and unhealthily bloated, his stomach shockingly so, more than the stoutly-balanced figure he'd seen here in Dendarii uniform just a few days ago, and far beyond the almost-duplicate of himself he'd tried to rescue from the raid on the clone crèche four months ago. In another person, Baron Fell for example, the near-obesity wouldn't have made him even blink, but Mark . . . could this be Miles himself, someday, if he slowed down? He had a sudden urge to swear off desserts. Elli was frankly staring, horrified and repelled.

Mark was smiling. A little control box lay under his right hand. His index finger kept pressure on a button.

Baron Fell saw the cold-box containing the hand, and started for it, crying, "Ah!"

"Stop," said Mark.

The Baron stopped, and cocked his head at him. "Yes?" he said warily.

"The object you are interested in is sitting in that sealed box on top of a small thermal grenade. Controlled," he lifted his hand with the remote in it, "by this dead-man switch. There is a second, positive-control switch in the hands of another person, outside of this room. Stun me or jump me, and it will go off. Frighten me, and my hand might slip. Tire me out, and my finger might give way. Annoy me enough, and I might just let go for the hell of it."

"The fact that you have made such an arrangement," said Fell slowly, "tells me you know the value of what you hold. You wouldn't. You're bluffing." He stared piercingly at Lilly.

"Don't try me," said Mark, still smiling. "After five days of your half-brother's hospitality, I'm in a *real* hostile mood. What's in that box is valuable to you. Not to me. However," he took a breath, "you do have some things that are valuable to me. Baron, let's Deal."

Fell sucked on his lower lip, and stared into Mark's glittering eyes. "I'll listen," he said at last.

Mark nodded. A couple of Duronas hurried to bring chairs for Baron Fell and Miles; the bodyguards arranged themselves standing. Fell's guards looked as if they were thinking hard, watching the box and their master; the Dendarii watched the green-clad guards in turn. Fell settled himself with a formal air, half-smiling, eyes intent.

"Tea?" inquired Lilly.

"Thank you," said the Baron. The two Durona children hurried out at her nod. The ritual was begun. Miles sat gingerly, and clamped his teeth together, hard. Whatever was going on here, he hadn't been briefed. It was clearly Mark's show. But he wasn't entirely sure Mark was sane, right now. Smart, yes. Sane, no. Baron Fell looked as though he might be coming to the same conclusion, staring across the tea table at his self-appointed host.

The two opponents waited in silence for the tea to arrive, sizing each other up the while. The boy brought in the tray, and set it beside the gruesome box. The girl poured just two cups, Lilly's finest imported Japan Green, for Mark and the Baron, and offered tea cookies with them.

"No," said Mark to the cookies in a tone of loathing, "thank you." The Baron took two, and nibbled one. Mark started to lift his tea cup left-handed, but his hand was shaking too badly, and he set it hastily back in its saucer on the arm of Lilly's chair before it could spill and scald. The girl slipped silently up to him, and lifted it to his lips; he sipped and nodded gratefully, and she settled down with the cup by his left knee to serve again at his word. *He's hurt one hell of a lot worse than he's managing to look right now,* Miles realized, his stomach cold. The Baron looked at Mark's trembling left hand, and more dubiously at his right, and shifted uneasily.

"Baron Fell," Mark said, "I think you will agree with me that time is of the essence. Shall I begin?"

"Please do."

"In that cold-box," Mark nodded toward the severed hand, "is the key to House Ryoval. Ry Ryoval's, ah, secret decoder ring." Mark cackled loudly, bit back the laugh, and nodded to the girl for another sip of tea. He regained control of his voice and continued. "Embedded in the ring's crystal are all of the late Baron Ryoval's personal code-keys. Now, House Ryoval has a peculiar administrative structure. To say that Ry Ryoval was a paranoid control freak would be a gross understatement. But Ryoval is dead, leaving his scattered subordinates at scattered locations without their accustomed direction. When the rumors of his death reach them, who knows what they will do? You've seen one example.

"And a day or two from now, the vultures will be flying in from all over to tear at the carcass of House Ryoval. Possession is rather more than nine points of the non-existent law around here. House Bharaputra alone has obvious congruent interests in House Ryoval's wares. I'm sure you can think of others, Baron."

Fell nodded.

"But a man who had Ryoval's own code-keys in his hand *today* could be at a considerable advantage," Mark went on. "Particularly if he was well-supplied with personnel to provide material backup. Without the tedious delays of cracking Ryoval's codes one by one, he could put himself in position to take immediate control of most or all of House Ryoval's current assets, from the top down instead of piecemeal. Add to that a well-known tie of blood to lend legitimacy to his claims, and I think most of the competition would sheer off without need for any expensive confrontation at all."

"My half-brother's code-key ring is not yours to trade," said Fell coldly.

"Oh, yes it is," said Mark. "I won it. I control it. I can destroy it. And," he licked his lips; the girl raised the teacup again, "I paid for it. You would not now be offered this exclusive—and it is still exclusive—opportunity if not for me."

The Baron gave a very tiny nod of concession. "Go on."

"What would you say the value of the Durona Group is, compared to the value of House Ryoval's current assets? Proportionally."

The Baron frowned. "One-twentieth. One-thirtieth, perhaps. House Ryoval has far more real estate. The, er, intellectual property value is harder to calculate. They specialize in rather different biological tasks."

"Leaving aside—or leaving behind—the real estate. House Ryoval is clearly enormously more valuable. Facilities, techs, slaves. Client list. Surgeons. Geneticists."

"I would have to say so."

"All right. Let's trade. I will give you House Ryoval in exchange for the Durona Group, plus value in a bearer-paid credit chit equal to ten percent of the assets of House Ryoval."

"Ten percent. An agent's fee," said Fell, looking at Lilly. Lilly smiled and said nothing.

"A mere agent's fee," Mark agreed. "Cheap at twice the price, which not-coincidentally is at least what you will lose without the advantages of Ry Ryoval's code-keys."

"And what would you do with all these ladies if you had them, ah, Mark?"

"What I wist. Wist, from *wistful*. I think I like the verb form better."

"Thinking of setting up in business here yourself? Baron Mark?"

Miles froze, appalled at this new vision.

"No," sighed Mark. "I wist to go home, Baron. I wist it real bad. I will give the Durona Group—to themselves. And you will let them go, free and unmolested and without pursuit, to wherever they— wist. Escobar, was it, Lilly?" He looked up at Lilly, who looked down at him and smiled, and nodded slightly.

"How very bizarre," murmured the Baron. "I think you are mad."

"Oh, Baron. You have no idea." A weird chuckle escaped Mark. If he was acting, it was the best acting job Miles had ever seen, not excluding his own wildest flights of scam.

The Baron sat back and crossed his arms. His face grew stony with thought. Would he decide to try to jump them? Frantically, Miles began trying to calculate the military options of a sudden fire-fight, Dendarii on deck, ImpSec in orbit, himself and Mark at risk, *the sudden bright muzzle-flare of a projectile weapon*—oh God, what a mess—

"Ten percent," said the Baron at last, "*less* the value of the Durona Group."

"Who calculates the value of that intellectual property, Baron?"

"I do. And they evacuate immediately. All property, notes, files, and experiments in progress to be left intact."

Mark glanced up at Lilly: she bent and whispered in his ear. "The Durona Group shall have the right to duplicate technical files. And have the right to carry away personal items such as clothing and books."

The Baron stared thoughtfully at the ceiling. "They may carry away—what each one may carry. No more. They may *not* duplicate technical files. And their credit account remains, as it has always been, mine."

Lilly's brows drew down; another whispered conference behind her hand with Mark. He waved away some objection, and pointed orbit-ward. She finally nodded.

"Baron Fell," Mark took a deep breath, "it's a Deal."

"It's a Deal," Fell confirmed, watching him with a slight smile.

"My hand on it," Mark intoned. He snickered, turned his control box over, and twisted a knob on the underside. He set it back down on his chair-arm, and shook out his trembling fingers.

Fell stretched in his chair, shaking off the tension. The guards relaxed. Miles almost fell into a puddle. *Cripes, what have we done?* At Lilly's direction, assorted Duronas scattered in a hurry.

"It's been very entertaining, doing business with you, Mark." Fell rose. "I don't know where home is for you, but if you ever decide you want a job, come see me again. I could use an agent like you, in my galactic affairs. Your sense of timing is . . . viciously elegant."

"Thank you, Baron," Mark nodded. "I'll keep it in mind, should some of my other options not work out."

"Your brother, too," Fell added as an afterthought. "Assuming his full recovery, of course. My troops could use a more active combat commander."

Miles cleared his throat. "House Fell's needs are mainly defensive. I prefer the Dendarii's more aggressive type of assignments," he said.

"There may be more assault work, upcoming," said Fell, his eyes going slightly distant.

"Thinking of conquering the world?" Miles inquired. *The Fell Empire?*

"The acquisition of House Ryoval will put House Fell in an interestingly unbalanced position," said Fell. "It would not be worthwhile to pursue a policy of unlimited expansion, and cope with all the opposition that must result, for a mere five or so years of rule. But if one were to live for another fifty years, say, one might find some most absorbing work for a military officer of capacity. . . ." Fell raised an inquiring brow at Miles.

"No. Thank you." *And I wish you all joy of each other.*

Mark gave Miles a slit-eyed, feline glance of amusement.

What an extraordinary solution Mark had wrought, Miles thought. What a Deal. Did a Jacksonian defy his upbringing by joining the side of the angels, rebel by becoming incorruptible? So it appeared. *I think my brother is more Jacksonian than he realizes. A renegade Jacksonian. The mind boggles.*

At Fell's gesture, one of his bodyguards carefully picked up the transparent box. Fell turned to Lilly.

"Well, old sister. You've had an interesting life."

"I still have it," smiled Lilly.

"For a while."

"Long enough for me, greedy little boy. So this is the end of the road. The last of our blood-pact. Who would have imagined it, all those years ago, when we were climbing out of Ryoval's sewers together?"

"Not I," said Fell. They embraced each other. "Goodbye, Lilly."

"Goodbye, Georie."

Fell turned to Mark. "The Deal is the Deal, and for my House. This is for me. For old times' sake." He stuck out a thick hand. "May I shake your hand, sir?"

Mark looked bewildered and suspicious; but Lilly nodded to him. He allowed his hand to be engulfed by Fell's.

"Thank you," said Georish Stauber sincerely. He jerked his chin at his guards, and vanished down the lift tube in their company.

"Do you think this Deal will hold?" Mark asked Lilly in a thin, worried voice.

"Long enough. For the next few days, Georish will be much too busy assimilating his new acquisition. It will absorb all his resources and then some. And after that, it will be too late. Regret, later, yes. Pursuit and vengeance, no. It's enough. It's all we need."

She stroked his hair fondly. "You just rest now. Have some more tea. We're going to be very busy for a while." She turned to gather up the young Duronas, "Robin! Violet! Come along quickly—" She hurried them into the interior of her quarters.

Mark slumped, looking very tired. He grimaced in bemusement at the teacup, switched it to his right hand, and swirled it thoughtfully before drinking.

Elli touched her half-armor helmet, listened, and vented a sudden bitter bark of laughter. "The ImpSec commander at Hargraves-Dyne Station is on the line. He says his reinforcements have arrived, and where should he send them?"

Miles and Mark looked at each other. Miles didn't know what Mark was thinking, but most of the responses that were leaping to his mind were violently obscene.

"Home," said Mark at last. "And they can give us a ride while they're at it."

"I have to get back to the Dendarii fleet," said Miles urgently. "Ah . . . where are they, Elli?"

"On their way from Illyrica to rendezvous off Escobar, but you, sir, are going nowhere near them till ImpSec Medical has cleared you for active duty," she said firmly. "The fleet is fine. You're not. Illyan would pin my ears back if I sent you anywhere but home right now. And then there's your father."

"What about my father?" Miles asked. Elena had started to say something—icy terror seized his chest. A kaleidoscopic vision of assassinations, mortal illnesses, and political plots all rolled together spun through his mind. Not to mention aircar accidents.

"He had a major coronary failure while I was there," said Mark. "They had him tied to a bed in ImpMil waiting for a heart transplant at the time I left. Actually, they should be doing the surgery right about now."

"You were there?" *What did you do to him?* Miles felt as if he'd just had his magnetic poles reversed. "I have to get home!"

"That's what I just said," said Mark wearily. "Why d'you think we trooped all the way back here, but to drag you home? It wasn't for the free holiday at Ry Ryoval's health spa, let me tell you. Mother thinks I'm the next Vorkosigan heir. I can deal with Barrayar, I think, but I sure as hell can't deal with *that*."

It was all too much, too fast. He sat down and tried to calm himself again, before he triggered another convulsion. That was just the sort of little physical weakness that could win one an immediate medical discharge from the Imperial Service, if one wasn't careful about who witnessed it. He had assumed the convulsions were a temporary snag in his recovery. What if they were a permanent effect? Oh, God. . . .

"I am going to lend Lilly my ship," said Mark, "since Baron Fell so-thoughtfully has stripped her of sufficient funds to buy thirty-six passages to Escobar."

"What ship?" asked Miles. *Not one of mine . . . !*

"The one Mother gave me. Lilly ought to be able to sell it at Escobar orbit for a tidy profit. I can pay back Mother and get Vorkosigan Surleau out of hock, and still have an impressive amount of pocket-change. I'd *like* to have my own yacht, some-day, but I really couldn't use this one for a while."

What? What? What?

"I was just thinking," Mark went on, "that the Dendarii here could ride along with Lilly. Provide her with a little military pro-tection in exchange for a free and fast ride back to the fleet. Save ImpSec the price of four commercial passages, too."

Four? Miles glanced at Bel, so very silent throughout, who met his eyes bleakly.

"And get everybody the hell out of here, as fast as possible," added Mark. "Before something else goes wrong."

"Amen!" muttered Quinn.

Rowan and Elli, on the same ship? Not to mention Taura. What if they all got together and compared notes? What if they fell into a feud? Worse, what if they struck up an alliance and colluded to partition him by treaty? North Miles and South Miles. . . . It wasn't, he swore, that he picked up so many women. Compared to Ivan, he was practically celibate. It was just that he never put any *down*. The accumulation could become downright embarrassing, over a long enough time-span. He needed . . . Lady Vorkosigan, to put an end to this nonsense. But even Elli the bold refused to volunteer for that duty.

"Yes," said Miles, "that works. Home. Captain Quinn, arrange Mark's and my transport with ImpSec. Sergeant Taura, would you please put yourself at Lilly Durona's disposal? The sooner we evacuate from here the better, I agree. And, um, Bel . . . would you stay and talk with me, please."

Quinn and Taura took the hint, and made themselves scarce. Mark . . . Mark was in on this, Miles decided. And anyway, he was a little afraid to ask Mark to get up. Afraid of what his movements would reveal. That flip phrase about Ry Ryoval's health spa was entirely too obvious an attempt to conceal . . . what?

"Sit, Bel." Miles nodded to Baron Fell's vacated chair. It put them in an equilateral triangle, he and Mark and Bel. Bel nodded and settled, its helmet in its lap and its hood pushed back. Miles thought of how he'd perceived Bel as a female in this room five days ago, prior to his memory cascade. His eye had always con-veniently interpreted Bel as male, before, for some reason. Strange. There was a brief, uneasy silence.

Miles swallowed, and broke it. "I can't let you go back to command of the *Ariel*," he said.

"I know," said Bel.

"It would be bad for fleet discipline."

"I know," said Bel.

"It's . . . not just. If you had been a dishonest herm, and kept your mouth shut, and kept on pretending to have been fooled by Mark, no one would ever have known."

"I know," said Bel. It added after a moment, "I had to get my command back, in the emergency. I didn't think I could let Mark go on giving orders. Too dangerous."

"To those who'd followed you."

"Yes. And . . . I would have known," added Bel.

"Captain Thorne," Admiral Naismith sighed, "I must request your resignation."

"You have it, sir."

"Thank you." And that was done. So fast. He thought back over the scattered pictures in his head of Mark's raid. There were still pieces missing, he was pretty sure. But there had been deaths; too many deaths had made it irredeemable. "Do you know . . . what happened to Phillipi? She'd had a chance, I thought."

Mark and Bel exchanged a look. Bel answered. "She didn't make it."

"Oh. I'm sorry to hear that."

"Cryo-revival is a chancy business," sighed Bel. "We all undertake the risks, when we sign on."

Mark frowned. "It doesn't seem fair. Bel loses its career, and I get off free."

Bel stared a moment at Mark's beaten, bloated body, huddled down in Lilly's big chair; its brows rose slightly.

"What do you plan to do, Bel?" asked Miles carefully. "Go home to Beta Colony? You've talked about it."

"I don't know," said Bel. "It's not for lack of thinking. I've been thinking for weeks. I'm not sure I'd fit in at home anymore."

"I've been thinking myself," said Miles. "A prudent thought. It strikes me that certain parties on my side would be less paranoid about the idea of you running around the wormhole nexus with a head full of Barrayaran classified secrets if you were still on Illyan's payroll. An informant—perhaps an agent?"

"I don't have Elli Quinn's talents for scam," Bel said. "I was a shipmaster."

"Shipmasters get to some interesting places. They are in position to pick up all kinds of information."

Bel tilted its head. "I will . . . seriously consider it."

"I assume you don't want to cash out here on Jackson's Whole?"

Bel laughed outright. "No shit."

"Think about it, then, on the way back to Escobar. Talk to Quinn. Decide by the time you get there, and let her know."

Bel nodded, rose, and looked around Lilly Durona's quiet living room. "I'm not altogether sorry, you know," it said to Mark. "One way or another, we've pulled almost ninety people out of this stinking gravity well. Out of certain death or Jacksonian slavery. Not a bad score, for an aging Betan. You can bet I'll remember them, too, when I remember this."

"Thank you," whispered Mark.

Bel eyed Miles. "Do you remember the first time we ever saw each other?" it asked.

"Yes. I stunned you."

"You surely did." It walked over to his chair, and bent, and took his chin in its hand. "Hold still. I've been wanting to do this for years." It kissed him, long and quite thoroughly. Miles thought about appearances, thought about the ambiguity of it, thought about sudden death, thought the hell with it all, and kissed Bel back. Straightening again, Bel smiled.

Voices floated from the lift tube, some Durona directing, "Right upstairs, ma'am."

Elena Bothari-Jesek rose behind the chromium railing, and swept the room with her gaze. "Hello, Miles, I have to talk with Mark," she said, all in a breath. Her eyes were dark and worried. "Can we go somewhere?" she asked Mark.

"'D rather not get up," Mark said. His voice was so tired it slurred.

"Quite. Miles, Bel, please go away," she said straightly.

Puzzled, Miles rose to his feet. He gave her a look of inquiry; her return look said, *Not now. Later.* He shrugged. "Come on, Bel. Let's go see if we can lend anyone a hand." He wanted to find Rowan. He watched them as he descended the lift tube with Bel. Elena pulled a chair around and sat across it backwards, her hands already opening in urgent remonstration. Mark was looking extremely saturnine.

Miles turned Bel over to Dr. Poppy, for liaison duty, and sought Rowan's suite. As he'd hoped, she was there, packing. Another young Durona sat and watched, looking a little bewildered. Miles recognized her at once.

"Lilly Junior! You made it. Rowan!"

Rowan's face lit with delight, and she hurried to embrace him. "Miles! Your name *is* Miles Naismith. I thought so! You've cascaded. When?"

"Well," he cleared his throat, "actually, it was back at Bharaputra's."

Her smile went a little flat. "Before I left. And you didn't tell me."

"Security," he offered warily.

"You didn't trust me."

This is Jackson's Whole. You said it yourself. "I was more worried about Vasa Luigi."

"I can see that, I suppose," Rowan sighed.

"When did you each get in?"

"I made it yesterday morning. Lilly came in last night. Smooth! I never dreamed you could get her out too!"

"The one escape was lock-and-key to the other. You got yourself out, which enabled Lilly to get herself out." He flashed a smile at Lilly Junior, who was watching them curiously. "I did nothing. That seems to be the story of my life, lately. But I do believe you'll all make it off-planet before Vasa Luigi and Lotus figure it out."

"We'll all have lifted before dusk. Listen!" She led him to her window. The Dendarii personnel shuttle, with Sergeant Taura piloting and about eight Duronas aboard, was lifting heavily from the courtyard of the walled compound. Point-women, going up to prepare the ship for the others to come.

"Escobar, Miles!" Rowan said enthusiastically. "We're all going to Escobar. Oh, Lilly, you're going to love it there!"

"Will you stay in a group when you get there?" Miles asked.

"At first, I think. Till it gets less strange for the others. Lilly will release us at her death. Baron Fell anticipates that, I think. Less competition for him, in the long run. I expect he'll have the top people stripped from House Ryoval and installed here by tomorrow morning."

Miles walked around the room, and noticed a familiar little remote box on the sofa-arm. "Ah! It was you who had the other control to the thermal grenade! I might have known. So you were listening in. I wasn't sure if Mark was bluffing."

"Mark wasn't bluffing about anything," she stated with certainty.

"Were you here, when he came in?"

"Yes. It was a little before dawn this morning. He came staggering in from a lightflyer wearing the most *peculiar* costume, and demanding to speak with Lilly."

Miles raised his brows at the image. "What did the gate guards say?"

"They said *Yes, sir*. He had an aura . . . I don't know how to describe it. Except . . . I could picture large thugs in dark alleyways scrambling to get out of his way. Your clone-twin is a *formidible* young man."

Miles blinked.

"Lilly and Chrys took him off to the clinic on a float-pallet, and I didn't see him after that. Then the orders started flying." She paused. "So. Will you be going back to your Dendarii Mercenaries, then?"

"Yes. After some R&R I guess."

"Not . . . settling down. After that close call."

"I confess, the sight of projectile-weapons gives me a new and unpleasant twitch, but—I hope I won't be cashing out of the Dendarii for a long time yet. Um . . . these convulsions I've been having. Will they go away?"

"They should. Cryo-revival is always chancy. So, you . . . don't picture yourself retiring. To Escobar, say."

"We visit Escobar now and then, for fleet repairs. And personnel repairs. It's a major nexus intersection. We may cross paths again."

"Not the same way we first met, I trust." Rowan smiled.

"Let me tell you, if I ever *do* need cyro-revival again, I'll leave orders to look you up." He hesitated. *I need my Lady Vorkosigan, to put an end to this wandering. . . .* Could Rowan be it? The thirty-five sisters-in-law would be a distant drawback, safely far away on Escobar. "What would you think of the planet Barrayar, as a place to live and work?" he inquired cautiously.

Her nose wrinkled. "That backward pit? Why?"

"I . . . have some interests there. In fact, it's where I'm planning to retire. It's a very beautiful place, really. And underpopulated. They encourage, um . . . children." He was skirting dangerously close to breaking his cover, the strained identity he'd risked so much lately to retain. "And there'd be lots of work for a galactic-trained physician."

"I'll bet. But I've been a slave all my life. Why would I choose to be a subject, when I could choose to be a *citizen*?" She smiled wryly, and came to him, and twined her arms around his shoulders. "Those five days we were locked up together at Vasa Luigi's—

that wasn't an effect of the imprisonment, was it. That's the way you really *are*, when you're well."

"Pretty much," he admitted.

"I'd always wondered what adult hyperactives did for a living. Running several thousand troops would just about absorb your energies, wouldn't it?"

"Yes," he sighed.

"I think I'll always love you, some. But living with you full-time would drive me crazy. You are the most incredibly domineering person I think I've ever met."

"You're supposed to fight back," he explained. "I rely on—" he couldn't say *Elli*, or worse, *all my women*, "my partner fighting back. Otherwise, I couldn't relax and be myself."

Right. Too much togetherness *had* destroyed their love, or at least her illusions. The Barrayaran system of using go-betweens to make marital arrangements was beginning to look better all the time. Maybe it would be best to get safely married first, and then get to know each other. By the time his bride figured him out, it would be too late for her to back out. He sighed, and smiled, and gave Rowan an exaggerated, courtly bow. "I shall be pleased to visit you on Escobar, milady."

"That would be joust perfect, sir," she returned, deadpan.

"Ow!" Dammit, she could be the one, she underestimated herself—

Lilly Junior, sitting on the sofa watching all this with fascination, coughed. Miles glanced at her, and thought about her account of her time with the Dendarii.

"Does Mark know you're here, Lilly?" he asked.

"I don't know. I've been with Rowan."

"The last time Mark saw you, you were going back with Vasa Luigi. I . . . think he'd like to know you changed your mind."

"He tried to talk me into staying on the ship. He didn't talk so well as you," she admitted.

"He made this all happen. He bought your passage out of here." And Miles wasn't sure he wanted to think about the coin. "I just trailed along. Come on. At least say hello, goodbye, and thank you. It will cost you nothing, and I suspect it would mean something to him."

Reluctantly, she rose, and allowed him to tow her out. Rowan gave them a nod of approval, and returned to her hasty packing.

CHAPTER THIRTY-ONE

"**D**id you find them?" Lord Mark asked.

"Yes," said Bothari-Jesek tightly.

"Did you destroy them?"

"Yes."

Mark flushed, and leaned his head back against Lilly's chair, feeling the weight of gravity. He sighed. "You looked at them. I told you not to."

"I had to, to be sure I was getting the right ones."

"No, you didn't. You could simply have destroyed them all."

"That's what I finally did. I started to look. Then I turned off the sound. Then I put them on fast-forward. Then I started just spot-checking."

"I wish you hadn't."

"*I* wish I hadn't. Mark, there were hundreds of hours of those holovids. I couldn't believe there was so much."

"Actually, there were only about fifty hours. Or maybe it was fifty years. But there were multiple simultaneous recordings. I could always see a holovid pick-up hovering, out of the corner of my eye, no matter what was going on. I don't know if Ryoval made them to study and analyze, or just to enjoy. A bit of both, I guess. His powers of analysis were appalling."

"I . . . don't understand some of what I saw."

"Would you like me to explain it to you?"

"No."

"Good."

"I can understand why you'd want them destroyed. Out of context . . . they would have been a horrible lever for blackmail. If you want to swear me to secrecy, I'll vow anything."

"That's not why. I have no intention of keeping any of this a secret. Nobody is ever going to get a handle on me again. Pull my secret strings ever again. In general outline, you can tell the whole wormhole nexus, for all I care. But—if ImpSec got hold of those holovid recordings, they would end up in Illyan's hands. And he would not be able to keep them from the Count, or the Countess either, though I'm sure he'd try. Or, eventually, Miles. Can you imagine the Count or the Countess or Miles watching that shit?"

She drew in her breath between her teeth. "I begin to see."

"Think about it. I have."

"Lieutenant Iverson was furious, when he broke in and found the melted casings. He's going to send complaints up through channels."

"Let him. If ImpSec cares to air any complaints about me or mine, I will air my complaints about them. Like, where the hell were they for the last five days. I will have no compunction nor mercy about calling in that debt on anyone from Illyan down. Cross *me*, will they . . ." He trailed off in a hostile mutter.

Her face was greenish-white. "I'm . . . so sorry, Mark." Her hand touched his, hesitantly.

He seized her wrist, held it hard. Her nostrils flared, but she did not wince. He sat up, or tried to. "Don't you *dare* pity me. I *won*. Save your sympathy for Baron Ryoval, if you must. I took him. Suckered him. I beat him at his own game, on his own ground. I will not allow you to turn my victory into defeat for the sake of your damned . . . *feelings*." He released her wrist; she rubbed it, watching him levelly. "That's the thing of it. I can shed Ryoval, if they'll let me. But if they know too much—if they had those damned vids—they'd never be able to leave it alone, ever. Their guilt would keep them coming back to it, and they would keep *me* coming back to it. I don't want to have to fight Ry Ryoval in my head, or in their heads, for the rest of my life. He's dead, I'm not, it's enough."

He paused, snorted. "And you have to admit, it would be particularly bad for Miles."

"Oh, yes," Bothari-Jesek breathed agreement.

Outside, the Dendarii personnel shuttle, with Sergeant Taura piloting, lifted the first load of Duronas to Mark's yacht in orbit. He paused to watch it rise from sight. *Yes. Go, go, go. Get out of this hole, you, me, all of us clones. Forever. Go be human too, if you can. If I can.*

Bothari-Jesek looked back at him and said, "They'll insist on a physical exam, you know."

"Yeah, they'll see some. I can't conceal the beatings, and God knows I can't conceal the force-feedings—grotesque, weren't they?"

She swallowed, and nodded. "I thought you were going to—oh, never mind."

"Right. I told you not to look. But the longer I can avoid examination by a competent ImpSec doctor, the vaguer I can be about all the rest."

"You have to be treated, surely."

"Lilly Durona has done an excellent job. And by my request, the only record is in her head. I should be able to slide right by."

"Don't try to avoid it altogether," Bothari-Jesek advised. "The Countess would spot that even if no one else did. And I can't believe you don't need . . . something more. Not physically."

"Oh, Elena. If there's one thing I've learned in the past week, it's just how badly cross-wired I really am, down in the bottom of my brain. The worst thing I met in Ryoval's basement was the monster in the mirror, Ryoval's psychic mirror. My pet monster, the four-headed one. Demonstrably, worse even than Ryoval himself. Stronger. Quicker. Slyer." He bit his tongue, aware that he was starting to say far too much, aware that he sounded as though he was edging into dementia. He didn't think he was edging into dementia. He suspected he was edging into sanity, the long way around. The hard way. "I know what I'm doing. On some level, I know exactly what I'm doing."

"In a couple of the vids—you seemed to be fooling Ryoval with a fake split personality. Talking to yourself . . . ?"

"I could never have fooled Ryoval with a fake anything. He was in this trade for decades, mucking about in the bottoms of people's brains. But my personality didn't exactly split. More like it . . . inverted." Nothing could be called split, that felt so profoundly whole. "It wasn't something I decided to do. It was just something I *did.*"

She was looking at him with extreme worry. He had to laugh out loud. But the effect of his good cheer was apparently not so reassuring to her as he might have desired.

"You have to understand," he told her. "Sometimes, insanity is not a tragedy. Sometimes, it's a strategy for survival. Sometimes . . . it's a triumph." He hesitated. "Do you know what a black gang is?"

Mutely, she shook her head.

"Something I picked up in a museum in London, once. Way back in the Nineteenth and Twentieth Centuries, on Earth, they used to have ships that sailed across the tops of the oceans, that were powered by steam engines. The heat for the steam engines came from great coal fires in the bellies of the ships. And they had to have these suckers down there to stoke the coal into the furnaces. Down in the filth and the heat and the sweat and the stink. The coal made them black, so they were called the black gang. And the officers and fine ladies up above would have nothing to do with these poor grotty thugs, socially. But without them, nothing moved. Nothing burned. Nothing lived. No steam. The black gang. Unsung heroes. Ugly lower-class fellows."

Now she thought he was babbling for sure. The panegyric of fierce loyalty for his black gang that he wanted to sing into her ear was . . . probably not a good idea, just now. *Yeah, and nobody loves me,* Gorge whispered plaintively. *You'd better get used to it.*

"Never mind." He smiled instead. "But I can tell you, Galen looks . . . pretty small, after Ryoval. And Ryoval, I *beat.* In a strange sense, I feel very free, right now. And I intend to stay that way."

"You appear to me to be . . . excuse me . . . a little manic, right now, Mark. In Miles, this would be normal. Well, usual. But eventually, he tops out, and finally he bottoms out. I think you need to watch out for this pattern, you may share it with him."

"Are you saying it's a mood swing on a bungee cord?"

A short laugh puffed from her lips despite herself. "Yes."

"I'll beware of the perigee."

"Hm, yes. Though it's the apogee where everybody else has to duck and run, usually."

"I'm also on, well, several painkillers and stimulants, right now," he mentioned. "Or I would never have made it through the last couple of hours. I'm afraid some of them are starting to wear off." Good. That would account to her for some of his babble, perhaps, and had the advantage of being true.

"Do you want me to get Lilly Durona?"

"No. I just want to sit here. And not move."

"I think that might be a good idea." Elena swung out of her chair, and picked up her helmet.

"I know what I want to be when I grow up, now, though," he offered to her suddenly. She paused, and raised her brows.

"I want to be an ImpSec analyst. Civilian. One who doesn't send his people to the wrong place, or five days late. Or improperly prepared. I want to sit in a cubicle all day long, surrounded by a fortress, and get it *right*." He waited for her to laugh at him.

Instead, to his surprise, she nodded seriously. "Speaking as the one out on the sharp end of the ImpSec stick, I would be delighted."

She gave him a half-salute, and turned away. He puzzled over the look in her eyes, as she descended out of sight down the lift-tube. It wasn't love. It wasn't fear.

Oh. So that's what respect looks like. Oh.

I could get used to that.

As Mark had declared to Elena, he just sat for a time, staring out the window. He was going to have to move sooner or later. Maybe he could use the excuse of his broken foot to inveigle a float-chair. Lilly had promised him that her stimulants would buy him six hours of coherence, after which the metabolic bill would be delivered by hulking bio-thugs with spiked clubs, virtual repo-men for his neurotransmitter debt. He wondered if the absurd dreamy image was the first sign of the approaching biochemical breakdown. He prayed he'd hold out at least till he was safely in the ImpSec shuttle. *Oh, Brother. Carry me home.*

Voices echoed up the lift tube. Miles appeared, with a Durona trailing along after him. He was skeletally thin and ghostly pale, in his Durona-issued gray suit. The two of them seemed to be on some kind of growth-reciprocal. If he could magically transfer all the kilos Ryoval had foisted on him the last week directly to Miles, they would both look much better, Mark decided. But if he kept growing fatter, would Miles attenuate altogether, and vanish? Unsettling vision. *It's the drugs, boy, it's the drugs.*

"Oh, good," said Miles, "Elena said you were still up here." With the cheerful air of a magician presenting a particularly good trick, he urged the young woman to step forward. "Do you recognize her?"

"It's a Durona, Miles," said Mark, in a gentle, weary tone. "I'm going to see them in my dreams." He paused. "Is this a trick question?" Then he sat up, shocked by recognition. You *could* tell clones apart—"It's her!"

"Just so," smiled Miles, pleased. "We smuggled her out from Bharaputra's, Rowan and I. She's going to go to Escobar with her sisters."

"Ah!" Mark settled back. "Ah. Oh. Good." Hesitantly, he rubbed his forehead. *Take back your coup, Vasa Luigi!* "I didn't think you were interested in rescuing clones, Miles."

Miles winced visibly. "You inspired me."

Er. He hadn't meant that as a reference to Ryoval's. Clearly, Miles had dragged the reluctant girl up here in a bid to make Mark feel better. Less clearly to Miles, though like crystal to himself, was an element of subtle rivalry. For the first time in his life, Miles was feeling the hot breath of fraternal competition on the back of his neck. *Do I make you uneasy? Ha! Get used to it, boy. I've lived with it for twenty-two years.* Miles had spoken of Mark as "my brother" in the same tone he'd use for "my boots," or maybe, "my horse." Or—give credit, now—"my child." A certain smug paternalism. Miles hadn't been expecting an equal with an agenda of his own. Suddenly, Mark realized he had a delightful new hobby, one that would provide entertainment for years to come. *God, I'm going to enjoy being your brother.*

"Yes," Mark said cheerily, "you can do it too. I knew you could, if you only tried." He laughed. To his dismay, it turned into a sob in his throat. He choked off both. He didn't dare laugh, or express any other emotion, right now. His control was much too thin. "I'm very glad," he stated, as neutrally as he could.

Miles, whose eye had caught the whole play, nodded. "Good," he stated, equally neutrally.

Bless you, Brother. Miles understood this, at least, what it was like to teeter on the raw edge.

They both glanced at the Durona girl. She moved uneasily, under the weight of this double expectation. She flipped back her hair, mustered words. "When I first saw you," she said to Mark, "I didn't like you much."

When you first saw me, I didn't like me much either. "Yes?" he encouraged.

"I still think you're funny-looking. Even funnier-looking than the other one," she nodded at Miles, who smiled blandly. "But . . . but . . ." Words failed her. As cautiously and hesitantly as a wild bird at a feeder, she ventured nearer to him, bent, and kissed him on one puffy cheek. Then like a bird, she fled.

"Hm," said Miles, watching her swoop back down the lift-tube. "I was hoping for a little more enthusiastic a demonstration of gratitude."

"You'll learn," said Mark equably. He touched his cheek, and smiled.

"If you think that's ingratitude, try ImpSec," Miles advised glumly. " 'You lost *how much* equipment?' "

Mark cocked an eyebrow. "An Illyan-quote?"

"Oh, you've met him?"

"Oh, yes."

"I wish I could have been there."

"I wish you could have been there too," said Mark sincerely. "He was . . . acerb."

"I'll bet. He does acerb almost better than anyone I know, except for my mother when she's lost her temper, which thank God is not very often."

"You should have seen her annihilate him, then," said Mark. "Clash of the titans. I think you'd have enjoyed it. I did."

"Oh? We have a lot to talk about, it seems—"

For the first time, Mark realized, they did. His heart lifted. Unfortunately, so did another interruption, via the tube. A man in House Fell livery looked over the chromium railing, saw him, and gave him a semi-salute. "I have a courier delivery for an individual named Mark," he said.

"I'm Mark."

The courier trod over to him, flashed a confirming scanner over his face, opened a thin case chained to his wrist, and handed him a card in an unmarked envelope. "Baron Fell's compliments, sir, and he trusts this will help speed you on your way."

The credit chit. Ah, ha! And a very broad hint along with it. "My compliments to Baron Fell, and . . . and . . . what do we want to say to Baron Fell, Miles?"

"I'd keep it down to *Thank you*, I think," Miles advised. "At least till we're far, far away."

"Tell him thank you," Mark told the courier, who nodded and marched out again the way he had come in.

Mark eyed Lilly's comconsole, in the corner of the room. It seemed a very long way off. He pointed. "Could you, um, bring me the remote-reader off that comconsole over there, Miles?"

"Sure." Miles retrieved and handed him the board.

"I predict," said Mark, waving the card around, "that I will be seriously short-changed, but not quite enough so that I would risk going back to Fell and arguing about it." He inserted the card into the read-slot, and smiled. "Spot-on."

"What did you get?" asked Miles, craning his neck.

"Well, that's a very personal question," said Mark. Miles uncraned guiltily. "Trade. Were you sleeping with that surgeon?"

Miles bit his lip, curiosity obviously struggling with his gentlemanly manners. Mark watched with interest to see how it would come out. Personally, he'd bet on curiosity.

Miles took a rather deep breath. "Yes," he said at last.

Thought so. Their good fortune, Mark decided, was divided exactly fifty-fifty; Miles got the good luck, and he got the rest. But not this time. "Two million."

Miles whistled. "Two million Imperial marks? Impressive!"

"No, no. Two million Betan dollars. What, about eight million marks, I guess, isn't it? Or is it closer to ten. Depends on the current exchange rate, I guess. It's not nearly ten percent of the value of House Ryoval, anyway. More like two percent," Mark calculated aloud. And had the rare and utter joy of rendering Miles Vorkosigan speechless.

"What are you going to do with it all?" Miles whispered, after about a minute.

"Invest," said Mark fiercely. "Barrayar has an expanding economy, doesn't it?" He paused. "First, though, I'm going to kick back one million to ImpSec, for their services the last four months."

"Nobody *gives* money to ImpSec!"

"Why not? Look at your mercenary operations, for instance. Isn't being a mercenary supposed to be profitable? The Dendarii Fleet could be a veritable cash cow for ImpSec, if it were run right."

"They take out their profit in political consequences," said Miles firmly. "Though—if you really do it, I want to be there. To see the look on Illyan's face."

"If you're good, I'll let you come along. Oh, I'm really going to do it, all right. There are some debts I cannot ever repay." He thought of Phillipi, and the others. "But I intend to pay the ones I can, in their honor. Though you can bet I'll keep the rest. I should be able to double it again in about six years, and be back to where I started. Or better. It's a lot easier to make two million out of one million than it is to make two out of one, if I understand the game correctly. I'll study up."

Miles stared at him in fascination. "I bet you will."

"Do you have any idea how desperate I was, when I started on that raid? How scared? I intend to have a value no one can ignore again, even if it's only measured in money. Money is a kind of power almost anyone can have. You don't even need a Vor in front of your name." He smiled faintly. "Maybe, after a while, I'll get a place of my own. Like Ivan's. After all, it would look funny if I was still living in my parents' house at the age of, say, twenty-eight."

And that was probably enough Miles-baiting for one day. Miles would, demonstrably, lay down his life for his brother, but he did have a notable tendency to try to subsume the people around him into extensions of his own personality. *I am not your annex. I am your brother.* Yes. Mark rather fancied they were both going to be able to keep track of that, now. He slumped wearily, but happily.

"I do believe," said Miles, still looking nicely stunned, "you are the first Vorkosigan to make a profit in a business venture for five generations. Welcome to the family."

Mark nodded. They were both silent for a time.

"It's not the answer," Mark sighed finally. He nodded around at the Durona Group's clinic, and by implication to all of Jackson's Whole. "This piecemeal clone-rescue business. Even if I blew Vasa Luigi entirely away, someone else would just take up where House Bharaputra left off."

"Yes," Miles agreed. "The true answer has to be medical-technical. Somebody has to come up with a better, safer life-extension trick. Which I believe somebody will. A lot of people have to be working on it, in a lot of places. The brain-transplant technique is too risky to compete. It must end, someday soon."

"I . . . don't have any talents in the medical-technical direction," said Mark. "In the meantime, the butchery goes on. I have to take another pass at the problem before someday. Somehow."

"But not today," Miles said firmly.

"No." Out the window, he saw a personnel shuttle descending into the Duronas' compound. But it wasn't the Dendarii one returning, yet. He nodded. "Is that by chance our transport?"

"I believe so," said Miles, going to the window and looking down. "Yes."

And then there was no more time. While Miles was gone checking on the shuttle, and couldn't watch, Mark rounded up half a dozen Duronas to help pry his stiff, bent, half-paralyzed body out of Lilly's chair and lay him on a float-pallet. His crooked hands shook uncontrollably, till Lilly pursed her lips and gave him another hypospray of something wonderful. He was perfectly content to be carried out horizontally. His broken foot was a socially acceptable reason not to be able to walk. He looked nicely invalidish, with his leg propped up conspicuously, the better to persuade the ImpSec fellows to carry him to his bunk, when they arrived topside.

For the first time in his life, he was going home.

CHAPTER THIRTY-TWO

Miles eyed the old mirror in the antechamber to the library of Vorkosigan House, the one that had been brought into the family by General Count Piotr's mother as part of her dowry, its frame ornately carved by some Vorrutyer family retainer. He was alone in the room, with no one to observe him. He slipped up to the glass and stared uneasily at his own reflection.

The scarlet tunic of the Imperial parade red-and-blues did not exactly flatter his too-pale complexion at the best of times. He preferred the more austere elegance of dress greens. The gold-encrusted high collar was not, unfortunately, quite high enough to hide the twin red scars on either side of his neck. The cuts would turn white and recede eventually, but in the meantime they drew the eye. He considered how he was going to explain them. *Dueling scars. I lost.* Or maybe, *Love bites.* That was closer. He traced them with a fingertip, turning his head from side to side. Unlike the terrible memory of the needle-grenade, he did not remember acquiring these. That was far more disturbing than the vision of his death, that such important things could happen to him and he didn't, couldn't, remember.

Well, he was known to have medical problems, and the scars were almost neat enough to look medical. Maybe people would let them pass without comment. He stepped back from the mirror to take in the general look. His uniform still had a tendency to hang on him, despite his mother's valiant attempts to make him eat more these last few weeks since they'd arrived home. She'd finally turned the problem over to Mark, as if yielding to superior expertise. Mark had grinned with amusement, and then he had proceded to harass Miles without mercy. Actually, the attentions were working. Miles did feel better. Stronger.

The Winterfair Ball was sufficiently social, without formal governmental or military obligation, that he was able to leave the dual dress sword set at home. Ivan would be wearing his, but Ivan had the altitude to carry it off. At Miles's height, the long sword of the pair looked damned silly, practically dragging on the ground, not to mention the problem of tripping over it or banging his dance partner in the shins.

Footsteps sounded in the archway; Miles turned quickly, and swung one booted leg up and leaned against a chair-arm, pretending to have been ignoring the narcissistic attractions of his reflection.

"Ah, there you are." Mark wandered in to join him, pausing to study himself briefly in the mirror, turning to check the fit of his clothing. His clothing fit very well indeed. Mark had acquired the name of Gregor's tailor, a closely-guarded ImpSec secret, by the simple expedient of calling Gregor and asking him. The boxy loose cut of the jacket and trousers was aggressively civilian, but somehow very sharp. The colors honored Winterfair, sort of; a green so dark as to be almost black was trimmed with a red so dark as to be almost black. The effect was somewhere between festive and sinister, like a small, cheerful bomb.

Miles thought of that very odd moment in Rowan's lightflyer, when he'd been temporarily convinced he was Mark. How terrifying it had been to be Mark, how utterly isolated. The memory of that desolation made him shiver. *Is that how he feels all the time?*

Well, no more. Not if I have anything to say about it.

"Looks good," Miles offered.

"Yeah." Mark grinned. "You're not so bad yourself. Not as cadaverous, quite."

"You're improving too. Slowly." Actually, Mark was, Miles thought. The most alarming distortions of whatever horrors Ryoval had inflicted upon Mark, and which he resolutely refused to talk about, had gradually passed off. A solid residue of flesh yet lingered, however. "What weight are you finally going to choose?" Miles asked curiously.

"You're looking at it. Or I wouldn't have invested the fortune in the wardrobe."

"Er. Are you comfortable?" Miles inquired uncomfortably.

Mark's eyes glinted. "Yes, thank you. The thought that a one-eyed sniper, at a range of two kilometers at midnight in a thunderstorm, could not *possibly* mistake me for you, is very comfortable indeed."

"Oh. Well. Yes, there is that, I suppose."

"Keep exercising," Mark advised him cordially. "It's good for you." Mark sat down and put his feet up.

"Mark?" the Countess's voice called from the foyer. "Miles?"

"In here," said Miles.

"Ah," she said, sweeping into the antechamber. "There you both are." She smiled at them with a greedy maternal gloat, looking most satisfied. Miles could not help feeling warmed, as if some last lingering ice chip inside from the cryo-freezing finally thawed, steaming gently. The Countess wore a new dress, more ornate than her usual style, in green and silver, with ruffs and tucks and a train, a celebration of fabric. It did not make her stiff, though—it wouldn't dare. The Countess was never intimidated by her clothing. Quite the reverse. Her eyes outshone the silver embroidery.

"Father waiting on us?" Miles inquired.

"He'll be down momentarily. I'm insisting we leave promptly at midnight. You two can stay longer if you wish, of course. He'll overdo, I predict, proving to the hyenas he's too tough for them to jump, even when the hyenas aren't circling any more. A lifetime of reflex. Try and focus his attention on the District, Miles. It will drive poor Prime Minister Racozy to distraction to feel Aral is looking over his shoulder. We really need to get out of the capital, down to Hassadar, after Winterfair."

Miles, who had a very clear idea just how much recovery chest surgery took, said, "I think you'll be able to persuade him."

"Please throw your vote in. I know he can't fool you, and he knows it too. Ah—just what can I expect tonight, medically speaking?"

"He'll dance twice, once to prove he can do it, and the second time to prove the first wasn't a fluke. After that you'll have no trouble at all persuading him to sit down," Miles predicted with confidence. "Go ahead and play mother hen, and he can pretend he's stopping to please you, and not because he's about to fall over. Hassadar strikes me as a very good plan."

"Yes. Barrayar does not quite know what to do with *retired* strong men. Traditionally, they are decently deceased, and not hanging around to pass comments on their successors. Aral may be something of a first. Though Gregor has had the most horrifying idea."

"Oh?"

"He's muttering about the Vice-royalty of Sergyar, as a post for Aral, when he is fully recovered. The present viceroy has been begging to come home, it seems. Whining, actually. A more thankless task than colonial governor I cannot imagine. An honest man gets ground to powder, trying to play interface between two sets of conflicting needs, the home government above and the colonists below. Anything you can do to disabuse Gregor of this notion, I would greatly appreciate."

"Oh, I don't know." Miles's brows rose thoughtfully. "I mean—what a retirement project. A whole planet to play with. Sergyar. And didn't you discover it yourself, back when you were a Betan Astronomical Survey captain?"

"Indeed. If the Barrayaran military expedition hadn't been ahead of us, Sergyar would be a Betan daughter-colony right now. And much better managed, believe me. It really needs someone to take it in hand. The ecological issues alone are crying for an injection of intelligence—I mean, take that worm plague. A little Betan-style prudence could have . . . well. They figured it out eventually, I guess."

Miles and Mark looked at each other. It wasn't telepathy. But the thought that perhaps Aral Vorkosigan wasn't the only over-energetic aging expert Gregor might be glad to export from his capital was surely being shared between them, right this second.

Mark's brows drew down. "How soon might this be, ma'am?"

"Oh, not for at least a year."

"Ah." Mark brightened.

Armsman Pym stuck his head around the archway. "Ready, milady," he reported.

They all herded into the black-and-white paved hall, to find the Count standing at the foot of the curved stairs. He watched them with delight as they trooped into his view. The Count had lost weight in his medical ordeal too, but it only made him look more fit, in his red-and-blues. He managed uniform and sword-set with unconscious ease. In three hours, he'd be drooping, Miles gauged, but by then he'd have made a lasting first impression on his many observers, on this his first formal outing with his new heart. His color was excellent, his gaze as knife-sharp as ever. But there was no dark at all in his hair anymore. Aside from that, you really might think he could live forever.

Except Miles didn't think that anymore. It had scared the hell out of him, retroactively, this whole cardiac episode. Not that his father must die someday, perhaps before him—that was the proper order of things, and Miles could not wish it upon the Count for it to be the other way around—but that Miles might not be here when it happened. When he was needed. Might be off indulging himself with the Dendarii Mercenaries, say, and not get the word for weeks. *Too late.*

Being both in uniform, the Lieutenant saluted his father the Admiral now with the usual tinge of irony with which they commonly exchanged such military courtesies. Miles would rather have embraced him, but it would look odd.

To hell with what it looked like. He walked over and hugged his father.

"Hey, boy, hey," said the Count, surprised and pleased. "It's not that bad, really." He embraced Miles in return. The Count stood back and looked them all over, his elegant wife, his—two, now—sons. Smiling as smugly as any rich man could, he opened his arms as if to embrace them all, briefly and almost shyly. "Are the Vorkosigans ready to storm the Winterfair Ball, then? Dear Captain, I predict they will surrender to you in droves. How's your foot, Mark?"

Mark stuck out his right shoe, and wriggled it. "Fit to be trod upon by any Vor maiden up a hundred kilos, sir. Steel toe caps, underneath," he added to Miles, aside. "I'm taking no chances."

The Countess attached herself to her husband's arm. "Lead on, love. Vorkosigans Victorious."

Vorkosigans Convalescent, was more like it, Miles reflected, following. *But you should see what the other guys look like.*

Not to Miles's surprise, practically the first person the Vorkosigans' party met upon entering the Imperial Residence was Simon Illyan. Illyan was dressed as usual for these functions, parade red-and-blues concealing a multitude of comm links.

"Ah, he's here in person tonight," the Count murmured, spotting his old Security chief across the vestibule. "There must be no major messes going on elsewhere, then. Good."

They divested their snow-spangled wraps to Gregor's household staff. Miles was shivering. He decided his timing had been skewed by this last adventure. Usually, he managed to arrange an off-planet assignment during winter in the capital. Illyan nodded and came over to them.

"Good evening, Simon," said the Count.

"Good evening, sir. All calm and quiet, so far tonight."

"That's nice." The Count raised a dryly amused eyebrow at him. "I'm sure Prime Minister Racozy will be delighted to hear it."

Illyan opened his mouth, and closed it. "Er. Habit," he said in embarrassment. He stared at Count Vorkosigan with a look almost of frustration. As if the only way he knew how to relate to his commander of thirty years was by making reports; but Admiral Count Vorkosigan was no longer receiving them. "This feels very strange," he admitted.

"You'll get used to it, Simon," Countess Vorkosigan assured him. And towed her husband determinedly out of Illyan's orbit. The Count gave him a parting half-salute, seconding the Countess's words.

Illyan's eye fell on Miles and Mark, instead. "Hm," he said, in the tone of a man who had just come out second-best in some horse-trade.

Miles stood up straighter. The ImpSec medicos had cleared him to return to duty in two months, pending a final physical exam. He had not bothered mentioning the little problem with the convulsions to them. Perhaps the first one had just been an idiosyncratic effect of the fast-penta. Sure, and the second and third ones, drug flashbacks. But he hadn't had any more, after that. Miles smiled diffidently, trying to look very healthy. Illyan just shook his head, looking at him.

"Good evening, sir," Mark said to Illyan in turn. "Was ImpSec able to deliver my Winterfair gift to my clones all right?"

Illyan nodded. "Five hundred marks each, individually addressed and on time, yes, my lord."

"Good." Mark gave one of his sharper-edged smiles, the sort that made one wonder what he was thinking. The clones had been the pretext Mark had given Illyan for handing over to ImpSec the million Betan dollars he'd sworn he would; the funds were now in escrow for their needs, among other things paying for their place in that exclusive school. Illyan had been so boggled he'd gone absolutely robotic, an effect Miles had watched with great fascination. By the time the clones were out on their own the million would be about used up, Mark had figured. But the Winterfair gifts had been personal and separate.

Mark did not ask how his gift had been received, though Miles was dying to know; but rather, drifted on with another polite nod, as if Illyan were a clerk with whom he had just concluded some minor business. Miles saluted and caught up. Mark was suppressing a deep grin, resulting in a smirk-like look.

"All this time," Mark confided to Miles in a low voice, "I was worried about never having received a present. It never even crossed my mind to worry about never having *given* one. Winterfair is an entrancing holiday, y'know?" He sighed. "I wish I'd known those clone-kids well enough to pick something right for each. But at least this way, they have a gift of choice. It's like giving them two presents in one. How the devil do you folks give anything to, say, Gregor, though?"

"We fall back on tradition. Two hundred liters of Dendarii mountain maple syrup, delivered annually to his household. Takes care of it. If you think Gregor's bad, think about our father, though. It's like trying to give a Winterfair gift to Father Frost himself."

"Yes, I've been puzzling over that one."

"Sometimes you can't give back. You just have to give on. Did you, ah . . . sign those credit chits to the clones?"

"Sort of. Actually, I signed them 'Father Frost.'" Mark cleared his throat. "That's the purpose of Winterfair, I think. To teach you how to . . . give on. Being Father Frost is the end-game, isn't it?"

"I think so."

"I'm getting it figured out." Mark nodded in determination.

They walked on together into the upstairs reception hall, and snagged drinks. They were collecting a lot of attention, Miles noted with amusement, covert stares from the flower of the Vor assembled there. *Oh, Barrayar. Do we have a surprise for you.*

He sure surprised me.

It was going to be huge fun, having Mark for a brother. *An ally at last! I think.* . . . Miles wondered if he could ever draw Mark on to love Barrayar as he did. The thought made him strangely nervous. Best not to love too much. Barrayar could be lethal, to take for one's lady. Still . . . a challenge. Enough challenges to go around, no artificial shortages of those here.

Miles would have to be careful about anything Mark might interpret as an attempt to dominate him, though. Mark's violent allergy to the least hint of control was perfectly understandable, Miles thought, but it made mentoring him a task of some delicacy.

Better not do too good a job, big brother. You're expendable now, y'know. He ran a hand down the bright uniform cloth of his jacket, coolly conscious of just what *expendable* meant. Yet being beaten by your student was the ultimate victory, for a teacher. *An enchanting paradox. I can't lose.*

Miles grinned. *Yeah, Mark. Catch me if you can. If you can.*

"Ah." Mark nodded to a man in a wine-red Vor House uniform, across the room. "Isn't that Lord Vorsmythe, the industrialist?"

"Yes."

"I'd love to talk with him. Do you know him? Can you introduce me?"

"Sure. Thinking of more investing, are you?"

"Yes, I've decided to diversify. Two-thirds Barrayaran investments, one-third galactic."

"Galactic?"

"I'm putting some into Escobaran medical technology, if you must know."

"Lilly?"

"Yep. She needs the set-up capital. I'm going to be a silent partner." Mark hesitated. "The solution has to be medical, you know. And . . . do you want to bet she won't return a profit?"

"Nope. In fact, I'd be very leery of laying any bet against you."

Mark smiled his sharpest. "Good. You're learning too."

Miles led Mark over and performed the requested introduction. Vorsmythe was delighted to find someone who actually wanted to talk about his work *here*, the bored look pasted on his face evaporating with Mark's first probing question; Miles turned Mark loose with a wave. Vorsmythe was gesturing expansively. Mark was listening as though he had a recorder whirring in his head. Miles left them to it.

He spied Delia Koudelka across the chamber, and made for her, to claim a dance later, and possibly cut out Ivan. If he was lucky, she might offer him a chance to use that line about the dueling scars, too.

CHAPTER THIRTY-THREE

After a most fascinating chat on the topic of Barrayaran high-growth economic sectors, Vorsmythe was reclaimed by his wife for some escort purpose, and dragged out of the window embrasure he and Mark had taken over; he parted with Mark reluctantly, promising to send him some prospectuses. Mark looked around for Miles again. The Count was not the only Vorkosigan in danger of over-doing it tonight while trying to prove his health to assorted observers, Mark had realized.

Mark had, by default, become Miles's confidant for self-tests he didn't want to share with his ImpSec superiors, checking knowledge bases, going over old material ranging from Service regs to five-space math. Mark had made a joke about it exactly once, before he realized the depth of terror that was driving Miles's obsessive probing. Particularly when they actually found some hole or another in Miles's memory. It bothered Mark deeply, this new hesitation, this desperate diffidence in his big brother. He hoped Miles's obnoxious self-confidence would return soon. It was another strange reciprocity, that Miles should have things he wanted to remember, and couldn't, while Mark had things he wanted to forget. And couldn't.

He would have to encourage Miles to show him around some more. Miles enjoyed playing the expert; it put him automatically in the one-up position to which he was addicted. Yeah, let Miles expand his highly-inflatable ego a bit. Mark could afford it, now. He'd give Miles a run for it some other time, when Miles was up to speed again. When it was more sporting.

Finally, by hopping up on a chair and craning his neck, Mark spotted his brother just leaving the reception chamber, in the company of a blonde woman in blue velvet—Delia Koudelka, Kareen's tallest sister. *They're here. Oh, God.* He abandoned the chair and went on a fast search for the Countess. He finally ran her to ground in a third floor lounge, chatting with some older women, obviously cronies. She took one look at his anxious smile, and excused herself to join him in a nook in the carpeted corridor.

"Have you run into a problem, Mark?" she asked, arranging her skirts on the little settee. He perched gingerly on the opposite end.

"I don't know. The Koudelkas are here. I promised back at the Emperor's Birthday to dance with Kareen, if I made it home in time. And . . . I'd asked her to talk with you. About me. Did she?"

"Yes."

"What did you tell her?"

"Well, it was a long conversation . . ."

Oh, shit.

"But the gist of it was that I judged you an intelligent young man who had had some very unpleasant experiences, but if you could be persuaded to use that intelligence to get your problems straightened out, I could support your suit."

"Betan therapy?"

"Something like that."

"I've been thinking about Betan therapy. A lot. But I dread the thought of my therapist's notes all ending up in some ImpSec analyst's report. I don't want to be a damned show." *Again.*

"I think I could do something about that."

"Could you?" He looked up, shaken with hope. "Even though you wouldn't get to see the reports either?"

"Yes."

"I . . . would appreciate that, ma'am."

"Consider it a promise. My word as a Vorkosigan."

An adopted Vorkosigan, even more so than he. But he did not doubt her word. *Mother, with you all things seem possible.*

"I don't know what details you told Kareen—"

"Very few. She's only eighteen, after all. Barely assimilating her own new adulthood. More, hm, advanced matters could wait, I judged. She has to get through school, first, before undertaking any long-term commitment," she added pointedly.

"Oh. Um." He wasn't sure if he was relieved, or not. "It's all out of date anyway. I've acquired . . . a whole new set of problems, since. Much worse ones."

"I don't sense that, Mark. To me, you have appeared much more centered and relaxed, since you and Miles got back from Jackson's Whole. Even though you won't talk about it."

"I don't regret knowing myself, ma'am. I don't even regret . . . *being* myself." *Me and the black gang.* "But I do regret . . . being so far from Kareen. I believe I am a monster, of some sort. And in the play, Caliban does not marry Prospero's daughter. In fact, he gets stomped for trying, as I recall." Yes, how could he possibly explain Gorge and Grunt and Howl and Killer to someone like Kareen, without frightening or disgusting her? How could he ask her to feed his abnormal appetites, even in some dream or fantasy play? It was hopeless. Better not to try.

The Countess smiled wryly. "There are several things wrong with your analogy, Mark. In the first place, I can guarantee you are not subhuman, whatever you think you are. And Kareen is not super-human, either. Though if you insist on treating her as a prize and not as a person, I can also guarantee you will run yourself into another kind of trouble." Her raised brows punctuated the point. "I added, as condition to my blessing on your suit, the sugges-tion that she take the opportunity during her schooling on Beta Colony next year for some extra tutoring. A little Betan educa-tion in certain personal matters could go a long way, I think, to widening her perceptions enough to admit, um, complexities without choking. A certain liberality of view an eighteen-year-old simply cannot acquire on Barrayar."

"Oh." That was an idea which had never even crossed his mind, tackling the problem from Kareen's end. It made . . . so much sense. "I'd . . . thought about school on Beta Colony for myself, next year. Some galactic education would look good on my record, when I apply here for the job I have in mind. I don't want to leave it all to pure nepotism."

The Countess tilted her head in bemusement. "Good. It seems to me as though you have a sound set of long-range plans, well-coordinated to advance all your goals. You have only to carry them through. I entirely approve."

"Long-range. But . . . tonight is right now."

"And what were you planning to do tonight, Mark?"

"Dance with Kareen."

"I don't see the problem with that. You're allowed to dance. Whatever you are. This is not the play, Mark, and old Prospero has many daughters. One may even have a low taste for fishy fellows."

"How low?"

"Oh . . ." The Countess held out her hand at a level about equal to Mark's standing height. "At least that low. Go dance with the girl, Mark. She thinks you're interesting. Mother Nature gives a sense of romance to young people, in place of prudence, to advance the species. It's a trick—that makes us grow."

Walking across the Residence ballroom to greet Kareen Koudelka felt like the most terrifying thing Mark had ever voluntarily done, not excepting the first Dendarii combat drop onto Jackson's Whole. There the resemblance ended, for after that, things _improved._

"Lord Mark!" she said happily. "They told me you were here."

You asked? "I've come to redeem my word and my dance, milady." He managed a Vorish bow.

"Good! It's about time. I've saved out all the mirror dances and the called reels."

All the simple dances he could be expected to do. "I had Miles teach me the steps to Mazeppa's Minuet last week," he added hopefully.

"Perfect. Oh, the music's starting—" She hauled him onto the inlaid floor.

She wore a swirling dark green dress with red trim, that set off her ash-blonde curls. In a sort of positive paranoia, he wondered if her outfit could possibly have been deliberately color-coordinated with his own clothes. Surely it must be a coincidence. How—? _My tailor to my mother to her mother to her. Hell, any ImpSec analyst ought to be able to figure out that data trail._

Grunt, alas, had a distracting and distressing tendency to mentally undress her, and worse. But Grunt was not going to be permitted to speak tonight. _This one is Lord Mark's job. And he isn't going to screw it up this time._ Grunt could just lurk down in there and build up steam. Lord Mark would find a use for the power. Starting with keeping the beat. There was even a dance—Mazeppa's Minuet, as it happened—where the two partners touched each other, holding the hand or the waist, for almost the entire pattern.

All true wealth is biological, the Count had said. Mark finally saw exactly what he meant. For all his million Betan dollars, he could not buy this, the light in Kareen's eyes. Though it couldn't hurt . . . what was that damned Earth bird or other, that built wildly elaborate nests to attract a mate?

They were in the middle of a mirror dance. "So, Kareen—you're a girl. I, uh, had this argument with Ivan. What do you think is

the most attractive thing a fellow can have? A lightflyer, wealth . . .
rank?" He hoped his tone suggested he was running some sort of
scientific survey. Nothing personal, ma'am.

She pursed her lips. "Wit," she said at last.

*Yeah. And what store are you going to buy that in, with all your
Betan dollars, boy?*

"Mirror dance, my turn," said Kareen. "What's the most important thing a woman can have?"

"Trust," he answered without thinking, and then thought about
it to the point of almost losing his step. He was going to need a
mountain of trust, no lie. *So, start building it tonight, Lord Mark
old boy. Hauling one bloody basket load at a time, if you have to.*

He managed to make her laugh out loud four times, after that.
He kept count.

He ate too much (even Gorge was sneakily sated), drank too
much, talked too much, and danced *far* too much, and generally
had a hell of a good time. The dancing was a little unexpected.
Kareen reluctantly lent him to a string of several curious girlfriends.
He was interesting to them only as a novelty, he judged, but he
wasn't inclined to be picky. By two hours after midnight he was
stimulated to the point of babbling, and starting to limp. Better
to call it quits before Howl had to come out and take charge of
his burnt-out remains. Besides, Miles had been sitting quietly in
a corner for the last hour, looking uncharacteristically wilted.

A word passed to an Imperial household servant brought the
Count's groundcar back for them, driven by the ubiquitous Pym,
who had taken the Count and Countess home earlier. Miles and
Mark took over the rear compartment, both sagging into their seats.
Pym pulled out past the Residence's guarded gates and into the
winter streets, grown as night-quiet as the capital's streets ever did,
only a few other vehicles prowling past. Miles turned the heat up
high, and settled back with his eyes half-closed.

Mark and his brother were alone in the compartment. Mark
counted the number of people present. One, two. Three, four, five,
six, seven. Lord Miles Vorkosigan and Admiral Naismith. Lord Mark
Vorkosigan and Gorge, Grunt, Howl, and Killer.

Admiral Naismith was a *much* classier creation, Mark thought
with a silent sigh of envy. Miles could take the Admiral out to
parties, introduce him to women, parade him in public almost
anywhere but Barrayar itself. *I suppose what my black gang lacks
in savoir faire, we make up in numbers. . . .*

But they all ran together, he and the black gang, on the deepest level. No part could be excised without butchering the whole. *So, I'll just have to look after you all. Somehow. You just live, down there in the dark. Because someday, in some desperate hour, I may need you again. You took care of me. I'll take care of you.*

Mark wondered what Admiral Naismith took care of, for Miles. Something subtle but important—the Countess even saw it. What was it she had said? *I won't seriously fear for Miles's sanity till he's cut off from the little Admiral.* Hence the desperate edge in Miles's drive to reclaim his health. His job with ImpSec was his lifeline to Admiral Naismith.

I think I understand that. Oh, yes.

"Did I ever apologize, for getting you killed?" Mark asked aloud.

"Not that I recall. . . . It wasn't altogether your fault. I had no business mounting that drop mission. Should have taken Vasa Luigi up on his ransom offer. Except . . ."

"Except what?"

"He wouldn't sell you to me. I suspect he was already planning to get a higher bid from Ryoval, even then."

"That would be my guess. Ah . . . thank you."

"I'm not sure it made a difference, in the end," Miles said apologetically. "Since Ryoval just tried again."

"Oh, yes. It made a huge difference, in the end. All the difference in the world." Mark smiled slightly, in the dark. Vorbarr Sultana's wildly assorted architecture passed by outside the canopy, snow-softened to a kind of unity.

"What do we do tomorrow?" Mark asked.

"Sleep in," murmured Miles, oozing down a little further in his stiff uniform collar, rather like paste being sucked back into a tube.

"After that."

"The party season ends here in three days, with the Winterfair bonfires. If my—our parents really go down to the District, I suppose I'll divide my time between Hassadar and here, till ImpSec lets me come back to work. Hassadar is slightly warmer than Vorbarr Sultana, this time of year. Ah—you're invited to come along with me, if you like."

"Thank you. I accept."

"What do you plan to do?"

"After your medical leave is over, I think I'll sign up for one of your schools."

"Which one?"

"If the Count and Countess are going to be mainly residing in

Hassadar, maybe the District college there."

"Hm. I should warn you, you'll find a more, um, rural crowd there than you would in Vorbarr Sultana. You'll run into more Barrayaran old-style thinking."

"Good. That's exactly what I want. I need to learn how to handle those hassles without accidentally killing people."

"Er," said Miles, "true. What are you going to study?"

"It almost doesn't matter. It will give me an official status—student—and a chance to study the *people*. Data I can get off a machine. But I'm weak on people. There's so much to learn. I need to know . . . everything."

It was another kind of hunger, this insatiable gluttony for knowledge. An ImpSec analyst must surely possess the hugest possible data-base. The fellows he'd met at the coffee dispenser in ImpSec HQ had conducted flashing conversations with each other over the most appalling range and depth of subjects. He was going to have to hustle, if he wanted to compete in that crowd. *To win.*

Miles laughed.

"What's funny?"

"I'm just wondering what Hassadar is going to learn from *you*."

The groundcar turned in at the gates of Vorkosigan House, and slowed. "Maybe I'll get up early," said Mark. "There's a lot to do."

Miles grinned sleepily, puddled down in his uniform. "Welcome to the beginning."

MILES VORKOSIGAN / NAISMITH: HIS UNIVERSE AND TIMES

Chronology	Events	Chronicle
Approx. 200 years before Miles's birth	Quaddies are created by genetic engineering.	*Falling Free*
During Beta-Barrayaran War	Cordelia Naismith meets Lord Aral Vorkosigan while on opposite sides of a war. Despite difficulties, they fall in love and are married.	*Shards of Honor*
The Vordarian Pretendership	While Cordelia is pregnant, an attempt to assassinate Aral by poison gas fails, but Cordelia is affected; Miles Vorkosigan is born with bones that will always be brittle and other medical problems. His growth will be stunted.	*Barrayar*
Miles is 17	Miles fails to pass physical test to get into the Service Academy. On a trip, necessities force him to improvise the Free Dendarii Mercenaries into existence; he has unintended but unavoidable adventures for four months. Leaves the Dendarii in Ky Tung's competent hands and takes Elli Quinn to Beta for rebuilding of her damaged face; returns to Barrayar to thwart plot against his father. Emperor pulls strings to get Miles into the Academy.	*The Warrior's Apprentice*
Miles is 20	Ensign Miles graduates and immediately has to take on one of the duties of the Barrayaran nobility and act as detective and judge in a murder case. Shortly afterwards, his first military assignment ends with his arrest. Miles has to rejoin the	"The Mountains of Mourning" in *Borders of Infinity* *The Vor Game*

Chronology	Events	Chronicle
	Dendarii to rescue the young Barrayaran emperor. Emperor accepts Dendarii as his personal secret service force.	
Miles is 22	Miles and his cousin Ivan attend a Cetagandan state funeral and are caught up in Cetagandan internal politics.	*Cetaganda*
	Miles sends Commander Elli Quinn, who's been given a new face on Beta, on a solo mission to Kline Station.	*Ethan of Athos*
Miles is 23	Now a Barrayaran Lieutenant, Miles goes with the Dendarii to smuggle a scientist out of Jackson's Whole. Miles's fragile leg bones have been replaced by synthetics.	"Labyrinth" in *Borders of Infinity*
Miles is 24	Miles plots from within a Cetagandan prison camp on Dagoola IV to free the prisoners. The Dendarii fleet is pursued by the Cetagandans and finally reaches Earth for repairs. Miles has to juggle both his identities at once, raise money for repairs, and defeat a plot to replace him with a double. Ky Tung stays on Earth. Commander Elli Quinn is now Miles's right-hand officer. Miles and the Dendarii depart for Sector IV on a rescue mission.	"The Borders of Infinity" in *Borders of Infinity* *Brothers in Arms*
Miles is 25	Hospitalized after previous mission, Miles's broken arms are replaced by synthetic bones. With Simon Illyan, Miles undoes yet another plot against his father while flat on his back.	*Borders of Infinity*
Miles is 28	Miles meets his clone brother Mark again, this time on Jackson's Whole.	*Mirror Dance*

Chronology	Events	Chronicle
Miles is 29	Miles hits thirty; thirty hits back.	*Memory*
Miles is 30	Emperor Gregor dispatches Miles to Komarr to investigate a space accident, where he finds old politics and new technology make a deadly mix.	*Komarr*
Miles is 30	The Emperor's wedding sparks romance and intrigue on Barrayar, and Miles plunges up to his neck in both.	*A Civil Campaign*
Miles is 32	Miles and Ekaterin's honeymoon journey is interrupted by an Auditorial mission to Quaddiespace, where they encounter old friends, new enemies, and a double handful of intrigue.	*Diplomatic Immunity*